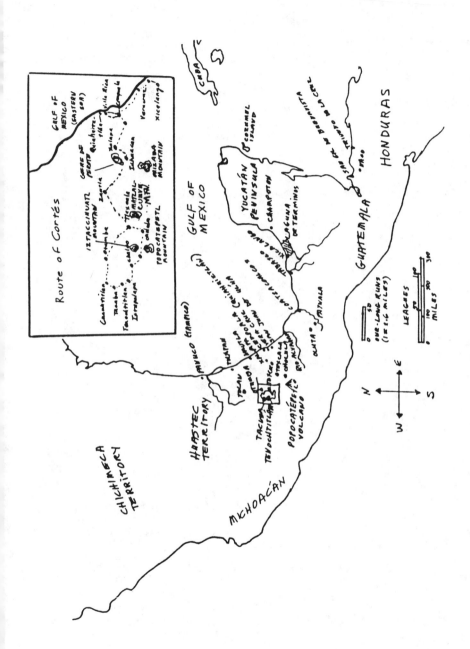

"You look so pretty tonight," Cortes said. "Maybe you should always wear yellow flowers in your hair."

"Thank you," Marina said softly, but her eyes were making inquiry, trying to anticipate what he wanted.

"I'll come right to the point," Cortes said. "You've had an offer of marriage. Juan Jaramillo wants to buy you from me."

Marina looked stricken. "Would you sell me?"

"Of course not!" Cortes snorted. He touched her cheek gently, stroked the shiny black hair falling so prettily on her shoulders. "Ironically, however, I'm prepared to give you away."

Marina's anxiety intensified. "Why would you give me away? Have I displeased you? What have I done?"

"You've never displeased me," Cortes said, reflecting as he said it that, even if they had quarreled at times, these words were quite true. "But I've been selfish, and I want to please you for a change. I need to know what you really want."

Marina's comprehension was functioning on two levels. His words sounded clear and simple, but what did they really mean? Had Cortes finallly come to realize how one-sided their love was, and would Juan's proposal stimulate Cortes into a similar offer? Or was her master angry with her, toying with her in some devious way? Had she exceeded the bounds of propriety by accepting a flower from Juan that morning? Had Cortes heard about it? She even began to question her own motives. Why had she decided to put the yellow flower in her hair? Was it to please Cortes, or to please Juan?

Her father's words came to mind once more. "Never want what you can never have, Malinalli." How unyielding was the fence those words had placed around her life? Would she be throwing away a chance for happiness by never daring to reach for it, imprisoning herself by never daring to ask for it? For a few seconds she pondered her predicament; then she answered . . .

As an avid reader of historical fiction, I found Helen Gordon's colorful and yet realistic novel about Dona Marina one of the best I've read! It is instantly mesmerizing—I couldn't put it down—and I found myself reading it until the early hours of the morning.

She skillfully humanized all of her characters, and transported me to the extraordinary era of the great Aztec civilization when Hernan Cortes and his small band of conquistadors invaded an empire!

—Phillip Mesel
Associate Professor, Bakersfield College

Que malinchista! This widely used expletive, so insulting to women, presumes unthinkingly to blame one woman for the fall of Mexico to Spanish invaders. Everyone "knows" that it was Malinche (corruption of *Malintzin*, mispronounciation of *Marina*) who helped Cortes form alliances with Moctezuma's Mexican foes by translating for him. Yet few of her detractors know she had been sold into slavery by her stepfather, then given to Cortes by defeated Tabascans.

If she could defend herself, how would Marina respond to the harsh accusations of treason? How would she explain pre-Columbian Mexico, where men ruled totally over women and the dreaded Aztecs dominated all other Mexicans? Would she bare her soul to us, explaining why the iron hand of authority could not dictate her behavior after loving words had won her loyalty?

Helen Gordon has reached through five centuries of male-dominated history to listen. She presents Marina the way authentic historical figures knew her to be: an intelligent, lovable, sensitive and courageous person who made the most of the few choices fate allotted her. Gordon carefully explores the historical forces that created such a central role for this exceptional woman and the socio-cultural factors that motivated her.

The story is fast-paced, entertaining, enjoyable fiction with interesting characters, based on well-researched historical facts. Gordon's timely re-examination of an era when two worlds collided, seen through a woman's sensibilities, may change many misperceptions that have clouded the intervening centuries. I hope all my students of Chicano history will read it.

—M.G.C. de DeLaRosa, Ph.D.
Professor of Chicano History

VOICE OF THE VANQUISHED

The Story of the Slave Marina and Hernan Cortes

by

Helen Heightsman Gordon

FIRST EDITION

Copyright 1995, by Helen Heightsman Gordon
Library of Congress Catalog Card No: 94-90752
ISBN: 1-56002-530-1

UNIVERSITY EDITIONS, Inc.
59 Oak Lane, Spring Valley
Huntington, West Virginia 25704

Cover by Bob Burchett

Dedication and Acknowledgements

This book is dedicated to my literature students, to Chicanas who wish to reclaim the heroines of their culture, and to all women everywhere who make the most of the choices life offers them.

My deep gratitude extends to all who have encouraged this project, but especially to my chief consultant and colleague Guadalupe de DeLaRosa, my student Maria Jiminez, her Mexican cousin Vicki Gonzales, and my husband Clifton Gordon, whose assistance has been generous and unflagging. Others who helpfully critiqued the manuscript include Karen Whicker, George Ellis, Phillip Mesel, Gabriole Zeviar-Geese, Frank Heath, Penny Embry, Caroline Webber, and Mary Anne Self. I appreciate research advice and travel tips from Sasha Honig, Clifton Garrett, and educators I met in Mexico and Spain. Deans David Rosales, Charles Carlson, and Robert Allison encouraged this work as my sabbatical project. My editor, Ira Herman, has combined his sound literary judgment and business acumen to bring the project to its first fruits.

I am indebited to many historians and other authors. I relied most on Hugh Thomas's recent comprehensive work *Conquest*, Jacques Coustelle's *Daily Life of the Aztecs*, Inga Clendinnen's *Aztecs*, Bernal Diaz Castillo's *True History of the Conquest of New Spain*, and Sandra Cypess' *La Malinche in Mexican Literature*. James Frey's *How to Write a Damn Good Novel* gave sound technical advice, as did members of California Writers Club. Friends too numerous to name, but too valuable to ignore, have sustained my enthusiasm over the past ten years. I thank them all.

—Helen Heightsman Gordon

Introduction

Marina's story has fascinated me since I first heard it fifteen years ago, but I'm convinced that past fictional treatments of her and Hernan Cortes do not do them justice. I've tried to place myself in Marina's sandals, to infer what kind of a world she lived in, what experiences she might have had, what personal traits might have enabled her to suffer traumatic hardships yet rise to great achievements.

To that end, I researched the tragic history of the West Indies and Cuba, the pre-Columbian societies of Aztecs and Mayas, and the way Mayan descendants live today. I traveled in the beautiful countries of Mexico and Spain. I read over fifty books about the Sixteenth Century milieu: anthropology, religion, history, art, biography, natural environment, geography, literature, and linguistics.

I've tried to be as true to historical events and characters as possible, while filling in the "blank spaces" with fictional characters and events that might explain why the lives of Marina and Cortes unfolded as they did. My historical sources differed in matters of spelling, terminology, interpretation of events, and even such facts as dates and genealogy. Therefore I made the following choices to keep the story readable but realistic.

In the novel, I use the familiar term *Aztec empire* although inhabitants on the Valley of Mexico called themselves "Mexica" (pronounced meh-SHEEK-uh). I reserve the term *Mexica* (plural) for the indigenous people of ancient Mexico, and *Aztecs* for the pre-Conquest citizens of the Triple Alliance city states of Texcoco, Tacuba, and Tenochtitlan (later renamed Mexico City). The term *Indian* is also a misnomer, but Europeans have so entrenched its second meaning in both English and Spanish that my characters have to use it at times to convey realistically the way in which they historically referred to indigenous people.

Another compromise is to use the name *Moctezuma*, as many historians have done, forming a hybrid of the original Nahuatl name *Motecuhzoma* and its Spanish corruption, "Montezuma."

To avoid distractions, I decided not to use accent marks and other diacritical markings on names throughout the book. For reference purposes, however, I supply them on the names of characters listed in the front of the book. Spanish and Nahuatl names without accent marks usually accent the next-to-last syllable.

Nahuatl and Mayan names may seem daunting at first glance, but to create a sense of the pre-Columbian culture, many names of characters are rendered in their Nahuatl or Maya forms (that is, *Anecoatl* rather than *Water Snake*, *Ah Cux* rather than *Weasel*. For reference, a pronunciation guide with examples is provided on the next page.

—Helen Heightsman Gordon

Pronunciation Guide

Though Nahuatl names may appear long and difficult, they are not hard to pronounce because the letters are sounded similarly in all words. Pronounce the consonants as you would in English except as follows:

tl is said as a unit, as in the English word *battle* (Tláloc = TLAH-loke; Cimátl = seem-AHTL)
x sounds like "sh" (Xilonen = shee-LO-nen) or sometimes like "s" (Xochimilco = so-chee-MEEL-koh)
z sounds like "s" (Tezcatlipoca = tess-kaht-lee-PO-kah)
hu sounds like "w" in *want* (Huitzilopochtli = weet-see-lo-POACH-tlee)
qu sounds like "k" before "e" or "i" (Quetzacóatl = ket-sahl-KO-ahtl) but "kw" before "a" (quachic = KWAH-cheek)

Pronounce vowels as you would in modern Spanish; also pronounce the "e" on the ends of words (Coatlicue = ko-aht-LEE-kweh)

a = ah as in *arm*, (Aztec = AHS-tek; Chac = chahk)
e = eh as in *set*, (Metzli = MEHTS-lee; Ome = OH-meh)
i = ee as in *eel* or *si*, (Xipe Totec = SHEE-peh TOE-tek)
o = oh as in *okay*, (Toci = TOE-see)
u = oo as in *pool*, (Yacatecuhtli = Yah-kah-tek-OO-tlee)

Maya pronunciation is similar, but Mayan words usually accent the last syllable. (Ix Chel is pronounced eesh-CHEHL, Ah Cux is ah-COOSH; Chichén Itzá is chee-CHEN eet-SAH). Accents in Nahuatl words usually fall on the next-to-last syllable (Tula is pronounced TOO-lah, and Tenochtítlan is teh-noach-TEET-lahn).

The Main Characters

The Spaniards: (All historical, but some embellished by fiction)

Hernán Cortés—conqueror of Mexico
Martín Cortés—son of Hernán Cortés and his slave Marina
Juan Jaramillo—captain under Cortés, Marina's husband
Pedro Alvarado—captain under Cortés, conqueror of Guatemala
Alonso Puertocarrero—captain under Cortés, Marina's owner
Diego Velásquez—conqueror of Cuba, mentor and rival of Cortés
Catalina Suárez—first wife of Hernán Cortés, married in Cuba
Juan Suárez—Catalina's brother, business partner of Cortés
Bartolomé Olmedo—Loyal friar on the Cortés expedition
Juan Díaz—chaplain assisting friar Olmedo
Gerónimo Aguilar—priest captured by Maya, Cortés' interpreter
Bartolomé de las Casas—priest, defender of Indian rights
Bernal Díaz—soldier of Cortés, historian of the Conquest who
  knew Marina personally
Pánfilo de Narváez—captain under Velásquez; rival of Cortés

Other important conquistadors: Juan Grijalva, Gonzalo de
Sandoval, Juan Velásquez de León, Andrés de Tapia, Cristóbal de
Olid, Diego de Ordaz, Franciso de Monteyo, Alonso de Ávila.

The Mexica: (Historical figures, in order of importance)

Malinalli Tenepal, later known as Doña Marina, Malintzin (mahl-
  EEN-tseen), or La Malinche—native girl who became an
  interpreter of Hernán Cortés
Moctezuma II—Uey Tlatoani or Aztec emperor of Tenochtítlan
Cuauhtémoc—Moctezuma's nephew, last emperor of Mexica
Cacama—King of Texcoco, nephew of Moctezuma
Ixtlilxochitl—"Black Flower"; brother and rival of Cacama
Cuitláhuac—King of Ixtapalapa, brother and successor to
  Moctezuma II.
Xicotenga the Elder—blind ruler of Tlaxcala, Cortés' friend
Xicotenga the Younger—warrior who opposed his father
Chicomácatl—fat cacique of Cempoalla
Olintetl—fatter cacique of Xocotla
Teudile and Cuitlálpitoc—ambassadors of Moctezuma

The Mexica and Mayas: (Fictional, in order of importance)

Itzamitl—"Flint Arrow"; Malinalli's father; tecuhtli of Paynala
Cimátl—"One Paper"; Malinalli's mother
Papalotl—"Butterfly"; Cimátl's sister
Anecóatl—"Water Snake"; Cimátl's second husband
Xiuhtetl—"Turquoise Stone"; son of Anecóatl and Cimátl
Callipopoca—"Smoking House"; macehual servant of Itzamitl
Chihuallama—"Old Woman"; healing woman, wife of
    Callipopoca
Atotl (Toto)—"Water Bird"; daughter of Chihuallama
Moyo—"Mosquito"; Chihuallama's youngest child
Acamapichtli—"Handful of Reeds"; first son of Chihuallama
Matlalquiau—"Green Rain"; sweetheart of Acamapictli
Opochtli—"Left Handed"; merchant friend of Malinalli's family
Metzli—"Moon"; daughter of Opochtli, friend of Malinalli
Chimalli—"Shield"; son of Opochtli, student warrior
Tlacatéotl—"Godlike Man"; eagle warrior and trainer of warriors
Tlacoch—"Spear"; son of Tlacatéotl, gambler
Toci—"Our Mother"; priestess-teacher in Coatzacoalcos
Huatl—"Jaguar"; merchant partner of Tlacoch and Opochtli
Nemon—"Bad Luck"; slave who befriends Malinalli
Ah Cux—"Weasel"; Mayan master of Malinalli
Quauhtlátoa—"Speaking Eagle"; fair youth sacrifice
Citli—"Rabbit"; son of Metzli by Quauhtlátoa
Quilitl—"Amaranth"; Cholula woman who befriends Marina

The Important Gods

Although pre-Columbian societies worshipped numerous
other minor deities, the gods below had greatest influence. All
are Aztec gods except Chac, Ix Chel, and Kukulcan. They are
listed in alphabetical order. For help with pronunciation, see the
pronunciation guide following the introduction. A few examples
of approximate pronunciation are given here, particularly where
the accent falls in an irregular place. (Most Aztec words stress
the next-to-last syllable; Mayan words stress the last syllable.)

Ayopechcatl—goddess of childbed, aspect of earth mother
Centéotl—corn god, husband of Xochiquetzal
Chac (CHOCK)—Mayan rain god, equivalent to Tláloc
Chalchiutlicue (chal-chee-oo-TLEE-kweh)—"Jade Skirt"; water
    goddess; wife of Tláloc
Cihuacóatl (see-wah-KO-ahtl)—"Woman Snake"; aspect of earth
    mother, magician, patroness of women who die in childbirth

Coatlicue—"Serpent Skirt"; earth goddess, mother of Sun God
Ehécatl (eh-HEH-kahtl)—wind god, aspect of Quetzalcoatl
Huitzilopochtli (weet-see-lo-POACH-tlee)—"Hummingbird of the Left or the South"; major god of sun and war
Ix Chel (eesh CHEL)—Mayan fertility goddess
Ixtlilton—"Little Black Face"; god of health and curing
Kukulcan (koo-kool-KAHN)—"Feathered Serpent"; Mayan equivalent of Quetzalcóatl
Metzli—Moon god
Ometecuhtli—"Dual Lord"; original creator, male/female unity
Quetzalcóatl (ket-sahl-KO-ahtl)—"Feathered Serpent"; god of learning, priesthood, and the arts
Tezcatlipoca—"Smoking Mirror"; god of night sky, patron of sorcerers; opponent of Quetzalcóatl
Tláloc (TLAH-loke)—major God of rain and agriculture; husband of Chalchiutlicue the water goddess
Tlazoltéotl—"Eater of Filth"; goddess of lust who receives confessions at the end of one's life
Toci or Teoinnan—mother of the gods
Xilonen—"Corn Doll"; goddess of young maize
Xipe Totec (SHEE-peh TOE-tek)—"Flayed God"; god of seedtime and planting
Xochiquetzal (so-shee-KETS-ahl)—"Precious Flower"; goddess of flowers, crafts, weaving, and sensual pleasure
Yacatecuhtli (yah-kah-teh-KOO-tlee)—"Guiding Lord"; patron of merchants and travelers

Table of Contents

Hernan Cortes meets Moctezuma's Ambassadors, and Marina translates for them.

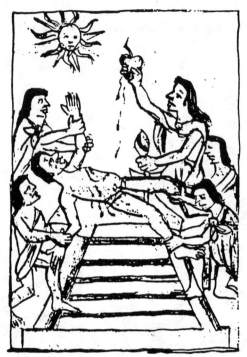

An Aztec artist depicts human sacrifice, offering the victim's heart to the Sun God, Huitzilopochtli. From the Florentine Codex.

La Malinche (Doña Marina), "the Tongue" of Cortes's conquest of the Aztec and the Maya, spoke both Nahuatl and Maya. She was given to Cortes in Tabasco, in 1519.

Chapter 1

A Life in Danger at Vera Cruz

Never want what you can never have, her father had said. She had accepted that as wisdom, the advice of an elder smoothing the rocky path of youth. But it could have been a command, his words like stakes driven into the ground to build a fence around her life. As she had peeped through the cracks in that fence, seeing her father's life as a warrior/chief, imagining its glory and excitement, she wished she had been born a boy, a son to bring honor to her father and glory to the gods.

That was a wish that could never be fulfilled. Yet her life as a woman had not lacked adventure or excitement, she mused on that day in Vera Cruz when she took her last leave of the country in which she had been born, the country whose destiny had been intertwined with her own in unpredictable ways.

A warrior's life contains much hardship and danger, her father had said, and she should be glad she was a woman, shielded from hardship by a protector. Her mother, too, had said a woman needs a protector, for women are weak and life holds many perils. Because her parents had spoken with such assurance and sweet reasonableness, she had believed them. She had learned to obey, as all women must, and to stifle the longings that could only bring unhappiness.

Yet the twenty-eight years of her life had unfolded in such an amazing way that even the wisest priest could not have envisioned her destiny. The priest who read her tonalamatl, or book of days, when she was born, had expected to predict her future based on the past; he could not have foretold a life so unique, such a mix of misfortune and triumph. She was no longer certain what she could never have, because she had already had adventures far beyond her childhood imaginings.

Such were the thoughts of Marina de Jaramillo in September of 1529 as she stood on the balcony of the inn at Vera Cruz overlooking the rain-drenched courtyard below. Her husband, Juan, had left before dawn with some tamemes hired to carry their trunks and several loads of trade goods to the sailing ship in

5

the harbor.

Her seven-year-old son, Martin, was still sleeping on the petlatl, his small form stirring occasionally under his tilmantli, his small breaths making regular and reassuring sounds. She must teach him to call the sleeping mat a *petate* and the tilmantli a *cape*, as the Spaniards did, for this day would mark the beginning of his life as an hidalgo's son, going to Spain for his education. Until Juan returned to take them to the ship, she would have a little time alone to think, to try to understand the fear she felt, a fear that seemed unreasonable.

Marina did not lack courage; if she could only understand the fear, she could conquer it. Her heritage as a Nahua woman had taught her to face the harshness of life squarely and to transcend pain by acknowledging it. Her courage had astonished most European men who met her, but it attracted them also.

She breathed deeply. If dangerous animals were near, she could recognize them by their smell. But the scents in the air spoke only of the salt from the sea, the dampness of rain-soaked leaves, and the musky smell of horses and mules in the innkeeper's stables. She remembered the first time she had smelled a horse, ten years before, when the strange animal and its bearded owner Hernan Cortes had both frightened her.

She listened intently to the birdsong filling the air. The birds would sense any danger to themselves, but she could detect no fear in them. She heard long, full-throated warbles, soft chirpings, a shrill thweet-thweet-thweet followed by laughingly rapid chuh-chuh-chuh-chuh, as if the birds surrounding her formed a chorus of competitors, each wanting to scrawl a signature of sound upon the morning hours before those hours passed into a whirlpool of irrecoverable losses.

A flock of small black birds pecked among the twigs that the night's rainfall had washed down from several tall trees. It was September, the end of the rainy season, when the rains still fell heavily but lasted not much longer than an afternoon nap. The early morning air felt moist and cool, and the red sky of dawn cast a soft light on the stone and adobe walls of the city named Villa Rica de la Vera Cruz, "The rich city of the true cross," which most people now called simply Vera Cruz.

A few puffs of clouds dotted the eastern sky, like playful children soon to be chased away by the hot rays of the sun. She could easily understand how her ancestors had seen the sun as the god Huitzilopochtli, had seen the red of the sky as the sacred blood that fed and sustained him in his long climb each day.

The metaphors of her first language, Nahuatl, had created for her a vision of the world full of imagination and mystery. Nahuatl speakers would see the shape of a thrown rabbit on the face of the moon, and the vanquishing of the stars by the morning sun as a triumph of the sword of the sun god. They

6

would see a mountain range as a sleeping woman, and nuggets of gold as "excrement of the gods." They would observe that the multitudes of people in a city were as numerous as the rushes on riverbanks, and would use the same word, *tollan*, for "place of rushes" and for "metropolis."

Her native tongue, Nahuatl, was a language of rhythm and repetition, through which she learned to feel the rhythms and cycles and renewals of nature. It was a language of compounded syllables, through which she learned that names and experiences bring new combinations out of old forms. The language lent itself to symbolism and interpretation of omens: everything could have more than one meaning, like a god who can take on many guises or send messages in mysterious codes. Anything was believable; nothing was ever purely what it seemed to be.

Marina's native tongue was a language spawned by a people whose uncertain lives held constant threats of disaster, a people whose earth could tremble under their feet, whose mountains could throw rocks, whose skies could withhold rain for many seasons or pelt the earth mercilessly and gouge it with deep barrancas when the downpour turned into fierce rivers cutting a path to the sea. Their crops could wither or drown unpredictably, and wildlife could disappear suddenly. Volcanoes and hurricanes could unleash an awesome and overpowering fury, seeming like the anger of a god. To the ancestors who had developed this tongue, magic was as necessary as grain, and belief in the supernatural was as real as a stone in the hand.

Marina heard Martin waking. Her attention turned to more urgent and practical matters; she must dress and feed Martin, pack a few items that had not been sent in the trunks, and be ready for Juan when he returned. As she moved, a bird cry pierced the air, and a flutter of wings emptied the courtyard below. Yet she saw nothing unusual.

* * *

As Marina turned back to the room and closed the shutter, a Spanish sailor walked out of the inn, carrying his belongings in a duffel bag slung over his back. He walked unsteadily and sniffed the air heartily, as if needing to clear his head after a night of revelry in port. His eyes squinted in the morning light as he started down the cobblestone street toward the harbor.

A tall and wiry friar, about sixty years old, approached from a side street and fell in stride beside the sailor. The friar's bare feet flexed confidently whether on stone or sand, and his bare head could have been either shaven for practical reasons or balding for natural ones. His robe of coarse maguey cloth hung loosely to his ankles, and a hemp rope around his waist served for a belt. He kept one hand in a deep pocket, clutching a thick letter with many pages.

"You are a Basque, judging from your clothes," said the friar to the sailor, pointing to the sailor's cap and boots. His voice, deep and friendly, nevertheless conveyed a sense of purpose and urgency.

"Aye, that I am. And so are you, father, judging from your speech," replied the sailor, removing his cap to show respect.

The friar nodded, elated to find a countryman from his own province. "I was born in Durango, and my first language was Basque. Your Spanish, too, carries the accents of the Basque tongue."

"Small world," said the sailor, his face beaming. "I come from Bilbao, very near your birthplace."

"We're both far from home," said the friar warmly, adjusting his steps to walk comfortably alongside his neighbor. "I've served here in New Spain for almost two years, and I hunger for news of Old Spain. Have you come from there?"

The sailor pointed a tattooed hand toward the harbor. "Aye, father, on that ship anchored there in the Gulf," he said. "The merchants are happy with trade these days. My ship brought a cargo of sheep and mules, steel knives and tools to this country, and we'll take back a cargo of silver, jade, cotton, rubber, and pottery." He grinned amiably as he added, "The nobles in Spain have become very fond of chocolate and tobacco; the merchants can sell all the cacao beans and yetl leaves they can ship over. I confess to a fondness for these luxuries myself."

"I'm glad for the merchants' prosperity," said the friar. His nose confirmed that the sailor had indeed smoked tobacco recently, and no doubt consumed some Jamaican rum as well. "And is the king prospering?"

The sailor laughed. "I'm a practical man. I know very little about royal affairs, but his majesty's subjects are loyal, and I hear he's launched many successful military campaigns. Of course, he sends missionaries to spread the holy word among all the conquered peoples."

The friar smiled in satisfaction; he had been given such a mission himself, though he had felt unworthy of it, after the king had seen his work at the convent of Abrojo, in Valladolid. He had taken part in the religious renewal of Spain after her triumph over the Moors, an effort to restore the simplicity and austerity of primitive Christianity to a generation of priests whose public piety often masked a greater concern for self-indulgence and power-seeking. The friar had read Erasmus and Sir Thomas More. In his new calling, he saw opportunity to bring to the Indians of New Spain, sometimes called Mexicans, a sense of the purity and simplicity that gave power to his own faith.

The friar had departed Spain even before being officially confirmed, a small matter in his eyes but one that his enemies were using to undermine his work. Even in this paradise of innocence, he had run into corruption among the men entrusted to govern New Spain while Hernan Cortes was away. Cortes had returned to Spain to visit the king, the pope, and the woman whom his father had arranged for him to marry. In his absence, the country had fallen into a chaotic state, and the friar wished passionately for the return of the conquistador, who had been a much better governor than those who followed him.

The friar had destroyed idols, to be sure, getting across a symbolic message that the old religions in the Valley of Mexico were superseded by a new faith, but he had not burned the manuscripts of the Mexica, despite what the rumors said. Nor had he treated Indians cruelly, despite what his enemies said. In fact, he had spoken out against the cruelties of those enemies when he could stand them no longer, but New Spain was not a place where one could speak freely without arousing antagonism.

"Are you a religious man, my son?" asked the friar gently.

"Aye, born and raised a Catholic, but more a sinner than a saint," the sailor replied good-humoredly. "I have a weakness for the Demon Rum, but I go to confession whenever I'm in port." He clapped a hand to his forehead, and turned bloodshot eyes to the friar. "My head is giving me a flogging today. My punishment for a wild night last night. If our ship hits a storm on the way back, I'll go into the arms of Saint Elmo with all my sins on my head. Would you hear my confession this morning?" He looked around to see if a church stood nearby.

The friar followed his gaze and guessed his intent. "I'm not from this mission," he said hastily. "I've walked 75 leagues from Mexico City to bring an urgent message to Spain." He had decided that this sailor was a man he could trust, and he suggested they walk on the beach where they could not be overheard. "I am Fray Juan de Zumarraga," said the friar, "and my life is in danger. You will have my blessing and that of God himself if you will help me to smuggle a letter to the King."

In a stunned voice the sailor asked, "What sort of danger?" He had never pictured himself as an instrument of God, but as a sailor he had always known himself to be in God's hands.

"It's a long story," Fray Zumarraga answered, "but briefly I can tell you this much: King Charles sent me here as First Bishop of Mexico and Protector of the Indians. For over a year and a half I have been witnessing cruel abuses against them. When Hernan Cortes left for Spain, these cruelties increased. My complaints were ignored by Beltran Nuno de Guzman, President of the Audiencia, because he himself has brutalized the Indians. He considers me and all of Cortes' supporters as enemies.

"Guzman tried to silence me and others in the pulpit on Whitsunday last June, and since then he has threatened our lives. I tried to send a letter to the King through the region of Panuca, but the spies of Guzman intercepted it and destroyed it. I have written another letter which I have brought with me." He fingered the bulky papers in his pocket. "Perhaps God has sent you to me so that this message can be delivered."

The two men walked along the beach, where the friar listened to the sailor's simple confession and absolved him. The sailor listened to Zumarraga as he told convincingly and specifically of the cruelties: the Indians had been enslaved and sold for profit—many shiploads of them—even though all the monarchs of Spain since Queen Isabel had forbidden enslavement of free Indians who had not resisted becoming Spanish subjects. The Indian vassals, laboring for low wages or to meet the demands of tribute, had been so overworked in the silver and gold mines that their life expectancy was reduced to 25 years. Although the encomiendas were supposed to be "trusts" granted to Spaniards to educate their vassals about Christianity in exchange for a portion of the natives' produce or labor, abuses had become rife. In some encomiendas, those who did not produce enough crops or gold to satisfy their masters were maimed or flogged or burned. To meet the demands for tribute, the poor Indians frequently had to sell their wives and children into slavery.

"Have you put all that in your letter?" asked the sailor, his reddened eyes wide with amazement.

"Yes, and more," Zumarraga answered. "The president is not the only abuser. Spanish settlers mistreat the Indians terribly. They load them like pack animals and take them wherever the Spaniards wish to go, without even feeding them. Some of the worst offenders are the gold miners, who load the Indians of their encomiendas and send them thirty, forty, or fifty leagues with heavy burdens. Many of them die along the way."

The sailor moaned. "Poor devils," he said. "My own sins seem small beside those you are telling me about."

"Indeed," agreed Zumarraga. "A friar in Puebla counted three thousand free men who have died on the road carrying supplies to the mines."

The sailor shifted his duffel bag forward on his shoulder as he tried to imagine humans as beasts of burden. "I can see why the king sent you here as protector of the Indians."

"When Guzman began to govern the province of Panuca," Zumarraga continued indignantly, "its Indians were subjugated and peaceful. He's sold 10,000 of his subjects as slaves, and consequently slave traders have raided the Panuca region. We know of three shiploads of slaves that have sunk. Many Indians abandon their villages, afraid they will meet the same fate. Some will not have intercourse with their wives, because they don't want to rear children under these horrible conditions."

"Is it like that everywhere in New Spain?" asked the

astonished sailor.

"Since Guzman began to govern, yes. In the valley of Mexico, he and his oidores have used 100,000 or more Indians that should be vassals of the crown, forcing the Indians to pay excessive tribute, pocketing the profits themselves. They have made the Indians build warehouses to hold the governor's stores of maize and textiles. They make the Indians bring their own materials, working them for months or years without holidays, and giving them so little maize to eat that many of them starve. Indians of Tlatelolco complained to me that Guzman's men demanded good-looking female relatives as tribute; they even carried off two pretty Indian girls from a convent in Texcoco. Guzman has enslaved eighty women for his own use as concubines."

The sailor, a rough but kindly man, had not been sheltered from the sight of suffering, yet he had not been hardened by seeing it. The atrocities described by this venerable friar seemed beyond belief, yet he spoke with such intensity and sincerity that the sailor was moved and thought the king should be informed.

The two men devised a plan: the sailor would imbed the letter in a cake of wax and hide it in an oil drum on the ship. He promised to take it personally to the court of King Charles I, who was also his spiritual leader as Emperor Charles V of the Holy Roman Empire.

The sailor knew that if that letter was discovered in his possession before the king received it, both he and the friar could meet their deaths. But he felt equally sure that when he faced Saint Peter at the golden gate, his sins would be forgiven.

Chapter 2

The Old World Impacts the New World

By the time Juan returned, Martin was awake and had eaten his bowl of atole and fresh fruit. Marina had adapted to the Spanish custom of eating early in the morning, again at midday, and again in the evening, though in her own childhood the morning meal had not been consumed until the sun was well on his way up the sky.

She was also raising Martin to adapt to the ways of the Spaniards, eating and dressing the way his father's people did, even though she believed children in Mexico were more comfortable going naked or wearing only a short loose garment until the age of ten or twelve years. That had been the custom among the people who were now being called Aztecs, the people from the ancestral lands of Aztlan. They had called themselves the Mexica, but the Spanish conquerors named them differently. Spaniards referred to the native population as *Mexicans* or *Indians*, reserving the name *Aztec* for the defeated nation once led by Moctezuma the Younger, the nation that had been crushed into oblivion in 1521, the year she remembered as 3-Calli or 3-House.

Even the word *Indians* was a curious one. Juan had explained that the erroneous name started when an explorer named Cristobal Colon, or Christopher Columbus, had mistaken some Caribbean islands for a country named India, but the word had been used so much it had become fixed in the language. Some of the friars who had begun studying the history of the native populations used the term *indigena* for those who had been born in Mexico. Juan was likely to tell other Spaniards that he had married an indigena woman, but his enemies would be more likely to call her an *Indian* in a scornful way. She had learned not to let such contempt bother her, for her Spanish friends had always proven to be more powerful than their enemies.

Expecting the day to be warm, Marina had dressed her son in a loose cotton shirt and short pants, garments that would allow for some air to get to his small body and yet would be acceptable to the Spanish people on board the ship. On his feet, as on her own, she put some woven hemp sandals called *cactli*, more practical than boots for warm weather, even though Juan would expect Martin to wear leather shoes and boots once they settled in Spain. She dressed for comfort, too, knotting a plain wraparound skirt at her waist, topping it with a traditional huipil that draped loosely from her shoulders to below her waist. The cotton fabric and elegant embroidered border would distinguish this dress from the rough garment of a peasant, but the shape of the garment would look much the same, at least to those for whom class distinctions were important. She was not one of those, and she did not dress to please such people.

In a *petlacalli*, or chest of woven reeds, Marina had packed a few garments for daily use during the 40-day voyage to Spain. They would get new garments in the port of Cadiz, Juan had promised, and new horses. He had sold their old horses at a good price; beasts of burden were much in demand in New Spain. After Juan had paid the innkeeper for their night's lodging, the travelers started on foot toward the dock.

The strip of shore on which they walked was still damp from the receding tide, so that each footstep squished a little puddle in the smooth gray sand. Martin eagerly trotted beside them, occasionally running ahead, and the spring in Juan's stride showed his happiness at the prospect of travel. Marina was silently saying goodbye to the land of her birth, knowing she would never return.

To the west the terrain rose sharply into high mountains covered with trees and bushes. To the south lay many barrancas carved by swift rivers, beyond those the coastal villages of her early childhood, and beyond those the thick, humid jungles of Maya country. To the north lay a wilderness, the land where the Chichimecs scratched out an existence by gathering wild plants and hunting small game. To the east, the morning sun glistened on the blue expanse of the Gulf of Mexico, each wave flashing tiny points of light as it flowed toward them, each breaking into a lacy froth on the gentle slope of the shore. Soon she would be going "beyond the mists," as the Mexica would say, beyond the eastern border of the land they had naively called Anahuac, "the One World," when they thought they knew where the world began and ended.

This strip of sand was like her life now, Marina thought. She could walk easily on the clear beaches, but mountains and deserts formed boundaries to the west, and the vast ocean to the east formed a tantalizing threat. In a sense, too, this thin strip of sand was separating her past and her future.

Her son, Martin, would live his life under different metaphors, Marina mused. His life could be seen as a bridge between the old, vanquished culture of the Aztecs and the new one of Spain. Or it could be seen as the flowing together of two powerful rivers, as the blood of his mother and father blended within his veins the best of two races, the mestizo. Martin was not the first mestizo, she knew. The friar Geronimo de Aguilar had told her about Gonzalo Guerrero, who had been shipwrecked with him many years ago in the Maya region. When the men were captured by a Maya tribe, Aguilar had been taken as a slave, but Guerrero had married a chieftain's daughter who bore him several children. And of course many children had been sired by the Conquistadors through their indigena concubines, or later by their indigena wives, as the missionaries began to insist that Spaniards set a good Christian example by either marrying their indigena women or bringing their legal wives from Spain.

Martin was one of the more fortunate sons, for he had been acknowledged by his father and recognized as legitimate by the Pope. Marina carried with her the precious letter from his father that affirmed Martin's status. It would stay beside her during the voyage, tucked into her reuzan, a bag woven of both traditional cotton and new wool fibers which might also be considered a metaphor for the blending of two worlds. The Otomi tribeswomen from the cold regions had adapted their weaving skills to the new fibers introduced over the past seven years by the Spaniards. Now they were selling woolen reuzans and serapes and mantles in thriving marketplaces, and few of them remembered how to use rabbit hair for spinning and weaving.

The coming of sheep and cattle had been one of many changes for the better since the Conquest, but Marina did not like to think of the bloodshed that had preceded these peaceful and beneficial exchanges. She had also seen harm done to the indigena peoples, for not all the rulers were as humane as Hernan Cortes, and not all the Christians from Spain had been as devoted to the Mexicans as the gentle friars from mendicant orders who kept faith with their vows of poverty. But no men were perfect, she had learned from experience, and no community of people could stamp out all the human flaws of greed and exploitation and cruelty. She also had seen that tyranny would not last forever, because something in the human spirit would always resist it.

Trotting beside his mother and Juan on the beach, Martin wanted to shed his sandals and run in the surf. "See the friar over there?" he pointed to a thin figure wearing the tattered habit of a Franciscan monk, talking earnestly to a sailor as they walked along the beach. "He has no shoes. Why can't I go barefoot, too?" He was becoming skillful at persuasion, Marina observed, like his father. The young Martin already knew that friars commanded respect, especially those that lived in poverty.

14

He spoke in Spanish, as he always did in Juan's presence, though he used the Nahuatl language when he and his mother were alone or with servants, never mixing the two languages.

"There's no harm in it," Juan said as Marina looked to him for approval. "Let him enjoy the beach while he can. Soon enough he'll be wearing shoes every day."

Marina untied Martin's sandals and slipped them into her reuzan. As Martin splashed in the surf, moving in the same direction his mother's slow walking, Marina raised her arm and measured the height of the sun's ascent with her hand. At arm's length, the sun stood one hand above the horizon.

Juan had not hired a tameme for this short trip, because the lightweight reed chest seemed a small burden on the broad shoulders of a former soldier. She considered him handsome now, with his curly brown hair and beard neatly trimmed for the long journey ahead, but in her girlhood she would have regarded curly hair and facial hair as defects. His tanned face bore pock marks from his childhood exposure to smallpox, but the scars endeared him to her as proof of his courage and strength. His cotton shirt spread open at the neck, but the warm and humid September day brought rings of sweat in circles below the sleeves. His heavy boots reached almost to his knees, and the pantaloons covering his legs also must have been warm, she thought. Europeans seemed always to wear too much clothing.

"Do you sometimes wish you were a boy again, to play barelegged in the water?" Marina asked Juan, although she kept a mother's watchful eye on Martin.

"I had very little playing as a child," Juan replied. "But I'm glad Martin's life will be different." He did not explain. He seldom talked about his childhood, and so Marina fell silent, thinking again about the anxiety she felt, and wondering why it seemed to blot out her pleasure in Martin's playful splashing or the pleasant anticipation of new adventures ahead.

When Martin ran back to them with a seashell, Juan set down the chest and hoisted the boy to his shoulders. "See that ship, Martin?" he said, pointing toward the Gulf where the three-masted vessel lay anchored. "That ship will soon carry us to Spain, where I was born. Her sails will puff in the wind, and she will fly across the ocean with all of us inside."

Martin's bare legs dangled on either side of Juan's thick shoulders. He clasped his hands under Juan's bushy brown beard and stared in amazement at the scene ahead. The dock was a busy place, with people scurrying about like ants in an anthill.

The passengers were forming a line to board the landing boats, which would carry them a few at a time to the ship. Some of them wore Spanish clothing, the women in long dresses, the men in plumed hats. Retinues of servants and slaves accompanied some of them, dressed in plain huipils and pants woven of maguey fiber. Marina was glad that Juan was taking no servants, and that he had freed his slaves some time ago.

Merchants from the inland villages were leading their heavily loaded mules, horses, and slave trains toward the dock, where the ship's crew were transferring the huge bales onto barges and then into the ship's cargo hold. Groups of sailors bustled past passengers and tamemes carrying their trunks and baggage. The tamemes, naked to the waist, carried their burdens on their backs in baskets or rope-bound bales, secured by leather tumplines braced against their foreheads. Their copper-brown skins, moist with sweat, glowed in the midmorning light.

"How will the ship know where to go, Don Juan?" Martin asked in Spanish, using the title *Don* to acknowledge Juan's rank as a Castilian knight.

"The captain and the pilots steer the ship," Juan said to Martin in the affectionate tones men use with children when explaining the obvious. "I'll show you the helm when we get on board. We'll have many days to explore the ship."

Marina shaded her eyes with her hand and stared at the flat horizon. "Would you tell Martin what you told me about the stars and the compass?" she asked. It still seemed incredible to her that sailors could follow a trackless path in the sea for as long as two Aztec months and be sure of their destination.

"The captain has a compass with a needle that points to the north," Juan said obligingly. "There." He turned and swept his muscular arm in a northerly direction. "And on a clear night, he can see the north star, so he knows which direction he's headed."

"What is Spain like?" Martin asked.

"You'll like it," Juan assured him. "Beautiful flowers grow there, but watch out for the bees because they have stingers, not like the bees here. Most boys have cats and dogs to play with; some even have horses to ride. They like to sing and play guitars." As Martin's eyes widened in excitement, Juan added playfully, "But all of them wear shoes."

"Oh," said Martin, disappointed. He squinted at the horizon, trying to imagine such a strange place. Then he tried to picture the man whose face he could not remember. "Will I see my father there?"

Marina looked quickly at Juan. His face had become stony, like one of the statues in Mayan temples, and she could not read his feelings. She pulled on Martin's arm and spoke to him in Spanish. "Come down now, Martin. You're too big for Juan to carry such a distance. Walk on your own strong legs."

"He needs to know the truth," Juan said. "He's seven years old now; he can understand." He lowered Martin to the beach, set him on the reed chest, and knelt to face him, his strong brown hands grasping the boy's thin shoulders. "Your father will be coming back to Mexico," he said, "and he wants you to go to a Christian school in Spain. So you won't see him. You'll live with me and my family in Castile."

"Won't I ever see him, then?" Martin asked, the inner corners of his eyebrows lifting, his jaw drooping.

"Perhaps when you grow up," Juan said with a gentle squeeze of Martin's shoulders. "It will be best if you don't see him until then, because he's married to a new wife. But in the meantime you can write him letters. You know he cares about you, because he's paying for your education. If you study hard, and learn to read and write, you'll make him proud of you."

Marina marveled at the prospect. She had always been amazed at the Spaniards' ability to send messages with marks on paper. And she knew that wisdom lay in the pages of books. She ached for access to such knowledge. "Could I learn to read and write?" she asked wistfully.

Juan looked perplexed. He straightened, brushing the wet spot on one knee of his pants where he had knelt in the damp sand. He hoisted the chest again to one shoulder as Marina took Martin's hand and resumed their walk. "You don't really need to learn reading and writing," he said. "Most Spanish ladies prefer to be good wives and mothers. Those who want to read books usually go into convents and become nuns."

Marina stiffened as she realized she had offended her husband. "I have so much to learn about Spain," she said apologetically. "I want to please you in all things, if only you'll teach me what I need to know." She knew she was fortunate to have such a husband—an affectionate man, though he sometimes drank too much rum or pulque. He could show outbursts of temper, but he was not quarrelsome. He loved adventure and excitement, and he could become restless after too much time in the comforts of home. She would have to understand this as he made the difficult transition from soldier to merchant. He had told her that merchants were not as highly respected in Spain as the *pochteca* were in the Mexican and Mayan territories.

Juan smiled tenderly and circled his free arm around Marina's shoulders. "You do please me, mi vida," he said. "You'll learn the ways of the Spaniards as quickly as you learned their language. You're beautiful, and you'll be even more beautiful when I find you a proper dressmaker in Cadiz." He stroked her long, straight black hair, securing a lock of it behind one ear. "A lace mantilla, a fan in your hand, black leather shoes with buttons, silk dresses with lots of ruffles and petticoats —you'll be an elegant wife. The other hidalgos will envy me."

Marina looked down at her loose cotton huipil, her ankle-length straight skirt, and her sandaled feet. Embroidered with colorful floral designs, the huipil had seemed elegant when she selected it for the voyage. So comfortably loose and cool in the land of the Mexica, it would seem foreign and perhaps not

17

respectable in the land of the hidalgos.

The feeling of fear returned, the rapid breathing, and she felt a moistness under her long hair at the back of her neck. She lifted her hair and let the breeze cool her neck, wondering again why she felt afraid. She did not fear physical danger, for she had survived jungles, deserts, and battlefields. She did not fear the unknown, for she had faced an uncertain future during most of her twenty-eight years. She should not fear carrying twenty pounds of petticoats, for she had carried as much as two arrobas when she was a slave, and she could still lift Martin when she had to. Surely Juan had in mind for her a life of luxury greater than she had ever known, yet she had never coveted that kind of luxury. If her father were still alive, what would he say to her now? Would he warn her against wanting too much, or would he understand what she was now learning—that unhappiness could come from being given riches one did not need or want?

They were very close to the dock when Martin became restless again. He brushed the sand from his legs and started toward some crates of caged birds waiting to be loaded. "Put on your sandals," Marina admonished. "There could be slivers in the dock or on the ship."

As they stood at the entrance of the dock, a train of tamemes arrived, straining under heavy loads. When one tameme slipped in the loose sand on the dock, Marina rushed to him, steadying his basket with her outstretched arms.

"Are you hurt?" she asked in Nahuatl. Sweat streamed down his body, and blood oozed from under the tumpline that crossed his forehead. His eyes rolled upward; then he collapsed on the ground.

Marina looked around for the tameme's merchant, crying "Help him," in both Nahuatl and Mayan. The merchant, who was checking his list of goods with a ship's crewman, turned to stare at her.

Juan leapt to her side. To her surprise he did not assist her, but pulled her angrily away. "This is not your concern," he snapped. "The tameme belongs to that merchant, not to you. Why can't you remember you're an hidalgo's wife? When you act without thinking, you act like a slave and embarrass me. Will you always think of yourself as a slave?"

Marina recoiled in shock, but before she could answer, the tall friar that she had seen earlier strode up to the prostrate tameme. "He's dead," said the friar, after feeling his forehead and listening for a sign of breath. Then he glared at the merchant, who had run nervously to the friar's side. "You must have burdened him with a load of seven arrobas," he said contemptuously, "and probably goaded him for more than a league's distance. In the name of God and King Charles, take these inhuman loads off the other tamemes, and give them rest

18

and food." His face had a stormy look, and his voice thundered with the indignation of one who speaks with power for the powerless.

* * *

Later that afternoon, when the small family had settled in their cabin, and Martin was exploring the ship with another passenger's son, Marina removed a bottle of rum from the petlacalli chest and poured a cup of rum for Juan. As he sipped it, she pulled Hernan's letter from her reuzan and asked him to read it to her. Juan stretched out along the bunk with his head on Marina's lap, and obligingly read it to her:

"My dear Juan and Marina: My heart is filled with gratitude as I write you this day. Most of the business that brought me to Spain has been brought to a satisfactory conclusion. King Charles and his court were delighted with the acrobats, the oddities, the jewels, and the fine featherwork I brought from New Spain. He has agreed to appoint me Marquess and give me generous territories in New Spain, though he did not appoint me governor as I had hoped.

"Of more immediate concern to you, the Pope was also delighted with the performers from New Spain, and he has issued a bull to legitimize three of my natural children, including Martin. The way is now clear for me to make Martin one of my heirs. I shall also give each of you an encomienda, the income from which should pay for Martin's education. That income will continue to support you if you live longer than I.

"I request that you bring Martin to Spain for his education. We have heard that Bishop Zumarraga has begun a good school for boys in Mexico City, but educational opportunities are greater in Spain. If he chooses, Martin could become a lawyer or scientist, or study theology under the greatest minds of the 16th century.

"The other matter I have attended to," read the letter from Hernan, "is to meet the bride selected for me by my father before he passed away. As you know, I have honored my father's memory by naming Martin after him, and I honored his judgment by giving him power of attorney to arrange my marriage. His choice of Juana de Zuniga, from a well-connected family, has proved excellent. She not only brings a generous dowry to the marriage, but has excellent personal qualities and is devoted to advancing my career. She is young and eager to start a family, so will be coming with me to New Spain as soon as she can make preparations.

"Please keep in touch with me and let me know if there is anything further I can do for you or for Martin. In boundless gratitude for your loyal support during the darkest hours and your contributions to the brightest hours of the conquest of New Spain, I remain your true friend, Hernan Cortes."

Juan folded the letter and returned it to Marina, who replaced it solemnly in her bag. She had heard the letter before and knew its contents. She tossed her head back so no tears would fall. Juan felt the shifting of her body, but he pretended not to notice, closed his eyes as if drowsy, and changed the subject. Feeling mellow with the effects of the rum, he decided to tell her more about the Old World that would be so new to her.

"You'll miss the trees," he told her frankly. "There is a saying that a bird can fly all across Castile without finding a twig to land on. Once there were forests, but all the trees have been used to build houses and ships."

Marina murmured softly to show she was listening. Although she was thinking that the Valley of Mexico could tell a similar story, she said nothing so that Juan would continue talking.

"Castilla means 'little castle' or 'little fort' because the land has been so much divided," he said, his deep voice paced a little faster and higher than usual. "When I left Castilla I was an hidalgo with the honor to bear arms, but no land and no wealth. Too proud to be a merchant, too poor to own land. Desperate enough to become a conquistador and trust everything to my fate as a warrior. But now I return with an encomienda. I have land, and Indians to work it. We will be a proud and prosperous family." He drained the cup and held it, empty, upon his muscular chest.

"What is a dowry?" Marina asked, remembering what Hernan had said in the letter. She was stroking Juan's face and curly hair, her fingers sensing the pock marks on his cheeks. He had survived many dangers; surely the Christian god had looked on him with favor.

"A dowry is the gift a bride's family gives to her and her husband when she marries," Juan replied. "If her family is wealthy, she is used to luxury, and the dowry will help to maintain a good life for her."

"What if a woman has no dowry?"

"Then she has fewer choices for a husband. Some men will not marry a woman without a dowry."

"But you did." She took the cup from him and returned it to the petlacalli chest.

"I'm one of the lucky ones," he said playfully, lifting his face to stare directly into hers. "I married for love."

Marina smiled contentedly down at Juan, remembering their impulsive decision to marry during a military campaign, on a night when Juan had been drinking pulque. Some friends thought he had been rash, that his judgment was impaired, but he had always steadfastly denied that. "I'm lucky, too," she said gratefully.

Juan had also been thinking of a question to ask Marina, and he took this occasion, while the ship rocked peacefully on the waves of the ocean, Marina was in a talkative mood, and Martin was occupied elsewhere. Juan had waited five years, since their marriage, hoping that in time her answer would incline in his favor. Even now it took courage, but he knew he would have no inner peace until he asked, "Do you still love Hernan?"

Marina did not answer immediately, and Juan began to regret having asked the question. It might be better not to know, if a truthful answer would be painful. Marina was usually truthful, though her cleverness in giving ambiguous answers had saved the lives of the Conquistadors more than once. This woman fascinated him with her complexity: soft but courageous, proud yet humble, ingenuous yet wise to the ways of a harsh world. She could also be vexatious at times, ignoring protocol and chatting with servants as if they were her equals. Her natural femininity brought out his own masculinity, yet she often asked unwomanly questions. She had her own ways of obeying him, too: she would do anything he asked but nothing he commanded.

"When a Spaniard speaks of love," she said, stroking Juan's chest and arms, "I'm never sure what he means. Fray Olmedo and Fray Aguilar speak about the love of God, about Jesus' love for humanity. Nahuatl has no word for that kind of love. Spaniards speak of the love of country, which a Mexica or a Maya would call 'loyalty.' Spaniards speak of love of family, which most Mexica would call 'duty.' The Mexica have a Nahuatl word for lust, and even a goddess of love, called Xochiquetzal or 'Precious Flower.' But she's a fertility goddess, and Spaniards don't seem to mean fertility when they speak of love."

"So-shee-KETS-all," Juan repeated in his best imitation of Marina's pronunciation. "Is she the goddess men confess to when they are dying?"

Marina was amused at Juan's pronunciation, yet it came as close as any she had heard from a Spaniard. "No, that is the goddess Tlazolteotl. Can you say her name?"

"Tloss-ol-tay-OH-tul," Juan attempted.

"That's close. She's sometimes called a love goddess, but her name means 'eater of filth' because she takes in all the sins men confess to her. Is that love?" She giggled as she pondered her own question. "Maybe that is a loving act."

Juan did not know how to answer. He had been trying to ask for love, not an analysis of love. He stood up, looked into a small mirror on the cabin wall, and began to comb his hair with his fingers. "Marina," he said seriously, "I must give you some advice. When you get to Spain, forget all this learning from your past. Speak only Spanish, and never give anyone doubts about your faith. Martin must do the same. I haven't told you about the

21

Inquisition, but thousands of people have been burned at the stake for heresy. Mostly they've been Jews who pretended to convert but secretly continued to practice their old customs. I know how sincere you are in your Christianity, but in the present mood of the country, suspicions can be easily aroused."

Marina looked puzzled. "I thank God every day for bringing me to the true faith," she said. "Won't the people of Spain believe that?"

"They will when they get to know you," Juan said. "You're the most devout Christian I've ever known. All I ask is that you watch your tongue until people get to know your heart."

Juan himself was a casual Christian who, having been born to the faith, was comfortably ignorant of its finer points. Marina, on the other hand, had drunk in her adopted religion as a thirsty person drinks water. At the mass baptism of twenty slave women in Tabasco, she had asked more questions than any of them. Juan had seen her animatedly discussing church doctrines with the chaplains on military expeditions, her face glowing in the campfires as they talked. As an interpreter for Cortes, she had participated eagerly in his campaigns to Christianize all the natives, bringing an enthusiasm and eloquence to her words that any priest might envy. He had seen her speaking to them, her hands ornamenting the air with graceful gestures. He had loved her then from a distance, and it seemed to him a divine miracle that he had come to possess her.

Marina stood and wrapped her arms around Juan from behind, snuggling her face against his back. "Thank you for the good advice," she said. "You can depend on my faith, my loyalty, and my devotion to you."

As Juan turned to embrace Marina, a bell sounded. "I love you Marina," he whispered. "I've loved you since I first saw you, and I always will. Someday you may love me as much as I love you, but I'll never ask you for more than you can give. Now let's find Martin. The bell is calling us to dinner."

Marina felt a wave of gratitude. She had a good man in her arms. She would do anything to please him, and since he had asked it, she would never again speak of her early life. But the memories were imbedded in her consciousness, and could not be banished either by a command of Juan's or a will of her own. Memories would come to her in dreams, as the first one did on that night in the year 1529, as the ship headed steadily into the pathless waters toward the Old World of the east, the north star burning on its port side in the bejeweled canopy of the Caribbean sky. In that sky the full moon, marked with the benign face of an old man which alternately resembled a thrown rabbit, looked down upon a world forever changed by the collision of two cultures and the passions of a few adventurers who had dared to explore, to question, to deny limits, and to expand the realms of possibility.

Chapter 3

Childhood Curiosity and Questions of Justice

No one in her birthplace of Paynala could have predicted that she would journey far, overcome great adversity, become the consort of a god, and return to the land of her birth bringing gifts to those who had rejected her. In the early years her tongue and curiosity seemed always to get her into trouble, yet later her tongue and quick wit acquired amazing power.

She had been called Malinalli in the years when she first wakened to awareness of the world, and her first memories were redolent with the scents of the soil and growing things. The rhythms of the seasons, of daylight and darkness, became the rhythms of her consciousness, and because they seemed as natural as breathing, she was not at first aware of their magical vitality. Her first playthings were pebbles and grasses; her first sensory pleasures were the songs of birds, the bright colors of flowers, and the smell of the earth after a cleansing rain. Her first entertainments were the dancing of butterflies, the darting of hummingbirds, the antics of frogs and lizards, and the labors of ants and spiders creating their hills and webs.

Paynala was a small village in the hotlands where the corn grew quickly enough to make a stalk for the slower bean vines, where the farmers prayed to the appropriate gods to send rain at planting time and to withhold it when it might spoil the ripening corn or the exploding cotton bolls. It had a small temple with some priests who watched the stars, alerting the village when the morning star signaled the start of day, advising the farmers when the planting season had arrived.

Marina would always remember the feeling in her childhood of being cradled between earth and sky, sheltered by trees and vines, warmed by a nurturing sun. She would always remember the distant mountains serrating the horizon like the saw-toothed edges of the maguey plants, the flowing river from which the macehualtin drew daily water, and the woods from which they gathered firewood, green boughs, cacao beans, and herbs. She would draw comfort from the solid, fertile soil under her bare feet, speaking to her as the earth does only to children and those who work it with their hands.

Yet nature's benign face could turn fierce, punishing with sweltering heat or shivering cold, hurricanes, earthquakes, undertows in the serene river. Her earliest lessons reinforced the dualities of pleasure and pain, nurture and nastiness, benevolence and brutality. Gods with dual or multiple natures ruled this unpredictable world, where the gifts of life could be bountifully granted or whimsically withheld. Much energy was devoted to divining the wishes of these fractious gods and seeking their approval. Ritual was as necessary as daily grain.

Malinalli had been named for the goddess Malinalli, or "Grass," who reigned on her natal day. She must have been about five years old when her father brought a macehualli home with him, because she was still being given only one tlaxcalli or corncake each day. Malinalli had been watching her mother, Cimatl, grind the corn for their evening meal and slice ripe tomatl fruit with an obsidian knife while the corncakes baked on the comal, filling their house with tempting odors. Cimatl made small rituals of her domestic tasks: she would breathe moisture onto the sacred grains of corn to strengthen them for the cooking-pot, and always she placed a few grains in the household shrine to thank the Corn God Centeotl and his wife Xochiquetzal for their blessings.

Malinalli ran to greet her father, as she usually did when he returned home around sunset. Seeing that he was in serious conversation with the stranger, she waited politely but curiously as the two men walked up a gentle sloping hill toward a piece of level grassy land. As their bodies became silhouetted against the twilight sky, she saw Itzamitl shift his tilmantli until both arms were uncovered, then with gestures of both arms appear to measure out an area of land. The macehualli, wearing only a maxtli around his loins, gestured also, his bare arms confirming those boundaries set by Itzamitl. Then the two men walked toward the house, both smiling. Itzamitl opened his arms to clasp Malinalli as she ran to him.

"This is my daughter, Malinalli," said Itzamitl to the stranger, and then as her mother stepped through the door he added, "and my wife Cimatl. This is Callipopoca, or 'Smoking House'; I've asked him to live here and work the land."

The macehualli kneeled, touching the earth with his finger and then his dusty finger to his tongue, by this gesture showing respect and also making a symbolic vow to speak truthfully. "Your daughter is as beautiful as your wife," he said with his head bowed. "I have a daughter, too, about Malinalli's age."

Cimatl invited Callipopoca to share their meal, but the macehualli declined. He was not worthy, he said, to eat in the house of a tecuhtli, and his wife would be waiting for him.

24

When Callipopoca left, promising to return the next day with his wife and children, Itzamitl hung his tilmantli on a peg in the wall and explained what had happened that day. He sat on an icpalli, a low-backed chair made of reeds, eating his corncakes and beans, his legs crossed at the ankles. Cimatl and Malinalli waited respectfully for him to finish before they would eat.

"I had to judge a case against Callipopoca and his wife today," said Itzamitl. "His wife is a tetlacuicuilique—a healing woman, knows a lot about herbs and medicines. A neighbor accused them of sorcery—said they had stupefied him by charms and stolen his maize while he slept."

"Are they sorcerers?" Cimatl asked, wide-eyed with fright.

"I don't think so," Itzamitl replied, "but it's hard to prove one way or the other. Their neighbor was convinced of their guilt, and he has a good reputation. It was the word of a Toltec jewelry maker against the word of a macehualli."

"I see," said Cimatl, kneeling beside a cloth-covered basket of warm corncakes and taking one out. "But both of them seemed honest to you?"

"Yes, both were convincing. The macehualli has never been in trouble before, and a judge can't favor a nobleman or artisan over a laborer. The Appeals Court at Texcoco has put judges to death for that."

"Sorcerers can be put to death, too. But what if the macehualli and his wife didn't do it? Could someone else have taken the maize?"

"Of course. The jeweler had no fastener on his door. He might be a heavy sleeper who couldn't hear a thief, or he might have just forgotten how much maize he had used already, or he might have drunk too much octli and got confused."

Cimatl smiled knowingly. "Is the jeweler over 50 years old?" She handed Malinalli a plate with sliced tomatl and more corncakes, which Malinalli offered to her father. The young girl was sitting near the hearth, listening intently to her parents, sensing from their solemn tones that their words were especially important that day.

"Yes, he's old enough to drink all the octli he wants. But there's no proof of that either, since no one saw him drinking. I wish I had Tezcatlipoca's smoking mirror, so I could see the whole truth."

"You're a good judge, my husband, but not a god. What did you decide?"

"I tried to give everyone some satisfaction. I required Callipopoca to give the jeweler the amount of maize he said was missing, but I wouldn't sentence Callipopoca to be hanged or sacrificed to the gods."

"And did that satisfy both of them?"

"The jeweler seemed reasonably satisfied, but Callipopoca

had no maize left for his own family. That's why I brought him here. I'll lend him some seed corn from our granary until he can grow some more, and then he can pay it back."

"What if they really are sorcerers?" Cimatl wondered uneasily. "Your kindness could work against us if they are."

"We'll know soon enough; watch them closely if you have any doubts," Itzamitl said firmly, a mild tone of annoyance in his voice. "You know I don't share your belief in black magic. Many things that are thought to be magical have simpler explanations."

Cimatl sighed. "So many things have no explanation; I know there are evil forces in the world."

"Yes, but don't look for evil where there is none, or you may plant it there yourself. I want you to treat our new workers with kindness. I've given them a plot of land, enough to build a house and grow a small garden. It's far away enough from the river so they won't be flooded in rainy season, but near enough to the fields so that Callipopoca can walk there every day."

"Whatever you wish," Cimatl said meekly. "I know you're a good tecuhtli, but sometimes people take advantage of you."

"A good tecuhtli helps his own family by treating his workers well," he said, scooping the last of his beans into his corncake. "Contented workers produce more food. They'll repay your kindness many times over."

"There's wisdom in what you say," Cimatl said. She never argued with Itzamitl even though she might be worried. Usually he did the right thing, but he could be tricked. She could detect his enemies intuitively, sooner than he could, because he always waited until they had actually done something harmful before he condemned them. Still, she felt lucky to have a husband with high principles.

She embraced Itzamitl from behind, nuzzling her cheek against his. "It might be nice to have a healing woman nearby," she said softly, "in case we need a midwife. And Malinalli could use a playmate her own age." Malinalli sensed that her parents were pleased with each other, but she felt left out until she snuggled against her mother's leg. When she felt her mother's arm on her shoulder and her father fed her a corncake from his plate, she knew that the circle of warmth surrounding them was large enough for three.

* * *

The next morning Itzamitl rose from his petlatl, as usual, before dawn. The wail of the conch shell and pounding of wooden gongs at the temple greeted the rise of the morning star in the east, before the sun rose. He was already wearing his maxtli, but he tied his deerskin cactli on his feet and knotted his tilmantli at his right shoulder. He wore the richly embroidered tilmantli not for warmth, since it was the sunny season, but as a symbol of his dignity as a tecuhtli. He did not eat, but walked to the administration building in the center of Paynala where his court and other offices would open at dawn. When he returned home at midmorning, breakfast would be ready.

Cimatl, too, arose before dawn, quickly slipping into her ankle-length cueitl (skirt) and huipil (blouse), tying her cactli on her feet. Then she began the round of tasks for making tlaxcalli, or corncakes. She had soaked dried corn overnight in lime and wood ashes to loosen the outer skin. After honoring the kernels, she crushed them on a stone metlatl with a grinding stone or mano; then she patted the mealy flour into thin cakes to bake on the comal. The comal rested on three large hearthstones, between which the wood or charcoal burned, under which an umbilical cord might be buried to bring luck to a newborn girl. Even the young Malinalli, sitting sleepily by her mother's side, knew that to step on these sacred hearthstones was forbidden. Cimatl believed such irreverence would bring disaster.

The hearthstones rested on firm earth, but the rest of the floor was paved with flat, reddish tezontli stones. Malinalli had not seen many other houses, so she did not know that theirs was the finest in Paynala, the only one with a stone floor and cedar beams to support their roof. It had a door made of deerskin stretched over a wooden frame, which Malinalli opened to look into the awakening courtyard. Birdsong resonated in the rosy pre-dawn air. Dew sparkled on the vines where morning glory blossoms hung unawakened, their petals closed into tubular shapes as if to ward off the forces of darkness.

Malinalli went alone to the temazcalli, or "bath house," a semi-circular structure built of reeds a short distance from the house, where she washed in cold water, making a lather from copal-xacotl, the fruit of the "soap tree." She urinated carefully in an earthenware jar so that her mother could use the urine later as a mordant for dyeing fabric; other wastes were collected in a hollowed log to be used as fertilizer in the gardens and cornfields.

Shortly after sunrise, when the morning glory blossoms had opened to the warmth of the sunrays, Malinalli saw Callipopoca and his family approaching from the direction of the river. His wife carried a small child wrapped in a shawl, and he carried a large basket on his back. A boy about nine years old trudged beside him, carrying a coa or digging stick and a rough reed cage containing a pair of fowls. A girl about six years old balanced a small basket over her arm as she led a small hairless dog by a rope. "There are the macehualli!" Malinalli exclaimed.

"Macehualtin," her mother corrected her, placing a gentle hand on her shoulder as they stood in their doorway. "There are five of them. *Macehualli* means one, *macehualtin* more than one."

"Macehualtin," said Malinalli slowly, imitating her mother's pronunciation perfectly. She focused excitedly on the children. "One of them is a girl."

Cimatl took Malinalli's hand and walked into the courtyard to greet them. "Good morning and welcome," she said to Callipopoca.

"Good morning, Cimatl-tzin," said Callipopoca, using the suffix *-tzin* that showed respect for the wife of a tecuhtli. "We are your new macehualli."

"Macehualtin," Malinalli giggled, noticing his error. "There are five of you."

Cimatl glared at Malinalli and spoke to her with annoyance. "Children do not correct the speech of adults," she said sternly. When Malinalli started to protest, Cimatl broke a thorn from a maguey plant in the yard and pressed it into Malinalli's hand. "This is a warning," she said. "Obey your mother or you will feel this agave thorn." Malinalli could feel the sharp prick, but she did not bleed. She felt wronged, but she soon forgot the scolding as she concentrated on the new family.

Her greatest interest was in the girl Atototl, or "Water Bird," who was a year older than she was and looked like a promising playmate. Atototl had work to do, however, helping her mother Chihuallama ("Old Woman") care for the toddler, two-year-old Moyo. Moyo's name, which meant "mosquito," had been affectionately given to him because he was the family pest. Chihuallama was still nursing him, welcoming the chance to rest every few hours as she sat on the ground and laid Moyo across her lap to suckle her generous breasts. Atototl, whose family called her simply "Toto" or "Bird," had the task of keeping Moyo out of the hearth ashes and teaching him to use the temazcalli.

The adults wore garments of ixtle or agave fiber, as poor families usually did, but the children were too young to wear clothing. All of them were barefoot, with deep brown skins as if blessed by the sun. The nine-year-old son Acamapichtli ("Handful of Reeds"), wore a bag of stones around his neck. "Every month I add weight to this bag," he told the curious Malinalli. "Soon I'll be able to carry 60 pounds, as much as my father."

"Today you can do some real carrying," Callipopoca said with obvious pride in his son. "Come with me to the woods for some saplings." The father and son took their flint knife and a copper axe out of the large basket, and before long they returned carrying two Y-shaped poles for the ends of their hut and a long thin log for a central roof support. Meanwhile, Chihuallama and Toto had cleared a space of grass and stones and swept the dirt to make a firm floor. Malinalli helped them as if they were

28

playing a game, so that her mother would not object to her doing the work of the macehualtin.

Chihuallama, a strong wide-hipped woman with a ready smile, worked as if she knew instinctively what should be done and what her role should be. She gathered palm fronds and cactus spears to dry while the males built a framework for the roof and bound it in place with dried vines. Then they covered the roof with the dried thatch and built the walls by tying thin saplings closely together. In between these larger tasks, Chihuallama managed the routine chores of making meals, nursing Moyo, and planting a few rows of corn and beans for their kitchen garden. Toto made many trips to the river with a pottery jug, often bringing water for the tecuhtli's household as well as her own.

When the structure was complete and the hearthstones in place, the family joined in covering the walls with mud, even Moyo, who got more mud on himself than on the walls. Malinalli joined the mudplastering with enthusiasm, pressing handfuls of wet clay into the cracks between the saplings and smoothing it. She considered this work more enjoyable than playing with dolls or bean games. She didn't realize that someday her willingness to work would help her survive.

Cimatl was kneeling in her own courtyard, one end of her loom strapped around her back, the other anchored to a pole in her patio. She was weaving and watching with amusement as her daughter learned to build a house with walls of wattle and daub. Although a tecuhtli's daughter would never be expected to do heavy work, she could learn something about how others lived. She could also learn to appreciate the superior structure of her own house.

In contrast to the daub walls of the macehualli's hut, the walls of the tecalli, or tecuhtli's house, were built of sun-dried adobe brick, then plastered with white lime. Cimatl had made decorative weavings to hang from the walls in the main room, where bunches of red and yellow peppers hanging from the cedar beams served for decoration as well as food. Unlike most of the one-room village houses, theirs had two separate rooms for sleeping. The petlatl or petates they slept on were the same reed mats that all the villagers used, though important guests were given two petlatls, stacked one on top of the other with cotton padding between them. Sometimes Cimatl slept in one of the sleeping rooms with her children; sometimes she slept with Itzamitl in his room. When a guest stayed in the house, the females all slept in one room and the males in another. Sometimes guests were housed in a special guest house not far from the tecalli. Itzamitl used the guest house for the emperor's tax-gatherers because his duties required him to be their host, but he did not share his own tecalli with them.

The main room of the tecalli was modestly furnished with two icpalli chairs and a petlacalli or "reed house," a chest in which they kept their valuables such as extra clothing and jewelry for special occasions. Pegs in the walls and on the cedar beams provided a place for hanging kitchen utensils like gourds or bowls or baskets. Pegs also served to hang the mantles of her father and his guests. After sunset, the tecalli was lighted with ocotl or pine torches, and the smells of burning pine resin mingled pleasantly with the charcoal smoke and the odor of baking corncakes. On special occasions, Cimatl burned copal incense in the recess on the west wall designated as a shrine.

Much of their daily living centered in the courtyard, where a tall huehuetl tree gave shade on hot afternoons and hosted the birds that sang at dawn. Morning glory vines, climbing the poles toward the thatched roof, shaded the patio and invited bees and butterflies when the blossoms opened. A patch of nopal cacti guarded one corner of the garden. Though ugly and thorny, the nopal provided edible leafy pads and seasonal blossoms and fruits. Maguey or agave plants, strangely ornamental with their spiked and twisted arms, provided thorns and thread for sewing, fiber for weaving, and sap to make sweetened syrup or the fermented drink called octli.

Cimatl was fond of flowers and had planted many herself around the courtyard, though she let the kitchen garden be tended by those of the villagers who owed her husband "wood and water" or other services. The villagers rotated these responsibilities, each serving for a few days each year. Cimatl did not keep fowls or edible dogs in her courtyard as the macehualtin did, because she considered the animals too messy, and the villagers usually provided some meat as their contribution to the support of the tecuhtli. In return, Itzamitl kept stores of corn and amaranth in his granary to distribute to the villagers in times of famine or when major feasts required large amounts of food.

Like the tecuhtli's house, the macehualli's hut had a little shrine to worship the gods and goddesses of corn and rain. For in the important respect of religion, the two families from different social classes felt similar gratitude and a similar sense of duty to the gods who they devoutly believed made their survival possible. In a world where great beauty existed but one's possessions or one's life could be swept away in a moment, every person needed to be attuned to the whims of the gods.

* * *

After the hut was finished and the males went off to plant and weed in the cornfields, Cimatl invited Chihuallama to bring her loom to the courtyard where the two women could work

30

together and talk. Cimatl was at first apprehensive and kept watching for signs of sorcery, omens, or bad luck, but soon the warm-hearted and practical macehualli woman won her confidence. Cimatl admired the fineness of the thread Chihuallama could spin from ixtle fiber, and Chihuallama admired the colorful creative patterns Cimatl could weave with cotton thread. "You must have been born under the sign 'ce xochitl' or 'one-flower,' to be such a skillful weaver," said Chihuallama, and that pleased Cimatl.

Their common experiences as mothers and homemakers bridged the lives of these two women, even though the chasm of their differences ran deep. Whether a woman was wealthy or poor in Paynala, her life was defined by similar duties and concerns: children, spinning, weaving, cooking, cleaning, and observing the religious rituals that affected the home. Both women knew how to dye yarn with vegetable dyes and to create individual patterns in their weaving; each took pride in her skills.

Yet it was not difficult to tell which woman had the more privileged position. Chihuallama often went naked above the waist while working in the sun, though she wore a huipil when she worked with Cimatl in the vine-shaded courtyard. She tied a square of agave fabric around her head to keep her long black hair out of the way, wearing it loose only on certain festival days. Cimatl, like other women in her social class, wore a plain huipil most days but made elaborately embroidered ones for feast days. She rolled her hair into a long roll on each side and wrapped it around her head, the two ends looped in front and sticking out like the little horns of a snail. Although all women dressed similarly in a long skirt or cueitl, Cimatl's was made of soft cotton and tied at the waist with a colorful narrow belt. Chihuallama's clothing was made of ixtle or agave fiber, though she had an embroidered huipil for feast days. Cimatl wore cactli every day, whereas Chihuallama went barefoot.

Cimatl, living in a small town like Paynala, avoided the extreme headdresses and jeweled ear cups that women of high rank liked to wear in larger cities. Here in Paynala her status was well known, and she needed no cumbersome ornamentation to set her apart as a woman of rank. Chihuallama, too, needed no reminders to keep her in her place as a servant or peasant woman. And so the two women worked companionably together, and were very friendly with each other although they could never be friends.

The two young girls, however, became friends, since they did not yet understand the ways that fate divides human beings from each other. Malinalli looked up to Toto, who had a year's more knowledge than she did, and who always seemed to be doing important things. If Toto had work to do, Malinalli helped her with sweeping or tending Moyo as if her chores were a game.

31

Malinalli enjoyed chasing the fowls and playing with the hairless dogs of the macehualtin, because her own courtyard had no such interesting inhabitants. Toto shared with her the mysteries of hatching chicks and puppy litters, which enhanced Toto in Malinalli's eyes, since Toto could predict and explain the marvels of nature to Malinalli's curious mind. It was Toto who explained that ants started a new colony whenever their anthills became too large; her parents said people often did the same.

One day the mothers agreed it was time for their daughters to learn to spin. They presented each girl with a thin clay spindle and small clay whorl, showing them patiently how to spin the tip of the spindle in the tiny hole of the whorl. At first the girls just practiced rolling the spindle, like a firestick, in two hands. Then they learned to spin the rod in one hand, twirling it between their fingers. Then they had to wind a piece of thread on it as evenly as possible. After some weeks of practice, they could take bunches of cotton or agave fiber and stretch them into a yarn. Toto seemed to enjoy this work and became very good at it, but Malinalli found it tedious and was always glad when her share of the work was done. She wondered if she could ever be as good at anything as her friend Toto.

* * *

Malinalli learned about healing powers when she had a stomachache. As she lay on her petlatl moaning, Cimatl walked to the house of Chihuallama and asked what to do. "Make some atole from the corn flour," Chihuallama advised, taking a jar of dried leaves from her cooking area. "Make it very thin, and crush these leaves into it, while I talk to Malinalli."

Chihuallama picked up one of her hairless dogs from the courtyard and took it into the sleeping room where Malinalli lay. She placed the wriggling dog on Malinalli's stomach. "Hold this warm little dog," she said, "while I pray to the god Ixtlilton."

"Who's Ixtlilton?" Malinalli asked, clasping the small dog and feeling its heat on her skin.

"He's the black-faced god who heals children."

"A god who heals children?" Malinalli was amazed.

"Yes. When no other cures work, children can go to his temple and drink the black water that his priests keep there. But his temple is far, far away. Now be quiet while I hold this black stone over you and pray." Chihuallama held the stone over the child, passing it rhythmically back and forth. "Oh Ixtlilton, let the magic of your stone draw forth the stones from the body of this child," Chihuallama chanted. Malinalli listened in fascination, but felt no movement of stones in her body.

After chanting this prayer several times, Chihuallama decided to try a different approach. She brought a deep bowl full of water, then bent Malinalli's head over it until her face was reflected in the water as if in a mirror. "Has this child lost her tonalli? Come, Chalchiutlicue, mother of the jade stone, you who have a jade cueitl, you who have a jade huipil, green skirt, green blouse, woman of jade, tell us the nature of this child's illness." She looked into the water intently. "If your reflection is darkened, Malinalli, that is a sign that your tonalli has been stolen."

Cimatl entered with the bowl of thin gruel. "Are you feeling better, Malinalli?" Malinalli lay back on the petlatl, curled on her side with her knees almost to her chin, and hugged the dog closely to her. The dog licked her arm, whimpered a little, and curled comfortably within the curve of her body.

"I don't feel good, Mother," she moaned. "Is my tonalli stolen?"

Cimatl looked at Chihuallama. "What do you think?"

"The reflection did not look darkened. She will probably get well. See if she can drink the atole now."

Malinalli sat up, still hugging the dog and feeling its warmth on her own small body. Cimatl fed her the gruel from a shallow bowl, telling her about the black dog that leads people to Mictlan after they die. "And there they don't have any more pain, but live in a paradise where they don't need food or water."

The pain slowly went away, and Malinalli slept. Chihuallama later said she was sure her chants and prayers had worked; Cimatl was sure that gruel and herbs had cured the stomachache; Malinalli always gave credit to a little dog who comforted her with its warmth.

* * *

"There is a famine in the Valley of the Mexicas," said the stubby merchant Opochtli, standing in Itzamitl's courtyard in his ragged, patched cloak and dirt-stained cactli. "They need corn and beans. Squashes don't travel too well, but I'll take any grain you can spare to Tenochtitlan."

"I'm sorry to hear that, Opochtli," said Itzamitl, walking with his pochtecatl friend toward the granary. "We've had good harvests here the last few years. We can probably spare five or six heavy baskets for your caravan."

"Will you have enough left for the village?" Opochtli looked around at the well-stocked granary with satisfaction.

"I think so. We'll have about the same amount in reserve." Itzamitl closed the granary and secured the door, then walked back toward the house with Opochtli.

"Fine. I'll be back with my tamemes tomorrow. I can pay you in cacao beans or quills filled with gold dust. Which would you prefer?"

33

"Probably the quills. The cacao beans might be useful in Tenochtitlan for food as well as for money."

"Right. The nobles would rather have chocolate to drink than turquoise or jade or quetzal feathers. What would you like me to bring from Tenochtitlan on the return trip?" Itzamitl laughed. "Then you'd get your quills back again, wouldn't you, my friend? But I'm glad you pochteca are willing to do travel and trading. If you go through Cholula, bring some of their wonderful pottery. Cimatl loves their red and black designs. And maybe a copper mirror for Malinalli."

"Ah, yes. Copper mirrors don't break as easily as obsidian. I prefer obsidian myself, but sometimes the edges flake off."

"Volcanic glass," Itzamitl concurred. "When it flakes the sharp edges can cut little girls' fingers."

Opochtli nodded and seated himself on the icpalli offered by Itzamitl. The two men smoked yetl in reed pipes as they talked.

"This famine has changed everything," the merchant mused. "Up until now, the traffic's all been in luxury goods—precious stones, tropical feathers, chocolate, rubber, gold dust, flower pastes for perfume, cosmetics, face-paint, embroidered mantles. I've never carried food before—never had to."

When he returned the following evening, Opochtli brought twenty tamemes, each carrying on his back a basket that would hold 60 pounds of food. He also brought five warriors, dressed in feathered headdresses and shields. They carried long spears, bows, and arrows. Opochtli spoke with Cimatl as his tamemes loaded their packs in the granary under Itzamitl's supervision.

"Why are you taking warriors?" asked Cimatl, as Malinalli inspected the row of solemn-faced warriors, touching their feathered shields admiringly. Malinalli was puzzled that the merchant in the ragged cloak seemed to be giving orders to these splendidly arrayed individuals. To her young mind, those who dressed well always seemed to be in charge. Perhaps Opochtli had a secret power over the warriors, she thought.

"We might be in danger," explained Opochtli. "We're carrying some tribute to Emperor Moctezuma as well as trade goods to sell. The emperor offers special protection to his pochteca to be sure the supplies for Tenochtitlan aren't stolen."

"Is there a lot of theft?"

"No, because the punishments are very severe. Death to a merchant who cheats the emperor or his nobles. If brigands attack a caravan, the emperor will send his own army to protect them. If his soldiers catch a would-be thief, they'll sacrifice him at the temple of Huitzilopochtli."

"What could be meaner than stealing food intended for hungry people?" Cimatl said. "Thieves deserve strict punishment."

Malinalli was listening to the conversation with great

curiosity. She wondered whether people who stole food were punished more than those who stole feathers or jewels. She wondered what it meant to be sacrificed at the temple of Huitzilopochtli, but she knew children were not supposed to interrupt grown-ups when they were talking. She stored her questions in her memory for a later time.

"Moctezuma has formed a guild for pochteca," Opochtli said proudly. "I'm going to be inducted as a member when I reach Tenochtitlan. Not every trader can be a member of the guild. In addition to the protection of his army, we have our own courts and our own religious ceremonies."

That night they witnessed the religious ceremony as Opochtli gathered his warriors around the hearth and prayed to the god Yacatecuhtli, "Lord Who Guides," the protector of traveling merchants. Opochtli burned incense and threw magic figures cut out of paper into the fire.

"We give to this fire these tokens of our veneration," said the merchant solemnly. "When we return, we will bring to this fire an even greater feast; we will share with this fire the good fortune that comes from our journey."

Malinalli watched in fascination as the flames licked and consumed the paper figures. The heavy smell of incense filled the room, and the fire threw shadows of the warriors onto the wall, making them larger than life. Then Opochtli signaled to one of the warriors, who left the room and returned with a blue cotinga bird in a cage of reeds. Opochtli reached into the cage, caught the bird in his hands, and twisted it by the neck.

"Yacatecuhtli, receive this offering," Opochtli prayed, throwing the crumpled bird into the fire. "Guide and protect us, your servants, so that we may accomplish our trade mission and return safely."

All eyes were downcast respectfully as the flames enveloped the blue feathers and the tiny clenched claws, and the smell of singed feathers mingled with the smell of pine and incense. No one noticed the downcast face of a five-year-old, its wetness shining softly in the dying firelight.

* * *

A few days later one of the villagers who brought wood and water also brought news that the calpixqui were coming. Cimatl and Malinalli hastily picked flowers and branches of foliage to decorate their main room. Then Cimatl made a chocolate drink of ground cacao beans, flavored with vanilla and sweetened with honey, whipped into a froth. This was the greatest luxury her husband could serve the tax-gatherers when they arrived.

"Is it time for the calpixqui to come again?" she asked her husband when Itzamitl arrived home for his midmorning meal.

Itzamitl drew a roll of bark-paper from the petlacalli chest. "They collected the usual tribute items only 40 days ago," he said. "Here's the list. I wasn't expecting them for another 40 days."

The noise of a conch shell and beating drum announced the arrival of the calpixqui and their caravan of tamemes and warriors. Itzamitl walked out into the courtyard to greet them, and Malinalli followed curiously.

The calpixqui—two of them—walked stiffly and held their chins so high that they appeared to be looking down when they were looking straight ahead. They wore rich embroidered tilmantli and maxtli; their cactli, like those of the warriors, were laced with criss-crossed thongs to the knee, and feathered bands circled the calves of their legs just below their knees. Their shining hair was bunched in a knot on their heads, held in place with a colored band. Each of them carried a bouquet of flowers, smelling it as he walked, as if disdainful of other smells of the countryside. Two tamemes whose baskets were not yet filled walked alongside the two calpixqui with fly-whisks, brushing away insects and flies.

"Welcome, ambassadors of Moctezuma," said Itzamitl. "Please come inside for food and chocolate." As they followed him inside and Malinalli served them hot drinks, Itzamitl apologized for not being quite ready to receive them. "We don't have all the tribute items ready for you yet," he said.

"Especially the embroidered tilmantli," Cimatl added. "It takes our women the full 80 days to make that many garments."

"Those can wait until our next trip," said the chief calpixque, sitting on an icpalli and sipping his cup of chocolate. "Your wife can leave now while we talk business. Today we're gathering food items. There's a famine in the Great Valley of the Mexica."

"Yes, I've heard of it," said Itzamitl. "We're praying to Tlaloc every day in our little temple to send you rain." He nodded to Cimatl, who left the room showing some irritation, but Malinalli sat quietly in a corner, ignored because she was a child.

"We thank you for your prayers," said the calpixque in a voice that, to Malinalli's ears, lacked warm tones. "But we also need food. Your tribute is being increased to include maize and amaranth, beans, fowls, and dogs. Anything that can alleviate the hunger."

"Of course we want to help." Itzamitl was sitting on the petlacalli, having given the two reed chairs to the guests. "We sent our surplus with a pochteca caravan a few days ago."

"In hard times, we all have to sacrifice for the good of the empire," said the calpixque with the flat voice. He waved the other one toward the granary. "See what is left in the granary, and take half of that," he ordered one of his men. "And take the fowls and dogs from the macehualtin huts."

Malinalli looked distressfully at her father. Surely he would stop these thieves, she thought. He has been a brave warrior. He is a judge who knows right from wrong. But he merely answered with his lips in a straight line and his eyes downcast, "Take what you need from the granary; those stores are for the common good. But the dogs and fowls belong to a poor family here who are also hungry. They've raised the animals to eat or trade for corn. I can't give them to you."

"Then the macehualli will give them up," said the calpixque, rising to his feet. "It's his duty to sacrifice for the empire. The farmers benefit when the emperor makes sacrifices to the gods so that the sun will keep shining and the crops will grow. Each farmer must carry his share of the burdens."

Itzamitl could see there was no point in arguing. "Then I ask you to make a record of the tribute on this bark paper and sign it with your hand print."

The calpixqui collected most of the remaining grain, beans, dogs, and fowls; then they signed the record made by Itzamitl, who accepted this fate with resignation. When they had gone, Malinalli dared to speak for the first time. "Why did they take the dogs and fowls from Callipopoca?" she asked in anguish.

"You heard the calpixque. Times are hard. We all have to sacrifice."

"Will they really eat the animals?" Malinalli asked, tears starting to flow. She regarded the domesticated creatures as pets, and had never considered what fate lay in store for them.

"Yes, of course, Malinalli. The animals would be food for someone even if they stayed here."

"Then are they stealing food from Callipopoca? Isn't it wrong to steal food from hungry people?"

"Maybe other people are hungry too," Itzamitl said irritably because he couldn't justify the actions of the calpixqui or his own apparent cowardice. "Why do you ask so many questions?"

"Because I want to know," Malinalli answered naively. "Is it true that the emperor keeps the sun in the sky? Is that why we send him tribute every year?"

Itzamitl did not answer directly. "I'll tell you all about that when you're older," he said. He lifted her gently onto his lap and stroked her hair. "You're getting to be quite a talker," he said. "I think I'll call you 'Tenepal' now that you're old enough to have a name of your own."

"What does Tenepal mean?" Her father's strategy of changing the subject was working; she wiped away her tears and looked at him expectantly.

"It means 'one who speaks much and with liveliness'—a perfect description of you."

Cimatl came into the room to clear away the cups. "Malinalli

37

Tenepal," she said. "Yes, that suits you. Now it's time for you to get to sleep."

When Malinalli's steady breathing indicated she was asleep, Cimatl asked her husband what had happened with the calpixqui. "They left us hardly any grains for emergencies," she complained. "And Chihuallama was very upset at losing her dogs."

"You can see why the Cuetlaxtecs once shut the Mexican tax-gatherers in a house and set fire to it," Itzamitl said bitterly.

"Are they exceeding their authority?" Cimatl asked. She, too, was upset with their greediness.

"I can't tell yet. But at least I have good records, and if they're acting without direct orders from the emperor they could eventually be put to death for fraud."

"I hope they won't do you any harm," said Cimatl, her instincts raising fear in her heart. "A man who reports fraud can put himself in great danger."

"I'm not afraid of them. I'm doing my job by sending all the required tribute through them. The courts at Texcoco will protect me if necessary."

"What shall I tell Malinalli? Malinalli Tenepal, that is."

"If she asks, tell her to be grateful for what she has. They could have taken much more than they did."

"What more?" Cimatl said angrily. "They left only a couple of jars of maize."

"They could have taken the children," said Itzamitl.

Chapter 4

Lessons of Life and Death

When Malinalli Tenepal turned six years old she began to receive a corncake and a half each day, a matter of pride with her because she seemed to be catching up to her friend Toto, who was seven and received the same amount. The girls had become involved that year in the cycle of maize growing, in all its tyranny and glory, by watching and helping Toto's father, Callipopoca, and her brother Acamapichtli, who was ten. The males cleared brush from a new milpa or field and piled it up to dry, their long arms swinging flint knives in rhythm before their strong stocky bodies. At the end of the dry season in the month of Tozoztontli (late March), they burned the dried brush and cactus spears, filling the air with thick smoke. Then they worked the ashes into the soil with their coas, or digging sticks, which Callipopoca said would help the corn grow.

After the first rain the males dug the holes for the maize, then let the girls drop four or five kernels in each hole and cover them with the damp, dark earth that smelled of roots. Malinalli liked this work better than the tedious spinning, but once the maize was planted the males sent the girls back to their feminine chores. They said men should take care of the weeding while the corn grew, bend the stalks to keep birds away when it began to ripen, and do the heavy work of harvesting in the month of Teotleco (late September). Callipopoca said the corn god was a hard taskmaster who demanded almost relentless toil in return for his bounty.

The growth cycle went especially well in the year 2 Reed [1507]. Malinalli Tenepal and Toto watched with satisfaction as the green shoots poked through the brown earth, unfolded into a leafy stalk, thrust upward into the blue sky. Within a month the weather-partners of sun and rain had turned the neat rows of plants into a forest higher than their heads, so that they could sit in the shade of the stalks or look at the sky through sun-drenched leaves topped with golden tassels. As the corn ripened, the fields gave off a sweet odor, luring birds and insects to share the bounty. At harvest time the men from the village gathered the ripe corncobs into big baskets. Soon the granary was filled with many baskets of golden corn dried on the cobs. The women of the village took what their families could eat and store in their own huts, then transferred the surplus corncobs to tall pottery vessels with lids, storing them in the tecuhtli's granary for future need. Chihuallama also sliced some of the fresh corn off the cobs to dry as kernels, and as she spread the golden kernels around her on the granary floor, the plump peasant woman looked as regal as a queen surrounded by piles of gold dust. There was amaranth, too, tiny grains shaken from their grassy stalks and collected into pottery vessels to be stored and used during the dry season. A sweet musky smell permeated the granary; general satisfaction pervaded the village.

The grateful farmers celebrated by offering a feast for Tlaloc the rain god in the month of Tepeilhuitl (late October). The girls worked beside their mothers making figures of amaranth paste representing the mountain gods, who served Tlaloc. His name, their mothers said, meant "He Who Makes Things Sprout."

Acamapichtli, learning to carve with a flint knife, made wooden snakes. He boasted that, although the girls' amaranth creations would be eaten, his snakes would endure after the feast. Chihuallama suggested burying the wooden snakes in the milpas to honor the mountain gods and bring rain for the next growing season.

Itzamitl and Cimatl hosted Tlaloc's feast, inviting everyone from the village over a two-day period. Guests wore their finest tilmantli, woven in intricate patterns or embroidered with brightly colored borders, and those who owned jewelry wore earcaps or bracelets. A few men and women flaunted their rank by wearing headdresses decorated with parrot or cotinga feathers. The guests feasted on roasted corn and fowl, beans, peppers, tomatoes, and cocoa. Children ate the amaranth figures they had baked. Musicians played flutes, drums, and the two-toned teponaztli gongs, as dancers performed to their rhythm with swirling feathers and rattles around their ankles. Student poets from the telpochcalli came to recite the poems they had composed.

Octli was provided for the guests, but no one became drunk, to Itzamitl's great relief, because he would have had to order punishment for public drunkenness. A macehualli convicted of that crime would have his head shaved in public while a crowd jeered insults at him, but if he repeated the offense, it could mean death. Distinguished personages like priests or government officials could meet with death for a first offense. No one exceeded the bounds of propriety, so the feast for Tlaloc was a happy feast, with no unhappy consequences following it. Life was good in Paynala in the year 2 Reed.

* * *

Visitors arrived in the year 2 Reed from two directions. Opochtli, the merchant, returned after a year of traveling to the great city of Tenochtitlan to the west, and Papalotl, Cimatl's sister, came from Coatzacoalcos to the east, the place where the land ended at the edge of the great waters.

Opochtli was just passing through; he was eager to get to his own home in nearby Oluta so he could bathe. His tattered and sloppily mended tilmantli gave off such a stink that Cimatl would not invite him inside the tecalli, so he talked to Itzamitl in the courtyard.

"I have an embarrassing problem," Opochtli told Itzamitl as the two men sat on the tezontli stones in the courtyard and smoked yetl.

"My nose tells me what that problem is," Itzamitl joked.

Opochtli smiled good-naturedly. "I vowed to Yacatecuhtli that I wouldn't bathe for a year if he would smile with favor on my trade mission, and he blessed me with great success. The emperor was most grateful for the goods I brought. He heaped gifts upon me and installed me in the guild of pochteca."

"Then what is the problem, friend?" Itzamitl asked.

"I can't go home with all this merchandise. If I do, my neighbors will think I'm rich. I left with 20 tamemes; now I have 30, as well as 10 slaves. All of them are loaded with valuable goods."

"Where are they now?"

"In a camp half a day's journey from here. I wanted to ask you a favor before I brought them in."

"What can I do for you?"

"Store these goods for me until I can arrange for a feast in honor of Yacatecuhtli, the patron god of merchants and travelers, in the month of Tlaxochimaco."

"That's twelve months from now, a long time."

"Yes, but I'll give you a choice of gifts from those I store with you, and you can present many gifts to the guests."

"Why don't you give them away yourself?"

"A merchant can't appear to be too successful, too wealthy. Then people will say he's acting like a tecuhtli, that he doesn't remember his place."

"I see," said Itzamitl thoughtfully. "It seems a bit deceitful, but your plan makes some sense. Since you and I don't have to pay taxes, we can redistribute some of the wealth we've acquired from the people who do."

"Then you'll help me out?"

"I guess I can do that. The granary is full, but I have a guest

41

house not far away that we could use. Can you leave a guard there for that length of time?"

"Of course. I'd be most grateful."

"I'd like to give you a gift in return," said Itzamitl. "Yet apparently you don't want fine mantles or jewelry."

"I couldn't wear them in public," said Opochtli regretfully. "But there is one thing you could do for me if you would."

"Anything one friend can do for another," Itzamitl said.

"Then I'd ask you to put in a good word for my son Chimalli and my daughter Metzli. I'd like them to be educated in the telpochcalli, along with the pilli, the children of the nobles. I can pay, of course, but the priests take only a few children who aren't born pilli. Your recommendation would carry much weight with them."

"I could certainly do that, if they want to go to the telpochcalli in Paynala where I have some influence. Are they old enough to attend?"

"Chimalli is ten; he could start when the next class enters. Metzli is just six, but she's been dedicated to the temple since birth. She might begin lessons with the priestesses when she's eight."

"She's the same age as Malinalli, then," Itzamitl said. "Is she quick to learn and talkative like Malinalli?"

Opochtli smiled and stood up to leave. "She doesn't talk as much, and she isn't so bubbly. But she's serious and obedient; she'll be a good student and probably a good priestess some day."

"Can you decide her fate so early? Suppose she wants to marry and have children?" Itzamitl stood also, and walked with his friend toward the road.

"It was in her tonalli at birth. We named her 'Metzli' after the moon god because she was born under a moon sign. The tonalpouhqui predicted her fate from the tonalmatl, but even if the prediction is wrong, she'll obey her father's wishes."

"You're lucky; my daughter Malinalli sometimes has a mind of her own. Did the tonalpouhqui foretell a warrior's life for Chimalli?"

"Yes, but that was a safe enough prediction," Opochtli laughed. "Every male must be a warrior at times. Merchants sometimes have to fight against brigands; farmers sometimes have to put down their coas and take up spears to defend their villages. But Chimalli wants to be a professional warrior; the desire overrides everything else. We named Chimalli after the shield we presented to him at birth. He clutched it in his tiny hand, and we thought that was a sign."

"Chimalli could certainly learning warrior arts in the telpochcalli here," said Itzamitl. "As for the girls, Cimatl would like Malinalli to go to the temple of Quetzalcoatl. Would Metzli consider that when she's old enough?"

"I think she'd like that," Opochtli replied with enthusiasm. "I've heard they really educate girls there—in history and rhetoric as well as weaving and cooking."

"When will I meet these youngsters?" Itzamitl gave his friend a parting touch on the shoulder as they reached the road.

"I'll bring them to the feast for Yacatecuhtli," Opochtli said. "I hope Malinalli will be there too. I'll invite her tomorrow when I bring the merchandise to store. Tell her I'll have a bath before I come tomorrow."

The merchant's optimism cheered Itzamitl, but after he left the tecuhtli wondered. Suppose the world came to an end before the following year? As the sheaf of years reached 52, astronomers predicted the end of the world. Cimatl had warned him that only very powerful magic could save it.

* * *

The next day as Opochtli brought his caravan of tamemes to the tecuhtli's house, he encountered a small group of travelers coming from the east.

"Make way for Papalotl-tzin," said a man in the regalia of a warrior, with a feathered shield, a headdress of red and yellow parrot feathers, and a lip-plug of jade that made his lower lip sag when he spoke. "She's coming to visit her sister, Cimatl-tzin, and the tecuhtli Itzamitl-tzin."

Opochtli bowed and gestured for them to go ahead, waiting as the couple and two servants, each carrying a full petlacalli on his back, moved ahead of them. "I'm in no hurry," said Opochtli with his eyes respectfully downcast, wondering for a moment if he should call his own warriors from the end of the caravan. But the travelers were obviously not concerned with robbing him, only with pushing past him quickly. The warrior pushed Opochtli aside with his spear, holding his hand over his nose.

Opochtli hurried to get his business done. He stored about half of the goods he had brought from Tenochtitlan—many quachtli of woven cotton, robes with rabbit-fur trim, various pottery vessels, many copper hatchets, cosmetic ointments and dyes, and even salt made from the salty waters of Lake Texcoco.

He saw Cimatl and Malinalli only long enough to give them presents he had brought for them and invite them to the feast he would be giving for Yacatecuhtli. He sensed that he might be intruding upon a family visit, because Papalotl's weeping red eyes made him suspect some grief had befallen her. He also heartily disliked the soldier who had escorted her, the man with the jade lip-plug. Such arrogance and hardness would surely bring the warrior to ruin if he were a merchant.

Cimatl and Malinalli were pleased with the copper mirrors Opochtli brought for each of them, and Cimatl liked the pottery

43

from Cholula. To Malinalli's great delight, Opochtli also left for her several clay dolls with arms that moved, and several more for the macehualtin, who might later bury them in the cornfields for good luck. Cimatl and Malinalli did not hold their noses, but thanked the ragged merchant for his kindness in remembering them. They did not urge him to stay, since he was eager to get home to his own village, but turned their attention to their newly-arrived guests.

Young Malinalli, awestruck with Papalotl's great beauty, instantly decided she wanted to be like this aunt she had never seen before. Her sad eyes, dark and shining like those of a deer, suggested tragedy and mystery; she carried her head erect with dignified grace. Although her name meant "Butterfly," Papalotl moved like a snail, every step hesitant and slow. Her shiny black hair was not twisted in the fashion of noblewomen, but hung loosely down her back to her waist. The wind blowing her hair, the sun shining on it, her hands brushing it back—all these attracted Malinalli's devotion, as if her aunt were a goddess, or certainly the most beautiful woman she had ever seen. Papalotl's plain white cueitl and huipil were made of fine cotton. Her cactli had only a hemp sole, with no deerskin leather at the back to protect her heels, but her feet were soft and pretty, not calloused like those of macehualtin.

She had traveled under the protection of Anecoatl, or "Water Serpent," who seemed to be taking charge wherever he went. "I saw Papalotl's husband killed on the battlefield," Anecoatl explained to Itzamitl as the two men ate their evening meal and the females served them. "Omehuatl died a brave death. I came to give the message to Papalotl, so she would know that her husband is now traveling every day with the sun god."

"Thank you for bringing her here, Anecoatl," said Itzamitl. "Cimatl will comfort her as only a sister can do."

"I was glad to do it, Itzamitl-tzin," said Anecoatl with a faint smile, which looked to Malinalli like a sneer when she combined the expression on his face with the tone in his voice. She had never before heard anyone use the suffix -tzin so much, as if he could not forget he was in the home of a tecuhtli.

"What battle did you serve in?" Itzamitl asked politely, not just to flatter his guest but to learn more about the death of his brother-in-law.

"It was one of the xochiyaoyotl, the flowery wars. You've heard about them, I suppose?"

"Oh yes, I served in some, when I was younger. They're holy wars. I wasn't supposed to kill my captives, just bind them and take them alive. I did take a few captives, but I didn't claim my right to their arms and legs. I don't like sacrifices."

"I didn't feel that way," Anecoatl said with a superior smile. "We know that a warrior who gives his life in sacrifice to the

44

gods will travel with Huitzilopochtli just as surely as one who dies in battle. Probably he has less pain, too, because yauhtli powder is thrown in his face when he's spread out on the stone." When Anecoatl spoke, Malinalli noticed that his lower teeth showed while his upper lip remained perfectly still. She also noticed that his way of talking didn't match his words.

"So you watched the actual ceremonies?"

"Of course," Anecoatl said proudly. "I followed my own captives up the steps of the great temple in Tenochtitlan. I watched while the priests took out their hearts and offered them to the sun god, proud to be the one who'd brought such offerings to Huitzilopochtli. Those are the fortunes of war; today my captive dies; tomorrow it could be my turn."

"Perhaps we should not talk about this in front of the women and Malinalli," said Itzamitl. This comment aroused Malinalli's curiosity, and she listened more carefully than before.

"Many women come to the ceremonies," scoffed Anecoatl. "The ceremony is quite spectacular. And the women know that Huitzilopochtli needs the food of human blood to make his journey across the sky each day."

"Let's go into the courtyard to smoke," Itzamitl suggested. "The women have been patiently waiting their turn to eat."

Malinalli was relieved when Anecoatl left the next morning, saying that he had to report for duty in Tenochtitlan. He spoke to Papalotl before he left, offering to return later to take her home, but she discouraged him, saying she would stay quite a while with her sister. Cimatl was the only family she had left, Papalotl told him, since her parents had died of illness shortly after she was married, and now her husband was dead also.

Papalotl had brought two servants with her, a married couple, and the woman did the grinding of the corn for the midmorning meal. But Papalotl sent the couple outside to sweep the courtyard while she worked with her sister at the hearth. The two women patted the corncakes into shape and baked them on the comal, talking softly as they worked.

"I don't feel much like eating," Papalotl said, patting a corncake half-heartedly.

"I'm not surprised," Cimatl commented. "You must be grieving over Omehuatl's death." She placed a corncake on the hot comal, concluding from the sizzling sound that the comal was about the right temperature for baking.

"Yes, I miss him," Papalotl sighed, tears forming in her almond eyes. "I don't know what I'll do without him."

"I'm sure you have many choices," Cimatl said consolingly, "but you shouldn't decide too soon. A grieving heart may not be able to choose wisely."

"Anecoatl has asked me to marry him," Papalotl said in a weary voice. "But I don't know."

"You don't have to decide now," Cimatl said. "He may not even return from the wars."

"Even if he did," Papalotl said, "I might not marry him. I know he's distinguished himself in battle, and he's handsome, but I'm not sure he'd be a good husband. I think he's the kind who'd never leave his wife alone. He keeps trying to touch me."

"Perhaps that isn't all bad," Cimatl said. "He's a virile man in top physical condition. He's attracted to you. That's natural at his age."

"I've been thinking of marrying one of my slaves," Papalotl said. "The man who's acting as my steward now, taking care of my home and my fields while I'm away."

"A slave?" Cimatl questioned.

"He's only a temporary slave. He has to work off a debt to my husband, then he'll be free again. He isn't the kind of criminal slave who could be sold in the marketplace."

"Well, I guess stranger things have happened," Cimatl said reassuringly. "I've heard about a king rewarding a good slave by making him a noble, and a queen promoting a commoner to knighthood then keeping him as her personal guard. Are you attracted to this slave of yours?"

"I get a real tickle in the loins when I look at him," Papalotl said, causing her sister to giggle.

Malinalli was just about to ask what that meant, but her aunt Papalotl suddenly rose to her feet, grabbed a bowl from a stack of clean dishes near the hearth, and vomited into it.

"Run quickly, Malinalli," Cimatl ordered, "and get Chihuallama. Aunt Papalotl is sick this morning." As Malinalli dashed from the room, Cimatl put her arms around her sister's shoulders and led her to the sleeping room. "No wonder you don't feel like eating this morning," she said soothingly as Papalotl lay down on the petlatl.

"Yes, now you know why I came here," said Papalotl. "I'm pregnant."

* * *

While Chihuallama made an herb tea for Papalotl, Malinalli stayed with Toto and little Moyo in the courtyard. She brought the clay dolls with movable arms that Opochtli had given her, presenting one to Toto and one to Moyo. Moyo tried putting the doll into his mouth, then made a face when he realized it did not taste good. The two girls laughed.

Their laughter came to a sudden halt when Moyo threw the clay doll down onto the courtyard floor. It broke into several pieces, scattering over several of the large tezontli stones.

"Naughty Moyo!" cried Malinalli. "That doll was a god figure. Now you may be in trouble."

46

"He's too little to understand," Toto said defensively. She had been a second mother to Moyo since he was born, and she defended him in a maternal way.

"I'm sorry. It's my fault for giving him the doll in the first place," Malinalli said apologetically. "I'll clean it up. It's supposed to be buried in a cornfield anyway, for luck."

"I hope it's good luck," Toto said wryly. "Anyway, thanks for giving us the dolls. It was very nice of you."

The girls were picking up the clay pieces when they heard the sound of the conch shell and the wooden drum announcing the arrival of the calpixqui. They started to run toward Toto's hut, but Moyo was too big for them to carry, and his stubby little legs could take only the tiniest steps.

He stumbled, and they stopped to help him to his feet. But as they looked up, they saw a pair of muscular legs, with golden thongs laced in crisscross fashion to the knees, planted firmly in their path. A dark brown arm encircled by a gold bracelet reached down and grabbed Moyo, lifting him wriggling and squalling into the air.

"Look at this child's hair," said the calpixque to his companion. "It has little whorls on the crown of the head."

"Perfect!" exclaimed the other, who was not a calpixque but a priest. "The sign of favor from Tlaloc. He'll be perfect for the ceremony of Atlcoualco, the stopping of the water."

Malinalli thought the priest smelled worse than Opochtli had; his long hair hung down in matted strings, and his black tunic was stiff with dirt and caked blood. She grabbed Moyo and tried to pull him away from the calpixque, but he laughingly held her down with one arm and handed Moyo to the priest. Toto stood helplessly by, crying and calling for her mother.

Chihuallama came running toward them, her short heavy body propelling her up the path as if she had sprouted wings. Cimatl was running close behind her, and both women were puffing, their breaths and their voices coming in short bursts of effort.

"Stop!" cried Chihuallama. "That's my child."

"Leave him alone," cried Cimatl.

"Shut up, women!" snarled the calpixque, standing between them and the priest.

Holding Moyo and trying to stifle his screams, the priest also spoke with considerable effort. "You the mother?" he asked Chihuallama. "Tell this child to stop squirming. He's being given a great honor. He'll be a gift to Tlaloc and go directly to the paradise of green gardens."

"No!" cried Chihuallama in great anguish.

"Please, kind lords," begged Cimatl. "Tlaloc has been kind to us this year; surely he's satisfied. We don't need to appease him with any more children."

"We'll hold the child until the month of Atlcoualco," said the priest firmly. "He'll be treated very well until then. He'll wear fine clothing and drink chocolate like a noble's son. Then he'll live forever in the land of flowers and warm rain."

"No, please," Cimatl sobbed, dropping to her knees and kissing the earth.

"Don't argue, woman!" shouted the calpixque. "You may not refuse the wishes of the gods."

Malinalli had never felt so powerless and angry. They were two women and two small girls. The men from their own farm were far away, working in the milpas; her father was working in the administrative offices in the town. These two intruders, who seemed like plain bullies to her, had a caravan of tamemes with them and the force of law and religion on their side.

The helpless females trudged slowly back to the tecalli, where Papalotl lay in ashen pallor on her petlatl, too weak to rise. Her servants had disappeared; they were later found cowering in the granary, which was just as well, since they might have been taken by the calpixque if they had been discovered. For when Itzamitl arrived home for his midmorning meal, the calpixque informed him of a new increase in the tribute which Paynala was to provide. Every 80 days, in addition to the regular tribute items of woven mantles, raw cotton, deerskin sandals, precious stones, and cacao beans, they were to provide ten slaves or children for sacrifice. Every province had to do its share, the calpixque explained piously, to keep the gods and the emperor contented.

When the calpixque had left, and Papalotl had muttered some angry words about him, Cimatl served her husband's midmorning meal tearfully. Itzamitl went into the courtyard, leaving his corncakes and beans untouched on his icpalli. Malinalli followed him outside, sensing that he, too, was angry at the calpixque.

"Can't we do something to get Moyo back, Daddy?" she asked hopefully.

"No," he said curtly. "I have to obey orders."

"But can't you talk to the emperor?"

"I said no!" he snapped. "Now leave me alone."

"Opochtli knows the emperor. Could he talk to the emperor and get Moyo back again?"

Itzamitl, angered by Malinalli's insistence, shook her by the shoulders. "I said leave me alone. Obey me!" He pushed her against a cactus until the thorns punctured her arm and blood ran down it.

"I hate you!" she screamed in pain.

"Learn your lesson, Malinalli. Hate me if you want to, but obey me." He shifted his tilmantli and stalked out of the courtyard.

Malinalli's tears flowed afresh, pitying herself because her father was angry with her, but crying also from rage that she could not express. While she was trying to pick the thorns out of her flesh and stop the trickles of blood running down her arm, she watched her father walk down the path toward the road, and then along the road until he became small in the distance.

The lesson she had learned that day was not what he thought it was. It was the hard lesson of a young idealist who once thought that her father could right any wrong, fix any unhappiness, soothe any hurt. He was human, after all, powerless in the face of some dangers. And she could not forgive his hurting her when she was only trying to help. She had not yet learned that people sometimes hurt the ones they care about instead of the ones who have hurt them, but in later years, when she saw that happen, she always remembered that scene, with the cactus thorns violating her flesh, the blood streaming down her arm, and her father becoming small in the distance.

Chapter 5

New Fire and New Life

Papalotl's belly had grown round by the month of Tititl, and Toto was the first to tell Malinalli the secret. "She's going to have a baby," said Toto. "That's how my mother looked before she had Moyo." The two girls were picking their way through the grasses and wild shrubs on the hillsides near Paynala. Toto was gathering some wild plants her mother used for herbs, and had taken Malinalli with her.

"Where does the baby come from?" Malinalli asked, amazed as always at Toto's wisdom, walking behind her through the tall grasses and leg-scratching bushes near the river. She was glad to be wearing cactli, though she usually envied Toto's freedom to go barefoot. Toto seemed as much at home in the wilderness or woodlands as in her hut with the hard-packed dirt floor.

"From the gods. They put a baby in your tummy and it grows there, just like a melon or squash." Toto gently picked some mushrooms and placed them in her basket. She had a secret envy, too, and by that time she was emulating Malinalli by wearing a similar skirt and huipil. Even though Toto's mother had clucked her tongue, saying that a girl didn't need to wear a skirt until she was older, Chihuallama understood her daughter's desire. She had spun as fine a thread as she could from the ixtle fiber and woven a garment for Toto that looked almost like cotton.

Malinalli wasn't satisfied with Toto's explanation, so when she returned to the tecalli, she sought her mother and Papalotl, who were working at their looms in the courtyard. Each woman had hooked the top of her loom to a post on the patio, and she knelt with the bottom rod on her lap, the loom strapped around her with a backstrap. Their hands nimbly pulled the shuttles through the warp and pressed each thread tight into the growing mass of fabric. Beside them lay several spindles filled with red, yellow, black, and green yarns, used for borders or embroidery.

Chihuallama had not come to weave with Cimatl since Papalotl had arrived, because she wanted to give the two sisters time to visit privately. Malinalli did not sense the same aura of easy comfort when Papalotl was there; instead she sensed a competition between her intelligent but compliant mother and her outspoken, strong-minded aunt. There was always some tension in the air; still, she noticed a bond of caring between the sisters that went deeper than friendship.

"Aunt Papalotl," Malinalli asked, seating herself by her aunt and taking up a spindle to make yarn from a basket of cotton puffs, "are you going to have a baby?"

"How did you know?" asked Papalotl, throwing a surprised look at Cimatl. Cimatl also looked surprised, so Papalotl quickly guessed the source of the information. "You've been with Toto. Did she tell you that?"

"Yes. She said her mother looked fat for a while, but got thinner after Moyo was born."

"That's the way life is," said Cimatl, realizing that the time had come for a mother-daughter talk, and not wanting Papalotl to do it for her. "Babies grow from a seed in a woman's tummy. Be glad you're a girl, so you can become a woman some day and have a baby of your own."

"Do I have a seed in my tummy now?" Malinalli asked innocently.

Cimatl and Papalotl laughed heartily. The laughter stung Malinalli so much that she remembered it many years later, when she was old enough to realize why they had laughed.

"No, sweetheart, you're too young yet," said Cimatl gently. "Be patient; you'll be a woman sooner than you think."

"When is the baby going to be here?" Malinalli was excited about the thought of a new cousin. Moyo was gone now, and she missed him. She had never stopped blaming herself for giving him a clay doll that brought him bad luck. If she had another chance, another baby in her house, she would try not to make any more mistakes.

"I think it will come in the new year, in the month of Atlcoualco," said Papalotl.

"You'll have to be especially careful during the 'useless days' of the nemontemi," Cimatl warned Papalotl, "so the child won't be born early."

"I remember the useless days last year," Malinalli said. "We couldn't do anything, or cook our food, or have any torches lighted in the house."

Cimatl was always amazed at what this child could remember. "Well, this year it may be even more difficult," she said to her precocious daughter. "Many people think the world will come to an end after the nemontemi this year."

Her mother tried to explain the atmosphere of doom to Malinalli, keeping her words simple so that a six-year-old would understand. "The world has come to an end four times in the

51

past, which were called the four suns. The first time it ended when people were devoured by jaguars, the great cats that prowl in the mountains and the caves."

"I think of it as the dark forces of the earth," interjected Papalotl. "The night sky is spotted with stars, just as the jaguar is sprinkled with spots. The world died because it was devoured by its own evil forces."

Cimatl frowned at her sister. "Don't get too abstract," she said. "Malinalli can't understand all that." She went on, her fingers threading automatically through the threads of her loom as her words spun a story for her daughter. "The second sun ended when a great storm destroyed the sun, and men were turned into monkeys by that magical storm."

"You see, Malinalli? When men become as foolish as monkeys, they bring about their own destruction," said Papalotl.

"I think I understand, Mother," Malinalli said, happy to be talking with grown-ups who treated her like one of them. Many times she had listened in the corner while adults talked around the hearth, wishing she could be part of the important exchange of words. She felt grown up when adults talked to her, even if she didn't understand everything they said.

Papalotl agreed. "Malinalli understands much more than other children her age. I've never seen such a curious child."

"She knew over 200 words by the time she was two years old," Cimatl added proudly. Then she continued telling the story to Malinalli. "The third time the world was destroyed by a big fire, or tlequiauitl, which came pelting down on the earth like a great thunderstorm, full of lightning and fiery coals."

"Like the coals in the hearth before we bake corncakes?"

"Yes, but a whole sky full of them. The earth shook terribly, and opened up great holes, and people and animals fell into them. The last time the earth was destroyed, a rainstorm lasted a sheaf of years and flooded the whole earth with water."

"Have you ever seen a thunderstorm or a flood?" Papalotl asked Malinalli, who didn't know how to answer.

Cimatl answered for her. "She's seen lightning storms, and she's seen the river rising after the rainy season, but she hasn't seen as many bad storms as we saw growing up near the water's edge."

"Well, I've seen earthquakes, hurricanes, and floods," said Papalotl. "I can easily imagine where these stories come from."

"They're sacred stories," Cimatl said defensively. "I learned them from the priestesses, didn't you? I believe they are all true."

"I'm sure there's truth in the stories, but they've been changed over the years as people passed them on from one generation to another. We have to work hard to get the grain of truth in each of the stories."

"I memorized them in the telpochcalli," she said irritably.
"I'm sure I got them right."

Papalotl tied the end of a red thread and started one of
yellow in the pattern on her loom. "It's nothing against you,
Cimatl. I just don't see the stories the way you do."

"What's happened to your faith?" Cimatl's tone was
accusatory. "Have you become bitter since you lost your
husband?"

Papalotl pondered that before answering. "That's part of
what changed me, I suppose," she said slowly. "The gods seem
cruel to me now, but I wonder how much of the cruelty is
caused by the priests and the rulers, not by the gods. Did my
husband really have to die in a silly flowery war? The only
purpose for such wars is to take captives. Why do we sacrifice
and kill by the thousands? Just because the priests and the
emperor say so?"

"Papalotl," Cimatl said in alarm, "You're speaking heresy!
The priests know more than we do. They spend their lives
studying the will of the gods. And the emperor speaks for all
people; that's why he's called Uey Tlatoani, 'revered speaker.' "

"Well, he's supposed to speak wisdom, not nonsense."

Malinalli interrupted what might have become a quarrel.
"Did something bring the world back after it was destroyed?"

"Yes, Malinalli," Cimatl answered. "Quetzalcoatl saved it.
His name means 'Precious feathered serpent,' because the quetzal
feathers are more precious and beautiful than any others, and the
serpent can renew itself each year by growing a new skin."

"How did he save the world?"

"He went down into the caves inside the earth, to the very
bottom where the bones of the ancient men lay in darkness, and
sprinkled his own blood over them to bring the bones to life. So
the old people who had died in one of the other suns, came to
life again. That's why we need to sacrifice our own blood
sometimes, to repay the god for the blood he gave for us."

Cimatl expected her sister to dispute the story or re-interpret it,
but Papalotl only sighed.

Malinalli spoke. "Can he save us if the world comes to an
end again?"

"Nobody knows. He promised he'd return, but it isn't time
yet. The year 1 Reed won't come again for twelve more years."

Papalotl had been weaving silently for some minutes. "My
husband was devoted to Quetzalcoatl," she said, her voice fervent
with emotion. "Quetzalcoatl taught us to sacrifice only snakes or
butterflies instead of humans. He accepted jade offerings instead
of little children's hearts. I'm praying for his return and the end
of flowery wars. I only wish he could have been here for
Omehuatl and Moyo."

"I'm sad about Moyo, too," said Cimatl. She measured out a

length of yarn and severed it with her knife. "But fate measures out our lives like this yarn. Some live long lives; some live short ones. Omehuatl and Moyo have both won great glory by giving their lives for others, so let's be grateful. Some babies never get a chance to live at all."

"Do you really believe the world will end before my baby comes, Cimatl?" Papalotl's voice became subdued, fearful.

"Oh, no, Papalotl!" Cimatl cried fervently. "The priests in Tenochtitlan will have a New Fire ceremony and make the right prayers and sacrifices. I believe they can change our fate. But we have to be very careful during the nemontemi, and do nothing that would anger the gods."

"I don't really believe these prophecies," Papalotl sighed, "but if it will make you happy, I'll go along with your ceremonies."

"That's sensible of you, Papalotl," said Cimatl, greatly relieved. "It can't hurt anything, and you might just find out that I'm right. I pray every day that everything will come out well for you and your baby. Perhaps you'll have a son, to take the place of Omehuatl in your heart."

Papalotl stopped weaving and reached over to touch her sister's hand. "I know you want the best for me. That's why I came here for the birth. I would do the same for you."

Unexpectedly, Cimatl's eyes filled with tears. "How I wish you could do the same for me," she said. "You'll never know how much I envy you this child. I'd give anything to have a son!"

The two sisters removed the backstraps of their looms, hugged each other, and cried. Malinalli stood looking puzzled. Why didn't the gods just plant another seed in Cimatl's tummy? The ways of the gods were difficult to understand, indeed.

* * *

The celebration of the month of Tititl was supposed to bring rain. On the first day, the children were made to cry, to simulate the water drops that were needed from the skies. Some children had their ears pierced with thorns, accepting the pain as stoically as they could. Others, like Malinalli and her friend Toto, had only to remember some earlier pain to supply the necessary stream of tears.

Then the women were made to cry. Chihuallama's tears alone might have moved Tlaloc to send the desired rain. In the night, when the wind blew through the trees, Malinalli heard a woman's cry. "That's the spirit of Coatlicue," said Cimatl, "crying for her lost children." But Malinalli thought the moaning cry sounded like her neighbor Chihuallama, crying for her little Moyo, who was far away in Tenochtitlan. Picturing him in a green paradise provided no comfort, because it was his absence from earth that caused her such pain.

* * *

The nemontemi, or five useless days, came at the end of the month of Izcalli (mid-February). In the year 2 Reed [1507], nemontemi was especially feared because it marked the end of the sheaf of years, or the 52-year cycle, which could mean the end of the world if nothing happened to save it. In Paynala, people tore up their furniture and put broken icpallis and chests outside for the gods to see. They destroyed their gourds and other household utensils which would be of no use if the world ended. They let their fires go out, did not cook, ate very little, and did not play music or games.

Chihuallama took Papalotl to the granary, because a pregnant woman could be changed into a wild animal if the evil forces found her unprotected. As a midwife, Chihuallama stayed right beside her client to make sure the baby did not arrive during that time. A child born during those days would surely have an unfortunate tonalli, a dark fate.

On the last night of the nemontemi, Cimatl marched all the children up and down, keeping them awake. Sleep on that fatal evening could result in children being turned into rats, she explained.

The priests at the little temple in Paynala imitated the rites that were being held in Tenochtitlan, because Paynala was too far away for runners to come from the great city. At sunset the priests gathered on the temple steps to scan the skies, wrapping their black robes around their knees as they sat in solemn observation. They watched to see that certain stars, Aldebaran or the Pleiades, reached the center of the heavens.

Normally the local priests did not make sacrifices at their small temple; they depended on the rites taking place in Tenochtitlan to generate good will among the gods. Yet on this important evening, they could not afford any risks. They must have their own New Fire Ceremony. So they used the student-warriors from their own telpochcalli as runners, and calmecac students imported from Cholula conducted the ceremony.

Youths from the calmecac, young priests in training, had prepared a sacrificial victim, first choking him by garroting his throat with a cord, then extracting his heart with a flint knife. The fire that normally burned in the altar had been allowed to burn out. Itzamitl walked around the temple grounds to play his role as tecuhtli, maintaining order as a crowd assembled to watch the priests and see the New Fire Ceremony.

At the moment when the significant stars passed the meridian, the priests seized a wooden fire stick and a small wooden board on which to twist it until it heated, creating a spark and kindling a new fire in the breast of the newly-slain victim. Cries of rejoicing pierced the air when the flames leaped up and the stars gave the sign that their world would continue. The priests gave thanks to the Fire God for beginning another sheaf of years. Then they lit the fire at the altar, and the youths from the calmecac lighted pine torches in that fire.

Runners with torches, darting through the night like fireflies, fanned out from the new fire to light the hearths of all the villagers in Paynala. The exhausted women in the household of Itzamitl watched the road for signs of a runner bringing a lighted torch. When they saw the bobbing light in the distance, growing brighter as it came down the road and turned into the path to the tecalli, Cimatl wept for joy that a new sheaf of years was beginning. She pierced her own ears with a cactus thorn, offering her blood to the hearth and the Fire God.

Toto ran to the granary, where Chihuallama and Papalotl were holding their vigil. Chihuallama led the exhausted Papalotl to the door of the tecalli to welcome the runner and see the hearth fire lit before taking her to her petlatl in the sleeping room. Papalotl was very much surprised, as were the other women, to see that the runner was a person they knew.

"I came personally to bring you the good news and to help you start your hearth fire," said the warrior dressed in full regalia with red and yellow parrot feathers in his headdress. He carried a feather shield on his left arm as he held the torch in his right hand. Malinalli, bleary-eyed from staying up most of the night, recognized the face first by the lip-plug weighing down his lower lip as he spoke. It was Anecoatl.

* * *

The next day dawned bright and sunny, and the village came to life, invigorated with a new sense of purpose. Even the birds chirping in the ahuehuetl tree seemed to be thrilling to the new beginning. The villagers gathered rushes and reeds to rebuild the destroyed furniture and mats; the women shaped new kitchen utensils from dried gourds. Cimatl and Papalotl directed their servants to sweep the floors and whitewash the walls; they gathered green boughs and redecorated the tecalli.

Anecoatl stayed a few days in the guest house where the merchant Opochtli had stored some surplus goods, but he joined Itzamitl for the midmorning meal. Malinalli served the men and listened as they talked. Anecoatl told stories of the battles he had fought and the palaces he had seen. The finest palace, he said, was that of the emperor Moctezuma II, which had many rooms, beautiful gardens, and a zoo of rare animals and birds. Anecoatl was traveling to the Maya lands as a guard for a group of pochteca who planned to purchase rare birds and feathers. Moctezuma II was also trusting him, he reported proudly, with protecting the emperor's interest in the rare birds and animals.

Anecoatl told Itzamitl that he had wanted to offer Papalotl an escort back to her home in Coatzacoalcos, but he could see she was expecting a child soon. He had not known she was pregnant when he brought her to Paynala just after her husband's death. The men agreed that Papalotl should be with her sister when her child was born. They also agreed that, if the child was a boy, it would be wise for Papalotl to marry again soon, so that the child would have a father to guide him. Itzamitl told Anecoatl that a steward was managing Papalotl's farm while she was away, because her husband had no brother to take over after his death. It was customary for a younger brother to marry his older brother's widow, but Papalotl was unfortunate and her life would be difficult unless she found another husband.

"That's sad," Anecoatl said soberly. "She'll probably marry again when she's had time to finish grieving. I'll check on her when I come back this way. It's the least I can do for my fallen comrade, Omehuatl." Anecoatl's lips curved into a closed smile while he talked of Papalotl. Malinalli didn't trust his smile, nor did she trust his words because he didn't sound sad when he said "That's sad." But she said nothing about her worries. She knew that her father was wiser than she, and if anything was wrong, he would surely detect it.

"She's a strong-minded woman, Anecoatl," said Itzamitl with a grin. "It will take a strong man to lead her."

Anecoatl agreed by smiling his closed smile.

* * *

Fourteen days after the New Fire ceremony, Papalotl went into labor, and Cimatl summoned Chihuallama. Although at first making the expected protests that she was just an old woman unworthy of such an office, Chihuallama took complete charge of the birth. She invoked the patroness of the midwives, Temazcalteci, or "grandmother of the steam bath," to guide her efforts to bring Papalotl's child into the world.

Chihuallama first banished all men from the household; this day belonged to the women, she said with such authority that even Itzamitl meekly obeyed.

She prepared special foods for Papalotl, filling the tecalli with the smell of rosemary and laurel leaves. She ordered her son Acamapichtli to cut wood and take it to the temazcalli, for soon they would need a fire for the steam bath. She took over the sleeping room for the birth and brought a clean new petlatl for Papalotl. She massaged Papalotl's back, abdomen, and hips, commenting all the while on how the baby lay in the womb and how active it was. She covered Papalotl with a mantle to help her perspire. She braided Papalotl's hair and advised her to bite one of her braids if the pain became intense, because too much screaming might make the child ascend instead of descend. She spoke proudly of the nobility of all women who undergo the pain of childbirth, telling Papalotl that this day she would join the honorable ranks of women who had faced great danger with courage and fortitude.

Papalotl retorted that she just wanted to get it over with, she wasn't interested in being noble. Yet she welcomed the healing-woman's soothing chatter; the presence of this competent, warm-hearted woman reassured her.

For several hours Malinalli wandered in the courtyard or sat around the hearth, watching the women go in and out of the sleeping room. She tried to play a bean game with Toto, but she couldn't concentrate when she heard her aunt's moans coming through the open door.

"I remember when my mama had Moyo," said Toto. "She was very sick, and said she'd never have any more."

Cimatl called for Malinalli and Toto to bring some wood and water to the hearth, then talked with them as they built a fire together. "The first childbirth is always the hardest," she reassured the curious girls. "It may take a day or two for the body to change so the baby can come out. But don't worry; Aunt Papalotl is doing fine. The baby is kicking strongly, and that's a good sign."

"Does it hurt a lot to have a baby?" Malinalli asked as another moan issued from the sleeping room. She couldn't imagine why a baby would kick its mother.

"My mama says you forget the pain very soon," said Toto.

"It does hurt a lot," Cimatl said frankly, "but women are naturally strong and brave. They can endure a lot of hardship without complaint. That's why a woman who dies in childbirth is treated the same as a warrior. She accompanies the sun god from the highest point in the sky down to the sunset, where the earth welcomes her. Then she becomes a ciuateteo, or 'divine woman.' The goddesses of twilight are women who have died in childbirth." Chihuallama came out to the hearth and overheard the discussion. "Your Aunt Papalotl won't become a ciuateteo," she assured Malinalli. "She's healthy and strong. But she could use a little help right now. Boil some water, and I'll make her a drink from ciuapatli."

Cimatl looked at Chihuallama anxiously. "Ciuapatli?"

"Yes, to strengthen the contractions. They're coming quickly but not lasting long enough."

The herb drink worked its magic, and soon the girls heard the groans of Papalotl followed by the squalling of a newborn infant. Chihuallama appeared carrying a small bundle wrapped in

58

a cloth, saying "It's a girl. You can watch while I tie her umbilical cord and bathe her."

She placed the swaddled infant on a petlatl on the floor and unwrapped her, revealing the cord still attached to the mass of dark-colored afterbirth that looked like a deer's liver on the white cloth. Then she took an obsidian knife and severed the cord quickly where it joined the afterbirth. She tied the cord in a knot close to the squalling infant's belly, then cut away the remaining cord so that only a stub remained. "This part we will bury in the hearth," she said to Malinalli and Toto. "You may dig the hole now if you want to."

Chihuallama chanted a poem as she bathed the child in a basin of cold water, the infant's indignant cries competing with her joyful tones. Her verse invoked Ayopechcatl, the goddess of childbed:

> "Down there, where Ayopechcatl lives,
> The jewel is born, a child has come into the world.
> Down there, where Ayopechcatl lives,
> The jewel is born, a child has come into the world.
> It is down there, in her own place,
> That the children are born.
> Come, come here, newborn child, come here.
> Come, come here, jewel-child, come here."

Then Chihuallama wrapped the infant in a soft clean cotton cloth and spoke soothingly to her. "You have undergone the hardships of birth and cold water, precious one. Life can bring no pains to you that you cannot bear. You have come into this world where your parents toil in weariness. We cannot know what your fate will hold, but you will live in duty and courage."

Cimatl had silently helped the girls dig a hole in the earth around the hearth for the umbilical cord and afterbirth. As they buried it, Chihuallama said another prayer:

> "Today we bury the cord that
> tied you to your mother,
> Your navel cord that ties you to your family,
> For you must always dwell within your home
> As the heart within the body.
> Your place is within the home,
> Even as part of your body lies within the home,
> Even as the ashes lie within the hearth."

Cimatl placed the swaddled infant in a basket with handles, so the baby could sleep comfortably yet be carried to her mother easily when she woke.

Then Chihuallama turned her attention to Papalotl, who lay

exhausted on her petlatl. With Cimatl's help, she removed Papalotl's soiled huipil and washed her entire body with a soft cloth dipped in warm water. She bound Papalotl's belly tightly, to "fix the organs back in place," she said. "Now you should rest for forty days," she cautioned. "I'll come every day for eight days to massage you and bind you with clean cloths. If the bleeding has stopped by then, we can begin your steam baths. You mustn't eat anything except thin atole for a few days, and stay in bed as much as possible."

"At least you aren't warning me not to sleep with my husband," Papalotl said, weakly attempting to joke, since Chihuallama knew that her husband was dead.

Chihuallama took her seriously. "Not with any man, for at least a year," she said sternly. "Stay here with your sister as long as you can, so no man can rush you into marriage. Your milk will dry up if you get pregnant again; your precious daughter needs your milk for a year."

"The last thing I want right now is a man," Papalotl said wearily.

"That's what they all say, right after giving birth," Chihuallama said with a chuckle.

Then Chihuallama left Papalotl in Cimatl's care, and taking Toto with her, walked heavily up the path to her hut, eyes downcast, wondering if she could ever again do a midwife's work without thinking of Moyo. Her own last labor had been difficult, but having a healthy child had compensated for the pain. Now she would never see that child grow up, and her heart ached with a pain greater than the agony of labor.

Then she recalled her own words to Papalotl's newborn girl: "Life can bring no pains to you that you cannot bear. We cannot know what your fate will hold, but you will live in duty and courage." She straightened her shoulders, gripped Toto's small hand gratefully in her own, and walked on.

* * *

The naming of a child was a matter of great importance, not to be done without consulting a tonalpouhqui, or soothsayer. Itzamitl brought the tonalpouhqui home on the day after the child's birth, so that he could consult the sacred book, or tonalamatl, before the fourth day.

The tonalpouhqui's long, thin hair and the sparse beard on his aging chin, together with an obvious indifference to the stains on his robe, gave the family the impression that he was a spiritual man concerned less with appearances than with scholarship. But they knew there were customary fees expected for his services. Chihuallama came with gifts of food for the new mother and a turkey-hen for the tonalpouhqui. Itzamitl presented him with a quachtli of cloth, and Cimatl prepared a special meal for him as part of the usual reimbursement.

After Chihuallama told him the day of the birth and the approximate time, he looked in the tonalamatl to find the sign for that day and the set of thirteen days to which it belonged. He traced the glyphs painted on the bark paper with a bony finger, sucking in his cheeks and furrowing his brow in deep concentration.

"The child was not born under a good sign," he said, pausing so that his words would generate the appropriate sighs of disappointment. Then in his smoothest professional manner he suggested a compromise. "In this series of days, however, there is another sign we can work with. It can correct the unfortunate influence of the principal sign. Figures greater than ten are always favorable. If we wait for the fifth day instead of the usual four, we can name the child on a day with the number 10."

Murmurs of appreciation and agreement followed, the day was set, and the tonalpouhqui was rewarded with his meal and gifts. Cimatl began assembling the food for the feast which would follow the ceremony, and in the absence of other relatives, she invited all of Chihuallama's family. Papalotl had her first steam bath on the fourth day after the birth so that she would be purified and cleansed. Chihuallama threw water on the hot stones outside the temazcalli, creating steam within the reed house; then she scrubbed Papalotl's skin with bunches of dried grasses.

The two families and Papalotl's two servants gathered in the tecalli courtyard before sunrise on the naming day. All of them wore new, colorfully embroidered garments. Acamapichtli looked almost like his father in a similar maxtli and tilmantli, even though boys usually didn't wear a maxtli until they were thirteen. Malinalli and Toto had brushed their hair with reed combs until it shone, hanging smoothly to their waists. Cimatl and Papalotl wore flowers in their hair.

Since it was the midwife's duty to conduct the actual ceremony, Chihuallama arranged everything with great care. She brought a tiny spindle, a miniature shuttle like those used by women on their looms, and a little box. These she would present to the newborn as symbols of her future. If the child had been a boy, he would have received a shield and arrows. Her husband, Callipopoca, had woven a reed cradle for the newborn, work which everyone admired.

As the sun broke through the morning mists, shining on the dew-drenched morning-glory leaves and making them sparkle, Papalotl carried the child in her arms to Chihuallama. Chihuallama dipped her fingers in the full water jar beside her and wet the mouth of the infant with a few drops. "Take and receive this," she said, "for it is with this water that you will live upon earth, and grow and become green and grow again. For it is by water that we have what we must have to live upon this earth. Receive this water, precious one." Then she touched the infant's chest with her wet hand. "Here is the heavenly water, the very pure water that washes and cleans your heart and takes away all stains." Touching a wet hand to the child's head, she added, "Let this water enter your body, and may it live there, this heavenly water, the blue celestial water." Then as Papalotl held the child, Chihuallama bathed her entire body with her wet hands, invoking the blessings of the goddess Chalchiutlicue. "Now this child is new-born and new-formed, born again with the blessings of the water goddess. Whoever might do this child a mischief, go away, for she is under the protection of Chalchiutlicue, goddess who wears the robe of precious jewels."

The relatives, each in turn, spoke to the cradle that Callipopoca had made, the cradle in which the little girl would lie, calling it Yoalticitl, "healer by night." They asked the water goddess once more to protect the girl who would rest there. Papalotl placed her daughter in the cradle, putting the tiny spindle in her hand. The baby, though she seemed sleepy and bored with the ceremony, gripped the spindle tightly. Papalotl placed the tiny shuttle and box beside the infant in the cradle. Then she announced her choice of name: Quetzal-xochitl, or "precious flower."

Cimatl cringed a little, wondering how the girl would like such a babyish and cumbersome name as she grew older, but she remembered the devotion of Papalotl and Omehuatl to Quetzalcoatl, also called the "Plumed Serpent." So it was appropriate that Omehuatl's posthumous child be named in his honor. And besides, Cimatl reasoned, it would be only a short time before other children began to call the baby "Xochi," just as they called Atototl "Toto." Time would take care of the problem.

The baptismal feast was a modest one, since it came at the time of the usual midmorning meal. But in addition to corncakes there were beans, tamales stuffed with chopped turkey meat, and chocolate for everyone, so the meal seemed festive enough.

Papalotl's servants had spread mats around the courtyard for the guests to sit on, in case the ground was damp. While the children gathered around the cradle and admired the tiny pink fingers of Quetzal-Xochitl gripping her tiny spindle, the adults served themselves at the banquet table in the patio. Itzamitl led Papalotl to a mat and told her to be seated, that he would bring her a plate of food. Papalotl kneeled on the mat and sat back on her heels, as if she were preparing to do weaving.

Itzamitl brought a plate of food for Papalotl and a cup of chocolate for each of them, placing the cups on the mat between them. He sat down beside her, knees doubled under his chin and feet flat on the ground, wrapping his tilmantli around so that it covered his knees. "You sit as the schoolboys do when listening to advice," Papalotl giggled. She took a bite of tamale.

Itzamitl smiled, took a sip of chocolate, and replaced his cup on the mat. "I want to give advice today," he said. "As your nearest male relative, may I do that?"

"Of course," Papalotl smiled. "Advice is expected on a naming day. I hope I can raise my daughter as well as you and Cimatl are raising Malinalli."

"Thank you. We're proud of Malinalli," said Itzamitl. "My advice does concern Quetzal-Xochitl as well as you. I'm thinking of your future."

"Mine, too? Well, then?"

"I have reason to believe that Anecoatl may make you an offer of marriage. When he was here, he spoke well of you, and he knows that a child needs two parents."

"Do you think I should get married again?"

Itzamitl laughed. "I wouldn't dream of telling you what to do," he said. "I'd only advise you not to marry too soon. Anecoatl seems to admire you, but he'll be away for several months. Don't feel that you must accept a lesser offer until he comes to see you again."

Papalotl's smile faded. "I know you mean well," she said, "but I'm not interested in a husband right now."

Itzamitl's eyebrows went up in surprise. "You think you don't need a man?"

Papalotl sipped her chocolate carefully as she formed her answer in her mind. She didn't want to insult her brother-in-law, but she didn't expect him to understand how she felt. "I need a man only to supervise the work of my farm. My steward is doing that for me while I'm away."

"But don't you want more children? Anecoatl could give you strong, healthy babies. He has a good future as a warrior. He might even become an eagle or a jaguar knight. He hunts well with arrows, too. He'll be a good provider."

"My husband Omehuatl provided for me by leaving me property and macehaultin to work on it. I like being independent. But perhaps I'm imposing on you by staying here too long."

"Oh, no," Itzamitl protested. "You're welcome to stay. Cimatl likes having you here. But think about what you're saying. Do you want to live alone after you leave us?" Seeing that she was unmoved by that argument, he added, "You may not get a better offer, Papalotl. Anecoatl wants a son, and you haven't proved that you can bear sons. He's willing to take a chance on you, but not every man would."

"Why would I want such a husband?" Papalotl said irritably. "A man who thinks he's doing me a favor to marry me!"

"You're absolutely impossible!" Itzamitl exclaimed. He had hoped he could avoid showing irritation at her stubbornness, but the words came out like sharp knives. "You have a temper, and you like to run things. You should be more like Cimatl."

"So my husband could order me about like a servant?" Papalotl heard her voice rising in spite of her efforts to control it. "Why are most men so bossy?"

"Women need our protection," said Itzamitl in a patronizing tone. "But we can't protect women and children if they aren't obedient. You'd have a much happier life if you became more compliant."

"That shows how little you understand women," Papalotl said contemptuously. "With all due respect, Itzamitl, you're a good husband to Cimatl, and she loves you enough to put up with your pompousness. But the happiest marriage I see here today is not your marriage—it's Chihuallama's and Callipopoca's."

"What do you mean?" Itzamitl was genuinely surprised. He considered himself the ideal husband, and Cimatl the ideal wife.

"Callipopoca may be just a macehualli, but Chihuallama sees that he has everything he needs. No king could be better served, because she serves him with devotion. And whatever she needs, Callipopoca sees that she gets it. She does her work, and he does his. They never argue about who the boss is. Look how proud he seemed to be of Chihuallama this morning."

"They're an older couple," Itzamitl explained, for he knew that what she said was true. "I've seen that happen with older couples. Once a man has proved himself as the head of the family, he begins to relax and let his wife take over."

"It works the other way around, too," said Papalotl. "Women get tired of being controlled by men, and after awhile they just do what they want without worrying about whether it pleases their husbands."

Itzamitl had finished his chocolate by that time, and he could see there was no point in arguing. "I'm glad Cimatl doesn't feel that way," he said, rising to his feet. "She understands men better than you do, Papalotl. She knows that the gods have ordained male and female spheres, with behavior that is proper to each. It's like the rhythms of night and day, of rain and sun, of light and darkness, of earth and sky."

"Perhaps so," said Papalotl with a smile. "But the day doesn't dominate the night, and the sun isn't more important than the rain." She heard a small cry coming from the cradle and rose to go. "It sounds as if Quetzal-Xochitl wants her food, too. Thank you for bringing me a plate. And thank you for your concern about me and my daughter."

"You're welcome, Papalotl," said Itzamitl sincerely. "And you're welcome to stay here; I really mean it. I thought you'd be pleased to hear of Anecoatl's interest in you, but I don't want to push you into anything you don't want." Teasingly, he added, "I feel a little sorry for Anecoatl, but he'll have to learn for himself if he wants to take on a strong-minded female."

A plan began forming in Papalotl's mind. "When will he return?"

"In about six months, I think."

"Then I have enough time," said Papalotl, but she would not say for what.

Chapter 6

The Spanish Thirst for Conquest

Although she did not know it until much later, Malinalli's fate was also being formed in a world far away, by forces she could not have fathomed as a child. It was the world of Spain, fired by ambition and greed, swelling with pride and confidence that their way of life was to become the destiny of the world, their god the only god worshiped in the universe.

The life with which her own would be inextricably linked began in Spain, in the small town of Medellin, in the Extremadura region, in 1485. But the forces that would bring them together began in 1492, the high point of Spain's Golden Age.

The year 1492 had been significant in the household of Martin Cortes de Monroy and his wife, Dona Catalina Pizarro Altamirano, in Medellin. Their only son, Hernan, a frail and sickly eight-year-old, had been cured of quartan fever by the miraculous intervention of St. Peter.

Once the danger to young Hernan had passed, the dinner table conversation of this Medellin family centered on other events of the time. With the defeat of the Moors at Granada on the first day of 1492, Spanish forces had ended eight centuries of Moslem domination over the Iberian peninsula. This event added luster to the reign of King Ferdinand and Queen Isabel, even as it changed the nature of their kingdoms. Many soldiers who had served in the wars were returning to their provinces with a restless spirit, unsure what to do with their lives. The sparsely populated region of Extremadura, with its bitter cold winters and hot, arid summers, offered little opportunity to create riches, and thus it became the cradle of conquistadors.

Many veterans, like Martin Cortes, were hidalgos, entitled to certain tax exemptions. The term *hidalgo*, from *hijo de algo,* meant the son of somebody, or an important person of good family, even though the family might have little material wealth. Since common labor and business were disdained by these men, they usually sought entrance into respected professions such as law, military service, or priesthood.

The lure of quick riches and adventure also tempted many veterans and hidalgos. They became a ready source of trained fighters for the expeditions of Cristobal Colon and other explorers after 1492. Having lived in a country that had been conquered by Romans, Visigoths, and Moors, then reconquered by Christians from Northern Europe, they accepted conquest as natural. They saw spoils and tribute as entitlements. They wanted glory; they wanted gold. They saw no contradictions between service to their country and advancement for themselves. They also wanted land, and were willing to settle for it. Or steal it from others. Or even kill for it.

The spirit of the time also involved competition against Portugal for the discovery of new trade routes and new lands which might be made subject to the Crown. The smell of conquest seemed borne upon the ocean winds, beckoning the adventurer. This spirit profoundly influenced young Hernan Cortes.

Also, the drive for political unity in a country comprising many small, antagonistic territories found an ally in religion. The marriage of Ferdinand and Isabel had formed a fragile bond between Aragon and Castilla that Isabel hoped to strengthen.

Religious fervor for expansion of the Catholic faith, championed by Isabel, was fueled by the forced conversion of many Moslems after their defeat. Discovering that religious zeal could rationalize the confiscation of property to support their monasteries, the rulers also ordered the expulsion of Jews from Spain between May and July of 1492, unless the Jews converted to Christianity. Inquisitors were appointed to make sure that the new "conversos" did not continue to practice their old faith in secret. Heresy was punishable by burning at the stake, and the accused were not told who their accusers were.

When Hernan was twelve, in 1497, his parents sent him to Salamanca to live with an aunt, to study Latin and law. In a few years he became literate and eloquent, but also bored and restless. As he matured, the once-sickly boy became a deep-chested, robust man about 5'4" tall. His hair and beard darkened from a light reddish-brown to a deeper hue, though his face remained pale. In character, he seemed a maze of contradictions: He chafed at genteel poverty, yet squandered what money he had on gambling. He seemed obedient, yet rebellious; patient, yet rash; ambitious, yet unfocused; chivalrous, yet cruel when provoked to anger. He took so much interest in the local senoritas that he spent much time in confession, in conflict over the pull of his masculine urges and the power of his faith.

By the age of twenty-one, in 1506, Hernan Cortes had become weary of temporary work as a notary, half-hearted studying, and aimless drifting. He had also heard stories about the wealth of the Indies and dreamed of living in paradisaical splendor. He boarded a merchant ship in a convoy sailing for the settlement of Santo Domingo, on the island of Hispaniola, which later became known as Haiti and the Dominican Republic. Finding some gold in streams as well as a grant of land he could cultivate, Cortes became a successful plantation owner in Hispaniola. But the Indian populations, especially the Arawaks and Tainos, were being decimated by warfare, enslavement, overwork, and disease. Settlers began importing slaves from Africa, but they also sought new conquests as sources of slaves. Spanish conquistadors expanded into Puerto Rico in 1508 and Jamaica in 1509, easily conquering natives who had few weapons and little military experience.

Then explorers began eyeing the larger island of Cuba and a tiny one called Cozumel. They were drawing ever closer to the territory that they would eventually call the New World. It was the same world whose inhabitants had for centuries called it Anahuac, which in their language meant "The One World."

Chapter 7

The Omens of Light and Darkness

The year 4 Calli [1509] brought a strange omen. For many nights in the month of Tlacaxipeualiztli a great brightness, shaped like a pyramid or temple, rose from the eastern horizon and reached the heavens. It shot out such brilliant sparks and flashes that it seemed to rain fire on the earth and to blaze like daybreak. It appeared at midnight and could still be seen at dawn, but in the daytime it was quelled by the force and brilliance of the sun.

Many villagers in Paynala turned to their priests in terror, beating the palms of their hands against their mouths, weeping and shouting and crying out. The priests bled their earlobes with thorns until their earlobes hung in scarred and ragged strips, and they told the villagers to bleed their own earlobes or arms in penitence. They also promised a human sacrifice to the god Xipe Totec, "Our Lord the Flayed One," because it was the month of seedtime and planting, when he was usually venerated.

"Perhaps it's a good omen," argued Itzamitl when two priests came to the administration office to request his presence at the ceremony. "No harm has come to us—no plagues or famines. Perhaps the gods are telling us how pleased they are."

The older priest shook his head, his matted locks of hair dragging across his bony shoulders. "Omens give warnings," he said in a booming voice. "If we don't heed them, our plantings may not bear fruit. We need to avoid famine before it comes."

"You must trust his interpretation," said the younger priest. "In matters of religion, the scholars who have studied for years at the calmecac have authority over civil authorities."

Itzamitl knew he was being chastened. "I don't mean to overstep my authority," he said. "But surely the gods send good messages as well as warnings. You teach us that greed among humans is wrong. Are the gods greedy for more and more sacrifices, never satisfied?"

"You can't apply human reasoning to the gods," said the younger priest in alarm. "We'll know Xipe is satisfied when the

69

corn is planted and he allows it to grow."

Itzamitl lowered his eyes in respect. He had meant to appeal to their compassion, but he could not argue with the priests. "Where will you find your sacrifices?" he asked. "We've been buying slaves from the Mayan traders, but all of them have been sent to the emperor for tribute. I hope you won't take any children from the villagers."

"We need an adult for this ceremony," said the older priest. "We have to flay his skin so a priest can dress in it."

"Yes, the symbolism is important," the younger priest agreed. "Xipe Totec is the god of regeneration. Just as a plant sheds its old leaves and grows new ones, the priest who represents the god will wear a new skin."

"Like a husk enclosing a new seed," said the older priest, smiling toothlessly at his young protege.

"Then I'll talk to my merchant friend Opochtli," said Itzamitl, resigning himself to the inevitable. "He may have bought some slaves on his last trip."

"Can we rely on you to be there?"

"Of course. Wherever a crowd gathers, it's my duty to be there to keep order." Itzamitl walked to the door with the priests, thinking how heavily duty falls on the shoulders of a tecuhtli at times.

* * *

Opochtli had just returned to Paynala from a trip to the Valley of the Mexica with important news. The omen of the pyramid of light had greatly disturbed King Nezahualpilli of Texcoco, whose great city rose on the shores of Lake Texcoco, and who was greatly learned in the sciences and astrology.

"His astrologers could not explain the phenomenon to his satisfaction," Opochtli told Itzamitl as they shared an evening meal at his tecalli. "The king concluded that his rule and his realm had amounted to very little. He ordered his captains and the commanders of his armies to cease waging wars."

Malinalli, as usual when Opochtli was visiting, had offered to serve the men so that she could eavesdrop. Opochtli had grown fond enough of her over the past two years that he always bathed before coming there, but he still wore his patched tilmantli and tattered cactli. She wondered who this King Nezahualpilli was, but she kept silent, hoping to ask her father later.

Itzamitl gave a soft whistle of amazement. "Stop the wars? How did Moctezuma react to that?"

"Not well, I'm told," said Opochtli. "He's been depending on all three cities in the Triple Alliance to subdue the provinces and keep the flowery wars going. But the relationship between Tenochtitlan and Texcoco has been strained ever since Nezualpilli put one of Moctezuma's sisters to death."

"I'm surprised that didn't start a war between Tenochtitlan and Texcoco," said Itzamitl.

"It might have, but she deserved death. Have you heard that story?"

"A little, in my training to become a tecuhtli. It's given as an example of justice in the punishment of adultery. But you may know more than I do." He noticed Malinalli beside the hearth and handed her his plate, then signaled to Opochtli with a slight toss of the head. "If you've finished, let's smoke out on the patio."

The men lighted their reed pipes at the hearth, then took chairs out into the patio. The quiet of the twilight was broken only by the sound of crickets and an occasional distant bark from one of Callipopoca's dogs. Darkness was settling upon them, but soon a half-moon lighted the courtyard. The eerie pyramidal light had not been seen for the past three nights.

"She was only a child of fourteen when Axayacatl gave her to Nezhuapilli for one of his secondary wives," Opochtli began, seating himself on his icpalli. "I guess the old emperor thought he'd cement an alliance with Texcoco by giving Nezhuapilli one of his daughters."

"Do you think she felt slighted by not being a first wife?" Itzamitl speculated.

"No, I don't think that mattered to her," Opochtli said, blowing a puff of smoke into the air. "She had every indulgence any girl could want. But she became more and more extravagant and outrageous. Whenever she saw a well-shaped young man whose form agreed with her tastes, she gave orders that he could enjoy her favors by coming to her apartment in secret."

"But she got caught," Itzamitl said, showing that he was listening by adding to the story.

"Not for quite a while," Opochtli said. "After she had fulfilled her carnal desires, she had the young men killed and statues made to resemble them—had the whole apartment decorated with those infernal statues."

"Didn't King Nezahualpilli suspect something at that point?"

"No, she told him these were her gods, and he believed her. But she finally went too far. She gave one of her young men a jewel her husband had given her. When the King recognized the jewel on the young buck, he paid a surprise visit to her apartment."

"A lot of people were being careless," Itzamitl said. "The young man shouldn't have flaunted his jewel, and the young lady's playmates should've also asked questions about the statues."

"It was only a matter of time before someone slipped up. When Nezahualpilli finally caught her, she had three young men from excellent families disporting themselves with her. So in justice, she was killed, even though she was a king's consort and the daughter of an emperor."

"The point is, my friend," Itzamitl said, "that in justice all four of them were killed. To kill only the girl would have been revenge, but it would not have been justice."

"Quite so," Opochtli said appreciatively. "I can see you're a good judge. You see deeper than most people."

"I've heard two other stories about Nezahualpilli's sense of justice," Itzamitl said. "According to one story, he had his own daughter killed when she disobeyed his rules and permitted a young man to speak to her."

"That does seem harsh."

"Perhaps so, but when others in the court attempted to intervene on her behalf, he told them he wouldn't break the law to save anyone's skin. He said if he did, he'd be setting a bad example to other lords and dishonoring himself."

"So a lord or tecuhtli isn't supposed to show any pity toward his own daughter?" Opochtli asked, incredulous. He wondered if Malinalli was listening, but he saw no sign of her when he glanced at the open door of the tecalli.

"That story was a warning to all tecuhtlis not to show favoritism," Itzamitl said. "The other story concerns his putting a favorite son to death—actually his heir, which makes the story even more tragic. His heir, Huexotzinca-tzin, had been writing poetical exchanges with his father's favorite concubine, the Lady of Tula. She was a merchant's daughter, by the way."

"I suppose that shows the great king had nothing against merchants," said Opochtli drily.

"He admired the merchant's daughter for her merits, so he overlooked her family connections," Itzamitl said jokingly. "She was skilled at poetry herself, and she responded to the prince's poetic satires with some of her own. But certain gossips in the court saw this exchange of poetic blows as the prince making advances toward his father's favorite, and they accused him of treason."

"And Nezahualpilli put his son to death for that?" Opochtli's voice mingled anger and contempt. "For court gossip?"

"Yes, even though he loved his son more than anyone in the world. He was setting an example of impartial justice, even though it hurt him personally."

"I really don't understand that," Opochtli protested. "It seems such a harsh punishment for such a small offense."

"Yes," Itzamitl said. "Sometimes the law may seem harsh, but that's why we have so little crime here. When everyone knows what the risks are, and how harsh the punishment will be, few people steal or commit adultery."

"And is there no place in the law for compassion? Shouldn't

a small crime receive a light punishment?"

"Of course. The law recognizes differences. It deals leniently with children and old people. It holds a tecuhtli to a higher standard than other citizens, too. For example, you could get drunk on octli and just pay a fine, but if I did it, my punishment would be death."

"And do you admire this king Nezahualpilli? Would you hold to some unreasonable law at the expense of your own wife and daughter?"

"Fortunately, Cimatl is very obedient," Itzamitl replied. "Malinalli can be stubborn at times, but once she understands why she must do something, she tries to please. I'm sure I'll never have to deal out punishments to the women in my family."

"My daughter Metzli is a fine girl, too," Opochtli said, deciding to change the subject to something they could agree upon. "She's eight years old—the same age as Malinalli. I worry about her as she approaches womanhood. Her mother died giving birth, so she has only me to guide her. How early should a parent warn a daughter not to encourage boys' attentions?"

"Eight-year-old girls aren't too young to need some protection," said Itzamitl. "By the time our daughters are ten, I think they should be enrolled in a telpochcalli under the guidance of a priestess. In fact, I'm thinking that Cimatl should formally dedicate Malinalli to a temple very soon."

"Protection? Do you mean from temptation? Or is there some danger in Paynala that I don't know about?"

"I'm worried about the priests," Itzamitl answered frankly. "I believe I can trust you, Opochtli, not to repeat what I'm saying to you now. The priests are growing more and more insistent on making human sacrifices. One year some of Moctezuma's priests and tax-gatherers took Moyo, Callipopoca's little son, to sacrifice at the temple of Tlaloc. They could come after Toto, or even your daughter or mine, any time they want, and I couldn't stop them."

"I see," mused Opochtli. "Ironic, isn't it? We protect our daughters' virginity, saving them for marriage, and their very purity makes them desirable targets for the priests to sacrifice."

"That reminds me," said Itzamitl. "I need to find a slave to sacrifice for the ceremony in honor of Xipe. Do you have any to sell?"

"No," replied Opochtli. "The slave traffic usually goes toward Tenochtitlan, and I've just returned from there. But I'm going to Coatzacoalcos day after tomorrow, and I could get one from the Mayan traders in the market there."

"Good idea," said Itzamitl. "Could I ask one more favor?"

"Of course," said Opochtli. "I certainly owe you a favor. You got my son Chimalli into the telpochcalli."

"I should've asked about him," said Itzamitl, slightly

73

embarrassed at his oversight. "How's he doing in his studies?"

"Fine. He's learning to play tlachtli, too. Made the top team this year. His hips are always bruised from practicing."

"Glad to hear it," Itzamitl said. "When they have a ritual game, we'll have to see it."

"Good. I'd like that. And what was the favor you wanted?"

"I'd like you to take Cimatl and Malinalli to Coatzacoalcos with your caravan. They can stay with Papalotl there for a few days."

"Until the flaying ceremony for Xipe is over?"

"Yes. I don't want either of them to see that. It would frighten them. Besides, Malinalli has been wanting to see the market in Coatzacoalcos. I think she's old enough."

"I understand. Then tell them I'll come for them day after tomorrow at sunrise." Opochtli said goodnight and left for his own home, where his daughter Meztli would be waiting under the care of a servant. He wished he could think of a way of getting her out of town for a while, too. If Itzamitl couldn't trust the priests, he thought, no one could.

* * *

Malinalli was excited about the trip to Coatzacoalcos. Cimatl told her she would see the great waters, and a market bigger than she had ever seen, as well as her aunt Papalotl and her two-year-old cousin Quetzal-Xochitl. But she was also warned solemnly that the trip would take all day long, and her legs would get tired. She was determined not to complain.

Cimatl, too, was looking forward to the journey, to see Papalotl again. Papalotl had left Paynala when little Xochi was just a couple of months old, and the sisters had not had any news of each other since that time.

Opochtli came for them at sunrise, with five tamemes in his party, carrying baskets of trade goods. They walked along the road, usually in sight of the river that ran past Paynala, stopping to eat when the sun was two hands above the horizon and again when it was directly overhead. Malinalli noticed fewer trees as they moved to the east, except alongside the river. She was glad when they did stop to rest and eat in shady places where the river ran cool, so she could wash the dust from her feet.

By late afternoon her legs were aching, and her nostrils were caked with road dust, but she didn't complain. She wanted to show her mother she was a big girl, old enough to make such an important trip. The sun was sinking low in the sky when Opochtli stopped and spread out a large blanket. He told her to climb into it, then folded it around her and pulled her up on his back. Rolled up like a snail in its shell, she happily rode the last part of the journey on his generous back.

"I just want to prove I can still carry a load with the best of my tamemes," Opochtli said to Cimatl.

"You have the strength of a much younger man," Cimatl said. "Apparently your traveling has kept you healthy." She knew that a man could receive that kind of compliment easily. She did not say what else she was thinking, because it might have embarrassed him. But quietly she admired, even more than his strength, his kindness to a young girl who was too proud to ask for it.

* * *

"You must meet my husband," Papalotl said eagerly as she greeted Cimatl and Malinalli with hugs. Her house was much smaller than the tecalli, but it was made of stone, not of sticks and mud. Although she had no guest house, she did have a sleeping room where the women could all stay together, separate from her husband's sleeping room. "This is Omecitli, 'Two Rabbit,' " Papalotl said proudly.

Omecitli, a muscular sun-browned man with work-stained hands, bowed his head and lowered his eyes in respect. He wore only a maxtli, but Cimatl recognized her sister's embroidered designs on the border that hung down to his knees. "You must be Cimatl and Malinalli," he said. "Welcome. Papalotl has told me a lot about you."

Cimatl and Malinalli also lowered their eyes in respect and said they were pleased to meet him. Then Omecitli excused himself and left to tend the farm. The farm was smaller than Itzamitl's, and Omecitli obviously did much of the work himself.

"Is this the man you were telling me about? Your steward?" Cimatl still wondered if her sister had done the right thing.

"Yes," Papalotl said happily. "He's an excellent farmer. We have bigger pumpkins and sweeter corn than any family around here. And he's wonderful with Xochi."

As if she had heard her name, Xochi appeared in the doorway of the sleeping room, rubbing her eyes. She toddled over to Papalotl and grabbed the hem of her cueitl. Papalotl patted her reassuringly. The sisters exchanged the usual remarks about how big their nieces had grown, and Malinalli proved how strong she was by lifting her two-year-old cousin.

After they walked around the farm and admired the evenly-spaced, well-weeded rows of vegetables and cotton Omecitli was cultivating, the sisters seated themselves on a petlatl in a vine-covered patio and made plans to visit the temple of Quetzalcoatl with their daughters. Papalotl, too, had seen the omen of the pyramid of light and considered it to be a good sign, a message of beauty and peace.

"During the month of Quecholli, the fourteenth month," said

Papalotl, "some of my friends took their daughters to the temple of Mixcoatl and spent the whole morning there talking to the old priestesses, dancing with their daughters in their arms."

"What a lovely holiday," Cimatl said enviously. She took Xochi on her lap and began stroking the toddler's hair.

"We'll have a holiday here, too, at the local temple. I know some of the priestesses there," Papalotl suggested. "Shall we both dedicate our daughters to Quetzalcoatl?"

"That's what Itzamitl wants me to do for Malinalli," said Cimatl. "She'll get a good education there, I'm sure, but would dedication mean she could never marry and have children?"

"Not necessarily. She would train as a priestess, of course, and live a life of chastity, but if she decides to marry later on, it can be arranged."

"What's chastity?" asked Malinalli, though her attention centered on a bee flitting among the blossoms on her aunt's vines.

The women laughed. "That means not letting boys or men touch you in private places," Cimatl explained.

"Private places?" Malinalli still seemed puzzled.

Cimatl placed her hand between Malinalli's legs. "Here," she said simply. "That is your private place. Don't let any boys or men touch you there until you get married."

"Then men can touch me there?" Malinalli was clearly disturbed by the thought.

Again the women laughed. "Your husband can touch you there, but don't let anyone else."

"I'm never going to get married!" said Malinalli, filled with disgust.

"Then you may want to become a priestess," said Papalotl. "Those are the only choices you have."

"Your father may make the choice for you," Cimatl cautioned. "If he chooses a husband for you, you can't refuse to marry."

"My father wouldn't do that," Malinalli said emphatically. "He wouldn't make me get married if I didn't want to."

"I hope you're right," Papalotl said. "Your father does dote on you, but he likes to be obeyed."

"We obey him gladly," Cimatl said in the tone of an older sister teaching a younger one a great truth. "By not defying him in small matters, we earn his consideration and kindness in larger ones."

"Again," Papalotl said, "I hope you're right. You place a great deal of weight upon your ability to persuade Itzamitl, but he places equal value on his right to command you."

"That's the way the world works," Cimatl said with an impatient sigh. "Men have their rights and duties; women have theirs. It does little good to complain about the way the gods made us. Let's just be grateful that we have kind husbands; many people have worse burdens to carry than we do."

"I'm grateful for my wonderful mother and my wonderful aunt," Malinalli said, hugging first Cimatl and then Papalotl. Xochi, not to be outdone, left Cimatl's lap and held out her arms to Papalotl. Both women smiled and turned their attention to their daughters, responding warmly to the children's affection. Malinalli did admire both women and, although she enjoyed listening to them discuss their differing ideas, she didn't want them to quarrel. She also sensed that both women were right, each in her own way, and each in her own way was a successful woman. She was beginning to internalize the truth that there are two ways to deal with the world of authority: to obey when necessary to survive or to please, and to resist when necessary to preserve a sense of dignity.

The next day the four of them—two mothers, two daughters —visited the temple and met several priestesses. Malinalli made no objection to the ceremonies dedicating the girls to the temple, because she thought becoming a priestess seemed preferable to marriage. As they had promised, the mothers took presents of food to the priestesses and for themselves as well. After a meal of tamales, fruit, and cactus candy, they danced with their daughters in their arms, whirling in the sunlight until they felt warm and sweaty, then cooling themselves in a well-tended temple garden, where a breeze from the ocean blew gently through the leaves of shade trees.

Butterflies fluttered around the gardens, and the girls made a game of trying to catch them. Malinalli remembered that Papalotl's name meant "Butterfly," and remarked that she thought all papalotls were beautiful.

Papalotl responded with a smile. "I'm glad to be named after a beautiful creature that never does harm to any other, just lives in peace and brings joy to all people."

Malinalli felt contented in the gardens of the temple, spiritually inspired. Ever afterward, when she saw a butterfly, she would remember this happy day, dancing in the sunlight with her mother and her aunt, chasing butterflies among the brilliant blossoms, and resting in the deep shade of trees as their leaves fluttered with the blessings of the Wind God.

* * *

Opochtli came for Cimatl and Mallinalli and took them to the market with him. This place seemed even more marvelous than the temple, much larger and more crowded than the village square in Paynala on market day, and Opochtli said that equal numbers of people came every day.

They wandered through rows of merchandise spread out on

reed mats. One section had only staple foods like beans, corn, and chick peas. Another section had meats—dogs and turkey fowls in cages, deer freshly killed and trussed on poles, hanging by their feet. Another had fabrics—squares of cotton and agave fiber woven with regional patterns. Pottery was piled in heaps in another section, and nearby were utensils for the home—spindles, shuttles, looms, icpallis and reed mats.

Traders from Mayan lands exhibited rubber balls, tzictli gum to chew, tropical fruits, and shell ornaments. Artisans spread out their collections of jewelry made from gold and silver, turquoise and jade. Guards wearing cotton armor stood near with long pointed spears, watching to discourage or punish thievery.

Most fascinating to Malinalli was the feather section. She had never seen anything so spectacular as the banners covered with bright feathers—white, yellow, red, black, green and blue—floating from tall poles. Feathers ornamented elaborate headdresses, bracelets, shields, and leg ornaments.

Opochtli traded the jewelry and pottery he had brought from Tenochtitlan and purchased many bundles of feathers, which were much in demand in the Valley of Mexico and were easy to carry. Then he went to the southernmost portion of the market and bought three slaves. He planned to use two slaves as porters, he told Cimatl, and sell them along the way as he sold off his goods. The third slave was for the priests in Paynala.

Malinalli felt sorry for the slaves. They stood passively beside small bundles, improvised by knotting the corners of a piece of cloth, that contained their belongings. The males wore only maxtlis, the women only plain, coarsely woven huipils and skirts. Most were barefoot, though a few had ragged hemp sandals fastened on with straps. Some had long poles attached to the backs of their necks. Opochtli told her the poles kept the slaves from running away, but the new owners would remove them.

"Did the slaves do something wrong?" Malinalli asked her mother. The poles looked like a punishment to her.

"Most of them have done something wrong at least three times," Cimatl said. "Then they can be sold."

"What did they do wrong?"

"They might have stolen from a temple, or sold some goods that didn't belong to them, or plotted against their king, or kidnapped children to sell them as slaves, or tried to help other slaves run away," Cimatl answered. "Or they might have refused to work for their masters after becoming slaves."

Opochtli added to the list. "Some people gamble themselves into debt and become slaves until they repay the debt. Or if they cause the death of another man's slave, they become slaves to replace the one they killed. But usually those slaves can earn their freedom back again."

"Why don't they run away?" Malinalli asked. She looked intently at the women slaves, trying to picture them kidnapping children or stealing from a temple.

"Some do run away," said the merchant. "But that's considered a crime like the theft of someone's property. If the master of a runaway slave catches him, he can sell that slave."

"What happens to the slaves that are sold?"

"Some of them will work in the milpas for their owners. Those who stole from a temple may become slaves for the temple, bringing wood and water or sweeping it for the priests. Some may be used for sacrifices. If they do, they'll be treated like warriors who died for the good of their tribe."

"Is death their punishment for doing wrong?"

"In a way," Opochtli answered. "But you can look at it another way. Their deaths in most cases will be better than their lives. They'll have as much glory as the warriors who die in battle. And eventually they'll come back to earth as hummingbirds, the birds sacred to Huitzilopochtli."

"Is death a good thing or a bad thing?" Malinalli asked. She was puzzled that death could sometimes be seen as the worst punishment for a crime, and other times as a glorious reward.

"It's a part of life," Opochtli said. "It happens to everyone sooner or later."

"We just have to do our best with the time we have on earth," Cimatl added. "None of us can change our tonalli; the gods have plans for us, even if we don't know what those plans are. Now don't ask any more questions."

Malinalli obeyed and stopped asking questions. But those questions about life and death never left her; they simply took up a silent residence in her mind, turning around and around in her thoughts as she tried to build meaning from her experiences.

* * *

Cimatl concluded that the omen of the pyramid light had been a good sign, and the dedication of her daughter to the temple a wise act, when she became pregnant. After she had missed her monthly bleeding for the second time, she summoned Chihuallama.

The midwife was overjoyed and immediately launched into a long list of proscriptions. Cimatl was to avoid chewing tzictli gum, for fear that the baby's palate and gums should swell and make feeding difficult. A pregnant woman should not look at red objects, or the baby might be born backwards. If she went out at night, she should put a few ashes in her blouse or belt to protect her against ghosts. She should not look at the sky during an eclipse, or the child would be born with a hare lip, unless of course the mother had taken the precaution of carrying an obsidian knife with her under her clothes, against the skin.

Chihuallama lectured to Itzamitl also. He was not to let Cimatl grow angry or be frightened. He must give her anything she longed for to keep her contented. And if he went out at night, he must also carry a few ashes because if he saw a phantom, the child might be born with a weak heart.

Itzamitl, hoping that this child would be the son he had been wanting for years, agreed that his wife should have the best of care. He cautioned Malinalli to be especially helpful and see that her mother did not get upset. He also brought in a servant girl to help with carrying water jugs, making fires, sweeping the house, and preparing meals.

The new servant girl's name was Matlalquiau, or "Green Rain." She was the 14-year-old daughter of a woodcutter who had sometimes sent her with a load of wood as his share of the tecuhtli's support. Strong and cheerful, she sang as she did daily chores. When the inside chores were done, she worked in the kitchen garden near the house, watering and weeding. She did not live in the tecalli but arrived every morning before sunrise and returned to her parents' home at sundown.

Cimatl was happy with the work of Matlalquiau, except for two things. For one, Matlalquiau left very little for Cimatl to do, except for the weaving and spinning. So Cimatl found herself wandering aimlessly around the house after she became bored with the only tasks permitted her. Even tending her flower garden, which had occupied her happily in the past, was considered too much physical labor for her now. She was allowed to walk, however, so she found herself walking rather often to the edge of the river and watching it swirl around the stones or eddy in small pools along the banks. But when the rainy season came, Itzamitl did not want her walking along the muddy paths for fear she might slip and fall.

The other problem was that Acamapichtli, who was now twelve years old, seemed to be hanging around the house to see Matlalquiau. Acamapichtli would hurry through his own work with his father, doing what Callipopoca considered slipshod work, and run to the tecalli to help Matlalquiau, who didn't need his help but who seemed flattered by his attentions. He began to bring her small presents—an egg, or a necklace made of dried corn kernels, or a smooth beautiful pebble from the river.

One day Cimatl walked with Malinalli to the hut of Chihuallama. The bulge of pregnancy caused Cimatl to walk awkwardly, but Malinalli was prepared to steady her. The air smelled fresh and clean after a heavy rain, and the cornstalks in the gardens by the houses reached tall into the blue skies. A few clouds still clung to the tops of the distant mountains, as if resting there until the little mountain gods could carry more rain from the clouds into the thirsty earth, watering the crops and filling the rivers.

As they neared Chihuallama's hut, Cimatl and Malinalli could smell the delicious odors of tomatoes and chili peppers simmering on the hearth. Toto heard them coming and pulled back the cloth that hung in their otherwise open doorway. Her hands were red with the stains of ripe tomatoes. Chihuallama, whose hands were also red with tomato juice, insisted that they have some of her corn soup flavored with tomatoes and peppers. They all sat on mats on the pounded clay floor, sipping the soup from clay bowls.

"Are you feeling well? Is the baby kicking?" Chihuallama exuded a neighbor's interest as well as a midwife's interest in the baby. She expected the birth in about sixty days, plenty of time yet to get ready.

"Yes, the baby and I are both doing fine," smiled Cimatl.

"Momma lets me feel the baby kick sometimes, and it doesn't hurt," Malinalli crowed to Toto. Toto looked envious.

"Itzamitl has hired a servant for me. He doesn't want me to do anything too strenuous."

Chihuallama pursed her lips thoughtfully and nodded. "You shouldn't lift anything too heavy, of course," she said. "But a little work never hurt any woman. Keeps the body in good condition for the labor."

"Do you know the girl my husband hired—Matlalquiau?"

"Oh yes," Chihuallama said knowingly. "Acamapichtli talks about her all the time. Wants to walk her home every evening."

"Then you know about her and Acamapichtli," said Cimatl, relieved. "She's two years older than he is, so I wondered how you felt about their being together so much."

"I worry about it," said Chihuallama. "She's a nice girl, and her family are honest hard-working folks. But I think they should find a husband for her soon. Acamapichtli is too young for her."

"I'm never going to get married," said Malinalli emphatically, addressing her comment to Toto but expecting the adult women to take note. "I'm going to be a priestess."

"I'd like to get married someday," said Toto dreamily.

"There's plenty of time for that later," said Chihuallama. "Girls don't usually get married before sixteen. Boys usually wait until they're twenty or twenty-one, when they can support a family."

"Do you want to go outside with Toto while Chihuallama and I talk?" Cimatl asked Malinalli.

"Let's go to the river, Toto," Malinalli suggested. "Maybe we can catch a frog."

"You can go, Toto," Chihuallama agreed. "You've done enough work for today."

When the girls had left, Cimatl confided in Chihuallama the

real purpose of her visit. "I don't want to worry Itzamitl or Malinalli," she said. "But I've been having some bleeding for a couple of days. Can you give me something to stop it?"

Chihuallama's eyes grew wide. "Have you had any pains?"

"A little cramping."

"That's not good," said Chihuallama. "I'll make you some herb tea to stop the bleeding. But if that doesn't work, you may have to spend the last two months lying flat on your petlatl and praying to the goddess Ayopechcatl."

* * *

Malinalli and Toto walked carefully to the river, avoiding the muddiest and most slippery spots. The path to the river had been well worn by the feet of villagers going down for water, and puddles formed easily in its depressions. The wet grass along the sides brushed their ankles as they skirted around the puddles.

They walked past several milpas where the corn was growing tall enough to play hide and seek, but since the stalks were still drenched with the recent rainfall, they decided not to play in the cornfields. Wet feet would be reason enough for their mothers to frown at them, but wet and muddy skirts would have to be washed, and the result would surely be a scolding or worse.

"I'm not supposed to do anything to upset my mother," said Malinalli. "The baby might not be born right if I do."

"Mothers get upset easily when they are having babies," Toto advised. "We'll be very careful."

As they neared the river's edge, they could hear a frog croaking. They approached silently so as not to frighten the frog, peeking through some bushes to see where he was.

To their surprise, they did not see a frog, but the figure of a naked young man in a clearing between clumps of bushes. They could see his buttocks, his bony shoulders, and the back of his head. Standing close and facing him was a girl, just a little taller than he, wearing the unadorned skirt and huipil of a peasant. Her skirt was pulled up around her waist, and the brown arm of the boy was vigorously moving in and out directly between her legs.

Malinalli gasped, and Toto giggled. The boy turned around, upsetting a water jug on the ground behind him. He cursed and picked it up. Toto stopped in the middle of a giggle and grabbed Malinalli's arm, pulling her backward through the brush. They crashed through the bushes, running back to the path, slipping in the mud but miraculously not falling in it.

They kept looking over their shoulders as they ran. When they were sure no one was following them, and their breathing was coming hard, they slowed down to a walk.

"That was Acamapichtli," said Toto disgustedly. "I'm going

to tell my father."

"And that was Matlalquiau," said Malinalli, still shocked. "She was not being chaste."

"What does that mean?" asked Toto.

"I learned about it when I went to Coatzacoalcos," said Malinalli, proud that there was at last something she knew that Toto did not. "When a girl lets a boy touch her private places, she isn't being chaste."

"Is that wrong?" said Toto, amazed. "I just thought Acamapichtli was playing instead of bringing the water home."

"You'd better talk to your mother about it," Malinalli said. "She probably wants you to be chaste, just like me, except with your husband, that is."

When the two girls burst into the hut, Cimatl had finished her tea and Callipopoca was there for his noontime meal.

"Daddy," Toto tattled, "Acamapichtli was playing at the river instead of getting the water like you told him."

"And Matlalquiau wasn't being chaste," blurted Malinalli to her mother.

Cimatl and Chihuallama exchanged looks of alarm. Then Cimatl grabbed Chihuallama's arm. "Take me home," she said, her face becoming pale. "I'm having a cramp."

Chihuallama slipped Cimatl's right arm over her own strong shoulders and supported her with an arm behind her back. She started toward the door with Cimatl, pausing only long enough to issue a grim command. "Callipopoca, find your son and see if the girls are right about him. I may be away for the rest of the day."

The look on Callipopoca's face made the girls tremble, but they stayed until Acamapichtli arrived with the water jug.

"What were you doing at the river?" stormed Callipopoca.

"Getting water," said Acamapichtli sullenly.

"Were you with Matlalquiau?"

"Yes," Acamapichtli said defiantly. "What did they tell you?" He looked angrily at his sister and Malinalli.

"Did you touch her?"

"She wanted me to."

"That's no excuse. You have work to do. You can't afford trouble. Fooling around with girls will just get you into trouble."

Acamapichtli hung his head and said nothing.

"Stop seeing her," said Acamapichtli.

"No," he said, his jaw rigid, his eyes blazing defiantly into his father's.

Suddenly the irate Callipopoca grabbed his son and turned him upside down over the flames of the hearth. "Give me that chili powder, Toto," he said. Trembling, Toto complied, and her father poured the powder onto the flames.

An acrid smoke puff enveloped the head of the writhing Acamapichtli, and he screamed in pain, coughing as if he would choke to death. The smell of the burning chili filled the hut and made the girls' eyes itch and burn. They ran outside, rubbing their eyes, tears streaming down their smoke-dirtied faces, coughing and gasping.

They gulped the fresh air outside the hut. The smoke still filtered slowly through the thatched roof, and Acamapichtli's screams turned to begging. "Please let me go," the boy cried. "I'll obey. I promise."

Toto and Malinalli were still crying outside the hut when Callipopoca came out, squinting his eyes but showing no tears, striding angrily toward the milpas. They could hear Acamapichtli sobbing inside the hut, multiplying their own misery.

"It's our fault," said Malinalli through her sobs. "We shouldn't have told."

Holding her nose and squinting, Toto went inside and brought her brother out, leading him as if he were blind. "I'm so sorry, Acamapichtli," she said. "I didn't know this would happen."

Acamapichtli didn't answer. He could only cough and wretch as if trying to vomit, rubbing his burning, tear-blotched eyes with his fists. He stopped crying very soon, and Toto never saw him cry again. When their father returned that evening he brought a maxtli for Acamapichtli and told him to put it on. "From now on," Callipopoca said gruffly but with pride, "wear this maxtli every day. You're taking some of the privileges of being a man, but a man must learn restraint. From now on, you are a man, Acamapichtli. From now on, act like one."

* * *

Malinalli was still crying from pain and shame when she arrived at the tecalli. She had borrowed a dog from Toto, remembering how a warm dog had comforted her when she had a stomachache. Chihuallama would not allow her in the sleeping room where her mother lay, but she accepted the dog from Malinalli and took it in, saying that it might help.

Matlalquiau had returned from the river and prepared the evening meal silently, not singing even one song. Malinalli stayed silent, also, thinking she had caused enough trouble. When her father returned at sunset, she didn't run to meet him as she usually did, but trudged down the path with heavy feet.

"What's the matter, Malinalli?" asked Itzamitl.

Tears flowed afresh. "I didn't mean to upset her, Daddy."

"Upset who?"

"Mommy. She has a tummyache. I didn't mean to hurt anyone."

"Where is she?" Itzamitl began walking more rapidly.

Malinalli ran behind him. "In the sleeping room.

Chihuallama is with her."

Itzamitl loped across the courtyard and into the tecalli. Chihuallama was sitting beside Cimatl, feeding her some broth. Cimatl was still clutching the dog to her stomach, but it whined, squirmed, and ran to Itzamitl, sniffing his feet. "I'm glad you're home," Chihuallama said simply. "I'm doing all I can."

Itzamitl took the dog outside and tied it to a post in the patio. He paced in the courtyard, his head bowed in prayer to one god after another, until the red glow had disappeared from the sky and clouds had covered the stars.

Matlalquiau timidly offered to stay, if she could be of help, but Chihuallama dismissed her curtly. "You've brought great trouble to my son," she said tiredly. "I'm too worried to scold you now, but if you care about Acamapichtli, leave him alone. He's too young for you. As for Cimatl, I'll stay as long as she needs me. You can come again in the morning." So Matlalquiau left with a heavy heart, wondering if she would ever see Acamapichtli again, feeling a pain in her heart that filled her chest to bursting.

Malinalli brought the dog some atole in a clay bowl; the dog lapped it up then curled into a ball and slept. She sat in the light of a pine torch and tried to keep busy by spinning cotton thread. She could hear Chihuallama chanting in steady rhythms, praying to the goddess Teteoinnan, mother of the gods, and Ayopechcatl, goddess of childbed. She felt consumed with guilt, sure that she had brought all this trouble into their house.

The chanting stopped. Malinalli could hear a few muffled groans, and then silence. The weary Chihuallama came to the door carrying a bundle of blood-soaked rags, her arms red with blood, her huipil drenched red. She spoke to Itzamitl. "This is a hard grief we bear. Cimatl will be all right, but the child is dead. It would have been a boy."

"Can I see them now?" Itzamitl asked, choking on his words.

"You can see Cimatl, but not the baby," Chihuallama said huskily. "I had to cut the child to pieces when he died within her. If I hadn't, she'd have died too. It's the hardest thing I've ever had to do." Then she left for her hut, carrying the bundle in her arms, leading Toto's little dog by its rope. Her shoulders sagged and her feet shuffled as if the tiny bundle she carried weighed more than she could bear.

Malinalli had never seen her father cry, and he did not cry then, but he could not speak. He went into the sleeping room and sat on the floor beside Cimatl, his arm across her sleeping form, his head bowed in ineffable sorrow. His grief suffused the room and the tecalli and stretched to the cover of clouds above until the whole night sky seemed to grieve. Tlaloc and the mountain rain gods wept for him as the rain fell and turned all the paths and gardens and milpas to mud. The sky was still weeping when

Malinalli awoke the next morning beside the cold, dead ashes in the hearth.

* * *

The gloom in the tecalli lasted many months. Itzamitl was saved from total despair by having to go to the village every day and take care of government business. Cimatl was saved by knowing that Malinalli needed her, and she devoted herself to her one remaining child as if to give her the mothering that two children normally take. Chihuallama was saved by the hard work that forms the framework of a peasant's life. There was no time for sadness when there were crops to harvest and children to feed and clothing to mend. Malinalli was saved only by thinking of the life of penance she would lead when she could begin to serve at the temple.

But there were moments when none of them could avoid the terrible grip of their loss. On Malinalli's ninth birthday in the year 5 Rabbit [1510], when the family had finished their evening meal, Itzamitl gave her a present from the market in Paynala. It was a three-legged bowl, one that could stand over glowing coals and keep the food hot. "Soon you'll be learning to cook," he said. "I'll be a proud father when my daughter serves me something she's made in this dish."

"Thank you," Malinalli beamed, taking the dish then handing it to Cimatl to put away for her. She felt important when her father took pride in her femininity. But then she remembered how much he had wanted the son he lost. "Did you want a boy when I was born?" she asked timidly.

"Not at all. I like girls. Especially those who can cook." He tried to smile, but he had gone so long without smiling that his face simply looked contorted. "I would have liked a son, Malinalli, as any man would. But that doesn't mean I don't want a daughter, too. Parents have room in their hearts for all their children."

Hearing her husband's words, Cimatl walked out into the courtyard to get control of her grief. She wished she could be as philosophical as Itzamitl, but her sense of loss was still acute; she was still angry with the gods who promise so much, only to snatch it all away.

For Malinalli, however, Itzamitl had said exactly the right thing. Tears of relief and pent-up anguish spilled out of Malinalli's eyes. Soon she was sobbing, "I didn't mean to upset Mommy. I didn't mean for the baby to die."

"Oh my dear little flower, my precious feather," Itzamitl said. "Are you blaming yourself? Come to me. I need to talk to you." He held out his arms and Malinalli plunged into them as if they were a cool river on a hot day. He lifted her onto his lap as he sat on the icpalli, holding her in his arms, speaking soothingly.

"It wasn't your fault the baby died. These things happen sometimes. It isn't anyone's fault."

Malinalli felt ashamed of her tears and wiped them away with her fist. "Did the gods take the baby so the sun will stay in the sky?"

"Maybe so. The gods give us the gifts of life, and food, and shelter, and children. But whatever they give, they can take away. You haven't done anything wrong, my precious daughter. Please don't cry."

"Big girls don't cry," she said, forcing a smile.

"You're a big girl, all right. This year you'll learn to cook, and when you're ten, you'll go to the telpochcalli and learn all about the gods and the history of our people."

"Did you go to the telpochcalli?" Malinalli asked, her curiosity now exceeding her grief.

"Yes, and to the calmecac after that. I learned self-discipline there, as all warriors and priests must do. We'd get up several times each night and bathe in the cold river. We learned to endure pain and hardship without complaint."

"Girls can do that, too," said Malinalli.

"Oh, yes. Women can endure as much pain as men. They can have just as much courage. Your mother's had a great deal of pain, but you never hear her complain."

"I wish I had been a boy," Malinalli said. "I'd be a warrior if I were a boy."

"Warriors have a hard life," Itzamitl said. "It isn't all glory and feathers and parades. Do you know what my father said to me when I left for the telpochcalli? He said 'listen, my son, you are not going to be honored, nor obeyed, nor respected. You will be looked down upon, despised, and humiliated. Every day you will harden your body by bathing in the cold pools. Every day you will cut agave-thorns and draw blood from your body with those spines. You will fast until you are weak with hunger, but through all this you will make the best of things.' He was right about all those things. We learned self-control and humility, the most useful lessons in life."

"Will I do all those things too?"

"Yes, but not as much. Girls don't have to cut wood or repair the ditches. They do cooking and weaving and make robes for the priests. Girls have an easier life in the telpochcalli."

Malinalli still thought temple life for girls sounded boring, but she did not argue. She went outside to find her mother standing beside the ahueheutl tree and staring silently into the darkness. Malinalli wondered whether a woman's life was truly easier than a man's. The wind was blowing hard in the tops of the trees, making a moaning sound, like a woman crying for her lost children.

Chapter 8

The Conquest of Cuba

The Viceroy Diego Colon, son of the deceased explorer Cristobol Colon, chose Diego Velasquez to head the expedition to Cuba in 1511. Velasquez, an hidalgo from the province of Cuellar, had served seventeen years in Spain's wars before coming to Hispaniola as a pioneer settler in 1493. Under the orders of former governor Nicolas de Ovando, he had obediently killed Indians by the hundreds if they were suspected of being rebellious or harboring rebels. Yet he killed as if he were cutting palm fronds with a machete, getting an unpleasant business out of the way, not taking much pleasure in it. Since Ovando had a similar reputation, the two men had worked well together, but Ovando held stern religious convictions, whereas Velasquez inclined toward hedonism.

Velasquez made a commanding figure, with a fair complexion, spacious forehead, a well-chiselled nose and mouth, and a narrow full-bearded chin. His large, clear eyes conveyed a pleasing intellectual expression, though the pursuit of profit pleased him better than the pursuit of learning. Although already a rather portly figure at forty-six, fond of food and drink, he presented an imposing presence when he went about elegantly attired as was his custom. These qualities no doubt endeared him to Maria de Cuellar, for they had become engaged to marry. Yet she was somewhat apprehensive; she had noticed his tendency to become jealous and easily angered. His outward amiability concealed a restless and suspicious nature.

Other members of the expeditionary force included Bartolome de Las Casas as chaplain; Panfilo de Narvaez as lieutenant; Hernan Cortes as clerk of the treasurer; and Pedro de Alvarado, as captain of one of the four ships that would carry 300 men to Cuba. Narvaez, a native Castilian of ruddy complexion and surly temperament, had entered military service at a young age and had become one of the first settlers in Jamaica. At thirty-three, he had a reputation for fierceness and had trained thirty Jamaican archers for this expedition.

Cortes, having served briefly in a few of Ovando's campaigns against the rebels, was getting bored with the life of a prosperous gentleman farmer and disappointed with the small amount of gold his Indians were finding in the streams of Hispaniola. At twenty-six, he was ready for new adventures. Alvarado, the same age as Cortes but more impetuous and hot-tempered, had arrived in Hispaniola the year before, in 1510. A handsome man with sunny blond hair, pointed beard, and slender face, he relished excitement and loved the privileges of command.

* * *

The natives of Cuba, mostly of the Taino tribe though the Spaniards called them Indians, possessed a few stone axes and crude spears to use as defensive weapons. These offered little resistance to the steel swords and the crossbows of trained archers among the Velasquez forces. Militarily easy, the conquest nonetheless generated some moral difficulties. The young Bartolome de Las Casas observed some scenes that would later haunt him with guilt and anger. These scenes would drive him into a lifetime crusade in which he became a voice that could not be stilled, a conscience that could not be denied.

As a hundred of Narvaez' soldiers approached Caonao in Cuba, they stopped to eat breakfast near a dry river. A few shallow pools were shriveling in the tropical heat, but many stones lay exposed in the riverbed. Using the stones as whetstones, the soldiers sharpened their swords before marching to the village. Those men who had horses rode; others walked along the banks of the parched stream until they reached the village. Some began singing loudly and swinging their sharpened swords with playful swishes through the air.

Several naked Taino villagers, busy at their tasks of making a canoe and simple pottery, were seated on the grass between the river and a large thatched hut. A few stood in the doorway of the large hut, one of several *bohios* erected around a small common area. Startled at the noisy Spaniards and their snorting horses, the Indians stopped their work and stared in fright.

Suddenly one of the Spaniards thrust his sword into the belly of an old man, testing its sharpness. The Taino grunted in disbelief, clutching his exposed bowels; his wife screamed in terror. Then all hundred soldiers drew their swords, attacking the screaming villagers. The soldiers followed women, children, and men into the large hut, slashing and stabbing until the ground was drenched with blood. One soldier cut a man in half and cried, "No one has a sword sharper than mine."

In a few minutes the massacre was over. The men cleaned their swords by dipping them in the shallow puddles of the riverbed, then wiping them on the grass. Quiet descended, broken only by the sound of a few steel blades being re-sharpened on the river stones and the buzz of flies attracted to the carnage. Las Casas stood in shock looking at the piles of corpses, arms, legs, disemboweled trunks, and severed heads strewn around the clearing. A few rats ventured timidly out of the grass, sniffing, then nibbling on the wasted body parts. A crocodile thrust his snout from a stand of bamboo on the bank, slowly looked around, then retreated to lie in wait.

Las Casas stepped behind one of the smaller huts, where a partially finished canoe and some pottery shards lay scattered on the ground. A tiny carved household idol, called a *zemi* by the Taino people, lay face down in the blood-soaked dust. Las Casas vomited until he felt weak. Then he followed the soldiers to their next campsite, keeping at some distance behind them.

Later that night Narvaez' men joined the others in a campsite on the beach. They ate some freshly netted ocean fish, shellfish collected from tidal pools, and potatoes scavenged from Indian gardens. Then they gathered around a campfire and told stories. Las Casas listened, still feeling sick, but fearful of drawing the men's anger upon himself. The light from the fire made shadows on their faces, giving them a devilish appearance. A few bats flapped overhead, like omens from the underworld,

The stars shone serenely as if the universe had not been disturbed. A warm breeze brought the smell of seaweed scattered randomly along the beach, castaway plants locked in a perpetual cycle of destruction and renewal.

"When I was in the Carib Islands," one soldier related, "we needed food, and the natives wouldn't bring us much. My dog got hungry. The bugger was whining at my heels. I saw an Indian woman on the road carrying a sucking baby. Since they wouldn't feed us, I thought their brats shouldn't be fed either. I tore the baby from the mother's arms and threw it to my dog. My dog ate better than I did that day."

"They're nothing more than animals themselves," another said contemptuously. "They go naked unless someone makes them wear clothes. Did you know the Caribs are cannibals? They'll eat you if they catch you alone in their territory."

"Disgusting beasts," agreed another. "The friars think they can turn them into Christians, but Indians can't ever understand religion. They're a bunch of idol-worshiping savages."

Las Casas felt himself growing tense and angry, prodded by his religious principles to speak out against evil. He said a quick silent prayer; then he spoke with restraint. "Perhaps we should set them a good example," he said. "A Dominican priest I know witnessed some Spaniards taking some Indian prisoners. Some of the Indian women had newborn children, and when the babies cried, the soldiers grabbed them by the legs and threw them against the rocks. Then they tossed them into the jungle so they'd die there. Was that good Christian behavior?"

"Listen to the sermon," responded one soldier mockingly. "You haven't seen much of war, have you?"

"You talk like a do-gooder," growled the soldier who had been in the Carib islands. "I guess that's what chaplains are supposed to be. But before you get holier-than-thou with us, remember how you got your own encomienda."

The soldier who hated savages laughed. "Through blood and guts, chaplain! None of the Indians just give up their lands to colonists. You're building your precious empire on the backs of fighting men with blood on their hands and mud on their clothes."

"True enough," replied Las Casas sadly. "None of us can have a perfectly clear conscience here. None of us can cast the first stone." He resolved to say nothing more about the soldiers' behavior, but just to be accountable for his own. He still felt nauseated, a sickness of the soul as much as one of the body, he felt sure.

Hernan Cortes, who had been with Velasquez' troops that day, had been leaning against a nearby palm tree, listening to the talk of the Narvaez troops. He stepped into the firelight, speaking in calm and conciliatory tones. "Some of you rode horses today. Did you consider them friends?" After some murmurs of assent he continued. "A horse or a dog is a friend when he works for us. Some animals show us a devotion that no human can match. Even if you consider the Indians animals, you'd be wise to treat them well."

"What good are the stinking Indians to us?" asked the soldier who hated savages. He spat into the flames.

Cortes' voice took on greater sternness. "I understand how you feel," he said. "You have to be able to hate an enemy who's trying to kill you, or you couldn't kill him first. I've been in battle. I know how it is. Lieutenant Narvaez won't reprimand you for killing in battle, and perhaps not even for killing in sport. But remember that we need workers to grow the crops that feed us. The king wants vassals, not corpses. Dead Indians don't work, and they don't pay tribute."

Cortes' words encouraged Las Casas to speak again. "Queen Isabel also wanted the Indians well treated if they don't resist," he said. "She dictated a codicil to her will."

"Yes," Cortes agreed, "and I obey her even after her death. She was a great Christian lady."

"She wanted to spread the Christian gospel," Las Casas added, glaring at the soldier who hated savages.

"A few words said by a priest don't make savages our equals," said the soldier angrily. He started to rise to his feet, as if to start a brawl, but Cortes restrained him with a hand on his shoulder.

"No one is your equal, Roberto," Cortes said with a mix of admiration and amusement in his voice. "I've never seen a better swordsman. I'd challenge you to some swordplay or some gambling right now, but I hate to lose either at swords or cards."

Roberto pointed to a scar on Cortes' chin, still red and healing, making a rift in his thin dark beard. "Is that wound proof of your swordsmanship?" he said in affable mockery. Cortes' response was quick and jovial. "No. From a knife. An irate husband's knife. I might add that my opponent won the fight, but he lost his woman."

The laughter that followed released some of the soldiers' tensions. The men went to sleep in good spirits, and Cortes had made his point without antagonizing the soldiers. He was getting some practice in leading men to carry out his wishes without seeming to command. Even Las Casas could claim a small victory in the incident, for these men stopped their wanton killing, and some even asked for absolution in their confessions.

* * *

In a few weeks' time the steel swords of the invaders had slashed their way through the tropical forests and brought many fearful natives into submission. Only one Indian resisted the Spaniards in Cuba, and his last words made him a folk hero, immortalized in the shrine of the often-told tale. His name was Hatuey; he had fled to Cuba from Hispaniola after a massacre that Velasquez had directed. There he was finally captured and condemned to be burned at the stake. A Franciscan friar urged him to be baptized as a Christian, so he could enter heaven after his death.

"Are there Spaniards in Heaven?" asked the Indian captive.

"Of course," the friar assured him.

"Then I would not want to go there," Hatuey said contemptuously. And he went to his fiery death with his pagan pride intact, never relenting even as the smoke filled his eyes and mouth and the flames blistered his flesh.

Chapter 9

Choices, Chastity, and Celebrations

In the year 6 Reed [1511], when she was ten years old, Malinalli experienced some foreshadowings of the distaste she would acquire for the Aztec rituals of cannibalism and punishment. That year Chihuallama began teaching her and Toto to cook. Chihuallama knew how to break the neck of a turkey, and she taught the girls to pluck its feathers and prepare it for roasting. But Malinalli was shocked when she saw Chihuallama kill one of her dogs to make meat-stuffed tamales, peeling away the animal's outer skin, gutting it like a deer, slicing chunks of the meat into a pot of boiling water. Malinalli had always considered deer meat a proper food, a hunter's prey. She had also seen Chihuallama kill frogs and lizards for their meat. But she thought of the dogs as part of the domestic scene, playful animals who served humans and deserved their protection. Toto, on the other hand, took the same unperturbed attitude her mother did, that the dogs had been raised as food; it was their destiny to become food for humans.

When Malinalli refused to eat anything made with dog meat, her parents scolded her sternly for her squeamishness, telling her she was being childish and unrealistic. When she still refused to eat, Itzamitl forbade Cimatl to feed her anything at all until she ate the dog meat. To make sure she didn't eat somewhere else, Itzamitl confined her to her own house and yard.

Toto, too, derided her friend's obstinacy, since they couldn't work or play together while she was being punished. "Don't be silly, Malinalli; it's only a dog."

"And you're only a servant!" Malinalli snapped. "Don't talk down to me!" She instantly regretted her outburst when she saw the look on Toto's face, but she didn't apologize. It was difficult enough to endure her parents' scolding; chiding was intolerable from a girl close to her own age. Her words had driven the wedge of class consciousness between them, and from that time on, Toto spoke to her in a deferential, aloof way. Malinalli felt a sense of loss, but her sense of injured pride proved stronger.

After three days of fasting, Cimatl pleaded with Malinalli to obey her father. Cimatl brought a tempting stew, steaming with the smell of spicy broth and vegetables. Malinalli relented, partly because she thought hunger may have made her snappish with Toto, but mainly to please her mother. She ate only a tiny bite of the dog meat along with many vegetables and much broth. By that time she had learned that hunger pains will disappear after the first few days of deprivation. Later in life she would be glad for that knowledge.

The lives of Malinalli and Toto had begun to diverge at adolescence. Although they would both be taught to do similar kinds of women's work, their prospects for education and for marriage were quite different. Toto was a macehualli's daughter; she could expect to remain a servant or perhaps to marry a farmer. Her tasks at the age of 11 were already preparing her for a life like her mother's, and she dreamed only of the man she might marry someday, not of a different kind of life.

Malinalli's future, however, was a matter of some discussion between her father and the men of the noble class in Paynala and Oluta. The age of ten was not too soon to decide the future of a tecuhtli's daughter, since arrangements should be made well in advance of her marriageable age of sixteen. Cimatl reminded Itzamitl that Malinalli had been dedicated to the temple of Quetzalcoatl, but he countered that such an agreement need not be permanent. Still, he reasoned, it might be best to let her spend about six years in the temple under the guidance of a priestess, away from the influence of impetuous macehual youths like Acamapichtli and Matlalquiau.

Acamapichtli, the son of Callipopoca and Chihuallama, had eloped with Matlalquiau that same year, when she turned sixteen. He was only fourteen, still too young to expect his parents' approval, but he was consumed with the fire of adolescent passion and fearful of losing Matlalquiau to some youth who had reached the approved age of twenty. Matlalquiau also preferred Acamapichtli to any of the older youths she knew, those that she might have been forced to marry. Her attraction to Acamapichtli became intensified when it became forbidden. So in furtive meetings in the cornfields they pledged to live with each other openly until such time as the adults in their world would acknowledge, however reluctantly, that the couple belonged together and should be allowed to marry.

The lovers began living together in Matlalquiau's village, where Acamapichtli's parents were not known and could not be disgraced by their son's unconventional behavior. Acamapichtli was learning the woodcutter's trade from Matlalquiau's father, so her parents accepted her choice without much fuss. Chihuallama, however, felt keen disappointment in her son and did not talk about him; in fact, Callipopoca had ordered her not to. But

Cimatl knew her macehual neighbor was grieving, and she hoped the lovers would one day reappear, beg their parents' forgiveness, and tie their tilmantli in a belated but acceptable union.

Fathers of the upper classes worried more than woodcutters did about their daughters' chastity, and Itzamitl cared greatly about his family's image in the community. He had issued the order to punish a pair of adulterers, and all the villagers in Paynala over the age of ten were obliged to watch. So Malinalli witnessed a stoning near the Paynala temple that year, along with other village youths, as a warning to them to live chastely. They formed a semicircle near the temple wall, the younger and shorter ones standing in front of their mothers to be sure their vision was not blocked.

The crime of adultery was a civil crime—that is, a crime against the village which Itzamitl administered, but it was also a religious offense, so the priests administered the punishment. Priests from the Paynala temple marched solemnly before the crowd wearing official black robes trimmed with embroidered white skulls. Their shaved foreheads shone in the morning sunlight; the long locks from the tops of their heads hung in matted strings down their backs. Their earlobes and arms showed scars from self-mutilation by thorns or flint knives.

Speaking with some difficulty, because his tongue had also been mutilated by having a thorn-studded thread drawn through it many times, a priest explained to the crowd that a crime had been committed. He said the whole community must join to see that justice was done, or the gods would surely punish them all. Because the accused woman was married, she was not free to be an auianime, or "pleasure woman" for the accused man. The priest compared the man to a thief who had taken a basket of corn from another man's field. "If a traveler merely satisfies his own hunger by taking from the first row of corn along the roadside," the priest explained, "then the farmer owes him that kindness. But if he takes a basket into the farmer's field to reap the benefits of the crop the farmer has watered and weeded and cared for, then he is a thief."

Then the priest picked up a stone from a pile near the temple wall. The other priests and villagers followed their lead, holding stones in readiness as the accused couple were brought in. The woman, led to the temple wall by a rope around her neck, wore a stoical expression and fixed her eyes on the ground, as if determined not to cry out. However, when a priest threw a flower-covered cord around her neck and tightened it quickly to strangle her, a gasp of pain escaped her stiff lips. As she crumpled in the dust, another priest lifted a heavy rock and dropped it on her head, crushing her skull with a cracking sound audible to the apprehensive crowd.

The man was first stripped naked by the priests, then his

96

head shaved with flint knives, then thrown to his knees while the villagers jeered and pelleted his back with stones. "You scorpions! A plague on you all!" he cursed angrily, picking up a stone and throwing it back at one of his tormenters, but his defiance only caused the villagers to rush upon him and beat him with sticks as well as pummel him with heavier stones. The priests crushed his head with a huge stone, and the villagers advanced, shouting, their faces twisted into wild rage, pummeling both bodies with stones. When the cursing and shouting stopped, the bloody masses of two bodies lay among the scattered stones. The villagers drifted away, vultures began to circle, and the blood-covered priests wrapped the bodies for cremation.

Malinalli again felt sick, not only at the blood and the suffering she had witnessed, but also at the memory of the gloating faces and vengeful cries of the villagers. These neighbors, decent hard-working people she had known for years, had been throwing stones as if they were rubber balls in a game of tlachtli, had been wearing satisfied smiles as they left the scene. She walked glumly back to the tecalli beside her mother, who was also unusually quiet. She ate very little that day, but Cimatl didn't eat much either.

* * *

The calpixqui were irritated when they learned of the stoning; they would have preferred to take the victims to Tenochtitlan as sacrifices. The priests of Tenochtitlan needed 12,000 human hearts to consecrate the great sacrificial stone at the temple of Huitzilopochtli that year, 6 Reed. But the priests of Paynala convinced them that stonings were occasionally needed to deter others from crime, especially impressionable youths.

Some of the necessary sacrificial victims were purchased from the Mayan traders coming through Paynala. These merchants spoke limited Nahuatl and were viewed with suspicion by the villagers. But the Paynala merchants found it necessary to do business with the Mayas, buying not only slaves but also rubber, salt, shells, and feathers from the tropical regions. They could use these items to satisfy tribute demands from the Emperor. As long as Moctezuma's calpixqui were satisfied with slaves, the Emperor would not provoke a battle to take captives.

* * *

When life is hard, ceremonies become necessities. In the month of Tlaxochimoco, or "Offering of Flowers," (late July) it was time for a feast to honor Yacatecuhtli, patron god of the merchants. It was a time of rejoicing, when mothers and children went into the fields and woods, gathering wildflowers to decorate their homes and public buildings. Cimatl and Malinalli joined Chihuallama and Toto in a lovely day of gathering flowers and fragrant pine boughs, one of their happiest days together.

The merchant Opochtli had been storing his surplus goods for nearly two years in the granary and guest houses of Itzamitl, and both men were eager to see the storehouses emptied in a grand display of generosity. The feast was held in a public hall in Paynala, where all the adult villagers from both Paynala and Oluta could assemble. When Opochtli arrived, he could see a group of "bumblebees" already beginning to gather—uninvited poor people who hoped to glean some leftovers. He considered the custom of "bumblebeeing" not only harmless but flattering to the host, because it enhanced his reputation for generosity.

People of high rank were served first, by macehualtin like Chihuallama and Toto, who dressed in the white garments typical of everyday wear for the servant and working classes. They knew Opochtli had provided food enough for everyone, and they would eat when the nobles had finished. His offerings included not only the foods everyone liked, but appetizing and imaginative ways of serving them. Every guest was given a present, and the presents were elegant: reed mats, baskets, pottery, deerskin cactli, deerskin pouches, beautiful woven blankets, mantles, huipils, feather-covered shields, and even jewelry made with precious stones and silver.

Since both Opochtli and Itzamitl had ten-year-old daughters, they arranged for the girls to meet each other at the feast. Malinalli and Metzli would both be attending the telpochcalli in the temple at Coatzacoalcos soon, and their fathers hoped they would become friends. Metzli, who had rather oddly been named after the moon god, was a frail girl whose huipil hung loosely on her bony shoulders. Her huipil, dyed red with the finest achiotl, was embroidered around the neck with a string of yellow hearts. Her bright costume made her skin look pale and yellowish, but her large eyes gleamed with intelligence. Malinalli and Cimatl wore huipils of dark blue cotton, which Cimatl had dyed with anil. She had trimmed their huipils with geometric designs of red cochineal dye, original designs on which Metzli complimented her. As the three of them sat together and chatted amiably, Cimatl observed Metzli's politeness and eagerness to please adults; she decided Metzli would indeed be a good companion for Malinalli at the temple.

Opochtli also brought his son Chimalli, who had been studying at the telpochcalli to become a warrior. Chimalli's colorfully-bordered tilmantli, knotted at one shoulder, revealed a right arm with splended curving muscles. His dark eyes looked out under a bang of hair cut straight across his forehead, but the hair on his crown was bound in a topknot. A long lock on one side of his neck indicated his status as a novice warrior; he would cut it when he had accomplished certain feats. His smile was broad and confident, his posture straight, his eyes alert and inquisitive.

Malinalli thought Chimalli was the handsomest youth she had ever seen, but Metzli had grown up with him and saw him only as a big brother who liked to have his own way. Chimalli was not introduced to Toto because her role that night was that of a servant, but she took every opportunity to serve him, as if he were the only guest present. Her eyes fastened upon the curves of his smiling mouth and powerful limbs as if to memorize them.

Chimalli paid little attention to any of the girls present. He walked around with a companion from the telpochcalli, a youth named Tlacoch, or "Spear." Tlacoch, who wore two tilmantli to display his wealth, was the pilli son of an eagle warrior who taught military skills at the telpochcalli. His well-built body revealed his physical heritage from his warrior father, but he walked with loose arrogance, not prideful carriage.

Tlacoch's father, the eagle warrior Tlacateotl, or "Godlike man," was Chimalli's idol. Tlacateotl was, indeed, an impressive figure. As one who had reached the highest ranks of knighthood because of brave feats of war, he could wear a xicolli or special tunic under his tilmantli, tied at the throat with a ribbon. His tilmantli was a simple white, but rich gold threads formed a border of stylized eagle's heads, and decorations of gold adorned his cactli. He could have worn a feather-covered headdress signifying his rank as an eagle knight, but instead he had modestly stuck two feathers into his topknot, the way a beginning warrior would do when entering his first battles.

In the background musicians played flutes and drums. A white-robed calmecac student stepped into the center of the hall and recited from memory a poem by the famous poet-king of Texcoco, Nezahualcoyotl or "Fasting Coyote":

All the earth is a grave from which nothing escapes.
Even perfect things descend into its tomb.
Rivers, fountains, and waters flow,
But never return to their joyful beginnings.
As they widen their banks, hastening to the
vast realms of the rain god,
They also fashion the urn of their own burial.
Once there were men of majesty and fortune,
Who sat upon thrones in praise and pride and power.
They decided cases, presided in council,
Conquered provinces and commanded armies,
Possessed treasures, destroyed temples.
Once their animate bodies were flesh and bone,
But now they fill the bowels of earth with dust.

Vanished are their glories, just as the fearful
smoke vanishes from the infernal fires
of volcanoes.
Nothing recalls them but the voice of the poet.

When sighs of appreciation from the guests rewarded the student, other students stepped into the center to recite poems they had written. Their sad poetry exuded dark images and symbols, themes of loss and fortitude. Yet clearly the guests were enjoying it.

While the musicians were still playing softly on their flutes and drums, Tlacoch introduced Chimalli to his auianime, Centli-xochitl, or "Corn Flower." She was dressed for dancing, with a fringed skirt that swayed as she moved, smiling through teeth tinted with a red dye. The axin cream she had used made her face look paler, so it glowed a soft yellow in the light of the pine torches. "You may dance with her," said Tlacoch, "but if you want someone to sleep with, you'll have to get an auianime of your own."

"I hope I can find one as pretty as yours," Chimalli said with more gallantry than honesty. So as not to offend Tlacoch, he joined the two of them in a dance, holding Centli-Xochitl's left hand high on one side as Tlacoch held her right hand on the other side. Chimalli was glad, however, that he had no real interest in the painted women that his fellow students spent their evenings with. Nothing excited him as much as the war games and training for battle that he excelled in at the telpochcalli. Women, to him, meant only distraction from his studies, a drain from the constant practice he would need to master the weapons and strategies for military success.

Chimalli and Tlacoch were asked to entertain the crowd with displays of their military accomplishments, and so they staged a mock swordfight with wooden swords. Their mock swords resembled the fearsome macahuitl that could cut enemies to pieces in hand-to-hand combat, but instead of the obsidian chips that a real maquahuitl would have glued into its edges, these had only feathers dyed red to simulate blood when they touched the opponent. Both young warriors danced around the stone floor with agile footwork that delighted their audience. Tlacoch waved his sword with grand flourishes, winning the applause of the crowd, but Chimalli moved with swift and certain thrusts, taking advantage of an opening in Tlacoch's gestures to pin his sword against his opponent's chest. His left hand grabbed Tlacoch's right wrist, gripping it so tightly that Tlacoch dropped his sword. Tlacoch scowled, but his expression changed into submissiveness when his father the eagle warrior raised an elegant eyebrow.

Chimalli laughingly went through the ceremony of the flowery wars: "You are my beloved nephew," he said to his captive, pressing the wooden sword on his shoulder until Tlacoch knelt before him.

"You are my beloved uncle," muttered Tlacoch. "Do with me what you will." If this had been a real flowery war, those words would have acknowledged the victor's right to sacrifice the captive to Huitzilopochtli.

Chimalli placed a friendly arm around his mock opponent's shoulders and led him to his auianime. "I bring you a captive," he said to Centli-Xochitl. "You may have his heart. Do with it what you will." Then he bowed respectfully to their teacher, Tlacateotl, who roared heartily in approval. Even Tlacoch laughed, waving a signal to the musicians to make dance music.

Toto brought a tray of chocolate drinks to the youths, and when Tlacoch began to dance with Centli-Xochitl, she decided to act boldly. "I would be your auianime," she said softly to Chimalli. "I am Atototl of Paynala, but people call me Toto."

Chimalli looked at her in surprise. "How old are you, Toto? Old enough to make a decision like that?"

"I'll soon be twelve," she said truthfully. "I'd look older if I braided my hair and dressed like the other auianime girls."

Chimalli smiled as a big brother might smile. "You honor me, little Toto," he said. "You're prettier in your plain white dress than the painted ladies are in their fringes and embroidery. Your plain face is more pleasing than their masks of yellow axin and their cochineal-dyed teeth. Believe me, you don't want to be anyone's auianime."

His words, though intended to discourage her, simply made her adore him more. His brotherly smile had revealed his even white teeth and the sensitive curves of his mouth, sparking a passion in Toto that, being new to her, seemed like the summons of an irresistible fate. "I would always dress to please you," she vowed.

Chimalli shook his head. "You're much too young, and I'm committed to becoming a warrior. Stay with your parents, little Toto; they need you, and one day you'll make a fine wife for a lucky farmer."

"May I come to the telpochcalli to see you?" Toto asked.

Chimalli pondered that question. "Don't grow up too fast, little one. Come and see me a year from now. Maybe by then you'll have changed your mind." He doubted that she would even remember this night a year later.

"I'll come," Toto promised ecstatically. Then she disappeared before her mother could come after her.

While Tlacoch had been dancing with his auianime, Tlacateotl had been surveying the daughters of nobles to select a wife for him. He watched Malinalli's graceful movements as she swayed to the music, observed the dainty way she held her food in her fingers, listened to her spirited conversation with Metzli, and then spoke to Itzamitl. "Your daughter Malinalli will be a beautiful woman soon," he said. "She resembles her mother."

"Thank you, Lord Tlacateotl," said Itzamitl, lowering his eyes in respect. "Your son Tlacoch is also a fine young man."

"He has the faults of youth," said the eagle knight candidly. "Rashness, insecurity, a little cockiness. But he's only 15; he has some growing to do."

"Oh, but he's got a fine model in his father," Itzamitl said tactfully. "Clearly he's had good breeding."

Tlacateotl smiled, and the feathers bobbed in his topknot. "He has promise, I admit," he said. "The telpochcalli has disciplined him; now a few years of military service will polish him. I'm thinking our two families might form an alliance, if you find him acceptable for Malinalli."

Itzamitl felt the blood of embarrassment warming his cheeks. "You honor us, great Tlacateotl," he said. "But Malinalli is only ten; we plan to send her to the temple of Quetzalcoatl for a few years."

"Excellent!" boomed Tlacateotl. "The priestesses will give her a fine moral education. By the time Tlacoch is twenty, she'll be fifteen—about right, I'd say."

"Malinalli says she wants to be a priestess," Itzamitl said hesitantly, "and my wife would approve of that. But I think she should stay at the temple only long enough to get an education."

"You're the head of the household," said Tlacateotl gruffly. "Your women obey you, don't they?"

"Yes, I can truthfully say they do," Itzamitl said.

Tlacateotl took this conversation to mean that an agreement had been reached between noblemen, but before Itzamitl had actually promised Malinalli to Tlacoch, Opochtli approached them with cups of octli.

Tlacateotl greeted Opochtli warmly as he accepted the drink. "Your son Chimalli is my prize student," he said to Opochtli. "He'll make a fine warrior."

"Yes," agreed Itzamitl. "A son to be proud of. No octli for me, thanks."

Opochtli lowered his eyes. In his plain brown tilmantli and scuffed cactli, he looked the picture of humility. "Thank you, Lord Tlacateotl. My friend Itzamitl here recommended him for your telpochcalli. I'm glad he hasn't disappointed his mentors."

"Quite the opposite," Tlacateotl said. "He's brave and skillful. One more year of study, then he'll meet the test of battle. He'll be an eagle knight someday if he keeps up the good work." Then Tlacateotl left to talk to Cimatl and Malinalli. The well-rounded arms of Malinalli, he thought, showed to good advantage next to the spindly arms of Metzli.

When Tlacateotl had gone beyond the range of hearing, Opochtli sat on the mat beside Itzamitl and commented, "Too

102

bad his son has so few of Tlacateotl's good qualities."

"What's the son like?" Itzamitl asked. "Would he make a good husband for Malinalli?"

"Aha. I wondered what Tlacateotl was up to," said Opochtli sagely. "Marriage, is it? If I were you, I'd wait to see how he and Malinalli get along. My guess is she won't like him."

"Why not? He seems well brought up."

"Yes, but he's had life too easy. Like so many of the pilli, he avoids work and seeks pleasure—just the opposite of his father. Chimalli brings Tlacoch with him for holidays in Oluta sometimes. From what I've seen, Tlacoch seems interested only in gambling and women."

"Chimalli seems to like him. Are they close friends?"

"Pretty close. But I suspect Chimalli befriends Tlacoch because Tlacateotl is his father. What young warrior wouldn't want to please his training master? But even a pilli must prove himself as good as his father if he wants to advance. Tlacoch will probably never earn the stature or the respect that his father has."

"We're thinking of an engagement between Tlacoch and Malinalli," Itzamitl said. "But I wouldn't want to make Malinalli unhappy, even if refusing the offer makes me look like a weakling."

"I'm not the best person to advise you," Opochtli said, locking his arms around his bent knees, pulling his tilmantli to cover his folded limbs until he looked like a brown bundle. "I have competing interests. I'd secretly been hoping that Chimalli and Malinalli would grow fond of each other. We're only a family of merchants, but Chimalli's wife will never lack any comforts I could provide."

Itzamitl assured Opochtli, "I regard your family as a most honorable one, and Chimalli has all the qualities I'd like in a son if I had one. But I know you better than I know Tlacateotl, and it wouldn't be fair to judge Tlacoch too hastily. I'll find out if Malinalli has a preference."

Opochtli grinned and clapped a hand on Itzamitl's shoulder. "Sometimes an apparent weakling is actually a jaguar. Consider Malinalli's happiness, by all means. I'll never tell anyone how soft-hearted you are with your womenfolk. It seems to me you're proceeding wisely. Now let's smoke a few pipes of yetl. The night is almost over."

Neither of the men noticed that Toto was clearing away some dishes nearby, and they had no idea that their words were causing her great anxiety.

* * *

A few days after the celebration for Yacatecuhtli, Itzamitl

103

invited Opochtli to bring his daughter Metzli to the tecalli. It was time, he told his merchant friend, for their daughters to experience the rite of passage to adulthood. He planned to deliver the usual fatherly advice to Malinalli, to tell her what is expected of a Nahua woman. Cimatl would be there, adding her motherly advice, and since Metzli had no mother, Itzamitl thought perhaps she would like to participate with his family. Opochtli gratefully agreed.

At sunset on the appointed day, the girls, dressed in their best clothing, with flowers adorning their shiny washed hair, faced their parents in the courtyard. Opochtli had bathed and dressed himself in a handsome tilmantli with a red border; he was even wearing new cactli in obvious discomfort. Itzamitl and Cimatl wore the same nice clothing they had worn at Opochtli's feast, and Cimatl had woven a ribbon into her twisted hair. Cimatl's flowers were blooming brightly in her garden, being visited by hummingbirds and butterflies, and the shadow of the huehuetl tree was spreading eastward over the tezontli stones.

Itzamitl spoke first, directing his words to Malinalli. "Here you are, my little daughter, my precious necklace, my human creation. You are my blood, my color. In you is my image."

Malinalli looked at her father's fine features, noticing the lights and shadows on his face, and felt proud to be seen as his image. She lowered her eyes in respect.

"Listen closely," Itzamitl continued, "while I speak to you of life. You were sent to earth by our lord, Possessor of the Near and the Close, maker of humankind. Now you are able to see for yourself that life is not all joy and pleasure. There is torment, worry, fatigue, and suffering."

Opochtli, too, had been taught the words that a father should speak to a daughter on such an occasion, and he spoke directly to Metzli. "My precious quetzal plume, my little daughter, my gift from the creator of people, I speak to you of life. Listen well, my dear child, for here on earth is a place of much weeping, where one's breath is exhausted, where affliction and pain abound. A cold wind blows and glides over us like obsidian blades."

Metzli, too, lowered her eyes in respect and stood solemnly, her thin arms dangling awkwardly at her sides.

"You heard the poets at the feast conveying the words of wise men," Itzamitl resumed. "We should not always go about groaning, or filled with sadness, because our lord gave humans laughter, sleep, food, strength, and lastly the sexual act, by which people are sown. There is nobility, eagles and jaguars. There is authority, kings and priests and fathers. There is satisfaction in struggle and work, desire for a husband or wife, and the will to live until it is time to die."

"All this gladdens life on earth," Opochtli added. "Even

104

when there is suffering, if life must be that way, we do not need to live in fear and weeping."

Itzamitl touched Malinalli's arm, and when she looked up, he pointed to Cimatl. "Here is your mother," he said proudly. "Look upon her serenely. From her womb you sprouted forth; from her body you were released; at her breast you were nourished. Like a little weed, you sprouted. As a leaf comes out, you grew, you flowered."

Cimatl smiled warmly at Malinalli, but it was not yet her turn to speak.

Opochtli spoke next. "You, too, my dear daughter Metzli, have grown like your mother, who rests now in the land of Mictlan, who watches us now from the red of the western sky. Your job, like Malinalli's, will be to get up early each day and prepare the meals, to sweep and clean with a broom, to make offerings to the gods and prepare incense of copal resin. Embrace the spindle and weaving stick, and learn the arts of featherwork, embroidery, and decorating of your home."

"Show respect for your parents and family," said Itzamitl to both girls. "Do not throw dust and rubbish on them; do not smear their good name or bring mockery upon them, on the red and black ink of their family name. If you disgrace them, it would be better that you perished immediately. You have reached the age when you will desire sexual things and seek a companion. Do not call to a man as it you were searching for him in a market. Do not stare at him or go about speaking your desire for him."

"Honor the choice of a mate that your father makes for you," Opochtli added. "Do not scorn or reject that man who should be your companion, for he may mock you, and you may become a harlot. Whoever your companion might be, you both together will have to finish this life. Do not leave him; hold on to him; even if he is a poor man, a little eagle, a little jaguar, a hapless soldier, a poor nobleman, or an exhausted farmer with little wealth; do not despise him for that."

Itzamitl's voice deepened as if in prayer. "May our lord, the knower of men, the inventor of people, see you, strengthen you. All this I give you with my lips and my words. Thus, before our lord I fulfill my fatherly duty."

"You daughters may cast away this knowledge if you choose," added Opochtli, "but now you know it. I have fulfilled my office as a father, my little girl, my daughter. May you be happy in life; may our lord make you happy."

Cimatl had been looking at each man as he spoke. When they had finished, she turned to Malinalli. "Little dove, little child, my little girl. You have received something rare and wonderful from the heart of your father. He has given you his blood; even though you are a little woman, one can see his image in you. He

105

has given you wise counsel, to which I can add nothing. But I will fulfill my office, too. Do not cast aside the breath and advice of your father. His words are like precious stones, like rounded and grooved turquoises, and in truth he speaks the wisdom of our ancestors. Save them, make them a painting in your heart. With this guidance you will bring up your children, make them men and women. You will deliver wisdom to them and tell them all that we have told you."

Then Cimatl turned to Metzli. "Dear child of Opochtli, all I have said to my daughter would be said by your mother to you if she could be with you today. Allow me to take her place this one time, to teach you the things a woman must know to make her way along the slippery path that is her moral road in life. We are traveling through a difficult place, walking here on earth. On one side of us is an abyss, on the other a ravine. Only in the middle does one live, only in the middle does one walk safely."

The fathers then lighted pine torches while the girls seated themselves on petlatl mats beside Cimatl. She gave advice on how a maiden should walk, dress, speak, apply makeup, and so on. Then, as the smell of pine and the glow of firelight gave enchantment to her words, she spoke of the divine mystery of sex. "To join your body to that of a man may bring you real joy, but do not take that pleasure lightly, for the gods give you power to create new life in that way. Do not give your body in vain, my little dove. If you cease being a virgin before you marry, you will become a lost woman, and you will never be under the protection of someone who truly loves you. If a lost woman marries, she will not live in peace, and her husband may always be suspicious of her.

"If you are already under the power of someone, do not permit your desire to lead you astray. And do not be disrespectful of your husband, to step vainly over him, to commit adultery with another man. If this transpires, there is no remedy, no going back. If you are seen, and your behavior becomes known, you will be put in the streets, dragged through the dirt. People will break your head with stones, turn it into pulp. You will create a bad name, a bad reputation for your family; you will disgrace the parents who gave you life. You will cast dung upon the books of paintings that are your family history. People will gossip about you and call you 'one sunken in the dust.' And even if nobody sees you, even if your husband does not see you, the Possessor of the Near and the Close will see you in his dark mirror.

"Do not disobey the gods, but live in calm and peace on earth, the short time that you live here. With respect to us, may we be glorified, and may you be happy. Draw near to Our Lord, the Possessor of the Near and Close. These are the virtues that will give you the face and the heart of a Nahua woman."

106

After many warm embraces all around, the girls retired with Cimatl to the sleeping room. Stimulated by the ceremonies and the attention they had received, they talked a long time before falling asleep.

Opochtli and Itzamitl lingered a while in the patio, smoking and talking about the perils of parenthood. Then Opochtli retired to the guest house, knowing that he and Metzli must get up early the next morning for the walk back to Oluta. For him, the ceremony had not only fulfilled his duties as a parent, but also formed a bond with Itzamitl and his family. Grateful for their friendliness to him and Metzli, he resolved that they would never lack for anything he could provide. He had also raised his hopes that, when the time came, Itzamitl would approve a union between Malinalli and his son Chimalli.

As Opochtli drifted to sleep in the guest house, he tried to remember whether his son's tonalli had predicted success both in war and in marriage. He couldn't remember, and the thought troubled him.

Chapter 10

Temple Life and Tempests on the Coast

Malinalli was still insisting that she never wanted to marry (not to marry Tlacoch in particular), so it was with some relief to everyone concerned that she and Metzli left for the temple of Quetzalcoatl in Coatzacoalcos. Opochtli conducted them with a trading caravan, leaving them in the hands of the priestesses, glad that neither girl had yet been pledged to marry.

Itzamitl, encouraged that Malinalli had bent to his will on the matter of eating dog meat, hoped she would tire of the austere life at the convent by the time she was sixteen and become more compliant in the matter of marriage. Cimatl, with a mother's concern for safety, felt relieved that Malinalli would be closely guarded and kept away from the calpixqui and the predatory priests from Tenochtitlan.

For Malinalli, the temple held new adventure that made the rigid discipline of the priestesses quite bearable. From the temple heights she could see the vast sweep of the ocean, the white froth of the lapping surf like a border edging a blue tilmantli. She never tired of watching the waves salute the shore, each one dropping a tribute of a few grains of sand. She delighted in the flocks of shore birds running in the surf, feeding on the gifts from the waves, and taking to the sky like troops of graceful dancers whenever a human approached.

There was not much time for walking on the beach, however, except when the girls occasionally gathered shellfish in the tidepools. Every morning the girls prepared a meal for the priests, always grinding corn and making cakes on the comal. For the evening meal, the priestesses taught them to make a variety of new dishes. To inland-bred girls, the most interesting dishes contained fresh fish and shellfish, often flavored with tomatoes and onions and peppers. Malinalli and Metzli watched the kitchen priestess closely as she cooked, and soon they could make many of the dishes from memory.

Weaving robes and blankets for the priests and calmecac students occupied the temple girls several days each month.

Although weaving was considered a higher art than spinning, reserved for girls old enough to do it properly, Malinalli found it as tedious as she had found spinning. She did her share each month, but she was always glad when the duty was done. The priestesses tried to invest the tasks of spinning and weaving with magic, saying that the earth goddesses spin life like a thread, winding it around a spindle as if to make a human body. A woman weaves the threads together, they said, as she weaves her life around the warp and the woof of necessity and celebration. All our individual lives, they said, like thin little threads, make the fabric of community, the solidness of group life. The poetry of their abstractions appealed to young Malinalli, but not enough to make the tasks less onerous. Metzli, however, absorbed every word unquestioningly and assigned a spiritual dimension to every mundane task.

A good portion of each day was devoted to study. Malinalli and Metzli learned how to speak well and behave with good manners, just as the young men did in the telpochcalli, where they were learning to be good citizens as well as warriors. The temple girls and telpochcalli boys learned the history of the Mexica (whose ancestors had come from Aztlan), the pantheon of gods and goddesses, the stories associated with many of the divinities, and the rituals appropriate for their worship. The feasts associated with the gods began to make more sense to Malinalli, and even the hated sacrifices began to seem more reasonable when the priestesses told them what divine purposes were served by these rituals.

* * *

The first year Malinalli and Metzli spent at the temple was measured in the ceremonies of the months, and their religious education centered on those.

Atlcoualco, or "stopping of the waters" was considered the first of the eighteen months in the Aztec calendar, the time period Spaniards called Febrero or late February. The priestesses taught them that children were sacrificed in Tenochtitlan to the rain-god Tlaloc and the Tlaloque, or mountain-gods, who sent flashes of lightning and booms of thunder when they were displeased. Tlaloc was important to peasants and farmers, just as Huitzilopochtli was important to warriors, and the priestesses said that two equally impressive temples to these great gods had been built in Tenochtitlan, the capital city of the Mexica, where the Emperor Moctezuma lived.

Malinalli's favorite instructor was the priestess Toci, whose name meant "Mother of Gods" or "Our Grandmother." Toci had taken the name of the goddess Toci when she entered service at the temple, and she never revealed her birth name to the girls.

Because Toci did seem motherly, Malinalli told her about Moyo, the child of Chihuallama and Callipopoca, who had been taken from his parents in Paynala to be sacrificed to Tlaloc. "That may have seemed unjust to you when you were small," Toci said reassuringly, "but think of it this way. Every warrior risks his life to save the rest of his people when they are in danger. Every mother risks her life bearing children to carry on the work of the society as a whole. A few will die from those risks, but many lives will be saved because those few lives were sacrificed. Moyo gave his life for his parents and his nation; he became our gift to Tlaloc in return for the many gifts Tlaloc gives us—the rain that waters our crops, the streams and rivers that we drink from."

Malinalli's eyes filled with tears as Toci explained so simply what had been a perplexing mystery to her.

"We don't practice child sacrifice here at our temple," Toci explained further. "Our temple is dedicated to Quetzalcoatl, but the priests say all Nahua peoples benefit from the ceremonies in the capital city of Tenochtitlan." Malinalli accepted Toci's reasoning and resolved to memorize everything she was taught so she could become as wise as Toci.

* * *

Toci had a gift for teaching complex ideas simply. On the first day of lessons to the young priestesses in training, she had explained the shape of the world by turning a clay bowl upside down inside a larger bowl filled with water. "The earth," she told her students, "is called *Cem-Anahuac* because it is 'the place surrounded by water' just as this small bowl is surrounded by water in the larger bowl. You have seen how the waters of the ocean bring us gifts from the gods, yet the waters keep their mystery. We are like ants crawling around on this bowl; we can go only a little way into the water. The water can bring us death as well as life." Ever afterward, Malinalli viewed the world that way, even after other men proved it was round.

To explain the gods that ruled the four directions, Toci had her students line up on the east wall of the temple room that served as their classroom and workroom. "Think of yourself as following the journey of the sun," she said. "You begin in the east, where you are born anew each day. To your left is the south, where the sun reaches its highest point. To your right is the north, where darkness rules because it is farthest from the zenith of the sun. Before you lies the west, where the sun dies each night."

At her direction, the girls walked across the room from east to west, each girl thinking of her place in the cosmos, her own journey through life. "As you move from the middle of the room

110

to the west," she said, "imagine that you are accompanying the sun god from the zenith to the end. That's what women do who have died in childbirth or given their lives in sacrifice." When they reached the western wall, she added, "Now you may rest, just as these brave women do."

When they were seated on the west side of the room, Toci folded a piece of cloth several times and presented it to the attentive young priestesses. "Is this one piece of cloth?" she asked.

"Yes," they replied in unison.

Toci unfolded the cloth. "Now you see twice as much," she said. "But is it still one cloth?"

"Yes," Metzli replied confidently. "We see more of it, but it is all one."

Toci unfolded the cloth one more time. "Now you see four times as much as you did. Yet is it still one cloth?"

"Yes," Malinalli said, wondering where Toci's questions were leading, but happily following her lead.

"Quite so," Toci said triumphantly. "Now remember that as I tell you about the four gods that all came from one. The first god Ometeotl, whose name means 'two god' or 'dual god' was both male and female, father and mother. So Ometeotl was self-created, and created everything else in the world. The union of male and female aspects created Tezcatlipoca, also called 'Smoking Mirror,' and his female counterpart Tezcatlanextia, 'Mirror Which Illumines.' Tezcatlipoca has the power to unify light and darkness, and it is said that when he looks into his smoking mirror he can see things that humans cannot see. He rules in the north, and his color is black, the color of night."

Toci pointed to the cloth, to the creases that showed where the folds had been. "Another unfolding or creation gave us the red Tezcatlipoca, who is Xipe Totec. Red is the color of the sunrise which creates the new day, and Xipe is the god who created corn, the holy grain that nourishes humans."

Malinalli remembered hearing about Xipe and the ceremonies associating him with corn. "Why do the priests call Xipe the 'flayed god'?" she asked.

"Because he is also the god of regeneration," Toci explained patiently. "We peel off the old, dead husks from an ear of corn, as if we are flaying the sacred grain. Yet even these husks decay and feed the new corn. The grains that seem dead when we plant them in the earth bring forth new life. That is the creative power of the god at work, the cycle of life and death."

Metzli, emboldened by the questioning that Malinalli had begun, asked, "Why do the priests sacrifice a person to Xipe and cut off his skin and wear it over their own?"

Toci's voice began to sound strained, but she answered as she had been taught. "The priests tell us that human death is also

111

necessary to bring forth life, the spiritual life beyond this earthly one. The priests are impersonating Xipe, by wearing a skin just as the new corn wears a husk."

"Is the person they sacrifice being punished?" Malinalli asked.

"No, no," Toci answered hastily. "He is playing the part of the seed. His death is like planting a seed so that other lives can be nourished. If Xipe is pleased with the offering, he will make the corn grow for us all. And he who has been freed from his earthly body will find a better life, a spiritual life."

"Where will he go?" asked Metzli.

"Ah, that brings me to the other aspects of Tezcatlipoca," Toci answered with a smile of relief. "Hold your questions until I tell you about the blue Tezcatlipoca, or Huitzilopochtli. When the sky is blue we can see the sun at its zenith, so that is the color associated with Huitzilopochtli. His name means 'Hummingbird of the left' or 'Hummingbird of the south,' because warriors go to the south after death. Those who die bravely in battle—or those who are sacrificed to a god—will accompany Huitzilopochtli, the sun god, to the zenith of his daily journey. After a time they return to earth, resurrected as hummingbirds."

Toci pointed to the folded cloth once more, holding it so that one of the corners pointed to the west. "There was also created a white Tezcatlipoca, a god known as Yohualli Ehecatl, whose name means 'Night and Wind' because he is invisible and intangible like his father Tezcatlipoca and his grandfather-also-grandmother Ometeotl. He was associated with the west and sunset. His other name is Quetzalcoatl, which means 'feathered serpent' or 'precious twin,' because the quetzal feathers are the most precious and beautiful on earth, and because the serpent sheds its skin to duplicate itself, to bring new life from old."

"Why is our temple dedicated to Quetzalcoatl?" asked one of the other girls who had been silent until that time.

"Quetzalcoatl is said to be the god who first made humans. He also made a great sacrifice to continue human life on earth," Toci explained. "I'll tell you all about it tomorrow." In that way, she kept the girls curious and eager for another lesson.

The following day, after the girls had made corncakes for the priests of the temple and the calmecac students, after the morning chores were done, Toci continued her basic lessons. Whether the girls actually became priestesses or left the temple to become mothers, she wanted them to be able to tell these stories to others. She could not read the sacred books of the priests, and she could not teach her young students to do that, but she could give them the stories to pass on to other women and children, giving meaning to their existence.

"According to priests who can read the red and black ink of

112

the sacred books," she began, "there have been four ages in human history, called the Four Suns. These four earlier ages all ended in disasters." Toci recited the Four Suns legend in greater detail that Malinalli's mother had, but the four apocalypses were similar: floods, jaguars, volcanic fires.

Of course Malinalli had a question: "Why didn't Tlaloc bring rain to put out the fires?"

"I've wondered that myself," Toci admitted. "The priests tell us we mustn't question the ways of the gods."

"Did all this really happen?" Metzli asked. "How do the priests know what happened so many years ago?"

"They have the sacred books, but even then these are only the stories that have been told for many generations, from mother to daughter, from father to son."

Toci handed each of the girls a spindle, a whorl, and a basket of cotton bolls. "Let's keep our hands busy while we talk," she said. "The priests won't approve of our talking so much, but they won't mind if we keep making thread or weaving."

Malinalli had seen the priests talking to the male students. The boys did not work while the priests talked. They looked like rows of beans or bundles of cotton, sitting with their tilmas wrapped around their knees, listening attentively to the priests. Malinalli accepted the spindle willingly and reached for a cotton boll, but she asked curiously, "Why do girls work as they learn, and boys only listen?"

The round eyes in Toci's round face narrowed in disapproval. "The boys can't weave and spin," she said defensively. "They do other work, like bringing wood to the temple. Their lives aren't easy here. They learn to endure suffering without complaint."

Metzli also frowned at Malinalli. "Don't fuss about it, Malinalli," she said. "Just do your work. Maybe life isn't fair, but I want to hear about the Four Suns."

"Me, too," said another girl. Another told Malinalli to be quiet, and three others echoed the disapproval.

Malinalli felt heat rising in her face. "I'm sorry," she said to the girls, and then to Toci, "Please go on."

The girls had already learned in their homes how to spin thread, so they began to work with no further instruction as Toci resumed her explanations. "Listen to the stories not only for what happens in them, but also for what they mean," she said. "I've thought often about the story of the Third Sun, which ended in fire and stones from the sky. I think it's trying to tell us that rain alone can't help men survive. The plants need water, but they also need the fire of the sun. Like water, fire can save us or kill us. Only when we have a balance, when we do not have too much water or too much fire, can humans survive."

113

"What is the story of the Fourth Sun?" Metzli persisted, her fingers twirling the spindle expertly as a cotton thread formed and wound around it.

Toci continued. "The Fourth Sun, called 4 Ehecatl or Four Wind, was ruled by Quetzalcoatl. That sun lasted 364 years, but in the year 1 Flint a devastating hurricane blew away all the trees and the sun itself. All who survived were turned into monkeys, and went into the mountains to live."

"Was that when Quetzalcoatl made the sacrifice to bring back human life?" Malinalli asked. Unlike Metzli, she stopped spinning to concentrate on what Toci was saying.

"Not yet. Not until the Fifth Sun. Be patient, Malinalli," Toci chided gently. "I'm coming to that. The Fifth Sun is the age we are living in now. Much of the work of the temples, here and everywhere, is done to keep the sun in its motion around the earth. The sacred books predict that the Fifth Sun will end in an earthquake."

Malinalli realized with a start that she was not doing her share of the work, so she picked up another cotton boll and pulled its soft fibers apart to begin twisting it into thread.

When Toci was satisfied that all the girls were working, she continued her story. "The gods were concerned that no humans were left to populate the earth," she said. "So they sent Quetzalcoatl to the great underworld of Mictlan, where the bones of all the dead humans were kept. The lord of Mictlan, called Mictlan-tecuhtli, challenged him by giving him an impossible task to perform. He gave Quetzalcoatl a conch shell with no holes in it and told him to blow it. But other living creatures came to help. Some worms drilled holes for him, and some bumblebees entered the holes to make sound inside.

"So Mictlan-tecuhtli gave Quetzalcoatl the bones, and Quetzalcoatl pierced the foreskin of his tepuli to drop his blood over them. The drops of blood infused life into the bones, so humans were reborn. Since his sacrifice was for those who deserved to live, it was done as a penance or *macehua*. Ever since that time, the people have been called *macehualtin*, which means 'those who deserve penitence.' "

"So that is why we do penance by bleeding," said Meztli.

"Yes," Toci answered. "We do for Quetzalcoatl what he did for us. But he doesn't want human blood; he's satisfied with small animals and butterflies."

"Why does Huitzilopochtli want human sacrifice, then?" Malinalli asked.

"Huitzilopochtli is the god of war as well as the sun. His priests say he needs blood to sustain him as he climbs the sky. The Aztecs believe they've won many wars because they feed him with the blood of their captives."

"Do you think Huitzilopochtli would be satisfied with small

animals, like Quetzalcoatl?" Malinalli asked.

Toci's reply took on a little sharpness. "You'll have to ask one of his priests about that," she said. "It's not for me to question the decisions of the high priests. I can't express any opinions different from theirs."

Metzli turned to Malinalli and spoke reassuringly. "If the people who are sacrificed go to live with the gods, perhaps they're better off there than they would be in this world."

"I'll try to remember that," Malinalli agreed softly. Sensing that she had made Toci uncomfortable, and wanting to put the priestess at ease, she added, "I'm glad we're at the temple of Quetzalcoatl, though."

"I'm glad, too," Toci responded, beaming at the girls. "You're all good workers; you'll make good priestesses. Tomorrow I'll tell you how Quetzalcoatl discovered maize with the help of a black ant and brought it to human beings."

Toci walked among the girls, examining their work and voicing approval. Then in a lowered mischievous voice she added, "I'll also tell you how Quetzalcoatl lured the goddess Mayahuel to earth and turned her into a maguey plant so that men could draw octli from her trunk."

The girls all clamored to hear the story, but Toci kept them in suspense until their chores were done the next morning. Then she made good on her promise. When the priests and the calmecac students had been fed, when the comal had been washed and the floor swept, when the girls had taken up their spindles and baskets of cotton, she told them more legends about Quetzalcoatl and Mayahuel.

"Mayahuel was very fruitful when she mated with Quetzalcoatl," Toci commented after she finished a story. "Some say she had 400 breasts; some say she had 400 sons."

"Could anyone really have 400 sons?" asked Metzli.

Toci laughed. "Remember I said to look at the meaning behind the stories," she reminded them. "We say 400 when we mean there are too many to count. That's why when a man gets drunk on octli people say he's drunk 400 rabbits. You all know that the maguey plant sprouts new arms when the old ones are cut back, don't you? And to get to the sweet juice inside the plant, we have to cut the top off. What is the story telling us?"

Malinalli spoke excitedly. "I think it's telling us that the maguey plant gives us gifts from the gods—too many blessings to count, like needles and thread, cloth, rope, paper, sweet juice, and medicines."

"But also a drink that can be a curse," Metzli added solemnly.

"Good thinking, girls," Toci beamed. "Now tell me this: Do you think Quetzalcoatl deserves credit for giving men the maguey plant, with all its benefits and troubles? Or do you think

115

Mayahuel deserves credit for finding a way to keep on living and giving even after her head was lopped off?"

Malinalli and Metzli burst into laughter, followed by all the other girls. Toci laughed too, confident they had understood her point: that men and women might interpret a story in different ways. When the merriment subsided, Toci resumed a serious tone.

"I've told you about Quetzalcoatl the god," she said. "But you should also know about the high priest Topiltzin Ce Acatl Quetzalcoatl. He was such an important prophet of the god Quetzalcoatl that many people confuse the man with the god that he served."

Toci had memorized the story from hearing and repeating it many times, so she embroidered while she talked, pulling a white thread through black fabric with a maguey thorn.

"Long ago in the ancient city of Tollan," Toci chanted in the rhythms of Nahuatl poetry, "lived a great priest named Topiltzin Quetzalcoatl. He was born in the year 1 Reed, or 'Ce Acatl,' so he was first called Topiltzin Ce Acatl. He worshiped only one god, the dual god Ometeotl, the father and mother of us all. This priest was guardian of Ometeotl's son Quetzalcoatl, who asked for no sacrifices except butterflies, bees, or birds.

"You know that the god Quetzalcoatl had a brother god, Tezcatlipoca, who opposed him as darkness opposes light, and who was also the darker side of himself. And though his priest rose to great heights, he fell to great depths, for he too had a darker side. Listen, my children, to his sad story of greatness and tragedy.

"His father was Totepeuh, the priest-ruler of Tollan, who was not supposed to marry. His mother was Chimalman, who caught an arrow one day where Totepeuh was hunting. When Chimalman swallowed a piece of jade, Topiltzin was conceived.

"He asked for his father when he was nine, but his father was dead. He found his father's bones and buried them in a temple mound at Quilaztli. At that time in Tollan, also called Tula, the people wore animal hides; they didn't know how to make tilmas or plant corn; they ate only raw meat from birds and snakes and deer.

"Topiltzin became a priest and fasted, bathed at midnight, did penance with thorns. He wandered from city to city, teaching and learning what others had to teach. He learned to plant corn and cacao and cotton of many colors. He could make dishes and pottery painted herb-green, white, yellow, and red. He lived four years in Tollan-tzinco, and built a turquoise house.

"When their old ruler Huactli died in the year 10 House, the Toltecs came to him. They asked him to be their priest and their ruler. He taught them the ways of Quetzalcoatl, and so he became known as Quetzalcoatl. He permitted no sacrifices except insects and small animals.

116

"The people thrived, and he acquired riches. Jade, turquoise, gold, silver, redshell, whiteshell—all these treasures, and the plumes of quetzal birds, cotingas, troupials, trogons, herons, and roseate spoonbills. He built houses for fasting and prayer, a house of red shell, of white shell, of quetzal plumes. He began a temple with columns shaped like serpents, but it was never finished.

"He kept to himself in guarded chambers, and did not go out in public. Even when they did not see him, the Toltecs followed his orders. They became skilled in arts and crafts. They prayed in his temples and obeyed the laws of the god Quetzalcoatl.

"But the sorcerers who followed Tezcatlipoca opposed him; they wanted human sacrifices. They decided to trick him, to bring about his downfall. First they sent to him a mirror in which he saw his own body as something ugly and shriveled. Then they tempted him to eat a delicious stew of greens, tomatoes, chilis, fresh corn, and beans, though he was fasting. Then they tempted him to drink octli or pulque, giving him five cups.

"When he was drunk with the octli, they sent for his sister. Though she was fasting, she came to his summons. They gave her five cups also, which they said was her portion. She slept with her brother that night, and when dawn came, they felt ashamed and disgraced.

"Quetzalcoatl wandered to the east, as far as the ocean. He wept and gathered his attire. He put on his head fan of feathers and his turquoise mask. Then he set himself on fire; he cremated himself. As he burned, his ashes rose into the air.

"The old people say these ashes turned into precious birds: green parrots, scarlet macaws, blue cotingas, white-fronted parrots, and all the other precious birds, rising into the sky.

"The old people say Quetzalcoatl disappeared for eight days. They say he made arrows in that time, arrows to shoot at the living when he returned. After eight days the Morning Star appeared in the East. The old people say that the star is Quetzalcoatl returning, sometimes in the east, sometimes in the west. He was born in 1 Reed and died in 1 Reed, so his span of life was one sheaf of fifty-two years. The old people say that he will return in the year 1 Reed."

When Toci finished the story of Quetzalcoatl, she had also finished embroidering a white flower on the black robe she was making for a priest. When she looked up at her students, they had all stopped spinning their thread and were listening to her, spellbound, sitting as motionless as a row of beans before her.

* * *

The rainy season was supposed to begin in Toxcatl, the fifth

117

month, but just to make sure it did, the Aztec priests in Tenochtitlan would sacrifice a handsome youth who had lived like a lord for a year personifying the god Tezcatlipoca, "Smoking Mirror." The priestesses were moved to tears when they told about this ceremony, which symbolized a god's willingness to be sacrificed for the good of the people. They considered the divine youth honored to be chosen for this symbolic act. Four lovely young girls, also much honored, would spend his last few months with him catering to his every need. Girls had important roles to play in the religious life, the priestesses said, and Malinalli and Metzli tried to imagine being among these heroines in the future. They determined to live such virtuous lives that they would be eligible for the honor.

The priestesses explained that women would have their turn to become goddesses in the seventh month, Tecuilhuitontli, and the eighth month, Uey Tecuilhuitl. Both months celebrated the "feast of the lords." First a woman would become Uixtociuatl, goddess of salt-water, and be sacrificed to celebrate those who make salt. Then one would become Xilonen, goddess of young maize, and her head would be lopped off while she was dancing, just as the ear of maize is plucked from its stalk. The priestesses said they would be proud if one of their girls should be chosen by the priests of Tenochtitlan for this honor. Malinalli and Metzli were awed by the prospect of such heroism, such devotion on the part of a woman. They could picture nothing more noble; they tingled with emotion as Toci described the ceremony she had witnessed in Tenochtitlan during the month of Uey Tecuilhuitl. While she was supervising the girls' weaving, she kept her tongue as busy as their hands.

"During the first seven days," she said rapturously, "the emperor had the whole population served with food and drink to show his good will towards the macehualtin. Every evening, at sunset, the songs and the dances began, in the light of torches and braziers, and sometimes even the emperor Moctezuma came out to dance. From sunset until the middle of the night the warriors and the women, holding hands, danced between the rows of glowing braziers and lighted torches, chanting rhythmically as the musicians played their gongs and drums.

"On the tenth day," she continued, "the maiden chosen to be Xilonen appeared, her face painted yellow and red like the maize kernels. She wore a headdress of quetzal plumes, a turquoise necklace enhanced with a golden disk, embroidered clothes, and red cactli. In one hand she carried a shield; in the other she rattled a chicauaztli of maize kernels to make magic.

"Everyone stayed up all night," Toci remembered with a blissful expression, "and the women sang the hymns of Xilonen. At dawn the dances began. All the men, even the war-chiefs and young officers, carried the maize-stalks that we call 'totopantli'

118

or 'bird flags.' Everyone joined the procession behind Xilonen (for we thought of her as being the goddess herself), threading our way to the temple of maize, Cinteopan. We carried the goddess forward with us, surrounding her, beating our two-toned gongs while the priests sounded their horns and conch shells. When the goddess stepped inside the Cinteopan, the officiating priest stepped forward with his gold-handled flint knife and swift as an arrow cut her head cleanly from her body.

"Then," Toci said with a satisfied sigh, "we all ate the cakes made of young maize that had never been dried, and the young maidens that had never looked at any man made maize cakes to offer to the gods."

Malinalli and Metzli had listened intently as Toci described the ceremony. "How could the maidens never have looked at any man?" Metzli asked, puzzled. "I've looked at my father and brother ever since I was born."

"Silly!" said Malinalli. "That just means the girls had been chaste. No man had touched their private places."

"That's right, Malinalli," said Toci. "They were virgins. You temple girls must be perfectly chaste to serve Quetzalcoatl."

"Have you always been chaste?" Malinalli asked Toci directly. Her tone expressed simple curiosity, not accusation, but Toci was a little startled by Malinalli's bluntness.

"You ask too many questions," said Toci a little brusquely, "but this one time I'll answer you. It may help you girls to know my story. I was an auianime once, but when my young warrior was killed I had nowhere to go. Some merchants offered me money to entertain them, but I wouldn't sell my body. Instead, I hired them as guides to bring me to Coatzacoalcos. I gave them my only jewel—a fine piece of jade my warrior had given me, to bring me to this temple. I've been here ever since, learning about herbs and medicines and teaching girls like you to weave."

Metzli looked at Toci with the adoration of a novice; Malinalli looked at her with the respect of an idealist. No longer would Toci seem like a chatty middle-aged woman to them, but like a heroine who had known great tragedy and survived it with dignity.

* * *

In the eleventh month, Ochpaniztli, when rain might spoil the harvest, the priests prayed for Tlaloc to withhold rain. Women swept the temples clean, and a woman incarnating the goddess Teoinnan was sacrificed. The Emperor made awards and gave promotions to warriors at the feast of Ochpaniztli, where eagle and jaguar knights entertained him with mock battles.

When the young trainees learned that the goddess Teteoinnan ("Grandmother of All") was also known as Toci, they made good-natured inquiries about their instructor's name. The priestess Toci admitted she had chosen that name, not to be sacrificed, but to become a mother to young priestesses like them. This explanation satisfied them, because they remembered what she had taught them about Quetzalcoatl, the priest who had taken the name of his god. Deeply impressed with Toci's devotion, Metzli attached herself worshipfully to the priestess, following her everywhere like a baby duck. The bond forming between the childless woman and the motherless girl seemed to satisfy a hunger in each of them.

Malinalli heard more about the ceremony of the feast of Ochpaniztli from Chimalli, who came to visit his sister Metzli in the following month, Teotleco. They had been at the telpochcalli for almost a year, and both of them had turned eleven years old by that time, though there had been no birthday celebrations. Priestesses said all celebrations should show piety to the gods.

"You've cut off your lock!" Metzli exclaimed proudly when the priestess Toci ushered her brother into the courtyard at the temple. "Have you seen battle already?" The girls were cutting harvested maize from the cobs, but they laid aside their flint knives to welcome their visitor. His long lock had been cut away, and his thick hair tumbled grandly over his right ear. "Look, Malinalli—he's a real warrior now!"

"Greetings, Metzli. Good to see you, Malinalli," said Chimalli with a respectful bow of his head and a flash of his handsome white teeth. "Lots of things have happened since I saw you last year. Some of the advanced students at my telpochcalli were allowed to help fight the war against the Tlaxcalans. We've already had some real battle experiences."

Toci excused herself and went into the temple to find some food for their guest.

"Are you an iyac, then?" Malinalli marveled. "Have you taken your first captive?"

"Even better than that," Chimalli beamed, pointing to the leather bracelets on his forearms. "I'm a tequiua—killed one enemy and took three captives. Now I can wear these bracelets."

"And feathers on your head?" asked Metzli eagerly.

"For ceremonial occasions, or in battle," Chimalli said with a modest smile. "I wouldn't wear them every day."

"Did the Emperor give you these?" Metzli said, admiring the bracelets.

"No, not personally," Chimalli laughed. "One of his commanders did—a quachic. I did see the Emperor, though, at the feast of Ochpaniztli."

"Moctezuma? In person?" Malinalli had never known anyone who had actually seen the Emperor. Even the merchant Opochtli had not seen Moctezuma in person, though the Emperor had sent gifts to him.

120

"I'll tell you all about it," Chimalli said, seating himself on the ground and pulling his tilmantli around his knees. "The emperor came in escorted by a long procession of eagle and jaguar knights. The back of his icpalli was covered with a jaguar's skin, and the seat was covered with quauh-petlapan, or eagle-feathers. At his feet the knights put all kinds of weapons and badges of honor—shields, swords, cloaks, loin-cloths, leather bracelets, feathered headdresses, gold medals. We all stood before him in even rows and saluted him."

"Did you get close enough to see his face?" Metzli sat in front of her brother and locked her arms around her knees, preparing to listen a long time.

"Of course not. If you get close to the Emperor, you have to keep your eyes down. It would be rude to look him directly in the face. Even the great chiefs looked down when he gave them their decorations. They went aside to put on their ornaments, then they formed ranks again in front of Moctezuma. At some distance, of course."

"Were any women there?" Metzli asked, "Wives and sisters?"

"Yes. Mothers, too. The old women shed tears and said 'here are our beloved children; will they ever find their way back?' They were afraid to say the word 'war.' They told each other not to say the words 'water' and 'burning' for six days or it would be a bad omen, but they really meant not to say the words 'blood' and 'war.' "

"Are you going to a battle now, Chimalli?" Metzli asked. "I'd feel bad if you were killed."

"Don't feel bad," Chimalli said, patting her hand gently. "If I die in battle, I'll become a quauhteca, a companion of the eagle. I'll climb with the sun, blazing with light every day." He made flapping motions with his hands.

Toci appeared with a basket of corncakes. "Eat these," she said to Chimalli. "You must be hungry after your long march from Tenochtitlan. Shall I put down a mat in the calmecac for you tonight?"

"Thanks, that'll be fine," Chimalli grinned. "I'm only here for a day. I'm on a mission for my superior officer."

"Can you tell us about it?" Malinalli asked.

"Yes, because it concerns you," he said. "My new superior officer knows your family. He sent me to Coatzacoalcos to find your aunt. Her name is Papalotl, I believe?"

"Papalotl?" Malinalli asked, mystified. "I haven't seen her for a long time. She lives on a farm outside the city, and I'm not supposed to leave the temple grounds."

"Hasn't she come to see you, then?"

"No," Malinalli said apologetically. "She knows we're concentrating on our studies. And she has to take care of Xochi."

"Xochi?"

121

"Her little girl. She's dedicated to the temple, too."

"Who? Papalotl or Xochi?"

"Xochi," Malinalli laughed. "Papalotl dedicated her when she was a baby."

"That's good," Chimalli said with relief. "Because my superior officer wants her for a wife. He was promoted to quachic at the Ochpaniztli ceremony and is ready for marriage now. He's sent me to escort her to Tenochtitlan."

Stunned, Malinalli took a few seconds to form her response. "I don't think she can come," she said. "She's married to someone else."

"Oh," said Chimalli, his forehead wrinkling in a frown. "Then he sent me here for nothing. He'll be very upset. He thought she'd wait until he sent for her."

"I'm glad you came to see us," Metzli said, gently touching her brother's hand. "It wasn't for nothing."

"Of course not," Chimalli agreed hastily, finishing his last bite of corncake. "I'm glad to see my little sister and Malinalli. Tell me, Malinalli, can you give me directions to Papalotl's farm?"

"I think I can remember," Malinalli said, creasing her brow. "You follow the road that leads along the river, and then take a side road to the north that has tall trees along it."

"Oh, yes. I think I passed such a road on my way here."

"You said your quachic knows my family," said Malinalli, with a puzzled frown because she couldn't think of any high-ranking warriors except Tlacateotl, who was retired in Paynala. "Tell me, Chimalli, who is your quachic?"

"Didn't I mention that?" Chimalli said in surprise. "His name is Anecoatl."

* * *

Panquetzaliztli, the fifteenth month, honored the great war god Huitzilopochtli and his little messenger-god Paynal. Malinalli wondered if Paynala, home of her parents, was named for that messenger-god. The ceremonies lasted all twenty days of the month, beginning with songs and dances. Again, Toci had stories to tell.

"In Tenochtitlan," said the priestess, "I saw even the sacrifice victims sing and dance for this feast. Nine days before the feast, they took ritual baths, and everybody—captives and captors together—danced the 'dance of the serpent.' On the last day of the month, the masters gave ornaments to the captives. The captives put on the ornaments and said farewell to their masters, then dipped their hands in ochre or blue paint to leave their hand-prints on the door jambs. Then singing as if their voices were going to break, as if they were hoarse, they formed a procession for the little god Paynal. They walked from the center of Tenochtitlan along the shores of the great lake Texcoco to Coyoacan and back again. When they arrived at the temple of Huitzilopochtli, they were sacrificed one by one on the great sacrificial stone."

"Were a lot of people sacrificed to Huitzilopochtli?" Malinalli asked.

"Quite a few," answered Toci. "The priests say he needs a lot of blood to keep his energy up. And each new Emperor seems to want to surpass the ones before him, with larger and larger ceremonies."

"Do there have to be so many sacrifices?" Malinalli asked. She was remembering fragments of a conversation between her aunt Papalotl and her mother, almost six years before. "Why isn't it enough to sacrifice one person at each festival?"

"You ask too many questions," Toci said curtly, dismissing the inquiry because she had wondered the same thing herself, and she had no answer. Still puzzled, Malinalli drew her own conclusions. If even gentle-spirited Toci could get excited at these festivals, perhaps all the subjects of Moctezuma could. Malinalli was glad Toci had explained the enigma of duality in Quetzalcoatl and his tragic priest-namesake, who struggled between good and evil, darkness and light. Toci herself seemed to have a dual nature: committed to a peace god, but apologetic for a war god. She spoke disapprovingly of sacrifices, yet her stories revealed a fascination with them. That observation did not diminish Toci in her eyes, for a noble struggle for virtue made Toci lovable. It was not the first time Malinalli had seen good people attracted to evil, nor would it be the last. But Malinalli yearned to find a way to spread Quetzalcoatl's teachings and diminish the power of the war god.

Thus passed the eighteen months of twenty days that created the cycle of a year. The five nemontemi days that ended the year, February 7 to February 11, were considered so baneful that nothing was done. Although there were no spinning and weaving tasks in the temple, there was no comfort from fires, flowers, or lively stories of the gods and their ceremonies from the facile tongue of Toci.

* * *

When Metzli discovered blood on her cueitl one morning during the nemontemi days, she was terrified. The bad luck of the nemontemi seemed to be focusing on her. "What have I done?" she asked Malinalli frantically. "Am I sick inside? Is this a sign from Huitzilopochtli that I should do more penance?"

Malinalli, who knew no more about menstruation than Metzli did, could only try to comfort her friend. "I'm sure you haven't

123

done anything wrong," she said, "but you may have hurt yourself. I'll go with you to see Toci. Maybe she can cure you."

"No, no, don't tell anyone," Metzli agonized. "I feel ashamed. I'll make an offering to Huitzilopochtli and Tlaloc."

"Maybe Quetzalcoatl too."

"Good idea. Help me pierce my ears."

Malinalli went to get some agave thorns while Metzli secretively washed her skirt in a bowl of cold water. Metzli spread the skirt on her petlatl and covered it with Malinalli's petlatl so it might dry slowly without being seen. Malinalli brought Metzli a piece of cotton she had just begun weaving, and the two girls tied it in place under the cord Metzli used as a belt. Then they found a clean cueitl to wear over it.

After three days of praying and puncturing earlobes, the menstrual bleeding stopped. Metzli explained her bloody ears to the priestesses as penance to get through the nemontemi. Since she had always been pious, they didn't question her motives, a few blood spots on her clothing, or Metzli's compulsive hand-washing. Metzli and Malinalli felt enormously relieved and grateful for the intervention of the gods.

When the problem returned the next month, in Atlcoualco, Metzli became worried enough to ask Toci after the other girls had left the classroom. "I've had pains in my chest and my back—sharp pains like a lightning flash, like being cut with a flint knife," she said. "I've found blood on my legs and my skirt. Are the mountain gods attacking me from the inside with their lightning?" Her voice trembled as if she expected punishment.

"Oh, my child," said Toci sympathetically, pulling a lock of Metzli's hair behind her scarred earlobe. "Or maybe I should say 'woman' and not 'child.' That's just your menses."

"My what?"

"Your menses. It means you're a woman now."

Metzli's eyebrows peaked in the center of her forehead. "Pain and bleeding mean I'm a woman?"

"Yes," Toci laughed. "Women have a lot of pain and bleeding, but a strong woman doesn't complain. Your breasts are tender, aren't they? And starting to poke out like little buds?"

"Yes, and they hurt."

"I know. They're getting larger, so they can make milk in case you have a baby. The bleeding will come every month as long as you take care of yourself. It's a warning to stay away from men."

"I don't understand," Metzli fretted. "How do I take care of myself?"

"Don't bathe or wade in the ocean while you're bleeding. Don't let yourself get cold, and don't eat foods from the cold group like beans and avocado. Wear a cloth under your cueitl to catch the blood, wash it out in cold water every night, and don't

124

let any dogs or rats get hold of it."

"But what if I don't want my menses to come every month?"

"You can't stop it, if you're a priestess," said Toci. "You have to be chaste, stay away from boys and men. They could stop it, but you wouldn't like the results."

Metzli's eyebrows peaked again in distress. "Why not?"

"Boys and men are filthy creatures," Toci said. "You don't need to know any more than that. Just follow the orders of the priestesses, and Quetzalcoatl will protect you from shame."

When Metzli relayed to Malinalli what Toci had said, Malinalli quickly interpreted Toci's puzzling words in the light of what she had learned growing up in Paynala. "She's telling us not to give our bodies to a man," Malinalli said. "Remember what our parents told us last year?"

"I remember," Metzli said miserably. "They didn't tell us we'd bleed every month."

Malinalli laughed at the irony. "They didn't, did they? They just told us what we didn't need to know and left out the more important things."

"What didn't we need to know?" Metzli asked.

"To stay away from men," Malinalli answered emphatically.

Metzli clasped her friend's hands in complete agreement. "We'll both stay away from men," she promised solemnly.

* * *

Although the weather was cold in the month of Atlcoualco, the dry season was an easier time to travel without trudging through mud. Opochtli had taken a small caravan to Coatzacoalcos to sell pottery and buy rubber. He stopped at the temple to take blankets to his daughter Metzli and Malinalli. He told the priestesses a family matter had come up—a matter of some urgency that justified a visit. Toci took him to one of the temple rooms where a brazier glowed and told him to warm his hands while she brought the girls to him.

"Chimalli sends greetings to you both," he said as Metzli and Malinalli came into the room. He gave them each a blanket, in which they wrapped themselves gratefully, thanking him enthusiastically. Then to Malinalli, he said, "Chimalli and I both offer condolences on your Aunt Papalotl's death."

"I didn't know," said Malinalli, shocked. "What's happened to her?"

"She and her daughter were drowned. Chimalli told us when he passed through Paynala on the way back to Tenochtitlan."

"How did it happen?" Malinalli asked, tears filling her eyes as memories flooded her thoughts. Visions returned of Papalotl when she had first come to Paynala, with her sad dark eyes and long shining hair. Visions of her holding her infant Xochi at the naming ceremony in the tecalli. Visions of her dancing with Xochi in the sunlight at the temple, her long loose hair blowing in the wind, the fine hairs catching the sunlight in a halo around her head.

"As you know, Chimalli went to see her on some matter of business," Opochtli explained. "From what Chimalli could gather, she and her daughter had gone to the river to get water. The child must have slipped on a mossy stone; Papalotl must have tried to save her, and the current pulled them in. Her husband became alarmed when they didn't come back and went to find them. He found them both downstream a short distance, lying in the shallows at the river's edge. Chimalli said when he arrived at their farm, the husband was quite overcome with grief, so he may not have told the story clearly."

Metzli moved immediately to comfort Malinalli with an embrace. "It's a noble death," she said sympathetically. "People who die of drowning go to the meadows of Tlaloc, and live forever in his paradise of green grass and blooming flowers."

Malinalli barely noticed her friend Metzli. She sat down on an icpalli and pulled her blanket around her. A confusion of questions whirled around in her head. Why had Chimalli gone to the farm anyway, after she told him Papalotl was married? Did he have to verify that for himself? How could Papalotl have drowned in a river she had known intimately all her life? A river she bathed in and gathered water from every day? Opochtli could not answer these questions, of course, so she kept them to herself. At length she asked Opochtli, "Did Chimalli see Papalotl before she died? Or was she already dead when he got there?"

"I think she was already gone. Why do you ask?"

Malinalli felt a weakness coming over her. Had she done anything wrong when she gave Chimalli directions to Papalotl's farm? Should she have trusted Chimalli just because he was Metzli's brother? She shivered but told herself her dark thoughts must be coming from grief. "Did Chimalli say why he wanted to see her?"

"Just that he had a message for her from his superior officer," Opochtli said. "And by the way, his commander knows your family. He was visiting them in Paynala when I left."

"Anecoatl," she said wearily. "Chimalli told us that when he came here, before he went to Papalotl's farm."

"Anecoatl's acting on your father's behalf with the calpixqui," Opochtli added. "One of them has accused your father of cheating on the tribute records. Isn't that crazy? An honest man like Itzamitl being accused?"

"Is he in trouble?" Malinalli asked anxiously.

"No, not really. I'm sure Anecoatl can intercede with the Emperor if necessary. He's a favorite of Moctezuma's—brought him the captive that will be the divine youth sacrifice next year." Opochtli rubbed his hands over the brazier. "You know," he mused, "I didn't like Anecoatl at first—almost ran me over when he brought Papalotl to Paynala years ago. But he's moving up in the world. He'll be a good person for Itzamitl to know." "Can I go back to Paynala with you?" Malinalli asked. "I think my mother may need me." "Of course," Opochtli agreed, "if the priestesses will give you a leave. Do you want to come home too, Metzli?" "The temple seems like home to me, father," Metzli said. "When you're away so much, and Chimalli is away on his campaigns, there's no family for me in Oluta, and I'd only be in the way in Paynala. I'm needed here." She tried to sound contented with her lot in life, but her tone carried a tinge of resentment.

"Metzli is our best student," Malinalli told Opochtli proudly. "She does everything better than the other girls."

Opochtli looked at Metzli paternally, but he spoke to Malinalli. "Of course she does," he said with a trace of awkward gruffness. "I'm just as proud of her as I am of Chimalli."

Metzli smiled, a thin pale smile, and lowered her eyes, a shadow of sadness clouding her face. "I'm needed here," she repeated, as if she had said that many times to herself.

Malinalli wondered fleetingly why Opochtli had not told his daughter directly that he was proud of her, but then her thoughts turned to more important matters. She left quickly to let Toci know she was leaving and to gather her belongings for the trip home. What was happening to her father in Paynala?

Chapter 11

The Suspicious Death of Itzamitl

Chimalli was staying in the guest house at the tecalli, making a stopover in Paynala on his way to Tenochtitlan, when Toto came to him shortly after sundown. He was alone, relaxing with a yetl reed after having taken his evening meal with Itzamitl and Cimatl. He was blowing his yetl smoke into the air, watching it rise lazily as he listened to the chirping of the crickets. He was thinking of the great city where he would be training, dreaming of its palaces and gardens and temples, when Toto appeared like a vision in the doorway.

She was taller than she had been when he first saw her, and she was taking on a woman's form. She had braided her hair around her head to look older, each braid holding a fragrant flower. She had knotted her skirt so that it pulled around her hips in soft folds instead of hanging straight down, and it revealed one shapely leg below the knot. Her huipil was embroidered as if for a feast, and the bulge of her firm young breasts caught the fading light and made a shadow between them. She wore no paint on her face or teeth, but her dark eyes and brows accented her pretty features.

"Do you remember me—Toto?" she asked timorously. "You said to come back in a year; it's been nearly two."

"Toto!" exclaimed Chimalli. "I didn't recognize you. Has it been more than a year?" His answer was true enough, but the whole truth would have been that he had not remembered her, so busy he had been with his studies and his first thrilling battle experiences.

Toto thought she had heard what she wanted to hear—that he remembered telling her to come back in a year. So she proceeded confidently, "I see you've cut off your warrior's lock," she said admiringly. "Have you chosen an auianime yet?"

"No," Chimalli laughed. "I didn't have time. I was sent into battle before I had completely finished my training. The Tlaxcalans had been refusing to send tribute to the emperor." Chimalli felt a stirring in his tepuli as he looked at the bare leg of the girl who was just becoming a woman. The dying sun made a rosy halo around her slender body as she stood in the doorway. Chimalli wondered if the gods had sent her to him, but he could not be quite sure.

"I'll be your auianime," said Toto with disarming trust and simplicity, stepping inside and letting her skirt drop to the guest house floor.

"Wait a minute," said Chimalli, staring at the puddle of cloth on the floor. "You're still pretty young. Does your mother know you're here?"

"I'm thirteen, almost fourteen," said Toto, moving closer. "I became a woman when I was twelve."

"Then you might have a baby if you sleep with me."

"My mother's a healing-woman. She told me all I need to know. I won't have a baby yet."

"Wouldn't she rather see you marry a local farmer than follow a soldier around?" Chimalli was growing more excited as he attempted to dissuade this girl. He found himself hoping she would resist his arguments.

Toto did not disappoint him. She stepped close enough to loosen his maxtli, just as she had once seen Matlalquiau do with her brother. "I told her how much I want to be with you," she said. "She understands, because she desired my father that way before I was born." When his maxtli fell to the floor, making a soft pile beside her skirt, she took his hand and pulled him gently down to the petlatl. Sitting beside him with her legs folded under her, she rubbed his chest and legs with her open palms. The rosy light was fading into purple shadows; the fragrance of flowers infused the room with magic.

As her hands flowed over his body, making his skin tingle, his tepuli became stiff with a hunger greater than he had ever known. He reached under her huipil and stroked her breasts, then her thighs. Their bodies joined, and neither spoke until the hunger had been satisfied. Toto's braids had loosened and lay limply on her bare shoulders; the flowers she had entwined in her hair lay crumpled on the floor, still emitting a strong and satisfying fragrance.

"I've never desired a woman like this before," he whispered against her cheek, still breathing heavily. "Now I know why the other students cared more about their auianimes than about their studies."

"Now I know why my brother couldn't think of anything except Matlalquiau," Toto said in a happy murmur. "They were always sneaking away into the cornfields or the bushes by the river." She giggled a little as she remembered spying on them. "They couldn't get married; he was too young."

"What happened to them?"

"They ran away to Matlalquiau's village. They still live there.

129

Papa doesn't want us to talk about them, but mama hopes they'll come back someday and tie the tilmantli."

Chimalli sat up, crossed his legs in front of him, and leaned his arms on his knees. "I'm too young to marry, too," he said. "And so are you. You know that auianimes don't always marry their soldiers, don't you?"

"Sometimes they do," Toto said dreamily. "My mother was an auianime for my father, but he didn't want to be a warrior all his life. He always knew he'd go back to farming after he did his military service."

"Bad luck for you, then. I'll always be a warrior."

Toto sighed and shifted to lie on her side, propping her head on one elbow. "I know. And maybe you'll marry Malinalli. I've heard your father talking to Itzamitl about it."

"What?"

"About marrying Malinalli. Didn't he talk to you about it?"

Chimalli snorted. "No. We've never talked about marriage at all."

"Maybe I shouldn't have told you, then," Toto said contritely. "I just want you to know that it won't matter if you do. You aren't expected to marry until you're twenty. If I can be your auianime for the next four years, I'll be content."

Chimalli folded his arms around her again. "You're sweet, Toto," he said. "So understanding. The gods are really smiling on me to send me a woman like you."

"And on me," she said. The room had grown dark, and the only light in the guest house was a ray of moonlight, which they believed had been sent by the moon god to bless them. They were still in each other's arms when the sunlight entered the same opening, brightening the walls that had enclosed a night of complete happiness.

* * *

Anecoatl, who had been staying in another guest house nearer the village center, gave his permission for Chimalli to take Toto with him to Tenochtitlan. Chimalli would receive more seasoning at the calmecac there, he said, and then he could aim for the highest military honors in the empire. It would be better for Chimalli to have an auianime while finishing his training, Anecoatl reasoned. Warriors were best for fighting and training just at the same age when their bodies roared for women and they craved large quantities of food. The urges of nature, like a jaguar in a cage, were easier to subdue when they were periodically satisfied.

Anecoatl also sent a message with Chimalli to his own superior officer, explaining that he had to stay in Paynala a while. The accusation against Itzamitl had not yet been fully

130

investigated, he said; it was probably false, but soon the truth would be known.

Chimalli felt uncomfortable about having brought the news of Papalotl's death. It had affected the entire household. He had hoped to tell Anecoatl only that Papalotl was dead, but his hosts had already informed Anecoatl that Papalotl had married her steward, and Anecoatl was behaving with a grumpy stiffness, as if his pride had been hurt. Cimatl, depressed over the loss of her sister and little niece, had gone into mourning by fasting and piercing her tongue with thorns. Itzamitl, even though he had considered Papalotl a bad influence on Cimatl, was worried about his wife. As that added to his worries about the investigation, he, too, was having difficulty eating and sleeping. He developed a high fever, which Anecoatl sent his own ticitl to cure.

Toto packed her small bag of clothing, said a tearful goodbye to her mother and father, and promised to return some day soon. Callipopoca would have objected to Toto's leaving, because Chihuallama still needed a daughter's help, but he dared not defy Anecoatl's wishes. Anecoatl represented the Emperor, and the Emperor could call upon citizens at any time to perform a duty.

Chihuallama assured Callipopoca that she would not be too busy without Toto. Then she assured Toto she would keep busy enough. Toto knew they would miss each other, and keeping busy would help her mother adjust. Toto remembered how sad her mother had been when little Moyo had been taken for a sacrifice and again when Acamapichtli had left to be with Matlalquiau. But Toto was very excited about her new relationship and her chance to travel. Her mother by then had become resigned to the impetuousness of youth and the perversity of fate. She also held a deeply personal philosophy that nothing in life is permanent, that all children are only loaned from the gods until the gods lead them away. So the couple departed, heading westward to the fabled city of Tenochtitlan.

Later that day Chihuallama brought some herb tea to Itzamitl, but Anecoatl met her at the door and set the tea aside. She asked to see Cimatl, but Anecoatl said Cimatl was sleeping and did not want to be disturbed. Frustrated and suspicious of the ticitl Anecoatl had brought with him, Chihuallama trudged back up the hill to her hut. "I think he is a sorcerer, not a healer," she said to Callipopoca. "And I don't trust Anecoatl."

"You might be a little jealous, my good wife," Callipopoca said gently. "You've been replaced in your daughter's life by a young man, and now you're being replaced as a healing woman by a ticitl."

"So—I'm just a useless old woman!" Chihuallama exploded.

"Not to me," Callipopoca said firmly. "Even if you are jealous, I was about to say, you're never wrong about people. I don't trust Anecoatl either."

* * *

When Malinalli returned to Paynala with Opochtli, the ticitl
was already hard at work to cure her father's illness. Itzamitl lay
on a petlatl in the main room near the hearth, trying to conjure a
vision from the peyote the ticitl had given him. Her father
recognized Malinalli and gave her a weak smile as she entered
and embraced him. Cimatl, her hair falling loosely around her
shoulders, also managed a weak smile for her daughter. Then
Malinalli sat on a petlatl beside her depressed mother as they
observed the ritual. Anecoatl sat on an icpalli near the hearth, his
eyebrows knotted as if he were deeply concerned, his lip-plug
dragging his lower lip into a pout. Opochtli sat on another icpalli
in the corner, his face so passive that no one could tell what he
was thinking, his dark eyes peering out over puffy bags of flesh
on his cheeks.

The ticitl, whose dark green tunic resembled a priest's except
that it was clean, crushed copal incense into a bowl and threw it
into the hearth fire, filling the room with a musky odor. He
crushed tobacco leaves into the same bowl, using a small
cylindrical stone for a pestle. Then he held up five fingers to
signify the healing power of his hands, chanting, "You, the five
tonalli who all look in the same direction, tell me who is the
powerful and venerable being who is trying to destroy our
tecuhtli? It is I who speak, I the ticitl, the lord of spells." Then
he spoke directly to the tobacco crushed in the bowl. "You who
have been struck nine times and crushed nine times, we will cure
this bewitched head with the red medicine, the root chalalatli. I
call the cold wind that he may cure this bewitched head." He
placed his hands on Itzamitl's temples, just above the ears, and
pressed them as he blew on the top of his head. "Oh wind," he
continued, "do you bring the cure for this bewitched head?"

"I see bright lights," Itzamitl said dazedly. "Many colors."

"Do you see towers, or stones, or worms?" asked the ticitl.
"Only colors, lights," mumbled his patient. "Clouds. I feel as if
I'm flying in clouds like the birds."

"That may be good," said the ticitl, rubbing his chin. "Then
you aren't sick from lust. We won't have to pull out worms or
stones from your body."

Itzamitl moaned. His forehead gleamed, and sweat ran in
little rivers down his neck. Opochtli shifted uncomfortably on his
icpalli, causing it to squeak. But he was no authority on healing,
so he said nothing.

Malinalli, deciding that her father needed some nourishment,
pulled some maize flour from one of the shelves and made a thin
mush of atole while the ticitl waved a quiauhteocuitlal, or "gold

of rain" stone over Itzamitl's body.

"This is good for those who are terrified by a thunderclap, and also for those who have inward heat as you do," said the ticitl. "It was dug from the mountains by the people of Jalapa after it fell from the sky. If the mountain gods have stricken you, they can cure you."

Cimatl sighed and looked at Opochtli with tear-filled eyes. "He's been getting worse every day for seven days," she said. "The gods must be angry with me. First Tlaloc takes my sister and my niece; then he makes my husband ill."

Opochtli moved to comfort her, sitting beside her on the petlatl. "It isn't your fault," he said. "The gods follow their own whims; they punish anyone who happens to be in their path."

Anecoatl walked over to Opochtli and extended his hand, pulling him to his feet. "I'll walk with you outside," he said. "Perhaps there are too many people here for the ticitl to do his work." Opochtli sensed that Anecoatl was annoyed with him, but he saw no reason to argue, so he accompanied the quauchic into the courtyard.

When the atole was ready, Malinalli started to feed her father, holding the bowl to his lips and tilting his head to ease the swallowing.

The ticitl grabbed the bowl from her. "I'll add some quanenepilli," he said. "The powder of passion flower will heal if the trouble is in the chest." He took a leather pouch from a pocket in his tunic, shook a powder from it into the mush, and stirred it with his finger. As Malinalli continued the feeding he resumed his chant: "I the ticitl, the lord of spells, I seek the green pain, the tawny pain. Where is it hidden? Enchanted medicine, I say to you, I the lord of spells, that I wish to heal this sick flesh. You must go into the seven caves of the lungs. Do not touch the yellow heart, enchanted medicine; expel from this place the green pain, the tawny pain. Come, you the nine winds, expel from this flesh the green pain, the tawny pain."

* * *

Cimatl and Malinalli maintained their vigil beside Itzamitl through the night, bathing his forehead with cool water, giving him sips of water when he woke with a raging thirst. The ticitl and Anecoatl retired to the guest houses, and Opochtli walked up to the hut of Chihuallama to seek her advice.

While her father lay asleep, Malinalli spoke softly to her mother. "I have a headache and backache, too. What tea should I drink?" She pulled her shoulders together tensely as a sharp pain shot through her abdomen.

"Do you have a cramp?" Cimatl guessed from the contortions that her daughter was suffering from menstrual cramps.

133

"Yes, in my private places," Malinalli said. "Metzli has had these pains too. The priestess Toci says it's her menses."

Cimatl noted the small bumps under her daughter's huipil and smiled knowingly. "Have you started bleeding each month?" she asked. She took some dried leaves from a jug and placed them in a cup. Then she took hot water from a clay pot that straddled the three stones of the hearth, pouring it over the tea leaves.

"No, but Metzli has. She started at nemontemi, and we thought it was a sign of bad luck."

"Yours could come any time," Cimatl said, stirring the tea leaves with a stick. "Don't be frightened. All girls start around your age. I'm surprised Metzli started so young; she's so frail and underdeveloped. But you never can tell by looking at a girl." She handed the cup of tea to her daughter.

"Did you start at my age?" Malinalli found it difficult to imagine her mother being a young girl, though the firelight verified her youthful beauty, even now.

"About that age. I don't remember exactly. What I do remember is that people had some wrong ideas about it. Girls used to get married when they were much younger—ten or eleven years old—and many people thought their husbands caused the bleeding. One of my mother's sisters asked if I'd been out in the cornfields with a man. It made me angry."

"Toci told Metzli not to get cold," said Malinalli, holding the clay cup in both hands and sipping her tea. "She said to stay away from men."

"Good advice for now," Cimatl smiled. "Save your private places for your husband. Don't speak to men you don't know, or they may think you want them to touch you."

Itzamitl shifted in his troubled sleep, and Cimatl bathed his forehead with a wet cloth. Malinalli went outside for more water, filled the clay pot, and replaced it on the hearthstones. "What did Toci mean when she said men and boys were filthy creatures?"

"Did she say that?"

"Yes. She told Metzli they could stop the bleeding, but not to let them do it because they were filthy."

Cimatl sighed. "Some women hate men," she said. "That's why they say those things. Some of them have been hurt by men. Try to understand why some women talk like that, but don't follow their example. Marriage is the best life for a woman. A woman needs a man to protect her and give her children."

"I don't want to get married," Malinalli said, as emphatically as she could while keeping her voice low. "I don't want a man to touch me."

"You still feel that way?" Cimatl picked up some embroidery to keep her hands busy as they talked.

"Yes. I'd rather be a priestess. Maybe even be sacrificed as a

134

goddess."

"I wouldn't object to your becoming a priestess," Cimatl said, "but your father wants you to marry a nobleman. Not all women can be priestesses; most women have a duty to become wives and mothers."

"That tea's helped already," Malinalli said gratefully, hoping to change the subject. "The pain seems to be gone."

"Now that you are a woman," Cimatl persisted, "you could have a baby. Remember when you were a little girl and wanted to know how a seed got into your tummy?"

"I remember you laughed at me," Malinalli recalled.

"A man plants that seed," Cimatl went on. "That man will be your husband if you're a chaste woman. His tepuli will fit inside your tipili cleft, and the seed will come from him in a white liquid from his body, his omecitl, white like octli but stickier."

"How awful," Malinalli shuddered.

"Not awful at all," Cimatl said dreamily. "If your husband is gentle, he can give you great pleasure." She looked fondly at Itzamitl and brushed his hot cheek with the back of her hand.

"Do you have to do that to get children?"

"Yes," Cimatl smiled, "it's the only way. But children are the best part of marriage. They are well worth any pain you have in giving birth."

"I remember when you lost your baby," Malinalli said. "I was afraid you'd die, you suffered so."

"Yes, I remember too," Cimatl said sadly, tears glistening in her lower eyelids, "life has heartbreaks as well as joy, pain as well as pleasure. When you have a child you will enter the space that only women can enter, and pay the price that all women must pay, no matter how rich or poor. You will be like a goddess creating new life; your pain will seem unbearable, but it will be quickly forgotten. Your courage and endurance through that pain will earn you the right to be respected, just as a brave warrior has a right to be respected. Your child is your gift to all humanity. Motherhood is what sweeps you into the cycles of life, brings you to a pool in which only women can bathe, unites you with all women who have preceded you to that sacred place."

Malinalli stared in wonderment at her mother. "Your words are like poetry," she said. "You have courage, like my teacher the priestess Toci. I admire her because she's been so strong when she lost the only man she ever cared about. But you're a heroine too."

"All mothers are heroines," said Cimatl.

Itzamitl moaned again and began to writhe on the petlatl. Cimatl laid her embroidery aside and prayed fervently, promising penances to any god or goddess that would cure her husband. Malinalli prayed to Quetzalcoatl, promising to devote her life to

135

his temple if he would save her father.

Itzamitl heard Malinalli's prayer and spoke to her in agonizing, gasping breaths. "I know I'm dying," he said. "So hear my last words. Take care of your mother for me."

"I won't let you die," said Malinalli fiercely, rubbing away her angry tears. Cimatl sobbed dejectedly but said nothing.

"If you were my son," her father continued hoarsely, "I'd tell you to become a fine nobleman, so you'd be chosen to take my place as tecuhtli." He paused, as if savoring a pleasant memory or dream. "I'd say learn to dance, enjoy the drums and the bells and the singing, for life will always bring duties, but we have to make our own joys."

"I'll be your son," Malinalli sobbed. "I can do anything a son could do."

"Be realistic, my sweet daughter," her father said, his voice barely whispering. "Never want what you can never have. That is the way to unhappiness. Marry a fine warrior like Chimalli or Tlacoch, and raise brave sons. Teach your sons to make things with their hands, so they won't depend too much on the labor of others. Teach them to cultivate their lands, because even a nobleman can't live on nobility alone. Only the land can nourish us; it feeds the Moctezumas and the macehualtin alike. Never lose touch with the land; never forget the land that sustains you."

"I'll remember your words," said Malinalli, "and I'll take care of mother." But she would not promise to marry, because she despised Tlacoch and could never be sure that Chimalli had not had something to do with Papalotl's death. None of the immature boys she had seen at the telpochcalli seemed remotely acceptable as husband material.

Cimatl broke in, her voice deep with grief. "Forgive me, my husband," she said, "for never giving you a son."

"There's nothing to forgive," Itzamitl rasped, then started to cough. "You've been a shining jewel in my life. I'm sorry I couldn't live long enough to clear my name."

Cimatl threw herself across Itzamitl's chest and sobbed uncontrollably. Itzamitl weakly placed his hand on her head and stroked the loose, lovely hair. Then his hand dropped. Malinalli withdrew with her private grief, leaving her parents alone. Only then did she begin to wonder what would happen to her mother after her father died.

When morning came, Itzamitl lay in the profound sleep from which no one could wake. Cimatl walked around in a daze, holding her hands folded across her chest as if afraid anything she touched might disappear. Malinalli felt barely awake, numb with the realization of her loss. Yet the sun shone warmly, the flowers in the courtyard bloomed colorfully, and birds were singing in outrageous impudence, as if the natural world could not sense that a wife's joy in living and a daughter's faith in prayers had just come to a bitter, premature end.

* * *

While her mother talked to the ticitl and Anecoatl about funeral arrangements, Malinalli trudged morosely up the hill to Chihuallama's hut to tell her and Callipopoca of Itzamitl's death. Chihuallama was preparing the corncakes, and Callipopoca was trimming his fingernails with a flint knife while he talked to the merchant Opochtli, who had spent the night at their invitation.

"Why didn't papa ask you to cure him?" Malinalli asked Chihuallama bitterly. "The ticitl didn't know what to do."

"Anecoatl sent me away," Chihuallama said sadly. "But maybe I couldn't have cured him anyway."

"Why did he send you away?" the merchant asked suspiciously.

"Want to know what I think?" interjected Callipopoca. "My guess is that Anecoatl didn't want him cured."

"Hush, my husband," warned Chihuallama, patting her corncake expertly. "We don't have any reason to think that."

Opochtli grew more suspicious. "Malinalli," he asked, "did the ticitl give your father any medicines after I left the room?"

"No," Malinalli said, puzzled. "No—or maybe yes. He added some passion flower powder to the atole I made."

"You're sure that's what it was?" Opochtli probed.

"That's what he said."

Chihuallama patted Malinalli's shoulder reassuringly. "Nothing to worry about, Malinalli. Lots of ticitli use that medicine. It's a good medicine; I'm just sorry it didn't work. You'd better run along now and stay with your mother. I'll come help wrap the body as soon as I've finished feeding the men." Malinalli trudged back down the path to her mother's house, a sense of foreboding mixing with her grief.

When Malinalli was out of hearing range, both Opochtli and Callipopoca expressed their distrust of Anecoatl.

"I'm suspicious too, but what reason would he have to want Itzamitl dead?" asked Chihuallama. She pulled a hot corncake from the comal and handed it to Callipopoca.

"I don't know," Opochtli answered honestly. "I thought he was trying to be helpful with that ticitl of his. Now I'm not sure. Chihuallama, can you keep an eye on him, and let me know if you spot any trouble?"

Chihuallama handed the merchant a corncake. "I'll try. But let's keep our suspicions to ourselves. We don't want to start any rumors or upset Cimatl and Malinalli without good cause."

Opochtli bit into the warm corncake, chewed it briefly, then spoke with his mouth full. "Okay, so we don't want to upset Malinalli or Cimatl. But what do you really think?"

"I think he was poisoned," said Chihuallama.

Chapter 12

Romance and Intrigue in Cuba

When the conquest of Cuba was over, Diego Velasquez rewarded himself well with choice lands in the island. He also rewarded Hernan Cortes with desirable land on the Duaban River. To provide labor to work it, he granted Cortes and Juan Suarez a joint encomienda—the Indians of Manicarao. The encomenderos agreed to live in Cuba and teach their Indians Christianity, as stipulated by the encomienda or "trust."

Many of Velasquez' followers complained that his methods of distributing the spoils of conquest were unfair and arbitrary—not according to rank, nor length of service, nor fitness for colonial life. Some soldiers received less than they felt they deserved; some got nothing at all. The birth of the first colony on Cuba, therefore, was attended by the midwife of discontent.

As treasurer's clerk for the expedition, Cortes had assured that tribute was paid according to established ratios—one fifth of the spoils to the Viceroy of the Indies, Diego Colon, and one fifth to King Ferdinand of Spain. Ferdinand had not remarried since Isabel's death in November, 1504, and he appeared superficially to be honoring the deathbed codicil to her will regarding the Indians. But Ferdinand cared only for the wealth that came to Spain from the Indies, so he allowed the colonists to do as they pleased with the natives.

* * *

Once Diego Velasquez had established military rule in Cuba, he turned to more practical matters—settlements, construction, and matrimony. He founded the town of Baracoa on the northeast shore, across the Windward Passage from Hispaniola. Using ships' carpenters familiar with Spanish houses, he built a grand house using woods from the island forests—mahogany, pine, and ebony. Its balconies overlooked a sandy beach and the aquamarine ocean. Red limestone blocks made a splendid patio for entertaining, especially when enclosed by flowering trees from Spain—royal poinciana, hibiscus, and bougainvillea. Following Spanish traditions, Velasquez made an agreement with his countryman, Don Cristobol de Cuellar, to marry his daughter Maria, who had accompanied him to Hispaniola. After satisfying himself that Maria was the Don's only heir and that her dowry would include some modest properties in Cuellar, Velasquez pronounced Maria a suitable bride for himself. The flattered Maria sailed across the Windward Passage to Cuba along with her father, who was to give her away at her wedding, and her two ladies in waiting, Leonor and Catalina Suarez. The mother of the Suarez sisters, La Marcayda Suarez, also came along to assist with the wedding in small matters such as decorations and refreshments. Their brother, Juan Suarez, had already taken his wife and children to Cuba, where he shared property with Hernan Cortes. The unattached females in the family were expecting him to shelter them, unless, of course, they could find husbands.

The Suarez sisters had spent two disappointing years in Santo Domingo without finding the rich husbands they hoped for. The dresses they had brought from Spain were becoming shabby, and importing new ones was difficult. In the absence of local dressmakers who could design fashionable dresses for Spanish ladies, they did their best with their own needles, scissors, and the fabrics that came across the seas in large bolts of undifferentiated quality and unimaginative textures. Still, having managed to create socially acceptable attire, the sisters came to the wedding with low necklines and high hopes.

The wedding was a sumptuous affair, an outdoor ceremony followed by feasting, music, and dancing. Bright lanterns festooned the patio of Velasquez's new hacienda, fragrant wild pig roasted on a spit, and bowls of rum punch lured the guests into gaiety. The sound of flutes and castanets mingled with that of Spanish guitars. Full-skirted ladies swirled around gentlemen in brocade doublets and colorful silk hose as they circled the polished wood dance floor. It was a fiesta fit for Spain—transported to the tropics. Most of the colonials from Santo Domingo attended, some as an obligation to Velasquez, who was expected to become governor of Cuba, others simply to see the new island they had heard so much about.

After the ceremony Catalina spotted a wedding guest clad simply yet elegantly in a doublet and silk hose that set off to advantage his broad chest and well-formed legs.

"Who is that gentleman?" she asked Maria, flipping her fan in his direction, then drawing it coyly alongside her cheek.

"Diego's friend, Hernan Cortes," Maria answered, spreading her white gown as she seated herself on a stone bench, like a lily in full bloom. "Hernan was treasurer's clerk for Diego when he came to conquer this island."

"Is he married?" Catalina tucked her pink gown under her and sat beside the new bride, like a rose blooming beside a lily.

Maria laughed. "Worse. He's had a string of native women. Diego says he's been taking the Indian cure for syphilis. Indians call it *guayacan*. Spaniards call it *palo santo*, or holy wood."

"Does it really cure?"

Maria smiled impishly. "They say it does. But the woman who catches him may catch something else in the bargain."

"Oh." Catalina's delicate lips pouted in disappointment.

"Well, Maria, aren't you glad you have a husband, so you can make sport of those who don't? You're lucky; not every girl has a father who can arrange a marriage for her. But don't get smug over your good fortune. In this place, fortune can be fickle."

Catalina left Maria in the hands of several well-wishers and wandered to the punch bowl, where her mother was functioning as an unofficial hostess. A woman who had a way of always seeming to be in charge, La Marcayda summoned servants to keep the punch bowl filled. Then she summoned her son Juan, with a gesture and an expression he had learned to obey early in life. She prodded him to make introductions.

Juan had already introduced his sister Leonor to the yellow-haired Pedro de Alvarado and left them chatting in a corner where a palm tree's shadow filtered the light from the lanterns. Then he fulfilled his filial duty by introducing his sister Catalina to Hernan Cortes, who bowed cordially and asked her to dance.

Catalina gave Cortes her arm and moved gracefully into the dancing area. She sized him up quickly: pallid face, but probably recovering from illness. Legs a little bowed, but probably a horse owner. Strong shoulders and arms. Good manners. Well educated, judging from his speech. Good sense of rhythm, though she could teach him a few graces in dancing. She concluded quickly that such a man could provide a woman like her with the means to become the great lady she deserved to be.

When Cortes returned Catalina to her seat, he promised her another dance. As a dutiful guest and astute politician, he paid his respects to the bride Maria. Then he courteously danced with Catalina's mother, La Marcayda, and her sister Leonor, who had been fluttering around Pedro de Alvarado all evening.

Catalina, too, danced politely with other gentlemen present, including the groom and the father of the bride. Her eyes never left Cortes for long, especially when he was dancing with Leonor. Even as she circled the floor with the handsome Alvarado, who had obviously captivated her sister's attentions, Catalina's thoughts tended toward striking a bargain with her attractive sister: don't maneuver in my territory and I won't maneuver in yours. Probably the gentlemen present would have been surprised if they had known how similar the ladies' thoughts were to those of military men planning a campaign.

140

The ladies, too, would have been surprised to know the contents of the conversation of Cortes and Alvarado as the two greeted each other during a quiet time when the musicians were taking a break. The two veterans of the Velasquez expedition met at the punch bowl, but as they sipped their punch, they walked out of the range of hearing of other guests.

"You look like quite the gallant tonight," Cortes said goodnaturedly to Alvarado. "Quite different from the fighting man I met in the campaign."

"And you," retorted Alvarado amiably, "are hardly recognizable without mud on your boots and sand in your hair."

"I'm sure I look quite different myself," Cortes chuckled. "I don't know which I enjoy more—the excitement of a campaign or the amenities of civilization."

"There's danger in both," Alvarado said sagely. "Here you might chase a woman until she catches you."

"I've noticed a certain lady in hot pursuit of you," Cortes joked. "Are you willing prey?"

"No," Alvarado answered seriously. "My heart belongs to a native woman. Haven't you discovered how loving and giving these Cuban women are? They make a man the center of their universe."

"Yes, I've found that too," Cortes said, "and they ask so little in return."

"It's strange how a perfectly docile woman can get a hook in you. My woman has never nagged me about being unfaithful, but now I feel guilty if I'm not true to her."

"You're fortunate to find true love under any circumstances. I wish you both much happiness," Cortes said. He wondered if he would ever feel that deeply about any one woman. He couldn't imagine giving up the thrill of conquest.

Cortes soon began feeling the effects of the rum punch and the scent of flowers in the tropical air. When the spirited music began again, he loosened his doublet to dance as exuberantly as a peasant. In this festive mood, he returned to Catalina, who was tilting her head provocatively and smiling at him from behind her lace-edged fan.

As they danced, the twirling, fair-skinned, delicate Catalina seemed doll-like, fragile, precious as a rare jewel. She knew some dance steps Cortes had learned in Salamanca, and he began to feel some nostalgia for his student days.

The dancers cooled themselves by sitting for a while on the patio, then strolling in the moonlit garden. Catalina kept up an animated conversation, with much smiling and flipping of her fan. She asked about his plans for his own hacienda—would it be like the Velasquez house? She listened to the tales of his youth in Extremadura, his experiences at Salamanca and Valladolid, his adventures in Hispaniola and Cuba. Cortes found himself talking easily and fluently, enjoying the intimacy of words. He had found native women attractive in an exotic way, but it delighted him to hear a woman speaking melodious Spanish and understanding all his words, appreciating his thoughts.

"It's so exciting to meet a gentleman like you in these islands," Catalina asserted as the guests began to leave.

"The pleasure is mutual," Cortes assured her, realizing that he had spent most of the evening in her company. "There are so few women like you in the West Indies."

By the time they said goodnight to their hosts, Cortes and Catalina had agreed to meet again. Catalina felt certain that her charms were working for her at last. Cortes recognized the traditional ploys of courtship, but he, too, felt excitement at this pretty girl's interest in him. She knew the games of flirtation, and he loved the adventure in such games. He hadn't realized how much he had missed that kind of gambling since he had left Spain.

* * *

A week later, the fortunes of the new bride, Maria Velasquez, had indeed changed. She was dead—of a fever, her grieving husband said. But no one ever knew for certain. What did become clear was that her dowry had already become the legal property of Diego Velasquez.

* * *

As an agent of Viceroy Diego Colon, Velasquez busied himself with building cities in harbors that might be used for commerce: Baracoa, Bayamo, Santiago on the southeast coast, and plans for Havana in the northwest. When Velasquez turned to the notary Hernan Cortes for assistance in legal work and planning, Cortes had an opportunity to observe how Velasquez worked. He was a man of dubious loyalties. While giving the appearance of obedience to his Viceroy, Velasquez was making every effort to switch his allegiance to the King of Spain. Nevertheless Cortes liked Velasquez, and he sensed it would be unwise to question his benefactor's strategies.

Under this wily mentor, who served himself while appearing to serve his chief, Cortes served an apprenticeship for several years. In that time Cortes was building his own hacienda and increasing his personal fortune by prudent management of his land and his workers.

Velasquez also included Cortes in his social life. After Maria's death, Leonor Suarez had quickly offered consolation, then companionship. Velasquez discovered that her charms were considerable, she was willingly available, and her passionate nature offered welcome diversion from the affairs of state. Soon Velasquez and Cortes were socializing on a first-name basis, and within a year after Maria's death they were being seen with the Suarez sisters as a steady foursome.

The two men had been in close association about a year when Velasquez invited Cortes to his home one afternoon. They strolled in his garden, then relaxed on his patio, watching colorful parrots flit among the flowering shrubs. An African in white servant garb brought tall glasses of pineapple juice—their favorite of the indigenous fruits on the island. Then the African stood impassively nearby and slowly waved a large palm-leaf fan, his bare black feet protruding from the loose legs of his pants like those of a gangling adolescent.

"Blacks make better servants than the Arawaks or the Taino Indians do," said Velasquez as he plumped into a wicker chair, crossed his stocky legs at the ankles, and stretched them out to their full length before him. One plump arm dangled over the back of his chair; the other reached for the glass of juice, his unbuttoned shirtsleeve retracting as he reached. "Better slaves, too. Working in the canefields doesn't bother them as much."

"Sugar cane is doing well here," Cortes commented. "Your idea, wasn't it?" He sat close to the table, one arm resting on it, relaxed but respectfully straight-spined. Even in his loose-fitting shirt, open at the neck, Cortes conveyed the air of a Spanish gentleman making a polite inquiry.

"My idea? Yeah—I'd seen some cane brought to Jamaica from the Canary Islands. If we can get a sugar business going here, we can make rum. Maybe even enough to export."

"Citrus trees from Valencia thrive here, too," Cortes said. "It'll be a long time before some of these crops mature, though." He sipped his juice thoughtfully.

"In the meantime," Velasquez said emphatically, "we need more labor. The Indians die from every disease they catch. Blacks have more resistance. There's real profit to be had in slaves, boy." Because Velasquez was twenty years older than Cortes, and much taller, he could speak in a paternal manner without seeming presumptuous.

"What about the King's prohibitions against slavery?"

"No laws against bringing slaves from Africa, my boy. Even in Spanish territories, you can get around laws if you know how. Who's going to enforce them? As long as King Ferdinand gets his Royal Fifth of the tribute, he won't complain."

"And the Viceroy?"

"Colon?" Velasquez snorted contemptuously. "The man's as incompetent as his father. You've heard the proverb *obedezco pero no cumplo*—'I obey, but I do not fulfill.' We just agree to everything he says, never defy him openly, but never do anything we don't think is best for our own territories."

"I can see you'll be an effective governor," Cortes said with a tactful nod. "I hope the Viceroy appoints you. You can count on me to help colonize the Santiago site. As to importing slaves, I couldn't oppose your plan in good conscience. I, too, have a few slaves—legal ones I've taken in battle."

Velasquez smiled approvingly. "And a few slave women, I'm told, who wouldn't go back to their villages if you let them."

"As a matter of fact, some of them have told me as much."

"What's your secret?"

"No secret. I've found that slaves work best when they're well treated. The most prosperous farmers all know that."

"Of course, of course!" Velasquez said impatiently. He signaled the servant to refill their glasses. "And now about another matter. You're twenty-seven years old now, right?"

"Right."

"When are you going to settle down and raise a family? You've recovered from the Clap, I suppose."

Cortes smiled and leaned back in his wicker chair. "I've been wondering the same about you. Settling down, that is. Are you thinking of marrying again?"

"No," Velasquez said. "It's only been a year since Maria's death, and her father's still alive. I should mourn his daughter at least a year, don't you think? He knew my family in Cuellar."

"You're in the public eye," Cortes acknowledged, stroking his neatly trimmed beard. "You have to keep up appearances." Cortes wanted to remain in the good graces of a man who could be a powerful friend but an implacable enemy. He was learning the arts of diplomacy, even as he sensed he was being manipulated.

"I'll be frank, Hernan," said Velasquez, gulping a swallow of juice and wiping his mouth with his sleeve. "Leonor knows I can't marry her right now, but she hopes I can persuade you to marry Catalina. Make an honest woman of her, you know."

"No offense, Diego," said Cortes, "but Catalina was no untouched maiden when I met her. I know she's been lonely, and she can't help coming from a poor family. I do find her attractive. Very feminine, delicate, intelligent. But I don't believe she cares about me as a man; she'd marry anyone that had an income to suit her."

Velasquez bristled. "You're insulting my lover's sister! If you think she's an opportunist, what are you? Didn't you come here looking for gold?"

Cortes rose and clapped Velasquez on the shoulder. "Of course, my friend. Didn't we all? Perhaps none of us are worthy of the women who marry us. Please excuse me now. I have to get back to the plantation."

"What's your hurry?" Velasquez said gruffly.

"I'll be frank with you, too, Diego," Cortes said. "You

mentioned my raising a family. I'm going to be a father. My natural child's mother is the Indian woman called Leonor Pizarro on my hacienda. She took my grandmother's name when she was baptized."

"Good God!" Velasquez moaned.

"I was going to ask you to be the child's godfather."

"Certainly NOT!" Velasquez roared. Juice spurted from his glass as he slammed it down on the patio table. "How can you even acknowledge the bastard? Use your head, Hernan! Don't throw away your future for a whore of an Indian."

"I'm sure you don't mean to insult the mother of my child," Cortes said with a chilly politeness, and left.

* * *

When the child was born—a daughter—Cortes named her Catalina Pizzaro, in honor of his mother. Thus there were three Catalinas in his life—his mother, his natural daughter, and Catalina Suarez. However, he had stopped seeing Catalina Suarez, and as a consequence his relationship to Diego Velasquez had become strained.

Shortly after his quarrel with Velasquez, Cortes was approached by a group of dissidents seeking legal advice. Many of them had participated in the conquest and felt slighted afterward. Others simply disliked Velasquez, complaining about his bad temper and unscrupulousness. The dissidents had requested a panel of judges to be sent from Spain to investigate the justice system in the Indies. While awaiting these judges, they held secret meetings, sometimes in Cortes' home. They drew up documents to show the judges, testifying to the unfairness of Velasquez. The group asked Cortes to carry the documents to Hispaniola and be their spokesperson.

Cortes agreed, though he began to regret it as he crossed the choppy Windward Passage in a native canoe in deep darkness. "Why did you get involved in this, you fool?" he asked himself as wind-whipped waves sloshed into his canoe and the small craft bucked in strong currents. Perhaps, he thought, because he found adventure as irresistible as gambling. Perhaps he was eager to test his skills in legal argument, or try his hand at daring leadership. Whatever the reason, he completed the journey. Even a fool's promise is a promise, he told himself.

When he stepped ashore on the return trip, a pair of rough hands grabbed him. He felt a bruising chain being thrown around him, a coarse sack being pulled over his head. He was tossed into a wagon and hauled to the jail in Baracoa. "We have orders to hang you," said the jailor. "Orders from Velasquez himself."

145

Chapter 13

Hazards and Escapes in Cuba

The Baracoa jail was small, dank-smelling, and crudely built, not intended to house criminals for long. Its only uses that first year had been to hold drunken nuisances briefly or to hold thieves until they could be hanged in the village square.

"You, on the other hand, are charged with treason," said Juan Suarez to Hernan Cortes through the bars of the tiny cell where Cortes had slept the night on a stone floor. "Velasquez wants you hanged for attempting to overthrow his government." Suarez, as Cortes's partner in an encomienda in Cuba, had told the jailor he was visiting Cortes on a business matter.

"Not exactly a fair charge," Cortes replied, rubbing his bruised arms where the chains had left their mark. "I was the legal representative of a group filing a legal petition."

"But you did it secretly, and Velasquez feels betrayed. I've seen him angry before, but never as angry as he is now."

Cortes moaned. "The dissidents knew he'd be angry. That's why they couldn't tell him. If they had, any investigation by the Crown would've been a sham."

"Some of your friends are interceding for you," Suarez said. "They are insisting on a trial before Velasquez hangs you."

"I can just imagine," Cortes said bitterly, "how much justice I'd receive from a jury picked by Diego Velasquez. Are you one of these friends trying to save my neck?"

"Not at all," Suarez said in disgust, "but my sister Catalina is. She still wants to marry you—though I can't imagine what she sees in you."

"Ah, Catalina!" sighed Cortes. A vision of their first dance together flashed through his memory, bringing a renewed desire to hold her, to smell the perfume of her warm body instead of the foul odors of his cell. "Where is she now?"

"Home, at my hacienda," Suarez replied. "I won't let her come to see you. She's been weeping and wasting away ever since you jilted her."

"Harsh words, my friend," Cortes said defensively. "I never

146

promised to marry her."

"Cad!" exploded Suarez. "You led her on, took advantage of her affection for you. When you slept with her, she had every reason to expect you to do the honorable thing."

"The honorable thing?"

"Yes, honorable. Remember honor? Or do you think civilization's rules are suspended out here?"

Cortes bristled, but since he was behind bars, Suarez had the advantage. "Strange you should say that," he retorted with a slight edge to his voice. "My priest thinks I should marry the mother of my child. I've been getting lots of lectures about honor lately."

"Well, why don't you?" Suarez challenged. "Some Spaniards are doing that. I personally think one should marry one's own kind, but the priest has a point, since you fathered a child out of wedlock."

Cortes began to pace his cell. "Don't think I haven't thought about it," he said defensively. "My Cubana is loving, loyal, and undemanding. Perhaps I should marry her, but every man has a dream, Juan. Mine has been to return to Spain in triumph and have my father select a bride for me. I've given him so much sorrow, I'd like to make him proud someday."

"You have an uncanny talent for doing rotten things and making good excuses for them," Suarez said contemptuously. "So let's make a business deal. What you really want is a woman with a dowry. And my sister wants you, God help her. So here's what I'm prepared to do. I'll give you my half of the Manicaro encomienda as Catalina's dowry, and we'll try to persuade Velasquez to drop the charges."

"You sound pretty cynical, Juan," Cortes said, but he was thinking that Suarez had matured a great deal since he had first come to Hispaniola. "What's in it for you?"

"If I'm cynical, that makes two of us," Suarez retorted. "And if I were as greedy as you are, I'd just let you hang. Then Diego would probably give me your half of the encomienda. But all I want is peace in my household. My crops are doing well enough to provide modest comfort, and my family doesn't crave riches. I'm tired of Catalina's moping, tired of my wife's complaining that Catalina doesn't help around the house."

Cortes laughed cynically. "Oh, so you want me to take her off your hands?"

"Don't be insolent, Hernan. I could leave you behind bars, you know. What do you say to my offer?"

Cortes decided that a penitent approach would work better than a defensive one. "Tell Catalina I'm sorry, very sorry. It was all a misunderstanding. Tell her I'd give anything right now to see her again."

"Anything?" Suarez's tone was caustic. "Including keeping

your implied promises?"

"Yes, I'm telling you the truth. I really am sorry. If I had no sense of honor, I wouldn't have kept my promise to the dissidents and I wouldn't be in this mess. I'll tell Catalina personally how sorry I am, if you'll just let me talk to her." Cortes gripped the bars and looked Suarez straight in the eye as he did when negotiating legal matters. "Tell her also," he said, "that a dead lover would be no good to her."

"Very well," Suarez said, "but I don't trust you, even if she does. I'm joining Baltasar Bermudez in a civil suit against you. He may have exaggerated some of the wicked deeds he claims you've done, but I'm on solid ground. I'm claiming you breached your promise to marry Catalina. If you get free and still don't marry her, at least you'll pay for trifling with her."

"This news overwhelms me, Juan," Cortes said sadly. "But I see your side of it. A brother shouldn't have to support his sister all her life."

"I have my hands full with my wife and my mother-in-law," Suarez agreed. "And you've reduced Catalina's chances to marry anyone else. You can see why I no longer consider you a friend."

"I deserve your contempt," Cortes said contritely. "If I go to the gallows, I beg you and Catalina to forgive me."

Suarez left seemingly pacified, but Cortes feared a trial with false witnesses. He had observed such mock trials at the hands of Diego Velasquez. So when his guard left that evening to get a meal, Cortes broke the flimsy padlock, seized a sword and shield he found lying in the outer chambers, pried open a window with the borrowed sword, and let himself down through the window. Then he ran to a nearby church to take sanctuary.

* * *

When Velasquez heard of Cortes's escape, he was furious. He accused the guard, Juan Escudero, of taking a bribe. He sent the chastened guard to try to force Cortes out of hiding. He pleaded with the priest to deny sanctuary. He prevailed upon Juan Suarez to lure Cortes out of the church. None of these measures worked. Cortes insisted he would speak to no one except Velasquez, and Velasquez refused to come to the church.

Cortes had been in sanctuary a week when Catalina appeared in the courtyard. Feelings for her arose in his heart: gratitude for her efforts to save him, desire that had not completely died. He stepped out into the churchyard to speak to her.

"Catalina," he said urgently, "I'm so glad you're here. Diego is threatening to hang me, and I don't want to die until I've begged your forgiveness."

Catalina turned to face him, her blue eyes filled with tears.

148

"I've missed you so much, Hernan," she sobbed. "Juan told me where you were, but he didn't send me here. He's so angry with you right now."

"I know," Cortes said. "I don't blame him. But I can't be sure of a fair trial here."

"I want you to know that my sister Leonor is trying to intercede for you with Diego. She's engaged to marry him."

Cortes murmured congratulations, but he winced at the thought that he and Diego Velasquez might become brothers-in-law. "I'm grateful for her help, and yours," he said sincerely. "If I can get free of my troubles, I want to marry you."

Suddenly from behind the church, the constable Juan Escudero appeared with a squad of armed soldiers. They surrounded the unarmed Cortes and, upon Escudero's orders, fastened a ball and chain on one leg to prevent Cortes's escape.

Catalina screamed and protested, but Escudero shoved her aside roughly. As the squad led him away, Cortes stared bitterly at the face of the constable who had tricked him. He resolved never to forget that face, and years later, when the tables were turned, Escudero would have cause to regret his scheming.

* * *

This time, the recaptured prisoner was taken to the hold of a ship, still wearing his leg chain. Aboard ship, the boy who served him told him that the ship would soon sail for Hispaniola, and Cortes would be tried before the same group of judges that had come from Spain to investigate Velasquez.

Feeling humiliated and desperate, Cortes managed to work his leg free from the shackles, though he injured his foot in the process. That same night he exchanged clothing with the boy who served him and slipped out a side door. Finding a skiff hanging alongside the ship, Cortes climbed into it and lowered it to the water. He also cut loose another boat to prevent pursuit.

The turbulent water of the river Macaniagua slapped at the sides of the tiny skiff and pushed it seaward as Cortes tried to row against the current. His arms began to tire, and he considered trying to land, but that might be dangerous if the skiff capsized. Instead, he risked swimming to shore, abandoning the skiff to the mercies of the winds and currents.

That night Cortes took several bold risks. He arrived at his home on foot, his borrowed clothing still dripping with river water, and entered without waking any of his household. Taking time only to change into dry clothing and boots, arm himself with a sword, and gather up some documents he had notarized that might incriminate Velasquez, he headed on foot for the home of Juan Suarez.

He did not wake Suarez, but left the documents with a

servant, along with a note for Suarez to meet him next day in the church. Then he walked to the church and took sanctuary there once more, this time with his sword at his side.

The next morning Suarez read the documents and put them away for safekeeping. He then rode his horse to the church where Cortes was waiting. Suarez was feeling more generous toward Cortes because Catalina had told him of Cortes's apology and promise at the church, and because other colonists had expressed some sympathy for Cortes's position. The general opinion was that Velasquez had been too harsh with Cortes.

At the church, Cortes's haggard face and rumpled clothing revealed his exhaustion, though he greeted Suarez cheerfully in the small library where the priest had left them alone. A picture of Christ's face glowed above them on the stone wall, but the room was otherwise furnished only with a bookshelf, a small table, and a couple of straight hard chairs.

"Why did you leave those documents for me last night?" Suarez asked, though he thought he knew the answer.

"To gain your trust," Cortes replied. "You can destroy them so they won't do damage to your future brother-in-law."

"Then you can't use them in your own defense," Suarez said.

"Precisely. I'm tired of fighting with Diego; I want a truce."

"Perhaps the time is right for that," Suarez suggested. "I'm also tired of the strife between my relatives and friends. Diego is assembling some men right now to quash a rebellion in the islands. He'd be better off with an ally than an enemy."

Cortes smiled, seeing an opportunity for both peace at home and adventure beyond. "Thank you, Juan. We all know that Diego has a keen grasp of whatever may be to his advantage."

"True," Suarez said, "but he's been generous with us, and we owe him something."

"I agree, and he can be reasonable after he calms down. I'd like to assure him of my loyalty. Where is he now?"

"He and his servants are quartered on a farm outside the city. I can take you there."

"First bring me a crossbow and some arrows," Cortes requested.

* * *

When darkness fell that night, Suarez appeared at the church with the crossbow, the arrows, and a fresh horse for Cortes. Then Suarez led him to the farm where Velasquez and his servants were staying. Velasquez's soldiers had already departed on their march against the rebels, and so the two armed men gained easy access to the hacienda. They pushed open the unlocked door and told a frightened servant to summon his master.

150

Velasquez entered the room, pale and quivering with anger, drawing a velvet robe over his nightshirt. "What are you doing here?" he demanded, looking more at Suarez than at Cortes.

"Hernan has something important to say to you," Suarez said.

"Then tell him to put down that crossbow," Velasquez fumed. "Only a coward would come here like that in the middle of the night. If you do anything to harm me, my servants and soldiers will track you down."

"If you put aside your pride for a moment and listen to him, you'll be glad you did," Suarez said. Then he turned to Cortes. "Give me your weapons, Hernan. You won't need them tonight." He took the bow and arrows from Cortes and laid them on a table.

"I brought a weapon only to make sure you would listen to me," Cortes said, extending his weaponless hand to Velasquez. "Now I offer you my hand in friendship, and I offer my good right arm in your service to quell the rebellion."

Velasquez looked surprised, but he also perceived a way out of his current dilemma. With the Indians rebelling in other islands, he didn't want to risk the rebellion of the townspeople who supported Cortes. Before accepting the proffered handshake, he turned to Suarez and asked suspiciously, "Is this a trick?"

"No tricks, Diego," Suarez answered. "Hernan has given me all the documents that might be used against you. I'm holding them in good faith, expecting both of you to drop all charges and bury all grudges."

"I offer you the documents as proof of my friendship, loyalty, and good will," Cortes said, still extending his hand patiently. "Also, I plan to marry Catalina as you wished. I've been proud and foolish, but I hope to make amends."

Velasquez took Cortes's hand but still asked suspiciously, "What changed your mind? How do I know I can trust you?"

Cortes's voice took on an aggrieved tone. "How can you still doubt me? I have more cause for grievance than you do. You passed judgment on me without hearing my side. You would have hanged me without a trial. You refused to come to the church to talk to me. I've given you all the evidence that could be used against you. And now, even after I've risked my life to come here and offer to serve you, still you doubt me!"

"I've checked the documents thoroughly, Diego," Suarez assured him. "Everything is there." He was watching Cortes's performance with some admiration. Cortes could talk his way out of any situation, Suarez thought.

"And how do you intend to deal with the dissidents now?"

"I'll tell them the plot failed, that you were too smart for us. I'll also tell them you're being generous in victory, and you'll grant them amnesty just as you are doing with me."

Velasquez appeared convinced. He embraced Cortes, laughing with relief, thinking how pleased Leonor and Catalina would be. "I don't need more proof, but I do need you on the battlefield. Stay for a late supper with me, both of you."

Suarez declined, since his mission had been accomplished, and he was needed on his hacienda. But Cortes accepted, and the two men talked until their grievances had been aired and reconciled. When Cortes became drowsy Velasquez invited him to use his bed for the night. The next morning, when a messenger arrived to tell Velasquez of Cortes's escape, he found the two men in the same bed.

* * *

During the next six years, Velasquez's confidence in Cortes appeared to be restored. Velasquez made a goodwill gesture by standing as godfather to Cortes's natural child, named after his mother, Catalina Pizzaro. His fiancee, Catalina Suarez, was contented to have Cortes living with her at her brother's house while Cortes constructed the first and finest house in the new colony of Santiago, where their marriage was formalized in 1515. Velasquez became governor of Cuba and married Leonor Suarez, having become prosperous enough so that he could forego the advantages of a dowry.

Of the thousand or so Spaniards living in Cuba at the time, Cortes became one of the wealthiest. His Indians found placer gold for him in the streams, and his hacienda produced profitable crops under the combined labors of legal slaves, encomienda vassals, and wage-earners. He spent his money lavishly, as a generous host and socially prominent citizen. He gambled often, losing and winning with equal grace. He chose clothing of quiet elegance, avoiding flashiness, but adorning his black velvet cloak with gold buttons shaped like knots.

He closed his eyes to the slave trade being carried out by his brother-in-law, Diego Velasquez, but even though Cuba's labor shortage became acute, Cortes avoided participating in slavery expeditions. In addition to his farming and mining operations, he made considerable profit by raising cattle and pigs, providing salt pork and bacon for outward-bound ships from his first plantation on the Duaban River.

* * *

Bartolome de Las Casas had given up his own Indian encomienda on a Sunday in 1514, after having a religious epiphany. He had been denied communion by a Dominican priest because he was an encomendero, and he felt unjustly treated until he read the words of Ecclesiastes 34:21, "the bread of the needy is their life; he that defraudeth him thereof is a man of blood."

In a fiery sermon, Bartolome pledged to devote his life to championing the cause of the Indians, but he was never able to earn their love, so bitter he became in trying to denounce their enemies. He was strangely silent on the matter of black slaves being imported and sold in Cuba, even as he was an eloquent messenger in detailing the abuses practiced by Spaniards against the Indians. Those who knew him best concluded that it was the eradication of sin rather than the love of the persecuted that had first place in his heart. That hatred of sin was to place him in opposition to his old friend Hernan Cortes for the remainder of their lives. Even though they were both deeply religious men, they developed widely divergent views about the best ways to serve their God.

* * *

By the age of thirty-two, Cortes had spent seven prosperous years in Hispaniola and five equally prosperous ones in Cuba. He seemed to have achieved all the success a man could want. But he recalled a dream he'd once had during a fever, a dream he had thought so significant that he told his friends at the time. In his dream he was wearing strange rich garments and being served by strange people who addressed him with great deference.

So it did not surprise Cortes's friends that, in 1517, when he heard news of lands to the west, Cortes realized he wanted more than a life of ease and affluence. He could never have imagined such a feeling during his impoverished years in Extremadura and Valladolid or his first struggling years in the West Indies. But now he recognized an ailment which for him had no permanent cure—the disease of restlessness.

Governor Velasquez, on the other hand, suffered from the disease of greed and its symptom of mistrust. He became intrigued by the tales of Francisco Hernandez de Cordoba, who had made a disastrous visit early in 1517 to the Yucatan Peninsula. Cordoba had lost most of his crew—three ships and 110 men—in clashes with the Indians of Yucatan, which he thought to be another island in the West Indies group. Cordoba himself died of his wounds in Cuba, but he had brought back tales of stone temples, walled cities with palaces, and natives possessing trinkets made of gold.

Velasquez immediately sent an agent to Spain to arrange a concession for future discoveries. At the same time he approached his nephew, Juan de Grijalva, to mount another expedition, this time with four ships and 200 men. One of his four ships was placed under the command of Pedro de Alvarado.

When Grijalva did not return at the expected time,

Velasquez became suspicious. Was the young captain trying to betray his uncle and claim the glories of discovery for himself? Velasquez sent another ship to search for him, this time under Cristobal de Olid. When Olid did not return, Velasquez became nearly frantic. He turned to an old friend, Baltasar Bermudez, who had once sided with him against Hernan Cortes. But Bermudez placed so many conditions upon his acceptance that Velasquez withdrew the offer.

Thus it was that Diego Velasquez turned again to his former rival, Hernan Cortes, to head an expedition to Yucatan in 1518. The fifty-four-year-old Velasquez had taught the thirty-four-year-old Cortes a great deal about conquest and administration of colonial territories. He had also taught him how to survive political intrigues. In some ways the two men were very much alike. For that reason they got along very well most of the time, and for similar reasons their relationship was doomed to a certain mutual distrust. That distrust would be put to a severe test in the years 1519-1521, two years that were destined to reshape not only the relationship of two former friends, but those of nations.

Chapter 14

A New Life for Cimatl and Metzli

Two weddings took place in Paynala in the year 8 House [1513]. One brought Malinalli pain; another brought joy.

"How can you do such a thing?" Malinalli asked Cimatl in great distress. "Daddy hasn't been gone more than a month, and you talk of marrying Anecoatl."

"Don't be impudent," Cimatl warned, "unless you want a thorn-prick. Twelve-year-olds don't tell their parents what to do!" Cimatl pulled down one of the dried pine boughs that had decorated the tecalli wall and tossed it out into the courtyard. "These branches have lost their fragrance," she said. "We'll get fresh ones today."

"But I don't understand," Malinalli objected as she cleaned the ashes out of the hearth. "Anecoatl wouldn't even let us bury Daddy as a tecuhtli should be buried. He ordered Daddy cremated like everyone else. How can you forgive him?"

"If you'll stop criticizing your elders," Cimatl said with rising anger, "I'll try to explain." She grasped Malinalli by the shoulders, gave her a firm shake, then hugged her tightly and changed her approach to a plea. "Dear daughter, please try to understand. It's natural to feel loyalty to your father. I grieve for him, too, but we have to be practical. What else can we do? How can we live?"

Malinalli wanted to suggest that they live in the temple of Quetzalcoatl and keep their family pride intact, but she held her tongue because she really wanted to know what her mother was thinking. With her hands she scraped the ashes into a pile and pushed them onto a flat board to carry outside.

Cimatl took a deep breath, pulled down another dry pine bough, and continued. "Anecoatl has been generous to let us live here until the new tecuhtli is chosen. He's being considered for the post because he's been the emperor's agent here, he knows the town, and he's learned enough about Itzamitl's work to carry it on."

"Will he live in this house if he's chosen tecuhtli?"

"Yes," Cimatl sighed. "If Itzamitl had a son, or even some brothers, one of them might be chosen. But even a close male relative would have to prove his worth. The emperor and his advisors make the final decision." She took some old boughs into the courtyard and piled them there.

Malinalli picked up a straw broom and swept into a pile the dry pine needles that the old boughs had shed. "What if the emperor doesn't choose Anecoatl?"

"Then he might choose Tlacateotl or someone else who knows this village and has been educated in a calmecac."

"Oh," Malinalli moaned. "I can picture Tlacateotl as a tecuhtli, but I wouldn't want to stay if Tlacoch was here."

"What have you got against Tlacoch?"

Malinalli had a ready answer. "He's conceited and lazy; I've seen him cheat in patolli games, too."

"Well," Cimatl said with a sly smile, "you just gave me an idea. You could marry Tlacoch! If Tlacateotl becomes the tecuhtli, we could all live here as one happy family." She pulled the last spent pine bough from the tecalli walls.

"Never! I'd rather live in the temple at Coatzacoalcos."

"And where would I live?" Cimatl reminded her gently, adding the last dried bough to her pile in the courtyard. "Our choices are getting more limited all the time. Now that your father is dead, we don't get a share of tribute any more. The villagers don't even bring us wood and water the way they used to. The only macehualtin who still do that are Callipopoca and Chihuallama. I can't afford to pay for your education at the telpochcalli any more—not unless I can remarry."

"Oh," said Malinalli. "I hadn't thought about that. Does that mean I won't be going back to the temple?"

"Let's wait and see. Anecoatl is in Tenochtitlan right now. He'll see the emperor and try to convince him that your father's not a thief. Will that change your opinion of Anecoatl?"

"I suppose so," said Malinalli reluctantly. She well remembered her father's deathbed wish to have his name cleared.

"Good. We're planning to have the wedding as soon as he gets back." Cimatl put her arms around Malinalli, hugging her tightly. "I'll be honest with you, Daughter," she said. "I know Anecoatl isn't the man your father was. No one can replace Itzamitl, either in my heart or in yours. But I'm grateful to Anecoatl for offering us a home. I'll be a good wife to him, and you must be a good step-daughter. Will you promise to respect and obey him as the head of the household?"

Malinalli still had suspicions about the healing man Anecoatl had sent when her father was terribly sick, but she couldn't be sure the ticitl had done anything wrong, and she didn't want to upset her mother with suggestions of foul play. Unable to promise respect for Anecoatl until it had been earned, however, she chose her words carefully: "I'll try for your sake."

"That's my good girl!" Cimatl said, greatly relieved. "Now let's walk to the woods and get some fresh pine branches."

* * *

The celebration upon Anecoatl's return was both a wedding feast and an installation into the office of tecuhtli. Anecoatl proudly flashed the presents given to him by the emperor: a new lip plug made of gold, armbands of fine feathers, several quachtli of fine fabrics. He told Cimatl and Malinalli the awards were for bringing to justice a corrupt calpixque who had stolen tribute goods and blamed Itzamitl. He did not make that announcement public, however, and Malinalli wondered why. She told herself she should give Anecoatl a fair chance to win her trust, but doubts hovered in her thoughts like clouds around a mountaintop.

His wedding day gave Anecoatl a chance to glitter as he interacted with the village officials and wedding guests at the social hall in Paynala. Watching him perform a host's duties, Malinalli began to hope she had misjudged Anecoatl, trying to see him from her mother's point of view. What had once seemed like arrogance seemed, on that happy day, like a man's affectionate pride in his glowing bride. What had once seemed like ruthless competitiveness seemed like desire for excellence in his work. What had once seemed like ambition to make useful connections might only be an interest in his new community. What had seemed like greed and materialism could be interpreted as a desire to become a generous host. Malinalli tried to understand the admiration in her mother's eyes when the priest tied the corners of Cimatl's and Anecoatl's tilmantlis and announced that they were man and wife. "I'll be happy for my mother, and not think of myself," she vowed silently.

Malinalli was delighted to see, among the people from neighboring villages who had been invited to the wedding feast, the young couple Acamapichtli and Matlalquiau. She had not seen either of them since Acamapichtli had quarreled with his father and left Paynala. While the drums and flutes played, hired dancers whirled around the room, their flamboyant feather costumes creating intricate patterns of color and motion. While the pine torches suffused the atmosphere with soft light and fragrant smoke, Acamapichtli approached his parents with Matlalquiau by his side.

For this wedding, Chihuallama and Callipopoca had come as guests, not servants. Cimatl had insisted they be treated as long-time friends. She had given them cotton mantles to wear, and Chihuallama had made deerskin cactli for her husband and herself, but their scrubbed feet still showed the callouses of hard, barefoot work. They were standing to one side a little self-consciously, as if unsure how to mingle with the nobles, village officials, and other dignitaries at the feast.

Acamapichtli approached them boldly, giving Callipopoca no time to avoid him. "You're going to be grandparents," he said proudly, putting his arm around Matlalquiau's waist. Under his arm, an arm sun-browned and thickened during two years of working as a woodcutter, Matlalquiau's huipil bunched up to reveal the bulge of early pregnancy.

"My parents have agreed to let us tie the tilmantli," said Matlalquiau, earnestly looking into the surprised Chihuallama's face. "They like Acamapichtli."

"We'd like your blessing, too," Acamapichtli said, looking first at his father and then, imploringly, at his mother.

Chihuallama looked quickly at Callipopoca, probing his face for his answer. She remained silent, but the hope in her eyes pulled on her husband's heart like a rope tugging a rock.

Callipopoca flipped his mantle behind his shoulders and placed his hands on his hips, bracing his strong upper arms proudly. He glanced briefly at Chihuallama's expectant face, then sternly fixed his eyes on their son Acamapichtli. "So," he said in a deep slow voice. "A sixteen-year-old can be a father before he's a man."

"I'm a man," Acamapichtli said defiantly, standing with feet apart and shoulders straight, ready to face any challenger. "I've done all the right things. I've learned a trade. I know how to girdle trees and cut them into firewood when they fall. I can support my wife and child. I've spoken to her parents, used all the right words with them."

"And they've spoken to all my relatives," said Matlalquiau with a giggle. "They all told Acamapichtli I'm much too stupid to be a wife. They can't understand what he sees in me." She smiled at Acamapichtli, her eyes crinkling merrily at the joke, because such bantering was traditional in her village. "Well, Matlalquiau, I can say the same about my son," said Callipopoca, a smile cracking the mask of his stern face. "You've lived with him for two years, so you know he's a poor catch. Since you have your heart set on it, and since you both are so stupid, I guess it can't be helped."

"Ah," Chihuallama sighed in delight. "We can tie the tilmantli as soon as the arrangements can be made. When is the baby due? Are you eating enough for two?"

As Chihuallama and Matlalquiau chatted excitedly, Callipopoca guided his son toward the mats where the banquet foods had been spread out profusely. "I haven't seen your mother so happy in many months," he said. "She needs children around her to be happy. So for her sake, I'll forgive you. But if you break her heart again, even if you are my son, I'll kill you."

Matlalquiau expected her child in the month Etzalquiztli, at the beginning of the rainy season, planting time. Chihuallama helped Callipopoca plant corn in their own garden, then left to attend the birth of her grandchild in Matlalquiau's village.

Callipopoca stayed in Paynala to finish planting in the milpas. He, too, was eager to see his new grandchild, but he thought men would only be in the way at a birth. A few days after Chihuallama had left, bubbling with anticipation, he was working alone in his milpa, missing her.

Suddenly Acamapichtli appeared and simply went to work beside Callipopoca, the son adapting to the rhythms of his father's movements as he had when he was a child. The macehual made no objection. Neither did he express gratitude, though he felt it, because Acamapichtli was simply behaving like family. The matter-of-fact acceptance of the giving and taking of help confirmed that the son had indeed resumed his place in the family.

"You have a grandson, now," Acamapichtli said proudly as he plied the earth with his digging stick. "I'll teach him all the things that you've taught me."

Callipopoca could not have put into words how he felt, but his work became easier and his heart lighter. Having his grown son beside him seemed to put strength in his arms and endurance in his legs, so that he had energy to swim in the river with Acamapichtli when the day's work was done. He was not one to nourish regrets about the past, but he did wish that he had taken more time for swimming when Acamapichtli was a boy.

When Chihuallama returned, she praised her daughter-in-law's strength and devotion to the baby. She expressed confidence that the young couple would be good parents. "That's how we know we've been good parents too, my husband." The truth of her statement validated all their years of dutiful effort. Realizing that their affection for their children had overcome all the troubles, uncertainties, mistakes, defiance, fears, and sorrows, Callipopoca felt successful. His mud-daubed hut breathed joy through the very walls, and the humble thatched roof covered the happiest pair of grandparents in Paynala.

Three months later, at the time of Tlaxochimaco, when the young green cornstalks were spearing the sky, Cimatl gave birth to a son. Although Anecoatl had resisted at first, Cimatl would have no other midwife except Chihuallama. Anecoatl had argued that this midwife had failed to bring Cimatl's last child safely into the world, but Cimatl merely looked at him icily and replied, "She saved my life when I lost my last child."

Anecoatl could not refute that statement, so he acceded to Cimatl's wishes. He did not like the way Chihuallama looked through him as if he were not there, nor did he like the way Malinalli looked down in deference but seldom spoke. Yet he knew this was not a proper time to impose masculine domination, for in the matter of childbirth, women had indisputable authority.

Malinalli kept a vigil with Chihuallama during the night, after Cimatl's first labor pains started. Remembering what had been done during the two other births in the house, Malinalli kept the hearth fire going to heat water in the clay pot. She held her mother's hands when Cimatl groaned in agony; she gave her a braid to bite on when the pain was intense. Remembering her mother's miscarriage many years before, she prayed silently that the child would be born as easily as possible, and that neither the mother nor the child would die.

Chihuallama strung a rope across the room and hung blankets on it to enclose Cimatl's petlatl in some privacy. She laid out her knife, her cloths, and her herbs in case they were needed. She sang softly and spoke to Cimatl in soothing tones, praying softly to the goddess Cihuacoatl to bless this event. When she could see the infant's head starting to push through the vaginal opening, she helped Cimatl to a squatting position to make the pushing more effective.

The baby was born in the dark of night, while rain fell steadily from dark clouds above. Shortly before the conch shell sounded from the temple, his cries of rage at the world's discomforts sounded from the tecalli. Chihuallama chanted a prayer thanking the goddess Cihuacuatl for the miracle—the son Cimatl and Anecoatl had wanted so much.

Tired but contented with the successful outcome, Malinalli wiped Cimatl's glistening face with a wet cloth. "You've been so brave," she said. "No warrior could be any stronger."

Cimatl smiled weakly. "You've been a big help to me, Malinalli. I'll do the same for you some day."

"Not if I can prevent it," said Malinalli. Though she spoke in a joking tone, she was quite serious.

"What do you mean by that?" Chihuallama asked as she severed the umbilical cord expertly with her knife and tied the stub at the infant's navel. Then she set the cord aside to be buried in a battlefield to bring luck to the future warrior.

"Malinalli often says she doesn't want to marry and have children," Cimatl explained sleepily. She closed her eyes as Chihuallama washed her legs and placed soft cotton cloths between them to absorb the discharge of blood.

Chihuallama then turned to bathing the child with confident, experienced hands. "You'll change your mind," she assured

Malinalli. "When you see this cute little one grow up and toddle around, you'll want a child or two of your own. Go and wake Anecoatl now. He'll want to see the welcoming ritual."

Chihuallama wrapped the squalling baby in a clean cotton blanket and placed him in Cimatl's arms until Anecoatl arrived. Anecoatl had been sleeping in the guest house to stay out of the women's way, but he showed great excitement when he saw his son. For the first time, Malinalli felt sympathy for Anecoatl, a man who was seeing the fulfillment of a dream. "He'll make a good father," she thought to herself. "He really wants this son."

Chihuallama took the swaddled infant and raised him toward the sky. "Precious son," she chanted, addressing him officially as she did all infant boys, "you must understand that your home is not here where you have been born. You are born to be a warrior, to travel far away. You are a quecholli bird, and this house where you have just been born is only a nest. Your mission is to give the sun the blood of enemies to drink and to feed the earth with their bodies. Your country, your legacy, and your father dwell in the house of the sun, in the sky."

Anecoatl beamed proudly. "I'll call him Turquoise Stone, because he's as perfect as a jewel," he said. "Make arrangements for the naming ceremony, Chihuallama."

* * *

The tonalpouqui looked at the sacred books and pronounced a favorable day for the naming. Despite its being a rainy month, the sun broke through the clouds enough that day so that people could chat in the courtyard between showers. The white blooms on the morning glory vines glistened with raindrops, like jewels in the clear light of the morning.

Those who had come to greet the baby brought presents—mantles and blankets from the wealthy, food and basketry from poorer neighbors. Callipopoca had carved the ceremonial gifts from wood—a small shield, a tiny bow, and four arrows symbolizing the four directions.

Chihuallama, in her role as midwife, conducted the ceremony at dawn. Standing beside her full water-jar, she addressed this new child in a way that reminded Malinalli of the naming of Xochi, Papalotl's baby. But the words were different because this child was a boy.

"Eagle, jaguar, valiant warrior, oh my grandson!" intoned Chihuallama. "Here you are come into this world, sent by your father and mother, the great god and the great goddess. You have been begotten in your own place, among the almighty gods, the great god and goddess who live above the nine heavens. Quetzalcoatl, who is in all places, has done you this kindness. Now be joined to your divine mother, the goddess of the water,

161

Chalchiuhtlicue."

Wetting her fingers, she placed some drops of water on the baby's mouth. "With this water you will live upon earth, grow and grow green again. It is by water that we have what we must have to live upon this earth. Receive this water." She sprinkled drops from her fingers on his chest, "to cleanse your heart," and on his head "that this heavenly water may enter into your body and live there, that this celestial water become part of you." Then she washed the child's whole body with water from her jar. "Now you are protected from evil," she pronounced. "Let no one do you mischief, for you are born again, new-formed and protected by our mother Chalchiuhtlicue."

She presented the infant four times to the sky, once in each direction, calling upon the sun, the astral gods, and the earth as the divine spouse of the sun, to protect this child. Then taking the shield and the arrows, she begged the gods that the boy might become a courageous warrior, and that his life might end where the brave who die in battle rest and rejoice. Then she announced the name chosen by the infant's parents: Xiuhtetl, or "Turquoise Stone."

Murmurs of approval rippled among the dozens of villagers in the courtyard. Then Cimatl took the infant, who was fretting by then, into the tecalli to nurse him. The old women of the village thanked Chihuallama solemnly, and she answered them with flowery words in praise of the parents and the child.

Tlacateotl, the retired eagle-knight who taught warrior-skills in the local telpochcalli, was considered an old man now that he was past fifty years old, so Anecoatl asked him to give a speech representing the town elders. The proud old warrior, determined to show his rhetorical training from the calmecac of his youth, pontificated upon the mysteries of life and fate. "Lord Anecoatl," he said, "this child is truly in your image, your likeness; you have a scion—you have flowered! You have begun a dynasty, to carry on your noble house as you administer the affairs of this fine community. And the mother, Cimatl—she is the peer of the goddess Cihuacoatl, a great beauty who graces your home, the house of the tecuhtli. Surely fate has brought you together for some divine purpose."

From time to time Tlacateotl excused himself for going on too long. "I am afraid of wearying you and giving you pains in your heads and your stomachs," he said, and then droned on with renewed vigor. Some visitors were relieved when a shower of rain gave them an excuse to go inside. "This celestial water," they joked, "has been sent from the gods to give us relief."

When the infant had been nursed and placed in a basket, Tlacoch, Tlacateotl's son, tried to get his attention with a feather. When Turquoise Stone ignored him in favor of sleep, Tlacoch became bored and wandered over to the mats spread with food and drink. "I'll take some octli to my father," he said to an old woman as he filled a cup. "He can celebrate all he wants today." But instead of taking the cup to his father, Tlacoch took one sip and then another; soon he had drunk the whole cup.

Tlacoch returned to the octli jar several times, using different pretexts. When he saw Malinalli walking toward the granary, his blurred vision turned the thirteen-year-old girl into a goddess walking in fields of light. His numbed senses thought he heard her calling his name. His unsteady feet followed her footsteps in the damp earth.

Malinalli had gone into the granary to pray. She felt exhausted by the work of the week before—caring for her mother and new half-brother, cooking meals for Anecoatl, preparing food for the naming ceremony, cleaning and decorating the tecalli. Even more exhausting were the emotions tearing her apart. Never before had she felt this gnawing new emotion of jealousy. Now that a son had come into the household, she felt displaced. She had tried hard to do her tasks well, but her work went unnoticed except when she could not get it all done. Even Cimatl, who had always treated her affectionately, had been preoccupied all week with nursing her son and taking steam baths in the temazcalli. On the naming day, while other people were lavishing attention on the baby, congratulating the parents, and praising the midwife, Malinalli felt ignored. She wanted some time to be alone.

She crumpled to the floor of the granary and indulged herself in some bitter tears. "Quetzalcoatl," she prayed aloud, "why did you take my father away? And Papalotl? If they were here, they'd be helping me. Now I feel like a servant—even worse, a girl servant. Why couldn't you have made me a boy?"

Tlacoch pushed open the deerskin door of the granary. "There ya are," he said thickly. "I'm here, pretty one. Who ya talkin' to? Wanna talk t' me?"

Malinalli jumped to her feet. "Tlacoch! You've been drinking octli!" Chills of fear ran up her arms, not fear for herself, but for Tlacoch. He was a pilli, a nobleman's son; if he became drunk in public, his punishment would be severe.

"I know why y'r a girl," Tlacoch said leeringly. He set the empty cup down on top of a large basket of grain and approached her. "To tempt men, tha's why. Y'r prettier than my auianime. She likes bein' a girl. I give her a good time. Ya wanna have a good time?" He grabbed at Malinalli, but she squirmed away and ran to the other side of the granary. He lost his balance and fell to the floor.

"Listen to me, Tlacoch," Malinalli said, loudly enough for him to hear, but she hoped not loud enough for anyone outside to hear. "I'm leaving. You stay here. Go to sleep. Keep out of sight. I'll come back in a little while and see if you're okay."

163

She grabbed a basket and filled it with corn, just in case anyone saw her leaving the granary, and opened the door. No one was looking. She closed the granary door and walked back to the tecalli, trying not to attract attention or to appear rushed. Tlacoch lay on the granary floor, unconscious.

* * *

Tlacateotl had discovered the octli, too, and was giggling with some of the older women when Malinalli returned. Malinalli could not think of a pretext to get Tlacateotl away from the other celebrants to speak to him alone, so she quickly decided that he could be of no help to her or Tlacoch that day.

Could she turn to Anecoatl? She wasn't sure. As the new tecuhtli, he was a judge and public administrator, charged with punishing public drunkenness. Her father, when he was tecuhtli, would have made no exceptions for friends or family. Anecoatl seemed like an entirely different sort, but she didn't want to put him in the awkward position of having to choose between doing his duty and helping the son of a man he wanted to impress.

She trusted Opochtli, but he was not available; he was away, traveling his trade routes.

Then she remembered Callipopoca. Her strong, reliable neighbor would surely help her. Malinalli looked for him and found he had already returned to his hut, leaving Chihuallama behind to finish her ceremonial duties. She walked up the path, found Callipopoca, and told him about Tlacoch.

"I'll take care of it," he said. He put a pot of water on his hearth and added wood to the embers. "I'll make some of the tea Chihuallama makes for me when I've had too much to drink."

"I've never seen you drink octli," said Malinalli, surprised.

"You never will," he grinned. "I don't do that in public!"

"It was foolish of Tlacoch to do it," she said.

"Yes, very stupid, in fact," agreed Callipopoca. "But he's young. About eighteen years old, isn't he?"

Malinalli nodded. "Five years older than I am."

"Well, he should be getting some sense by now," Callipopoca said. "He's almost old enough to marry. Some boys never learn responsibility. Or they have to learn it the hard way."

"Shouldn't he be forgiven the first time, though?" Malinalli asked. She remembered how stern Callipopoca had been with Acamapichtli as a boy, remembered the smell of the burning chili powder and Acamapichtli's choking as his father punished him. Yet now the grown son and the father seemed very close, as if they had been tugging on opposite ends of a rope all those years, and had finally used that rope to bind themselves together.

"Forgiven? Yes, but also punished, so he learns never to do it again." In a way, Callipopoca spoke for all Mexica fathers, who were expected to show their affection by providing for the basic needs of their sons, especially self-discipline. "Whatever hardships lie ahead, he will need discipline to meet them."

"I see," Malinalli nodded. "You're a wise father, a good neighbor. And you're a kind person to help Tlacoch." Greatly relieved, she walked down the path toward the tecalli.

Callipopoca arrived at the granary a short time later carrying a pot of tea and a cup—nothing unusual, since Callipopoca often carried items for his wife. When he looked in the granary for Tlacoch, the young pilli was gone. He must have awakened and found his way out, Callipopoca thought, so he turned and walked back to his hut. There was probably no need to worry.

* * *

The next morning Anecoatl followed Malinalli to the granary. While she was gathering corn, he opened the deerskin door and stood beside the tall basket where Tlacoch had left his cup. He picked it up, sniffed it, and held it out to Malinalli.

"Can you explain this?" he asked accusingly.

Malinalli stopped filling her basket. A feeling of discomfort ran down her spine and along her arms. She wasn't sure how much Anecoatl knew, or even how much he should know for his own protection. She answered guardedly, "Someone must have left it here yesterday, during the feast of the naming ceremony."

Anecoatl advanced slowly. "It smells of octli," he said. "Who would come to the granary just to drink octli?"

"It wasn't me," she said, hoping that her reply would protect herself and Tlacoch too.

"But you did come to the granary yesterday, didn't you?" Anecoatl's tone was becoming more and more inquisitorial.

"Yes," Malinalli admitted, looking directly into Anecoatl's eyes. "I gathered some corn and took it back to the tecalli."

"Did anyone ask you to do that?"

"No," she answered, stepping backward as Anecoatl advanced. "It was my own idea. I just wanted to be alone."

"Alone?" Anecoatl had backed her against the granary wall. "Or did you meet someone here?"

"Someone followed me," she said desperately. "I don't want to say who it was."

"Followed you? Or did you lead someone here? What were you up to?" Disbelief and suspicion colored his voice.

"I didn't lead anyone here," she said, angry tears starting to burn in her eyelids.

"I think you're lying, Malinalli. I think you took advantage of one of the guests."

"No, no. It wasn't like that at all."

Anecoatl was close enough so that she could smell his breath

165

in her face. He pinned her right shoulder against the wall with his left hand. His right hand rubbed up and down her legs, then he forced his fingers between them, pressing hard. "Are you putting your tipili into service already?" he leered. "Can't wait until you have a husband?"

Malinalli tried to twist away, but Anecoatl's strength overpowered hers. "Please," she begged. "I haven't done anything wrong. Let me go."

"You could serve me, too, Malinalli," he said in what he considered a persuasive tone. "The father of a newborn baby loses his wife's attentions while she's giving milk."

Malinalli shook her head desperately, rubbing the back of her head against the wall. "Please, let me go!"

Anecoatl's tone became unctuous. "I wouldn't tell on you," he bargained. "I wouldn't tell your mother you've been cavorting with Tlacoch. Instead, I'd tell her how pleased I am with you." He pressed his body against hers. She could feel the bulge of his tepuli, hard against her own soft flesh.

Angrily, with all her strength, she pushed him away. "You saw Tlacoch! You saw him follow me here."

"You slut!" Anecoatl spat out the words. "I found him here on the floor after you'd had your way with him. I took him down to the river and dunked him in the water until he sobered up. He said you tempted him, first with octli, then with your body."

"He's a liar!" Malinalli yelled. She ran toward the door, shoving Anecoatl away and knocking him temporarily off balance.

Anecoatl recovered his balance and ran after her, grasping her arm and whirling her around to face him.

"I think you're the liar," he said. "And if you come into my court I'll deal with you as harshly as I would any other liar, even if you are Cimatl's daughter."

"Let me go," Malinalli raged, kicking at him with her feet. "I'll tell my mother!"

"Calm down," Anecoatl said in low determined tones, his hands pressing brutally into her shoulders. "You won't tell your mother anything, and neither will I. She wouldn't believe your word against mine, especially if I tell her you seduced Tlacoch."

"Let me go!"

"Not until you promise."

Malinalli summed up her options quickly. She was in this man's power; she couldn't escape. Perhaps she could avoid the worst effects of his anger by agreeing to keep his ignoble secret. She would surely feel compromised, with her honor and integrity being challenged, but she had little choice. When she stopped struggling, Anecoatl relaxed his grip.

"All right, then," she said. "I'll promise if you will."

"Then we have an agreement," said Anecoatl. "Your secret will be safe with me as long as you don't try to cross me." He pointed to the cup, which lay on the floor near her discarded basket. "Take the cup back to the house with you in your corn basket," he said. "Wash it and put it away. Let it remind you that I've made an exception for you, just because you're Cimatl's daughter. Don't ever forget how generous I've been with you, and don't try any trickery."

He stalked out of the granary as Malinalli obeyed him. She trembled as she put the cup in her basket and covered it with corn. She felt anger more than fear, but one worry began at that moment and continued growing through every subsequent contact with her step-father. Her anger was turning to hatred, hatred like a raging fire in her heart.

* * *

Metzli had grown more devout in the two years after Malinalli's departure from the temple of Quetzalcoatl. She sought excuses to work alongside Toci when she was cooking or weaving for the priests, seeking the priestess's advice. Metzli yearned to make some grand sacrifice, to give her whole life and being to some noble cause. Toci willingly offered suggestions.

"A life of service to the priests and the temple is a noble life, a humble life," Toci said, kneeling on the stone floor and twirling the firestick in a pine board to start the fire between three stones. It was just before dawn, in the month of Toxcatl, in 10 Reed [1515]. Because no rains had yet begun, they were starting their usual morning preparations outdoors.

Metzli supplied Toci with dried pine needles to catch the sparks. "Have you ever wanted to be a sacrifice, Toci?" Her breath caught as she pictured the pageantry Toci had told her about in Tenochtitlan. "Wouldn't it be marvelous, to be chosen over all other maidens and sacrificed as the corn goddess?"

Toci exhaled with a snort. "Do you want to be a shining moon standing out in the sky? Or just a faint little star giving your humble light to keep the world from total darkness?" As the fire caught hold and licked around the dried branches between the hearthstones, she set the comal across them to heat.

Metzli hung her head and fixed her eyes on the floor. "My wish must have sounded proud and vain," she said contritely. "I should be humble and serve where I'm needed." She took some corn from the soaking pot and began to mash it on her grinding stone.

Toci smiled. "It's only when you talk that way that you'd be suitable for a holy sacrifice," she said. "Girls who want glamour or glory for themselves aren't virtuous enough."

Metzli sighed. "Humility is hard, isn't it?" she pondered,

taking some corn meal and patting it expertly, making soft slapping sounds in perfect rhythm. "If I ever achieve it, I'll be proud of myself."

Toci laughed. "Now you're getting the idea. If you want to be the center of attention, you don't deserve to be. The only girls who are perfect enough to be sacrifices are those who don't think they're good enough."

"That's a puzzling thought, but so true," Metzli said. "I'm not perfect enough to be chosen, but sometimes I do wish for excitement; I just can't help it."

"A peaceful life isn't so bad," said Toci. "I've known the storms of passion, the pain of excitement, the thrills of battle, and all the heartache of losing the warrior I hoped to marry. Believe me, you're better off here, in a life of serenity, serving in humble ways."

When the first batch of corncakes was ready, Metzli carried them, covered with a cloth, into the hall where the priests were gathering after their morning prayers. As she placed the dish of corncakes on the mat, she saw a jaguar knight enter the hall with a prisoner. He wore padded cotton armor dotted with spots to represent that animal and that high military rank, but not the jaguar head covering. His topknot was bound by a bright red cloth, his sandals stained with the blood of recent battle.

His prisoner, a youth about eighteen years old subdued by a rope around his neck, also wore the padded cotton armor of a warrior. His forelocks hung in loose bangs straight across his forehead; the rest of his locks were held in place by a cord made of two cloths of different colors twisted together. His strong cheekbones rose high under his deep-set eyes, and his full lips curved into a gentle expression as he stared impassively into space. Metzli began to feel a pull inside as she stared at the handsome prisoner. She thought he might be destined for sacrifice, so she secretly envied him.

"Who are these men?" Metzli asked one of the priests, but he glared her into silence instead of answering her.

The oldest of the priests strode over to the newcomers, spoke quietly with them in Nahuatl, then brought them to the mat in the center of the room. Metzli picked up the dish of corncakes and offered it to the soldier. When he had taken one, she offered one to the prisoner, keeping an eye on the priest to see whether his expression registered approval or disapproval. He simply ignored her, so she again held out the plate of corncakes to the prisoner. The young man glanced at his captor, and seeing no disapproval, took another corncake and began to chew it.

When she felt his eyes upon her, Metzli lowered hers as she did for priests, then in confusion raised them again. She wasn't sure what behavior was proper with a prisoner. When her eyes met the gaze of the young prisoner, she stood motionless as if pierced by an arrow. His chewing stopped and his square jaw loosened as he returned her gaze. Self-consciously, she fingered her long dark hair, tucking it behind her ears. Then she turned, and in embarrassed silence, served the last corncake to a priest. Toci entered the hall, bringing another plate of hot corncakes. She, too, stared at the impressive knight and his prisoner; then she motioned to Metzli. "I left some corncakes baking on the comal," she said to Metzli. "Bring them here when they're done."

By listening to the priests talking among themselves, the two priestesses gathered information while they served food. The prisoner was a Tlaxcalan. Aztec forces had attacked Tlaxcala in a flowery war, attempting to burn their temple, which would have symbolized victory and entitled the victors to take prisoners for sacrifice. But the Tlaxcalans fought with such ferocity that the Aztecs had retreated with only a few prisoners. The retreating soldiers, carrying a number of their own wounded, had run too short of supplies to feed prisoners along the route back to Tenochtitlan. So they had left their few prisoners at the friendly temple of Cholula until another army could be assembled to bring the prisoners to the capital for sacrifice.

The jaguar knight, recovering from a spear wound, had been left in Cholula to guard the prisoners. A surprise attack from the Tlaxcalans had caused him to flee, keeping only one prisoner. Because his prisoner was exceptionally brave and handsome, the jaguar knight wanted to give the emperor this prize. If the emperor approved, this fair youth might be sacrificed at the feast honoring Tezcatlipoca. The knight asked the priests if he could leave the youth with them for a year, to be treated like a lord, fed well, and given whatever comforts he desired.

After the priests had agreed and the jaguar knight had left, the captive was put in Toci's charge. He was not to be tied or guarded at the temple unless he tried to escape. Toci asked Metzli's assistance in making him comfortable, so she prepared a private room for him with a special petlatl: two mats, with a layer of duck feathers between them.

When Metzli carried his food to his room, she talked with him. He spoke a dialect of Nahuatl unfamiliar to her, but similar enough to hers that she could understand him. She learned that his name was Quauhtlatoa, or "Speaking Eagle," and he learned hers.

"You should be comfortable here," Metzli said to him. "Toci says we're supposed to treat you like a lord." She placed the meal tray on a reed mat, but Quauhtlatoa ignored it.

"All I want is a warrior's death," he said, sitting on an icpalli, leaning back, and folding his arms. He had shed the ugly suit of padded cotton armor and looked more relaxed in a maxtli and deerskin sandals, but he still wore the headband of red and white twisted cloths. "It makes no difference to me whether I die

169

on the battlefield or in sacrifice to Tezcatlipoca. I don't need a year of coddling."

The statement troubled Metzli, partly because she hated to see anything beautiful die—even a butterfly—but also because the words sounded hauntingly like those she had said to Toci only a few days earlier.

"It's a great honor to be chosen," she said. "You must be brave and noble. Toci says you'll become Tezcatlipoca himself."

"You seem intelligent," Quauhtlatoa said with mild amusement. "You know that's just an illusion, don't you?" He leaned forward and tucked his feet behind the legs of the icpalli. With his left hand braced on his hip, right arm draped casually over his right thigh, the lean lines of his body showed a sinewy grace that even his enemies would see as beautiful.

"I suppose it is," Metzli said agreeably. "We can't really make you a god just by treating you like one. But after you die, you'll become Tezcatlipoca."

Quauhtlatoa spoke contemptuously. "Impossible! I couldn't become Tezcatlipoca; he already exists. My father warned me that you Mexica think pretty fuzzily. No wonder you can't defeat an army of Tlaxcalans half the size of your own."

Metzli was startled by the vehemence of his remark but decided his anger was understandable. "Was your father a warrior like you?" she asked, trying to change the subject. "My father is a pochteca, a traveling merchant. I see him once or twice a year when he comes to the market in Coatzacoalcos."

"My dad's an artisan. Makes arrows and shields. Becoming a warrior was my idea." Again he tipped backward against the wall, balancing the icpalli on two legs.

"Careful," Metzli said in genuine alarm, reaching instinctively to catch his arm and balance him. "You'll fall and hurt yourself." Then she laughed as the irony of her remark struck her. "We have orders to keep you safe and healthy for a year. Then you can have your wish for a warrior's death."

Quauhtlatoa laughed too, then quickly sobered. "I think about death all the time," he said. "Death will be easy; it's life that's hard."

Metzli thought about that for a few minutes as she smoothed the lumps out of the upper petlatl and laid a blanket over it. "I was thinking about death the other day," she said pensively. "I told Toci I wanted to be sacrificed to the corn goddess. But she says I'm not good enough."

"Aren't you a virgin?" asked Quauhtlatoa, surprised. "You look as if you couldn't be more than fourteen."

"I *am* fourteen," Metzli said primly, "and of course I'm a virgin. But I have selfish desires; a virtuous person always puts other people first."

"Why would you want to end your life so young?"

170

Quauhtlatoa asked.

"Why would *you*?"

"To be a hero, I guess."

"Well, I'd like to be a heroine."

"Maybe we're both actually cowards, afraid to live," said Quauhtlatoa. He stood and began to pace the room. "Maybe I didn't fight as hard as I should've. Maybe that's why I let myself be taken prisoner."

Quauhtlatoa's thoughts went too deep for Metzli, but at least he hadn't ridiculed hers. As she listened to him talk, she was glad he was alive, glad he had been taken prisoner, glad just to be sitting on the stone floor in his room, talking about what was important in their lives. When Toci came to the doorway, Metzli was looking up at the pacing Tlaxcalan as a midwife would look up to the heavens when naming a child.

"Come, Metzli, you have other work to do," Toci said gently.

Quauhtlatoa whirled to face Toci. "It's my wish to have Metzli serve me at every meal," he said, sounding like a young lord accustomed to ordering servants about. "It's my wish to have her teach me about your religion."

"As you wish, favored son of Tezcatlipoca," Toci nodded. "Metzli's a priestess in training. She can teach you very well."

Quauhtlatoa then turned to Metzli. "Your lord is hungry now," he said. "You can begin teaching me while I eat."

* * *

For many months the cynical young Tlaxcalan and the naive Mexica maiden found pleasure in each other's company. They talked around the hearth in the rainy season, when the winds made a chorus as background to their voices, and studied each other's eager faces as the firelight flickered on them. When the rains abated, they walked together along the beach, made small fires at night when the ocean breezes blew softly, felt the salt spray on their tongues, and watched the moon climb into the sky with the murmur of the surf in their ears.

Toci arranged the work of the temple so that Metzli would be free to spend time with Quauhtlatoa; making him contented was considered part of her duties. Metzli began to understand her own religion better as she explained to Quauhtlatoa the peaceful principles of Quetzalcoatl. Quauhtlatoa had a keen mind and grasped concepts quickly, but if anything she said seemed illogical or contradictory to him, his piercing questions would send her back to the other priestesses for explanations. She could feel an attraction growing, because she thought of him whenever they were apart. But she remained faithful to her vows of chastity and never slept with him.

171

Toci had observed gradual changes in Metzli. The fourteen-year-old no longer seemed like the serene and philosophical child she had been. At times she dripped sadness; at other times she radiated happiness. Toci understood the causes of these changes in Metzli. Hadn't she herself known such joy, as uplifting as birdsong, and such sadness, as deep as a well?

As the days of nemontemi passed and Atlcoualco began the new year, the priests brought three maidens from the village to stay with Quauhtlatoa. It was normal procedure for the "fair youth" sacrifice to spend his last four months in the company of beautiful maidens who would cater to his every desire. He dutifully slept with them, but his dissatisfaction grew greater each day. The only maiden he really wanted was Metzli, perhaps because she was bound by her vows to resist him. Nothing whets desire so much as that which is forbidden.

Metzli, too, was experiencing desire, all the more intense because she was determined to fight the impulse. The virtue of chastity became more difficult to achieve when tested by temptation. Was she becoming more worthy to be a sacrifice, she wondered, by experiencing emotional pain? She began to wonder what she really wanted most, because undeniably she envied the maidens who could sleep untroubled with the most beautiful young man in the empire.

* * *

When Opochtli came to Coatzacoalcos on his next trading journey, he hardly recognized his daughter. Whereas he remembered a skinny girl with bony arms and an ethereal face, he saw a vibrant girl with round arms, a radiant smile, and the poise of a woman. Her smile would flash brightly, then be replaced by lines of sadness around her mouth. As they walked along the beach and talked, even an empty shell could send her thoughts floating away into sadness.

"Something about you seems different," Opochtli said, puzzled. "Are you taller? I've never seen you wear blossoms in your hair before. They're very pretty."

Metzli smiled, thanked him, and abruptly changed the subject. "I'm thinking of leaving the temple, Daddy."

"You want to come home to Oluta?" asked Opochtli.

"I didn't mean that, exactly," said Metzli. "Nobody's there for me. You're still away a lot, and Chimalli is still in Tenochtitlan, I assume."

"Not any more. He's been sent to fight in Tlaxcala. The Tlaxcalans still refuse to pay tribute to Moctezuma, and the Aztecs have cut off all trade with them, so the war's becoming rather nasty."

"So I've heard," said Metzli, with only a slight catch of her breath.

"Don't worry; Chimalli's a first rate warrior; he'll be all right. Might even get enough prisoners for a promotion." Seeing the look of consternation on Metzli's face, Opochtli ventured another suggestion. "Would you rather go to Paynala and stay with Malinalli? She's there helping her mother with Turquoise Stone."

"Turquoise Stone?"

"Her baby brother. He's a toddler now, full of energy, getting into everything."

"Ah, yes, Anecoatl's son. How is Cimatl?"

"Happy, as far as I can tell. Malinalli isn't happy, though. I could be wrong, but I think she could use a friend."

"I'd like to see Malinalli again," Metzli said. "Maybe I can stop in Paynala on my way to Tenochtitlan."

Opochtli registered surprise. "Tenochtitlan? Why do you want to go there?"

"To say goodbye to a friend," Metzli explained, "at the feast of Tezcatlipoca."

"What friend? I'm not following you."

"Daddy," said Metzli, "I hope you'll understand. You've always been willing to listen to me, and Chimalli's been a good brother to me. Now you say the Tlaxcalans are his enemies, but I have a friend from Tlaxcala that means a lot to me."

"A man friend?"

"Yes, a warrior—a captive."

"Metzli," Opochtli said in growing irritation, "are you consorting with one of our enemies? How can you do this to Chimalli and me? I forbid it!"

"Daddy, you haven't let me explain."

Opochtli grew more excited. "Some things can't be explained. I don't know where you found this friend. The priestesses are supposed to watch over you in this place."

"He's just a friend, Daddy. I'm not planning to marry him, or anyone else, ever," said Metzli. "I told you I just want to say goodbye."

"You don't have to go all the way to Tenochtitlan for that," Opochtli said, still fuming. "You can find friends in Oluta; some might make good husbands."

"I'd drown myself before I'd marry any of the boys I knew back home," Metzli said passionately, defying her father for the first time in her life.

"Then drown yourself! I don't know what's got into you, Metzli!" Opochtli strode away angrily, leaving a tearful Metzli standing on the beach.

* * *

173

When the jaguar knight arrived to take his prisoner to Tenochtitlan, Metzli had packed a small bundle of belongings. "I'm coming with you," she announced to Quauhtlatloa, who had been waiting patiently at the temple door for the captor he had once called "uncle."

"Stay here, where you're safe," Quauhtlatloa pleaded, holding Metzli tightly. "Strange, isn't it?" he said tenderly into her ear. "When I wanted to die, they made me live another year. Now that I'd give anything to live, they'll make me die."

Metzli buried her face in his neck so that her tears wet her own face as it pressed against his flesh. "Strange, isn't it? When I wanted to be virtuous enough to give myself to the gods, I didn't qualify. Now that I've maintained my high principles, I'm bitterly sorry that I did. Now I only wish I had slept with you. I wish I were having your child."

"Oh, Metzli, my moon goddess," said Quauhtlatoa with a sigh of great agony, "I worship you."

"You've made me a goddess, then, by the way you treat me." Remembering their earlier conversation about transformations, she added, "It's no illusion."

"And you've made me a god, for a whole year. I didn't believe it could happen, but it did. Who would've guessed that illusions can become truths?"

The jaguar knight broke into their agonized conversation. "You two love-birds are making me sick. I've never seen such mooning." He turned to Metzli and picked up her small bag of belongings. "For heaven's sake, woman, come along. We'll be on the trail for at least a month, and you'll have several days in Tenochtitlan before the ceremony. If he hasn't made you pregnant by then, I'll have to do it myself."

Toci watched in aching contentment as the happy trio departed on foot heading directly west. Ghosts swirled in her consciousness, and a sad realization overwhelmed her. Each new generation had to learn its own lessons, feel its own pains. That was the way of the world; what had happened before would surely happen again. The sun would rise and bloom in the sky, then be swallowed by the earth's dark caves each night. The rains would come and go, descending in showers and ascending in mist. The crops would grow tall, bear fruit, wither, and die. Every fifty-two summers a sheaf of years would be bundled up and another would begin, as long as the gods were not displeased. And Quetzalcoatl, her patron god, would come again, before her time on earth had expired. When was it he had promised to return? Yes, she knew: in 1 Reed. She must prepare for that year, the year when everything would change, and the spirit of peace would rule again.

Chapter 15

Changing Fortunes for Malinalli

The old Eagle Knight Tlacateotl had waited a decent length of time before speaking to Anecoatl about a marriage between his son Tlacoch and Malinalli. It was the year 11 Flint [1516]. Anecoatl had been tecuhtli for nearly three years; he had proved himself an able administrator although he was not as well liked as Itzamitl, Malinalli's father, had been. Anecoatl's marriage to Itzamitl's widow, Cimatl, appeared successful, especially since the birth of their son. Little Turquoise Stone was already talking, and his sturdy plump body gave everyone reason to believe he would indeed become a great warrior. Malinalli had helped rear her half-brother for two years, until he was weaned.

In short, Tlacateotl reasoned, Malinalli should soon be free of responsibilities to her mother and half-brother. She was fifteen years old and should expect to be married by sixteen. Tlacoch was twenty years old, expected to be married by twenty-one or twenty-two. They both came from good noble families, the best bloodlines in the little village of Paynala. The match seemed so obviously appropriate that Tlacateotl was surprised when Tlacoch reacted unenthusiastically to his suggestion.

"Don't you find her attractive?" said Tlacateotl to his son.

"She's okay," replied the pilli. "Everyone says she's the prettiest girl in Paynala."

"Then we should make arrangements before some other family does."

"With all due respect, Dad," Tlacoch said, "I don't want to get married. I have Centli-Xochitl to sleep with, and she doesn't nag me like a wife would."

Tlacateotl scowled. "Afraid of the responsibility? You'd rather spend all your time gambling on patolli games and hanging around tlachtli ball courts?"

Tlacoch looked down in respect, but he pressed his lips into a thin line and hunched his shoulders as if to endure his father's scolding or preaching with as little pain as possible.

Tlacateotl placed a reassuring hand on Tlacoch's tensed

shoulder and tried gentle persuasion. "You could become the next tecuhtli some day," he said. "You need a wife who can manage your household while you're away, plan entertainments for your guests, bear children for you, and raise them properly."

Tlacoch knelt before his father, touched the dirt with his fingers and then placed some upon his tongue. "I respect you as I do the earth," he said. "Forgive me for disappointing you, Dad, but I don't want to be a tecuhtli. I'm not interested in going into battle to prove my manhood, and I think being a judge would be a bore. I'd rather be a calpixque and travel around the empire collecting tribute for the emperor."

Tlacateotl winced. He had known for some time that Tlacoch had no taste for battle, but like old warriors everywhere, he had hoped his son would, in time, grow into a replica of himself.

"I've spoiled you, haven't I, Tlacoch?" Tlacateotl said, patting the topknot of his only son. "I've given you everything you ever wanted. But now I want something from you. I want grandchildren I can be proud of."

"Centli-Xochitl can give you grandchildren if that's what you want."

"That's not what I want," Tlacateotl thundered, pushing Tlacoch off balance so that he tumbled onto the floor. "I want grandsons with warriors in their bloodline. Real men, if their father can't be one. I won't give you permission to marry your auianime, and if you expect to keep on living here with me, I'll pick a wife for you who'll give me grandchildren!"

Tlacateotl stomped out, heading straight for the tecalli of Anecoatl. He had made a mistake, he told himself as he walked down Anecoatl's path. It was a mistake to consult young people about what they wanted for their future. Very few of them could see what was good for them. Yet he still hoped Tlacoch would listen to reason once the marriage was arranged.

Anecoatl received him warmly, but when Tlacateotl made his offer of marriage between Tlacoch and Malinalli, Anecoatl's smile faded and his manner cooled. The men were smoking reed pipes in the courtyard under the huehuetl tree, and Anecoatl took several puffs before making a reply.

"You honor our family," Anecoatl said in a cool, smooth voice. "But we'll have to think about your offer."

"The dowry wouldn't have to be much," Tlacateotl said, anticipating Anecoatl's possible objections. "I'd even help with the wedding feast, since I have no daughters."

Anecoatl smiled thinly. "We should all be lucky enough to have only sons. Daughters and stepdaughters can be a problem. Malinalli says she wants to return to Coatzalcoalcos."

"It's a mistake to consult young people," Tlacateotl grumbled. "They don't know what's good for them."

"I wasn't thinking that," Anecoatl said. "I was thinking that

Cimatl should be consulted, since Malinalli is her daughter, not mine."

"Yes, yes, I see," Tlacateotl hastily agreed. "It's wise to consider her feelings, even though the decision should be yours."

"It will be," Anecoatl said with a mysterious wink, then rose to let his guest know that the visit was terminated. "Just let me handle this in my own way."

* * *

Tlacateotl returned to an empty house, since Tlacoch had gone to be with his gambling friends from the House of Song. As Tlacoch gambled far into the night, his eyes became glazed with excitement. When the conch shell blew to acknowledge the beginning of day, he gathered his winnings and headed for Tenochtitlan. There he could gamble in the marketplace every day and attend occasional tlachtli ball games where the wagers would be high. If he could only win enough money gambling, he thought, he would not have to depend on his father's largess nor suffer the indignity of parental control. Money, money, money. Money was the key to an independent and worry-free existence. All he needed was money.

* * *

A few weeks later, another father approached Anecoatl. This time it was Opochtli, the pochteca merchant, who proposed a marriage between Malinalli and his son Chimalli. He and Chimalli chose to come at sundown, when Cimatl and Malinalli had cleared away the dishes of the evening meal and were lighting pine torches in the tecalli.

Chimalli had returned to Paynala in triumph, wearing the costume of an eagle knight, a remarkable achievement for a young man only 19 years of age. Feathers dotted his armor; his dark eyes peered from under a headdress resembling the head of an eagle, as if his face were being swallowed by a bird with a great beak. His skin had become more deeply tanned by living outdoors most of the year, and his black hair was cut warrior-fashion.

Chimalli wore his full regalia when he came with his father to the tecalli. The warrior costume greatly impressed Turquoise Stone, now almost three years old, who eagerly asked to hold Chimalli's shield. The toddler stroked the feathers and strutted around with the shield over his head, laughing whenever he bumped into anyone with it.

Toto also arrived with them, hoping to see her parents, who still lived in the hut near the tecalli. As the auianime of Chimalli, she had followed him adoringly through many campgrounds where he had battled the Tlaxcalans. Toto looked more like a woman, now, with her hair rolled in the style popular among women in Tenochtitlan. Her eyes gleamed with the worldly knowledge of a traveler; she carried her shapely shoulders as proudly as a young recruit. Cimatl hardly recognized her. Anecoatl did not recognize her at all, but envied Chimalli's access to her beauty. Malinalli especially wanted to hear the adventures of her old friend Toto, which she imagined must have contrasted dramatically with her own dreary existence of cooking and cleaning in Paynala, but after a very brief greeting to Malinalli and her family, Toto ran up the hill to the hut of her parents, the macehaultin couple Chihuallama and Callipopoca.

"You've grown so handsome," Cimatl exclaimed to Chimalli, but her remark was really intended to please his beaming father. "I can hardly believe you're the same boy who used to run around Paynala with wooden toy swords and reed shields."

"Tell us about the battles with the Tlaxcalans," urged Anecoatl, hoping to swap war stories about his own victories.

"No, tell us about Tenochtitlan," urged Cimatl. "Is it truly as spectacular as most travelers say it is?"

"I'll do both, if we have time," said Chimalli with the broad smile that had endeared him to Toto and many others. Then he turned to Malinalli. "Which would you like to hear first?"

"I'd rather hear news of your sister Metzli," Malinalli replied. "She stopped here briefly last year, on her way to Tenochtitlan with a jaguar knight and a young man named Quauhtlatoa. Did she see you when you were in Tenochtitlan?"

Chimalli's smile faded. "I did see Metzli, only for a few moments, at the feast of Tezcatlipoca. She was one of the four maidens who accompanied Quauhtlatoa to the steps of the temple of Huitzilopochtli. I was part of the honor guard for the priests. What a spectacle that was! I watched him say goodbye to Metzli and the other maidens at the foot of the great temple; then he climbed the stairs, breaking a flute at the top."

"Why did he break the flute?" asked Cimatl. Turquoise Stone heard the word "flute" and ran to the reed chest that held his toys, pulling out a small reed pipe of his own and blowing it until his father took the toy away.

"The flute is part of the ceremony," Chimalli continued. "The Fair Youth is always educated like a lord for a year, taught to play the flute and dance and speak with a flowery tongue. His merriment ended with the broken flute. The priests dressed him as if he were indeed the God Tezcatlipoca sacrificing his body for the people. The priests gave him yauhtli powder to dull the pain; then they cut open his chest, held his beating heart to the four directions, and left it to burn in the sacred eagle-bowl. They carried his body carefully down the steps; they didn't fling it down as they would have with other captives, because he was the embodiment of the god. His head was placed on the tzompantli rack beside others who had served the gods this way. His year of adulation was finished, and he met his death bravely."

Opochtli snorted. "He was a dirty Tlaxcalan!"

"He was still very brave," Chimalli said firmly, looking at his father directly but not disrespectfully. "No Mexica warrior could have met his fate more courageously."

"What happened to Metzli after that?" Malinalli asked earnestly.

"She told me she was going into service at the temples of Quetzalcoatl and Tlaloc, near the temple of Huizilopochtli. Tlaloc's temple is just as grand as the war god's temple, and it needs just as many priests and priestesses. Many of them live in the smaller temple of Quetzalcoatl."

"I've heard Tlaloc's priests are not doing sacrifices any more," Anecoatl added.

"Maybe that's why Metzli chose to serve Tlaloc," Malinalli mused. "The god of rain and water and tears."

"Metzli might well pray for tears," Chimalli said. "When the Tlaxcalan died, she looked quite radiant through her tears. I don't know how to explain it."

"Well, it's over now," Opochtli said heavily. "She's gone from us; we'll speak no more of her."

"If you see her again at the temple," Malinalli said to Chimalli, "bring news of her whenever you come this way."

"She's dead to us!" Opochtli exploded. "Dead! She betrayed her own family by consorting with that enemy."

An awkward silence fell over the room. Cimatl looked at Anecoatl; Malinalli looked at Chimalli.

It was Chimalli who finally broke the silence. "Let's walk down to the river, Malinalli. Our parents have important matters to talk about. I'll tell you all about Tenochtitlan."

Grateful to have a reason for leaving, Malinalli walked outside with Chimalli. Turquoise Stone had recovered his flute, but Cimatl came for him and took him to bed. Malinalli strolled beside Chimalli down the path to the river. They could hear the distant murmur of water on the evening air, blending with the croaking of frogs and the chirping of crickets. "Do you think Metzli was wrong to do what she did?" she asked.

Chimalli spoke gently. "Forgive my father's intolerance," he said. "His words were too harsh. Metzli can't be considered a traitress when she was just following orders. She was told to make the Tlaxcalan happy for a year, so he could be the fair youth sacrifice to Tezcatlipoca."

"Do you think she was wrong to break her vow of chastity?"

"Don't ask me to judge my own sister," Chimalli said sorrowfully. "She couldn't obey two conflicting commands. The priestesses told her to be chaste, and then they said to grant him every wish. She couldn't do both."

"You're very understanding," said Malinalli. "I think most men would just condemn her."

"I understand because I'm in conflict myself," Chimalli said. "My father came here today to arrange a marriage between you and me. He's talking to Anecoatl and Cimatl about it right now. I want to obey my father, but I don't want to hurt Toto."

"The solution is quite simple, really. I've told everyone I want to be a priestess," Malinalli said firmly. "Toto wants to marry you. I hope she does."

"It isn't that simple," Chimalli said in a troubled tone. "You and I are both duty-bound to obey our parents. Metzli has upset my father, and I can't disappoint him too. He couldn't accept Toto's family as in-laws for me."

Malinalli's frustration was growing with every step. "Your father has been good to me, but his disappointments and prejudices are his problems, not yours and mine. Chihuallama and Callipopoca are fine people with high moral standards."

"Can't you understand?" Chimalli protested. "He accepts them as friends; he just wouldn't want them as relatives. Toto understood that when she became my auianime."

"What more is there to understand?" Malinalli retorted, her voice rising in anger. "I don't want to marry anyone, and I don't want to hurt Toto either. I'm committed to the temple in Coatzacoalcos. I came here only to help my mother, but now that my half-brother is weaned, I think I'll walk to Coatzacoalcos and serve in the temple there again."

They were almost to the river bank, close enough to feel the damp air and hear the water's gurgling. The moon had risen like a slice of melon in the sky, casting a pale light on the path. A sudden memory of her drowned Aunt Papalotl surged into Malinalli's mind, providing another reason why she could not trust Chimalli. She stopped in the middle of the path.

"Let's go back now, Chimalli," she urged.

"Is something wrong?"

"Yes. Everything's wrong. Let's go back."

Malinalli ran back toward the tecalli. Chimalli ran after her, but he did not know the path as well as she did, and he stumbled over a stone. He picked himself up and dusted off his warrior costume. Feeling disgusted with himself for falling, he walked slowly back to the tecalli, arriving just as his father was preparing to leave.

"Did Malinalli get here safely?" Chimalli asked. "She was racing me back to the house, and I fell."

Opochtli laughed heartily. "Some protector you are, my boy! She got here way ahead of you; now she's gone to see Toto." He was clearly in high spirits, so Chimalli assumed he had made the bargain he had come for. After bidding their hosts goodnight, they walked toward their own home in Oluta. Opochtli told Chimalli that Anecoatl had invited them back in ten days' time for an answer. Having every expectation of a favorable reply, Opochtli began singing, not loudly, but happily as they walked through the moonlit darkness.

Chimalli thought of Toto, wondering if he had been too harsh with her in reminding her they could never tie the tilmantli. He thought of Malinalli's disinterest in him as a husband, even though she had never rejected him as a friend. He thought of his devotion to his father and the duty of a warrior, who was expected to marry at twenty and to father brave sons for a new generation of warriors. He took deep breaths and long strides as his thoughts tied themselves in knots. He began to dream of going back to a simple, uncomplicated battleground.

* * *

The following ten days produced events that changed many lives permanently, so Opochtli never did get a direct answer. Instead, a calpixque appeared at his door with orders from the emperor. Chimalli was to go immediately to Tlaxcala, where the battles were raging fiercely and the emperor's forces were in grave danger of defeat. Chimalli solemnly said goodbye to his father, expecting that he would never return from this battle, for he knew firsthand of the fierceness with which Tlaxcalans always fought against Moctezuma's domination. These days, he sorrowfully told his father, few of Moctezuma's warriors returned alive from those battlegrounds.

Although Opochtli suspected that Anecoatl had something to do with these sudden orders, he knew warriors cannot question their assignments. He no longer felt comfortable around Anecoatl, and assuming that the question of marriage was now irrelevant, he resolved not to visit the tecalli any more.

* * *

Toto became ill, and Chihuallama could not cure her with herbs, or chants, or atole, or any of the magic charms she knew of. She had seen sickness of the heart in some older people when they lost the desire to live. Toto's illness seemed like that to her. If Toto ate even a few bites of food, she became nauseated.

Malinalli spent two days at Toto's side in the macehualli hut. She bathed Toto's feverish forehead with cotton cloths dipped in cool water. To cheer her friend, she sang some of the songs and recited some of the poetry she had learned in the temple of Quetzalcoatl. When the fever seemed to break on the second day, she spoke encouragingly to Toto.

181

"You must get well, dear Toto," said Malinalli softly, close to Toto's ear. "You must know that Chimalli cares for you more than any woman in the world, and I will never come between you."

"Where is Chimalli now?" Toto asked weakly.

"Opochtli sent word that he was called by the emperor to the battlefields of Tlaxcala," Malinalli replied, soaking a cloth in a basin of water and wiping Toto's face as she spoke.

"Tlaxcala?"

"Yes, high in the mountains north and west of here."

"He's in danger," Toto moaned. "He may never come back."

"A warrior learns to face danger," Malinalli said. "You're in danger, too, if you don't start eating again. Make yourself strong for Chimalli. Eat the atole your mother made for you."

Toto responded in short, labored sentences. "Don't worry about me, Malinalli. Do what you must. Women have no choice. Chimalli says he has no choice either. He'll never tie the tilmantli with me."

Malinalli looked up at Chihuallama, who hovered over them with a bowl of atole in her hands. "What can we do for her?"

Chihuallama spoke to her daughter with mingled concern and disgust. "This is the folly of passion," she said. "Why set your heart on a man above your station? Only grief can come of it. Now that Chimalli is an eagle knight, of course he won't mate with a chicken."

"Maybe none of us chickens will mate with *him*," Malinalli said flippantly. "Believe me, Toto, I care more about you."

"Hear that, Toto?" her mother remonstrated, kneeling beside her with the atole. "No man is worth such heartache."

Toto tried to drink a few sips of atole from the clay bowl Chihuallama held to her lips, but then her head fell back on the petlatl. Her forehead again felt hot to Malinalli's touch, and when Toto's eyes closed in sleep, Malinalli rose to her feet. She felt so weary that she, too, wanted rest, but she promised to return the next day.

When Malinalli had gone, Chihuallama put down the bowl and sat quietly beside her sleeping daughter. For some time, her hands lay folded in uncharacteristic stillness, doing nothing.

When Toto stirred and opened her eyes, Chihuallama sat with Toto's head in her lap, gently stroking her face and hair. "You haven't told me everything, have you?" she asked softly.

Toto closed her eyes again. "I didn't want you to know," she said in a whisper, "but you can always see through me."

"You show signs of a woman who has taken too much ciuapatli root," Chihuallama said. "Did you want not to have a child?"

Toto shivered; her voice caught. "Whatever Malinalli says, I know Chimalli doesn't want me. He didn't want our child."

182

"Did he know?"

"When I told him, I thought he'd be happy, but I was wrong. He wasn't angry or upset; he just didn't care."

Chihuallama's face showed the pain of a parent who believes she has failed. "So you tried to use a child to do what you couldn't do yourself, to hold a man. Then you killed the child to punish Chimalli. What can you be thinking?" Her voice became stern. "A child is not a tool to use against others. A child is not a magic charm. Why didn't you come to me? I would have helped you raise your child."

"I know, Mother," Toto said wearily. "I knew exactly what you'd say. I just didn't want to be a woman with a child and no husband, living with my parents until I grew old."

"Would that really be so bad?" Chihuallama argued. "We have a good life here. We choose happiness; you choose misery."

"You have what you want, because you want very little," Toto said with some bitterness. "I'm not like you; I want a different kind of life."

"So you risk your life because you want some other kind of life?" Chihuallama chided. "Does that make sense? The only difference between you and me is that you only appreciate what you can't have, and I appreciate what I have."

"You think young people should just accept their fate and obey the rules, even wrong and cruel ones? Why should our fathers tell us who to marry? Why can wealthy people choose, but not poor people? Don't you see the injustice?"

"You think I don't get angry at injustice?" Chihuallama sounded angry at the thought. "I wanted to kill the Toltec man who accused your father of stealing, but that wouldn't have done any good. Hating other people doesn't hurt *them*; it only hurts the person who hates. Things turned out all right anyway, because Itzamitl was kind to us. For every unkind person, you can find ten kind ones."

Toto sighed, knowing her mother spoke wisely. "You're a wonderful person, Mother. I wish I could be more like you, but I can't. My heart tells me your words ring true, but my head tells me life isn't always that simple."

Chihuallama gathered Toto in her arms and pulled Toto's head against her own motherly breast, as she had done when Toto was little. Affectionately she said, "What's done is done. Learn from your own mistakes, not from what I say to you. You'll find life is good, if you give it a chance. Sleep now if you can. The world will look brighter tomorrow."

* * *

When Malinalli returned to the tecalli, she found Cimatl very agitated.

183

"Toto doesn't seem to be getting well," Malinalli said to her mother.

"I'll go to her right now," Cimatl offered, her voice sounding high-pitched and tense.

"She's sleeping now. That's why Chihuallama sent me home." Irritably, Cimatl repeated her intention to go to the macehualli hut. "I have to see Chihuallama today anyway. I'll do what I can for Toto. You stay here with Turquoise Stone."

Malinalli sighed. She would get no rest while watching her three-year-old brother, but her mother left without further word, so she took Turquoise Stone into the courtyard. She lay wearily on a mat and watched him as he chased some butterflies and dug with sticks in one of the flower beds, pretending to plant some seeds as he had seen his mother do.

* * *

Cimatl burst into the yard of Chihuallama's hut, scattering the dogs and turkeys that usually clustered around the open doorway looking for food. As soon as she entered the hut she cried out, "Anecoatl has sent me to warn you. There's trouble in Paynala. You and Callipopoca must leave immediately, and never come back."

"What kind of trouble?" Chihuallama asked in alarm. She looked quickly at her sleeping daughter, but Toto did not seem disturbed, her breaths coming regularly but heavily through her slightly open mouth.

"Some of Itzamitl's old enemies have made threats. They've told Anecoatl they have proof that your husband conspired with mine to steal some of the emperor's tribute. The punishment could be death."

"Callipopoca would never do such a thing!" Chihuallama exploded. "His accusers are liars."

"I'm sure Callipopoca is innocent," Cimatl assured her. "Itzamitl would never do that either. It's terribly upsetting. I thought those charges had been cleared up years ago."

"Does Anecoatl believe these lies?" Chihuallama set the clay bowl of cold atole outside the door, where her dogs could finish what Toto couldn't eat.

"He says he doesn't," Cimatl said. "He says he's only concerned for your safety."

"And do you believe what he says?" Chihuallama's voice had taken on an unaccustomed cynicism.

"Of course I do," Cimatl said defensively. "He'd help if he could, but these enemies are powerful people. Their word has some weight with the emperor."

"We know all about the power of lies," Chihuallama said. "Remember when we first came here, ten years ago? Itzamitl

184

knew Callipopoca wasn't a thief, but he made him give the lying Toltec some corn anyway, just to keep him happy."

"I remember," Cimatl said slowly. "You were accused of sorcery, weren't you? It's hard to prove your innocence against a charge like that."

"Itzamitl understood that. He gave us this land to make up for what he took away. We've always been grateful to him."

Cimatl's eyes filled with tears. "Itzamitl was a kind man, a good husband. I know Anecoatl isn't quite as good a man, but he's doing his best, and it isn't fair of me to compare them."

"I suppose a woman has to defend whatever husband she's got," Chihuallama said cynically. "I don't trust him, but I won't speak ill of him to his wife. He's the tecuhtli now, and if he wants us to leave, we'll go, but not until Toto is well."

"You'll have to leave today," Cimatl said. "Anecoatl says it's urgent."

"I can't leave Toto. Suppose Malinalli was the sick one. Could you leave her on a moment's notice?"

Cimatl's voice trembled in desperation. "I'd feel just as you do—I'd try to protect my daughter. You can leave Toto with me, but you really must get away."

The fear in Cimatl's voice told Chihuallama there was more to the story than Cimatl was allowed to reveal. Reluctantly the healing-woman agreed to be ready when her husband returned from the milpas. Working in silent sadness, the two women packed what few belongings Callipopoca and Chihuallama would be able to carry, as well as a bundle of clothing that belonged to Toto.

* * *

When Callipopoca returned from the milpas, he listened carefully to his wife's explanations, and though his face showed anger, he spoke only a few words in restrained tones. He took a slow walk around the yard that had been his home for ten years, saying a silent goodbye to the hut he had built himself, the garden Chihuallama had planted, the distant forest and the grassy hills. Then he gathered his daughter into his arms, carrying the sixteen-year-old as he had carried her when she was an infant, slowly down the hill to the tecalli. He carried her into the main room and put her limp body on a petlatl beside the three hearth stones, where she would be warm until she woke.

Cimatl had explained the situation to Malinalli, and the two of them stood solemnly beside the hearth as Callipopoca settled his daughter gently on the petlatl. Anecoatl had taken Turquoise Stone to the village, to get the boy's hair cut, he said. Even if that was only an excuse to avoid a confrontation with Callipopoca, the women were relieved that Anecoatl was not there to make the emotional scene more difficult.

"Where will you go, Callipopoca?" Malinalli asked anxiously, while Cimatl tried to manage a weak smile.

Callipopoca turned to face her. His wet cheeks shone in the light of the hearth fire. "I don't know yet," he said simply. "We leave our daughter in your care. When she's well, tell her to get in touch with her brother Acamapichtli. He'll know where to reach us."

"Goodbye, Callipopoca," Cimatl said tearfully. "We'll miss you and Chihuallama."

Callipopoca did not answer, nor did he look into Cimatl's face or put his eyes down in respect. Instead he stared straight ahead and walked out of the tecalli as if he were in a trance.

* * *

Malinalli fell into a troubled sleep that night. Before the conch shell had sounded or the first light rays appeared, she was awakened by her mother's touch and her urgent whispering.

"You're in danger, too, Malinalli," Cimatl said, "just like Callipopoca. You must leave right away, and not try to come back."

"What's wrong, Mother?" Malinalli sensed her mother's great fear. Instantly she became fully awake.

"Your father's enemies have threatened your life," Cimatl answered tearfully. "I can't tell you more than that. There's no time to waste. Disguise yourself in this huipil." She pulled Malinalli's cotton huipil over head and upheld arms, as if her daughter were still a child. Cimatl then slipped the coarse maguey fiber garment over Malinalli's arms and head. She put cactli on Malinalli's feet—woven hemp cactli, not deerskin.

"You can travel with a Maya trader, disguised as a slave, until you reach Coatzacoalcos. Then you can seek sanctuary at the temple. Don't try to come back to Paynala. It will never be safe for you here. Do you understand?"

Malinalli searched Cimatl's face for a sign, but she could see nothing there except fear and desperation. "Yes, Mother. I understand." Then Cimatl gave her a tight, hurried embrace.

Cimatl led Malinalli by the hand as they crept through the main room, past the sleeping form of Toto lying beside the cold ashes of the hearth, through the courtyard bathed with a ghostly moonlight, down the path to the road that led to Coatzacoalcos.

A caravan of traders waited for them at the road. Several tamemes were sitting on their loaded baskets, resting before resuming their long journey. As they approached, the women could also see a group of slaves roped together, sitting on the dirt road as they waited. A stocky Maya man, apparently the caravan leader, held out his open palm to Cimatl. He said a few words in

Mayan, a tongue neither Cimatl nor Malinalli understood. Cimatl placed a piece of jade in his hand, and he smiled.

"The jade was a gift to me from your father," Cimatl said to Malinalli. "It should pay for your safe passage to the temple at Coatzacoalcos. If I never see you again, please believe that I'm trying to save you. I'll do everything I can for Toto, too."

Malinalli embraced her mother, the tears on her own cheek blending with the tears on Cimatl's cheek, their two hearts pounding against each other's breasts. Then the stocky Maya trader nudged her into the line of slaves, who traveled ahead of the tamemes. He did not tie her to the rope that joined the other slaves, because Anecoatl had assured him, when the two men had made their arrangements, that this slave was perfectly docile and would not try to escape.

The leader barked a command. The tamemes hoisted their tumplines to their foreheads, adjusted their loads on their backs, and faced the eastern sky where the faint gray pre-dawn color announced the beginning of another day's struggle between the forces of light and darkness.

* * *

After the funeral pyre had been lit, and Toto's body had been consumed by the flames, Anecoatl could breathe a little more easily. The scheme had worked even better than he had foreseen. Since the corpse had been dressed in Malinalli's clothing, no one had questioned whether this body had indeed been the body of Cimatl's daughter. Cimatl's undiminished flow of tears, enough to rival the tears of the water goddess Chalchiuhtlicue, had been interpreted by everyone as the natural grief of a woman who had lost a beloved daughter to a sudden illness.

If anyone from the village had seen Toto come there with Chimalli, they might also assume that she had left with Chimalli, continuing her services to him as his auianime in the war camps near Tlaxcala. Her parents had left Paynala in great fear of ever returning, so they could never raise doubts in Paynala as to the identity of the body purported to be Malinalli's. Nor could they raise questions as to the fate of their daughter. Even Toto's brother Acamapichtli, if he should ever ask, could be told that his sister had recovered and followed Chimalli to the wars.

Chimalli would probably never return from the battles, Anecoatl told himself. He also congratulated himself on having bribed the calpixque to take the false orders to Chimalli at Opochtli's house. Chances were slim that this calpixque would ever come this way again, and even slimmer that he would have any incentive to reveal the secret and thus incriminate himself as well as Anecoatl. Anecoatl warned himself not to be smug, however; he would have to be careful never to boast of his cleverness or let this information slip to Cimatl. She had been difficult enough to persuade as it was; she didn't need to know that Chimalli's doom had come about from design, not from the vagaries of fate or the stubbornness of Moctezuma. Cimatl would probably believe quite confidently for a long while that her daughter had been sent to Coatzacoalcos to take up service there as a priestess. If Cimatl ever did travel to Coatzacoalcos, she would learn that Malinalli had never arrived at the temple there. Hazards of travel might explain that situation, if questions should ever arise.

Again, he must be very careful not to let it slip that he had tricked the Maya trader into paying him for a slave. He chuckled to himself at his own cleverness. After all, the trader had received good value for his ten gold quills—a female slave in good health, who knew how to cook and weave, who couldn't run away because she didn't know her owners' language, and probably a virgin as she had always said she was.

He felt exceptional paternal tenderness after the funeral rites, as he smoked a reed pipe and watched his healthy young son playing in the patio. Turquoise Stone was throwing pieces of corncake on the tezontli stones to attract the birds and then waving his arms to make them fly away.

"We have a wonderful son," he said proudly to Cimatl, touching her shoulder affectionately. "Now he is almost assured of becoming the next tecuhtli."

Seated on her petlatl near his feet, Cimatl said nothing and did not look up at him. Her eyes focused closely on her work as her fingers pulled a maguey thorn through the fabric of a huipil, drawing red embroidery thread along with it.

"You're a wonderful wife, too," he said to Cimatl. "You did your part to make sure our son will have a good life. Of course you made some sacrifices, but parents do make sacrifices for their children. Turquoise Stone will be grateful, you'll see. He'll take care of us in our old age."

Again Cimatl said nothing.

"I know what you're thinking," Anecoatl said. "You wanted to keep your daughter here, but that was impossible. She might have run away to the temple anyway. Worse still, she might have married a warrior like Chimalli. That boy was always flattering his superiors to make them like him. He could've become the next tecuhtli if he'd married Malinalli; he would've been closely related to Itzamitl as well as to you and me. Then what kind of life could Turquoise Stone look forward to?"

Cimatl fastened the thread she had been working with by tying a knot on the underside of the fabric, then sliced off the surplus thread with her obsidian knife. She picked up another thorn with a different colored thread—yellow, this time—and began another portion of the design. Again, she said nothing.

"Can you picture that grimy merchant Opochtli in the tecalli if his son became tecuhtli? I don't see how he could have even asked to tie the tilmantli with our family."

Cimatl said nothing. She knotted her yellow thread.

"We couldn't have refused Tlacateotl, though," Anecoatl continued as if talking aloud to himself, "not a man of his stature, not if a distinguished personage like him wanted to marry into the family. Malinalli shouldn't have been so critical of his son; Tlacoch would have been a better match for her. She tried to seduce Tlacoch once, you know. I never could understand why she hated him after that. Maybe he was just too drunk to perform."

Cimatl looked sharply up at her husband, a quizzical look on her face.

"It was at the naming ceremony," Anecoatl hastily explained. "You didn't know about it; you were busy with the baby. Malinalli must've been jealous of all the attention Turquoise Stone was getting. She was leading Tlacoch on, luring him into the granary. She even tried to lead me on." Anecoatl stopped talking and looked into his wife's puzzled, pained eyes. "I didn't tell you about it because I didn't want to upset you. Now it doesn't matter, I suppose. Soon you'll get used to her being gone. Soon you'll be glad she's gone."

When Cimatl spoke at last, her words were enigmatic. "I'm glad you told me that," she said to her husband. "It hurts me to hear it, but now I understand more than I did."

"Then I'm glad, too," Anecoatl said with relief. "You can trust that I have good reasons for everything I ask you to do, even if you don't see the whole picture."

"You first asked me to poison her," Cimatl said dully. "I couldn't understand why you wanted her dead." Her hands stopped pulling the embroidery thread and lay limply in her lap.

"You see how weak I am in your hands, precious flower?" Anecoatl said, stroking Cimatl's cheek with the back of his hand. "You persuaded me that it wouldn't be necessary. I've yielded to your soft wiles and your feminine tears, even against my better judgment. I wouldn't want other people to know how often I give you your own way in things."

"No one would ever guess," Cimatl said, suppressing an ironic laugh in her throat. She had seen the lust in her husband's eyes when he looked at Malinalli. She could make a very good intuitive guess as to who had been trying to seduce whom in the granary three years before. She comforted herself that Malinalli would have a better life ahead of her than she could have had in Paynala, even if her future life kept her celibate and childless within temple walls, shut away from the evils of the world.

Chapter 16

A Slave Among the Mayas

Her mother's frantic instructions and the mysterious passing of a jadestone into the hands of the Maya merchant had convinced Malinalli that her survival depended on escape in the guise of a slave. She outwardly acted the part for three days, inwardly consoling herself that she was really just a traveler accompanying the Maya traders as far as Coatzacoalcos.

At first she rubbed her shoulders when the rough agave fiber irritated them. At first she resented the rain that drenched her hair, soaked her shivering body, and made her muddy cactli slip off her feet. She felt assaulted when swarms of mosquitoes assailed her, too many to brush away. But then she became resigned to the discomforts, assuring herself they were only temporary. Removing her cactli, she slogged along barefoot, carrying them or tucking them under her rope belt. When the rain began again, she welcomed temporary relief from mosquitoes.

For three days she had not heard any words she could understand. She thought nostalgically of her friends in the temple of Quetzalcoatl, anticipating a warm welcome in the familiar and comforting rhythms of Nahuatl. Meanwhile, she did whatever the other slaves did when the traders spoke or motioned to them. She slept on the ground, wearing the only clothing she had. She ate the meager handful of corn allotted each slave, and gratefully drank water from a bowl passed among them by a guard. He used a willow switch on any slave who spoke to another, so Malinalli inferred that talking was forbidden.

She could not understand the slaves and tamemes anyway. They all seemed to be Mayas, with broad faces, arched noses, and slanted eyes, their hair cut short and straight just below their ears. They carried large baskets or bundles, braced upon their backs by a tumpline strapped across their foreheads. She was not asked to carry anything, but she assumed it was not expected because her passage had been paid for.

Nonetheless she felt uneasy as the traders' caravan followed the road eastward along the river. The river, probably the same one that flowed serenely near Paynala, roared threateningly as it swirled swiftly over rocks and gnarled tree roots. When they came to a place where the river widened and slowed, she saw two long dugout cedar canoes sitting partially in the water, partially grounded along the river bank.

A group of Maya men were huddling around a small campfire, drying their mantles on nearby bushes. As the traders approached, the Mayas with short hair gathered their damp mantles and took positions in the front and rear of each canoe, each grasping an oar. One man with long, braided hair and tattooed arms, apparently the leader, greeted the traders in the melodious language Malinalli could now clearly recognize as Mayan.

Malinalli's guard pointed to a canoe and motioned to several slaves to climb in. As if accustomed to this routine, the slaves arranged their bundles in the middle and knelt at the two ends of the boat, near the oarsmen. The ends of the canoes were narrower but carved with higher sides than the middle, so passengers could cling to the sides. When Malinalli hesitated, the guard shoved her roughly into the canoe, pushed it into the river, then jumped in beside her. Malinalli protested, but her Nahuatl cries were met only with Mayan curses. Her frantic gesturing and pointing toward Coatzacoalcos were ignored.

It was then she first realized she had been betrayed, perhaps by her captors, perhaps by her own family. Whatever the explanation, she had really become a slave. As she clung to one side of the canoe, the river licked it like a hungry jaguar seeking prey. As the oarsmen steered into the swift current, Malinalli tightened her grip, her heart pounding.

When the canoes reached the mouth of the river they continued out to the open sea, dark and foreboding. Could this be the same ocean whose gentle white-laced waves had once bordered the eastern boundary of her world, bringing gifts of fish and shellfish to the temple? Terror gripped Malinalli as the canoes slipped further away from the shore. Dark waves slapped at the sides of the small craft, and stone-gray clouds hung ominously overhead as the distance widened between them and the shore. The oarsmen stayed within sight of land, heading southward along the coast. She prayed silently to Quetzalcoatl for their safety. Then she prayed to Tlaloc not to drown them and to Teoinnan to soften the hearts of the traders and let her go free.

When the traders pulled their canoes into the mouth of another great river, beached their crafts, and led her and the other slaves ashore, she knew her first two prayers had been answered. But when the traders herded the slaves toward the great market at Xicalango, she knew that her prayer for freedom might never be answered. One trader fastened a slave collar

191

around her neck, then threaded a rope through a hole in the collar to connect her to the other slaves. Thus secured, she was led past stone warehouses, along roads bustling with people in strange costumes and tattoos, with lordly men carried in rich litters, with women carrying small children on their hips.

The collar and rope around her neck humiliated Malinalli and angered her even more than the miserable weather, annoying insects, or lack of food. She fought back her tears, because she knew crying would do no good, and she might be beaten for showing weakness or anger. Inside, however, her tears formed a great waterfall, a fountain of anger at being betrayed, a downpour of self-pity as great as any rainstorm that Tlaloc and his wife Chalchiuhtlicue together could send to earth.

She gazed bitterly at the heels of the slave in front of her as they trudged toward the market, wondering if her own feet would become like his—yellow and calloused with deep dirt-stained cracks. Silently observing, she resolved to find some way to escape, but the surroundings disheartened her: swamps to the south, oceans to the north and east, jungles to the west.

She had heard her merchant friend Opochtli speak of Xicalango, "the place where the language changes," and she knew this must be that fabled place where merchants came from near and far, highlands and lowlands, to exchange goods. The Xicalango market, larger and busier than that of Coatzacoalcos, presented a medley of sights, smells, and sounds. A warm breeze, slightly salty from the ocean and nearby swamps, also carried odors of human sweat, animals in cages, seafood and shellfish, chili peppers and other seasonings, fresh vegetables and fruits. She heard the clamor of people bargaining in many dialects, dogs barking, fowls and parrots squawking, children whimpering. Yet the eyes of a slave saw the market differently than had those of a curious child. Instead of inviting her inspection and approval, the produce and products mocked her. Instead of suggesting what she might possess, they reinforced her status as possession. In addition to the usual sacks of grain and beans, reed and leather products, the merchants here offered honey, beeswax, and a fermented drink called *balche*. Dried fish and fowl, copal, cotton fabrics in bundles, drums and other musical instruments, clothing and sandals, dyes, cosmetics and herbs—these marvels were not for slaves.

At some stations craftsmen were creating beautiful ornaments from feathers, shells, precious stones, and metals. Artisans were pounding bark strips into paper or gold into very thin sheets. Potters were coiling ribbons of clay into shapes of practical beauty. These marvels, too, were not for slaves. Painfully Malinalli recalled her father's words, "Never want what you can never have," and felt the pangs of poverty.

Her guard led her past the stalls to the slave section at the

192

far edge of the market, near a stone wall. Here stood the male and female slaves in plain ragged garments, many with long poles attached to their collars. Most had small bundles at their feet; most were barefoot. The smell of human sweat mingled with the animal smells from other sections. Flies buzzed around the slaves, crawling over their clothing and arms. Occasionally a slave lifted a hand wearily to brush them away from his eyes.

The guard motioned her to stand beside the other slaves. He removed the rope from her collar and remained with her as the trader led his other slaves and tamemes, with their bundles and baskets, toward a warehouse. Later one of the tamemes returned with a jug of water and two balls of ground corn wrapped in leaves. After he departed, the guard shared the water and food with Malinalli. She ate hungrily, in silence.

Like the other slaves, Malinalli stood in the sun, glad to feel its warmth after the rains of the past few days. She studied the people in the marketplace, hoping to see a familiar face, hear a comforting sound. Instead, buyers' and merchants' eyes skimmed over her without seeing her. Some officials strolled around keeping order and settling disputes, but they, too, ignored the slaves.

Although she could recognize the typical shabby garments of some pochteca from the Aztec territories and heard a few snatches of Nahuatl speech, most of the buyers and sellers dressed and spoke like Mayas. Some young men walked by whose faces and bodies were painted black. Others wore armbands and painted their bodies red, or mixed red and black; she assumed these to be warriors because they purchased arrows and shields. Some men had tattoos of many colors on their arms, legs, and faces.

The Maya men wore more elaborate loincloths than the Aztec maxtli. They were wound around the waist several times, and the ends hung down in front and back, decorated with woven patterns and embroidery. The men also wore sandals of deerskin or tapir, and capes like tilmantli, not knotted at the shoulder, but fastened in front with shell or copper ornaments. Many men wore pendants hanging from their earlobes, and some older ones had stretched their earlobes enough to hold huge ear-caps. Unlike the short-haired slaves, these prosperous men had long shiny black hair, braided around their heads, with the ends hanging down like a tassel onto which obsidian mirrors had been tied.

The bodies of Maya men appeared shorter but thicker than those of Aztec men, and their faces rounder. Folds of skin on their eyelids gave them a slant-eyed appearance, and many had lustrous dark eyes that seemed focused toward their noses.

The women she saw looked small and fragile; their skins were darker than the men's, a deeper copper color. They, too, dangled pendants from their ears and tattooed their skin. Many women had painted their faces with red achiote, and almost all of them had filed their teeth to points. They wore their hair long and intricately braided, but they did not ornament it with mirrors as the men did. Their huipils had plain, square neck openings, but their skirts were decorated or fringed, and large necklaces drooped across their shapely breasts. Around their shoulders they draped a length of cotton cloth, fastened with an ornament in front. Many of them carried bouquets of flowers which they smelled from time to time. As they walked past, fragrant perfumes emanated from their hair and skin. Unlike the men who wore leather sandals, the women she saw were barefoot. Their calloused feet contrasted curiously with their cosmetics, perfumes, and other evidence of pampering.

Malinalli watched several traders purchase slaves, counting out one hundred cacao beans for each. She listened to the Mayas counting, comparing their numbers to those she knew in Nahuatl, thinking the knowledge might be useful if she could escape. During the day some shoppers approached her guard and pointed to her, but after some bargaining, they went away. She assumed that her mosquito-bitten face and dirty, stringy hair had discouraged potential buyers. When her guard motioned for her to sit on the ground and offered her some water, she realized how little it took to make her grateful.

Yet the anger remained just below the surface of her impassive mosquito-bitten face. She imagined herself breaking free, finding her way back to Paynala, and stabbing her step-father with a flint knife. She imagined confronting her mother in rage, waving the bloody knife at her: "Look what you've done, you traitress! How could you sacrifice your daughter for your husband?" Reason told her that the traders could have been the culprits, but her hatred of Anecoatl caused her to believe he had arranged her fate. Why had he not just killed her? That might have harmed his reputation or brought about the swift Aztec retribution of death to himself. Untangling the knots of her emotions kept her mind occupied through a long afternoon.

During that long hot afternoon, a merchant walked by carrying a cape trimmed with hummingbird feathers, stimulating Malinalli to imagine a conversation with a hummingbird. She was surprised at the bitterness in her thought-words: "So there you are, Father! Resurrected as a warrior from the southern sky, come back to mock me with your fast-beating wings, darting around to flaunt your freedom while this earthly prison traps me here. It was you who taught me to obey, never to question authority, always to do what I'm told. But now see what obedience has done for me! Look how I'm rewarded for serving you, my mother, my brother, my step-father. How could you do this to me? How could you die and leave me so helpless?"

Late in the afternoon, a caluac arrived, sporting a wand that identified him as agent for an important lord, the manager of the lord's household and purchaser of his supplies. Two servants accompanied him, carrying heavy chests full of cloth, dried fish, salt, and other supplies. Though it was time to start homeward, he still needed an attractive slave for his batab, or lord, in Tabasco. Grumbling about the price, he counted out one hundred and twenty cacao beans.

The guard pinched several cacao beans to make sure they were not filled with sand. Then he nodded to the caluac and handed him a rope to put through the collar around Malinalli's neck. Malinalli vigorously brushed aside the rope, saying "No" in Nahuatl even though she knew she would not be understood. Surprised, the caluac returned the rope to the guard. He motioned to Malinalli to follow him and started to walk away. Because she followed dutifully a few paces behind, he felt sure she would not run away. She was still wearing the loathsome collar that marked her as a slave, and Mayan officials would deal harshly with runaways.

Observing that Malinalli had no bundle of personal belongings, the caluac purchased another garment for her before he left the market. If she were washed and dressed in clean clothing before his master saw her, he thought, she might look as if she was worth the price. As he handed the garment to Malinalli, her eyes filled with tears. He touched her shoulder gently and spoke in soothing tones, noticing that her hands and feet were not calloused like those of other slaves. He suspected this girl could tell some secret sorrows, if only she could talk.

She didn't look strong enough to carry much weight, but to his surprise, she took a basket of supplies from a servant who also carried a reed chest on his back. The servant tried to pull the basket back from her, but she tugged insistently until the caluac intervened, speaking a few words to the servant. The caluac guessed that his new slave wanted to prove her worth by carrying her share, so he handed her the basket and placed within it the garment he had purchased for her. Then he removed the collar from her neck. For the first time in many days, a smile of relief and hope lighted her face.

She noticed that the servants as well as the caluac wore sandals for protection from cobblestones. She was glad to have her own cactli as the small group started down the white limestone road toward Tabasco, the city-state where her new master lived, where a new kind of life awaited her. She tried to think of it as an adventure, but the well of tears in her chest pressed against her ribs and made breathing difficult.

* * *

The road to Tabasco was level and smoothly packed with limestone gravel, even though much of the territory they passed through rose into hills of limestone rubble or sank into gullies and depressions. The caluac, carrying a censer of burning copal to earn the protection of the god of travelers, set a brisk pace for his servants, but he stopped at the resting places spaced at regular intervals along the roadside. At sunset the travelers stopped at a merchant's inn, where they slept on mats in a room with bare walls and a palm-thatched roof.

The next morning, the caluac smeared his own face, then Malinalli's face and the servants' faces, with a sticky red substance. After a meager meal of maize gruel, they continued their journey. When they came to a river, Malinalli heard mosquitos whining around her ears, but the red substance repelled them. The caluac counted out five cacao beans to a boatman, who ferried them across the river.

The caluac and his slaves had been passing through territory thick with thorn bushes and scrubby trees not much higher than their heads. But along the river many kinds of trees grew tall and close together, vines climbed on some of them, and she could hear the screeching of monkeys and squawks of tropical birds in the treetops. The heat and moisture in the air fatigued the travelers, but the caluac let them stop fairly often to rest. As they approached their destination, Malinalli saw groves of cacao trees planted in regular rows. Men shouldering baskets were gathering the cacao pods from clusters on the tree trunks.

When the travelers arrived in Tabasco, the caluac led them to a large house made of polished red stones, with a rich tapestry hanging across the arched doorway, a string of copper bells dangling alongside it. He led them around to the rear of the house, to a patio where the servants set down their bundles. As he began sorting his purchases, a full-breasted woman came out, carrying a suckling child about six months old.

After a few words from the caluac, who called her "Ix Kukul," (which he pronounced EESH kooKOOL) the woman took her child inside. Soon she brought a jug of water and plates of food for the travelers. Malinalli ate hungrily, using her corncake to scoop the cold beans into her mouth. Then Ix Kukul took her by the hand and, carrying a basket with soapberry root and two clean garments, led Malinalli past several other houses to the edge of their village. When they came to a large cenote, or natural well in the limestone, the woman removed her own clothing, then Malinalli's, and showed her how to bathe in the cenote.

Several other women were filling water jugs and washing clothes at the cenote, some with young children who splashed as they bathed in the water. Malinalli noticed dark spots above the children's buttocks, which at first looked like bruises. As she got closer, however, she could see the spots were too similar on all children to be caused by injuries, and the mothers seemed to be treating them well. A white bead adorned the top lock of each small boy's partly-shaven head, and each little girl wore a seashell tied with a string over her genital cleft. One older girl, who appeared to be about Malinalli's age of fifteen, wore no shell. After she dressed, she hoisted a toddler to her hip and carried him away like that. Malinalli wondered if the girl was the toddler's mother or his older sister. No men came to the cenote while she was there that day, so she assumed the men bathed at a different time. She slid her legs gradually down from the limestone rim into the dark water, letting them adjust to the coolness before she immersed the rest of her body.

The cool fresh water tingled pleasantly on her skin as Malinalli washed the red substance from her face and arms. While Malinalli washed her hair, Ix Kukul emerged from the well and dressed herself in a clean huipil. She washed the garments they had worn to the cenote, rubbing them with the soapberry root, flipping them against the stone to beat out the dirt, rinsing them, then wringing water from them with an expert twist.

When Malinalli emerged, Ix Kukul handed her the new garment the caluac had purchased at Xicalango. "Kub," she said, pointing to it. Malinalli was not sure whether "Kub" meant the garment or a gift, so she touched the huipil Ix Kukul was wearing.

"Kub?" she asked, fingering the cloth.

"Kub," Ix Kukul repeated emphatically, with an approving smile. Her teeth had been filed to points, which looked like the fangs of a dog to Malinalli, but Malinalli gave no indication that she saw anything unlovely about Ix Kukul. She sensed that this woman might be a friend in a frightening world of strangers. "Kub," Ix Kukul said again as she slipped the new garment over Malinalli's head. Then she examined Malinalli's head for lice, parting the hair with her fingers and scratching the scalp in places. She found none, so Malinalli did not learn the word for lice.

Ix Kukul put the clean wet garments in the basket, and Malinalli carried it. As they began the walk back to the batab's house, Ix Kukul touched her chest and said "Ix Kukul."

Malinalli pointed to Ix Kukul and repeated her new friend's name. Then she touched her own chest and said "Malinalli Tenepal."

"Malinalli Tenepal," said Ix Kukul, struggling with the length of the name.

"Malinalli," the new slave corrected herself, remembering that her father had given her the name *Tenepal* because she talked so much and with such liveliness. That name would not be appropriate for a slave. She pointed to grass growing alongside their path. "Malinalli," she said. "It means 'grass'." Then she pointed to herself again and repeated "Malinalli."

When they returned to the house, Ix Kukul led her into the cooking room. She pointed to the three-stone hearth, saying "Koben." She picked up a feather that had been plucked from a turkey-fowl. "Kukul," she said, holding it up. So Malinalli knew that her name meant "feather." She also pointed to her baby, asleep in a cradle, and said "Ah Tok." Then she took a flint knife from a chest, saying "tok" as she held it up. So the baby's name meant "flint knife." With a pang, Malinalli remembered her father's name, Itzamitl, which meant "flint arrow." It was probably only coincidence, but Malinalli did believe her father would return some day, would find some way to watch over her. Could he be watching through a baby's eyes? Already she was regretting her vengeful thoughts about her father in the slave market, wishing she could see him again and hear his wise counsel.

Ix Kukul then taught her some useful kitchen words: *cum* for a rounded cooking pot, *ic* for a red chili pepper, *buul* for beans, *kum* for squash, *iz* for sweet potato. Because corn formed the basis for every meal, among the first words she learned were those dealing with maize: *chim* or *nal* for corn, which in Nahuatl was *centli*; *pozole* or *za* for the porridge she had called *tole* in Nahuatl; *kah* for the cornmeal she had called *pinolli*; *uah* for the corncakes she had known as *tlaxcalli*.

In the next few days, helping Ix Kukul with cooking, she learned the names of some vegetables and fruits that were new to her. Within the gardens and orchard that surrounded the house, fruit trees grew *haaz* (papayas) and *u cheel* (avocado). A vine yielded a fruit called *chayote*, cooked like a squash. The garden also provided root vegetables: a small round root called *chicham*, and *dzin*, a sweet cassava root that made a flour finer than pinolli. Chili pepper bushes, planted like ornamental shrubs around the house, provided food as well.

Although she and Ix Kukul could eat only the foods left over after the batab and his family had eaten, Ix Kukul knew enough to cook such generous amounts that there was always extra food. Malinalli tasted such luxuries as stews made with *tzimin* (tapir meat), *ac* (turtle meat), *baclam* (manatee or sea cow), and even *zub* (armadillo), which Ix Kukul considered a great delicacy. Ix Kukul taught her to add the fruit of the achiote to stews, giving them both flavor and red color. She also made stews of the dried fish and meats the caluac had brought from Xicalango.

Working as a cook's assistant, Malinalli felt more fortunate than other slaves of the batab. The male slaves worked in the cornfields or in the groves of cacao trees that grew so profusely in the hot climate of the Maya lowlands. Male slaves carried heavy loads such as the limestone rubble used to build roads. Or they tied ropes to heavy stone blocks and pulled them on rollers to build houses and walls. Female slaves had lighter, but more tedious, work. Many of them had to kneel in one position for many hours of the day, weaving cotton or rabbits-wool mantles with a backstrap loom. Washing clothes, cleaning, sweeping, and caring for children also filled their days. Malinalli remembered the similar kinds of work she had done at the temple and for her family in Paynala; she remembered seeing her mother and Chihuallama doing spinning and weaving side by side. It seemed that women led similar lives everywhere, no matter how rich or poor, no matter what country or city they lived in, no matter whether they married or became priestesses or lived as slaves.

Not all women lived under the protection of households or temples, however, as Malinalli learned from a bewildering experience she had one morning. She was walking to the cenote with Ix Xtzul, a slave from the batab's household whose name meant "centipede." They passed the local temple and the nearby house of young men, a structure open on one side with three whitewashed walls and a palm-thatched roof, furnished with low cots made of reeds and vines. She had seen blue-painted young men there before, assuming they were students at the temple, like those she had known at the calmecac and the telpochcalli.

That morning there were no young men in sight, but a skinny young woman lay unconscious on one of the cots, tied to it by two loincloths wrapped around the bed and her torso. Her clenched fists were clamped against her naked thighs, and her bare legs showed several dark bruises as well as smudges of blue paint.

"Guatepol," said the slave Ix Xtzul in disgust, setting down her water jug and going to the side of the prone woman. Malinalli set down her jug and began untying knots in the cloths that bound the girl's arms and shoulders. Ix Xtzul did not help Malinalli untie the knots, but instead unclenched the unconscious girl's fist and removed five cacao beans from its grasp. "Guatepol," she said again, spitting on the girl's bare legs. Then she picked up her jug and left, still gripping the stolen cacao beans in one hand.

Malinalli finished loosening the knotted cloths and used them to wipe spittle and smudges from the girl's legs. The guatepol moaned and stirred, murmuring something in Mayan. Malinalli could not understand her, nor could she say anything to comfort the poor creature. Unfolding the cloths to their full width and length, Malinalli used them to cover the unfortunate girl as best she could. Then she retrieved her water jug and ran to catch up with Ix Xtzul, who had been well named because she moved as quickly as a centipede with a hundred legs.

When they had filled their water jugs, the girls retraced their steps past the temple and the house of young men. The guatepol was gone, as were the cloths that had bound her. Malinalli never saw her again. To avoid the house of young men after that, Malinalli found another path to the cenote. She also tried to avoid Ix Xtzul the slave, as well as any young man with blue paint on his body.

* * *

Even though she was well fed and not badly treated in the first couple of months, loneliness overwhelmed Malinalli. She could not learn the language fast enough to express herself, and the chatting of Ix Kukul with the other servants and slaves made her feel isolated. She saw the caluac occasionally, when he came to the cooking room to give instructions to Ix Kukul, but he maintained a distant authority and did not attempt to teach her his language. Ix Kukul, too, taught her only enough so that she could obey commands, not enough to have a real conversation.

Ix Kukul called the caluac "Ah Balam," which Malinalli later learned meant "Jaguar," and she treated him with such deference that Malinalli was surprised to learn that he, too, was a servant, though one with considerable authority over the household. He was also Ix Kukul's husband, the father of little Ah Tok. Ah Balam served as a deputy to the batab, who was a tax collector as well as a city administrator, and although Ah Balam was not unkind to the servants under his supervision, he had a sense of importance. He treated his wife, as he did the other servants, with condescension.

At night, when Malinalli and the other women slaves retired to their mats in a common sleeping room, she cried silently in the darkness. The worst part of her enslavement was not the work, but being unable to communicate. Immersed in sadness, she thought of Toto, her childhood friend, wondering if Toto had died or recovered from her illness, but since going home to Paynala was impossible, she would never know. Malinalli also thought of Toci, the priestess at the temple of Coatzacoalcos who had told her stories about the gods and explained the meaning of existence. She wondered how far away Coatzacoalcos was from Tabasco, and whether she could find the temple if she ran away. How could she travel, though, without money or protection, not knowing the language, even if she could find out which direction to go? Dense forests surrounded the Tabasco area, thick brush, steep gullies, deep rivers. Thinking of these natural barriers, she always fell asleep exhausted from the day's work and the heavy burden of her own unhappy thoughts.

After she had counted forty days among the Mayas, Malinalli stopped counting, became more reconciled to her fate, and cried less often. She no longer felt shock at the filed teeth of the Maya women, the tattooed bodies and stretched earlobes of the men. She had been astonished when she first saw Ix Kukul feeding a coati at her breast after feeding her baby Ah Tok, but when she saw other women doing that also, she realized that they were raising these animals the way Chihuallama had raised her turkeys and dogs on the Paynala farm. She no longer felt pity for Ah Tok, strapped in his cradle with a board against his forehead to flatten it, a beeswax ball dangling before his eyes to cause him to become cross-eyed.

As she adapted to the Maya customs, she became more interested in the people. She even became bold enough to want to share some of her own knowledge with them, confident enough to teach Ix Kukul some of the simple but flavorful dishes she had learned to make at the temple in Coatzacoalcos. Ix Kukul seemed surprised at this young girl's knowledge, but it did not offend her to be taught by a fifteen-year-old girl.

Ix Kukul now trusted Malinalli enough to let her go alone to the cenote, fill a jug with water, and carry it back to the batab's house. She bathed in the cenote each time she went for water, having learned that if her skin did not smell sweaty, fewer bees and flies would annoy her. She was also allowed to serve the batab and his wife, after she had watched the other servants do this and had learned enough of their language to understand simple requests they were likely to make.

The batab, whose name was Ah Hoh or "crow," was a shriveled older man with flaccid arms, yellow skin, and wrinkles that cut into his face like dry rivers. Around his home, or when supervising the workers in his orchards, he dressed in embroidered garments but wore no jewelry or head ornaments except a wooden plug where one side of his nose had been pierced. When he went on a trip to collect taxes or visit other noblemen, he dressed elegantly, wearing jeweled earplugs, an amber noseplug, jeweled armbands, and decorated sandals. His wickerwork headpiece, topped with swirling masses of blue-green quetzal feathers, seemed to double his height. Over his loincloth he put an ankle-length skirt trimmed with the fur of a jaguar. He took four slaves to carry him on a litter, and several others to carry tribute he collected or gifts he would make to his friends. The servants in his retinue carried beautiful feather fans to create a breeze for him or wave away the blood-sucking flies and sweat-loving bees. These servants also scattered people along the roads to make way for him, and when he arrived at a destination, spread mantles for him to walk on.

The batab's wife always dressed in white, the color of mourning. She walked with a stoop, her rounded upper back curved like the side of a hearthstone. She spent her days embroidering loincloths for her husband or supervising servants

201

who dyed the colored threads she used. Only on very grand occasions did she wear embroidered garments herself, and she seldom went outside except for an occasional walk in her garden.

When Ix Kukul told Malinalli that the batab wanted her to serve food and drinks at an important banquet he would be giving to celebrate his son's marriage, Malinalli felt she was being rewarded for good work. She remembered the feasts Opochtli had given, entertaining his guests with music and dancing, poetry reading and juggling. She looked forward to the event with pleasant anticipation, even though she would not be a guest there, only a serving woman.

She did not realize that this feast day would also mark for her that difficult passage from innocence to experience, from childhood to womanhood, that divides most women's lives into partitions of before and after. For the bride and groom, that passage would be marked with ceremony, congratulations, and camaraderie. For her, however, the path would be walked alone, without ceremony or caring, not even consolation.

* * *

Preparations for the batab's party, which was to announce the arrangement of his son's marriage, took several days. The caluac Ah Balam assembled an array of gourmet foods—fruits, deer, ducks, turkeys, armadillos, and coatis. Ix Kukul also gathered cacao and vanilla beans to make chocolate drinks. Ah Balam bought large quantities of balche, a drink made of fermented honey and the bark of the balche tree. Servant women applied colorful paints to dried gourds, making them into festive cups. They swept the courtyard, spread out reed mats for guests to sit on, and placed pine torches in holders.

The serving women, especially selected for their beauty to please the guests, were given new kubs for the occasion, and when the day arrived they took turns braiding each other's hair in a single strand down the back. They helped with last-minute food preparations, then spread the various dishes in tempting arrangements on mats centrally placed in the courtyard.

The musicians arrived with three kinds of drums: a *tunkul* or kettledrum that reached to the beater's chest as he pounded the deerskin top with his hands; a smaller one like the Aztec teponaztli, made of hollowed wood and beaten with rubber-tipped beaters; and one which sat on the ground while the drummer straddled it and beat it with his hands. They also brought gourd rattles and lacquered tortoise shells that made mournful sounds when struck with the palm. Together with deer-bone whistles, silver bells, and reed flutes, the drums made hypnotic music that carried through the evening air for great distances.

Guests arrived, elegantly adorned with brightly colored mantles and loincloths, embroidered huipils, amber nose plugs, feathers and jewelry, each bringing to the host a beautifully woven mantle and a ceramic vase of fine quality. Clowns and jugglers entertained the guests while they ate and drank. A Holpop set the pitch and taught songs to the guests, later taking a place of high esteem at the head of the circle of mats. Dancers performed with rattles and copper bells, urging the guests to dance also.

When the musicians rested, the batab introduced his son, Ah Cux (which sounded like AW COOSH to Malinalli), and the son's bride-to-be, Ix Chan (EESH CHON). He congratulated the girl's parents, who also spoke briefly to the guests. Malinalli could not understand the words, but the air of happiness around her, the music and festivity, stimulated her. She carried a trayful of colorful gourd cups filled with balche, which the guests drank so quickly that she could not bring refills fast enough. Soon the guests were dancing in pairs or groups of four, then refreshing themselves with more chocolate and balche. Although the women drank less balche than the men, Malinalli was amazed to see guests of all ages drinking freely in public.

Malinalli had not seen the batab's son before. His name, Ah Cux, meant "weasel." By Mayan standards he was handsome, with a nose-bridge arched like the beak of a graceful bird, broad shoulders and muscular arms, long loops of braided hair ornamented with obsidian mirrors. The black body paint which marked his unmarried status was the subject of many jokes that evening, as people tried playfully to rub it off. A few stripes of red body paint also marked him as a warrior. Like other males around twenty years old, Ah Cux lived in the house for young men near the temple where he was a *chilane*, or student, studying the arts of war.

Conscious of the presence of his prospective bride and in-laws, Ah Cux did not drink as much balche as the other young men. Malinalli could see the two faces of this drink that night: first it brought great merriment, then great mischief. After some of the men had drunk many cups of balche, a fight broke out. Ah Balam, whose official duties prohibited drinking at his batab's feast, intervened and sent the intoxicated men home under the care of their less intoxicated wives, urging them all to come again when they had overcome their headaches.

Some of the men began dancing with women who had arrived with other men, and a number of these pairs slipped away into the fruit orchard. Remembering the punishments she had witnessed in Paynala for adultery, Malinalli worried about the fate of guests who were dallying in the orchard, but since drunkenness was permitted among young people, adultery might also be tolerated. She shrugged as she gathered dirty cups and dishes onto her tray. She had much to learn besides language in this strange new world.

* * *

Ah Cux, the batab's son, had been watching the serving girls while his bride-to-be basked in the attentions of well-wishers. When Ix Chan left with her parents at the end of the evening, and the other guests had departed, Ah Cux approached his father and asked about the newest girl, who had attracted him with her graceful movements and shiny hair. The elder man steered his son toward the orchard, where they could talk privately, walking under the light of a nearly full moon.

"Ah Balam bought her from a ppolm in Xicalango," said the batab.

"From traders? She's a slave, then?"

"The ppolm said so. They found her in some village to the west. Speaks only Nahuatl. They claim she's a virgin, but she might be a concubine some jealous wife wanted to get rid of."

"Do you want her for a concubine?" asked Ah Cux with a grin.

Ah Hoh laughed. "Too late for that," he said amiably. "I'm too old. We just wanted some pretty girls to serve the guests."

"May I take her to the house of young men with me?" asked Ah Cux, confident that his doting father would deny him nothing.

His father's face grew stern. "That wouldn't be a good idea. I've seen how bedraggled some of the young women get after they've spent a night ministering to the animal spirits in the house of young men."

Ah Cux lowered his eyes. "You're fond of her, I can see. I must apologize for asking."

"I only meant she's a good slave," Ah Hoh said gruffly. "Cost us 120 cacao beans. I don't want her roughed up."

"I understand," said Ah Cux agreeably, though he still thought his father showed unusual concern for this slave.

The batab did not want to seem ungenerous, especially since his son's marriage would be uniting two prosperous families. He had an idea. Clapping a hand on his son's shoulder, he said warmly, "Tell you what I'll do. I'll give you Malinalli for a wedding present."

"Is that her name, Malinalli?"

"That's right. You'll inherit all my slaves anyway, when you become batab. If you want her now, you can take her to our guest house tonight."

"I'd like that," Ah Cux said eagerly, his male member tingling at the prospect. He was glad he had not been drinking excessively, so his blood was not sluggish.

204

"After you're married," his father continued, "she can cook for you and Ix Chan. Ix Kukul has taught her how."

"That should make Ix Chan happy," replied Ah Cux, but he was not really thinking of his future wife's happiness.

* * *

The batab himself escorted Malinalli to the guest house. Ah Cux awaited them there, sitting on a low bench called a *canche* and removing his sandals. He rose to greet them, bowing his head to his father.

"I give you this slave," said the batab to Ah Cux, taking one hand of Ah Cux and placing it on Malinalli's shoulder in a gesture of command. Then he spoke to Malinalli. "Ah Cux is your master now. Do as he asks." Then he disappeared into the night.

Malinalli understood his command, and she had read the faces of the two men, discerning their intentions. She began to tremble from a mixture of fear and excitement, as Ah Cux untied her skirt and pulled her kub up over her head and arms.

The moonlight through the open door revealed a bed made of small saplings laced together with vines, covered with a woven grass mat. Ah Cux removed his manta and spread it on the mat. Then he removed his *ex*, or loincloth, tossing it onto the reed chair. He lay down on the bed, pulling Malinalli's two hands toward him as he leaned back so that she lay on top of him.

For a few minutes they lay together that way. The touch of his bare skin on hers was not unpleasant, although a hint of balche fermented his breath. She could feel his hard tepuli under her belly—but that was a Nahuatl word. She didn't know the Maya word for it. Nothing very bad was happening, so she relaxed. Even as he pulled her legs apart so that she straddled him, she was thinking that the dire warnings of the priestesses might have been exaggerated.

Then he tightened his arms around her and rolled over on top of her. Surprised, and with his full weight on her, she gasped. She felt the jab of his body, a sharp pain, then the thrusting like the beat of a tunkul drum. The saplings under the grass mat yielded and swayed. She clenched her teeth to endure the pain, remembering the time she had given her mother a braid to bite on when the labor pains shot through her body like knives. "Women have strength and courage," she reminded herself. "They bear pain without flinching." She steeled herself, not wanting the heroic goddesses of the twilight to hear her cry out.

Yet she also felt revolted and degraded. Her parents and the priestesses had issued many dire warnings about a girl's responsibility to stay chaste until marriage. How could this intangible, precious quality of chastity be bought like a vessel of cheap pottery, sold for a handful of beans, used or misused at the whim of its purchaser, even given as a vulgar gift from one crass buyer to another? Feelings of anger and betrayal again surfaced, again were beaten down in practical necessity. Yet the question persisted: Why had she been educated to value honor, chastity, and justice, when the very people who made the rules could make a mockery of these virtues?

After Ah Cux fell asleep, she put on her kub and skirt and quietly walked back to the servants' sleeping room. Still trembling, she curled into a ball in a corner of the room, glad that she had not awakened anyone, relieved that the long day was over. The relief of tears eventually enabled her to fall asleep, but not until she had calmed herself with an angry vow—to learn all she could of the Mayan language so that someday she could make her escape. If she failed to reach Coatzacoalcos, then even the jungles seemed preferable to her miserable fate as a slave.

Chapter 17

Malinalli Meets Nemon the Slave

Ah Cux left Malinalli in the household of his father, the batab, when he married Ix Chan and went to live with his father-in-law. It was customary for a Maya man to serve his bride's family for five years, insuring that the marriage would be permanent, that the families would get along.

Not understanding that custom, Malinalli thought she had displeased Ah Cux when he left without summoning her to his bed again. She remembered her night of pain and dreaded a recurrence, but what would happen to her if the batab's son disliked her? Would she be sent away, perhaps turned out of the house to become a guatepol—a "public woman" who served the houses of young men for a few cacao beans? When she went to the cenote for water, she bathed as usual but lingered afterward in the shade of a tall cedar tree, crying and praying silently to Quetzalcoatl and Teoinnan.

A voice speaking Nahuatl surprised her. "Don't cry, little sister."

She looked up to see a macehual youth around nineteen years old, carrying a Mayan jug, but wearing an Aztec maxtli. His well-shaped legs supported a lean, agile body, and his skin was smooth, free of scars or tattoos. His deep-set dark eyes gave his face a shadowed, melancholy look.

"You speak Nahuatl," she marveled, her tears stopping abruptly.

"The language of the Nahuatlaca, the men who explain themselves and speak clearly," said the youth with a trace of self-mockery, showing that he knew the definition of Nahuatl given by those who spoke it. He grinned cheerfully but tensely, as if he were not accustomed to smiling. "Why are you crying? Look at the blue sky and the cool green water of the cenote. Listen to the birds. Look at the butterflies flitting among the blossoms. Give thanks to Huitzilopochtli—or should I say Tezcatlipoca or Quetzalcoatl?"

"Quetzalcoatl," said Malinalli, wiping her cheek with the flat of her hand. "Patron of the artisans, lover of birds and butterflies."

"Aha, I was right!" said the youth. "You're a Nahua girl. I could tell by your face and skin color. I'll bet you've been to a telpochcalli. What's your name?"

"Malinalli Tenepal," said Malinalli, realizing she had not used her full name in many months. "What's yours?"

"Nemon. I was born in the days of the nemontemi. Doomed to bad luck all my life."

"I've had bad luck, too," Malinalli said.

"I can see that. You're dressed like a slave, but you don't talk like a slave. You don't have a slave's hands and feet."

Malinalli looked at Nemon's hands and feet, browned from the sun, calloused from hard work. His short-cut hair also showed his status. "You're a slave too," she observed.

"I'll be free in two more years," Nemon declared, "after the family debt is paid. Three years ago a famine struck Cholula, so we had nothing to eat. Someone had to give five years of service to buy grain from the Maya traders."

"So you made that sacrifice for your family?"

"I was the logical choice," Nemon said. "Just my luck to have two sisters and a small brother—too small to work. My family's better off without me, anyway. I'd probably bring them bad luck."

Malinalli sighed as she thought about bad luck, good luck, and the mysteries of causation. She remembered the broken clay doll just before little Moyo had been taken for sacrifice by the calpixque in Paynala. "Do we bring bad luck on ourselves?" she asked. "Did you do anything to cause the famine?"

"I don't think so. The gods decide. Nothing we can do makes any difference. Some of us are born unlucky." Nemon began filling his water jug in the cenote.

Reminded that she had come for water, not for talking, Malinalli lifted her full water jug to her shoulder. "I have to get back to the batab's house," she said. "Will I see you again? No one else here speaks Nahuatl, and I don't know Mayan yet."

"I speak both," said Nemon. "I've been here three years, learning the language the way children learn it. I'll come to the cenote for water again in two days, when the sun is as high as it is now."

* * *

Two days later Malinalli went to the cenote early and bathed quickly, so that if Nemon appeared they would have time to talk. Then she began braiding her wet hair, delaying her return as long as possible. She began to worry that Nemon might not come.

208

But he did. "How long have you lived among the Mayas?" he asked when he appeared with his jug.

"About three months," she said, then hastily added, "—about 60 days."

"Months here are twenty days long, just like the Aztec months," Nemon said. "But here they call a month a *uinal*. A day is called a *kin*. Eighteen uinals and five useless days make a *haab*, which you call a year or a *xiuhmolpilli*. Lots of things are the same here, but lots of things are different."

"I've noticed some differences," Malinalli agreed. "Did it surprise you to see young people getting drunk here?"

A sunny smile crossed Nemon's shadowy, sensitive face. "It surprised me, but I like it. The Mayas are happier people, more carefree. Take the nemontemi days, for instance; the Mayas call them *uayeb*. Aztec people are afraid of them, expecting bad luck and maybe bringing it about. Here they just consider the uayeb as useless days, an excuse to get drunk instead of working."

Malinalli laughed. "Then the useless days can be useful after all."

Nemon smiled, looking directly into Malinalli's eyes. "That's better," he said. "You laughed. You're happier today."

"Yes," she agreed. "It's good to have someone to talk to. I'm trying to learn the Mayan tongue, but it's hard. Can you teach me?"

"Not much time for that here," said Nemon, stepping aside as an old woman approached the well with a water jug. "Sometimes it gets crowded here, too."

"Could you come to the batab's house? Would your master give his permission?"

"My master is Ah Hoh's friend," said Nemon. "During the growing season my master needs me, but when the harvest is over, he might let me come as a favor to his friend. I'll ask him."

Malinalli returned to the batab's house with such a light heart that the water jug she carried felt light also. She noticed the tall palm trees with sunlight shining on their swaying fronds, heard birds singing in the thorn bushes, and smelled the fragrance of blossoms she had never noticed before.

* * *

The batab Ah Hoh had no objections to Malinalli's learning to speak Mayan, and Nemon's master was glad to do a favor for the most powerful man in the community, so the lessons were arranged. Nemon began coming every day at sunset in the month of Cumhu (December), after the harvest, talking to Malinalli as she scraped ashes from the hearth and put dried corn to soak for the next morning's meal. Then there was time to sit and talk in the light of a pine torch or in the moonlight on clear nights.

Nemon always arrived with wet hair, fresh from his evening bath in the cenote. He enjoyed these talks so much, and Malinalli glowed so much in his presence, that Nemon continued to come even as the seasons of hard work approached, even though he walked home very tired at night and slept very little.

On one of his early visits, he told her with some pride that he was mastering all the tasks of farming, hoping some day to have his own *hun uinic*, or family-sized plot of land. The months of Pop and Uo, January and February, were the times of light rains, the time to cut down trees to clear new land for corn and beans. He could fell a tree in an hour with his stone ax, but he arrived feeling tired after chopping all day, so Malinalli urged him to keep his visits short in Uo. From Zotz to Mol, March to May, the weather became hot and dry, the best time to burn the felled trees, a time when Nemon was not so tired after his daily work. Yax, Zac, and Ceh—June and July—were the months for planting, when the rains would fall heavily if the god Chac granted their prayers.

"Here the rain god is called Chac," Nemon explained to Malinalli. "You call him Tlaloc, but Chac is another name for him. We pray to Chac when we're planting."

"What if Chac doesn't send rain?" Malinalli asked.

Nemon looked uncomfortable. "He's sent rain every year that I've been here," he said. "Farmers tell me that sometimes in the past a sacrifice was necessary."

"What kind of sacrifice? Human hearts?"

"A long time ago, they would paint a slave blue, tie him to a post and dance around him as they shot arrows into him. Then they cut out his heart, and put it in the Chac Mool's bowl at the temple," Nemon said. "They haven't done that for a long time."

"Then what do they do now?"

"I haven't seen it myself," Nemon said, uncomfortable under Malinalli's barrage of questions. "I only know what the other slaves tell me, but I've heard they drown a woman or child in one of the sacred cenotes."

"I see," said Malinalli, disappointed. "Does Chac keep a beautiful green garden for anyone who drowns, like Tlaloc?"

"I don't know much about the gods," Nemon said with some irritation. "I haven't been to the telpochcalli like you. I'm only a macehual, a farmer. When you learn the language better, you can ask the priests here. The *Ah Kin* can answer religious questions better than I can."

"I'm sorry," Malinalli said with a crestfallen look. "We won't talk about religion if you aren't interested. We can talk about anything you want to."

"I've been a slave longer than you have," Nemon explained patiently. "You know slaves can't ask questions. We learn by

210

watching and listening, so all I know about religion is what my master thinks is important. My master's a merchant, a *pplom*, what you would call a pochteca. He gives a feast every year for Akyantho, the god of foreigners and trade. He sends me to the temple sometimes with offerings of food."

"For Akyantho?" Only after the words were out did she realize she had asked another question.

"Usually for Kakoch, the greatest god, the creator of the earth and the sea and the sun," Nemon answered, not noticing that he was explaining religion a little. "Sometimes for the corn goddess, Ix Kanleox, so the harvest will be good. We know the priests eat the food, but the gods don't seem to mind sharing."

"Do you believe priests can talk to the gods?" Malinalli asked, then she added hastily, "You don't have to answer."

"Sometimes I wonder," Nemon said frankly, looking around to see which household members might hear him. Confident that none could understand him, he expounded in Nahuatl, "There are good priests and bad priests. Most people think the priests help us when they read the book of days, but none of them could find a favorable day for naming me. That's why I have this bad-luck name of Nemon. Maybe the *Ah Men* can divine what's causing a sickness, with their crystal beads and roots and bones and sacred beans, but when I get hurt or sick I'd rather go to a woman who knows plants and herbs—an *ix alanzah*."

"That makes sense to me, Nemon," Malinalli said. "In Paynala we had a healing woman, Chihuallama. We always went to her first if we had a fever or pain or sickness."

"I'm a simple man," Nemon said, "a common man, a *yalba uinic*, very powerless in the hands of the gods. I feel afraid sometimes when the black clouds gather in the hurricane season, when the lightning flashes, or when the earth dries up and the crops wither. So I just pray to the rain god Chac and the sun god Kin to help grow my crops. When the corn grows tall and ripe, I always take a few grains to the temple out of gratitude."

"Those are deep thoughts, Nemon," Malinalli said. "You're as wise as any priest, I'm sure. Of course, I haven't talked to many priests. They don't like to answer girls' questions."

"You do ask a lot of questions, for a girl."

Malinalli sighed. "I've always been full of questions," she said. "That's how I learned when I was at the temple. I can't seem to change, even if my life has changed."

Nemon's manner softened. "I'll answer as many questions as I can," he said. "Just remember that I'm not a scholar or a priest. I respect priests for telling farmers when to plant, but farmers who take food to them deserve as much respect as the men who paint their bodies blue and stare at the stars."

"That's what my father said," Malinalli recalled. "Never forget our ties to the land, that's what he told me. It's the land that nourishes us; even proud and wealthy people with soft hands and quetzal feathers depend on the land and the farmers."

Pleased at that, Nemon asked about her father. He listened sympathetically to her story of being educated at a temple, seeing her father die and her mother remarry, and being sold into slavery, which she blamed on her step-father, Anecoatl.

Nemon noticed that Ix Kukul was making many trips past them, bringing a bowl one time, putting away a broom another time, scowling at them because they had talked for a long time in Nahuatl. Nemon thought she was probably annoyed because she couldn't understand what they were saying. "Let's talk in Mayan now," Nemon said in Mayan. "You need the practice. You can still worship Quetzalcoatl if you want, but here he is called *Kukulcan*. The name means the same: 'feathered serpent.' In Mayan a feather is *kukul*, a serpent is *can*."

Over the months when he came to see her regularly, he taught her many useful things. Unlike most of the teacher-priestesses at the temple of Quetzalcoatl, who had recited long passages for the temple girls to memorize, Nemon gave Malinalli general principles that she could apply to many words. He taught her the singular forms and plural forms of words at the same time, so she could see that the endings of many plural words were similar. "Your master is a *batab*," he said. "Two or more are called *batabob*. You walked here on a *sacbe*, or 'white road' made of limestone. There are many *sacbeob* leading to other cities. Nobles are called *Ah Mehenob*, slaves are called *ppentacob*, and common men or farmers are called *yalba uinicob*."

Another suffix he taught her was *om*, meaning "he who does"; after learning that *cay* meant "fish" and *pat* meant "clay pot," she could guess that *cayom* meant "fisherman" and *patom* "potter." He taught her a game played with reeds or straws, *colomche*, which meant "he who withdraws a reed, a sliver," because *col* meant "to withdraw something" and *che* meant "wood, tree, sliver."

He also taught her that a Mayan word could have more than one meaning. Building on her knowledge that *kin* was the name for a day, he taught her that it also meant "sun," and "sun god," so she could easily learn the word for priest, *Ah Kin*, meaning one who could read the "count of days," the *Tzolkin*.

Similarly, she learned that *pop* was a reed mat, like a petlatl, but it could also be the word for "throne," or seat of importance. Pop was the name of the first month of the Mayan calendar, and a *holpop*, "he who sits at the head of the mat," an official of great authority.

"So that's why the word *Chac* can mean the rain god or an old man," Malinalli observed.

Nemon was pleased that she caught on so quickly. "Yes," he said, "because calling a man *chac* means his age is respected."

To her perplexity, Malinalli also learned that a thing could have more than one name. Some people referred to corn as *nal*, some as *chim*, some as *ixim*. Nemon said you could tell the region a person had come from by the word he used for corn.

He had a sense of humor about language. "Everyone thinks his own language is the right way to speak," he said, "and his own tribe is the true race of men. The Nahuatlaca call themselves 'the people who speak clearly,' but they call others *popoloca*, meaning people who speak nonsense, or *totonac*, which means 'crude persons, rustics.' "

Malinalli smiled. "Or Chichimec, meaning people who live like dogs."

"I'll bet the Chichimecs don't call themselves that," Nemon said with twinkling eyes. "They probably think they're the ones who live right, that the Mexica are the strange ones. People think like that everywhere, though. The Maya call their greatest king *Halach Uinic*, which means 'true man'; the Mexica call the speakers of Maya *chontalli*, which means 'foreigner,' but those who live around here call themselves *Putun*."

Nemon insisted that Malinalli speak Mayan as much as possible, so that after she had lived a year in Tabasco, she could talk to Mayas in their own tongue. She readily complied, because to break the language barrier was to break the walls of loneliness. When he had known her a year, Nemon sensed Malinalli would not need him much longer. Yet he had grown fond of her, and he tried to think of a way to continue seeing her.

He formed a plan in his mind. The batab had told everyone in his household that Malinalli was the concubine of his son, Ah Cux. But Ah Cux never came to see her, so Nemon deduced that her owner cared little for her. Nemon had to serve one more year to pay off his debt to the merchant. When that year was over, Nemon would be free and twenty-one years old, the right age to obtain a *hun uinic* farm and a wife. He planned to grow enough cacao beans to come back and make an offer that Ah Cux could not refuse—200 cacao beans, an unheard-of price to pay for a slave.

Nemon did not discuss his plan with Malinalli. To do so might have brought bad luck. Even more important, it might have offended the man or men who owned her, if they should hear of it and suspect a plot.

* * *

The seasons which Nemon measured in terms of planting cycles were measured in festivals in the cooking room of the batab. As with the Mexica, the Maya festivals were linked to the seasons and the growth cycles, celebrations of life and propitiation of gods and goddesses. As Malinalli worked alongside

213

Ix Kukul, she tried to converse with her about the meanings of the festivals and the special dishes the servants prepared for each feast. Ix Kukul good-naturedly corrected Malinalli's mistakes in Mayan, telling her how she would say what Malinalli was trying to say, but Ix Kukul was not the skillful teacher Nemon had been. Still, she saw no harm in women's talking as they worked, and as Malinalli became more adept in Mayan, she became a better companion for Ix Kukul. After a few months the women began to exchange stories as they chopped vegetables and stirred stews or baked amaranth cookies for festivals.

"My mother told me the story of man and corn," said Ix Kukul as she flipped her hands, flattening a corncake which she called *nal*. "In the beginning there were no men or animals, not even mountains and caves, only sky. But there was a great creator, Lord Strong Snake. He created the earth, the mountains, the plains, and the rivers. Then he created the animals, but they didn't worship him, so he created a superior being, a man. The first man was made of clay, but he was weak and clumsy. The second man was made of cork, *tzite*, and a woman was made of the pith of the bulrush, *sibak*. But they had no gratitude or intelligence. So the gods destroyed the earth and all the creatures in it. Then they made a man of corn. He could think and speak, and his eyes turned toward the skies in gratitude. That's why we worship Yum Kak, the god of corn."

Malinalli responded with the Mexica story of the four suns, and how each had been destroyed with a calamity, and how Quetzalcoatl or Kukulcan had saved the human race for the fifth sun. "We have a corn god, too," she said. "We call him Centeotl, because the corn is called *centli*. He's the husband of Xochiquetzal, or 'flower feather,' goddess of arts and crafts."

Ix Kukul had been listening with interest, but she cautioned Malinalli not to say 'we' when talking about the Aztecs. "You can never be happy here if you think of yourself as belonging with other people somewhere else," she said. "You can never go back to the land you came from, any more than a wife can stay in the home of her mother and not go live with her husband. Make the best of it."

Malinalli saw the merits of Ix Kukul's advice. She would follow that advice and make the best of things. She had much to be grateful for: plenty of food, shelter from storms, a daily bath at the cenote, clean garments to wear. Other slaves did not fare so well. But even as she reminded herself of her relative good fortune, she sighed with a deep sense of loss. With the decision to accept this fate, she no longer thought about escaping. She had become a slave in her own mind, the most permanent and devastating kind of bondage.

* * *

When Malinalli had been in Tabasco for a year, she was skillful enough in Mayan to tell Ix Kukul the story of the tragic love affair between the princess Morning Star and the prince Young Deer, who had been turned into an orchid plant that yielded the sacred vanilla.

She could also understand Ix Kukul's stories. As Ix Kukul was sprinkling salt into a tamale filling one day, she told Malinalli the story of a man who married a witch without knowing what she was. "One day he asked her to crush two measures of salt, which she did," said Ix Kukul. "Then he followed her into the woods, where she undressed under a great Ceiba tree. Then she shed her skin, and wearing only her bones, went into a moonlit clearing and ascended into the sky. When she returned, he sprinkled the salt on her, so she could not rise again."

Malinalli thought that was a strange story, as if Ix Kukul had forgotten to tell the end of it, but Ix Kukul was satisfied just as it was.

Ix Kukul had even stranger stories for Malinalli on another day. Her husband, the caluac Ah Balam, had returned from another trip to the market at Xicalango the evening before. He said he had seen houses floating on the ocean, houses with tall white banners that moved with the wind. These strange sights had caused much excitement in the marketplace, he said. Artists were painting pictures of them on bark paper to send to their rulers, even some artists of the Aztec emperor in Tenochtitlan. Everyone was talking about them.

"That's a strange story indeed," Malinalli said. "But if Ah Balam saw it himself, it must be true."

It was true. The time was early in the year 12 House [1517], and the floating houses were the ships of Francisco Hernandez de Cordoba from the island of Cuba, exploring the shores of the Yucatan Peninsula, scouting for new territory, looking for slaves, thirsting for gold.

* * *

Nemon learned similar news from the slaves who had accompanied his master the merchant on a recent trip to Xicalango. "My master heard amazing news," Nemon said to Malinalli and Ix Kukul as they washed gourd cups after the evening meal. He spoke in Mayan so Ix Kukul could also understand. "He talked to men who saw mountains floating on the waves. They saw men with white faces and beards coming out of the mountains—*dzules*, foreigners."

"Where?" Ix Kukul said, her eyes widening in fear.

"Near Tulum, near Xicalango, even here in Tabasco," Nemon said, his voice growing more emphatic as he named a distant city, then a closer one, then their home territory.

"The men must've come from the floating houses Ah Balam saw," Malinalli reasoned, looking at Ix Kukul and then Nemon.

Nemon went on breathlessly. "The *dzules* came in canoes from the floating mountain to the shores, but the Halac Uinic's soldiers shot them with arrows until they went away."

"Halach Uinic has true magic," sighed Ix Kukul. "He has the favor of the gods; he's a god himself."

Malinalli nodded, amazed at what she had heard. She had never seen the great king that her batab served, and because she was a slave, she could never hope to.

* * *

Other amazing things happened in the year 12 House. A flaming omen, shaped like an ear of corn, a fiery signal, appeared in the sky every night for almost the whole year. It seemed to bleed fire, drop by drop, like a wound in the eastern sky. It blazed at midnight and burned till the break of day, then vanished with the rising sun. People spoke of it at the cenotes and marketplaces, clapping their hands over their mouths, amazed and frightened, asking each other what it could mean.

A fire also appeared one day in the middle of the sky while the sun was still shining. It forked into three prongs, flashed out from the sun straight into the east, giving off a shower of sparks like a red-hot coal.

Nemon saw this strange phenomenon, and was afraid.

* * *

Little Ah Tok, or "Flint Knife," the infant son of Ix Kukul and Ah Balam, had learned to walk several months before the fire omen appeared. Although he was still nursing at his mother's generous breasts, he was growing up. The cradle boards had done their job of shaping his head properly, and the ball of wax that dangled from his forelock was continuing to attract his eyes to the center. His parents were concerned about possible impending disaster, especially since they had seen the omens, and they knew it was time for the ceremony of *hetzmek*, when the child is ready to be carried on the hip.

The ceremony was simple enough, with the batab's wife dressed in her usual plain white huipil, and the batab Ah Hoh in comparatively modest finery, both promising to care for the child in their household if any evils should befall the parents. Then Malinalli served everyone a cup of chocolate, and she was permitted to drink what was left over. It was a happy day.

That night, however, she was awakened by the sound of a woman's weeping. Then the weeping turned into moaning and

216

faded away. Was it only the wind in the trees? Was it Quetzalcoatl in his guise of Ehecatl, god of wind, sending a message? The next morning she asked Ix Kukul if she, too, had heard strange sounds.

Ix Kukul replied curtly, "I didn't hear anything," and quickly changed the subject.

The next night Malinalli was again awakened, this time by a woman's voice crying "My child, why did you leave me? Where have they hidden you?"

And again the next morning she spoke to Ix Kukul as they patted corncakes together. "Do you believe in omens, Ix Kukul?" Ix Kukul admitted she did. Encouraged by that, Malinalli said, "You've seen the strange omens of light in the sky. I think I heard another last night."

"The woman crying again?" asked Ix Kukul.

"Yes. The legend of the earth mother Cihuacoatl is that she wanders the earth at night, weeping and searching for her lost children. She's the goddess of childbirth, and death, too; she gives life but also takes it away."

Ix Kukul snorted. "What a silly story. I can't think of any silly stories to tell you about our goddess of childbirth, Ix Chel. How can you believe in a goddess who creates children then kills them and mourns for them? Putun Mayas are not that silly."

"Maybe I'm imagining things," Malinalli said lightly, though she still felt concerned. She could see that Ix Kukul did not want to discuss the legend, so she changed the subject.

Something awakened her again that night, so she slipped out of the slaves' sleeping room and stood in the faint light of a quarter moon, listening intently. A wind whispered through the leaves in the orchard, carrying also the faint suggestion of crying. As Malinalli walked softly toward the sound, she heard the rhythms of a Mayan poem being chanted.

At the base of an avocado tree, she saw a figure in white, sitting in ghostly stillness, weeping and chanting softly:

Little flower of my womb,
portrait of your mother,
why do you leave me in loneliness?
Did I not give you life
with great pain and suffering?
I gave you to suck at my breast,
I protected you from birth.
Where is your saintly soul?
Why did you go away from me?
My heart grows weak and heavy.
Your leaving is destroying me,
my little flown-away bird,
little flower of my womb.

My heart is lonely
and cries for your return.

The weeping woman repeated the verse over and over, like a prayer or incantation. Clearly she was addressing a daughter who had died at birth. Suddenly Malinalli recognized the chanter, a woman in a white dress of mourning—the batab's wife.

Moving with deliberate slowness and as quietly as she could, Malinalli retreated to the slave quarters. At last she understood the household secret, the one Ix Kukul could not talk about. Ix Kukul could not admit this secret, not only out of loyalty to her mistress, but because she felt some guilt. It might have been the hetzmek ceremony for her boy Ah Tok that stirred the buried longings in her mistress's soul.

Malinalli pondered the irony of a batab's wife who seemed to have everything, yet could find no contentment in anything, not even her other offspring, her grown son. Malinalli had seen grief before; she herself had experienced grief so deep that she could not feel sunshine or hear birdsong. Yet this woman sounded like one who had gone through all nine hells of the Maya religion without catching a single glimpse of the thirteen heavens. Hers was a grief akin to madness.

* * *

Not long after that eerie night, the batab was found dead in his bed, his face more yellow than ever, his mouth open like that of a gasping fish. His wife dissolved in tears, wailed that a widow is unclean, complained that a death complicates other lives intolerably, and repeatedly expressed a desire to go to the other life with her husband and the daughter who had flown away, the little bird that had flown away too soon, so long ago, so far away. The stone house with its painted walls and elegant tapestries resounded with her lamentations and overflowed with her gloom.

When their son, Ah Cux, received the news of his father's death, he came quickly, bringing his wife of one year, Ix Chan. He ordered that a death statue be carved immediately, that his father be cremated quickly, that his remains be placed in the statue. No sooner was this done, than he found his mother hanging by a rope in the orchard, determined to go to the sacred place of suicides, ruled by the goddess Ix Tab. She was cremated also, and her remains buried in the garden, as Ah Cux thought that would have been her wish.

* * *

Ah Cux became batab, overwhelmed by the duties he was

not yet ready for and the shock of losing both parents within a short time. His wife, Ix Chan, proved difficult to please. She felt cheated by having to leave her own parents' home long before she expected to. Only one year had elapsed out of the five years of service her husband was expected to give her father. Since she could not complain about her husband's duty to his own parents, she complained constantly about his servants and slaves. She brought her own servants to Tabasco, favoring them over those that had served Ah Hoh.

Before long, the servant couple Ah Balam and Ix Kukul left to work for another lord, taking their young son with them. Ix Chan persuaded Ah Cux to elevate one of her servants to the position of caluac, but since she had no cook in her retinue, Malinalli had to do the work that had formerly been done by two persons—herself and Ix Kukul.

To make matters worse, Ix Chan banished Nemon from the household, saying he was wasting the time of her servants and slaves. She wouldn't even let him say goodbye to Malinalli, so Malinalli thought she would never see Nemon again.

* * *

The next two years proved as difficult for Malinalli as her years with her step-father and her half-brother had been. Exhausted from the cooking work that began before dawn each day and ended after sundown, unable to get the supplies she needed from the lazy new caluac, she wished that she, too, could leave as Ix Kukul had done.

No matter how tired she was, she could not refuse Ah Cux if he called her to his bed after sundown. She knew that each time she obeyed her new master, her new mistress would heap extra work on her and abuse her with a constant stream of criticism. As Ix Chan grew more shrewish, Ah Cux turned more frequently to Malinalli, partly for respite from his wife's sharp tongue and partly to irritate her further. Malinalli felt trapped in a joyless round of fatigue and marital feuding.

* * *

When the year 1 Reed arrived, Ah Cux had acquired warehouses full of tribute, much more self-confidence, and several new slave girls. Malinalli was then eighteen years old, a competent cook, able to speak Mayan well enough for most practical purposes. Even if Ah Cux had known she was still lonely, even if he had cared, he was preoccupied with more important matters.

The troublesome omens had continued, and Ah Cux was getting reports that the floating houses had emerged again from the east. In military emergencies the batab was expected to assist the nacom, or elected general, by going to battle and commanding soldiers if necessary. Remembering the way Maya soldiers had defended their shores in the year 12 House, the Halach Uinic had assembled his batabob, "they of the axes," ordering them to take command and drive away the intruders. The Halach Uinic had heard reports that some white men with beards had come ashore in canoes from the floating houses, that they had filled barrels with water and given beads to the natives who brought them corncakes and fowl and other foods. He had also heard that some Maya traders had tricked the white men by exchanging useless gold trinkets for some unusual green stones as beautiful as jade. The dzules, the foreigners, could come back, and they might be angry about being cheated, but fortunately there were not very many of them.

The Halach Uinic gave orders to the batabob to be prepared to fight if the white men came back. They were to assemble large numbers of warriors, huge amounts of cotton quilted armor for them to wear, and as many weapons as they could find—bows, arrows, atl-atl spear throwers, lances, knives, slings with rocks, and other weapons. They were to station these warriors all along the coast, but especially near rivers and wells where the dzules would be likely to come ashore for water.

* * *

Malinalli had been preparing large amounts of food for several days after the attacks began. First the thousand soldiers had to be fed, most of whom were yalba uinicob who left their farms temporarily to defend their territory. Women and slaves who were left on the farms and in the homes had to provide the food and take it to the military camps. Later she was troubled to hear that food was being sent to appease the foreigners who came ashore in canoes from their floating houses in the sea. What could that mean?

While Ah Cux was away, Nemon returned, much changed after a two-year absence. He jangled the string of copper bells at the front entrance and stood with his legs braced confidently apart, adjusting his expensive mantle to make a good impression. His long hair was braided with an obsidian mirror glistening on the tassel. His richly embroidered *ex* (esh), as the Mayas called their loincloth, hung almost to the tops of his tapir sandals.

One of Ix Chan's servants pulled back the door tapestry and permitted him to enter. Nemon asked for Ah Cux, but since the batab was away, the servant summoned his mistress, Ix Chan.

"I greet you, great lady, as a free man, owner of a farm," Nemon said with a courteous bow of his head. "I'll make my business brief. I have two hundred cacao beans in this pouch to purchase a slave. I offer that to you for Malinalli."

"You've changed indeed, Nemon," said Ix Chan, who found that the changes pleased her eyes. She knew she would have to think quickly. "My lord is away now, fighting the intruders," she said. "Personally I wouldn't object to such a sale, but he might drive a hard bargain with you."

"What price would he ask?" Nemon said coolly. "I'm offering twice the usual amount for a slave."

Ix Chan's eyes traveled up and down the body of the twenty-one-year-old, well-built young man. "He might consider a few years of your service here in exchange," she said in a cooing voice, her eyebrows lifting slightly, her mouth curving into a sly smile. "We could give you a good position here. We need a more efficient caluac to oversee the household. You'd have authority and respect here."

Nemon's mouth straightened into a hard line across his expressionless face. "That wouldn't interest me," he said coldly. "I have a farm to tend. I need a wife to help me there."

Ix Chan's voice also turned cold. "You'll have to see my husband, then. I won't intercede for you. You'll find him at the camp near the River of the Sacred Monkey." With a gesture of dismissal, she turned and left the room.

Nemon glanced quickly into the cooking room. Malinalli was not there. He strode out the tapestry-covered door and walked toward the temple with a determined gait. Once out of sight of Ix Chan's servants, he turned toward the path to the cenote.

He found Malinalli at the cenote, filling her water jug, her hair wet and shiny from her morning bath. His heart leaped to see her, and he rejoiced that she was alone. He stood in the path where she would see him when she turned around.

"Nemon!" she cried when she saw him. "How wonderful you look!"

"You, too," he said happily. "As beautiful as ever." He took the water jug from her hands and set it on the ground. "We haven't much time," he said, holding her two hands in his. "I've come to buy you from Ah Cux, to make you my wife."

Hope leaped in Malinalli's heart. "Have you seen Ah Cux? Did he agree?"

"No. He's away. I saw Ix Chan, but she was no help."

Malinalli sighed. "Most of the men are away to fight the dzules. Will you be drafted to fight too?"

"I won't fight for my former masters," Nemon said defiantly. "I'd run away first. My farm is in a remote place, far from the rivers and the coast. They'll never find me. Will you run away with me, now?"

Malinalli had never faced greater temptation. Her eyes radiated joy. But then she reflected on the punishments. "To take a slave from a batab is theft," she said. "You could be tortured

221

and killed for that."

"I'll leave two hundred cacao beans in payment," Nemon said. "That's more than a fair price."

From behind a thorn bush two women stepped out. One was Ix Xtzul, "centipede," the slave that Malinalli most despised, who grabbed Malinalli's arms and held them behind her back. The other was Ix Chan, who had asked Ix Xtzul to lead her to Malinalli.

Ix Chan spoke with haughty anger. "Your offer has been refused, Nemon. If Malinalli disappears, you'll be caught and killed. My husband will see to that."

With her arms still in the grip of "Centipede," Malinalli turned to Nemon with anguish on her face. "Go, Nemon! I don't want to go with you." Her voice choked on the lie she was telling.

Nemon's eyes sought hers. "I'll see Ah Cux at his camp near the river," he said intensely. "I'll pay whatever he asks."

Malinalli's voice became more desperate. "Please go, Nemon! You could be killed! I'll be safe here. Why should I want to be the wife of a farmer, when I can live in a batab's fine stone house and have fine foods to eat?"

Nemon reeled back, the color in his face draining into pallor. He pulled his shoulders back like a soldier ready to march and took a deep breath. "Goodbye, Malinalli," he said stiffly. Then without another word, he turned and walked away.

* * *

Ix Chan was angry because Malinalli had become so stubborn, refusing to cook or clean, refusing to eat, staying in the slaves' quarters on her mat all day, pretending to be sick. Even the threat of a whipping had no effect on her.

"You can kill me," she said wearily, "but you can't beat me." She closed her eyes and laid her head back on the mat.

"Who says I can't?" Ix Chan raged, standing over her and swishing a willow in the air threateningly. "While Ah Cux is away, I'm in charge here."

"I say you can't," Malinalli said defiantly, looking up at her mistress with loathing. "Because if you beat me and leave me alive, you'll wake up dead some morning."

Despite the brittle humor in those words, Ix Chan could tell that Malinalli was serious. Ah Cux, when he returned, might even take sides with his intransigent concubine and further undermine Ix Chan's authority. That would set a bad example for other servants and slaves. Feeling angry and humiliated, she began to wish she had taken Nemon's offer in Ah Cux's absence, even if Ah Cux might have disapproved when he returned.

After brooding in this manner for two more days, Ix Chan

saw her chance to get rid of a troublesome slave. A messenger came from the Halach Uinic with bad news. The Maya soldiers had been defeated at the River of the Sacred Monkeys, he said. The dzules had long knives harder than flint that could cut a man in two and not break. They had shields that arrows could not penetrate. They could make thunder and smoke and throw big balls as hard as hearthstones. Some of them rode on the backs of huge deer, or perhaps they were demons with a human torso and a deer's legs. The dzules were demanding food and mantles as tribute, and they wanted twenty slave women to cook and clean for them.

Ix Chan believed his words, for she had heard some of the distant battle cries and thunderous sounds. "I'll do my part for the good of my people," she said sweetly. "You can have Malinalli to give to the dzules."

Chapter 18

Cortes and his Yucatan Adventures

While the Mayas had been trying to decipher the meaning of omens and to drive away the men who came in floating houses, interest in their lands had been growing in Hispaniola and Cuba.

Diego Velasquez, Governor of Cuba, had become upset in 1518. "Who can I trust?" he thundered at his old friend and brother-in-law Hernan Cortes in the governor's office at his official residence in Santiago. "That coward Cristobal Colon never even went ashore when he had the chance. Just chatted with the natives in their dugout canoes and traded a few trinkets. Then my own nephew goes to explore the territory, and he's been gone much too long."

"To be perfectly fair," Cortes said in his most persuasive gentlemanly manner, "Colon was sent on a different mission—to find a sea route to Cathay. Personally I wish he had left the door open so others could enter the Yucatan territory, but I can see why he pushed on. As for your nephew, everyone trusts Juan Grijalva. He's probably just been delayed."

Velasquez, who had grown so portly during his prosperous years in Cuba that he needed an especially large chair, continued to fume, hitting his mahogany desk with his fist. "Then I sent Cristobal de Olid, supposed to be the best captain around. He went to find Grijalva, and now he's lost, too."

"Maybe they've run into trouble. Isn't that why you asked me to assemble a fleet of ships?" Cortes said with the annoyance of one who has heard all this before.

"Yes!" Velasquez exploded. "You agreed to hunt for them, didn't you? Not to pursue some agenda of your own?"

"I agreed to that," Cortes said impatiently, "and to all your other stipulations." He counted on his fingers as he recited them: "to look for the castaway Spaniards from the Vivaldia shipwreck seven years ago, to watch out for Amazons, to treat the natives well and teach them about Christianity, never to venture inland away from the coast, to trade for gold and keep valuables in a locked chest, not to take anything from the Indians by force, and not to consort with Indian women."

"And what did I say about settlements?"

"You said King Charles is not permitting them, yet he wants us to take possession of any new lands in his name."

"Right. His highest priority is to spread Christianity and the fame of Spain."

"I have the same goal," Cortes assured the governor. "I owe Saint Peter my life; I'll spread his holy word whenever I can."

"If that's your goal," Velasquez said, "why are you acquiring war supplies? I've heard you're storing gunpowder and lead, crossbows, muskets, bronze guns—who knows what else."

"Surely you know," Cortes said patronizingly, "a captain may need to defend his ships at any time."

"And horses!" Velasquez exclaimed as if playing a trump card. "Why are you taking so many horses with you?"

"To impress the natives, of course," Cortes promptly replied. "You know how the horses frightened the natives on Hispaniola and Cuba. What makes you so suspicious?"

Velasquez countered that accusation with one of his own. "Why are you going so far in debt?"

The vein in Cortes's throat stood out as it often did when he grew angry. "What's this all about, Diego? Of course I've gone into debt—spent about 20,000 pesos buying pigs, chickens, bacon, beans, oil, wine, water kegs, beads, trading trinkets, and all the other things I'll need."

"Are you thinking of establishing a settlement in the new territory? You've had black-and-gold banners made, inscribed with the motto 'follow the sign of the Holy Cross and through it we will conquer.' "

"I wouldn't go against the King's orders," Cortes answered in a controlled voice. "We'll conquer the spirit of darkness, the evils of Satan, as we spread God's word. But why needle me like this? Don't you want your share of any gold we find?"

Velasquez rose and walked to the window, looking out through the palm trees to the sunny sea, the frothy edges of the waves on the sandy shore. "I wish I were younger," he said wistfully. "I'd go myself. I wouldn't have to worry about people I hired keeping more than their share."

Cortes stood up to leave, putting on his cape. "I swear by this beard, Diego, your suspicions are groundless. Grijalva and Olid are as loyal to you as I am. But let me give you some advice as an old friend. Don't vacillate this way, giving us positions of trust, then changing your mind. What reason would I have to go to all this trouble, outfitting ships, finding crews? I have my hacienda, plenty of money for gambling, a pretty wife, a certain prestige here in Cuba. Because you asked me to, I've spent a lot of time and money making preparations. I'm determined to succeed, for my King and my god. Trust me; I care about your advancement as well as my own."

Velasquez continued staring out the window. "Where could they be?" he muttered, as if he hadn't heard anything Cortes had said.

* * *

Before Cortes had finished his preparations, a ship from the Grijalva expedition sailed into port. Pedro de Alvarado, the captain, brought a cargo worth 20,000 pesos in gold obtained from the natives in the Yucatan territory. He said that Grijalva would be back a little later, after he had explored further north along the coast. When Velasquez questioned him closely, Alvarado grumbled that Grijalva had not let the men form a settlement.

Grijalva and Olid both returned shortly thereafter, bringing tales of visiting an island called Cozumel, of seeing stone cities like a "little Cairo" on the Yucatan coast, of being received with friendliness and gifts in Tabasco, of sailing to the north where some finely dressed Indians had presented them with gifts of beautifully wrought golden jewels and ornaments.

On his expedition, Grijalva had taken as interpreters two Indian prisoners Cordoba had captured at Cape Catoche who had learned a little Spanish—Melchior and Julian. When the interpreters asked the natives of Tabasco where more gold could be found, the Indians pointed to the west and said "Cholula" and "Mexica." The reply sounded like gibberish to Grijalva and his men, but it convinced them that more gold could be obtained further inland.

Fortunately, Cortes was able to recruit thirty-eight experienced crew members who had sailed with Grijalva and Cordoba. Melchior agreed to come as interpreter. Alvarado, eager for adventures and gold, agreed to command another ship and to bring three brothers. Cortes also recruited an excellent pilot, Antonio de Alaminos, who had been a cabin boy on Cristobol Colon's fourth journey and navigated the gulf stream while serving Grijalva and Cordoba. Even two former commanders, Cristobal de Olid and Juan Grijalva, agreed to come.

Unfortunately for Grijalva, his uncle the governor chastised him severely for not establishing a settlement in Yucatan, even though Grijalva's explicit orders had been to confine his mission to trade. Confused and broken-hearted, Grijalva served under the less experienced Cortes, who had been given similar instructions, but who had learned that Diego Velasquez sometimes gave orders which he hoped would be discreetly ignored.

* * *

Cortes stepped up his recruiting. He began dressing elegantly to give an impression of confidence and prosperity. He wore a plume of feathers with a medal, a gold chain, and a velvet cloak buttoned with knots of gold. He sent a crier throughout the town promising that all who accompanied him would receive a share of the captured riches and a grant of land and Indians in the new country. Soon he had three hundred men from the Santiago area and had chartered a fleet of ships. He had also borrowed considerable sums from friends who considered the loans as investments. Velasquez's suspicions deepened; he accused Cortes of behaving as if he "had been born in brocade."

Fearing that Velasquez might change his mind, Cortes hastily departed from Santiago on November 18, 1518. Sailing westward along the southern coast of Cuba, he gathered more men and ships, including some of exceptional merit: Gonzalo de Sandoval, Alonso Puertocarrero, Andres de Tapia, Bernal Diaz del Castillo, and even Juan Velasquez de Leon, a disenchanted cousin of Diego Velasquez. Cortes used the gold-knot buttons from his cape to pay for horses when he could find the costly animals for sale on the island. Twice Diego Velasquez sent messages to ports along the route ordering Cortes to turn back, but they only made Cortes more determined to proceed.

When ten of his eleven ships met at Cape San Antonio, on the southern tip of Cuba, Cortes held a muster. He counted more than five hundred fighting men, a hundred sailors, seventeen horses, and an arsenal that would sustain quite a war if they were attacked by Indians as Cordoba had been.

It was then February of 1519. Cortes addressed his recruits with a stirring speech: "My friends and companions," he shouted to the multitude, "we are engaging in a just and good war which will bring us fame. Almighty God, in whose name and faith it will be waged, will give us victory. We shall do as we shall see fit, and here I offer you great rewards, although they will be wrapped about with great hardships. I shall make you in a very short time the richest of all men who have crossed the seas. God has favored the Spanish nation. We have never lacked courage and strength and never shall. Let us go our way contentedly, and make the outcome equal to the beginning."

The hardships he had in mind came from the picture he had pieced together from reports of earlier voyages. In many places the warriors wore quilted cotton armor which could stop an arrow or a spear. The natives were reported to be skillful archers, but they did not use poison-tipped arrows. In addition to spears, they had heavy two-handed wooden swords edged with razor-sharp inlays of obsidian, or volcanic glass. They had been known to remove the jawbones of men they killed and wear them as trophies on their upper arms. They were said to worship hideous idols, to sacrifice their captives in huge stone temples, and then to eat their flesh. Some said that Amazons—huge warlike women—inhabited the unexplored regions. Some said the natives practiced sodomy, though it was unclear how they knew this.

The eloquence of Captain-general Cortes' speech was followed by a solemn mass, led by the expedition's ecclesiastics, Father Bartolome de Olmedo and the licentiate Juan Diaz. Olmedo was the rare kind of man whose character combined a merry disposition, fervent zeal for his work, charity towards all people, and the good judgment to offer wise and benevolent counsel. Diaz was dutiful, but sometimes sullen. Placing the expedition under the protection of Cortes's patron saint, Saint Peter, the ships weighed anchor and sailed on February 18, 1519, pursuing the allure and mystery of Yucatan.

* * *

Pedro de Alvarado, the impetuous, high-spirited, yellow-haired captain of one ship, had been too impatient to wait for the other ten. Instead of meeting the other captains at Cape San Antonio, as Cortes had ordered, he sailed ahead to the island of Cozumel, arriving two days before the others. By the time Cortes arrived at Cozumel, Alvarado's men had entered two towns, scared away the inhabitants, and consumed forty fowls they had left behind. The undisciplined crew had looted a house of worship, taking some altar cloths and small chests containing diadems, idols, and other sacred objects made of a low-grade mixture of copper and gold.

Cortes was furious. He publicly upbraided Alvarado, put some of his crew in chains as punishment, and made an apology through his interpreter to the natives in hiding. He also invited them to the Spanish camp, promising to return the sacred objects. When some of them timidly ventured into the camp, he returned the objects and, in exchange for the forty fowls his crew had devoured, gave them gifts of bells, scissors, and knives. He gave each man a Spanish shirt and befriended them with cheap green beads, which the natives thought were the precious stone they called *chalchihuitl*, or jadeite.

Through Melchior, Cortes and the two missionaries tried to persuade the gentle natives to give up their idols and embrace Christianity. Fearfully, the natives protested that if these gods were profaned, they would send lightning and hurricanes in vengeance. To convince them of the error in their thinking, Cortes ordered his men to roll the idols down the steps of their temples. Although the natives' groans and lamentations filled the air, no lightning or storm occurred.

Hastily, the ships' carpenters erected an altar, crosses, and a shrine to the Virgin Mary. Father Olmedo and Juan Diaz performed mass for the first time within the walls of a temple in the land that would come to be called New Spain. For the rest of the time on the island, the two missionaries tried to pour the light of the gospel into the bewildered natives, but the light went through a dubious channel in the person of the interpreter Melchior, who understood only a little Spanish and almost nothing of Catholic doctrines. At length, however, the compliant natives were convinced of the impotence of their own deities and were willing to embrace new concepts and rituals.

Although Melchior's linguistic skills were mediocre and his loyalty to Spain doubtful, Cortes did succeed in using him to inquire about the Spaniards who had been shipwrecked eight years before. The Cozumel natives had heard of some white men who were held captive by the Mayas, across the channel from Cozumel. The Cozumel natives feared the more warlike Mayas on the mainland, but finally one man was persuaded by a quantity of the magic green beads to carry a letter signed by Cortes.

"Noble lords," the letter read, "I departed from Cuba with a fleet of 11 vessels and 550 Spaniards, and arrived here at Cozumel where I am writing this letter. The people of Cozumel have assured me that in your country there are five or six bearded men who look like us. I suspect that you are Spaniards. I beg you within six days from the time you receive this letter, to come to us without delay or excuse. We shall recognize and reward the favor. A brigantine will be waiting to pick you up."

The Indian courier placed the letter in his rolled-up hair, sailed to the mainland in a brigantine, and disappeared into the scrubby trees of Yucatan. After waiting eight days for a reply, the brigantine's captain, discouraged, returned to Cozumel.

Cortes, also discouraged, bid farewell to the Cozumel tribe and took his fleet out to sea. It was already March of 1519; the captains had to proceed even if they could not accomplish the task of finding the Spanish survivors.

When one of the ships developed a leak, Cortes ordered all ships back to Cozumel so the defective ship's seams could be caulked. While waiting, some of the men began to hunt for wild pigs.

Andres de Tapia, hunting with two companions, noticed something unusual: a large canoe had arrived at the town from the direction of Cape Catoche. He sent a messenger running to tell Cortes that the canoe might be carrying the missing Spaniards. Six men, wearing Indian garments and carrying oars, stepped out of the canoe and walked toward them. Tapia felt disappointed; clearly these were Indians, not Spaniards. Then one spoke in badly articulated Spanish: "Dios y Santa Maria de Sevilla." Tapia moved quickly to embrace his countryman.

"Where is the Spaniard?" asked Cortes when Tapia approached with the Spaniard at his side.

The Spaniard squatted down on his haunches, as an Indian would, and said, "I am Jeronimo de Aguilar." Aguilar was carrying an oar, wearing a ragged cloak and loincloth, with a sandal hanging on one foot and another tied to his rope belt. His hair was shorn in the manner of an Indian slave. With his naturally brown skin, he was indistinguishable from the Indians he had hired to row him to Cozumel.

Cortes ordered Tapia to bring Aguilar a shirt, a doublet, pants, stockings, and shoes. He ordered food and drink for Aguilar and the Indians who had brought him from Cape Catoche. When the Indians had left, bearing gifts of green stones, Cortes took Aguilar to the captain's quarters to hear his story.

Pronouncing Spanish with some difficulty, for he had not used it in eight years, Aguilar related his adventures. He was a native of Ecija who had taken holy orders. He and fifteen other men and two women had left Darien for Santo Domingo eight years before. When the ship struck on the Alacranes and could not be floated, the passengers launched a small boat hoping to reach Cuba or Jamaica. Strong currents carried them instead to Yucatan, where they were captured and divided among several chiefs. Some of his companions had been sacrificed to idols; others had died of disease. The women, made to grind corn and do other domestic tasks, had soon died of exhaustion. Only he and one other Spaniard had survived: Gonzalo Guerrero.

"How did you manage to survive?" Cortes asked with keen interest, taking a map from a shelf and unrolling it.

"I was going to be sacrificed, but I escaped and fled to another chief who took me in and kept me as a slave," Aguilar explained. "I've been chopping wood, carrying loads, and working in the fields."

"Can you tell us about this country?" Cortes inquired eagerly. "How many towns? How well defended?"

Aguilar looked downcast. His new shirt, a size too large, drooped from his thin shoulders. "I know very little because I was a slave," he replied sorrowfully. "Once I was sent four leagues from home with a load, but it was too heavy, and I fell sick. I think there are many towns, but I haven't seen them."

Cortes patted his shoulder sympathetically. "It isn't important; you'll see many towns with us. We're glad we found you. What about Guerrero?"

"He's living in a Maya village five leagues distant from my master's village. When the messenger brought me your letter, I was overjoyed. I gave my master the ransom of beads and begged him to release me, which he did. I took the letter and some beads to the village of Gonzalo Guerrero, but he didn't want to leave his family."

"He has a family?"

"Yes, he married a chief's daughter and had children by her.

230

When I read him the letter he said to me, 'Brother Aguilar, I have a wife and three children. The natives here look upon me as a lord and a captain in wartime. You go, and God be with you, but I've tattooed my face and pierced my ears. What would the Spaniards say if they saw me like this?' Then he told me how proud he was of his sons, how handsome they were. He said he'd take the green beads I brought and give them to his sons. He said he'd tell them they came from his own country."

"You say he's a captain in wartime?"

"A valiant warrior. That's how he won the heart of the chief's daughter. She begged her father to spare his life, so he could teach the young men the arts and strategies of war."

"I'd like to have him in our hands," Cortes said. "He could tell us a lot about the way the Indians fight."

"I'd like that too," Aguilar said, "but his loyalties may have changed. Guerrero organized many warriors from Maya tribes when a ship full of hostile soldiers came two years ago."

Cortes stroked his chin. "So it was Guerrero who routed Cordoba. I wish my men had been more insistent about finding Guerrero and bringing him to me. We almost missed finding you, and it will never do to leave Guerrero here."

"His wife wouldn't let him come anyway," Aguilar said with great seriousness. "She complained that I was bothering a great warrior with my foolish words, and he shouldn't listen to a mere slave like me."

Cortes laughed. "I can see he's come up in the world," he said. "Gone from being a captive slave to a great commander of men, but soft as clay in the hands of a woman. I guess we don't need to worry about him after all."

* * *

With all ships in good repair and their newfound interpreter with them, the fleet left Cozumel on March 4, 1519. After good weather that day, a fierce wind came up at night and almost drove the ships ashore. It abated by midnight, but one ship had been separated from the others, and nothing could be done until they located it. To everyone's great relief, they found it anchored in a bay. There they explored for two days, marveling at the maize plantations, the temples, the statues of tall women that natives worshiped there. So they named it Punta de las Mujeres, the Cape of the Women.

On March 12, 1519, the Cortes fleet arrived at the river near Tabasco which Grijalva's men had named after him. They anchored the ships at sea and took all the soldiers by boat to the Cape of the Palms, about half a league from the town of Tabasco. Grijalva and the veterans of his earlier expedition expected another friendly welcome, but greatly to their surprise,

231

the river banks and mangrove thickets were swarming with Indians in red and black war paint.

A long canoe approached, filled with Indian chiefs carrying shields and lances. Aguilar asked them in his Mayan dialect what they were disturbed about. He told them the Spaniards meant no harm, that they wanted to exchange gifts for fresh water and to engage in trade. As Aguilar talked, the chiefs became angrier. They threatened to kill any soldiers that entered their town or crossed their barricades of fences and tree trunks.

Cortes responded the next morning by sending boats filled with cannons and soldiers with crossbows. He sent a hundred soldiers under Alonso de Avila to maneuver along a footpath and attack the city from one side while he and his men approached from the river by boat. The Indians were waiting in the swamps, brandishing their weapons, pounding drums, and sounding conch shells to frighten the invaders away. Cortes ordered his men not to fire their cannons or crossbows until he made one more appeal for peace through Aguilar. He said he wanted to tell them about God and the King of Spain, but if they made war on his men, and the Spaniards defended themselves, the fault would be theirs.

The Indians replied that they would kill anyone who landed on the shore. They underscored their intentions by sending hails of arrows and stones, noisily thumping drums, and trumpeting conch shells. They launched canoes and engaged the Spaniards in man-to-man combat, some of them waist deep in the muddy water. While fighting, Cortes lost a shoe in the mud but kept on fighting with one bare foot.

Avila arrived with reinforcements, his foot soldiers having broken open many of the barricades. Together they forced back the Indians, whose arrows and fire-hardened lances were no match for the Spaniards' steel swords, crossbows, and cannon fire.

When the advancing soldiers captured a temple where the Indians had stored the town's most valuable possessions, Cortes halted the battle and told his men not to pursue the enemies in flight. Wearing both shoes, having recovered the one he lost in the mud, Cortes took possession of the land for His Majesty, making a sign of possession by three cuts of his sword in a huge silk-cotton tree that stood in the temple square. He declared his intention to defend that land for the King of Spain, using the sword and shield he held in his hands. The soldiers cried out their approval, waving their swords in support, in the presence of a Royal Notary. This done, they all slept in the great temple square, with sentinels on the alert.

* * *

The next morning Cortes looked for his interpreter Melchior,

232

planning to send him with Pedro de Alvarado to explore the inland territory. Melchior had disappeared, but the Spanish clothes he had worn were found hanging on a tree in the palm grove.

Cortes, much annoyed at the desertion of Melchior, thanked God and St. Peter that he still had Aguilar. He feared, and later confirmed, that Melchior had gone to inform the Indians how many Spaniards there were, thus increasing the confidence of the Indians that they could overwhelm the invaders.

Skirmishes went on for several days, warriors on each side fighting valiantly—the Spaniards against thousands of Indians fiercely defending their homeland, the Indians against weapons and military strategies they had never experienced. Pedro de Alvarado fought so bravely that he redeemed himself in his general's eyes for his earlier misconduct.

Diego de Ordas and his foot soldiers were engaged in battle on a plain near Ceutla, where eight thousand Indians from the entire region had assembled. The heavily armed foot soldiers, advancing across a cultivated plain cross-hatched with drainage canals, often stumbled and fell in the ditches and loose earth.

Meanwhile, Cortes had brought thirteen horses from the ship and transported them to land, assigning them to his best horsemen. After a day of exercise, the stiff animals could move as well as ever. Cortes and his horsemen approached from wooded areas, hidden from the Indians' view. When the horsemen came thundering into the plain, bells ringing on the breastplates of the horses, the riders yelling "Santiago" and pointing their lances directly into the faces of their enemies, the terrified Indians fled. They had never seen horses before. They were not sure whether the rider and horse were one creature or two.

The horses and cannons finally won the day. Because the Indian warriors tended to group closely together, a cannon shot easily devastated their ranks. Three hundred Indians lay dead on the plain, and many more had been wounded. Because this victory took place on March 25, the Day of Our Lady to the Spaniards, they named the site Santa Maria de la Victoria.

The Spanish soldiers buried two of their own who had died of their wounds, one in the ear, one in the throat. Many others had been wounded. Having no other medication, Bernal Diaz and the other foot soldiers cut up the body of a dead Indian and used the body fat to sear the wounds of their own men and their horses.

* * *

The Spaniards had taken two warriors as prisoners. They gave the captives green and blue beads and sent them back to their chiefs with a message from Cortes, translated by Aguilar.

233

The next day the chiefs sent fifteen slaves, with dirty faces and ragged garments, carrying baked fish, fowls, and maize cakes. Cortes accepted the food graciously, but Aguilar denounced the slaves. He told them Cortes would talk only to their chiefs, and only if they were clean and well dressed, like diplomats.

The next day thirty well-dressed chiefs, called *caciques* by the Spaniards from an adopted Arawak word meaning "prince," came to Cortes with gifts of food. They asked permission to gather their dead for cremation, so the bodies would not smell bad or be eaten by jaguars. The *caciques* told Cortes through Aguilar that eight hundred of their men had been killed, many more wounded. Cortes gave them permission to cremate their dead, but asked them to return the next day with more food.

The *caciques* returned with thirty tamemes bearing food, as well as incense with which they perfumed the air and fumigated the soldiers around Cortes. He learned from them that the cacique of Tabasco had been taunted by his neighboring caciques for giving presents to Grijalva two years before. He also learned that his interpreter Melchior had betrayed him by revealing information about the Spaniards.

To teach the Indians a lesson and render them fearful of him in the future, Cortes decided to play some tricks on them. He told them through Aguilar that the war had been their fault because they insisted on fighting instead of peaceful trading, and the cannons might still be angry with them. Secretly giving a sign, he caused a cannon to go off noisily. The cannonball zoomed over the hills, reverberating like a thunderclap, terrifying the caciques.

About that time a soldier led in a stallion and tied his reins near the place where Cortes and the caciques were talking. Catching the scent of a mare who had been tied up behind the Cortes quarters, the stallion began to paw the ground, neigh loudly, and grow wild with excitement. Again, the caciques were terrified, but Cortes led the stallion away and reassured them that the horse would not be angry if they would make peace.

Much relieved, the caciques said they would return the next day and bring presents. They kept their promise, bringing four gold diadems and some ornaments shaped like lizards, little dogs, and ducks. They brought a pair of sandals with gold soles, two masks with Indian faces, and several loads of the quilted cotton with which they made armor. Cortes valued the cotton armor because it offered more protection and was more comfortable in the hot climate than the heavy metal armor from Spain.

The most valuable present from the caciques, however, was one they thought to be of little worth. They brought twenty slave women to cook for the conquerors, to launder and mend their clothes, and to provide whatever other comforts might be desired. One of the slaves was named Malinalli Tenepal.

* * *

To give his captains a taste of the rewards he had in store for them, Cortes promised a slave woman to those who had particularly distinguished themselves in battle. Much to the surprise of his subordinates, Cortes commanded them not to have sexual relations with their slaves. He quoted Velasquez's stipulation that members of the expedition must not consort with pagan women. When the men grumbled predictably, Cortes promised to solve the problem within a few days.

"Suppose we convert the women to Christianity?" Cortes asked his spiritual adviser, Father Olmedo. "They wouldn't be pagan any more, would they?"

"They wouldn't be pagans if they become Christians," Olmedo assured him. "Of course, fornication is still a sin, even with a Christian woman."

"That sin would be on the heads of the men who commit it," Cortes said. "You might be very busy at your confessionals, Father, but at least I would have kept my word to Velasquez."

"I make no judgment on that point of honor," Olmedo said. "I want to do the work I was brought here to do, to teach the natives about Christianity."

Cortes smiled. "Then let's begin tomorrow. I'll order my men to bring their slaves to hear God's holy word."

"Also order them to hear mass on Palm Sunday," Olmedo suggested. "And invite all the caciques to the ceremony, too."

* * *

When the morning meal was finished, the slaves sat dutifully on the sand, beside the huge cross erected by Cortes' carpenters the day before. They listened intently as Father Olmedo and Juan Diaz explained the rudiments of Christianity, interpreted by Aguilar.

One of the slaves asked questions. The others looked amazed at her temerity, but Aguilar and Olmedo answered her questions enthusiastically. She seemed genuinely awestruck at their words.

"Did Jesus Christ care about all people, even slaves?"

"Yes," Olmedo answered after Aguilar had translated Malinalli's question into Spanish. "God sees even the sparrow that falls, but He cares even more about men and women."

"And Jesus Christ was sacrificed for all men and women?" Her eyes glistened and her voice quivered at this thought.

"Yes," Olmedo answered through Aguilar, "by the sacrifice of the one, the many are saved. All those who believe in Him shall have everlasting life."

"Even those that did not die in battle or childbirth?"

Olmedo nodded solemnly. "Anyone who believes in him."

235

Malinalli still marveled at this revelation. "He was born to a poor woman, in a bed of straw?"

"Yes, but his mother was chosen for her virtue; we call her the Virgin Mary, or Santa Maria."

As Malinalli learned about Christianity from the friars, Olmedo and the Spaniards learned much about religious beliefs among the Mexican Indians. Knowing that such knowledge would be highly valuable in the future, Cortes watched and listened with pleasure and began planning his strategy for winning over the Indians to his faith. His captain Alonso Puertocarrero nudged him and pointed to Malinalli. "I'll take that one," he said, "the one asking all the questions."

Then all twenty women were baptized as a group. The baptism with holy water reminded Malinalli of the naming ceremonies she had heard in Nahuatl. She was told that baptism was a kind of rebirth, into a new spiritual life. She was not surprised, therefore, when she was asked to take a new Christian name.

She liked the name of the Christian mother goddess, Maria. That goddess must be like Toci or Teoinnan, the mother and grandmother of the Mexica gods. She wondered if the name Maria was too sacred for a slave to take, so she asked Aguilar, who could understand her Mayan words.

"If a slave took the name of Maria," she asked earnestly, "would the name become worn out?"

Aguilar knew why this girl, presumably a Putun Maya, had asked such a question. He knew that Maya people have four names—a common name, a sacred name used only by intimates for special purposes, a name from the mother's side, and a name from the father's side. Mayas use the common name so that the sacred name will not get worn out.

"Christian names don't wear out," he assured her. "Lots of women have the name of Maria, though. Why don't you take the name of Marina? It can mean 'little Mary,' or it can mean "of the seacoast.' "

Delighted, Malinalli adopted the Christian name of Marina. When the soldiers of Cortes came to know her well, they gave her the additional courtesy title of *Dona*, meaning "lady" in Spanish. Later the soldier and historian Bernal Diaz del Castillo would write that Dona Marina was the only one he could remember of the twenty slaves, but she was unforgettable. He would also praise her great inner virtue and courage despite mistreatment and hardships. He would admit in his memoirs that the Spaniards could not have achieved what they did without her.

At that moment, however, Marina could not see her future. Swept along in the present, she was fascinated by the concept of exciting new gods even more powerful than Quetzalcoatl, coming as prophesied in the year 1 Reed. Slaves whispered among themselves that the hairy-faced Spaniards might be gods. One in particular seemed godlike as he commanded the others, assigning each slave to one of his captains. He assigned her to Puertocarrero, who led her to his horse and showed her how to stroke the animal's neck and nose. The animal smell of the horse permeated the clothing of her new master, making her wonder if he ever bathed, but soon she learned to like the smell of horses. The stallion nuzzled her hand when she stroked his nose, tossed his mane with a snort when she stroked the sleek coat of his long, graceful neck. She sensed the power and grace that have always bonded men and horses into a mutual affection akin to passion.

When Captain-General Cortes rode past, guiding his mount confidently as if horse and rider had blended into one powerful creature, she wondered what kind of master such a commander would be. But her father's words echoed in her mind: "Never want what you can never have; that is the way to unhappiness."

Chapter 19

Cortes Discovers Marina

Early on Palm Sunday the caciques came to the temple square with their wives and children, as Cortes had requested. Also at his request, they brought canoes to help the Spaniards board their ships after mass. The pilots had warned Cortes that a dangerous gale, a "Norther," could imperil them if they delayed much longer. The caciques and their families stood in the temple court watching curiously as Cortes and every person in his company picked up a palm branch and marched in devout procession toward the Christian icons. Each participant kissed the cross and paid homage to the statue of Santa Maria. Then the two clerics, clad in their vestments, said mass.

Marina, standing respectfully among the other slaves, watched her new master, Captain Alonso Hernandez Puertocarrero, join other Spaniards of every rank in expressing devotion to the cross and the statue of a halo-crowned woman. As Aguilar interpreted mass, she listened intently to the story of the crucifixion and the man-god who gave his life that others might live. It reminded her of Quetzalcoatl's story.

When Marina heard the words of the lowly carpenter from Nazareth, "Father, forgive them, for they know not what they do," she wept openly. Father Olmedo observed Marina's tears, but not knowing how much of her own grief flowed into her weeping, he took great satisfaction in the power of the holy word to touch the heart of a slave.

After mass, the caciques presented Cortes and his men with baked fish, fowls, and vegetables. Through Aguilar, he thanked them and exhorted them to care for the image of the Virgin and the crosses in Tabasco and Ceutla. If they would deck each cross with garlands and reverence it, he told them, they would enjoy good health and bountiful harvests.

The ships set sail for San Juan de Ulua in fine weather, skirting along the coast where the soldiers who had previously seen it could point out features they remembered. They passed the towns the Indians called Ayagualulco and Tonala, towns Juan de Grijalva's expedition had renamed La Ramba and San Antonio on Spanish maps. Further on they passed the river of Coatzacoalcos, where Bernal Diaz excitedly pointed out the blue mountain ranges to the west and the two towering volcanic peaks, which he said were always topped with white snow. They sailed past the river called Papaloapan by the Indians, renamed "Rio Alvarado" by Grijalva's men because Alvarado had impetuously dashed into it ahead of the others. His audacity had earned both a reprimand from Grijalva and the personal fame that made the scolding inconsequential, except that it gave Alvarado a grudge against Grijalva. Cortes also named a river after Juan Grijalva, the mighty river flowing through Tabasco. Cortes thus honored Grijalva for discovering the territory and at the same time did a little mischief to Grijalva's uncle, Diego Velasquez, whose name adorned nothing in the new territory.

On Holy Thursday, 1519, the fleet arrived in the Port of San Juan de Ulua, which the pilot Alaminos knew well from his earlier expedition with Grijalva. He told the captains where to anchor their vessels so the northerly gales would do no damage.

Once anchored, the flagship hoisted her royal standards and pennants. They flapped in the warm breeze, rippling with sunlight and shadow against a blue, cloud-dotted sky. Within half an hour after the pennants went up, two large canoes filled with Indians approached the flagship. When they boarded it, the leader asked for the tlatoani.

Cortes turned to Aguilar. "What did they say?"

With an anguished expression, Aguilar said in Spanish, "They're not speaking Mayan. I don't understand their language."

Marina, standing on the deck beside Puertocarrero, had been listening with great curiosity. The Indians who had just come aboard spoke a Nahua dialect, close enough to her native tongue so that she knew they were asking for the leader, the one who "speaks for the others." Sensing that Aguilar had not understood them, she stepped forward, pointing to Hernan Cortes and saying in Nahuatl, "This great man is the tlatoani."

Then she turned to Aguilar and spoke in Mayan. "These men speak Nahuatl; they want to know which man is your leader." She glanced at Puertocarrero, trying to read his expression. Would he disapprove of her stepping forward to volunteer information? Taking such an initiative was certainly unusual behavior for a slave, but Puertocarrero smiled as if pleased by the scene. Marina relaxed, fairly sure she would not be punished.

The natives made signs of deference to Cortes, scraping the sea slime from the bow of the ship and touching it to their lips. Though puzzled by this strange gesture, Cortes gave them presents of blue beads. Marina explained to Aguilar that the natives' gesture meant respect in Nahua cultures, as if they were pledging with earth to speak the truth. Aguilar explained to

Cortes, and both men smiled appreciatively at Marina. "Greetings and welcome," Cortes said in Spanish. Aguilar translated the greeting into Mayan, which Marina quickly converted into Nahuatl, adding assurances to the natives that the Spaniards were expressing friendly intentions.

The Indian leader introduced himself as an agent of the Great Moctezuma. "My lord sent us to find out what kind of men you are and what you are looking for. If you need anything for yourselves or your ships, tell us and we will supply it."

Supplementing her words with improvised hand gestures, Marina translated this statement into Mayan and Aguilar repeated it in Spanish. Although a bit awkward, this system worked satisfactorily. Cortes ordered food and wine served to the Indians, taking some himself to assure them the food was wholesome. After they had consumed the meal, Cortes spoke again. "We come to trade peacefully with you," he said. "Tell your lord not to be uneasy at our arrival, but to see it as good fortune."

Again this friendly message was translated twice. Cortes noticed that Aguilar seemed to labor at the task, whereas Marina delivered her words fluently, with a cordial demeanor that caused him to wonder: where had this slave acquired such skill in rhetoric, such knowledge of the natives' customs, such gracious mannerisms to put their guests at ease? He concluded that Puertocarrero's slave would be an asset to the expedition, but he did not yet realize she would become indispensable.

One of the Indians had been painting a picture of Cortes on bark paper—the pale face, the long beard, the red cap, the strange coat with long sleeves, the puffed pantaloons and buckled shoes. He included an image of Marina, with her long loose hair, her bare feet, her mantle clasped in front in the Maya manner. His lord Moctezuma would be interested in this woman as well as in the tlatoani who spoke through her tongue. Then, contented with their information, their beads, their pictures, and some wine for their chief, the Indians departed.

Cortes thanked Marina in Spanish and took off his hat to her. Aguilar explained that this gesture was what a Spanish gentleman would do in the presence of a Spanish lady. Then, because he had no hat to remove, Aguilar bowed to her, explaining that this, too, was a gesture of respect. Glowing with pleasure, Marina said she had been glad to help. She had wondered if her intrusion into her masters' affairs would seem presumptuous for a lowly slave. The opposite had occurred; she had been thanked. What kind of masters, she wondered, would thank a slave? What kind of warrior would take off his headdress to honor a woman?

* * *

The next day, Good Friday on the Spanish calendar, the men took their horses and guns ashore. There was no level land, only sand dunes that rose to considerable height, so the artilleryman placed the guns where he thought best. Then the soldiers set up an altar, Father Olmedo said mass, and the building began. Three hundred soldiers searched for wood in the swampy area west of the beach. With this and some palm fronds, they devised makeshift huts for themselves and shelters for the precious horses.

The horses were suffering in the heat and slipping in the loose sand as their riders tried to exercise them. One horse died shortly thereafter at San Juan de Ulua, leaving them only sixteen for the inland march Cortes was planning. The wind whipped the sand dunes, shifting them and filling the air with grit. When the wind abated, clouds of insects arose to bite and sting the men and horses. From the stagnant swamps behind the dunes, decayed marine life emitted a stench. Definitely not a good place for a settlement, Cortes decided.

The next day, Saturday, many Indians arrived carrying fowls, corn cakes, and plums, which were then in season. They brought stone axes and saplings which had been stripped of their branches to make huts. As their leader talked to Cortes, the Indians showed the Spaniards how to tie saplings together with vines and hemp rope to make sturdy shelters. They covered the shelters with large strips of cloth, for relief from the hot sun.

While this work was progressing, the leader of the Indian group spoke to Cortes through Marina and Aguilar. "I am Teudile, governor of this province," he said. "I come as emissary from the great lord Cuitlalpitoc, who sends you this gold jewelry."

Cortes accepted the gift and thanked the emissary. "When may I see Lord Moctezuma, the ruler of all the Mexica?" he asked.

"Lord Cuitlalpitoc wishes to see you," said the emissary evasively. "He will come with us tomorrow."

* * *

On Easter Sunday Teudile arrived with Lord Cuitlalpitoc, heading a procession of three or four thousand Indians dressed in finely woven mantles and carrying no weapons.

When Cortes came to greet them, accompanied by his two interpreters and several officers, the two leaders kneeled on the ground, touched their fingers to the sand and then to their mouths. They swung clay censers with burning copal incense around Cortes, his officers, and the interpreters. Marina told Aguilar the incense would bring relief from insects, but she tactfully refrained from saying that it would bring relief to the

241

noses of the Indians from the smell of unbathed Spaniards. Many of the Indians carried baskets filled with fruits, vegetables, corncakes, fish, and fowls. At a signal from Teudile, the bearers pricked their earlobes, tongues, and lips with cactus spines, sprinkling their blood over the food. Marina explained to the startled Cortes, through Aguilar, that the natives meant to sanctify the food with their precious blood.

Other bearers brought flowers for the Spaniards and food for the horses. They found that horses refused roasted turkeys but would accept corn. As the food and flowers were distributed, Cortes's carpenters built an altar. He explained to the two lords, through his interpreters, that his men were Christians, vassals of the great King Charles of Spain. He invited them to observe Easter mass, which they did with great politeness, as Father Olmedo chanted the service in his fine singing voice.

When mass was over, Cortes dined with the envoys in his shelter, seating them on benches around a table. They admired the table and benches while Cortes complimented them on the food. When the table had been cleared, he renewed his attempt to make contact with their emperor. "King Charles ordered us to come here," he said, "because he has heard rumors about this country and the great prince who rules it. I wish to befriend your great prince and tell him many things that will please him."

Teudile considered the request presumptuous. "You have just arrived in this country, and already you ask to speak to our prince. Many of our own high-ranking citizens have never spoken to the Tlatoani Moctezuma, and he may not be willing to see you."

After translating these words, Marina asked Aguilar to explain to Cortes that the Aztecs had many levels of authority, "Advise him," she said, "to follow the protocol suggested by the governors, or he might offend them."

Aguilar passed on the governor's words and Marina's information about levels of Aztec authority, but he did not dare offer advice to his commander. Marina, of course, had no way of knowing what Aguilar said in Spanish, nor did Cortes know that his insistence on seeing Moctezuma might offend his guests.

"The emperor Moctezuma has sent you many gifts," said Cuitlalpitoc, who had also met the Grijalva expedition as the emperor's ambassador. He signaled for bearers to bring a petlacalli chest full of gifts and ten loads of fine cotton cloth. From the chest Teudile withdrew a turquoise mosaic mask in the form of a serpent's head, a headdress made of turquoise quetzal feathers, leg guards decorated with green stone beads and golden shells, a necklace of green stones supporting a golden disk, a sleeveless jacket, and a voluminous cape. The envoys adorned Cortes with these gifts and also presented him with a polished stone mirror, pretty obsidian sandals that were impossible to walk in, and a shield decorated with gold, seashells, and quetzal feathers.

Cortes received these gifts with many smiles and expressions of gratitude. Then he ordered one of his men to bring an arm chair from the flagship, a richly carved chair inlaid with woods of different colors. Seated in this chair as on a throne, he again tried to impress his visitors. He gave them stones with intricate designs that the Spaniards called *margaritas*, a string of twisted glass beads packed in cotton scented with musk, and a crimson cap to which was pinned a golden medal engraved with a figure of St. George on horseback, slaying a dragon.

Then Cortes rose from the ornate chair and, with a flourish, said to Teudile, "Send this chair to Moctezuma. Tell him to be seated in it when I come to visit him. Tell him to wear the red cap on his head when he welcomes me."

Teudile accepted the presents and said courteously, "Our emperor is indeed a great prince. He might want to know more about your great king. I will carry the present to him at once and bring back a reply."

While Alvarado and other cavaliers showed off their mounts and demonstrated their horsemanship, and the artilleryman sent a cannonball zooming over the dunes, the Aztec artists were busily plying their brushes on bark paper. They painted Cortes, the ships, the firearms, the interpreters, the horses, and even the two greyhound dogs that had been left behind by the Grijalva expedition in 1518 and had rejoined the Cortes expedition as expert rabbit-hunters the following year.

While the artists were trying to capture the effect of the cannonfire on paper, Teudile noticed a helmet worn by one of the soldiers. It was partially gilt, somewhat rusted and dented, but it reminded Teudile of a helmet he had seen on a carving of their war god, Huitzilopochtli. Pointing to it, he said, "That helmet might please the emperor."

Cortes seized the opportunity. "Take the helmet to your emperor, by all means," he said heartily. As the soldier dutifully yielded it to Teudile, Cortes continued, "And so that we might learn if the gold of your country is the same as in our rivers, please return the helmet filled with gold so we may send it to our great King Charles."

Teudile agreed to do so, but he was puzzled. "Why do you ask for gold instead of beautiful stones like jadeite? Here we think very little of gold. We call it 'excrement of the gods' although some of our artisans like it for decoration."

Cortes smiled. "We Spaniards suffer a disease of the heart that can only be cured with gold."

Teudile had no reason to doubt the foreigner's explanation. It seemed like a harmless comment at the time.

* * *

Cuitlalpitoc remained in the Cortes camp while Teudile journeyed to Tenochtitlan carrying the news, pictures, and gifts for Moctezuma. He stayed with several attendants in huts not far from those of Cortes, and his servants brought food to Cortes and his most valued subordinates, including the Alvarado brothers, Alonso Puertocarrero, and his interpreter-slave Marina. The rest of the four hundred Cortes men, however, had to gather shellfish or catch ocean fish for sustenance. In the humid environment, their cassava bread had turned sour from the dampness, had become moldy and filled with weevils, unfit to eat. They bartered for a few fowls from Indians who came to them from the towns, but mostly the Indians brought jewelry and stones of little value to trade for the beads of the Spaniards. Feeling hungry and deprived, some of the men began to grumble that they wanted to return to Cuba.

* * *

Six or seven days later Teudile returned with over a hundred Indians, laden with gifts from Moctezuma. They spread the gifts on mats covered with cotton cloths, dazzling Cortes and his troops with their magnificence. The first was a golden wheel, the size of a cart wheel, carved with many symbols and pictures. Those who weighed it afterwards declared it worth a fortune in pesos. Another wheel, even larger, made of silver to represent the moon, was so heavy that five strong men could barely lift it.

Faithful to his promise, Teudile also brought the helmetful of gold nuggets Cortes had requested, just as they had come from the mines. Because these nuggets proved there were gold mines in Mexico, Cortes valued them even more than the beautiful articles of cast or beaten gold shaped like jaguars, monkeys, ducks, dogs, and other animals. The bearers brought thirty loads of beautiful cotton cloth, woven in various patterns, decorated with colored feathers. The Spaniards admired these gifts in absolute awe.

Cortes again pressed his request for an audience with the emperor, but Moctezuma's reply was disappointing. Teudile relayed Moctezuma's many flattering remarks about the valiant men who had come to Tabasco and their great king whose fame had spread over so many lands, but he said they should not worry about an audience with the emperor. It was not necessary, and the emperor wished them to stay where they were.

Cortes protested, through Aguilar and Marina, that he and his men had come from distant lands across many seas experiencing great hardships. He said if they returned without having seen the emperor personally, they would not be well received in the court of King Charles. The king had specifically charged them with the responsibility of meeting the emperor, he argued.

Cortes' arguments contained exaggeration bordering on falsehood. In fact, King Charles had never heard of Moctezuma, but Cortes had become adept at persuasion and relished the challenge of changing people's minds, even if he had to stretch the truth. The trick was in convincing himself first; then others would get caught up in his convictions. His strategy did not work this time, not with underlings. So he became even more determined to see this shy Mexican monarch and to discover his sources of gold and silver. Ironically, the gifts intended to pacify the invaders had only whetted their appetite for more.

Trying not to show his disappointment, Cortes said many flattering things about the envoys and their generous emperor. Apologizing for their relative poverty, since they had little space on their ships to carry treasures, Cortes gifted the envoys with shirts made of Holland linen and sent the emperor a gilt-edged glass cup made of Florentine ware, engraved with trees and hunting scenes. He begged the envoys to ask once more for an audience with the emperor. They agreed to convey that request but made it clear they considered it futile. Their emperor or tlatoani, "the one who speaks for all," had spoken.

* * *

As soon as the messengers had departed for the Valley of Mexico, Cortes sent two ships to explore the coast and find an area suitable for establishing a port and settlement. They turned back when strong currents made their navigation too hazardous, creating another disappointment for the adventurer.

More disappointments ensued. The hungry Spanish soldiers complained that Cuitlalpitoc's Indians were leaving them to their own devices to find food. Soldiers who had been bartering with sailors for fish began bartering for gold from the Indians, and strife arose among them as to who should be allowed to trade for gold. Cortes listened to the complaints and settled the disagreements in a show of strong leadership, but he was unhappy with the malcontents, and they knew it.

The biggest disappointment of all came when Teudile returned for the last time. He brought ten loads of fine feather cloth and four green jadestones, esteemed more valuable than emeralds by the Aztecs. He brought more gold items, estimated to be worth thousands of pesos. But as to the personal interview with Moctezuma, the answer was an unequivocal "no" and a command not to send any more messengers to Mexico.

Because it was time for the Ave Maria, a bell sounded and the soldiers fell to their knees before a cross planted in a sand hill. Cuitlalpitoc and Teudile looked at each other in amazement, and Teudile, the more talkative one, voiced their curiosity. "Why do your soldiers humble themselves before a tree cut in this particular way?" he asked.

Cortes saw an opportunity. He turned to Father Olmedo and said, "Father, we have our interpreters here. This would be an excellent time to explain to Moctezuma's people the essential precepts of our faith."

The padre agreed, but seeing that Cortes wanted to do it himself, he invited Cortes to deliver the discourse on his faith to the Mexican envoys. Using the full range of his voice and gesturing with hands and arms to add force to his message, Cortes impressed his own troops with his eloquence as well as the envoys. With missionary zeal, he told them he would give them an image of the Virgin Mary that they could place alongside a cross in their capital city. "Then you will see how things go well with you," he promised.

Then he turned to exhortations. "Our great King has sent us to your country to tell you to abolish human sacrifices and other evil rites you practice," he said in great earnestness. "Also, do not rob one another, and do not worship those cursed images of your pagan gods."

Marina found herself in a dilemma at that moment. She had translated the words of Cortes dutifully except that she left out the word "cursed," which had no true equivalent in Nahuatl and could have been interpreted as an insult. She could see the puzzlement on the faces of the Mexican envoys, who were clearly intelligent men. They did not seem insulted by this criticism of their beliefs, but they looked at each other quizzically. Teudile commented to Cuitlalpitoc, "I think there is no difference between worshipping an image of Huitzilopochtli and honoring an image of the Virgin Mary."

When Aguilar asked Marina what Teudile had said, she hesitated to translate the cynical remark, so she chose a more tactful version: "He said he is thinking about all this," she said. When that comment was relayed to Cortes, he smiled pleasantly at Teudile, and each man believed his wisdom was appreciated by the other.

* * *

As he began to realize Marina's worth and to think about marching to Mexico contrary to Moctezuma's wishes, Cortes instructed Alonso Puertocarrero to keep Marina beside him every night for protection, not to let her sleep with other slaves. Even though the soldiers as a group treated her with great respect, Cortes realized that some of his men were becoming disgruntled and restless to return to Cuba. If any harm came to Marina, his loss of her would benefit his enemies.

Marina felt privileged that she and Puertocarrero had a shelter of their own, even a cloth cover to provide a barrier to mosquitos and a little privacy. Puertocarrero was a man of exceptional self-discipline who carried out every order promptly and unquestioningly. He expected the same degree of obedience from her, but he did not mistreat her. His frequent use of profanity confused Marina as she compared his language to Olmedo's, but she quickly deduced that her master's oaths were quite meaningless.

She sought ways to be helpful to Puertocarrero when she was not needed for interpreting. She cut a suit of armor for him from some of the quilted cotton they had received as tribute. At first she used a flint knife, but Puertocarrero showed her how to use metal scissors. He gave her a metal needle, so much more durable than a cactus thorn that it became a prized possession. She had no need to cook while the natives were supplying them with food, but she did wash her master's clothes.

Actually, he changed clothes very infrequently compared to other men she had known, except of course the pochteca or certain priests who went without bathing as a penance. Marina thought Puertocarrero smelled bad, but no more so than most Spaniards. They considered bathing a weakness because of the emphasis placed upon it by the Moors they had recently driven out of Spain. As a purely practical matter, moreover, the soldiers often slept fully dressed so they could spring into action if they were suddenly attacked. On the swampy coast, clothing also gave some protection from stinging and biting insects.

Marina, too, covered her body with her mantle at night to discourage mosquitos. When Puertocarrero reached under it to touch her intimately, she understood his need without words and removed her skirt obligingly. She learned to breathe in such a way that unfamiliar odors did not bother her. She continued to practice the slave skills she had learned while living with her Mayan master: to pretend she was somewhere else, to think about other things, until her duty was done and her master satisfied.

* * *

One morning the Spanish soldiers awoke to find every Indian gone from their camp. Teudile had brought word that Moctezuma was no longer concerned about the invaders, commanding his subjects to ignore the foreigners' teachings about the cross and the Virgin Mary. He said Moctezuma's gods and priests had answered his prayers and questions about the Spaniards, assuring him they were not gods after all, despite the perplexing omens. If the Spaniards did not take their ships and leave, Moctezuma intended to have them captured and sacrificed to the Sun God.

247

Fearful that the Indians' departure meant they were planning war, the guards at the camp became especially alert. Three days later, Bernal Diaz and another soldier were positioned on a sand dune as lookouts when five Indians came along the beach. Because they were dressed differently than the Indians who had decamped, and they carried no weapons, Diaz let them approach without sounding any alarms. He noticed large holes in their lower lips, some containing small disks spotted with blue, others containing thin leaves of gold. Some had elongated pierced ears, from which pendants hung down weighted with gold or decorative stones.

Smiling and making gestures of respect, the Indians, who were from a Totonac tribe, indicated their wish to be taken into camp. Diaz left the other soldier on guard and led the Totonacs to Cortes. Then he summoned Marina and Aguilar.

"Lope luzio," said the Totonacs repeatedly as they made gestures of respect to Cortes. Neither Aguilar nor Marina could understand Totonac dialects, but they inferred these words to be terms of respect.

Marina asked in Nahuatl, "Are there any Nahuatlaca among you, who speak the language of Mexico?"

Two of the Indians replied that they understood Nahuatl, and through Marina they delivered a message from their chief. "Our chief has sent us to welcome you and learn about you," said their spokesperson. "He would have sent greetings sooner, but you were surrounded by our enemies the Cholulans."

Cortes was intrigued to hear that Moctezuma had enemies nearby. Their village, he learned, was called Cempoala. Even more important, their cacique hated Moctezuma, despised the Mexica in Tenochtitlan far away, and mistrusted the Cholulans nearby, who were vassals of Moctezuma.

Cortes said complimentary things to the messengers and gave them presents for themselves and their cacique. He promised to pay them a visit soon. Apparently, he thought, animosities and alliances characterized all human societies, and he might use the schisms among the Indian tribes to his advantage, once he had dealt with the schisms developing in his own army.

* * *

When Cortes proceeded with plans to build a permanent settlement, the loyalty of his subordinates was put to a test. He had already chosen a name for the city—Villa Rica de la Vera Cruz, the "Rich City of the True Cross"—to reflect his two primary goals, riches and religion, in the country he was already calling New Spain.

Only one site had been located that seemed suitable for a permanent settlement. About twenty-five miles to the northwest,

Francisco de Montejo had found a place with a source of fresh water, a large rock that could provide wind shelter for the ships, and enough flat land to build housing. A neighboring Indian village, Quiahuitztlan, could supply food and a labor force. Cortes ordered the captains to sail to that site, which they did, but with some reluctance. He planned to take the horses overland, with a sizeable number of armed men, toward the fortress-like town of Quiahuitztlan, meeting the sailors at the site proposed for Villa Rica de la Vera Cruz.

Certain critics of Cortes began to meet in secret and spread complaints that he was exceeding his authority, that Velasquez had not given permission to settle but only to trade, and that Cortes was supposed to return to Cuba as soon as he had acquired as much gold and wealth as he could by trade. These men thought they had wealth enough to return to Cuba and put an end to their hardships. Thirty-five men had died of wounds incurred in the Tabasco battles, and many others were demoralized.

Supporters of Cortes also met in secret, formulating a plan that would circumvent their orders from Diego Velasquez not to build a settlement. These included Alonso Puertocarrero, Marina's owner; Bernal Diaz, who later wrote his memoirs of the conquest; Cristobal de Olid, commander of an earlier expedition to Yucatan; Alonso de Avila; Juan de Escalante; Francisco de Lugo; and the five Alvarado brothers—Pedro, Jorge, Gonzalo, Gomez, and Juan. These men feared that if they returned to Cuba, Diego Velasquez would claim all the gold they had won, just as he had done from the Grijalva expedition, leaving nothing for the men who had risked their lives. Under the initial agreement, Velasquez was entitled to one-fifth of the expedition's profits, as was King Charles, but supporters of Cortes thought his risk-taking entitled him, rather than Velasquez, to have the second fifth. They thought the balance of the treasure should be divided equally among the conquistadors and investors.

The plan involved a transfer of allegiance from Velasquez directly to the King. Since Cortes had claimed the territory in the name of King Charles, his supporters repudiated Grijalva's earlier claim in the name of Velasquez, who had been merely a lieutenant governor of Cuba at the time, subordinate to Governor Diego Colon of the West Indies. They voted to name Hernan Cortes Captain General and Chief Justice of the new territory, Pedro de Alvarado as captain of expeditions, Cristobal de Olid as quartermaster, Juan de Escalante as chief Alguacil Mayor (High Constable), Gonzalo Mejia as treasurer, and Alonso de Avila as accountant. Cortes also insisted that a few high offices be given to men who had shown some resistance to him in the past, because he wanted to win them over.

When the relatives, friends, and other supporters of

Velasquez heard of this plan, they expressed outrage. Complaining that they had not been consulted, they demanded to return to Cuba and refused any obedience to Cortes.

Cortes took a bold step. He resigned as leader of the expedition, severing all responsibility to Velasquez. He placed the most intransigent of the Velasquez men in prison aboard ship, but he released them as soon as he was able to persuade them to support his plans, through cajolery or bribery or both.

Then Cortes, with well-armed soldiers and horses, began his march toward Quiahuitztlan, to explore the territory, to seek food supplies, and to pay a visit to the cacique of Cempoala, whose city they would pass along the way. They marched along the shore some distance through sandy stretches and dunes, enjoying occasional glimpses of the magnificent mountain Orizaba, but finding little to eat except a large fish they found thrown ashore by the waves. They reached a large river, which they named Rio de la Antigua. They crossed it with difficulty, some by swimming, some with the aid of broken canoes found on its banks, some on makeshift rafts contrived for the horses.

The countryside became greener as they marched north and westward along the river. They passed groves of feathery palms and cacao trees, also wide rolling meadows where they found some deer grazing. Alvarado and some of the horsemen chased one deer and wounded it, but did not succeed in killing it. The men were also encouraged by the sight of pheasants and wild turkeys, which reminded them of peacocks, but they were growing hungry after two days with very little food.

* * *

Entering the deserted Indian town of Cotaxtla looking for food, Pedro de Alvarado and a hundred soldiers under his authority, mostly dissidents that Cortes wanted to keep busy, found a shocking sight. In the *cue*, or stone temple, lay the bodies of men and boys who had been sacrificed that morning. Most of the bodies consisted of armless and legless torsos with dark red holes gaping in their chests where the hearts had been torn out. The hearts had been deposited in stone receptacles before the idols. The receptacles, walls, and stone altars were stained with blood, as were several stone knives strewn about. The sight sickened even battle-hardened soldiers.

Searching through the deserted village, Alvarado discovered plentiful amounts of vegetables and poultry abandoned by the inhabitants. He could find only two Indians to carry maize, so he loaded each soldier with whatever food items he could carry back to Villa Rica. Although they helped themselves to the food, Alvarado's men did no other damage. Under strict orders from Cortes not to repeat the offenses Alvarado had sanctioned in

Cozumel, they left the temple as it was, strewn with the corpses of sacrifice victims.

This grim scene at Cotaxtla was repeated in several other small towns in the area. All had been deserted that same day; all showed evidence of ritual sacrifices that morning. When Alvarado returned to camp, located interpreters, and questioned the two Indian carriers, one of them said that the victims' arms and legs had been taken away to be eaten. He said the natives had fled because they were frightened by the horses and strange men they had seen coming toward them. They offered sacrifices before leaving so the gods would protect them.

Rumors of the cannibalism spread quickly throughout the camp, horrifying the soldiers and increasing the desire of some discouraged men to go home. In that way these findings worked against Cortes, but on the other hand, they convinced the Spaniards that the Mexican religion was akin to devil-worship, making them eager to destroy it with a sense of rectitude. Also, the food Alvarado brought back filled their bellies and made them more content than they had been in some time.

* * *

As they continued their march through lush fields and forests, the soldiers found several more deserted villages with evidence of recent sacrifices, the gore contrasting markedly with the beauty of the countryside. Following the orders of Cortes, however, they left sacred objects intact in the idol houses, including books made with folded bark paper containing strange painted images and incomprehensible glyphs.

While they were making camp one night in a meadow near the stream, twelve Indians approached carrying food. They told Cortes through his interpreters that their cacique had sent them to lead the Spaniards to Cempoala. Early the next morning, Cortes sent six Cempoalans ahead to inform the cacique they were coming, keeping the other six as guides.

Encouraged by the hope of warm welcome, the soldiers became more aware of the tropical beauty around them. They marched past stately trees adorned with grape-bearing vines and brilliant flowering parasites. They chopped their way through undergrowth of prickly aloe, wild rose, and honeysuckle. They heard the excellent songs of scarlet cardinals and mockingbirds. Marina, riding behind Puertocarrero on his horse, was especially charmed by the colorful parrots and dancing swarms of butterflies.

As they came within a league of Cempoala, twenty Indian officials came to welcome them for their cacique, bringing cones filled with bouquets of bright flowers to give to each horseman. As they walked into the city, the soldiers marveled again at the

251

gardens, which they called a "terrestrial paradise," and thanked God for having discovered such a country.

Two scouts had been sent ahead on horseback to see that quarters were being prepared for the army. They had not gone the full distance before turning and galloping back in great excitement, exclaiming, "The houses' walls are made of silver!"

Marina laughed when Aguilar translated that message to her. "Surely the walls are just whitewashed with lime, and polished until they shine." Aguilar and Puertocarrero laughed too, and from that time on they joked with the scouts that everything white looked silver to them.

When they reached the white buildings, a fat cacique came to welcome them in the courtyard. He was so heavy that two men stood beside him to hold him erect. He bowed deeply to Cortes and waved a censer of copal around him. Cortes and all his soldiers were then escorted to large apartments and fed corncakes and ripe plums, hospitality which the ravenous travelers heartily welcomed.

When they had finished eating, the fat cacique came to their quarters accompanied by a number of minor officials, all wearing rich mantles, their lower lips ornamented with gold labrets. He presented Cortes with a few pieces of jewelry and several pieces of cloth.

"Honorable Lord," said the fat cacique in Totonac, "accept this small gift with my best intentions. If I had more I would give it to you, but the calpixqui of Moctezuma have carried off all my family's jewels and gold."

This cacique's words underwent three translations: from Totonac to Nahuatl, then to Mayan, and then to Spanish. Although this process took considerable time, Cortes gained important information. The Cempoalans and their affiliated towns had recently fallen under the yoke of the Aztecs and felt grievously oppressed. They did not dare oppose Moctezuma because he ruled over countless vassals and huge armies.

Cortes conveyed through the interpreters that he wished to repay the kindness of the Cempoalans with good deeds, and that once he was settled in his new headquarters, he would consider how best to help his generous hosts. The cacique was satisfied with this promise, and the exhausted Spaniards retired.

The next morning, to the great delight of the soldiers, four hundred Indian tamemes were waiting to carry their backpacks, their food supply, and other provisions. Marina explained to Aguilar and Cortes that, in times of peace, a cacique was expected to provide tamemes for his guests, as a courtesy. Once aware of this custom, the Spaniards felt free to ask for tamemes whenever they left a hospitable village.

* * *

252

Unsure what resistance they might encounter when they approached the fortress-city of Quiahuitztlan, Cortes positioned his artillery in front of the column of soldiers and ordered his musketeers and crossbowmen to keep their weapons ready. They reached the city on the second day after leaving Cempoala, but to their surprise, it was almost deserted. Entering cautiously, Cortes found fifteen Indians in the plaza, well dressed and ready to welcome him with incense braziers.

One of these officials who spoke Nahuatl explained that their citizens had fled in fear of Spaniards and their horses, but after a messenger arrived from Cempoala to reassure them, they decided the Spaniards were welcome to stay and rest. The officials said they would encourage their people to return that night, because the cacique from Cempoala would be coming there with caciques from other towns.

The cacique arrived that afternoon as promised, carried in a litter by several husky tamemes, accompanied by a number of other important personages. Again that evening Cortes listened to grievances from many caciques whose sufferings moved him and his interpreters to pity. With tears and anguished voices, the aggrieved leaders told of being conquered by Moctezuma's warriors, then forced to send many of their sons and daughters every year for the Aztecs to use as sacrifices or slaves. In addition, Moctezuma's tax-gatherers, the infamous calpixqui, carried off and ravished any wife or daughter they desired.

Cortes responded sympathetically, "Our great King Charles is the earthly head of the Christian faith. He has sent us to help you, to prevent these robberies and cruel practices, and to teach you about our powerful faith."

The caciques seemed somewhat reassured, but their glances toward each other showed lingering uneasiness. While this conversation was going on, some Indians from the town rushed in with great excitement, saying that five of Moctezuma's calpixqui were approaching. Trembling with fear and deserting their guests, the caciques hastily began to prepare chocolate for the tax-gatherers, to cook food for them, and to decorate the room with flowers and fragrant branches.

Marina observed the fervid activity and commented to Aguilar, "Whatever fears these people may have of Spaniards or horses, they fear the calpixqui more. The calpixqui don't even carry weapons; their greatest weapon is the fear in the hearts of their victims."

Chapter 20

Marina Becomes Indispensable

The five calpixqui swaggered into the fortress-city of Quiahuitztlan smelling nosegays of fresh flowers as if the stench of this town, home to 20,000 vassals of Moctezuma, offended their nostrils. Each calpixque carried a crooked staff in one hand, symbol of his authority as the emperor's tax-gatherer. They wore their shining black hair tied in an authoritative top-knot, their richly-woven mantles fastened at the shoulder with golden clasps. Servants walked beside them, fanning the air with fly-whisks. Arrogantly they breezed past the Spaniards as if the foreigners were too worthless to deserve notice.

The tax-gatherers were immediately shown to their quarters in a shining white building. As soon as they had eaten the food brought to them by the villagers, they summoned the caciques and scolded them for hosting Spaniards in their houses. Moctezuma would be displeased, they said, to learn that these foreigners had been sheltered without his permission.

The caciques made no defense, but silently endured their chastisement. They winced, but did not protest, when the calpixqui announced the punishment for such a breech of loyalty: twenty men and twenty women must be provided as sacrifices to Huitzilopochtli, god of war and the sun.

"Every year they demand more," the fat cacique Chicomacatl complained later to Cortes and his interpreters. "They use your presence here as an excuse to demand more captives. They say Moctezuma needs Huitzilopochtli's favor so he can capture all the Spaniards and make slaves of them."

Cortes snorted like a horse. "Ha! They've never fought a Spanish army, I can see that."

"Be careful, my friend," warned the cacique. "They have thousands of warriors, enough to overpower your small force."

"One Spanish soldier is worth a hundred of theirs," Cortes boasted. "But tell me, could we join forces with the people they've been persecuting? Have the caciques in this region tried to unite against the tyrants?"

"There are fifty towns in this region. We could probably gather ten thousand warriors, but some would be young boys."

"That's quite an army."

"Not enough. Moctezuma can rally two hundred thousand from the towns he controls."

"Does he control every town and city in Mexico?" asked Cortes in exasperation. "Surely some people have resisted him."

"The Tlaxcalans, high in the mountains to the west. Their terrain is easier to defend than ours. They fought so fiercely for so long that Moctezuma's forces just gave up."

"What one brave group does, another can do," Cortes said emphatically. "You must resist the oppressors. I've told you our king sent us here to help you chastise evil doers. We'll back you up with our cannons, our muskets, our steel swords, and our fine cavalry forces."

Chicomacatl looked hopeful, then downcast. "We don't have time," he said. "They'll send an army to crush us if we don't deliver forty slaves to the calpixqui tomorrow."

"You have five unarmed Aztecs here now," Cortes argued. "You could easily arrest them and imprison them for their crimes. Send a proclamation abroad to all the Totonac leaders to refuse to pay any more tribute to Moctezuma."

The two leaders debated the suggestion for some time, Cortes urging, Chicomacatl worrying. But in the end the cacique was convinced. He left the apartment, leaning his weight on two attendants, and ordered the imprisonment of the calpixqui. As a special humiliation, since further insult would not increase his punishment, he had them put in collars attached to long poles, as they would do with captured slaves, so they could not run away.

* * *

Cortes detained Marina and Aguilar after Chicomacatl had left. "I have a plan," he said, "but I need your cooperation."

Both interpreters pledged to do whatever was needed. Marina, excited about resisting the hated calpixqui, could feel the blood surging in her arms and head. She told Aguilar and Cortes about her childhood experience of seeing the calpixqui snatch little Moyo away from his parents, the macehual couple who had served her father.

Cortes listened attentively. He began to understand the complexity of Marina's background, how she had been raised with servants and taught the customs of the Aztec ruling classes by her parents. He observed her facial features closely: her fine smooth skin, arched eyebrows, curved lips. He realized that, if she had been dressed more elegantly, she would be regarded by any healthy man as a beautiful woman.

"I can see why you hate the calpixqui," he said after he had heard Marina's story. "That may make it more difficult for you to understand my plan, but trust me and you'll be happy with the outcome." Then he addressed both Marina and Aguilar. "When you translate tonight, it may seem to you that I'm telling some falsehoods. Don't appear to question anything I say, either by your words or your faces."

Marina and Aguilar agreed, and that night they made their faces as inscrutable as stone. So well did Marina learn to convey the words of Cortes to others without showing any reaction to them, that most of the Indians came to think of the translated words as her own. The time was not far off when the Indians would think of these two as being so inseparable that they spoke with one voice.

* * *

Cortes had offered two of his own soldiers to guard the calpixqui because the nervous cacique had wanted to kill them to keep them from revealing what had happened. At midnight, when everyone else was asleep, Cortes sent Aguilar to summon one of these Spanish guards. Cortes told the guard to select two of the five Aztecs who seemed most intelligent, to loosen their bonds in such a way that the Indians of Quiahuitztlan would not detect it, then to bring the two Aztecs to his quarters.

When this was done, Cortes pretended to know nothing about the prisoners and to be curious about them. He asked them through his interpreters who they were and what country they came from. Marina and Aguilar, as agreed, gave no sign or expression of surprise at what Cortes was saying or pretending.

When the prisoners told Cortes who they were, adding that they had been unjustly imprisoned by conspiring Totonac chiefs, Cortes sympathized with them and had Marina bring them food. He told them he would sneak them aboard a boat with six of his trusted sailors and have them rowed to a safe place several leagues away from the angry Totonacs. In return for helping the Aztecs escape, he asked that they go immediately to their lord Moctezuma, tell him that the Spaniards were his good friends and would place themselves gladly in his service, if he would but make his wishes known. Cortes also promised to see that the remaining three prisoners would be set free and returned safe from harm. The Aztecs, relieved and grateful, thanked him for his mercy and promised to carry his message to Moctezuma.

* * *

When morning came and Chicomacatl found two of the Aztecs missing, he was determined to sacrifice the remaining three.

"I'm disgusted with my men for letting the prisoners escape," Cortes said, feigning anger. "What kind of guards would do such a poor job of watching? I'll discipline them in my own way. Have the other three prisoners taken in chains to my ship, where I can guard them myself. Who can be trusted?" The cacique, who had already sent word around the Totonac territories that the Spaniards must be gods because of their power to defy tyrants, yielded to the silver tongue of Cortes. Once aboard ship, however, unknown to the caciques on land, Cortes ordered the chains removed from the three Aztecs. They were allowed to move about the ship, but he kept them on board in case they should be needed as hostages.

Later, when the group of caciques assembled and wondered what they would do if Moctezuma launched an attack, Cortes reassured them in his most cheerful, confident manner. "King Charles is a much more powerful lord than Moctezuma," he said. "If you were to pledge your loyalty to him, he would protect you from Moctezuma or any other ruler who does you harm."

Therefore, as the scribe Diego de Godoy recorded their oaths, the caciques pledged obedience to his majesty King Charles of Spain. They further agreed to form an alliance with Cortes' forces against Moctezuma, and to obey all orders of the Spanish captains. They went away quite happy, certain they would never again pay tribute to the Aztecs. Unable to envision a future time when the swords and crosses of Spain would crush the entire Indian population, the oppressed along with the oppressors, the Totonacs congratulated themselves on overthrowing a tyrant. They felt very fortunate to have powerful friends like the Spanish god-men, the *teules*.

* * *

After the federation of twenty hill towns had been cemented, Cortes proceeded with building Villa Rica de la Vera Cruz. Although normally as averse to hard labor as any hidalgo, he set an example for his own men, carrying earth and stone on his back, digging foundations, placing stones in walls. His carpenters turned logs into usable lumber; his two blacksmiths made nails. Every man had a task, either making bricks and tiles, working in the lime kilns, or fishing for food. Aided by the donated labor of Indians from nearby towns, the Spaniards erected the rudiments of a town within a few weeks. They built a church, a stockade, an arsenal, a marketplace, a meeting hall, and even a gallows.

The women slaves, including Marina, did cooking and laundry, as they had always done. They also made suits of quilted cotton for their masters, all of whom had come to prefer the lightweight quilted armor over the heavy metal suits from

Europe.

At night Marina stayed near Puertocarrero, enjoying his protection, though by then he had other slaves to satisfy his sexual needs. She thought he had grown tired of her, but perhaps it was just as well, for the sex act held no pleasure for her. Actually, Puertocarrero was attracted to her, but he feared the possibility of getting her pregnant. A child would demand her attention and care, putting her in conflict over traveling with the Spaniards. Puertocarrero could see how necessary to the success of the expedition her linguistic talents would be. He could not explain that to her, because she did not yet speak his language, and he could speak neither of hers.

* * *

In Tenochtitlan, Moctezuma heard the news of the rebellion by the Totonacs and the capture of his tax-gatherers. Furious at such effrontery, and especially angry with the meddlesome foreigner Cortes, he assembled a great army to march against the Totonacs and capture the Spaniards. Just at that time his two tax-gatherers arrived, saying they had been rescued by Cortes. They were so sincere in their gratitude that Moctezuma's anger subsided, and he resolved to learn more about this unpredictable bearded white man.

The emperor sent two young nephews, high-ranking pilli who had already distinguished themselves in military matters, to present Cortes with gifts of gold and cloth and thank him for freeing his calpixqui. Cortes accepted these gifts, worth thousands of pesos, and embraced the envoys. As proof of his good will toward Moctezuma, he released into their care the three Aztecs he was still holding aboard his ship. He also entertained the young envoys, along with four elder warriors who had accompanied them, by having Pedro de Alvarado gallop his sorrel mare and skirmish before them in a meadow.

The caciques of the Totonac towns were astonished to see these envoys of Moctezuma bringing presents to Cortes instead of sending an army against him. As they buzzed with gossip about these events, the reputation of the Spaniards as wizards or teules was greatly enhanced. The Totonacs were certain Cortes had worked some kind of magic upon the Aztecs.

* * *

Cortes was not the only clever manipulator in that land. Chicomacatl, the fat cacique from Cempoala, urged him to march against an old enemy, the cacique of Cingapacinga, who was reportedly harboring Mexicans from Cholula and plotting against the new federation of rebel Totonac towns. Cortes assembled two

258

thousand soldiers, Spanish and Totonac, but when they arrived at Cingapacinga, the town leaders came to Cortes and tearfully denied any wrongdoing. They accused the Cempoalans of trying to settle old grudges and boundary disputes with false charges.

By the time Cortes realized, through Marina's translation, that he had been tricked, the Cempoalans had begun looting the Cingapacinga farms. Cortes angrily demanded that all the loot be returned to the farms. He threatened to leave none of the Cempoalans alive if anything of this nature occurred again. His discipline blended thunder and justice.

Because of his integrity in that matter, the citizens of Cingapacinga came to trust Cortes. As they conversed with him, they complained bitterly about Moctezuma just as the Cempoalans had done. They were also willing to listen to Cortes and his interpreters explain Christianity to them and urge them to give up their idols. The Cingapacingans also influenced neighboring towns to think of the Spaniards as friends.

Marina marveled at Cortes's ability to make friends on both sides of ancient disputes, and even to get former enemies to cooperate with each other. Surely, she thought, even if he is mortal, the Christian god has given him special powers.

Marina was becoming adept at delivering the standard speech on the fundamentals of Christianity, infusing as much feeling into the words as did Cortes himself. Cortes listened to her melodious voice with fond approval and watched her animated face as she translated. She had also begun to memorize the Spanish version, and by the time she had been an interpreter for six months she could anticipate, from Cortes' Spanish words, what Aguilar would be relaying to her in Mayan.

Marina very much wanted to learn enough Spanish so that she could translate directly, without the cumbersome intermediary of a third language (sometimes a fourth, because several of the caciques spoke only Totonac). Also, since she had no one to talk to in Mayan except Aguilar and other slaves, she thought she would feel less lonely knowing Spanish. Spanish would open the door to conversation with Father Olmedo, a wise and kindly man who might teach her more about the new religion she had embraced. She had been baptized hastily, before she understood much about Christianity, but after translating the story of Jesus Christ many times, she became fascinated. His message of peace reminded her of Quetzalcoatl, who had also urged his followers to live peaceably together. But the differences were great, and they made Christ especially appealing to Marina. Christ had been born in a manger; he went about barefoot; he had no servants or fine houses as did the high priest Quetzalcoatl. Unlike the disheartened Quetzalcoatl, who had sailed away in disgrace with a promise to return, Christ had never lost heart. He had made sacrifices for others and had actually overcome the forces of death and darkness. With noble words he had forgiven his enemies, thus achieving an ironic triumph over his persecutors, the triumph of patient meekness over violent arrogance.

What a wonderful god-man this Jesus Christ must be, Marina thought, to care about women and children and slaves! She ached to learn more about his teachings. Since she had no one to teach her Spanish as Nemon had taught her Mayan, she listened carefully to the Spanish expressions used by Aguilar and Cortes. Aguilar, on the other hand, took no interest in learning Nahuatl, because he hoped soon to return to Spain where he would not need it.

On the way back to Cempoala, the Spanish soldiers stopped to rest, for the heat of the sun and the weight of their backpacks and muskets had wearied them. A soldier took two chickens from a nearby farmhouse, not realizing that Cortes was watching and that he had just scolded the Cempoalans harshly about looting. When Cortes saw his own soldier's thievery, he became so angry that he ordered a halter put around the thief's neck. The soldier might have died from hanging by the halter, but when the poor man was nearly half dead, Pedro de Alvarado took pity on him and cut the halter with his sword. Cortes ignored Alvarado's intervention because he had made his point, and his temper never lasted long. When they arrived in Cempoala, Chicomacatl and other Cempoalan lords awaited him remorsefully. Fearful that the Totonacs might lose the Spaniards' friendship over this incident, they provided especially nice quarters for the Spanish soldiers. To make further amends, they brought eight young cacicas, daughters of caciques, as gifts to Cortes and his men. The maidens were clothed in rich garments, beautifully woven with regional designs. Each cacica wore a golden collar and earrings. Each came accompanied by a servant to serve her after marriage.

The fat cacique Chicomacatl said to Cortes, "Seven of these women are for your captains, to have children by them and cement our friendship. But this last one, who is my niece, is for you. She is the mistress of towns and vassals."

Marina hid a smile behind her hand, because she had never seen Cortes so embarrassed. Chicomacatl's niece was the least attractive of the group, a girl with big ears, a flat face, and dull, stringy hair. Marina wondered how Cortes would extricate himself from this delicate situation without offending his host.

Cortes was equal to the challenge. "I thank you for this generous offer," he said solemnly. "My captains may not accept, however, nor can I, because all of us have sworn not to have children by women who aren't Christians." Cortes then launched into his pet grievance. Every day, he told the caciques, his men saw four or five Indians who had been sacrificed, butchered, and their limbs devoured in an evil practice related to idol worship. Cortes said if the lords and their daughters gave up these evil practices and became Christians, they would not only keep the Spaniards' friendship but become lords over other provinces. One cacique protested that they could not give up their idols. These gods, he said, gave them everything they needed for health and good harvests. A priest who was present became angry at the idea of abolishing sacrifices, for he was certain all good things came from faithful adherence to such rituals. Others joined the chorus of disapproval.

Much irritated by their resistance, Cortes decided the idols would have to come down to prove how ineffectual the carved images were. He ordered his men, who were armed and prepared for battle, to ascend the temple stairs and push over the idols.

Immediately fifty soldiers clambered to the top of the cue, knocked over the huge idols, and rolled them down the steps. When the caciques and priests saw their idols splintering into pieces, they wept and prayed, begging their gods to pardon them, for they were unable to resist the overpowering teules.

Cortes commanded the soldiers to gather the pieces and splinters, take them out of sight and burn them. As they began this work, eight priests came out of a chamber and took over that task, showing solemn reverence for the fragments. They wore black cloaks like cassocks and long gowns covered with caked blood. Some of them had hair hanging to their waists, some to their feet, all of it matted and blood-caked. They smelled like sulphur or carrion. Marina explained that they abstained from women as well as from bathing. Cortes and his men could well believe it.

The next morning Cortes ordered all the masons in the town to bring plenty of lime to the cue, to cleanse the walls of blood and whitewash them. He ordered four of the priests to cut their hair, change their dirty black garments for clean white ones, and to keep themselves clean thereafter. He had a stone support built and plastered over, then a tall cross placed on it by his carpenters. As the caciques watched this process with sadness, Cortes explained that they were brothers now and allies against Moctezuma, so would leave with them a lady who would protect them—the Virgin Mary, mother of Jesus Christ their savior.

The next morning, which was Sunday, Father Olmedo said mass at the new altar. He burned incense near the image of the Virgin and the sacred cross. Olmedo and his chaplain, Juan Diaz, showed the Indians how to make candles from the native bees wax, and advised them always to keep candles burning on the altar.

Parents and uncles then brought forward the eight Indian maidens who were to be made Christians. After hearing much advice and instruction in the faith, the girls were baptized.

Chicomacatl, when his niece was asked to choose a Christian name, asked Cortes what his mother's name was, that his niece might honor her. "Catalina," Cortes replied, and so the ugly girl became Dona Catalina, the fourth woman in his life to be named Catalina. Carried in his litter, Chicomacatl led his niece by the hand and presented her to Cortes, who tried to look pleased.

Then Cortes did another clever thing. After assigning six maidens to various captains, he presented the most beautiful one to Alonso Puertocarrero. The lovely cacica, who had taken the Christian name of Francisca, was the daughter of the respected cacique Cuesco. Puertocarrero had no difficulty looking pleased.

"Keep Dona Francisca with you each night and have children by her to cement our friendship with her father," said Cortes. What he did not say, but what was clearly understood between the two men, was that Marina would be replaced by the beautiful Francisca in Puertocarrero's quarters. From that time on, Marina would serve only one conquistador and be entitled to his personal protection: the Captain-General and Chief Justice of the new settlement of Villa Rica de la Vera Cruz, Hernan Cortes.

* * *

By the end of July, 1519, Puertocarrero and Montejo had been dispatched to Spain with their share of the expedition's profits, about two thousand pesos' worth of gold. They were given the best ship in the fleet and the most experienced pilot, Alaminos. They were entrusted with an important mission: to convey to King Charles all the gold and precious goods that had been collected thus far by the Cortes expedition, to dazzle the King with this treasure and persuade him to favor the claim of Cortes over that of his rival, Governor Velasquez of Cuba. Cortes hoped the King would name him governor of the new territory.

Cortes had persuaded all the conquistadors to sign an agreement to send the entire treasure, not just the one-fifth the king was entitled to, convincing them that more treasure lay ahead. He said it was more important to secure the king's permission to make permanent settlements than to divide the treasure among them all. By relinquishing his own share, Cortes set an example. His arguments prevailed, but supporters of Velasquez became irate over this decision, demanding louder than ever to return to Cuba.

Cortes had been struggling with the Velasquez faction in his own ranks for many months, each time persuading the dissidents that great riches lay in store if they would stick with him and march inland to Tenochtitlan, where Moctezuma ruled, where gold could easily be had.

Within four days after the departure of Puertocarrero and Montejo, some relatives and friends of Velasquez tried to seize a ship to return to Cuba. One of them repented the last minute, however, and informed Cortes. Cortes had the rebels arrested, and after they confessed, severely punished. One of two men sentenced to be hanged was Juan Escudero, who had once arrested Cortes for Velasquez in Cuba. Cortes had not forgotten.

The rebellious sailors were flogged two hundred lashes apiece, the pilot was sentenced to have his feet cut off (though Cortes later relented), and the chaplain Juan Diaz, apparently one of the chief instigators of the plot, was given a great fright before he was pardoned by Cortes as a favor to the church.

In order to leave no source of trouble behind, Cortes took another bold action, first discussing it with his captains so it appeared to be their idea. After removing from the ships everything that would be useful in the new settlement, from fishing nets and rowboats to cables and sails, Cortes scuttled the ships. He had holes drilled in them so they would sink slowly, leaving one of the five ships afloat until the others had foundered. He told those who insisted on returning to Cuba that they could take that last ship, for he would hold no man against his will. When he had a list of those whose homesickness would render them untrustworthy, when he knew which men would bear watching, he had the last ship scuttled also.

When the bulk of his soldiers, who were stationed in Cempoala five leagues distant, heard the ships had been sunk, many were alarmed to be cut off from retreat. Cortes was in great danger of rebellion by his men, but his eloquence again saved the day. Speaking to them after mass, he appealed to their religious faith, their patriotism, their pride, and their greed.

"My friends and companions," he said, "we have been together on this important expedition for over six months. We knew when we undertook the venture that we would face battles and hardships, discouragement and despair. At times we had nothing to rely on but our strength, our quick wits, and our faith in our savior Jesus Christ. Yet we endured, we persevered, we triumphed in ways the world has never seen before.

"Our journey is not yet done, my friends. God has sent us here to spread his holy word, to end the evils of idol worship and human sacrifice. He has rewarded us with treasure and territory, vassals and friends. He has given us a glimpse of the future, which holds glory for us, for Spain, and for the Christian faith. Our future lies in the west, over a landscape of high mountains and deep rivers.

"Some of our ships have become unseaworthy, and they had to be salvaged and sunk. But we will have no need of ships when we travel across land to the source of the greatest treasure in the world. I say to you that we can still rely on our good swords and stout hearts. We can conquer our hardships and our enemies, with the help of God and his Son and the Blessed Virgin. There is no turning back, no way to retreat with honor, but there is no doubt of our success if we stand by each other."

After that honied speech, doubts faded. All the soldiers were again ready to serve God and their king. "To Mexico!" they shouted. "To Mexico!"

Marina, listening to her master speak to his followers about the adventure and riches to come, felt a great thrill. It was not the gold that excited her, or even the prospect of travel to exotic lands, but the fact that she understood almost everything Cortes had said—in Spanish.

* * *

Cortes left a capable officer, Juan de Escalante, in command at Vera Cruz. The sailors from the scuttled ships were to keep busy fishing with their nets, and a few soldiers who were too old or weak to travel would remain also. Cortes contacted the caciques of the twenty neighboring towns for labor to continue the construction work under Escalante's direction.

These matters accomplished, Cortes departed for the town of Tlaxcala on August 16, 1519. The Cempoalans gave them directions and provided two hundred tamemes. They warned him against going through the city-state of Cholula, because even though the road was easier and more level, the Cholulans were loyal to Moctezuma. The road to Tlaxcala would take them over steep mountains, but the Tlaxcalans were known for fierce independence and refusal to submit to Aztec tyranny. Forty caciques from the Totonac towns accompanied the Cortes forces as guides and advisers.

Cortes headed the column of 400 foot soldiers, 15 horsemen, a thousand Totonac warriors commanded by three caciques, and 200 tamemes carrying artillery and supplies. The first few days they followed the Chachalacas river, enjoying the lush greenery, the heavy fragrance of hot country fruits and flowers, the color and music of tropical birds.

After traveling several leagues, the soldiers began the gradual ascent toward the tablelands, entering a subtropical zone where colorful flowers still abounded, but trees were taller—oaks, cedars, fragrant pines and gum trees. They passed Jalapa, named for the morning-glory vines whose roots could be used as medicine, and wound their way upward toward Naulinco.

Stopping at small towns along the way, the caciques in their company told the inhabitants that the Spanish were teules with powerful magic. In each town, after requesting food for the troops, Cortes gave his missionary speech and offered to leave a cross and a virgin for the villagers. The friendly natives of Naulinco accepted this offer, as did those in some other towns. Father Olmedo sometimes cautioned Cortes not to leave these symbols, if he perceived that the Indians were not ready to receive them and care for them properly. Olmedo had developed a kindly sensitivity to the Indians he converted; his thoughtful advice often tempered the ardor of Cortes, often saved him from making rash mistakes.

Continuing their climb, the soldiers wound around the spur of an extinct volcano, where acres of lava and cinder residue testified to its ancient convulsions. Shrubs and tree trunks growing in the crevices gave evidence of the regenerative powers of nature. Their path led often along precipices whose sheer depths of two or three thousand feet filled them with awe and made any slip of footing a precarious matter.

As they entered a rugged pass, cold winds blew down the mountainsides, mingled with rain. As they climbed higher, the rain turned to sleet and hail, drenching their garments. The Spaniards weathered the abrupt change of climate with only the discomfort of soaked cotton jackets, but several of the thinly clad tamemes died from exposure. Marina pulled her cape tightly around her and clenched her teeth in the cold as Father Olmedo said a prayer over the bodies of their fallen comrades.

After several days of travel they reached the great tableland, seven thousand feet above sea level. Signs of cultivation appeared, fields of maize, hedges of various cacti, and aloes with rich yellow clusters of flowers on tall stems. The climate was more temperate, but the elevation too high for cotton plants or cacao trees.

Ahead lay more mountain ranges, their slopes thick with forests. They saw occasional green valleys and high deserts spotted with the twisted gray-green arms of maguey plants. They came to Xocotla, a large town with handsome white buildings and thirteen temples, one of which appalled them with its skull rack displaying thousands of victims of past sacrifices. The cacique of Xocotla, named Olintetl or "shaking stone," was even fatter than the cacique of Cempoala; the slightest movement caused his flesh to quiver like jelly. He commanded twenty thousand vassals, thirty wives, a hundred concubines, and two thousand other attendants. He received Cortes with cool arrogance, an unfriendly demeanor, and a meager allotment of food.

When Cortes asked Olintetl whether he was a vassal of Moctezuma, he replied cynically, "Who is not?" When Cortes spoke of the greatness of King Charles, Olintetl countered that Moctezuma was even greater, that he commanded thirty lords each of whom could field an army of 100,000 men. His indifference to the *requerimiento*, or discourse on Christianity, led Father Olmedo to caution Cortes not to leave a cross or image in their town lest it be profaned after they left. Cortes wanted to destroy the idols in the temples where sacrifices were made, but again Olmedo dissuaded him.

Olintetl advised the travelers to go to Tenochtitlan by way of Cholula, a large center for trade and religion, not far from the Aztec capital. However, the Totonac caciques accompanying the Cortes forces did not trust Olintetl or the Cholulans, so they decided instead to follow the road to Tlaxcala.

The column of Spaniards and Totonacs threaded its way through heavily wooded mountains and then emerged into a valley six miles wide. Blocking the nearest end of this valley, and marking the borders of Tlaxcala, stood a huge stone wall, nine feet high and twenty feet thick, with battlements at regular intervals. Though undefended, this wall spoke forcefully of the determination to keep foreigners out of the territory.

Indians from other towns had carried news of the Spaniards' movements, so that the cacique of Tlaxcala and his warriors were lying in wait, prepared to fight. Since Cortes' army had gone through territory populated by vassals of Moctezuma, the Tlaxcalans assumed they were agents of Moctezuma trying to gain entrance by deception.

Two scouts who spoke Nahuatl were sent ahead with a message from Cortes and a fluffy red Flemish hat as a gift, but they were seized and imprisoned. After waiting two days for an answer, Cortes decided to proceed into the city anyway. As his army approached the town, the terrified scouts, who had just escaped, ran to Cortes in panic. "They are determined to kill those who call themselves teules," said one.

The other added, "They threaten to eat any person they kill. They will kill the horses too."

Considering the threat a challenge to his military prowess, Cortes unfurled his banner with the Holy Cross, warning his men to prepare for battle and pray as they marched. Two leagues further, they came upon a stone fortress so strongly cemented that even an iron pickaxe would not break it.

The Tlaxcalans, who had been spying on them as they advanced, attacked with great fury, using lances with fire-hardened points, arrows, stones, and the most fearsome weapon the Spaniards had seen in all Mexico—the *macana* or macahuitl. The macana was a wooden broadsword, wider at the top than near the handle, with pieces of sharp obsidian or flint imbedded in the edges of the top and sides.

With a macana, one Tlaxcalan wounded a rider and then slashed at his mare's neck. The horse's neck was severed so completely that her head hung by the skin, and she fell dead. Later the Tlaxcalans cut the horse to pieces and offered its horseshoes to their idol, along with the Flemish hat and the letters the scouts had brought from Cortes.

The Spaniards managed to drive the Tlaxcalans back. Then they took refuge in a deserted town with some high temples, which were strongly built and provided a good vantage point. There they dressed the wounds of fifteen men and five horses, using the grease from the body of a dead Indian, but one Spaniard died.

Marina endured this battle and several others while the four hundred men under Cortes struggled against a force of fifty thousand assembled by the captain-general of Tlaxcala, a man called Xicotenga. During the attacks stones flew like hailstorms from the slings of the warriors, and javelins lay on the stones of the cue like corn scattered on a granary floor. Cortes developed a fever, yet fought all day on his horse in spite of it. Messages from Xicotenga, delivered with food and insults, galled Cortes even more than the ambushes. The Tlaxcalans had proved to all the Indians of Mexico that these pale bearded men and their much-vaunted horses were mortal. Though thwarted by the Tlaxcalans' skill and determination, Cortes grudgingly admired such tenacious and challenging fighters.

Although Cortes kept her away from the battlefront as much as possible, Marina took on the role of pacifier. To a pair of captured Indians who were later freed, she spoke in friendly tones, giving them beads and asking them to convey messages of peace from the teules who wished to treat them like brothers.

After several more days of fighting, the Spaniards counted forty-five men dead and almost all of them wounded several times. Marina dressed the wounds and spoke comfortingly to the soldiers, earning their deep respect for her courage. She had never shown fear, though she heard every day that the Tlaxcalans outnumbered the Spanish forces and were coming to eat them. The soldiers grew weak, hungry, and tired. They began craving salt, which was in short supply. Cortes decided to send a messenger to Xicotenga offering to negotiate for peace, boldly adding a threat to exterminate them if they preferred. Marina and Aguilar translated calmly, making sure their words showed no signs of desperation, though they too had become weak and hungry.

The messengers arrived while Xicotenga the Elder, father to the captain-general Xicotenga, was discussing the possibility of peace with a council of chieftains. The elderly man, thought to be 140 years old, was blind and frail, but venerated by all the caciques in his territory. He told his allies to consider that because the Spaniards had helped the Totonacs, those tribes no longer had to pay tribute to the Aztecs. Although the younger Xicotenga would have preferred prolonging the war, his father's arguments proved more persuasive.

* * *

Moctezuma, whose spies had informed him of the battle

between the Spaniards and Tlaxcalans, thought he would be rid of one enemy or the other. When he heard the two sides were making peace, however, he sent five emissaries to Cortes with gold treasures worth a fortune. The emissaries warned Cortes about the dangers of trying to travel to Tenochtitlan. They also warned him not to trust the Tlaxcalans.

When the Tlaxcalans made peace, however, they gave advice quite the opposite. They welcomed Cortes's army with flowers, copal incense, and a parade of about fifty chieftains wearing cloaks of red and white, the national colors of Tlaxcala. They apologized for making war on the Spaniards, saying they were surrounded by territories subject to Moctezuma, and they had to be on guard against his treachery.

Xicotenga the Elder said they were a poor people, "rich only in our spirit of independence," so he could offer only a few poor gifts to the Spaniards. Their mountain-ringed valley contained a river and fertile land; in fact, corn grew so abundantly there that the territory was called Tlaxcala or "land of bread." But they had no source of salt, and Moctezuma kept them so confined that they could not go out of their territory for it.

Cortes welcomed confirmation of reports that the Aztecs and Tlaxcalans mistrusted each other. He learned to play one against the other, listening to their complaints and professing a partiality for whichever one he was talking to. Marina faithfully translated, making no judgments about what her master said, recognizing that diplomacy may require duplicity at times.

The ability of Cortes to change alliances at will, and to make friends out of old enemies, could be seen as either skillful diplomacy or insincerity. Marina listened to this unique man almost every day as he guided, encouraged, cajoled, persuaded, manipulated, outwitted, defended, scolded, and charmed the people around him. Like most other people, she was inclined to trust him, assuming that if he said something untrue, he had good reason for doing so. She understood better than anyone else what a complex person he was. He seemed a bundle of opposites—gentle and harsh, demanding and lenient, humble and arrogant, greedy and generous, cautious and daring. His complexities held as much mystery for her as had the whimsical gods of her childhood. It did not seem impossible to her that Cortes, like Quetzalcoatl, could be both a man and a god.

* * *

The battles had lasted three weeks, leaving the Spaniards with fifty-five dead men and two dead horses. To recuperate, the survivors stayed another three weeks as guests of the two Xicotengas and other Tlaxcalans. The Tlaxcalans proved to be as staunch in their friendship as they had been ferocious in their

268

opposition. They had come to respect the valiant Spanish soldiers and their shrewd captain-general, just as Cortes had come to respect them.

Cortes wrote a letter to King Charles comparing the city of Tlaxcala to Granada, though it was larger (about 150,000 families), with stronger buildings, and better supplied with the produce of the land such as bread, fowl, wild game, fresh-water fish, and vegetables. Every day, he told the king, nearly 30,000 people came to the marketplace to trade for food, clothing, footwear, and ornaments. Their pottery equalled the best to be found in Spain. In the marketplace, he wrote, "There are establishments like barbers where they have their hair washed and shaved, and there are baths."

Cortes and his men took advantage of the baths and barbering facilities. Marina found the men's appearance much improved, and she too felt much better when she had bathed, washed her hair, and changed into clean clothing provided by her host.

* * *

It was Xicotenga the Elder who first called Cortes "Malintzin," which in Nahuatl meant "Marina's Lord." Hearing him repeat this name affectionately throughout the Spaniards' stay, the other Indians adopted the name. By the time Cortes reached Tenochtitlan the pronunciation had been altered to "Malinche," and it was applied to both Cortes and the woman who spoke for him as if they were one person.

It was also the Tlaxcalans who gave Pedro de Alvarado the nickname *Tonatiuh*, which meant "the sun" in Nahuatl. That appellation seemed to fit his fair skin and blond hair with reddish tints. More important, the Tlaxcalans gave him a wife, who as time went on would give him two children. The young woman, Tecuilhuatzin, was the daughter of the younger Xicotenga, the battle-scarred captain who had nearly defeated Cortes. She was one of five maidens given to Cortes and his captains to seal the truce between the two armies. The country was too poor to offer luxury goods, Xicotenga said, but they could offer their guests some beautiful young women.

Just as he had done in Cempoala, Cortes placed conditions on accepting the women. He insisted that all idols be destroyed, human sacrifice abolished, and Christianity adopted. Most Tlaxcalans, like the Cempoalans, bristled at ideas that would offend their gods. Again, the prudent Father Olmedo persuaded Cortes to be more tactful and patient in promoting his faith.

As a compromise, although the Tlaxcalans would not give up their gods, the five women were baptized and took Christian names. Cortes gave a woman to each of four captains: Cristobal de Olid, Alonso Davila, Juan Velasquez de Leon, and Gonzalo de Sandoval. Then Cortes presented Alvarado with Xicotenga's daughter, baptized as Luisa.

"I had hoped you would take my daughter as a wife for yourself," said the disappointed Xicotenga.

"She is a great beauty and a gracious lady," Cortes replied. "I know you honor me by your generous offer. But I'm already married, and a Christian man may take only one wife."

After Marina had translated that, Cortes added, "While I am here, I need no woman other than Marina." Aguilar translated that comment to Marina in Mayan, but she had already understood the Spanish words. She felt a warm glow in her cheeks as she looked gently at Cortes.

Xicotenga looked expectantly at Marina for the rest of the translation. Carefully she chose suitable words in Nahuatl and delivered them with her usual serenity: "My master says he has a Christian wife, and he needs no other woman."

* * *

When she was alone with Cortes that night within the whitewashed walls of the room in Xicotenga's stone house, Marina took off her sandals and her skirt, leaving her huipil as a modest covering from her shoulders to her knees. Cortes wore a shirt of fine holland linen, brought from Spain; she wore a huipil of agave fiber, given to her by the Tlaxcalans who used only home-grown fabrics. They were seated on reed chairs that, other than the sleeping mats, were the only furnishings. She held out the skirt and said to him in Spanish, "Do you need me in this way?"

"I need you in every way," Cortes said, pulling off his own boots. "Do you understand my words?"

"Si," Marina replied, imitating his accent perfectly.

"I'll teach you three other Spanish words," he said. "*Yo te amo*." He touched his own chest when he said *yo* and hers when he said *te*. He rubbed his heart with his palm when he said *amo*. "That is what a Spanish man says to a woman when he desires her and values her above all other women."

Marina looked puzzled because there was no exact translation for the words "I love you" in either Nahuatl or Mayan. She sensed the desire in his voice, saw tenderness in the way he looked at her. He had taken her in the sex act before, though not frequently, and she had complied dutifully. Something was different on this night in Tlaxcala. She tried to read his face, his voice, the language of his body. What was it he wanted?

She made a guess. "Do you want to take off my huipil as Captain Puertocarrero did sometimes?" she asked in Spanish.

"Would you like me to do that?" he asked in response. His

eyes did not flicker as they did when he was pretending; they looked steadily at her, and he made no motion to touch her.

Again she was perplexed. Was this commander of thousands, this master of many vassals and servants, asking a slave what she wanted? Unsure if she had understood his words clearly, she said with lowered eyes, "I want to please you, my lord. Tell me what you wish me to do."

"You're learning Spanish words very well," he said approvingly. "I hope you'll also learn some Spanish customs. In Spain we see a difference between the sex act and love. A man can pay for the sex act. He can force a woman in the sex act." He pulled off his stockings and stretched both feet outward, wriggling his toes as if celebrating their release.

Marina nodded agreement as she had see Cortes do when he talked with his captains. "Si," she said. "I have seen this done many times."

"When a man loves a woman," Cortes continued, "he wants her heart, not just her body. He wants to hear that she desires him as much as he desires her. Do you understand this much?"

"Si," Marina said, folding her hands quietly in her lap. "That is the desire a woman has when she can choose her own husband. My mother had such feelings for my father. My aunt Papalotl had such feelings for her husband Omecitli, though other people thought she should marry the eagle warrior Anecoatl. Anecoatl married my mother instead, but I don't think he loved her. He married for ambition, perhaps even to spite Papalotl."

"I envy those who can marry for love," Cortes said with a faint sigh. "You know I'm a married man, a Christian. I married Catalina under pressure from Diego Velasquez, so I'm guilty of ambition too, and I've often regretted it. I have to admit Catalina's been a dutiful wife, but I don't love her." He rose and pulled his shirt off over his head. The light of their single candle molded with shadow the sinewy strength of his back.

"Have you loved other women?" Marina asked curiously, grateful that her master was taking her into his confidence.

"Many times. Too many," Cortes replied, smiling as he reminisced, tossing his shirt onto the icpalli. "In my youth I gave my heart away too much. I got into trouble with some angry husbands, and my heart was broken often by ladies who didn't return my love."

"Don't the Spanish ladies have to accept the men who love them? Can a Spanish lady say no?"

"Certainly she can," Cortes explained. "But courtship is like a game. If the gentleman persists, and uses his charms, sometimes he can overcome her resistance and win her heart."

"Just as you've done with the Tlaxcalans," Marina laughed, her dark hair shifting on her shoulders as she tossed her head back. "They fought you ferociously. Now they admire you and make a fuss over you."

Cortes smiled, admiring Marina's ability to analyze and compare situations. He sat beside her and took her two hands in his. "There is some similarity between strategies of warfare and games of love," he agreed. "Love is more satisfying when a man wins a woman by persuading her. His greatest thrill is when she tells him she is ready for love, that she wants him."

At last Marina understood, not only his words, but what her lover wanted from her. To verify her comprehension, she probed, "Yet you say she can tell him not to come to her?"

"That's right," Cortes said. "She can tell him she doesn't love him. Tell him to go away."

Marina turned her head slightly and looked at Cortes from the corners of her eyes. Teasingly, she asked, "If I tell you to go away, will you do it?"

"If that's your wish," Cortes said with a shrug, releasing her hands. He stood and turned as if he intended to leave, but he took slow steps.

Marina reached out and grasped his wrist to stop him. "If I tell you to stay here, will you stay?"

"Of course I will," he said merrily, turning quickly around. He knelt on one knee before her in exaggerated submission. "I will do whatever you command. You have won my heart as a soldier wins a battle."

Seeing him kneeling, Marina was reminded of mock battles she had seen between student warriors. She touched his shoulder with the tips of her fingers. "You are my captive," she said in her best imitation of an Aztec warrior, "my precious nephew."

Cortes looked puzzled, so Marina explained. "Among the Mexica, surrender is a ritual. The captor says 'you are my precious nephew.' The captive then says to his captor 'you are my esteemed uncle' and then he must obey his captor in all things."

"Uncle," said Cortes with an obliging grin. Impishly he added, "What is your command?"

"If you grant me my greatest wish," she said in sudden seriousness, "you'll teach me your language and tell me whatever is in your heart."

Cortes took her hand and kissed it. "Te amo," he said. "Now you know what is in my heart."

"What does a Spanish woman say to a man when she desires him and values him above all other men?" Marina felt her body tingling, her heart beating faster.

"The same thing. *Yo te amo*, or just *te amo*."

"Te amo," Marina said. She knelt beside him and kissed his hand as he had hers.

Cortes wrapped both his arms around her and rolled her over

playfully onto the pile of petlatls which their hosts had layered with soft feathers and covered with cloth. When he lay on top of her he smiled triumphantly. "Say uncle," he said.

"Uncle," Marina laughed. "Tell me, precious uncle, why do Spaniards always wear too many clothes?"

Then they played the games that lovers have always played, undressing each other and learning the secrets of each other's bodies and souls. It was Marina's body that craved a lover for the first time that night, but it was her soul that surrendered to him completely. Having learned the language that could connect her heart intimately to his, she expressed her passion as wordlessly as the soaring of birds, as intensely as the brilliance of fire.

For Hernan, the sexual surrender to feminine power transcended any dalliance he had ever initiated. He felt the magic of the cosmos coursing through his veins, enlarging him until he became all men and his lover all women, their union as mystical as the rotation of the stars in the seasonal skies, as majestic as snow-topped mountains, as serenely turbulent as the rocking seas.

* * *

While the Spanish army recuperated in Tlaxcala, Xicotenga tolerantly permitted them to erect a cross at one temple, though holding fast to his own religious beliefs. Then he told Cortes and Marina about the Tlaxcalan religion, including the belief shared with the Aztecs and Mayas that Quetzalcoatl would return from the east some day. He told them much they would need to know about the city of Tenochtitlan, Moctezuma, and those who were the emperor's friends and enemies.

While they were there, another envoy arrived bringing loads of cotton cloth, jewelry, and other finery. He also brought a message from Moctezuma. The emperor would be glad to see the valiant commander Cortes, but he should come to Tenochtitlan by way of Cholula, where a welcome was being prepared.

When the envoy from Moctezuma had left and Cortes was making preparations to march again, Xicotenga warned him. "Don't go to Cholula. It's a trap."

Chapter 21

The Fathers of Paynala Seek Their Sons

"I want you to find my son for me," said the aging eagle warrior Tlacateotl to the merchant Opochtli as they met in the marketplace in Paynala. Market day in Paynala came three days after market day in Oluta, so people from both towns could go to both. Tlacateotl leaned on a crutch to ease the pain of gout in his swollen right foot. He had been carried to market in a litter by four youths who also wanted to do some shopping.

"That might be difficult," replied Opochtli, picking up a skinned rabbit from a vendor and counting out payment in cacao beans. "I haven't seen Tlacoch for several years. He must've changed a lot." Opochtli himself had changed in that time, too, he knew. The bulge around his middle had grown rounder, and his legs often pained him when he traveled.

"He'd be twenty-three now," Tlacateotl said. "He's been gone three years."

Opochtli did some quick calculating. It was now 1 Reed [1519], and Tlacoch had been gone since 11 Flint [1516]. "That's quite a while," the merchant said, thinking that his own son Chimalli had been gone almost that long. "I wouldn't know where to start looking for him."

"All these years I've been hoping he'd come home," said the old warrior, looking wistfully toward the road with eyes covered by a whitish film. Deep creases lined his face. "I thought he'd get tired of gambling by now."

"Want me to check at the gambling houses and tlachtli ball courts?" Opochtli asked. "That might narrow the search a bit."

"You have many merchant friends," Tlacateotl suggested. "They travel everywhere. Perhaps some of them have seen him."

The suggestion startled Opochtli, because surely a man of Tlacateotl's experience would realize how impractical it was. The merchant friends he spoke of wouldn't know Tlacoch if they saw him. Tlacoch had probably gone to a big city to gamble, where he could have been swallowed up in crowds of 100,000.

"You speak more with hope than with practical solutions,"

Opochtli said. "I understand that. I'm a father, too—or was." He put his rabbit carefully in a net bag, which he slung over his shoulder. "Come to my house for dinner tonight," he said. "Maybe we can think of something."

* * *

Opochtli's servants cleared away the rabbit bones and vegetable dishes and left the two fathers alone to smoke and talk. Tlacateotl's litter-bearers waited for him at a respectful distance, playing a game of patolli.

"Chimalli was one of my best students at the telpochcalli," said the eagle knight to Opochtli. "You must be proud of him."

"Yes, I'm proud of my son," Opochtli said sadly. "But I haven't heard from him since he left three years ago."

"If he's living, he'll surely come back to Paynala," said Tlacateotl.

"If," Opochtli echoed, leaving the word hanging in the air like the smoke from the yetl pipes.

"He's a year younger than my son," Tlacateotl said. "About twenty-two now, isn't he? Remember when the two boys played patolli games and fought with wooden swords?"

"Those were happier times," Opochtli reminisced. "Remember the mock battle they staged at my feast? Great entertainment!"

"Chimalli won, as I recall," said Tlacateotl. "He always paid more attention to what I taught him than Tlacoch did."

"Isn't that typical of sons?" Opochtli's question was only a comment; he did not expect an answer. "Daughters are even worse. It's a fortunate man whose daughter listens to him."

"I never hear you speak of Metzli," said the old warrior, puffing on his reed. "Have you heard from her?"

"No, and I don't expect to. I disowned her when she ran off with a Tlaxcalan captive who was going to be sacrificed in Tenochtitlan as the 'fair youth.' "

"Shameful," clucked Tlacateotl. "When her own brother was fighting the Tlaxcalans! I thought she'd become a priestess."

"She did, too—studied at the temple of Quetzalcoatl for awhile, then lost her senses. I consider her dead. I don't think about her any more. I think about Chimalli all the time, though. He may have died fighting the Tlaxcalans, but I keep hoping he's alive, that someday he'll find his way home."

"It's sad when a parent outlives a child," said Tlacateotl. "Seems as if the natural order of things is all upset. You were away when Malinalli died, weren't you? Cimatl has never been the same since. That's why I want to find Tlacoch. I was angry with him when he left, but my anger has faded now. I want to make peace with my son before I die."

Opochtli summoned a servant who was lighting pine torches. "Bring us a patolli game and some octli," he ordered, then turned to Tlacateotl. "What was the trouble between you and Tlacoch?"

"He was rebellious, undisciplined. I wanted him to marry Malinalli and settle down, or at least become a warrior. All he cared about was his auianime and his tlachtli games. We quarreled about that, and he left without saying goodbye."

Opochtli realized from that remark that Tlacateotl had been his rival in seeking a match between Malinalli and his son, but there would be no point in mentioning that. To bring up events of the irrecoverable past might strain the present friendship. Instead he said sympathetically, "Tlacoch's probably more mature now. It might be worthwhile to try to find him, see if he's had a change of heart."

The servant returned with a jug of octli, two cups, a bag of beans, and a board with painted lines. Opochtli spread the game on a mat and sat beside it, motioning to Tlacateotl to sit opposite him and play as they talked.

"Things have changed here, too," Tlacateotl admitted. "Now that Malinalli's gone, there's no point talking about marriage."

"I'm sorry I missed Malinalli's funeral," Opochtli said sincerely. "I heard about Cimatl's grief; she cried for months. I should go to see her more often, but I don't get along with Anecoatl." He did not admit that Anecoatl had rejected Chimalli as a mate for Malinalli, though the thought still angered him.

"At least Cimatl has her husband and son to comfort her," Tlacateotl said. "Young Turquoise Stone is growing well, has a fine healthy body. He'll be a fine warrior someday."

"Probably the next tecuhtli," Opochtli muttered, as he tossed some beans onto the game board.

"Anecoatl has already enrolled him in a telpochcalli," said Tlacateotl. "Too bad my own teaching days are over; I'd like to have the boy as a student." He, too, took a handful of beans and scattered them on the board.

Opochtli poured two cups full of octli and handed one to his friend. "Let's drink to the past," he said, "to happier days."

* * *

The two fathers had not been particularly good friends over the years; there was no special reason for Opochtli to expend a great deal of effort helping Tlacateotl find his lost son. At first he intended only to make casual inquiries in the course of his other business, but soon he took up the search as if it were a personal goal.

Opochtli decided to follow Tlacateotl's suggestion, crazy as it seemed. He asked his merchant friends, at their next feast to honor Yacatecuhtli, whether they knew of any men from Paynala who had surfaced in cities with great ball courts. None of them could say for certain if they had seen Tlacoch, but they had some suggestions.

"Find Tlacoch's auianime," one suggested. "He may have gone to live with her."

"Ask the slave merchants," suggested another. "They're always getting new slaves who couldn't pay gambling debts any other way."

The first suggestion did not bear much fruit, but it did lead to another piece of information. After digging in his memory awhile, Opochtli recalled the auianime's name—Centli Xochitl, "Corn Flower." He found her still living in Paynala, recently married to a stonemason. She said she had not seen Tlacoch since he left three years ago, but he had told her he was going to Tenochtitlan, where ball games were played every day. He hoped to get rich and send for her, but she had tired of waiting and married another man.

The second suggestion, added to the first, produced some valuable information. A month later Opochtli found a slave merchant traveling westward from Xicalango who had traveled back and forth to Tenochtitlan many times. He usually bought slaves as carriers in the Aztec capital and sold them after he sold off their loads in Xicalango. He remembered having bought a debtor-slave who came from a territory about one day's distance from Coatzacoalcos. He didn't remember the slave's name, but he did remember thinking it strange that the youth didn't want to be sold near his home territory as most debtor-slaves did.

"That could have been Tlacoch," Opochtli nodded. "Where did he go after that?"

"I used him on the return trip to Tenochtitlan," said the merchant. "I sold him to one of the pochteca there."

The slave merchant gave Opochtli the name of the pochteca who had purchased the debtor-slave in Tenochtitlan: Huatl, or "Jaguar." Opochtli had not been to the Aztec capital for a long time, because he felt the age in his legs when he climbed tall mountains. As he thought of Tlacoch and Chimalli, however, he decided to make one last trip to the Valley of Mexico.

At that point Opochtli realized why this search for Tlacoch had become important to him. If he could get to Tenochtitlan, he might find some military official who would know whether Chimalli was still alive. Opochtli was ready to face the truth, whatever it might be. Hope was no longer enough to sustain him. The hardest burden to bear was the burden of not knowing.

* * *

The House of Pochteca in Tenochtitlan smelled of yetl and

reed pipes, pine torches, and sweat-stained garments. The two-story inn served as a waystation for merchants to sleep and store their goods, also providing a place to exchange information about roads, weather, and other traveling conditions.

The pochteca guild in Tenochtitlan welcomed Opochtli to their meeting as a fellow merchant. Since he also brought with him many luxuries from the coastal lands—rubber balls, chewing gum, rare tropical feathers, cacao beans, and shells—they were eager to trade with him. Just before dawn, when the drums and conches of the temple announced the rising of the morning star, they assembled and burned paper images in their communal fire.

Sitting on mats around the hearth of the firelit meeting room, the pochteca shared news with Opochtli that had not yet reached Oluta or Paynala—that the Totonac villages had rebelled, that they were no longer paying tribute to Moctezuma.

"Why didn't the emperor send warriors to crush the rebels?" asked Opochtli in amazement.

"He started to," one pochteca said. "He gathered thousands of warriors and got them ready to march. Then he disbanded the armies. No one is quite sure why."

"There's speculation," said another, a broad-shouldered man in a yellow tilmantli. "Remember how rumors flew around here two years ago when a messenger arrived from the coast lands? He'd seen houses floating on water, and strange men with pale hairy faces coming out of the houses and catching fish from canoes."

"What does that have to do with the revolt of the Totonacs?" Opochtli asked politely.

"My informers tell me that more floating houses have arrived carrying foreign warriors who advised the Totonacs not to pay. Some of them ride animals like huge deer, and they have spears and arrows stronger than our atl-atls and macahuitls. Some people think the invaders are teules because their magic is so great."

"Nonsense!" said a gruff-voiced pochteca. "These so-called gods fought with the Tlaxcalans last month. I heard about it in Huexotzingo on my last trip there. The Tlaxcalans killed two of those deer the invaders call 'horses'—cut off their heads with macahuitls! They killed a few invaders, too, so that proves they're mortal. After the battle, the Tlaxcalans saw the invaders eating, sleeping, and taking women like any other men."

"I hear Moctezuma is upset," said the pochteca in the yellow tilmantli. "Just last year he lost Huexotzingo to the Tlaxcalans. He was so angry he stripped his officers of their rank and took away all their insignia—wouldn't even let them wear cotton."

Another spoke up. "He's sending his brother to investigate. He's talking to his astrologers and priests, every day."

"What do they know?" said the gruff pochteca. "They turn

278

their eyes to the sky, put their noses in books, and fail to see what's under their own feet." He imitated these actions of priests as he spoke, and much laughter followed.

Another defended the emperor. "Moctezuma's a smart man. He worked his way to the throne as a warrior, not just a dreamy-eyed astrologer or fuzzy-headed scholar. He seeks advice from seers and those who know the ways of the gods. Is that so bad?"

"Perhaps not," said the gruff one, "but a person can take too much advice, think too much, study too hard. What if he has to make a decision quickly?"

"Is a quick decision better than a good decision?"

"Not always, but a bad decision is sometimes better than no decision at all."

The head of the guild interrupted. "Gentlemen, I hope you're discussing decision-making in general. We wouldn't want you to be misunderstood. Some people might think we're being critical of the emperor here."

Realizing that he was the only newcomer there, Opochtli quickly assured them he had heard no disloyal words spoken, and in any case he would never repeat what had been said there. He changed the subject. "I am looking for a merchant named Huatl," he said. "Is the mighty Jaguar here?"

"I'm Huatl," said the gruff man. "What do you want of me?"

"I'm told you purchased a slave named Tlacoch two or three years ago. He comes from my region. Do you still have him?"

Huatl thought a few minutes. "I do remember him. Good body, but lazy. Sickly, too, it turned out."

"Sickly? Is he still alive?"

"Probably dead by now. I gave him to the temple of Tlaloc," said Huatl. "I would've given him to Huitzilopochtli, but he got skin rashes and was covered with scabs and scars. Not very pretty for a sacrifice."

"One more thing," said Opochtli. "If you were trying to find out whether a soldier had been killed in battle, who would you ask?"

"You might get some information from the tlacateccatl, 'he who commands the warriors,' if he'd see you. He's pretty busy now keeping track of the invaders. His office is in one of the emperor's new official buildings near the palace. If you want to try seeing him, I could take you there in my canoe. Was the soldier in a recent battle?"

"All I know is my son was sent to Tlaxcala, almost four years ago. I haven't heard anything from him since then."

"Then I can save you a trip, my friend. There were no survivors of those battles in the Tlaxcala region. The emperor was so determined to bring the region under his domination that the warriors were commanded to fight to the death. Any who

279

returned to the city were sacrificed."

Opochtli's jaws and shoulders sagged. His voice was low and hoarse when he spoke again. "They all became quauhteca, then." Huatl spoke solemnly, the gruffness gone from his voice. "Brave warriors all. You can be proud." "My pride is drowned in sorrow," said Opochtli. As the truth finally broke through the wall of his denial, he turned to face a wall, leaned against it with one arm bent to brace his head, and wept until the mix of anger and grief drained out. All the pochteca, in sympathy, left the room quietly until Opochtli could compose himself.

* * *

Later that morning Huatl took Opochtli by canoe through the canals to the center of the city where two great temples rose into the sky like twin gods serenely surveying their domain. The 114 steps leading to these temples had been newly washed by a night rain, leaving them shining in the morning sun. The temple painted blue and white was dedicated to Tlaloc, god of rain and green growth; the one with carved skulls painted white against a red background was dedicated to Huitzilopochtli, god of sun and war. A wavelike design made of seashells encircled the roof of Tlaloc's temple. A ring of butterflies, to suggest sunlight and fire, decorated Huitzilopochtli's. Black-garbed priests were hoisting great white feathered banners on long poles from the roofs to prepare for a feast day.

From the canal Opochtli walked along a wall carved with stone serpent-heads, through the gate leading to the complex of religious buildings, and eastward to the temple of Quetzalcoatl, a modest building curved like a giant snail shell. This building, humbly situated at the rear of the more imposing major temples, housed the priests and priestesses, a small hospital for the sick, and an orphanage. Opochtli carried a pouch full of cacao beans and gemstones under his mantle, ready to pay for any information he might receive.

He walked past a gardener who looked familiar, but he knew how the senses can trick travelers into seeing familiar lines in the faces of strangers. He was surprised, therefore, when he asked the gardener for directions, and the gardener answered in a familiar accent—the dialect of the region around Paynala and Oluta. He squinted and looked more closely. "Callipopoca! I'm surprised to see you here!"

The next thing Opochtli said surprised himself even more. He had fully intended to ask for the priest Quetzalcoatl-Tlaloctlamacazqui, the high priest for the temple of Tlaloc, who could give him information about a debtor-slave named Tlacoch. Instead, the words came out differently. "I want to see Metzli," he said. "Is she here?"

* * *

Either Opochtli's guess had been correct, or he had retained some dim memory of what Chimalli had said three years before about seeing his sister in Tenochtitlan. Metzli was indeed at the temple of Quetzalcoatl, serving the god she had been dedicated to, close to the great temples where the sacrifices took place in Tenochtitlan.

Callipopoca took him to the barren room where the priestess Metzli kept a sleeping mat, a wash basin, and a bowl. "My wife and I came here when Anecoatl drove us out of Paynala," he explained as they walked to her cell. "The priestess Metzli had already been accepted here to serve Quetzalcoatl. Everyone thought highly of her, so she helped us to get a place here."

"Then Chihuallama is here too?"

"Yes. She cares for the sick and the orphans. I plant trees and flowers. Wait here. I'll get Metzli; then I'll find Chihuallama for you." Callipopoca started out the open door of the cell, then turned toward Opochtli and said reassuringly, "They'll both be glad to see you. Metzli has prayed that you'd come someday, and Chihuallama will be eager for news of home."

Opochtli seated himself on the mat and waited. When Metzli came in, she seemed thinner than ever, draped in a loose black robe of agave fiber. Her earlobes had been pitifully shredded by the cactus thorns in penance, but her lips had not been scraped. She walked with purpose and confidence, as if these barren walls had given her serenity. Still, Opochtli felt pained to see her. Austere garb seemed all right for a pochteca, but his sons and daughters ought to present a finer appearance.

She smiled at her father and kneeled beside him on the petlatl. "I'm glad you came," she said simply. Then she chatted as if there had been no pain at their parting over three years ago. "I'm very busy this morning, preparing for the feast of Ochpaniztli, but since you've come a long way, the other priestesses have excused me for a while."

"Ah, yes, Ochpaniztli," Opochtli said. "The feast of brooms. Are you sweeping the temples this month?"

"Others do that," Metzli replied matter-of-factly. "My work is to prepare the prisoners, to hear their confessions."

"Their confessions?" Opochtli repeated in surprise.

"Yes. They confess to me as the agent of Tlazolteotl, the Earth Mother. You know the rule. One time before they die, they can be forgiven for all their sins."

"The earth mother eats the sins, I'm told," Opochtli said wryly, wondering if Metzli's thin frame had absorbed such a diet.

281

"In a sense. Some people call Tlazolteotl the 'eater of filth.' I've certainly heard some terrible stories. It's strange what happens, though, as we talk. I often see that the sins have been eating the man for a long time. Once that process is reversed, the slave or warrior can face death peacefully."

Opochtli listened to his daughter as if she were a woman he had just met. "You've changed, Metzli," he said with respect.

"Of course. I'm grown up now—eighteen years old."

"Not only that. You've changed your views of sacrifice, haven't you? I thought priestesses of Quetzalcoatl abhorred human sacrifice. You seem to be facilitating it."

"You don't understand, Father. I can't prevent the practice here; all I can do is comfort those who are facing it."

"I see," said Opochtli a little brusquely. "Well, it looks as if you've found a place for yourself here. I want you to know you can come home to Oluta, if you wish."

"Thank you for the kind offer," Metzli said evenly, not with the gratitude Opochtli expected. "Is that why you came?"

"I don't know why I came," Opochtli said irritably. "I was on another errand, but Quetzalcoatl may have been guiding my feet after all. I suppose it's only right that I be the one to tell you. Your brother Chimalli is dead, killed in battle."

"I thought so."

"How did you know? I just learned myself this morning."

"Maybe it's only right that I tell you something as well. Three years ago Chimalli came to me to confess his sins. He knew he was going into a battle from which he'd never return."

"So you do know, after all. Funny. I can't imagine Chimalli having anything to confess. He was a model son in every way, a model warrior, too."

"You see only what you want to see, Father. Chimalli was brave and honest and loyal, but he had the sin of ambition."

Opochtli snorted. "Ambition? That's a sin?"

"Not always, but if ambition and loyalty are carried too far, they can become great faults."

"I don't see what you mean."

"Forget it, then. Try to remember him the way you've idealized him."

Opochtli trembled with anger. "I haven't idealized him! You're tearing him down, speaking disrespectfully of the dead."

"Not at all. I've forgiven Chimalli all his sins, and he can never be punished for them. He went to his death serenely."

"You were always jealous of Chimalli," said Opochtli indignantly, rising to leave. "You act superior to him now, and I find that disrespectful. Still, I'm alone now. I don't travel as much as I once did. I'm willing to take you back to Oluta with me, where you'd have a better life."

"I could never replace Chimalli in your heart, Father,"

Metzli sighed. "Besides, my place is here, near my son."

"You have a son?"

"Yes, and you have a grandson. He's as handsome as his father was."

"The Tlaxcalan—is he the father?"

"Yes. He was sacrificed about three years ago, but his image lives on in his son."

"May I see the boy?"

"He's with the orphan children. Chihuallama watches over him while I work. She'll take you to a gate in the wall so you can see him playing, but don't speak to him. He doesn't know I'm his mother."

At that moment, Chihuallama and Callipopoca arrived. Chihuallama, huffing for breath because of extra weight she had added in recent years, welcomed Opochtli in great excitement. After much bowing and apologizing that she had nothing to offer him to eat, she asked anxiously for news from home. "When we left Paynala so hurriedly, our daughter Toto was very sick. Cimatl was caring for her. We haven't dared to go back. Tell us, have you seen Toto? Is she all right?"

Opochtli looked stunned. "I haven't seen Toto in many years," he said. "I didn't know she'd come back to Paynala; Cimatl never mentioned it to me. I thought she'd gone with Chimalli to be his auianime when he went to war."

"Ayeee," wailed Chihuallama. "What has become of her?"

Callipopoca rubbed a hand across his forehead. "Something isn't right. It isn't like Cimatl never to mention Toto to you. She knew Toto was your son's auianime."

"I'll ask Cimatl about Toto the next time I'm in Paynala," Opochtli said. "To tell the truth, though, I don't see Cimatl very often since Malinalli died."

Chihuallama gasped. "Malinalli died?"

"You hadn't heard that either? I was away when Malinalli took sick. The cremation was over by the time I got back."

Metzli looked shocked. "How did she die?"

"Cimatl said she had a sudden attack of pain in her chest," Opochtli replied. "She collapsed before a ticitl could be summoned. Everyone believes it was the mountain airs that caused it, blowing down on her and turning her blood cold in the night." Callipopoca's face contorted into a frown. "Something isn't right. I don't trust Anecoatl." He was also wondering whether Cimatl had told the whole story, but Cimatl had been good to him when he worked for her, and he would say nothing ill of her.

Metzli said in a conciliatory voice, "Perhaps we're all just upset; it can make us suspicious. Illness takes people away all the time; we have to accept death."

"We have to investigate death under mysterious

circumstances too," Opochtli said reprovingly. "I want to know why Anecoatl and Cimatl never told anyone what happened to Toto."

"I'm sad about Malinalli's death," said Metzli; I wish I'd known earlier. We get very wrapped up in our work here. The priests do try to send me any captives taken in the Coatzacoalcos region, but we rarely see people from Paynala."

Chihuallama rubbed her eyes and face with her work-worn hands. "The only person I've seen from Paynala is that slave with the scabs I've been treating. He's been away too many years. He couldn't tell me anything."

"Scabs?" Opochtli asked intensely. "Skin disease?" When Chihuallama verified that, he added, "Can you take me to see this slave? That might be Tlacoch, the man I'm looking for."

"It is Tlacoch," Metzli said in surprise. "What concern do you have with him?"

"His father wants him to return. He's ready to forgive Tlacoch's immaturity and defiance."

"Tlacoch has already confessed to me," Metzli said firmly. "His sins of gambling, betrayal, and theft have been eaten. He knows he deserves death, but he has a chance to die with honor."

"How?"

"He's being groomed for the Ochpaniztli feast. He'll fight in an exhibition against some of the eagle and jaguar knights."

"I've seen some of those exhibitions in the past," Opochtli said grimly. "What chance does the prisoner have, when he's tied to a stone disk, with only dummy weapons against the real weapons of the eagle and jaguar knights?"

"He expects to lose the fight," said Metzli calmly. "It's a ritual fight, with the stone disk representing the sun or life, and the knights representing the battle against the forces of darkness. We all eventually lose the fight for life, but we pass into another plane of existence. What matters is the courage we show during our earthly life."

Opochtli stared at his daughter in silence, long enough to make an awkward break in the conversation. Then he said, "You talk as if you worship death. The priests here have really got to you, haven't they?"

* * *

Chihuallama took Opochtli to the gate where he could see his grandson at play. The two-year-old was digging industriously in a sand pile, ignoring several older orphans who were butting a ball as if practicing for a tlachtli game. Chihuallama was still in shock from the news of Toto's and Malinalli's deaths, but she tried to be philosophical. "The gods are hard to understand," she said. "They take our children away, but they give us others.

284

These little ones have lost their parents, so Callipopoca and I try to take their places."

"You have a big heart, Chihuallama," said Opochtli. "Do you ever see your own grandson?"

Chihuallama smiled wistfully. "It's better not to. We have sanctuary here, so we never travel back to Paynala where Anecoatl could make trouble for us. We know our grandson is well cared for; Acamapichtli and Matlalquiau are both good parents. These little ones here need us much more."

Then Chihuallama took him to the exercise yard near the infirmary where Tlacoch was being held. Tlacoch was exercising with a wooden club, gripping it with both hands and swinging it through the air. He wore only a maxtli, so Opochtli could see the strength in his arms and legs.

"You might win that battle tomorrow after all," Chihuallama complimented her patient. He came over to her, at first not recognizing Opochtli. "Here is a friend to see you," she said, taking Tlacoch's hand to examine the skin between his fingers.

"Opochtli!" said Tlacoch. "What are you doing here?" Then he turned to Chihuallama, who had knelt to examine his feet. "The itching has stopped, Chihuallama. You make good medicines."

"I might ask you the same thing," Opochtli said. "What are you doing here?"

"It's a long story," Tlacoch said. "I came here with a merchant's caravan, earning my way as a tameme. The trip was harder than I expected, but I was proud of doing it on my own, without my father's help. I picked up a few cacao beans playing patolli with the merchants; sometimes I cheated to win. When I got to Tenochtitlan I started betting on tlachtli games. Do you have any idea how much money people throw away on those games?"

"I've heard," Opochtli nodded. "Some men get so carried away they'd bet their houses and the tilmantli off their backs."

Tlacoch smiled. "It's true. I did pretty well at first. Had a few ups and downs, but found lots of people willing to part with their jewelry or empty their warehouses. The game's more exciting if you have a wager on it."

Chihuallama completed her inspection. "Keep putting that lotion on, Tlacoch," she said. "And keep yourself clean. Most men get this problem when they haven't been able to bathe—usually soldiers or slaves."

"How did you get into trouble?" Opochtli asked.

"I made the mistake of gambling with a rich man who doesn't like to lose," Tlacoch said. "After he paid me what he owed me, he accused me of stealing it. He sent a constable to my house, and of course all the stuff was there—several mantles with unusual patterns, jewelry that other people recognized as his, lots of evidence against me."

"Surely you had witnesses too," Opochtli said.

"Strange how those witnesses disappear when they're bribed," Tlacoch said cynically. "It was a disillusioning experience, but I learned something important. I realized I had no true friends, no family I could turn to, no women I could trust after I lost my wealth. I'd even lost touch with Centli-Xochitl."

"I saw her before I left," Opochtli said. "She married someone else."

Tlacoch ground the toe of his sandal into the soil. "I'm glad for her sake," he said. "I wouldn't have been a good husband. All I really cared about was gambling and money."

Chihuallama interjected a comment. "You've changed a lot," she said. "Metzli has been a good influence."

"So have you, Chihuallama," Tlacoch said. "But there's more to my story. The judge took everything I had, and ordered me to pay a big fine, but he said I could work off my debts."

"So that's how you became a debtor-slave? Sounds as if you're a victim of injustice."

"I thought so, too, at first," Tlacoch said. "I was angry and bitter. I tried to do as little as I could while I was working off my debt, and once when a merchant sold me I stole several pieces of jade from him."

"I didn't know that," said Chihuallama.

"Metzli knows," said Tlacoch. "I confessed to her, and even asked her to take the tainted jade from my guilty hands. She taught me to see that I stole out of anger, not out of need. I vented my rage not against the one who had injured me, but against the one I could injure most easily. That was my worst crime, but I'd been lying and cheating for years without getting caught. Tomorrow I'll pay for my real crimes, not the ones people think I committed. In my own mind, though, I know I can enter the world of Mictlan with some honor."

Opochtli was moved by this talk. "Perhaps I can find a way to pay off your debts and save your life," he said.

Tlacoch looked at Opochtli in disgust. "Did my father put you up to this?"

"Not at all. He just asked me to find you. He has swollen feet now and can't walk far. His eyesight is failing. He wants to see you before he dies."

Tlacoch looked sorrowful for a moment. "Please be kind to him, and for his sake, don't tell him how badly I turned out."

Sympathetically, Chihuallama offered a suggestion to Opochtli. "You could tell Tlacateotl that his son died a warrior's death," she said. "That will be the truth."

* * *

286

The following day, Chihuallama and Metzli did not go to the festival of Ochpaniztli, but they could hear the roaring of the crowds, the beating of the drums, and the blaring of the conch shells coming from the temples of Huitzilopochtli and Tlaloc. Inside the temple of Quetzalcoatl they bowed before a small shrine, burned some incense, made offerings of corn and fruit.

"Quetzalcoatl," Metzli prayed, "please send a divine wind to speed Tlacoch's journey through the nine hells and thirteen heavens; send a black dog to befriend him along the way as he crosses the mountains and deserts to Mictlan, as he suffers the freezing winds and rains. When he has climbed with the sun enough times, let him come back to us as a hummingbird, for that was his father's wish for him."

"Quetzalcoatl," prayed Chihuallama, "this day we enter a period of mourning. For eighty days we will wear white garments and eat only one meal each day. In this way we accept the loss of our friends Tlacoch and Malinalli, and my daughter Atototl, my little 'water bird' that never learned to fly."

As the women were kneeling in reverent silence, two burly male figures entered the shrine, carrying a litter with a covered body lying on it.

Chihuallama recognized her husband Callipopoca and the merchant Opochtli. "I see you've brought Tlacoch's body," she said. "I'll prepare him for cremation."

"Not just yet," said Opochtli, huffing from the exertion of carrying his own plump body and the litter as well.

"He's still alive," said Callipopoca. "Quickly, Chihuallama, take care of his wounds."

Metzli sprang to her feet. "A miracle!" she exclaimed. "How did he survive the battle?" She pulled back the cloth covering Tlacoch's body. An ugly gash bloodied his left arm, numerous smaller scrapes bloodied his face and arms, and one leg lay at an awkward angle. Chihuallama rushed to get powdered obsidian to stop the bleeding and a splint for the broken leg.

"He was magnificent," said Opochtli, and with many gestures to embellish his tale while the women tended the wounds of the unconscious Tlacoch, he related what had happened at the ceremony. "Tlacoch stood tied to that sun stone as if he owned it, holding his wooden club like a tecuhtli holding a rod of authority. The emperor was watching Tlacoch while the jaguar knight strutted in his fur costume and the eagle knight paraded in his feathers. When the jaguar knight rushed against him, Tlacoch knocked the macahuitl right out of the warrior's hands. When the eagle knight came at him, raising his macahuitl to strike, Tlacoch thrust his wooden sword right into the eagle's gut. The jaguar came at him with a spear, but he stepped aside. When the spear hit the ground, he jumped on it with all his weight and broke it. The eagle knight had crumpled to the ground, but the jaguar caught Tlacoch several times with a slash of his macahuitl. Tlacoch wouldn't stop swinging his wooden club, and he had already wounded a prized warrior, so the emperor stopped the fight. The whole crowd roared its approval."

Callipopoca added, "The crowd appreciated bravery. I thought I would be carrying out a corpse, but Tlacoch surprised me. Maybe he wanted to live, after all."

"A miracle," Metzli kept murmuring over and over again as she threw yauhtli powder into the unconscious man's nostrils. "A miracle. A miracle."

While Tlacoch was thus anesthetized, Chihuallama's skillful hands straightened the broken leg, braced it with wooden splints, and wrapped clean cloths around the splints. When the wounds had stopped bleeding, she bound a cloth around the wounded arm. Then she spoke to Metzli as if Meztli were a foolish daughter instead of a priestess. "Now aren't you glad," she said with cheerful impudence, "that you didn't get what you prayed for?"

* * *

When Chihuallama and Callipopoca had taken Tlacoch to the infirmary, Opochtli spoke once more to Metzli.

"I'm a proud man," he said, "and I know that's a fault, but I've also been called kind and generous. I'm willing to help you raise your son, to give him servants and a fine education. I'm willing to overlook the Tlaxcalan side of him, even though I'll think of Chimalli every time I look at him."

Metzli shook her head sorrowfully. "I see pain in your face when you offer that," she said. "I don't mean any disrespect, but my son and I don't need your help."

"Now who's the proud one?" Opochtli chided. "This isn't a good place to raise a boy. Don't deny him opportunity just because of your own pride."

Metzli's voice took on an edge like flint. "You speak of pride," she said, "when you've never learned real humility. Just listen to yourself; try to hear what others hear. How generous is your offer to take me away from a place where I have important work to do, where I am respected, and into a place where a woman has no respect? How generous is your offer to raise my son if you teach him to feel ashamed of his father?"

"Well, what can you offer your son?" Opochtli retorted. "He doesn't even know who his mother is, not to mention his father."

"He'll know some day," Metzli said defensively. "He has all he needs here—plenty of food, playmates, an education better than most children will get."

"He needs his family," Opochtli said stubbornly.

288

"He has a family, right here," Metzli insisted. When her father made no response, she continued more gently, "If you can forgive my defiance of your authority, I can forgive your rejection of me. Most fathers favor their sons, so perhaps you can't help it. Yet the truth is, you always put Chimalli ahead of me; you might even resent me for being alive when he's not."

"There you go again with that nonsense," Opochtli said.

"I'm afraid we'd cause you unhappiness, and you'd cause us unhappiness, despite your good intentions. Perhaps you want my son to take Chimalli's place," Metzli continued, "but I don't think that would be fair to him. He's a different person."

"You don't understand boys. Every boy wants to become a warrior."

"Every boy wants to please his father; many of them only *think* they want what their fathers want for them."

"Your son could do worse than to be like Chimalli," said Opochtli, sensing that the discussion was going in circles.

Metzli stared at the ceiling before she spoke again. "I've been wondering whether I had the right to tell you what Chimalli told me. Now I think I must, because you could be in danger."

"What kind of danger?"

"Chimalli knew he was being sent to his death by Anecoatl. He felt betrayed, but as a warrior he had to obey."

"Did he accuse Anecoatl?"

"Not directly; that would have been treason against his superior officer. Remember that if he had to die, he wanted to die a death of honor."

"I know he did. But why would Anecoatl want him dead?"

"After Anecoatl had a son of his own, he didn't show Chimalli as much favor as before. If Chimalli had married Malinalli, he might have become the next tecuhtli. Anecoatl wanted his own son to succeed him, not Malinalli's husband."

Opochtli looked stunned. "By the thirteen heavens!" he cried. "Could I have brought this tragedy about by approaching that snake about marriage?" His forehead wrinkled; his nose twitched. "No one would believe this," he said. "It's too bizarre. Did Chimalli offer you any proof?"

"Chimalli had the matter pretty well thought out," Metzli said. "I'm telling you what he believed because you already suspect Anecoatl of foul play in Malinalli's death. If you confront him about that, you might be in danger yourself."

"What makes you so sure of that?"

"Because Chimalli told me about another death Anecoatl caused."

"Whose death?"

"All I can tell you is that Chimalli's part in the matter has been confessed and forgiven. His honor is secure; that's all I care about."

289

"What about Anecoatl?"

"He's not my concern," Metzli replied calmly. "You are. Just be careful. Don't let your grief or your suspicions lead you into any actions you'll regret."

"I'm not the only suspicious person," Opochtli said. "Have you ever talked to Chihuallama and Callipopoca about the death of Malinalli's father?"

Metzli looked puzzled. "No. Why?"

"Because the three of us suspected he was poisoned. We had no proof, so we didn't say anything. But when I get back to Paynala, I intended to get to the bottom of this."

"Do be careful, Father. I don't know much about Anecoatl, but I have a feeling he could be dangerous."

* * *

Metzli spent as much time as she could with Tlacoch while his wounds healed. She had tender thoughts of him, wondering if he might have been sent to her by the gods and goddesses to take the place of Quauhtlatoa, or "Speaking Eagle," the fair youth who had come with her to that very place three years before and had become one of those gods in a sacred ceremony. Everything works in cycles, she believed devoutly; when the sun seems to disappear, it returns; when a plant drops its leaves, new ones later appear; when one loses a friend, another comes to take his place. All this is mysterious, but certain enough.

Then she dismissed those thoughts. Hadn't she just chided her father for wanting a grandson to replace Chimalli? Besides, she had no time for the selfishness of friendship. Her work at the temple was greatly increasing as the priests of Quetzalcoatl were called to the emperor's palace almost every day. The priestesses not only had their usual work to do, but much of what the priests usually did.

Of course, the year 1 Reed had special significance for these priests. The high priest Topiltzin Quetzalcoatl had been born in the year 1 Reed and died when the year 1 Reed came again, completing a perfect 52-year cycle, a sheaf of years. The emperor Moctezuma kept asking the priests what prophecies they knew about Quetzalcoatl. Would he return in the year 1 Reed?

The priests busily consulted their books and charts, for none wanted to displease the emperor. Moctezuma had been seeing omens for the past ten years, each time growing more anxious. When he had seen a blazing comet in the sky a decade before and demanded an explanation from his priests and astrologers, all they could say was that they had not seen it. Enraged by their incompetence, he had them thrown into cages and left to starve.

Now Moctezuma was getting almost daily reports and pictures of strangers who had come from the east. He knew this much: the priest Topiltzin Quetzalcoatl had died by taking a raft into the mists where the sun rises; eight days later he reappeared as the Morning Star. Sometimes he would appear in the east, sometimes in the west, as if teasing astrologers. Had the high priest become transformed into the god he served? Had he become the star as legends explained it? Would he return to earth? The sacred books were not clear on that point, according to priests and astrologers, yet everything that happens must have happened at some other time. Anyone can clearly see that time moves in cycles, so the clue to the future must lie in the past.

Moctezuma fretted and walked moodily in his aviary and zoo. He thought of running away, hiding, but he knew destiny cannot be escaped. His priests wanted very much to set his mind at rest. They could never question his piety or his desire to serve the gods, if only he knew what was wanted. But the priests could only suggest that he make offerings in the House of the Sun or pray in the Temple of Centli, the Corn Goddess. Their words dispirited him further, so that he could make no decision. All he could do was meditate, meander listlessly in his gardens, and wait.

* * *

Metzli thought often of her brother Chimalli, now that she knew he was dead, and she wore the white robe of mourning for eighty days. Her first memories were happy ones; she recalled Chimalli's radiant smile as he caught a fish in the river or successfully balanced himself while walking on a stone wall. The last memory was that of a tormented soul who had asked her, as the agent of Tlazolteotl, to hear his confession.

"I've worshipped my quauchic as if he were a god," Chimalli had said in bitter anguish. "I tried to be his right arm, to do whatever he would want done, without question, as an arm obeys its owner. If he wanted me to kill for him, I would do it."

Metzli remembered the chill she had felt when Chimalli said those words, but she had showed no emotion. A priestess must be willing to listen to any confession, no matter how painful.

"I tried to be like him, act like him, think like him," Chimalli had said. "Now I wonder if the deeds I did were my own or his. Is an arm to blame when it shoots the arrow that kills?"

"Tell me about the arrow," said Metzli.

"Actually, it was a drowning," said Chimalli. "I don't know if I'm guilty or not. Every year the thought torments me more. And now I too am going to certain death, on the orders of the man I served so loyally."

"Were you obeying orders? A warrior must obey an order, even if he would not do the deed on his own."

"The orders were not specific. But Anecoatl had said he would rather see this woman dead than have anyone else have her. I thought he was suggesting a way for me to please him, even though he couldn't order me directly to kill her."

"A woman?"

"A woman he admired and wanted to marry. She had her child with her at the river when I went to talk to her. While her mother was talking to me, the child wandered into the river, slipped on a mossy stone, and fell into the current."

"Could you have saved her?"

"Maybe. I don't know. I just stood there, like a statue."

"Did the mother try to save the child?"

"Yes. She ran into the water, grabbed the girl, and tried to pull her out. But the rocks were slippery underfoot, and the current pulled her down as well."

"Why do you feel guilty? Because you did nothing?"

"I did nothing, nothing," he said, as if chanting the phrase. "Even when the woman caught a branch, and the waters were boiling over her head as they do over a stone, and she cried out for help, I did nothing. She clung to the branch with one hand, and her daughter with the other, but the water filled her mouth and swirled over her head. Her hand slipped off the branch, and she went down again."

"Why didn't you help her?"

"I remembered Anecoatl's words. I was trying to think as he would think. He would not want her to be saved."

"Who was this woman?"

"Her name was Papalotl. She was Malinalli's aunt."

"Oh," said Metzli. "I vaguely remember. You came to see Malinalli and me when we were in training in Coatzacoalcos. You asked for directions to Papalotl's farm, and Malinalli told you Papalotl was already married."

"You do remember," Chimalli said in amazement. "I didn't think you'd paid much attention."

"I didn't think much of it at the time, but tell me, Chimalli, did you really *have* to go to Papalotl's farm?"

"Maybe not. I thought at the time I had to see for myself. I couldn't return to Anecoatl with second-hand information."

"And when you did return, was Anecoatl pleased to learn she was dead?"

Chimalli hung his head. "He praised me for letting her drown. He said he had other plans anyway. I was so crazy with ambition at the time, I thought pleasing my superior officer was the highest form of service to my country."

"And shortly afterward, he recommended you for knighthood."

"Yes," Chimalli had said glumly. "I was honored. But I've never been sure I was honorable."

292

* * *

As soon as Opochtli was sure Tlacoch was out of danger and the broken leg was healing, he planned his departure. Even if he didn't bring Tlacoch or Metzli with him, he had good news for Tlacateotl. When he said goodby to Chihuallama, she said something puzzling to him. "Metzli may not always remain a priestess," she predicted. "A woman like her can hardly resist a reformed sinner. Keep up your hopes, old man; you may have other grandchildren yet."

Opochtli planned to accompany the pochteca Huatl in the long trek over the mountains to Oluta, a march they wanted to complete before the cold weather set in. Before they began their journey, he settled some unpaid debts.

"Here are the five pieces of jade I promised," Opochtli said as he counted them out in Huatl's hand. "That should settle the account for the stones Tlacoch stole from you. Now how much do I owe you for the payments to the knights?"

"The jaguar was happy to get a rubber ball and chewing gum for his sons and 500 cacao beans," Huatl said. "The eagle gave me a little more of a problem, since he doesn't have children, but his wife looked so lovely in the shell necklace and the quetzal plumes that he felt obliged to do me a favor. Neither of them could figure out why I wanted my former slave back, so I told them he had stolen from me and I wanted the pleasure of working him to death."

"That was imaginative, Huatl!" said Opochtli. "The gladiators could certainly understand a motive like that. They won't get in any trouble over this, will they?"

"Not really. They gave the crowd a good show, and that's the whole point. They haven't done anything illegal."

"Clever, weren't they?" Opochtli said with a sly smile. "They acted so fierce, they even fooled me for a while."

Then the two pochteca joined their caravan and marched off down the causeway, across the waters of Lake Texcoco, past the chinampas floating on the serene waters of Lake Xochimilco, and finally eastward along the route to Cholula, where the blue cone of Popocateptl smoldered. When they noticed several columns of warriors also heading in that direction, they felt secure. It looked as if Moctezuma had the military situation well in hand.

293

Chapter 22

Betrayal and Retribution in Cholula

Opochtli and Huatl became concerned when they tried to follow the road to Cholula but found the usual passage between two volcanos blocked by logs and boulders. A company of Aztec warriors stopped the pochtecas' caravan and wanted to purchase small items such as drums and flutes, armbands and earrings.

"Sell us what you can now," said one of the warriors. "We don't recommend that you linger in Cholula."

"We're always happy to trade," said Opochtli. "What's going on in Cholula now? Are the markets open for business?"

The Aztec with the highest rank, a *tequiua* whose leather armbands indicated he had taken at least four captives, motioned Opochtli and Huatl to pass on. "We have no time to talk," he said. "We advise you not to stop in Cholula. There could be some trouble. You'd be wise to keep moving."

The two pochteca thanked the Aztecs for their advice. As they hastened through the city, they noticed several archers climbing into positions on rooftops. When they saw a number of women walking along the road carrying baskets, children following their mothers like baby quail, the pochteca hastened their own steps eastward through the city. The city reminded Opochtli of an anthill when a stone has been dropped on it, people scurrying like ants in all directions.

"That's odd," said Huatl, as they passed a temple whose altar and steps showed the blood of recent sacrifices.

"What's odd?" asked Opochtli. He had seen many such temples; this one seemed no different.

"The sacrifices. Cholula is a holy city, dedicated to Quetzalcoatl. They haven't sacrificed anything larger than a frog here in all the years I've been traveling through it."

Opochtli looked to see if the temple had a *tzompantli* or skull rack. Seeing none, he walked up the steps to the stone receptacle beside the altar. Several small hearts lay in the bowl of the *quauhxicalli*, their dark red color indicating they had been recently deposited there. A few flies, attracted by the odor, buzzed in circles or crawled along the stained stones. Opochtli quickly rejoined Huatl and urged the tamemes to move along quickly. "You're right, Huatl," he said. "Something's made these people awfully scared. Those hearts in the *quauhxicalli* were the hearts of children."

* * *

"I warn you, it's a trap. If you insist on following the route through Cholula, I insist on sending ten thousand warriors to assist you," Xicotenga the Younger said to Cortes after the conqueror announced he was preparing to leave Tlaxcala.

"So many?" Cortes was studying a map, paying little attention to his host. "Looks as if we could get to Cholula in a day's march," he said to Marina, who was looking over his shoulder. Then he looked up at Xicotenga. "I'd think half that number would be plenty. We still have most of the Totonac warriors with us." Marina translated directly from Spanish to Nahuatl; she no longer needed Aguilar.

"You are underestimating the forces of Moctezuma and the deceptiveness of the Cholulans," said Xicotenga. "Moctezuma's emissaries suggested you take the road through Cholula, didn't they? That ought to make you suspicious."

"Perhaps, but Moctezuma might be sincere. He's sending messages and gifts quite frequently now."

"Hah!" Xicotenga exclaimed, waving a frail hand impatiently. "One day he wants you to come; the next day he wants you to go away. How can you take his messages seriously? The friendship he professes is false; his courtesies are hollow."

"I have other reasons for establishing a base in Cholula," Cortes responded patiently. "This map shows it lies in a direct line between Tenochtitlan and the coast. With friendly contacts in Cholula, I could communicate faster with Vera Cruz or Cempoala if I need more supplies."

"That may be so, but the Cholulans are allies of Moctezuma. Didn't you wonder why no expressions of good will came to you from Cholula, only six leagues away, when more distant villages sent congratulations? Didn't you wonder why the first emissaries from Cholula were people of low rank, as if to insult you?"

"I'm glad you pointed that out to me, but the second delegation consisted of real nobility, I believe."

"Only because we demanded better treatment for you. Cholula is a proud city, thriving with trade, a center for many religions. The businessmen and priests always bow to Moctezuma's will as long as their routines aren't disrupted. Whatever he tells them to do or say, they'll do."

"The nobles said they didn't invite me sooner because I was staying with you, their enemies," Cortes said. "Doesn't that

295

sound plausible?"

"They can explain anything with honeyed words," Xicotenga said with a snort. "How do you explain the military activities around Cholula in the last few days? Messengers have come to tell me a powerful Aztec force is gathering near Cholula, preparing to defend the city. You might not get the welcome Moctezuma promised."

"I'll keep your advice in mind," Cortes said, rolling up the map. "I do appreciate your concern, my honorable friend. I've already told the Cholulan delegation I'm coming to their city, so I can't tactfully back out of my agreement. Also, I can't afford to look hesitant or weak."

Xicotenga shrugged. "As I said, if you are so foolish as to travel by that route, we will send ten thousand men with you."

"Six thousand will be plenty," Cortes replied, not wanting to offend Xicotenga by refusing his offer completely. "We don't want to alarm the Cholulans by bringing too large an army."

Before leaving, Cortes presented Xicotenga with many of the gifts Moctezuma had sent to him, including cotton fabrics and mantles, which had been difficult to procure in Tlaxcala because of the Aztec embargo. Xicotenga was much pleased. In just forty days Cortes had won so much affection from this former enemy that he wept when Cortes said farewell.

Cortes also presented Marina with a gift: a golden clasp that became her favorite possession. Rectangular and carved with good-luck designs, it secured her mantle around her shoulders. Similarly, the gift of his love secured her confidence, wrapping her in a shawl of protective adoration. Whenever she felt lonely or frightened, touching that clasp reassured her of her value and worth. During their restful stay in Tlaxcala, she had bloomed like a bride, opening her heart as the morning glory opens at the warm touch of the sun. The joy in Hernan's eyes when he embraced her assured her of her power to please him, that fragile power of love which paradoxically strengthens those who yield to it.

When they departed for Cholula, Marina walked with a sure, buoyant step alongside her master's horse. Yet as soon as they reached the open road, Cortes lifted her onto his horse where all of his followers could see her cling to his back, conveying without words her closeness and her importance to him. Indeed, the Spanish soldiers had already seen her value to their army and their commander, for they were calling her "Dona Marina," as if she were a high-born Spanish lady.

* * *

The large army of Spaniards, Totonacs, and Tlaxcalans moved rather slowly, crossing some rough and hilly ground before coming upon the wide plain which spreads out for miles around Cholula, a tableland six thousand feet above sea level. The cone-shaped mountain of Popocatepetl was sending puffs of smoke into the air. Cultivated fields of corn, chili peppers, maguey or agave plants, and aloes covered the plain, irrigated by numerous streams and canals. Woods and waterways also suggested to the practical eye of Cortes that this city was rich in resources.

Cortes decided to camp beside a small stream for the night, not wanting to enter Cholula after dark. Marina was getting water from the stream when she saw several caciques from Cholula approaching. From their clothing, she could see they were high ranking nobles. She ran to Cortes' shelter, wanting to be near him if he needed an interpreter.

The caciques said they had come to welcome Cortes but were displeased to see so many of their Tlaxcalan enemies in the camp. They expressed a fear that large numbers of idle soldiers could cause disorder in their city. Cortes answered that he did not wish to abuse their hospitality, and accordingly asked his Tlaxcalan volunteers to remain in this camp while he went into Cholula with his own men and his Totonac volunteers. The Tlaxcalans agreed to wait there, parting with Cortes the next morning with expressions of affection and good wishes. Alvarado and Olid stayed in the camp with the Tlaxcalans, offering to teach them some military strategies the Spaniards had used against them successfully in their own territory.

As the smaller division of the army approached Cholula, many ordinary citizens lined the roads, full of curiosity. They marveled at the huge prancing horses, the bearded men in strange costumes, the glinting steel weapons.

The Spaniards, too, were impressed by the Cholulans: the nobles in their fashionable cloaks, the women and children who threw flowers and wreaths to them. They admired the wide streets, systematically laid out and well maintained. The sturdy stone houses, the gardens, the numerous temples with awesome spires and towers—these impressed Cortes so much that he wrote to King Charles that night, saying he had not yet seen a city better suited for Spaniards to live in. Neither he nor the King had any qualms over the idea of conquering their Cholulan hosts, for to them conquest was a way of life. The entire history of Spain had been a struggle for military dominance by Moors, Romans, Visigoths, and other civilizations clustered around the Mediterranean Sea, whose name meant what they believed it to be: "Center of the World."

The Cholulan nobles escorted Cortes to a large building with several courts near a temple, where they housed the whole army comfortably. Servants arrived and fed them well with turkeys, vegetables, fruit, and the flat corncakes which the Spaniards were now calling tortillas. On their first night there, more caciques paid them a visit, some bringing their wives.

One wife was particularly charmed by Marina, who asked her many intelligent questions about Quetzalcoatl. The wife, whose name was Quilitl or "amaranth," was pleased to learn that Marina had been taught many of the tenets of the venerable priest-god. Proudly Quilitl informed Marina that Quetzalcoatl had resided in Cholula, where he had taught artisans and architects as well as priests and public administrators. The whole city, she said, was dedicated to Quetzalcoatl, although many other religions were tolerated there. She invited Marina to visit her at her house.

This cordial welcome by Cholulans made Cortes and his captains believe that the accusations made by Tlaxcalans were unfounded, that their suspicions could be attributed to long-standing hostilities between rival city-states. After the second day, however, no food was brought to the Cortes army. When he requested food from the priests at the temple, they said they had no corn, and they sent only wood and water.

The nobles did not call on Cortes again, and when he sent a messenger to make inquiry, they all gave excuses of illness. Alarmed by this turn of events by the third day, Cortes sent his Totonac volunteers and his servants into the marketplaces to see what they could learn. He also advised Marina to accept the invitation of the cacique's wife to pay her a visit.

That same day, before Marina could leave, some ambassadors arrived from Moctezuma. Their manner was haughty, their speech abrupt. "Our prince has sent us to say that he does not want you to come to Tenochtitlan," said the senior ambassador. "He says he cannot feed you and your army; he will be very upset if you disregard this request."

"Please tell your prince I'm very disappointed," said Cortes in his most courteous manner. Marina translated his message into courteous Nahuatl words that conveyed his diplomacy as well as his meaning. "I've heard such amazing things about your great prince that I can't wait to meet him. Why does he vacillate so, first bidding me to come, then telling me not to?"

The ambassadors stiffened. "Prince Moctezuma has asked us to return directly to Mexico with your reply."

"Then you should leave tomorrow," Cortes said in the same courteous manner, "but please stay with us tonight, and we'll accompany you. I'm leaving for Tenochtitlan tomorrow myself."

The ambassadors looked at each other. Cortes gave each of them a string of beads, and they agreed to stay overnight. He ordered Bernal Diaz to keep a close watch over them and to detain them if they tried to leave.

* * *

When Marina arrived at the home of the cacique's wife, Quilitl, she was greeted by the woman and one of her sons, a boy about fourteen years old. Then Quilitl sent her son away so the women could talk privately. They walked through her garden, where she pointed out her favorite flowers for Marina to admire.

"I have an older son," the cacique's wife said, "who needs a wife. As you can see, our family has some position in this community, and he could provide well for the wife we choose."

"Your younger son is quite handsome," Marina said tactfully, realizing that Quilitl intended to suggest a marriage. "I'm sure your older son is a man of distinction."

"I'll come right to the point," said Quilitl. "When I met you three days ago, I could see you didn't belong in that group of foreigners. You have beauty and breeding. How did you get mixed up with them?"

"It's a long story," Marina said. "I'll be as brief as I can. I was sent away with some Mayan traders after my father died; I thought I was being taken to the temple of Quetzalcoatl, but instead I was sold in the slave market at Xicalango. When the Spaniards came to Tabasco, my owners gave me to them."

Quilitl was visibly moved. "You've suffered many wrongs in your young life," she said. "How old are you?"

"Eighteen years old," Marina replied.

"Too young to die," said her new friend.

"Am I in danger of dying?" asked Marina, shocked.

"Much danger, indeed. Moctezuma has sent 20,000 warriors here. They're camped outside the city in ravines where your captains can't see them. They plan to kill all the Spaniards and their allies, except for a few to use for sacrifices."

"Oh!" cried Marina. "I could be killed along with them! How kind of you to warn me! Are you sure what you heard is true? How did you hear of this plan?"

Quilitl pointed proudly to a drum decorated in gold that stood nearby. "My husband received this drum from an Aztec warrior for helping prepare the city's defense. Three other captains received rich cloaks and jewels with instructions to bring the Spanish captains to Moctezuma, bound and ready to be sacrificed."

"Then it must be true. We're all in danger."

"You can stay with us," said Quilitl. "If my older son approves, perhaps you could marry him and join our household."

Marina did some quick thinking and responded warily. "I'd gladly stay, but my master expects me soon. If I don't return, he'll surely send soldiers to look for me. Besides, I have a few possessions I wouldn't want to leave behind."

"Could you get them and sneak away, without alarming the others, and come here?"

"An excellent plan," Marina agreed. "I could gather my few

belongings and some jewels my master has given me. If I come early tomorrow morning, will that be soon enough?"

"Probably," said Quilitl, "but don't delay any more than necessary."

"Thank you so much, Mother," said Marina, addressing the woman with a term of great respect. "Please tell my brother goodbye for me." She had not used the words *mother* and *brother* for many years; the terms sounded strange as she spoke them.

Walking toward her quarters, Marina pondered the honor Quilitl had offered her. Marriage to a man of rank would give her security and status she could never know as a slave. She liked this devotee of Quetzalcoatl, this gracious Cholulan, even though the Cholulans were allies of Moctezuma, who had oppressed her village of Paynala. Still, she felt no loyalty to the present tecuhtli of Paynala who had tricked her into slavery. Her impulses of gratitude pulled her instead toward the Spaniards who had treated her with kindness for many months. Loyalty and gratitude placed high in her list of ideals, but she could not always be sure where to place them in the real world.

* * *

The Totonac volunteers had spent most of the third day wandering around the city; they returned with bad news. They had seen several streets barricaded. Many of the flat roofs of the houses had been stacked with huge stones and other missiles. They had found several large holes in the streets, covered with branches and loose earth. Upright stakes had been braced inside the holes to wound any horses that fell upon their sharp points.

When Marina had translated these alarming tidings, she told Cortes she had something confidential to tell him. When he had dismissed the Totonacs, she told him what the cacique's wife had told her that afternoon.

"I don't want to leave you, even if I die at your side," she said, and added, "Te amo."

"I love you, too," Cortes said, "but neither of us will die tomorrow, I promise."

"Promise me, too, that no harm will come to Quilitl. She wanted to save my life; I want to save hers."

"No harm will come to her from my hands," Cortes promised. "Casualties of war can't always be prevented, though."

Cortes then sent Marina to the temple nearby, loaded with gifts of fine cloth for the priests. She persuaded two of them to return with her to Cortes' quarters. He questioned them thoroughly as to why no food had been sent that day.

The embarrassed priests said they had received contradictory messages from Moctezuma. First he had told them to show the visitors much respect; then he said not to feed them. The two

300

priests, much irritated by the emperor's conflicting orders, confirmed that Moctezuma had sent 20,000 warriors, half of them stationed around the city, the others camped in nearby gullies. Cortes thanked them for their truthfulness and gave them another present of richly embroidered cloth, telling them not to disclose what they had told him, or he would have them killed when he returned. He then asked the priests to contact all the caciques and have them meet him at dawn in the temple court, bringing a thousand porters to induce the Spaniards to leave Cholula. He told Marina to get some sleep, to be ready to interpret for him early the next morning.

Then Cortes consulted with his captains and devised a plan for a counterattack. He placed guards over the two ambassadors from Mexico, intending to use them as guides when the battle was over. He ordered his men to sleep in their armor, with their horses all saddled and bridled, in case of sudden attack. Then he dispatched a messenger to Alvarado, Olid, and the 6,000 Tlaxcalans still camped by the stream about two leagues away.

* * *

When his meetings were finished and his captains had left, Cortes lay down on a mat beside Marina. She stirred, wakened, and embraced him. In the quiet of that time alone with her, he marveled at her loyalty and devotion. She had been offered marriage to a cacique's son, yet she chose slavery. She could have saved herself, yet she chose to take her chances with him. He made love to her with great passion, not even removing all his clothing, because he knew the danger facing them in just a few hours would be great, and life's sweetest moments must sometimes be fitted into a crack between the hard stone walls of reality.

* * *

At dawn Cortes' plan went quickly into effect. The caciques arrived, bringing the requested porters with them so that they filled the temple court to overflowing. Some of these porters looked more like warriors, and some carried weapons, but Cortes had anticipated that. Many of them could be innocent tamemes or slaves, he knew, but a general cannot be concerned with sorting out the innocent in wartime. Spanish soldiers with swords and shields stationed themselves at the three gates to the walled court, so not a single Indian could pass unnoticed. Others, swords buckled on their thighs, took their places all around the sides of the court. Archers, lancers, and crossbowmen sidled quietly into their assigned positions.

301

Cortes, on horseback so all the caciques could see and hear him, delivered a stinging rebuke to them. Marina, standing on some steps nearby, translated his words and reflected his anger. He told them he knew of the schemes they were hatching against him, piling up stones, digging holes, evacuating their families. He asked why they treated his army this way, men who had come to benefit them by telling them about the great Spanish king and the powerful Christian God. He knew about the Aztec soldiers, he said, who had already started a stew pot to cook the Spaniards with salt and pepper and tomatoes.

"Such treachery as that must not go unpunished, by royal decree," Cortes concluded emphatically. "For that you must die." When he ordered a musket fired, the soldiers he had stationed around the court drew their swords and began the massacre.

Artillery fire plowed into the center of the court where bunches of Cholulans huddled together. Screaming and pushing, some rushed for the gates, only to be impaled on the pikes of the guards. Those who tried to scale the walls made easy targets for the archers and crossbowmen. Steel swords flashed in the morning sunlight, then turned red with the blood of the surprised Cholulans. As the swordsmen and cavalrymen sliced and stabbed, piles of maimed bodies littered the court, half-naked bodies defenseless against steel blades and cannonballs, savaged by weapons whose power they had never seen before, destructive power their imaginations could not stretch to comprehend.

Shortly afterward the 6,000 Tlaxcalans arrived, yelling and fighting fiercely in the streets against the warriors assembled by Cholulans and Aztecs. Soon the Tlaxcalans had crushed their enemies, including some Aztecs who had rushed in from camps in the ravines. Within three hours, over 3,000 Indians lay dead in the temple yard and littered the streets of Cholula.

The Tlaxcalans began looting, plundering, and taking prisoners for slaves. The Spaniards could not stop them from venting their deep, ancient hatred for the Cholulans who had betrayed them to the Aztecs. The next day more men arrived from other towns in the Tlaxcala province, doing more damage to the wounded city, taking whatever they could carry, destroying what they could not take. Only by appealing to the Tlaxcalan captains did Cortes finally bring the rioting under control.

Several of the Spanish captains discovered some "fattening" prisons, filled with Indians and boys who had been captured and were being fattened for sacrifice. With great relish the conquistadors opened the prisons and released the captives, sending them back to their native territories. The released captives, too terrified to be grateful, simply ran away like frightened deer.

* * *

On the second day after the massacre, Cortes decided to make peace. He had ordered the survivors of the Cholulan armies to clean up the messes and cremate their dead, which they did. Then, as the fires of human cremation mimicked the smoke rising above the green valley from the deep blue, white-capped volcano Popocatepetl, he held a public meeting. Several caciques from districts of the city that had not been involved in the plot asked not to be held accountable for the treachery of the others; these Cortes willingly sent back to their homes, saying the traitors had paid with their lives, and he had no wish to punish the innocent.

Then he publicly exonerated the two priests who had disclosed the secret plot and Quilitl, the woman who had wanted to be Marina's mother-in-law. Quilitl's husband had been killed in the slaughter, for he had been one of the traitors, but her sons stood beside her, and Cortes asked them to comfort her.

The ambassadors of Moctezuma were summoned, and Cortes made a speech to them for everyone else to hear. He said the whole city deserved to be destroyed, but out of respect to their lord Moctezuma, he would pardon them. In future, he warned, they must be well behaved, and never employ such treachery again.

Then Cortes addressed the chiefs of Tlaxcala, who had been summoned from their camps outside the city. "You have taken many Cholulans captive, to use them as slaves," he said. "Now return them to their families—every man, woman, and child."

A moan rippled through the ranks of the Tlaxcalans. One of the Tlaxcalan chiefs spoke out in protest. "You suffered one treachery, and you punished it very harshly. We have endured many treacheries, over many years, from the Cholulans. They have spied on us and sent information to Moctezuma; they joined his embargo and would not trade with us for salt. They deserve more punishment. We don't want to return our prisoners."

"You must give back all the captives," Cortes repeated firmly. "In return for their lives and their freedom, I am asking all the Cholulans to be grateful for your mercy, to make peace with you, and to trade with you in the future." Again a murmur ran through the ranks, but this time one of surprise.

"Finally," Cortes said to the Tlaxcalans, "you may keep the goods you removed from the homes and markets. I know you need the salt and cotton. These items can be considered as fines against Cholulans for letting the Aztecs use them as traitors, and as rewards to the soldiers who risked their lives here."

Grudgingly, each of the Tlaxcalan chiefs agreed to return his prisoners, and the caciques of Cholula agreed to resume trade with the Tlaxcalans. Cortes also delivered a speech about giving

303

up their idols and sacrifices and converting to Christianity, but Father Olmedo again dissuaded him, urging him to be patient. "You've taught a great lesson in Christian forgiveness," he said. "If these two feuding cities can learn to befriend their enemies, they will come to the arms of Christ soon enough. Let them do it gradually, so they come with willing hearts."

* * *

Although Cortes revered Father Olmedo and was inclined to follow his advice in matters of faith, his own convictions were so strong that he had difficulty understanding why other people did not convert to Christianity immediately upon hearing the gospel. To him the benefits of his faith seemed so obvious, and the pagan religions so hellish, that even when Olmedo restrained him he considered his compliance to be only a matter of strategy, perhaps of pacing. He had no doubt, however, that God was on his side, that eventually the forces of right would triumph over wrong, and that he personally could speed the process.

About ten days after the massacre, Marina told him of a tradition she had learned from the priests who had revealed the plot. They said Quetzalcoatl had left a legend: if his city was ever threatened, certain stones should be pried loose from his pyramid. Torrents of water would then gush out and flood the invaders, drown them, quench any fires of battle.

Cortes was delighted to hear this tale. Just as he had proven to the natives in Cozumel that their idols were false by sending them down the steps in splinters, just as he had convinced the Cempoalans how impotent their idols were, he wanted to convince the Cholulans. He took Marina with him to see the temple and determine just which stones the legend referred to.

The temple of Quetzalcoatl stood atop an imposing pyramid on a high mound in the valley. Like other teocallis in Mexico, it was oriented with four sides toward the four cardinal points and divided into four terraces. The base, built of stone and mortar, extended for an amazing 423 feet. The top was flat, not pointed like Egyptian pyramids Cortes had seen in paintings. His letter to the king had described groups of pilgrims wending their way to this temple to offer devotions, much as peoples of the Mideast gravitated to Mecca. Although many of the pilgrims looked ragged and beggarly, the atmosphere of the temple was sanctified, capable of inspiring reverence even in non-believers.

The image of Quetzalcoatl in the temple flaunted a collar of gold, ear pendants of mosaic turquoise, a headdress with flame-shaped plumes, and a jewel-studded scepter in one hand. To signify his rule over the winds, he held a shield painted with symbols of his authority. Marina stood in awe before this image and begged Cortes not to let his soldiers destroy it.

304

Cortes asked the priests in the temple near his quarters to rally as many people as they could to make a pilgrimage to the temple of Quetzalcoatl. There he would speak to them of the Christian god, who was also a god of peace. He particularly asked them to bring the widow Quilitl, who had wanted to be Marina's mother-in-law, thinking it would please Marina to see the kindly old woman embrace a new faith as Marina had.

On the appointed day the crowd of priests and citizens assembled at the pyramid and climbed its hundred and twenty steps. Many of them sat on the temple steps as Cortes gave his usual talk about Christianity. This time, however, he stressed the similarities as well as the differences between the religion of Christ and the religion of Quetzalcoatl.

Marina translated, glowing with a conviction that she had been chosen by God for important work. Certainly no other person there could have explained both religions so clearly. She looked at the mass of attentive faces and felt a power growing within her, as if God were commanding her to move mountains and giving her the strength to do it.

Then Cortes spoke of the legend, pointing to the stones it referred to. "Remove those stones," he commanded. The pilgrims, priests, and citizens emitted a chorus of gasps and murmurs. Again Cortes spoke, directing his remarks to the priests. Three of them moved toward the stones, and several of the citizens joined them in their endeavor to loosen the stones.

Marina then noticed Quilitl. She was wearing a white robe of mourning, and Marina remembered that her husband had been killed along with the other caciques involved in the plot. Marina stepped over to Quilitl, who stood at the edge of the crowd while others watched the removal of the stones. "How are things with you, Mother?" she asked.

Quilitl turned dark-circled eyes toward her. "Not well," she said. "My sons have turned against me. They blame me for their father's death."

"You pitied me once," Marina said sympathetically, "and now I pity you. Tell your sons you were not to blame. My master had many sources of information. What happened that day would have happened regardless of what you or I said to each other."

"It wouldn't matter what I said to them," the woman replied. "They feel angry over their father's death; it's easier to blame me than to admit they're powerless to avenge it."

"The new faith might bring you comfort, Mother. Jesus Christ has taken our sins and burdens upon himself."

Quilitl laughed bitterly. "I came here today hoping to see you destroyed by a flood of water when the stones are removed and Quetzalcoatl takes his revenge. You have betrayed my trust; the blood of thousands of my countrymen stains your hands."

Marina was taken aback by the stinging criticism. "Surely,

Mother, if you were unhappy as the object of undeserved blame, you would not subject another woman to that same injustice."

Just then the stones gave way. A roar exploded from the crowd, followed by disappointed silence. Cortes picked up the stones, one at a time, and threw them down the steps with a great clatter. No water came forth. Only dust.

Quilitl spat on Marina. "You Christians have no honor," she said. "You'd rather be your master's whore than an honest man's wife. You Christians accepted our hospitality but rewarded it by robbing our homes and killing innocent people. You've taken away my husband, my sons, my city. Now you would take away my faith." Marina fell tearfully to her knees, touched the stones of the court and then her tongue with the dust. "Forgive me, Mother," she begged contritely, her head bowed, expecting to feel a blow or at least to hear a prolonged scolding.

No answer came. Marina looked up only in time to see the white-robed figure throw herself over a parapet, certain to crash in a bloody death on the stones below. Then a rash of other suicides followed hers in spontaneous acts of despair.

Marina felt hollow as she walked back to the quarters she shared with Cortes. She would have much to ask Father Olmedo about, and much to tell him in her next confession.

* * *

For several days Marina brooded around the court. The words of Quilitl kept echoing in her thoughts, and she could not shut out the picture of this woman throwing herself from the top of the temple of Quetzalcoatl.

She sought Father Olmedo, asking him what Christians believe about punishment. He quoted the old testament: "an eye for an eye and a tooth for a tooth." He quoted the new testament: "If a man smite thee, turn the other cheek." She told him she would ponder those words well.

She was still pondering them when she ate privately with Cortes in his quarters that night. Cortes bragged that he intended to replace every temple in Cholula with a Christian church. Her depression and grief over the massacre of the Cholulans made her bolder than usual, and she confronted him. "Is it true that a Christian forgives his enemies?"

"Of course," Cortes replied confidently. "That's why many former enemies are now my friends."

Marina spoke petulantly. "You asked the Cholulans to forgive their enemies, yet you destroy their temples and kill people who have never harmed you."

Cortes spoke patronizingly. "Those are the casualties of war, Marina. We bring the cross and the blade. The blade makes way for the cross. That may seem harsh to you, but the history of the

306

world has been one of conquest. It can't be otherwise."

"Did you have to kill so many of the Cholulans? Couldn't you punish only those who plotted against you?"

The vein stood out on Cortes' neck; Marina recognized this sign of growing anger. "Well, that's just great!" he said ironically, throwing a tortilla down on his plate. "Not only do I have to consult my captains in matters of military strategy, but now I have to consult my interpreter! What do you know about the problems of leadership? How do you think we could have judged all the people individually before we struck? What do you know about the element of surprise in winning a campaign? What do you know about the need to establish a reputation for boldness to pave the way for future military successes?"

Marina felt her own anger rising, but she spoke with control. "I'm only an ignorant slave," she said. "I know nothing of military strategy, but I know the hearts of the people of Maya and Mexico. What does it gain you to conquer a city and bring inhabitants to their knees, if you lose the battle for their souls?"

"You aren't my religious adviser, either!" Cortes exploded, throwing his goblet against the wall. "What makes you think you can judge me and question my motives? Who do you think you are?"

"Just an ignorant slave," Marina answered icily. "I know my place, master." She picked up the soiled dishes and carried them out to the servants' quarters. She remained there, talking to the other women, until she thought Cortes would be asleep. Then she crept into his quarters and curled up in a corner, as far away from his sleeping mat as she could get.

For the rest of the time in Cholula, Marina spent most of her time away from Cortes' quarters on the pretext of helping Dona Luisa, who was pregnant with Pedro de Alvarado's child.

Alvarado had joined an expedition headed by Diego de Ordaz to explore the volcano Popocatepetl. Ordaz returned with a tale of adventure and good news. Although Indian porters had been afraid to accompany them higher than a certain point, the Spaniards had scaled the peak to its top, braving the icy winds and snow, finally able to peer from the rim of the crater into its smoldering cauldron of lava.

From that breathtaking height, the explorers could also see the towers and temples of Tenochtitlan to the west, its gemlike splendor gleaming in the midst of a shimmering pale blue lake, as tantalizing as a kingdom from a fable. They were overjoyed to find not only a source for sulphur, which greatly pleased Cortes, but also an easier road leading to Tenochtitlan—a smooth and relatively level one leading through Huexotzingo—which pleased Cortes even more.

Something else was displeasing him, however. He was troubled that Marina spoke to him only when he spoke to her, and then only with the briefest possible answer. If he asked her to sleep with him she obliged, but she lay as passively under him as a Spanish whore and seemed relieved when his lovemaking was over, as if it had been an ordeal. When he said *te amo* she replied simply *gracias*, without enthusiasm. She performed translating duties as efficiently as ever, but her voice held no ardor, and she never volunteered advice or information as she previously had done. When he asked her if anything was wrong, she simply answered *nada*, yet she never smiled.

Cortes turned to Father Olmedo. After making his usual confession, Cortes asked the wise friar's advice. "What is wrong with Marina?" he asked. "She's so moody these days."

"Have you asked her?"

"Yes, of course. But she won't tell me anything. We did have a few cross words several days ago. She thought I'd been too hard on the Cholulans, but she's never questioned my decisions before. Why has this campaign bothered her so much?"

"I can't tell you anything she's told me in confession," Father Olmedo said thoughtfully. "You might talk to her friend Luisa, however."

Cortes thanked Olmedo for the advice. Then he asked for more. "Do you think I was too hard on the Cholulans?"

"I know you have good intentions," Olmedo answered tactfully. "I also know you have difficult military decisions to make. Since you asked my opinion, I'll admit I thought the revenge against the Cholulans was excessive. We should be concerned with the example we set as Christians. No more than an eye for an eye. No more than a tooth for a tooth. To inflict more than that is not justice, but wrath."

"A deadly sin," Cortes acknowledged contritely. Again he thanked the friar, not only as his religious adviser, but as his friend. He then spoke to Luisa, as the good friar recommended, and she told him to ask Marina about the death of Quilitl.

"So that's what's troubling her," Cortes said with relief. "She's grieving for Quilitl. Why would she be angry with me, though? I did pardon the woman."

"You pardoned Quilitl in public," Luisa said. "You pardoned her even though she had committed no crimes—her husband had. You pardoned her in the presence of her sons, in public, as if they should feel some kind of shame about their parents. That's why Quilitl killed herself. She had nothing to live for."

"Are you judging me too, Luisa?" Cortes said sorrowfully. "First Marina, then Olmedo, and now you?"

"Not at all," Luisa said brightly. "I'm just telling you what you need to know to recapture Marina's affection. I care nothing for politics or religion, but I care for Marina. I can accept your imperfections more easily than she can. I'm not in love with you."

* * *

The message that went forth to Moctezuma, first from the remnants of his army that had fled home from the ravines, and later from the spies he sent to Cholula, was that the Spaniards must indeed be teules, not just men. They seemed invincible in battle, wrathful when displeased, generous in pardoning some of their enemies, and magical in their ability to mediate friendship between bitter enemies like Cholula and Tlaxcala. These teules had also demonstrated greater magical powers than the priests of Quetzalcoatl.

The good news for Moctezuma came from an envoy sent by Cortes, who relayed this message: the Spaniards did not blame Moctezuma for what had happened; they were inclined not to believe the lying Cholulans who had tried to blame the emperor for their misdeeds; and they offered their friendship, as always, to the great Moctezuma. They had been delayed twenty days by the mischief encountered in Cholula, but they were ready to press onward and hoped he would be gracious enough to receive them.

Greatly relieved, Moctezuma sent an envoy immediately with his response. He said he was glad his friends the Spaniards had not been taken in by the deceits of the Cholulans. They were totally untrustworthy people, the emperor said, who were always looking for someone to blame.

* * *

On November 1, when Cortes prepared to leave Cholula, he sent back all the Tlaxcalans except a thousand to serve him as porters. He also said farewell to the Totonacs, because they had no wish to enter the domain of their ancient enemies the Aztecs, and they had been gone from home since August 16. The volunteers returned laden with treasures, including many of the fabrics and mantles Moctezuma had sent to Cortes, as well as the spoils of conquest acquired in Cholula.

Marina took her place among the other women, servants and slaves who would cook and sew for the company of soldiers. Cortes sent a soldier to bring her to his side. She insisted her place was with the other women, but Cortes would not leave until she consented to ride with him on the back of his horse.

"I can't take any chances of losing you," he said to her as one of his attendants boosted her up onto the horse's back. "Hold tight!" He galloped for some distance, Marina clinging to his back, until they were far enough from the others so they wouldn't be overheard. Then he slowed his steed to a walk.

"I want to apologize," he said. "If you wish, I'll say that before my men, but I'd rather keep our disagreements private."

"Whatever you say," Marina said compliantly. "You don't have to apologize to me at all."

"I apologize for my insensitivity," he said. "I didn't realize you were grieving for Quilitl when we quarreled."

"She made me face some painful truths," Marina said. "When I thought about what she said to me, I realized I'm to blame for her death."

"I'm the one who's to blame," Cortes insisted, glad that Marina was speaking freely to him once more. "You had to tell me what you learned from her. You did the right thing, probably saved our lives. I thought I could protect her by pardoning her, but I guess I shouldn't have done that in public. It was a stupid blunder."

Marina had never heard Cortes admit to making a blunder. If Cortes could have seen her face then, he would have seen an expression mingling surprise and relief at the fulfillment of a frail hope.

"I've confessed to Father Olmedo," Cortes continued. "I was carried away by my bad temper when I heard about the ambush. The friar told me to set a good example of Christian behavior, and I said I'd try. A good Christian isn't a man who never makes a mistake, Marina. He isn't a man who never loses his temper. He's a man who takes responsibility for his behavior."

"And repents for any hurt he causes," Marina added. She had heard enough sermons to know what came next.

"I repent," Cortes said. "And there's something else I regret. When I became angry with you for criticizing me, I said something rash. I wish I could take it back, but words are like birds that never return to the nest."

"I shouldn't have criticized you," Marina said. "It's not my place to judge my master."

"That's what I thought at the time," Cortes said. "A proud man doesn't like criticism, but a big man learns to take it. I said you were nothing but a slave; now I could bite my tongue. You're much more than that to me. I couldn't have come this far without you. I need your criticism; I need your advice."

"Thank you for telling me that," Marina said gratefully. Her eyes were beginning to sting as those words opened a heart she had tried to lock.

"I love you, Marina," Cortes said gently, "even though I'm a married man and a very imperfect one. Father Olmedo constantly has to forgive my pride, my hot temper, my adultery, and now even my excessive zeal for victory. I know I don't deserve your love, but I'm willing to beg for it. Can you forgive me?"

Cortes could feel the wetness on the back of his shirt and the pressure of Marina's cheek against his shoulder blade. From her answer, he knew she had been talking to Olmedo. "Seventy times seven, if need be," she said with deep emotion.

310

Chapter 23

Tenochtitlan and Moctezuma

The citizens of the Aztec city-state, Tenochtitlan, gathered in groups bordering the sides of the causeway or paddled around the bridges in their canoes to see if the amazing rumors were true. Coming from the city of Ixtapalapa on the eastern edge of Lake Texcoco, a company of about seven thousand foreigners were marching into their city, escorted by some Ixtapalapan tecuhtlis. Heading the column of aliens came four stags without horns, called horses. These horses pranced, turned their heads to either side, and jingled little bells on their shining breastplates. The horses neighed and snorted loudly, dripped foam from their mouths, and sweated so much that water ran down their sides. When they ran fast, they made a great clattering as if someone were throwing stones. When they raised their feet, they stirred up the dirt and left rounded tracks in it.

On the horses' backs rode men in strange colorful clothing, some made of metal, hard and shining, covering their heads and breasts and legs, making clanking sounds. One of them, slightly ahead of the other three, carried a colorful banner on a long stick. He shook it and made it move, first in circles, then from one side to the other. The others carried shields on their shoulders and held unsheathed iron swords that glittered in the midday sun. At the heels of the first four men came two greyhound dogs, noses sniffing the ground, panting heavily.

The second group of riders wore cotton armor and carried shields covered with leather, their iron swords hanging from the trappings of the horses. In their midst rode a deep-chested man, about 34 or 35 years old, wearing leather boots and a red hat from which a long feather curled elegantly. Two persons without armor or weapons walked beside his horse, one of them a Nahua woman with glossy black hair descending to her waist. A third group of men carried crossbows and baskets full of iron arrows. From their hoods of cotton armor, quetzal feathers radiated on all sides. Then came the musketeers, shouldering iron weapons.

Most of the first four hundred men had pale or light brown

311

skin and bushes of hair on their faces, hair of different colors such as brown, black, yellow, and red. They were the Spaniards, who many said were teules. These were followed by several thousand natives dressed like people from the Tlaxcala region, carrying loads of supplies or wooden bows and arrows.

* * *

For the Spaniards, their first views of Tenochtitlan seemed equally astonishing on that historic day of November 8, 1519. They had already been impressed with the beautiful city of Ixtapalapa, where they had been welcomed by King Cuitlahuac, a nephew of Moctezuma, on the previous day. Its sweet-scented orchards and bird-filled gardens, its fine buildings of stone and cedar wood, fresh water ponds, and canals for traveling by canoe—nothing so magnificent existed in Europe. If Ixtapalapa was so marvelous, what must be in wait for them in Tenochtitlan, the greatest of all Aztec cities?

The causeways, too, had no parallel that the Spaniards had seen. Broad enough for eight horsemen to ride abreast, level and sturdily constructed of earth and stone, these roads connected the cities on three sides of the large salty Lake Texcoco and separated it from the fresh waters of Lake Xochimilco. On the east appeared occasional salt flats where workers were evaporating the saline waters to extract minerals. On the west, the sweet water teemed with fish and ducks. On both lakes, many canoes were ferrying produce and trade goods to and from the great lake-bound city. The native boaters stopped to stare at the strangers before resuming their routines.

At intervals the causeways had gates to control the flow of water, and at a major junction a fortress controlled access to the main causeway leading to Tenochtitlan. Cortes noted the strategic location of this Fort of Xoloc with its twelve-foot wall and towers at each end, where the main causeway branched into smaller ones leading to Coyoacan and Ixtapalapa. This fort could be used to cut off a retreat as well as to block the main entrance to the city. Cortes' captains noted this arrangement also, realizing that this lovely city could easily become a trap for their daring little band of four hundred Spaniards.

A delegation of a hundred dignitaries met Cortes's army at the junction near the Fort of Xoloc. These caciques and lords, all wearing richly decorated robes and feathered headdresses, crowded the causeway. Heading the delegation were four important personages, all related to Moctezuma: his brother Cuitlahuac, who ruled Ixtapalapa; his nephew Cacama, king of Texcoco; and the kings of Coyoacan and Tacuba. Two of these kings had already met Cortes. Cacama had been sent to meet Cortes and discourage him the day after he left Cholula;

312

Cuitlahuac had hosted Cortes's troops in Ixtapalapa after Cortes, undiscouraged by Cacama's pleadings, had pressed onward. The four kings knelt courteously before Cortes, touched the ground and then their tongues, and welcomed him with a Nahuatl greeting. Marina translated the familiar greeting directly into Spanish, which was understood by both Cortes and the other interpreter, Geronimo de Aguilar.

While the welcoming delegation took turns bobbing their feathered heads and kneeling in welcome, the Cortes army waited on the causeway. The four kings walked back toward Tenochtitlan, which lay half a league to the north, to accompany their emperor. The emperor Moctezuma made an entrance suited to his exalted rank, carried in a richly decorated litter, accompanied by numerous lords, officers, and other attendants. Cacama and Cuitlahuac, who had changed their garments and now wore even more splendid cloaks, supported Moctezuma with their arms as he stepped down from the litter. On a cotton cloth laid on the ground by servants, the emperor placed his golden-soled sandals adorned with turquoise stones. Four other lords held over the monarch's head a canopy decorated with blue-green quetzal feathers, embroidered with gold and silver threads, studded with pearls and precious chalchihuite stones.

Marina suggested that Cortes should observe how all the emperor's attendants, except the four kings, kept their eyes downcast. She explained that it was considered discourteous for people of lower rank to look directly into the emperor's face. Cortes thanked her but boldly decided to look Moctezuma in the eyes, as if speaking to a person of no greater importance than his own.

Dismounting from his horse, Cortes paid respect to Moctezuma with a deep bow. Simultaneously, Moctezuma said words of welcome. The emperor, about forty years old, stood a little taller than his brother; his body, although thin, showed an experienced warrior's wiriness. His narrow face was framed with black hair cut to reach just below his ears; his chin bore a scanty, but well-shaped, beard. His expression, primarily cheerful, could change in an instant to one of seriousness or gentleness. He wore no head ornament other than a panache of quetzal feathers, which descended down his back in a radiant string of deep turquoise. His white cotton tilmantli with its border of shimmering hummingbird feathers was clasped at his shoulder with a gem-encrusted pin. His copper-colored skin, immaculately clean, showed no traces of sweat as did the skins and clothing of the Spaniards.

Cortes offered his right hand to Moctezuma, who ignored it until Marina explained this courtesy to the emperor. Then Moctezuma reluctantly extended his own right hand, which Cortes held briefly in his fingertips as if it were the hand of a

European king. Then Cortes brought out a necklace of margarita stones, strung on a golden cord and scented with fragrant musk, placing it around the neck of the emperor.

Because Moctezuma appeared pleased, Cortes moved to embrace him, but Cacama and Cuitlahuac quickly grabbed Cortes's arms to restrain him. When Cortes gave Marina a puzzled look, she explained. "The emperor's lords are protecting him," she said. "You offend him when you attempt to touch him. They consider that gesture an unwarranted intimacy, perhaps even an indignity."

Cortes quickly recovered his poise and said many flattering words to Moctezuma through the mouth of Marina. Aguilar was present, and at times Marina verified her understanding of Spanish by translating Nahuatl into Mayan as well as Spanish for Aguilar's approval, but most of what was said Marina could understand without the need of a third party. She was also aware that Aguilar made some mistakes in translating from Mayan to Spanish, but she would say nothing critical of him because she did not want to hurt his feelings. He had been her friend for almost a year, sharing and enduring some difficult times.

When the emperor addressed him as "Malintzin," meaning "Marina's Lord," Cortes accepted the appellation in good humor. From then on, the Aztecs followed the custom adopted by most of the Indians of Mexico, using the same name for both Cortes and the interpreter who spoke for him, the woman whose voice had almost magically become blended with his. That name became altered within a short time, taking the form of "Malinche." Occasionally, however, if it became necessary to distinguish between them, Moctezuma would address Cortes as "Senor Malinche" and speak about Marina as "La Malinche."

Names have power, as the Mayans knew. In a Mayan religious rite, a name could represent the person himself. Language has power, as the Aztecs knew. Their priests were those who could speak to the gods; a leader was either a *tecuhtli* or a *tlatoani*, "one who speaks," and the most revered person in the realm, the emperor, was called the *Uey Tlatoani*. The name of *Malinche* began to accrue great power on that eventful day in 1519, because the Aztecs realized that an interpreter can have profound influence over those who depend upon her. Later they realized further that the combination of her loyalty and her linguistic talents gave Cortes an advantage even more awesome than steel swords, or mighty horses, or gunpowder. Yet no one would have been more surprised than the dutiful slave who stood barefoot beside her master's horse that November day, if she could have seen into the future. Her name was destined to become one of the most respected in Mexico while she lived, one of the most famous in Latin American history after her death. Also, through a peculiar process of mythmaking and demonizing, her name would become a synonym for "traitress" to generations yet unborn. The coming generations would hear her name spoken often by voices that would malign her, yet rarely by those voices that would speak on her behalf. Language, like power itself, is a tool not always used in the service of truth or justice.

* * *

Cacama and Cuitlahuac escorted the Cortes army to the palace of Axayacatl, Moctezuma's deceased father, and installed the emperor's guests in its spacious apartments. Along the way they had been dazzled by the city's most beautiful buildings, the homes of nobles, made of polished stone and carved woods, many decorated with feathered banners or festooned with flowers and vines. From the flat roofs or *azoteas*, children peered at them curiously. Many boatmen followed their progress along canals that interlaced the city, and well-behaved crowds gathered along the well-swept streets. Cortes estimated the city to hold about 300,000 people, but again he could find nothing in his own experience to compare with it.

Axayacatl's palace contained many statues of various gods, for Moctezuma had generously permitted assorted expressions of religion in his territories. He believed all gods could be honored without bringing any dishonor on his own. The palace had also been used as a convent for young priestesses and as a storehouse for the imperial treasure Moctezuma had inherited from Axayacatl. This treasure had been sealed up in a hidden room and its entrance quickly plastered over before the Spaniards were quartered there, for Moctezuma had concluded that his guests were as greedy for gold as monkeys for scraps of food.

The walls, ceilings, and floors were highly polished and spotlessly clean. Tapestries of cotton and featherwork delighted the eyes of the soldiers, and sweet-smelling smoke from braziers pleased their nostrils. Their sleeping mats, woven of palm-leaf, had coverlets of soft cotton, and many apartments also had a type of chair carved from a single slab of wood.

Moctezuma, arriving ahead of the slower column of Cortes's army, met Cortes at the palace and personally showed him to his quarters. He placed two necklaces around Cortes's neck, chains of red seashells from which dangled several life-sized shrimps made of gold. Then he told Cortes and his escorts to make themselves comfortable; he would send food and whatever servants they needed. A splendid meal endeared him to all the soldiers; gifts of fine fabrics and silver ornaments pleased Cortes.

* * *

The following day Cortes took his two interpreters, Father

315

Olmedo, and several captains to visit Moctezuma's recently completed palace. Like the Spaniards, Marina had never seen any building as magnificent as this. Though similar in style to his father's palace, Moctezuma's was more elegantly constructed and more luxuriantly furnished. Finely carved cedar beams and other woods, joined cleverly without nails, formed the ceilings. The visitors walked across floors of marble and jasper, through three great courtyards around which clustered innumerable rooms.

In one of the courtyards, where a fountain sent fine sprays of water into the air and many exotic birds flitted about, Moctezuma received his guests. He took them into an audience room and requested chairs for all of them. His attendants, who always walked barefoot in his presence and never looked directly at him, were much annoyed with the audacity of these guests who wore shoes or sandals and looked into the emperor's face. Nevertheless they obediently brought chairs, and Moctezuma seemed not the least offended by his guests' bad manners.

Seated in a carved wooden chair facing Cortes, Moctezuma explained his interest in the observations of Spanish activity in the Mexican and Mayan territories. "For several years I've seen omens and heard reports of bearded white men coming in floating houses from the east, where the morning star appears and the sun rises. Are you connected with these men who came before you?"

Cortes replied through Marina, "The explorers Cordoba and Grijalva came from my own country of Spain. They serve the same great king and the same God as I."

"You are the explorer who came in the year 1 Reed," said Moctezuma. "Have you heard of our god Quetzalcoatl, who was born in the year 1 Reed and died in a year with that same number?"

"I know a little of him through Marina," Cortes answered; then he tried to shift the subject. "Some of his teachings remind me of the teachings of our one true god, Jesus Christ."

"We have other more important gods," Moctezuma said, not yet willing to yield control of the conversation to his guest. "Our sacred books predict that Quetzalcoatl will return, just as the Morning Star disappears and returns. Some of my advisers think you may be a descendent of Quetzalcoatl; some think you might be the god himself returning; but others say he didn't promise to return in person, only as the Morning Star."

Cortes saw an opportunity. "I only know that God has sent me to you, to tell you about the Christian faith, so you will give up your idols. He's made me an instrument to do His will; He has the power to make this prophecy come true."

Father Olmedo cringed at the mention of idols, a topic he considered premature. "My captain general is a man of great faith," he said through Marina. "He means no offense, but only to share the joy of Christianity with others."

Marina detected the slight tension between Olmedo and Cortes. Many times she had heard Olmedo plead with Cortes to exercise patience, yet Cortes seemed unable to restrain himself from attacking the religious beliefs of the natives and thus alienating a great many. She realized how important it would be to convert Moctezuma. She translated faithfully what Olmedo had said, but added these words to facilitate the discussion: "Before we tell you about our religion, please tell us something of yours." Her plan worked; the emperor was pleased.

"I'm happy to explain," said Moctezuma, who took some pride in his piety and scholarship. "Our ancient ancestors came from a land far away called Aztlan. They wandered many places in search of food and a homeland. When other tribes tried to drive them away, their God Huitzilopochtli helped them win their battles and survive. Through his priests, he told them they would find a homeland where an eagle perched on a cactus with a snake in its beak. They found such a place, here in the valley of Mexico, in the swampy regions around Lake Texcoco, and settled here. At first they subsisted on snakes and frogs, but Huizilopochtli told them through his priests that if they would give him the sacred food he needed, he would make them into a great nation. He's made Tenochtitlan the greatest city in Anahuac, "The One World," and in return we provide him with the food he needs to climb the sky each day—the sacred blood of life."

Cortes shuddered at this reference to blood sacrifice, but he recognized the need to be tactful once Olmedo pointed it out to him. "We are Christians," he said, "who worship the one true god, Jesus Christ. He was crucified on a cross, where he died for our sins, but he was resurrected and is now in Heaven."

Olmedo interjected a correction. "We worship God the Father, his son Jesus Christ, and the Holy Spirit—that is, a holy trinity," he said.

Cortes smiled amiably. "I'm not as learned as Father Olmedo," he said. "I hope to send you many holy men some day who can explain more of the details of our faith. I can only tell you in the simplest outlines how God created the world, and gave it to Adam and Eve, but they brought death into the world by disobeying His commandments. Then it was necessary for Jesus Christ to come to earth and bring the gift of eternal life."

Cortes loved this kind of discourse so much that he never realized when he was being tedious. He went on talking for over an hour, ending with his usual plea for the natives to give up their idols and the human sacrifices. Olmedo gave Marina a frustrated look, but he said nothing.

At that point Moctezuma stood up, indicating his wish to end the interview, speaking more stiffly and formally than he had before. "Senor Malinche, I have understood all you said about three gods and the cross. We have heard about the things you have said in other towns, but we have not disputed any of these things because you are entitled to your beliefs.

"Here in this land we have always worshipped our own gods and thought them to be good. No doubt your gods are good also, but we do not want to hear more about them. We have our own beliefs about the creation of the world; we have believed them for many sheafs of years.

"As for your being teules like our revered Quetzalcoatl, I'm convinced that you are not. You have flesh and bones as we do, eat and drink as we do, become ill and die as we do. Yet you are valiant men, and as such we honor you. Please excuse me now; it's time for my afternoon bath. Take with you these tokens of my appreciation for your visit."

With that, Moctezuma signaled a servant to bring more gifts. The captains were especially pleased to receive individual gifts, because Cortes had not yet shared any tribute with them. They accepted rich mantles from Moctezuma with much appreciation for his generosity, and whenever they saw him after that, they doffed their quilted cotton caps to show him respect.

As the group walked back to their quarters, Cortes appeared dejected. "Converting Moctezuma is going to be more difficult than I thought," he said to Olmedo, but he had no intention of giving up. He was already planning to write King Charles that night, telling him that Moctezuma had assumed him (Cortes) to be the god Quetzalcoatl, who had promised to return in 1519. He would explain to the king that Moctezuma believed in a prophecy that men who came from the east were destined to rule over the Mexica. Later, some of his critics would accuse Cortes of stretching the truth for self-glorification; Cortes, however, actually hoped to deliver to King Charles, as a gift, this splendid city with thousands of willing vassals and converts.

Olmedo comforted him. "You did your best. There'll be other opportunities. When you talk to Moctezuma again, remember you're talking to a well-educated man. He'll be more likely to demand proofs and explanations than a peasant would."

"I tried to rush him too much, didn't I?"

"Probably so, but take heart," Olmedo said. "I've noticed Moctezuma's Achilles heel; you can take advantage of it to win him over."

"What's that?"

"He's lonely."

Marina had never heard of Achilles' heel, but she had understood the rest of the conversation in Spanish. She was sure Olmedo understood the best way to win Moctezuma's favor, for she too had noticed how much he welcomed a conversation eye to eye with Hernan Cortes. The emperor, who had probably two

318

thousand servants and two hundred concubines, was indeed a lonely man.

* * *

Four days after they had entered Tenochtitlan, Cortes sent Marina and Aguilar as messengers to Moctezuma, requesting permission to visit the famous market of Tlatelolco and the great temples that crowned the skyline of Tenochtitlan. The interpreters took with them one of Cortes' pages, Orteguilla, who had begun to learn a few words of Nahuatl.

"My master sends Orteguilla to serve you as an interpreter," said Marina. "Orteguilla is learning your language and would like to improve his mastery of it. He would also like your permission to see the great *tianguiz* of Tlatelolco and the *teocallis* of Huitzilopochtli and Tlaloc."

Moctezuma accepted Ortequilla's services gratefully and ordered a servant to prepare an apartment for him in the palace. He also granted Cortes' request to visit the temples, but only if accompanied by Aztecs. He provided guides to lead them to Tlatelolco and agreed to meet them later at the temples.

Those who accompanied Cortes on this excursion began to hear the sounds of music, animal noises, and bargaining voices while still some distance away. They found the marketplace bustling with noisy activity, yet clean and well ordered. It reminded Marina of the market in Xicalango, especially when she saw slaves attached to long poles being offered for sale, but Tlatelolco was larger than any markets she had seen. Bernal Diaz assured her it was also larger than any he had seen in Europe. He estimated that 40,000 to 80,000 people were thronging the market that day.

As in other markets, different sections had been assigned to artisans, pottery makers, basket weavers, feather workers, woodcarvers, clothing and fabric vendors, cotton producers, slave merchants, fur dealers, tanners, butchers, herbalists, and food growers. Lapidaries cut and polished precious stones or chipped pieces of obsidian and shaped them into flint knives or razors while spectators watched. Barbers cut hair and trimmed the sparse beards of older men with flint razors. Some merchants provided a kind of money exchange, using stacks of roasted cacao beans and goose quills filled with gold dust.

In addition to a variety of local vegetables, fruits had been brought from the temperate highlands and the tropical lowlands. Unusual delicacies included breads made with eggs, a cheese-like curdled scum from the lake, and sweet-tasting cactus fruit that would turn the urine red. Learning about the cactus fruit caused much joking among the Spaniards. They were also amazed at the abundance of medicines and herbs—even an herb guaranteed to kill lice.

Roving guards maintained order in the stalls and arcades; if quarrels arose, a tribunal of judges settled them on the spot. Deeply impressed with the abundance of goods and the vitality of the commerce, the Spaniards and Marina returned to Tenochtitlan to meet Moctezuma at the white temple trimmed in red.

* * *

Moctezuma had already arrived and was making his devotions at the top of the pyramid. He sent several attendants to help Cortes up the hundred and fourteen steps, but Cortes rejected their offer and bounded to the top, bragging to Moctezuma that Spaniards never became tired from overexertion. Marina, Olmedo, and his chaplain Juan Diaz followed at a slower pace, with Diaz commenting in Spanish that the vile smell of blood overpowered even that of copal incense.

Moctezuma ignored Cortes' bragging and pretended not to notice the Spaniard's heavy panting after he bolted up the stairs in defiance of the high altitude and the thin air. Moctezuma took Cortes to the edge of the pyramid and pointed out the features of the landscape: to the south stood Chapultepec, the "hill of the grasshopper," the source of water that flowed into Tenochtitlan through a great aqueduct. The three causeways were plainly visible, linking Tenochtitlan to cities on the west, north, and south of Lake Texcoco. He pointed out the two other cities that formed the powerful "triple alliance" or federation with Tenochtitlan: Texcoco and Tacuba.

Cortes was amazed at the trusting nature of Moctezuma, who was giving him information a conqueror would find as valuable as a map of fortifications. Taking the emperor's naivete as a sign of malleability, he said to Olmedo, "It seems to me, Father, that we might make some inquiries asking the emperor to allow us to build a church here."

Olmedo again urged patience and caution. "That might be a good idea later on, but Moctezuma doesn't seem inclined to give up his old gods yet. It doesn't seem like a suitable time to bring up the subject."

Following that advice, Cortes abandoned the thought and instead requested permission to see the inside of the temple. Moctezuma spoke to a blood-caked priest who allowed them to enter. A sacrifice had taken place that morning at the temple of Huitzilopochtli. Three new heads had been placed on the skull rack, which Diaz estimated held over 60,000 skulls in varying stages of decay. Three hearts, sprinkled with copal incense, were burning in the braziers. A mournful drum beat accompanied the sights and smells with a depressing rhythm.

Inside the temple, the stench of blood-stained walls revolted their nostrils as much as the statues revolted their eyes. The gigantic image of Huitzilopochtli, god of sun and war, stared at them with monstrous eyes. Its body, girdled with snakes made of gold and precious stones stuck on with amaranth paste, seemed to writhe in the dim light. The stone image of Tezcatlipoca, god of the Here and Now, projected a bear-like face and shining mirror eyes. This god's skirt, decorated with figures like little devils with snakes' tails, caused Diaz to pronounce that this was a god from Hell. In another recess they beheld an image of Xipe Totec, half man and half lizard, the god of seed time and harvest, which also seemed repugnant although it was artfully carved and ornamented with gems.

As they exited the temple and again stood atop the pyramid overlooking the valley, Cortes yielded to his earlier temptation. "Surely, Lord Moctezuma," he said with a voice tinged with supercilious amusement, "a great prince and wise man such as you must have come to the conclusion, at least in your own mind, that these idols of yours are not gods but devils."

As Marina translated these words, she could see Moctezuma's expression change. She had not tried to find a more tactful way to express Cortes' convictions. Remembering the slave market she had seen that morning, she wondered how many of those wretches would eventually be torn apart on these altars so their heads could become permanently grinning skulls, strung like beads to adorn an insatiable deity's heartless breast. She knew Cortes was being tactless, but she thought he was also quite right.

Moctezuma's words were squeezed between stiff lips. "Senor Malinche, do not say any more to dishonor our gods."

Cortes plunged on. "So that you may know and all your priests may see it clearly, do me the favor of letting me place a cross here on the top of this tower. And between the images of Huitzilopochtli and Tezcatlipoca, let me place an image of Our Lady, the Virgin Mary. When you see the fear your idols will have of this holy image, you will know they are deceiving you."

Moctezuma's angry reply was reinforced by the glowering faces of the two priests who stood beside him. "Senor Malinche, if I had known you would say such derogatory things about our gods, I would never have brought you into our sacred temple. We know our gods are good, not evil. They give us health and send us rain and growing seasons. They give us victories over our enemies, everything we could wish for. We are obligated to worship them in return for these benefits. I insist that you say not another word to dishonor them."

Cortes looked at Olmedo, but Olmedo was staring out across the broad valley with its shining lakes. Cortes tried to change the subject, saying it was time to return to their quarters.

"You return," Moctezuma said sulkily, pointing a finger

toward the palace. "I must stay to do penance for the great offense I committed in allowing you to come to this temple and speak evil of our gods. I must pray and worship here awhile." Cortes said apologetically, "I ask your pardon for any offense I may have uttered or any pain I have caused you." Then he descended the steps with his friar, his interpreters, his captains and soldiers. Some of his men had tumors and abscesses, so their legs suffered more in the descent than the captain general would admit.

* * *

Although they had urgent matters to discuss, Cacama and Cuitlahuac knew that Moctezuma did not like to be disturbed during his evening meal. He ate alone, observing a ritual that his intimates and servants knew well. For each meal, thirty different dishes had to be prepared and placed in three-legged pottery braziers with coals under the food to keep it warm. He would inspect these dishes along with his chefs and stewards, who would point out the most interesting delicacies. The chefs would tell the emperor whether each dish contained venison, wild duck, quail, rabbit, turkey, pigeon, partridge, or pheasant. They had been told not to mention any human flesh used in their cooking, since that meat was supposed to be donated to the priests at the temple. Besides, since Cortes had arrived and condemned the practice, Moctezuma had ordered his cooks not to use human meat. Cacama worried that this decision showed an unhealthy influence the Spaniard had on his emperor.

After the emperor had made his selections, the food was placed on plates of red or black Cholula ware and taken to his private quarters by four beautiful women who had just bathed and put on clean garments. The remainder of the prepared food could then be distributed among the other palace residents.

The women placed the food on a low table with a white tablecloth. As Moctezuma sat beside the table on a low stool with an embroidered cushion, the four women brought painted gourds, some filled with water to pour over his hands and some empty ones to catch the water below. They brought him towels, napkins, and fresh corncakes. Around his table they placed a wooden screen painted gold, so no one could see him eating. If the weather was cold, as it was that night, they also built a fire of smokeless wood in his quarters.

While the emperor ate, the serving women stood aside, remaining very quiet, as did the guards in the emperor's suite. At times the emperor might request dancers or dwarfs or jesters to entertain him, but if he did not, his close relatives could join him while he drank the chocolate that invariably ended his meal. This drink was served in great reverence in a golden cup,

322

because it was supposed to give him great powers over women.

Cacama and Cuitlahuac had gone through all the preliminary protocol to show respect. They had removed their sandals and replaced their fine cotton mantles with coarse ones made of agave fiber. They had lingered outside the emperor's suite so as not to make a rude, hurried entrance. As kings of city-states appointed by their kinsman Moctezuma, they held sufficient rank to speak to him after his meal, but they would act humble in his presence to make him appear exalted. Cuitlahuac was Moctezuma's younger brother, a well-built man thirty-five years old.

Cacama was a nephew to both Cuitlahuac and Moctezuma. His proud ancestry included his father Nezahualpilli, also known as the sorcerer king of Texcoco, and grandfather Nezahualcoyotl or "Fasting Coyote," the famous poet-king of Texcoco. As he waited barefoot on the marble floor outside Moctezuma's quarters, Cacama thought of his ancestors. His father, Nezahualpilli, had taken great pride in the predictions of his fortune-tellers, who foresaw a time when the Mexica would be ruled by strangers. Moctezuma had contested that pronouncement, insisting that his own fortune-tellers, who had predicted otherwise, were more skilled. Nezahualpilli had proposed they settle the matter by playing a series of ritual ball games, the winner of three to determine who was right. He had also waged his whole kingdom on the outcome, against only three turkey-cocks waged by Moctezuma. When Moctezuma's teams won the first two games, Cacama feared the entire city-state of Texcoco would have to be forfeited, but Nezahuapilli's teams won the last three games in succession, and Moctezuma laughingly delivered the three turkey-cocks he had wagered. Cacama thought his uncle had accepted his gambling loss with gracious good humor, but was that same good-naturedness a trait the Spaniards could use against him?

When Cuitlahuac and Cacama saw the serving women entering Moctezuma's room with chocolate and small golden pipes for his tobacco, they entered politely, barefoot on the marble floor, walking backward until the emperor chose to recognize them. Moctezuma did so, feeling quite cheerful after a satisfying meal.

Cuitlahuac spoke first, keeping his eyes on the floor. "My dear brother, we have serious concerns to discuss with you."

Moctezuma signaled to the servants. They removed the cloths and dishes and disappeared quickly, leaving only the golden pipes and the golden cup of chocolate on the emperor's table.

"You're one of my heirs, Cuitlahuac," Moctezuma said as he sipped his frothy drink. "As my brother, you're a likely candidate to become the next Uey Tlatoani. Your opinion carries weight with me. Feel free to speak to me about your concerns."

323

"I'll be brief rather than rhetorical," Cuitlahuac said. "You know Cacama and I both opposed your bringing the Spaniards here. We thought they might do some harm once inside the city."

"True, you both objected," Moctezuma said. "But didn't we finally agree it was best to get to know them, find out what powers they had, and kill them once we learned what we needed to know? You remember that, don't you, Cacama?"

Cacama spoke up. "It may be time to kill them now. You've learned they aren't gods. They defiled our temple."

Moctezuma drained his cup and placed it on the low table. "Senor Malinche has apologized for his irreverent words. He wanted to put an idol of the Goddess Mary in the temple, but I refused. Instead, I'm allowing him to build a shrine in the palace of Axayacatl where his men can do their devotions. That ought to satisfy him."

"It may look that way," said Cuitlahuac, "but they started building their shrine near the wall we cemented up—the one that sealed off the royal treasure. Now we've heard bad news from the steward who serves the Spaniards' meals. He says the plaster has been tampered with; he's sure they've opened it and sealed it up again."

"With all due reverence, Uncle," said Cacama, "we think you've shown these intruders too much courtesy. No matter how many gifts you give them, they crave more and more."

Moctezuma stood up, emitting a belch before speaking. "I'm sure our vassals in the conquered territories say the same thing about us," he said philosophically. "We collect tribute so we can secure the favor of other rulers, and King Charles may be a powerful monarch we should befriend. Rulers show their own greatness by giving gifts to other rulers and special guests."

Cuitlahuac sided with his nephew Cacama. "Remember, my dear brother Moctezuma, we have only the word of these bad-smelling soldiers that they serve a powerful king. They could be lying, intending to grab what treasure they can for themselves."

"I understand your point," Moctezuma said. "You know we tried many times to discourage the teules or block their way. I didn't want them here any more than you did, but none of our strategies worked against their magic. As to their truthfulness, how can we judge that unless we talk to them? As to their insatiable greed, I acknowledge that, yet they do seem to appreciate what I give them, especially the soldiers."

"But now," said Cuitlahuac in exasperation, "you've given them permission to build two boats here. Our calpixqui have seen Spanish soldiers and tamemes bringing materials from their city in the Totonac territory."

"Yes," Moctezuma said with growing annoyance, "I know that. I told them they could bring materials salvaged from their old boats on the eastern coast. They want to build sailing craft here, to take pleasure cruises on the lake. No harm in that."

"There's harm in their staying here so long," Cuitlahuac said angrily. "How long will they be spying on us while they build their boats? How do we know they won't use their boats for spying after they're finished?"

"And there's another thing, Uncle," said Cacama. "We've just heard that the army you sent to fight the Totonacs has put down the rebellion in Cempoala and the surrounding territories. If Malinche learns that his allies in Cempoala have become your vassals again, he could go on quite a rampage."

"Then we can't delay much longer," Moctezuma said. "I'm not worried about their finding the treasure stored in the palace. They couldn't steal it without our knowing, could they? But participating in a rebellion of the Totonacs is an outrage we can't tolerate. We'll kill them tomorrow." He lighted a golden yetl pipe in the flames of his smokeless wood fire and inhaled the yetl smoke. "Too bad, in a way," he added. "They've shown courage, like brave warriors willing to die for their country and their gods. I was beginning to like them."

* * *

While Moctezuma had been talking strategy with his royal advisers, a similar kind of plotting was taking place in the quarters of Cortes. He was approached by four of his captains—Pedro de Alvarado, Diego de Ordas, Juan Velasquez de Leon, and the young Gonzalo de Sandoval, who was only twenty-two but already earning the respect of his subordinates and the other captains for his gentlemanly manners, humane disposition, and admirable self-discipline. The captains brought a dozen soldiers they trusted, including a veteran of many campaigns and an astute observer, Bernal Diaz del Castillo.

"We find ourselves in a trap," said the feisty Alvarado, who was always eager for excitement. "We could see the layout of the causeways when we stood on the pyramid."

Ordaz, who had led the expedition to the top of the volcano Popocatepetl and discovered the best road to Tenochtitlan, spoke next. "Moctezuma could pull up the drawbridges and cut us off from retreat," he said. "We're like sitting ducks here."

Sandoval also expressed concern. "Moctezuma has shown us great kindness and hospitality, but his attitude could change any time. I'm afraid you've offended the emperor by challenging his gods. From what I've seen of human beings, nothing puts fire into their blood faster than the idea of defending their gods. I've noticed that the stewards have been rather surly in the last couple of days when they brought our food."

Velasquez de Leon made another observation. "Remember all the warnings we got in the towns we passed through? People said the Aztecs would lure us into a trap and kill us. We're vastly outnumbered by palace guards, and even if our Tlaxcalan friends wanted to send help, they couldn't get across the lake."

Cortes listened patiently to all of them, making sure each captain felt he had been heard. "I share your concerns," he said. "Please don't think I've been so blinded by the treasures here that I've lost my senses. Everything you say is true; I feel as anxious as you do. The question is, what can we do now?"

"We need a hostage," Alvarado suggested. "We've already discussed this among ourselves, and we think we should seize the emperor himself."

"That's a bold plan," Cortes said. "Wouldn't his guards kill us on the spot?"

"Not if we threaten to kill him first, and we should be prepared to carry out the threat," said Ordaz.

Sandoval suggested a strategy. "You've got a honeyed tongue, Captain General Cortes," he said. "If you can lure Moctezuma away from his guards on some pretext, we can take him by surprise. His subjects have such great respect for him that they'd let us escape rather than see him come to harm."

At that moment a trusted soldier appeared with two Indian messengers who had come secretly from Tlaxcala, carrying a letter for Cortes. Cortes read the letter quickly and then, in an anguished voice, shared its contents. "This letter is from Vera Cruz," he said. Our Alguacil Mayor Juan de Escalante and six of his soldiers have been killed by an Aztec army. His horse was killed, and so were many Totonac warriors trying to defend their towns. They've succumbed to Moctezuma's forces again; now they're forbidden to bring food or supplies into Vera Cruz. The survivors are asking me what to do next."

The vein on Cortes' neck was standing out, revealing his anger. He buckled a sword onto his thigh and said to everyone present, "Sleep in your armor tonight and keep your swords at your side, in case of a surprise attack. First thing tomorrow, I'll take five of you with me to see Moctezuma. Our plan is so outrageous, it might just work."

* * *

When Moctezuma received the message through Marina that Cortes wished to see him about the Totonac rebellion, he granted permission. Shortly afterward, Cortes arrived with five captains and his two interpreters. After his usual salutations, Cortes launched into a complaint. "Senor Moctezuma, I'm astonished that a valiant prince such as you, after saying you were our friend, have sent your army to take arms against my Spanish soldiers at Vera Cruz and Cempoala. These towns and the other Totonac towns are under the protection of King Charles of Spain.

326

How could you betray us like this, after I ordered my captains to serve you?"

Moctezuma protested. "Senor Malinche, I only learned of this revolt myself last night. I didn't order it done. I'll have the matter investigated."

"This isn't the first time I've had to forgive you," Cortes went on, growing more emphatic with each sentence. "Your army attacked us at Cholula, and we heard reports that your captains had frequently plotted to capture us and kill us. All this I've forgiven because of my great regard for you. I'm willing to forgive even this latest insult if you'll come with us silently and without protest."

Moctezuma gasped. "What are you saying, Malinche? Are you taking me prisoner in my own palace?" His face drained into the color of ashes; his hands trembled.

"You'll be as well treated there as you are here," Cortes said. "I give you my solemn promise, which I will keep more faithfully than you have kept yours to me."

Moctezuma started to move toward the entrance of his apartment, but two of the Spanish captains barred his way. He decided to try persuasion. "Senor Malinche, I cannot leave my own palace. All the household would be disturbed. Official business would be disrupted. What you ask is impossible."

"If you don't come," Cortes insisted, "my captains here will kill you on the spot."

"Then my guards would hunt you down and kill all of you," Moctezuma said angrily. "How dare you threaten me this way?"

"We take that risk," Cortes said. "Now will you come peaceably, or shall I give the order?"

Velasquez de Leon twisted one arm of the trembling emperor behind his back and held the point of his steel knife against Moctezuma's throat. "Why waste time talking to him?" he snarled. "If we have to die, let's take this tyrant first."

Marina did not translate that threat because Moctezuma had clearly felt the captain's knife and heard his angry voice. Instead, she spoke gently, as if offering advice to a friend. "Senor Moctezuma, I advise you to go at once with these men without making any protest, and you will be treated with all the honor a great prince deserves. If you refuse, you'll remain here a dead man, but if you accept, you'll learn much from them."

Moctezuma tried one more ploy: he offered his son and two legitimate daughters as hostages in his stead. Cortes remained firm; the emperor must come himself; there was no alternative. When Moctezuma reluctantly agreed to accompany them to their quarters, he was surprised that the captains and Cortes all welcomed him with that strange Spanish custom they used to show affection to each other: an embrace.

327

King Cuitlahuac came again to see his older brother, but Moctezuma refused to see him alone. A Spanish guard had to be present, as well as the bilingual page Orteguilla who knew enough Nahuatl by then to understand what Moctezuma was saying to his own people. Moctezuma insisted that he wanted to spend some time with his Spanish friends; he would conduct his official business from the palace of Axayacatl. Cuitlahuac's suspicions deepened, but so ingrained was his respect for authority that he found it unthinkable to question anything his emperor said. Thus the very obedience the emperor had demanded from his subjects worked to the advantage of his enemies.

Moctezuma was allowed to wander in his marvelous gardens and aviary, to enjoy every beautiful flower and remarkable bird he had collected, and to walk around the zoo that had horrified the Spaniards when they learned what his caged animals fed on. Although still attended by his women servants, he took his meals in the palace of Axayacatl and slept there each night. Cortes spent most evenings with him, and the emperor was somewhat mollified when Cortes learned to play some of his favorite games, patolli and totoloque.

Moctezuma was especially fond of totoloque, which involved some gambling. He would bet a stake of jewels or gold, as would his opponent. They would then toss smooth golden pellets for some distance and move golden tiles along a board to keep score. Each player had five tries to outscore his opponent, and the winner claimed the jewels or gold that had been wagered. Cuitlahuac kept score for his brother, and Alvarado for Cortes. When it became obvious that Alvarado was cheating, adding more points than Cortes had earned, the emperor joked that Alvarado made too much *yxoxol* when he marked the score. The cheating didn't matter much, because Cortes always gave his winnings to Moctezuma's attendants, and Moctezuma gave his winnings to Cortes' men. To Moctezuma, the loss seemed a small price to pay for entertainment he found rather enjoyable.

Every day Moctezuma gave presents to the soldiers who guarded him and their captain, Juan Velasquez de Leon. Usually he gave them cloth or small gold jewelry, but he gave Bernal Diaz a pretty concubine when the soldier requested one. These gifts and his genial manner endeared him to his Spanish guards.

Despite the amiable evenings together, Cortes demanded that Moctezuma punish the warriors who had re-conquered the Totonac territories and killed Escalante in Vera Cruz. Accordingly, Moctezuma summoned his captain Cuauhpopoca, "Smoking Eagle," and the fifteen men who had served under him in the reprisals against the Totonacs, including his only son.

When Cortes interviewed them, he extracted a confession that the attacks had been conducted by order of the emperor.

"They have implicated you in this affair," Cortes reproached Moctezuma. "By Spanish law, you should die for your part in this rebellion against a Spanish protectorate. I've grown so fond of you I'd rather die myself than see you harmed. Instead, I'll make an example of your captain and all his subordinates so this will never happen again; they must be burned at the stake."

Cortes ordered Moctezuma put in chains while the burning was carried out in front of Moctezuma's palace. The emperor reacted with tears to the humiliation of being shackled, knowing that he could no longer keep up the pretense that he was staying with the Spaniards voluntarily. He had been disgraced forever in the eyes of his countrymen.

When the executions had been completed, and the smell of burning flesh and hair had permeated even into the palace hallways, Cortes returned to remove the shackles personally. "Your captain Cuauhpopoca, his son, and his officers have paid the price for your sins," Cortes told Moctezuma. "They accepted their fate with resignation. Not one of them cried out in pain." He spoke in admiration, yet he also felt some pity for men so resigned to ritual sacrifice that they yielded to it without the least sign of protest.

Moctezuma wept quietly, wishing that he, too, could accept without flinching the bewildering treatment his gods were inflicting on him. For in his belief system, nothing was accidental; everything depended on the gods. Nothing could happen unless the gods willed it. Was their anger still smoldering over the disrespect shown them when the Spaniards entered their sacred place? He decided he would go again to the temple, do more penance, prick his own penis with the barbs of a stingray imported from the coast, and try to regain the good will of Huitzilopochtli.

On the wall above Cortes' head, Moctezuma could see an ornament comprising the carved figure of a man with arms spread out on a cross, wearing only a maxtli and a crown of thorns, his head drooping in deep sorrow and suffering. His own people knew that kind of suffering, Moctezuma thought. It was the suffering of people who wonder why their gods have forsaken them.

* * *

The people of Tenochtitlan had witnessed the public burnings and knew the Spaniards could be fearsome; however, they were also quite tradition-bound and not accustomed to defending themselves against tyranny. Fishermen, farmers, and merchants went about their business, trying not to become

329

involved in power struggles of the ruling classes. But unrest was brewing among the nobles.

In several other cities surrounding the lake, including Texcoco and Ixtapalapa, a growing alarm became mixed with a growing disgust for Moctezuma's weakness. Seeing Moctezuma's spirit ebbing, Cacama and Cuitlahuac increased their own determination to oust the invaders, but they were cautious not to say anything in public that might be considered treason.

Unknown to them, they had an ally in Cuba. Governor Velasquez, former friend and rival of Cortes, was also assembling an army of soldiers under Panfilo de Narvaez, with orders to capture Cortes, discredit him, and reclaim the lands he had usurped by pitting the interests of Cuba against those of the Spanish crown.

Chapter 24

The Death Throes of an Empire

The defiant king of Texcoco, Cacama, was ferried across the lake to Tenochtitlan in an elegant acali with awnings to protect him from the April sun and many oarsmen to ply the waters swiftly. When he disembarked, a rich litter awaited him, ornamented with jewels and gold embroidery. Yet he was a prisoner, he well knew, by order of his uncle Moctezuma.

Ushered into the reception hall of the palace of Axayacatl by Moctezuma's officers, Cacama confronted his uncle with the same anger he had shown in his earlier message of defiance. Also in defiance, he did not remove his sandals.

Moctezuma, seated in a carved chair, looked too thin and frail for a man only 41 years old. Seeing him this way convinced Cacama further that he had been right—Moctezuma's fighting spirit had been broken. The once-proud emperor had fallen completely under the domination of the greedy Spanish general Cortes and the two interpreters who stood beside him, conspirators who were scheming to gain total control of the empire. Also present were several Spanish captains, including Pedro de Alvarado, at whom Cacama glared with undisguised hatred.

Moctezuma said courteous welcoming words but soon began to chide: "Why did you refuse to send tribute to Senor Malinche? The kings of other city-states have agreed to show fealty to King Charles of Spain and sent their share of treasure. You not only refused, but you called me an old woman, an old hen!"

Cacama responded by glaring disrespectfully into his emperor's face. "You're acting like a weak old woman—not the brave warrior you once were! I begged you not to bring these foreigners here. They've abused your hospitality and turned you into their vassal, a slave to do their bidding!"

"They show me respect and kindness," Moctezuma said defensively. "Malinche had a soldier flogged who spoke disrespectfully to me."

"And in return you opened up the treasury and gave it all to the men who hold you prisoner! Was that brave? Or smart?"

Marina and Aguilar were finding it hard to keep up with the translating of this heated quarrel into Mayan and then Spanish. As the words came faster, Marina began translating directly into Spanish, giving Aguilar an apologetic smile. Aguilar shrugged his acquiescence; he had less work to do when Marina translated directly. He listened and made mental notes to discuss with her later any errors she made in pronunciation or grammar, but he was satisfied that she was getting the main ideas across to Cortes.

"It's the will of the gods," Moctezuma said to his nephew with conviction. "They've sent these men here just as they send earthquakes and floods and droughts. We can't question what the gods do. They want us to acknowledge the greater power of Spain. What use is the treasure to us?"

"Uncle, I beg you, don't listen to these conniving invaders! They use your religious beliefs to rob you and trample on your people. While they take you on pleasure cruises around the lake, they are sending men to Coatzacoalcos to set up a fortress and a port for more of their accursed ships. While they take you hunting or play games with you, they are sending men into all the provinces to look for gold."

"Gold is a trifle!" exploded Moctezuma. "What good is gold to us? Will it feed us? Give us shelter? Heal our wounds?"

Cacama threw back his mantle and exposed many scars on his arms, burns just beginning to heal as whitish and pale pink splotches on the normal copper color of his skin. "Gold may not heal wounds, but it can cause them," he said, thrusting both arms toward his uncle's surprised face.

"What's this?" Moctezuma said, touching the scars and then looking quizzically toward Cortes.

Cacama pointed angrily to Alvarado. "This evil man came to Texcoco demanding gold. When I told him we had no more, he poured hot tar on me!"

Moctezuma turned to Alvarado with a scowl. "We call you Tonatiuh because your yellow hair reminds us of sunlight. We revere the sun and treat you well. Why have you done this?"

Alvarado's pale face turned pink, as if sunburned. He looked at Cortes, who nodded at him to answer but remained silent himself. "He could have saved himself that pain if only he'd given us what we asked for," he said to Cortes. "I was only obeying your orders to find more gold."

Cortes gave Alvarado a disapproving look but hesitated to upbraid him in the presence of the Aztecs. He thought it best to do that privately, later.

"I apologize for my captain's excessive zeal," Cortes said to Cacama. "We'd heard so much about your organizing a rebellion among the other kings that Captain Alvarado thought this was just one more act of defiance. I sent you a conciliatory message, and you replied haughtily that you didn't know anything about King Charles of Spain and didn't recognize his authority here. This country was claimed in the king's name over a year ago; we've told you that, but you wouldn't listen. Can we depend on you to be more cooperative now, so this won't happen again?"

"I'm not impressed with your honey tongue, Malinche!" Cacama sneered. "Your words are false as cacao beans stuffed with sand. You've lied to my uncle and tricked him. Whatever you may do to me, thousands of our people are growing angry over your cruelty, your abuse of our leaders, your contempt for our gods and our way of life. You and all your minions will die for your crimes!"

"Seize this rebel!" cried Cortes. His captains grabbed Cacama by the arms; he did not resist, but threw his shoulders back and his chest out proudly, like a captured warrior.

Cortes turned to Moctezuma. "You've heard your nephew's threatening words," he said angrily. "If you don't punish his treason, we'll have to do it in the name of King Charles."

Moctezuma, badly shaken, rose from his chair with as much dignity as he could muster. "Cacama, my beloved nephew, I'm grieved to hear you talk this way. I placed you on the throne of Texcoco even though your brother Ixtlilxochitl challenged you. I fought on your side in the bloody war he started. Now you rebel against me and my friends; you defy my orders; you force me to remove you from the throne."

"Uncle," said Cacama desperately, "can't you see who your friends are? Don't you know your enemies? Ixtlilxochitl is your enemy, not I. He went to the foreigners when they first reached our shores and offered to join forces against you. The Spaniards are your enemies, not I. They would steal your empire as well as your treasures. The priests are your enemies, not I. They advise you to destroy yourself; I am trying to save you."

"My decision is made," Moctezuma said, his voice quivering with anger. "I obey the will of the gods. Your younger brother Coanacoch will henceforth be king of Texcoco, and you will be imprisoned until you come to your senses."

Cacama focused a look of pity upon his uncle and a look of loathing upon the Spaniards. He was then dragged away and put in chains. Cortes also prevailed upon Moctezuma to order the arrest of the five other kings, including his brother Cuitlahuac, who had conspired with Cacama. When these kings also had been put in chains, Cortes had achieved his major objective: complete control of the governments of the Aztec dominion.

Cortes was not satisfied, however, for he still hoped to gain control over the souls of the Mexica. He persuaded the reluctant emperor to permit him to place a cross and an image of the Virgin Mary between the temples on the great pyramid in the city center. When Moctezuma had compromised to that extent,

333

Cortes pressed him further. Against the protests of Moctezuma and the sensible advice of Father Olmedo, Cortes decided to turn one of the two Aztec temples into a Christian shrine.

Had Cortes been willing to follow Olmedo's advice and use persuasion rather than force, he might have saved the lives of hundreds of his own followers and many thousands of natives. But such patience was not in his nature, and in April of the year 1520, he delivered the one outrage that the conquered people could not tolerate, the last insult they would endure before amassing all their fury against him. By cleansing the Sun God's temple, smashing a cherished image, and mocking their faith, he laid the foundation for revolt and his most humiliating defeat.

* * *

Dona Marina had become friends with Dona Luisa, Alvarado's woman, who had an appealing way of taking life as it comes without letting its injustices perturb her. The two women stood together at the foot of the great pyramid while their men worshiped in the newly-cleansed temple above. The hundred and fourteen steps had also been scrubbed and cleansed thoroughly. Cortes had joked that Moctezuma could walk up the steps without having cloths spread before his feet. A number of Spanish soldiers were filing into the temple or standing in small groups talking amiably, but the temple grounds had been deserted by natives, and the priests had disappeared into the temple of Quetzalcoatl to avoid mingling with the Spaniards.

"It does look better, doesn't it?" Luisa said. "Smells much better, too, now that the dried blood is chipped off." She spoke in Nahuatl, Marina's native tongue, so their conversation flowed easily. The bulge of pregnancy protruded under Luisa's huipil; she stood with her legs slightly apart and folded her arms across the shelf of her midsection.

"It certainly looks better to me," Marina agreed. "Tell me, Luisa, do you think Christianity is a better religion than the ones we grew up with?"

Luisa looked at her warily. "I suppose so. I don't think much about it."

"I think about it all the time," said Marina. "Father Olmedo tells me stories from the Bible when he has time. I like the story of the good Samaritan especially, but also the stories of a wise king named Solomon and an ambitious king named David."

"I don't know Spanish well enough to understand Father Olmedo," Luisa said. "My Pedro thinks it's better for me not to learn any more than he teaches me."

"What does he teach you?"

Luisa giggled. "I know the Spanish words for 'bring me my dinner' and 'take off your clothes,' " she said.

Marina laughed, remembering that she, too, had learned those words from her first Spanish master, Puertocarrero. "I can see why he thinks that's enough for his purposes. Does he also say he loves you?"

"No," Luisa replied. "I don't understand most of what he says anyway. He kisses me, though—all over my face and neck and even on my mouth. Does Hernan kiss you? Does he pucker his lips like this and make little noises?" She illustrated by pursing her own lips and kissing her hand with a little smack.

"Oh, yes," Marina said dreamily. "He kisses my face and caresses my whole body with his hands. He makes me feel as if I'm the only woman in the world that matters to him. I get so excited that I pull him to me; I feel as much desire as he does."

"Pedro does that too," Luisa said. "I've never had sex with an Aztec man, but some native women have told me they don't get much pleasure from it. Perhaps we're lucky to have Spanish men for masters."

"It depends on the man, not the nationality," Marina said. "When I was young in Paynala I saw a neighbor boy giving his girlfriend great pleasure in the rushes by the river or in the cornfields by his house. I had a Mayan master once named Ah Cux and a Spanish master named Alonso Puertocarrero. Both of them satisfied themselves and cared nothing for me. Hernan is the only master I've had who makes me feel loved."

"Does it bother you, then," asked Luisa candidly, "that Moctezuma has given one of his daughters to Cortes?"

"A little," Marina admitted. "Life seldom gives a woman exactly what she wants, so it's useless to complain. I'd like to be a Christian wife whose husband is completely faithful, but Hernan already has a wife in Cuba. He says he confesses his sins every week to Father Olmedo, but when a soldier is far away from home the sin of adultery is easily forgiven."

Luisa smiled knowingly. "I'm sure Pedro's conscience doesn't bother him a bit," she said. "He's not married, but he's had a child by a Cuban woman as well as the one I'm carrying."

"Hernan says most marriages in Spain are arranged by the parents," Marina said. "He says a man can marry one woman and love another, even though adultery is considered a sin."

"So what's unusual about that?" Luisa said cynically. "The men here have concubines as well as wives. I can't believe men anywhere would settle for one woman if they could have more." Tired of standing, Luisa brushed her hand over one of the stone steps to see if dust had settled there. Satisfied that she would not soil her skirt, she sat down on the well-scrubbed step. Marina sat beside her, wrapping her arms around her knees.

"It doesn't make much difference for women, anyway," said Marina. "I've never forgotten the stoning I saw when I was a child. The woman was married to someone else; that's why she was being punished for adultery. The man was stoned, too, but he wouldn't have been punished for using a concubine or a slave."

"It's a hard life for women," Luisa acknowledged. "I try not to think about it. No point in making ourselves unhappy. I'm just glad Pedro is kind to me most of the time. He has a bad temper, but he only beats me when he's drunk."

"Hernan never beats me at all," Marina said gratefully. "He says he loves me too much."

"Lucky you!" Luisa exclaimed. "I hope it lasts. Hernan has a temper, too, and I've seen him lose it. Now that he has Moctezuma's daughter for a concubine, he may grow tired of you."

"He says he loves me more than Dona Ana. He accepted her only because Moctezuma let her be baptized. He hopes Moctezuma will be converted, too, if he sees how it benefits Ana."

Luisa laughed so hard that she had to lean back and brace herself against the stone steps. "Is that what he told you? And you believe it? What a golden tongue that man has!"

Marina laughed too, but quietly, since some of the soldiers nearby had turned to stare. "He does have a golden tongue," she agreed. "You shouldn't be surprised that he's charmed me. I think he could charm a butterfly out of its cocoon. He's talked kings out of their treasure chests and persuaded thousands of people to give up their idols and their sacrifices. I believe what he says because I believe in what he does."

"We both have to be loyal," Luisa said soberly. "No matter what our men do, we have to accept it and not criticize."

Marina nodded agreement. "But in your heart, Luisa, did it bother you when Pedro poured hot tar on King Cacama? I'll never forget those badly burned arms, the splotches on his skin."

"Of course it bothered me," Luisa admitted; "that's why I don't like to think about it. Don't Hernan's actions bother you sometimes? Didn't it bother you when Hernan distributed the treasure among his soldiers so unfairly? Pedro got a double share because he's a captain and a horseman, but he was still pretty unhappy, and he says the foot soldiers were really upset. By the time Cortes had taken out the royal fifth for King Charles, and a fifth for himself, and deducted all his expenses for the settlement at Vera Cruz, the soldiers only got a hundred pesos apiece. That's out of treasure worth more than six hundred thousand pesos!"

"Yes, I was a little concerned," Marina admitted, "but I can't judge how fair the shares were. He pacified the men by explaining that greater wealth lies ahead."

"The golden tongue again!" Luisa said. "He also promised them a reward in Heaven, if they'll help him spread crosses around Mexico. Now they seem very happy, don't they?"

"They seem fairly contented, but I sense that something bad is about to happen," Marina said. "When Moctezuma pleaded with Hernan not to destroy the idols, just to allow the priests to carry them down gently, Hernan ignored him. He grabbed an iron bar and smashed the face of Huitzilopochtli's image."

"Why worry about it? You don't believe in Huitzilopochtli any more, do you? The Christian god seems much more powerful."

"I want to believe that Christianity makes men better, more loving, like Father Olmedo. It seems unnecessarily cruel to torture Cacama, or even to hurt Moctezuma's pride that way."

"Especially," said Luisa with a tinge of mockery, "since Hernan didn't want to hurt Moctezuma's feelings by refusing to take his daughter to bed. Rather inconsistent, isn't he?"

"I know Hernan's faults," Marina said, "just as you know Pedro's, but I love him anyway. It distresses me when he doesn't live up to his beliefs, but at least I feel free to tell him so. He listens to me and Father Olmedo, too, but even when he knows our advice is good, he can't seem to change his ways."

"You can't reform a man anyway," Luisa said. "Stand by him even when he's in bad trouble. Hernan will have his hands full if there's a revolt, and some of his own men are grumbling that Moctezuma has treated them better than Cortes has. Don't tell him I said that; I just thought you should know."

"I won't say anything," Marina promised, "but thanks for the information. You know what troubles me about this day? It's too quiet. The people are all hiding in their houses. The priests have deserted the big temples. Something's going on."

Luisa stood up as she saw Alvarado approaching. "Don't let things worry you so much, Marina," Luisa said affectionately. "Most people are probably just staying out of trouble. The priests are probably sulking because other people don't respect them the way they used to. Some people take religion too seriously. Try not to think about it."

"I'll think about that," Marina said, but as soon as she realized what she'd said, she laughed at herself.

"Some people just can't change their ways," Luisa said teasingly as she hugged her friend. Luisa departed with her master, and Marina started up the steps toward her own master, who was still greeting the soldiers who had come to pay homage to the newly constructed cross and image of the Virgin.

From the top of the steps Marina surveyed the sprawling city, gleaming like a jewel in the midst of the silvery Lake Texcoco. Her eyes swept over the complex of buildings surrounding the temple, including a snail-shaped one that must be Quetzalcoatl's temple, its walls rounded to allow winds to flow freely through it. A small boy ran out of the temple of Quetzalcoatl chasing a rubber ball. A large woman in macehual

337

dress ran after him, swiftly picked him up, and carried him inside.

Marina felt haunted by that scene. The woman resembled Chihuallama, the macehual woman who had taught her to spin, who had healed her illnesses, who had attended her mother in childbirth. The little boy reminded her of Moyo, Chihuallama's child, who had been taken away by Moctezuma's calpixqui to be sacrificed. With a shudder, she resolved to help Cortes in any way she could to stamp out the evil of human sacrifice. Christians didn't always live up to their ideals, she thought, but at least their ideals seemed worth trying to live up to.

* * *

As Marina and Cortes walked with Moctezuma in the royal gardens one day, Cortes surprised Moctezuma by offering to leave Tenochtitlan. He said he wouldn't stay where he wasn't wanted, provided he could build three ships. He requested that Moctezuma send some native labor to Vera Cruz to cut timber for the ship-builders. He promised that, when his carpenters had finished the ships, he would take Moctezuma to Spain to meet the king. Moctezuma dispatched the laborers as Cortes had requested, even though he doubted that Tenochtitlan could ever return to normal after the devastation the Spaniards had brought.

Soon afterward, Moctezuma showed Cortes a piece of linen-like cloth he had just received from the Gulf Coast. "See these pictures?" he exclaimed in delight. "They show a fleet of eighteen Spanish ships anchored in a bay. These symbols here indicate there are eight hundred men, eighty horses, and twelve pieces of artillery."

Cortes looked closely at the linen as Moctezuma stretched it out fully in the light. "Blessed be the Redeemer for His mercies!" he exclaimed, trying to sound pleased, but Marina could tell he was worried.

"Now," Moctezuma crowed with great satisfaction, "you can leave with your countrymen on these ships. You don't need to wait for new ships to be built."

Soon afterward, Cortes' fears were confirmed. A messenger arrived bringing a letter to him from Gonzalo de Sandoval, his captain stationed at Vera Cruz. Sandoval's report said the fleet that had anchored there on April 23 was commanded by an old enemy, Panfilo de Narvaez. The tall red-bearded Narvaez, an hidalgo from Valladolid, had been commissioned by Diego Velasquez, Governor of Cuba, to seize Cortes, bring him to Cuba to be prosecuted for treason, and reclaim Mexico as a conquered territory that properly belonged to Velasquez.

The other bad news was this: Velasquez had convinced Bishop Fonseca, Spain's powerful administrator over the West

Indies, that Cortes's envoys, Puertocarrero and Montejo, were mutineers against the authority of the Cuban government. Fonseca ordered the ship and its treasure seized in Sevilla. The two envoys had tried to petition King Charles, but he was on his way to Germany where he was to be crowned as successor to Maximilian I.

Gonzalo de Sandoval, though only twenty-two years old, had a reputation for showing excellent judgment. When Narvaez sent a priest, a notary, and four soldiers into Vera Cruz to demand surrender, the calm commander demanded proof of authority from the Spanish king. When Narvaez' men could not produce it, he had them seized, trussed in net hammocks, and sent on the backs of tamemes to Cortes in Tenochtitlan.

The Totonac porters, staunch allies of Sandoval and Cortes, covered the distance of several hundred miles from Vera Cruz in only four days. When a scout saw them approaching, Cortes sent a welcoming committee with horses for all of them. He greeted them warmly, apologized for the rough treatment they had received, and gave them some gifts from the treasure store.

Pacified by Cortes' kindness, the men relayed some important information. A smallpox epidemic had arisen in Cuba, keeping Governor Velasquez busy. Velasquez was also in trouble with the audiencia in Hispaniola, the body of administrators that governed all the West Indies. Velasquez had been so zealous about recruiting men for the Narvaez expedition that he had forced some men into service against their will. As a result, many of the Narvaez crew were restless, and at least one of them, a black slave who had been forced into service, had become sick with smallpox on board the ship.

Cortes learned that the Narvaez forces had invaded Cempoala after they discovered how inhospitable the sand dunes were at San Juan de Ulua. In Cempoala they had behaved like pigs, taking over the temples as their quarters, wresting food away from the Cempoalans, even grabbing for themselves some of the young women who had been offered to Cortes's men but who had stayed with their parents when the Cortes forces left.

Cortes also learned that Moctezuma had sent gifts and encouragement to Narvaez, so Narvaez was hoping to make allies of the Aztecs. In Coatzacoalcos, Narvaez had tried to enlist the cooperation of Juan Velasquez de Leon, a kinsman of Diego Velasquez, but the captain had remained steadfastly loyal to Cortes. Velasquez de Leon even offered to fight a duel with anyone who spoke ill of his commander.

After much thought, Cortes devised a daring plan to halt Narvaez. He would leave Alvarado in charge of Tenochtitlan with a force of one hundred forty men, including all who might have a tendency to support Diego Velasquez. He would take only five horses and seventy loyal men, whose loyalty would be further secured by large gifts of gold from his fifth of the treasure.

Moctezuma offered to send along five thousand of his own warriors, but Marina warned Cortes that Moctezuma was only pretending to be sad at the thought of the Spanish forces leaving. She cautioned that Cortes could not depend on the loyalty of Aztec warriors. Since Marina had confirmed his own suspicions about Moctezuma, Cortes firmly declined the offer, using his usual diplomatic language so the emperor would not be offended or become suspicious.

Cortes was much heartened to learn of the loyalty of his captain stationed in Coatzacoalcos, Juan Velasquez de Leon, whose ties to Diego Velasquez must have tested that loyalty sorely. Cortes sent a messenger asking Velasquez de Leon to join him at Cholula with a force of his own subordinates and two thousand warriors from Chinantla who hated the Aztecs. The Chinantla warriors had been taught to make copper-tipped lances twelve feet long, which they could wield with great accuracy. Sandoval, too, brought all the men he could spare from Vera Cruz and many Totonac Indians with whom he had maintained good relations.

This army assembled at Cholula and marched toward Cempoala along a river swollen high against its banks from the late spring rains. They endured downpours that soaked their quilted cotton armor, and when darkness fell, they stretched out on the soggy ground to rest. Their evening meal consisted of deer and wild pigs killed during the long day's march, but eaten raw so as not to reveal their presence with a fire.

Cortes walked among his men, keeping his voice at a normal level, exhorting them to prepare to defend their honor as well as their lives against these enemies who had come to rob them. He spoke to the men by name, indicating appreciation for all the battles they had fought together, the hard times they had endured for the glory of their king and country and God.

"I place my life in your hands now," he said, "because we all know you could gain easy rewards by turning against me and giving me over to Narvaez. I've had similar temptations at times, but I refused any offers that would have been to my own advantage if they would have been disadvantageous to you. Some of you might now prefer to seek peace rather than fight. Whatever your inclination, speak freely and no one shall hinder you from doing as you wish. Say whatever is on your mind."

Several men swore their loyalty and told him to go on.

"I'm deeply moved by your courage and patriotism," Cortes responded. "There's a saying in Castile: 'Let the donkey be killed or else the one who goads him.' I say let it be so, for if any of us falters now, it will mean disgrace to us all."

The men gave shouts of joy, but Cortes quickly hushed them

by pointing in the direction where the enemy lay sleeping. His soldiers lifted him on their shoulders and passed him from one to another until he begged them to stop. Then he gave them specific instructions for their attack on Narvaez, to be accomplished by stealth, under cover of darkness.

* * *

Taken by surprise, the Narvaez artillerymen could not even get the protective wax plugs out of their cannons before they were overcome and their own weapons turned against them. Some of the Narvaez men were confused by fireflies, thinking the flashes of light from these insects were emanating from the matchlocks of a huge force of musketeers. Sandoval dashed to the top of the main temple where Narvaez had his quarters, throwing a torch atop a thatched roof along the way. In the light of that fire, Narvaez fought until a pike struck him in one eye, blinding him on that side ever afterward. He cried out, "Holy Mary protect me! They've destroyed my eye! I'm dying!"

With their leader incapacitated, though he did not die, the Narvaez forces quickly capitulated. Narvaez had lost seventeen men in the fighting; Cortes lost only two. Some of the Narvaez men were already inclined to switch their allegiance. Several had already been approached by Juan Velasquez de Leon during his earlier visit, when Narvaez had tried to win his support. The gallant captain had impressed the Narvaez men by wearing a gold chain on one shoulder doubled twice under his arm and had secretly given some of them gifts of gold nuggets and chains from Cortes. Cortes had said, "Gold can break rocks," a saying which Velasquez de Leon had found to be true.

"Congratulations, my Lord Cortes, for capturing me," Narvaez sneered as he surrendered. "You must consider it a great feat."

Cortes replied with bravado and contempt. "Congratulations are due more to the God who gave us this victory and the gallant comrades and gentlemen who shared in it. Capturing you is the least significant thing I've done in this land. You should be ashamed of mistreating Juan Velasquez de Leon, the captain I sent to reason with you. Even worse, your actions have distracted us from our important work here. You've shown disloyalty to King Charles by attacking us, and you really ought to be hanged. Lucky for you, we are merciful captors." Narvaez and his captains were then put in chains and sent with Sandoval to be imprisoned in Vera Cruz.

Shortly after dawn, though he had not slept all night, Cortes donned a long orange robe over his armor and sat in an armchair as if it were a throne. From this position he set about persuading the Narvaez men to join forces with him, to conquer new worlds, to seek honor and glory and treasure. He showed them great magnanimity, asking his soldiers to return to them any weapons or horses that had been confiscated during the fighting. If his own fighting men grumbled about that, Cortes reminded them that they were outnumbered and would be wise to make friends.

By capitalizing on their discontent with Narvaez, by placing a few gifts of gold in some avid hands, and by using his considerable persuasive powers, Cortes won over Narvaez' entire fighting force. One by one the men kneeled before the orange-robed conqueror, kissed his hand, and pledged their loyalty. To make sure they did not conspire against their new leaders, however, Cortes divided them into four groups of two hundred or less, to be sent in four directions with different captains. Soon, however, those orders would be rescinded and the entire force redirected, for trouble was brewing in Tenochtitlan.

Cortes had barely sent news of his great victory to Pedro de Alvarado when four of Moctezuma's chieftains arrived, weeping, from Tenochtitlan. They claimed Alvarado had launched a massacre against unarmed worshipers at the feast of Tezcatlipoca, although Cortes had given permission for the celebration. The Mexica had risen in revolt and were attacking the Spaniards. Alvarado was besieged in his fortress and quarters, where the Mexica had set fires in two places. They had also set fire to the three brigantines Cortes had planned to use for retreat if necessary. Seven of Alvarado's men had been killed and many more wounded; all were fighting for their lives against overwhelming odds.

The first thought Cortes had upon receiving this message was not of Alvarado's safety, nor of his own fatigue. Marina was in Tenochtitlan, in the same palace that Alvarado was defending. She was in danger! Quickly he barked orders to his captains to follow him with all their troops by forced marches. Then he mounted his horse and galloped off for Tenochtitlan, as fast as his strong chestnut steed could fly, accompanied only by two trusted cavaliers.

"Dear God, Dear Jesus, Dear Mary, Dear Saint Peter," Cortes prayed fervently as the horses thundered along the shortest path toward Tenochtitlan. "Keep her safe for the good work she does in your Holy names, keep her safe for the good work yet to be done." He had repeated that simple prayer several times before he admitted to himself and his God what was really uppermost in his heart: "Keep her safe for me."

Chapter 25

Revolts and Reversals in Tenochtitlan

Tlacoch had become restless while his wounds were healing, while he had so much time to think about what he should do with his life. More and more, he could not imagine a future life without Metzli in it, yet she was dedicated to the cloistered life of the temple. Metzli had nursed him tenderly, cauterizing his wounds with hot sticks and spreading salves on his scratches. She brought him a staff to lean upon while his leg was healing after his gladiatorial combat at the feast of Ochpanitztli.

Half a year had passed since that time; he could limp around the complex of temple buildings and soon would have no reason not to walk away. The rainy season had begun with a few short bursts of showers, leaving the air clear and clean, the ground damp until the sunrays drew the mists upward from the stones of the walkways and the topsoil of fields and gardens. Metzli was already busy preparing for the feast of Toxcatl, to honor the major gods Huitzilopochtli and Tezcatlipoca.

On the evening before that ceremony, Metzli invited Tlacoch to walk with her as she inspected some of the work being done in preparation. "Everything seems so different this year, with the Spaniards here," she said. "At first we weren't sure we'd be able to have the ceremony at all; now we think it might be the best one ever."

"Why is that?" Tlacoch asked. Their steps had carried them to the doorway of a workshop where several women were grinding amaranth seeds. They entered, smelling the musky scent of the seeds and the sweat of the workers. Two sour-faced Spaniards, dressed in their strange pantaloons with swords strapped to their thighs, were watching as the native women ground the grain and formed a framework of reeds for the paste. Without speaking to any of the workers or Metzli, the Spaniards strode out of the building, muttering in their strange barbaric language.

Metzli stood aside and let the Spaniards pass before answering Tlacoch's question. "Did you see the man with yellow

343

hair and beard?" she asked in a low voice. "That was Pedro de Alvarado, the captain in charge here while Senor Malinche is away. You asked why we might not be able to hold the festival. That's because Spaniards don't like ceremonies involving human sacrifice. Moctezuma asked permission to hold the festival and attend it. Captain Alvarado thought about it and said we could hold the festival. He wouldn't let the emperor come, but he said some of his own men would be here. The priests want to make this festival the best ever, to impress the Spanish guests."

"I wouldn't call them guests," Tlacoch said wryly. "I've heard they took the emperor prisoner, but he won't let anyone rescue him." He and Metzli were walking slowly behind the grinding women, a shriveled group with faces wrinkled like dried plums and wiry arms. They concentrated on their tasks like priests sworn to silence and paid no attention to the visitors.

"Our priests have talked to Moctezuma about that," Metzli said in matter-of-fact tones in case the workers were listening. "He's convinced these men were sent by Quetzalcoatl. They came to our coast last year, in 1 Reed, so some people think they came to fulfill a prophecy that Quetzalcoatl would return."

"Does that make sense to you, Metzli?" Tlacoch asked. "Surely if Quetzalcoatl had sent them, they'd be peaceful teules. Have you heard about how they slaughtered the people of Cholula?"

Metzli gave him a warning look and ignored his question. "See how hard these women are working?" she said with an uneasy smile. "They've fasted for at least a hundred days, taking only water and one meal of thin atole each day. Now they're eligible to make the sacred model of Huitzilopochtli and assist in the ceremonies. May we watch you work, venerable mothers?"

Seeing Metzli's priestess robe, the women made no objection to letting her and Tlacoch watch the procedures. One of the women showed them a framework of reeds and sticks in a manlike shape. Others began plastering upon the frame a paste made from the ground amaranth seeds mixed with liquid from birds' eggs. When the statue was finished, they dressed it in rich feathers and painted crossbars over and under its shiny obsidian eyes. One woman extracted three jewelry items from a bag and placed them upon the image: a gold noseplug shaped like an arrow and inlaid with precious stones, earrings of turquoise mosaic shaped like serpents with golden rings dangling from them, and wristbands of coyote skin fringed with strips of blue paper.

Next, they placed feather ornaments on the model: a belt of feathers, a necklace of yellow parrot feathers fringed like the locks of a young boy, and the magical headdress of hummingbird feathers. Over the entire model they placed a nettle-leaf cape, painted black and decorated with five clusters of eagle feathers.

The model's maxtlatl was painted with vertical stripes of bright blue and decorated with images of severed limbs and fringed with amatl paper. Its tilmantli was painted with skulls and bones; its vest was painted with dismembered human parts such as ears, hearts, intestines, torsos, breasts, hands, and feet.

At its shoulder the women placed a red paper flag, on its head a flint knife of red paper resembling a knife steeped in blood. In one hand the image held four arrows; in the other a bamboo shield decorated with fine eagle feathers. A pendant made of blood-red paper hung down from the shield.

Tlacoch watched the construction of the god figure half-heartedly, for his eyes were drawn to Metzli. She felt his eyes on her but concentrated on the model while she thought of the words she wanted to say to Tlacoch. When the task was finished, Metzli praised the women for their excellent work and walked outside with Tlacoch. They walked toward the temple of Quetzalcoatl, past the towering pyramids standing in readiness for the festivities and ceremonies of the next ten days.

Darkness had fallen, and stars overhead formed a jewel-studded canopy. The half-moon threw a feeble light on the edges of a few clouds. The air carried a fragrance of early blossoms responding to the first rains of the month Toxcatl. Metzli felt the presence of Tlacoch driving out all other sensations, so she chose her words carefully.

"The feast of Toxcatl always reminds me of my one and only passion," Metzli reminisced. "The father of my son was the fair youth chosen for sacrifice four years ago, when I was fifteen. He was a Tlaxcalan, captured in the wars between Tenochtitlan and Tlaxcala." She laughed softly, remembering her own defiance. "I gave up my vows of chastity for him, but I have no regrets."

"Was that the reason you became estranged from your father?" Tlacoch stopped at a stone bench beside the path and took Metzli's hands, pulling her gently toward him until she was seated beside him. They were quite alone in the temple complex, since all the priests and workers had retired early in anticipation of the day ahead.

Metzli looked at the stars overhead. "If you mean my vows of chastity, Father didn't care much about that. He just couldn't stand my getting involved with a Tlaxcalan while my brother Chimalli was fighting against Tlaxcala."

"I've been a disappointment to my father, too," Tlacoch said solemnly. "He wanted me to be like your brother Chimalli, but I had no interest in wars and fighting."

"I guess fathers want the best for their children, at least the best they know of," Metzli said. "It's sad that so few of them really get to know their children, so they give them all the wrong things."

"I used to blame my father for that," Tlacoch said, "but now I blame only myself. I was a lazy spendthrift, throwing away my life on pleasantries because I was bored. Now that I've faced death, I'd like to make better use of my second chance at life."

Metzli sensed that Tlacoch was preparing to say goodbye; she felt as if the tiny space between them was stretching into a chasm, a gulf that would separate their lives permanently. "What will you make of your life? You're probably eager to start seeking your fortune, but I'll be sad when you leave here."

"I thought first I'd have to work off my debt to Huatl, the pochteca, but when I talked to him he said someone else has paid my debt. He wouldn't say who."

"I wonder," Metzli mused. "Perhaps it was a patron who saw you fight. My father and Callipopoca said you were magnificent."

Tlacoch felt the stirring of desire for this woman he could never have as the pale moonlight softly defined the folds of her priestess robe. "What about you? Will you always live at the temple? Or have you ever considered marriage?"

Metzli looked down humbly, as if in the presence of a revered lord or priest. "Fortunately, I've never been forced to marry in order to live. I'm grateful that the priests and priestesses here took me into service when I was carrying the child of an enemy warrior," she said. "They were kind enough to let my son stay in the orphanage here. You may think it strange, but I've been afraid of marriage. Most married women are little more than slaves; they desire bonds but receive bondage."

"Most people are slaves in one way or another," Tlacoch mused. "I've been a slave to money; Chimalli was a slave to ambition; our emperor is a slave to power. The worst bonds are not those others put on us, but those we put on ourselves. Even you, Metzli, are a slave to the priests here. Why is it better to cook and clean for them than for a family of your own?"

"You reason very well, Tlacoch. I've wondered that myself at times, but there is a difference. I want to be useful, but I don't want to be used. I'm assigned other duties here besides cooking and cleaning. I can teach or nurse patients in the infirmary." She added in a self-mocking tone, "A fallen woman has other uses, too. Because I've broken my vows of chastity, I make a good agent for Tlazolteotl, the goddess of lust."

"Suppose I became a great warrior," Tlacoch said earnestly. "Could I inspire your lust? Would I be good enough then to offer myself as a husband to you and a father to your son?"

Metzli felt her chest and throat fill with joy, for she had become quite attached to Tlacoch by tending his wounds, and she admired the depth in his conversation. He had matured from the shallow youth he had been in Paynala, and as she began to love his mind, her body yearned for him also. "I could lust after you, easily," she said happily; "I've learned something about that from Tlazolteotl." Then her tone became solemn. "We still should seek the approval of our fathers in Paynala and Oluta. My father would probably be as pleased as yours would if you became a warrior, but I wouldn't be. I might never see you again."

Tlacoch spoke in even greater earnestness. "I'm not blind to the world around me," he said. "The foreigners in this city are becoming a menace. Soon every able-bodied man will be pressed into service, including those with healed wounds like me. Every farmer and tradesman and artisan will have to put aside his trade, at least until the foreigners are ousted. If I have to be a warrior, I should be as good a warrior as I can be."

Metzli grasped both his hands. "War is for fools!" she cried. "Even if you didn't have a weak leg, why should you fight and die for Moctezuma?" She looked around cautiously, but seeing no other people within hearing range, she continued, "Do you know what he did to the priests from this temple three years ago?"

"No," Tlacoch said frankly. "Three years ago I was gambling or drunk most of the time. What was happening here?"

"Moctezuma sent for the priests of Quetzalcoatl when he heard about the houses floating on water. All the priests came and knelt on one knee before him, to do him great reverence. He asked if they had seen strange omens in the sky or in caves, in the lakes and streams. He wondered if they had seen visions or heard Chihuacoatl crying on the night wind."

"That was in the year 12 House?"

"Yes. They had seen some strange omens like a light in the midnight sky, but the priests couldn't tell Moctezuma how to avoid any disasters to come. They just said that whatever mysteries the gods had in mind would happen very soon."

"That didn't satisfy the emperor, of course."

"Moctezuma was furious. He asked them if they had heard the prediction of Nezahualpilli's sorcerers, that strangers would come to rule Mexico. They could only answer that if the gods willed it, it would surely take place, and he could do nothing except wait."

"Did the emperor punish them when he didn't like their answer?"

"Not only the priests, but their families as well. He had the priests thrown in prison, but some of the palace servants took pity on them and helped them escape. So Moctezuma sent his chiefs to their villages with orders to ransack and destroy their homes, strangle their wives with ropes, and dash their children's heads against the walls."

Tlacoch took a deep breath. "I can see why you hold a grudge against Moctezuma, but he's also done some good things, like building temples and canals and roadways."

"I didn't say he's all bad," Metzli said. "I only said he isn't worth dying for. Why don't you become a silversmith or featherworker? Or even a pochteca like my father?"

"What good would a trade like that do me, if our whole civilization is destroyed? Don't you remember what the Spaniards did to Cuauhpopoca and his son, burning them and fifteen nobles to death in front of Moctezuma's palace?"

"It was horrible," Metzli said. "Immoral acts are committed by warriors on both sides of a conflict. How can you know which side is the right one?"

"Maybe that doesn't matter," Tlacoch said. "Maybe the only thing that matters is which side your own countrymen are on."

* * *

Early the next morning, Tlacoch and Metzli joined the huge crowd on the temple steps to watch the fiesta in the Sacred Patio below. The sun was rising unobstructed in a cloudless blue sky, which Metzli said was a good sign for the dancers. Tlacoch observed several Spanish "guests" mingling among the natives, but no one seemed as concerned as he was that the Spaniards were carrying spears and swords.

The paste model of Huitzilopochtli was placed before his temple, standing on the ground where everyone could walk past in single file and offer gifts of round seedcakes or bits of dogmeat or incense. Certain men who had fasted twenty days or more assumed their duties as "Brothers of Huitzilopochtli" to control the crowd. They carried pine wands to guide the celebrants and dancers, keeping them in single file and in proper order .

All the young warriors, wearing clusters of heron feathers on their maxtli, filed into the patio doing the Dance of the Serpent. First came the bravest or *tequiua*, those who had captured four or more enemies, wearing cotton tufts atop their heads to show the number of captives they had taken. The *iyac* youths, who had taken some captives with the help of others, had cut off their long locks and wore feathered headdresses. The youngest or *piochtli*, their hair gathered into a long lock showing they had taken no prisoners yet, followed at a distance.

The warriors had sworn to dance and sing with all their hearts, hoping the Spaniards would marvel at the beauty of the rituals. As the dance became more spirited and the feathers bobbed and swirled to the sound of throbbing drums and trilling flutes, the warriors did not even stop to urinate, but simply loosened their maxtli and separated their clusters of heron feathers for the purpose. If anyone fell out of step or lost his place, the other dancers struck him on the hips or shoulders and pushed him so hard he sprawled to the ground. The "Brothers of Huitzilopochtli" would drag the offender outside the circle by his ears, and no one questioned the punishment because these officials were regarded with fearful veneration.

At the high point of the festival, when the dance was liveliest and song was following song in rapid sequence, the armed Spaniards suddenly sprang up and ran forward as if for battle. They closed the entrances and gateways, posting guards so no one could escape. Then they began slaughtering the celebrants in the Sacred Patio, stabbing them, spearing them, beheading them, splitting their skulls with their swords, or disemboweling them as they fell to the ground.

Two Spaniards forced their way to the musicians, cutting off the arms of a man who was drumming. The music stopped abruptly as the other drummers and flute players fled and scattered. The drummer's head then rolled across the patio floor, severed by a Spanish sword.

Some of the celebrants tried to run away after the swords slashed their abdomens, but their intestines dragged as they ran; their feet became entangled in their own entrails. Some tried to force their way through the gates, but Spanish spears impaled them. Others tried to climb the walls, but Spanish swords severed their legs. Some ran to the temples atop the pyramid, but the Spaniards eventually hunted through all the rooms until they found the hidden ones and killed them.

Tlacoch grabbed Metzli's hand and tried to pull her towards a gate, but seeing that escape cut off, he forced her to the ground near a slaughtered warrior. "Lie very still," he commanded, and Metzli was so terrified that she made no move or sound as Tlacoch pulled the body of the dead warrior over her. Even as the blood of the dead warrior soaked into her robe and hair, she made no motion except the trembling she could not control and the shallow breathing that was keeping her alive.

The blood of the dancers flowed from their severed limbs and gathered into pools on the ground. As these pools grew wider, the stench of blood and entrails filled the air. As a final indignity, the Spaniards combed over the corpses, removing all jewelry and other valuables. The only people who survived, like Metzli and Tlacoch, were some who wore no jewelry to tempt a Spaniard into discovering them. They survived only because they had fallen under the bodies of others and become so drenched with blood that the Spaniards had taken them for dead.

* * *

The sun had climbed to its zenith in the bright blue sky, sending warm rays to dry the blood of the massacre victims that stained the Sacred Patio. The Spaniards had returned to their quarters in the palace of Axayacatl, leaving an ominous quiet to replace the song and dancing of a few hours before.

A few priests who had not been present at the dances were rummaging among the bodies, trying to fit the arms and legs and torsos together if possible, so they could carry the whole bodies of the victims in bags to their homes before cremating them. The cloths that covered the faces of the priests to keep out the stench also hid their downturned mouths and absorbed their tears. They had been inured to the sight of blood, but not to a slaughter they considered unnecessary and totally lacking in purpose. This blood could not have honored Huitzilopochtli, the priests angrily assured each other, because the image of the god also lay in pieces, fractured and trampled by the Spaniards who had come ostensibly to do honor to the god but instead had mutilated him and robbed him of his jewels.

Other workers and warriors gradually joined the priests in this grisly duty, seeking the bodies of their family members or comrades in arms, clearing away the entrails to prevent pestilence from developing. They had their orders: those bodies that could be identified were taken to their homes and then to the House of Young Men for burning.

When Metzli and Tlacoch heard the familiar accents of Nahuatl spoken around them, they stirred and allowed themselves to be rescued. Tlacoch stayed to help with the work of bagging the bodies, but Metzli returned to the temple, sick at her stomach, barely able to remove her bloody garments and bathe her shaking body before collapsing in a heap upon her sleeping mat.

* * *

A groundswell of anger ensued among the Mexica of Tenochtitlan, building to rage before the day was over. Those who spread the word of the massacre also issued a call to arms. "Come running, all you Mexica! The foreigners have murdered our warriors. Bring your spears and shields, your atlatls and slings, your knives and stones. Our captains are gathering at the palace of Axayacatl. Death to the murderers!"

Marina and Luisa had felt some premonition when Alvarado had refused to let them attend the festival. When they saw him and his men return to the palace covered with blood, bruised with stones, they both became alarmed.

"No time to explain," Alvarado said to the women as he rushed in. He began issuing orders to servants and guards: "Have the cannon placed in the parapet facing the street, and tell all musketeers and archers to bring their weapons." Then he ordered Luisa and Marina to go up to the second floor, where they might be relatively safe from the arrows and stones already assailing the palace. He ordered a guard to take Moctezuma upstairs also, and to place him in chains until the battle was over.

In the streets around the palace, mobs of angry citizens mingled with warriors under the command of a determined nephew of Moctezuma, a son of the great emperor Ahuitzotl, named Cuauhtemoc. Cuauhtemoc, whose name meant "Descending Eagle" and symbolized the glory of the setting sun, had once supported his uncle Moctezuma's efforts for peace, but the events of this day had galvanized him into permanent opposition to anything Spanish.

Over the next few days, the Mexica maintained a steady stream of rocks and arrows aimed toward the Spaniards' quarters and set fire twice to the parts of the stone palace that could be burned. They burned the three brigantines Cortes had built, watching with great satisfaction as the flames and smoke carried their wrathful message to the parched blue skies, for even the gods were cooperating by withholding rain.

Determined to starve the eighty Spaniards under Alvarado's command, the Aztec army closed the market at Tlatelolco and stationed sentries to prevent any porters from carrying supplies to the palace of Axayacatl. They even killed anyone they suspected of being a porter. When Itzcuauh or "Flint Eagle," one of Moctezuma's lords, appealed to them from the palace rooftop to cease the fighting and return to their homes, the citizens shouted insults and war cries at him. "Who is Moctezuma to give us orders? We are not his slaves." A hail of arrows, stopped only by a Spanish shield hastily inserted between the archers and Itzcuauh, drove the disheartened lord inside.

Then a messenger brought bad news to Cuauhtemoc. Cortes had defeated Narvaez and was bringing a force of 1300 men with him from the coast. Cuauhtemoc ceased the hostilities temporarily, but kept the markets closed. Then he waited, confident that the vaunted "teules" would starve to death like any other mortals.

* * *

Cortes rushed into the Spanish quarters in Tenochtitlan to find Marina and Luisa in the upstairs rooms, frightened and hungry but otherwise unharmed. He embraced Marina so passionately that Luisa started to leave the room, but Cortes called her back to stay with Marina, because he had urgent matters to attend to. He kissed Marina once more, fervently on the mouth, and promised to return as soon as he could. Then he posted a guard outside the women's room.

Cortes found Alvarado badly shaken but defensive, insisting that he had heard rumors of a trap like that set for the Spaniards in Cholula and had acted in preventive self-defense. Though he admitted destroying the amaranth image of Huitzilopochtli, he claimed to be following the example set by Cortes a few weeks

351

earlier. Cortes could not deny having indulged his own anger and revulsion at the idols in the great temple, so he could only chide Alvarado for bad judgment.

"You didn't have to walk into a trap; you could have simply forbidden the ceremony and kept the peace," Cortes scolded. "If I can rely on you at all, Pedro, I can depend on your behaving rashly without thinking first. Now we have no hope of converting these natives peacefully. Now we have no choice but all-out war, with much loss of life."

Alvarado bristled, but replied calmly. "Blame me if you will, but credit my men with their bravery and forbearance in defending your position here. If they'd been an ounce less courageous, you'd have no base here, no soldiers here, and probably no interpreters either."

His anger subsiding, Cortes put an arm around Alvarado's shoulder. "I know your virtues, my friend: intelligence, great skill in battle, courage. I do appreciate your protecting Marina and Aguilar and Moctezuma. I won't be completely happy with you, though, until you develop some self-control."

With a relieved smile, Alvarado agreed. "I see the need of it, my General. The sight of you is so welcome to me that I'll do anything you ask." Then the two men embraced like the old friends they had become over the years. Cortes often had to discipline Alvarado but seldom could bring himself to do it. He relied much on this volatile captain, so disciplined militarily, so undisciplined personally, who had no equal for horsemanship and swordsmanship, who took quick and decisive action when danger required it. So Cortes muted his disappointment with Alvarado and took out his anger on Moctezuma.

Moctezuma, released from his chains, tried to welcome Cortes, but Cortes was uncustomarily curt. "You dog!" he snarled. "You've been trying to cut a deal with Narvaez to join forces with you. You, who profess to be my friend! I'm sick of your treachery—with the Cholulans, the Totonacs, and now with my own countrymen!"

Moctezuma protested, but feebly, because the wrath of Cortes could scorch cornfields like the sun in a drought. Bearing the heat of Cortes's anger, Moctezuma felt withered like the brown husks that shrivel and blow in the drying wind.

"Furthermore," Cortes continued, "you're keeping the markets closed and bringing us no food. These are acts of war! When you see your precious temples and idols destroyed now, remember how you provoked us!"

* * *

When he was alone with Marina that night, Cortes removed all his clothing, spread himself face down on the mat he now

352

called a "petate," and allowed her to bathe him by dampening a cloth in a small bowl of water and rubbing it over his body.

"Water is very precious now," Marina said as she stroked his back and arms. "The supply from Chapultepec to the palace has been cut off, and the lake here is too salty for drinking." She bent her face to kiss his back and the side of his neck that she could reach. "You, my lord, are even more precious than water."

"I've been four days on the road," Cortes said. "You can imagine how good that water feels to me." He rolled over to let her stroke his chest, savoring the cool sensation as the water evaporated on his skin. Then he reached up and pulled her head down to his, kissing her on the mouth. "You, my princess," he said in imitation of her, "are more precious to me than water."

He removed her huipil as he had done in Tlaxcala, and they spoke of their pleasantest memories as they lay together, creating a nest of happiness like birds in a tree about to be consumed by beasts of prey. "We're going into battle tomorrow," he said. "My desire always increases just before a battle."

"I've noticed that," Marina responded. "My desire will match yours tonight, no matter how many times you want me." She nuzzled her face against his neck. "It's been so long. You've been away twenty days, and before that you were sleeping with Dona Ana."

"Oh, my love," Cortes moaned, "were you hurt by that? I thought you understood why I was doing it—only because Moctezuma wanted a grandchild sired by me. I should have explained."

Marina touched his lips with her finger, as if to seal them. "No need to explain, my lord. Men and women are both bound by our duties. Men are prodded by their manly nature; sometimes that corresponds with their duties and sometimes it conflicts. A woman's nature prods her as well. I'm nineteen years old now; by that age most women have had at least one child. Luisa is younger than I am, and she's expecting a baby in a month or two. Would you give me a child too, as you did for Ana?"

"That's a sweet request," Cortes said tenderly. "You'd make a lovely mother. You can't imagine how many times I've wanted to stay inside you and make that happen."

"You can make it happen tonight."

"Even though I'm going into battle?"

"Especially because you are. I always pray for your safety, but if you should be killed, it would comfort me to have your child."

"Someday," Cortes said with emotion, "I want more than anything else to grant that wish. It's my wish, too, but I have to be practical. If you should become pregnant, I couldn't take you with me into dangerous territory."

"I'm strong," Marina said. "I never complain about

hardships."

"I know. You're the most amazing woman I've ever known," Cortes said, and even though he had used those words before in youthful flirtations, he knew they had never been as absolutely true as they were that night. He also knew he could never say those words to any other woman again.

Marina took her lover's compliment as evidence of agreement. "Then you'll stay with me every night, until I conceive?"

Cortes laughed and kissed her again. "Not yet," he said. "The time isn't right. I need your other talents too much right now. But I promise you by all that's sacred, I swear by this beard," and he stroked the brown bush on his chin, "when the fighting is done and we've won the peace, you'll have your wish."

* * *

Cortes had seen some of the pictographs of the Aztec conquests drawn on bark paper. The glyph for victory was a burning temple, drawn from the custom of taking possession of the central institution in a village, whether or not it was burned, and claiming fealty from the villagers thereafter. Marina had told him how that happened in Paynala, a bloodless conquest. The Aztecs had simply taken a squadron of warriors to the undefended temple one day, and her father had agreed to pay tribute to the Aztecs rather than risk the lives of his subjects. The strategy of the Spaniards, therefore, once they obtained reinforcements from the Narvaez forces, was to take the great temples of Tenochtitlan once and for all, bringing the subject population under control by force and by employing the power of their own customs against them.

In the meantime, while some Spaniards were preparing for the battle, others were busily gathering treasures and piling them near melting-pots in a courtyard. By building a hot fire and blowing on the coals with long reeds, they could melt down gold and silver into a molten mass, pour it into a mold, and let it cool into transportable ingots. Marina was dismayed to see the fine artistry of jewelry turned into ugly bricks, but she said nothing. She knew her place; she knew the risks of overstepping that place; she must ignore the small irritations and save her energies for larger concerns.

Moctezuma was even more dismayed at the destruction of his fine gifts, especially when the Spaniards tore down a shield or banner of beautiful featherwork simply to snatch off a gold clasp or trim. Fine featherwork required many hours of skilled labor. The artisan had to stretch a piece of fine cotton over a frame, sketch a design on it, select each feather for the proper color and shape, cut off the thicker part of the quill, and glue each individual feather in place with a dab of oli. The Aztecs took great pride in the artistry of their feather shields and banners, yet the Spaniards tossed away this work as if it were cornhusks. Moctezuma could no longer take pleasure in his meals, his garden, his zoo, or his aviary. His former friend Cortes was treating him with contempt, refusing to speak to him or to let Marina talk to him. He sunk further and further into depression, so that not even prayer comforted him.

Feeding an army of approximately 1300 Spaniards and approximately 8000 Tlaxcalan warriors, as well as nearly a hundred horses, presented a major challenge for Cortes. The water shortage had been temporarily solved by digging a well in the palace grounds near a small spring, but the drought continued, and the food shortage became more acute.

The ranks of the Aztec army and irate citizens continued to grow outside the palace, filling the whole complex of temple buildings at times. As Cortes peered from the second story windows, he could see a more formidable army taking shape than he had seen before. Many of the warriors carried the dreaded *macana* or *maquahuitl*, a two-handed wooden sword with sharp pieces of obsidian wedged into the sides. Many carried spears with fire-hardened tips. Even farmers and boatmen had joined the crowd carrying slings and stones. In addition, he saw people gathering on the azoteas, piling up stones to throw down upon any porter or canoe that tried to bring food into the Spanish quarters.

To make one last effort at pacifying the menacing crowd, Cortes decided to release Cuitlahuac, the brother of Moctezuma who had been imprisoned for conspiring with his nephew Cacama against Moctezuma and his Spanish friends.

Cortes was watching with Marina from the upper story when Cuitlahuac was released. The crowd let out a shout of joy as they recognized the king of Ixtapalapa. Marina darted out onto the rooftop to take advantage of the joyful moment. "Mexicanos, come forward!" she shouted. "The Spaniards need your help! Bring them food and pure water. They are tired and hungry, almost fainting with exhaustion! They have mercifully sent King Cuitlahuac to you. Be merciful with them, too! Forget your anger and let them be the brothers they want to be!"

A hailstorm of stones and arrows flew at Marina, accompanied by angry shouts. The barrage might have killed her if Cortes had not swiftly stepped out onto the roof and interposed his shield. "Get inside, Marina, for God's sake," Cortes yelled, pulling her arm with his right hand and holding his metal shield with his left to deflect all the missiles whizzing through the air. Once inside, he spoke sharply to her. "Never do such a foolish thing again!" he scolded. "Never trust your own safety to the decent inclinations of a mob!"

Sobbing, Marina clasped her arms around her lover. Stung by the intensity of the hostility, she also sensed the loss of what had once seemed an almost magical power to persuade. "They hate us!" she said brokenly. "They hate us all, not just the ones who injured them!"

"Hate needs no justification," Cortes said grimly as he tried to comfort her. "All it needs is a target."

* * *

Tlacoch stood in awe at the scene he had just witnessed. Wearing a warrior costume, he stood behind several others who, like himself, were new recruits. Several of them had just sent arrows flying toward the parapet on the rooftop of Axayacatl's palace, but he had only gripped his maquahuitl in readiness for hand-to-hand combat if necessary. The more experienced warriors, the tequiua, rushed forward to welcome the King of Ixtapalapa as he stumbled out of the palace door. Tlacoch stepped aside as they pushed through the crowd to escort the king to safety.

"Who was that woman on the rooftop?" he asked an older warrior standing beside him.

"La Malinche," said the warrior, spitting on the ground as he said the words. "The man was Senor Malinche, the chief of the conquistadors, the one who imprisoned Moctezuma. It's a pity our stones and arrows missed them."

"I thought he called her *Marina*," said Tlacoch, "but I didn't understand his other words. Strange. She was dressed like a Maya woman, but she spoke Nahuatl."

"She has two tongues, like a snake, they say," the older warrior snarled. "Malinche talks through her."

"I thought I'd seen her someplace before," Tlacoch said.

"We've heard she came from the Maya territories," said the old warrior. "You been there?"

"Nope. Guess I was mistaken. Anyway, she couldn't have been the girl she reminded me of. Malinalli's been dead for at least four or five years."

* * *

The Aztecs had grown in numbers and also grown tired of waiting for the foreigners and their Tlaxcalan allies to starve. They formed an aggressive attack, with a ferocity that Cortes was ill prepared to deal with. Just before dawn, with the shrieking of a conch shell accompanied by drums and yelling, a column of well-armed warriors, most of them wearing quilted cotton armor, advanced upon the Spanish quarters.

The Spaniards attempted to discourage them by sending out their cavalry with lances and by shooting off a cannon they had installed behind the parapet on the palace roof. The horses were plagued by clouds of arrows and stones, which fretted them like stinging insects despite their protective coverings. A squadron of Aztec warriors fell under the assault of a cannonball, but another squadron climbed over their bodies and attacked the parapet with a battering ram. Some attempted to scale the parapet, but they were struck down by the bullets of a Spanish marksman or the maquahuitl of a Tlaxcalan.

Though the weapons of the Aztecs were less massively destructive than the technology of the Spanish muskets and cannons, Aztecs had been trained in warfare since childhood and used weapons with great skill. From a distance, they used slings to send rocks whizzing like bullets straight to their mark. Closer up, they could use their atlatls to throw spears with devastating speed and accuracy. Closer still they could use their flint-edged macahuitls or a three-pronged dart with a cord attached for its retrieval. It was a battle of primitive fury against technological superiority, but Cortes had clearly underestimated the power and skill of his opponents.

Flaming arrows arched over the palace walls and into the thatched roofs of the huts erected in the courtyard to shelter the Tlaxcalans. The flames spread rapidly in the parched thatch, and soon some of the wooden parts of the palace had also caught fire, including part of the protective wall surrounding it. Because no water was available, men threw dirt on the flames. To contain the spread of the fire, Cortes made a breach in the palace wall, hoping to protect the gap with musketeers and crossbowmen, but soon the Aztecs pushed their way through it. Overwhelmed by sheer numbers of Aztecs, who kept up an incessant volley of arrows and spears from their atlatls, the Spaniards were relieved when night came and the enemy stopped fighting.

The following morning Cortes himself led a cavalry charge at full gallop to surprise the Aztecs. The Aztecs, though thrown into some disorder, regrouped behind barricades of timber and earth to send more clouds of arrows and well-aimed stones. As the Spanish forces cleared away the barricades, losing momentum in the effort, the enemy nipped at them relentlessly.

The canals came alive with canoes full of warriors with razor-sharp macuahuitls that did great damage to the unprotected bodies of the Tlaxcalan warriors and also found chinks in the Spaniards' armor. Stones rained down on the Spanish forces from the azoteas, and the battered Spanish men retaliated by setting fire to the houses. Since each house was separated from the others by canals, however, the fires did not spread. Wooden drawbridges between the houses were raised so Spanish soldiers had to wade waist-deep to cross a canal. Even so, several hundred houses went up in flames that day, killing the occupants as well as the combatants on their roofs.

The day went on with attacks and counterattacks, reprisals and retreats, defeats and renewals, rallying and stubborn resistance. At the end of the day, exhausted with fighting and hunger, the Spaniards retreated to their fortress. Though the Aztecs kept to their custom of not fighting at night, they kept the Spanish forces awake with shrieks, yells, and drums.

After several days of fighting, the Cortes forces became demoralized. Bernal Diaz remarked that the arrows and javelins that fell in a single day resembled wheat on a threshing floor. No matter how well the Spaniards fought, a hundred Aztec warriors sprang up to replace every ten they killed. The Spaniards' armor was battered, their helmets dented or split. Some of their favorite weapons had been shattered or rendered useless; the supply of gunpowder was running low.

A body of five or six hundred Aztecs had placed a barricade at the top of the great pyramid, permitting themselves a grand view of the temple grounds and the besieged palace of Axayacatl. Cortes decided to lead an assault party up the steps of the pyramid, although he was suffering from a wound in his left hand. Tying a shield to his left arm, he started off with three hundred cavaliers and several thousand auxiliaries. When the horses slipped on the blood-covered stones of the temple courtyard, his troops dismounted and proceeded on foot.

The stair steps, twice as high as they were wide, so narrow that a man's foot must be placed sideways, could discourage even a climber who carried no heavy weapons. A steady hailstorm of missiles from above further hindered the Spaniards. The climbers had to circle the huge structure at each terrace to reach the next flight of stairs, so they had climbed nearly a mile when they reached the top, breathless and panting in the thin atmosphere. Immediately the Aztecs pounced on them in hand-to-hand combat. As they grappled, many of them tumbled down the steps in the arms of their enemy, to be crushed on the pavement below. All morning the fighting raged. The platform at the top was thick with blood before the Spaniards' steel had overcome the Aztecs' flint knives. The cost to both sides was dear: hundreds of Aztecs, and forty-five of Cortes' most prized fighting men.

The victorious cavaliers rushed to the sanctuaries, to find that the cross and the image of the Virgin Mary had been removed. The grim figure of Huitzilopochtli, however, still leered at them over his censer of smoking hearts. With shouts of triumph, the victors tore the statue from its niche and tumbled it down the bloody steps, to the great horror of the citizens who had gathered at the base of the pyramid.

Then the flames set by the Spaniards devoured the great

teocalli, just as the rituals in that structure had devoured so many human hearts in the past. The smell of burning blood rose with the smoke. The sacred ashes floated, then descended to earth again, falling upon fragments of the statue once revered as the image of the greatest god in the One World. The descending sun continued to cast lights and shadows on the anguished faces of men and women who believed they could not live without the sun god, and who felt sure they would never see another dawn.

* * *

The dawn did arrive, but the first rays of light did not reveal to Cortes a defeated or deserted city. Instead, the first rays played upon rows and rows of other Mexica in war costumes, gathering around the temple grounds and the palace of Axayacatl where his exhausted men had retired to dress their wounds and recover from the emotional highs and lows of the previous day.

Cuitlahuac had placed himself at their head, wearing the regalia of an eagle knight and flanked by guards carrying a feathered banner with royal designs. After a conch shell trumpeted and a drum roll wakened anyone who might still be sleeping, Cuitlahuac shouted to Cortes. "Your end is near, foreigners! You imprison our leaders, but new ones arise to take their place. You slay our warriors, but we will fight on even if twenty-five thousand of us die for every Spaniard we kill."

As Marina translated those words to Cortes, she could see the despair in his face. "They've never yet defeated you," she reminded him. "They won't defeat you now, no matter how many thousands they send. Even if they're as numerous as grains of sand, they can't stop the ocean."

Cortes put his arm around Marina affectionately, looking out a window at the legions of enemies who were heating up for battle by shouting insults. "Your faith in me is touching, dear Marina. You can inspire me to fight to the death."

"Not to your death, to a long life!" Marina exclaimed, as cheerily as she could to disguise her own discouragement.

"I'm ready to leave this country, Marina. Narvaez's men are complaining and maligning me; I don't know how long they'll hold out. The Tlaxcalans are dying by the hundreds because they have no armor. I should send them home. Some men who came with me from Cuba over a year ago are getting homesick and battle-weary. I'm going to ask Moctezuma to speak to the Indians out there. He can tell them we'll leave, if they'll just put down their drawbridges and let us pass along the causeways."

Marina went to Moctezuma with that proposal, accompanied by Father Olmedo and Cristobal de Olid. The unhappy monarch glared at the trio and replied, "What more does Malinche want from me? I won't listen to his false words or talk to him. My

359

fate has been sliding downward ever since he came into my life."

"He wants to get out of your life," Marina said. "Just say that to the people who are gathering outside. They're hungry to hear their tlatoani speak once more." Then she translated what she had said to the two men who accompanied her.

"They've chosen another leader," Moctezuma said dejectedly. "They follow Cuitlahuac; they won't listen to me."

"You're still their emperor," Marina said. "Show them you are. Tell them you can get the Spaniards to leave peacefully if the warriors will let them pass without more fighting."

"Ask Cuitlahuac to have the drawbridges replaced on the causeways," Olid said to Moctezuma. "If we have bridges, we'll take our horses and all our men across the lake and away from here forever."

"Also," Father Olmedo added, "You can stop much of the suffering. If we have to stay here and fight, many more people will die. You can save many of your countrymen's lives."

A hopeful look crossed Moctezuma's face. He called for his page Orteguilla and requested some royal robes. Shortly afterward, he emerged from his room wearing a tilmantli bordered with white and blue, clasped with a beautiful pin of green jade set in gold. A copilli, or diadem, ornamented the proudly-held head of the man who could still walk tall, who still carried the golden scepter as the symbol of his authority. With a firm tread, he planted his golden-soled sandals on the stone floors and climbed to the roof, accompanied by several Spanish guards and his own Aztec attendants.

As he appeared on the battlements in his splendid garments and raised the golden scepter to make himself known to the crowd below, a hush fell over the raucous mob. Many of the Mexica dropped to one knee and bowed their heads respectfully to their emperor. Others stared in open-mouthed wonder at seeing the man who had once forbidden anyone to look into his face.

"Why have you come here, my people, bringing arms to the house of my father?" Moctezuma asked in a paternalistic manner. "Have you heard that I am a prisoner here, and come to demand my release? If so, you act upon good instincts, but as you can see, I am not a prisoner. The strangers at whom you aim your arrows are my guests. I remain with them by choice. They would like to leave now and return to their own homes. Let them pass freely; that is my wish."

For a few moments the crowd stood silent, torn between two conflicting but equally powerful loyalties: to their emperor and to their religion. Could their devotion to the monarch who symbolized their country overcome their sustained anger over insults to statues that symbolized their gods?

Then a single voice called out, "Moctezuma, you debase

yourself and your countrymen. You've let the Spaniards turn you into a woman, fit only to weave and to spin!"

Cuitlahuac spoke sharply. "Silence! Let the Uey Tlatoani speak!"

Then another Aztec captain with four cotton balls on his topknot rose from his bent knee and stood before the emperor. "Revered Speaker," he said, "we have prayed for your safety and will honor you as much as ever when our prayers are answered and you have returned to your former glory."

"No!" cried the voice of the first man. He stepped forward, holding his shield before his face. "We no longer recognize Moctezuma the Younger, except as Moctezuma the Coward. Our new tlatoani is Cuitlahuac, King of Ixtapalapa."

Then Cuitlahuac spoke again. "This is a sad day for me, my brother, but you must hear me now. The Spaniards have tricked you. They've had many chances to leave; instead they stayed and imprisoned their hosts. Cacama, our nephew, still lies in Spanish chains. We can't let any Spaniards leave here alive, or they'll come back in greater numbers. Don't aid them any more! Become again the dauntless warrior you once were!"

From a nearby rooftop, an arrow whizzed through the air, almost striking Moctezuma in the arm, breaking its force against the stone wall behind him. The Spanish guards quickly interposed their shields between the emperor and the crowd, but a storm of stones had already begun to shower the hapless ruler. Three stones actually hit him on the head and the arms, knocking him senseless to the ground.

The guards carried Moctezuma's limp form to his room, where he lay in semi-consciousness for three more days, neither eating nor allowing anyone to tend his wounds. Despite the affection of the Spanish soldiers who visited him and doffed their quilted hoods or helmets to him, he made no response. Despite the tender ministrations of his two legitimate wives and their weeping daughters, he did not recognize them. Despite the presence of his devoted nobles who served him faithfully to the last, he made no effort to live. Despite sincere exhortations of Father Olmedo to embrace Christianity and save his soul, he chose to die in the faith with which he had lived. Then on the day the Spaniards called June 30, 1520, in the year the Mexica called 2 Flint, the unhappy prince breathed his last.

No one could say whether his brain had been injured by the stone that struck it or whether his mind had suffered the intolerable indignity of a Uey Tlatoani plunged into disgrace like a plummeting eagle dropping from the sky with an arrow in his heart. Marina understood the irony because she understood the culture. This broken man had risen to the highest rank any mortal could attain in the One World of the Mexica, then had been brought down by a stone, the most primitive possible weapon in the hands of his lowliest subjects. His death marked a low point for the Aztecs, yet it was not the lowest point either for them or for the Spanish conquistadors who seemed, for the moment at least, to have triumphed.

* * *

Moctezuma's death made evacuation even more imperative by giving the Aztecs one more grievance to avenge. Cortes had been laying plans for several days. His carpenters had been building a portable bridge which could be laid down then taken back up to enable them to cross any gaps in the causeways. He had organized the army in a marching order of three divisions: the vanguard of two hundred foot soldiers would go first, commanded by Gonzalo de Sandoval and supported by twenty cavaliers. The rear guard was entrusted to Juan Velasquez de Leon and Pedro de Alvarado; they commanded most of the infantry and artillery. Appointing Juan Jaramillo as his assistant, Cortes took charge of the center, including the baggage and two fifths of the treasure placed on the strongest horses. Under their watchful eyes would travel his interpreters and four prisoners he might need as hostages: a son and two daughters of Moctezuma, and the rebellious Cacama, deposed king of Texcoco. The Tlaxcalan warriors were divided equally among the three divisions, many serving also as porters.

The remaining treasure, after Cortes had secured a fifth each for the king and himself, was left to the soldiers. Cortes told them to take whatever they could carry from the pile of gold ingots and precious stones, but he warned them not to overload themselves. Most of the soldiers already wore gold chains, and the more experienced ones like Bernal Diaz took only a few jadestones that would be easy to carry and useful for barter. The naive Narvaez men, however, loaded themselves with gold ingots and other bulky items that glittered only slightly more than the eyes of their avid acquisitors.

Because he thought the Aztecs would expect him to take the more familiar route to the south, Cortes planned his exit to the west along the shorter causeway leading to Tacuba. Knowing the Aztecs' disinclination to nighttime fighting, Cortes planned to march in darkness. Just after midnight, on July 1, Father Olmedo said mass to invoke the Almighty's protection on their perilous journey. Then the gates were eased open and the army marched forth into a drizzling rain. Although the mist hindered them with poor visibility, they made their way through the city and approached an open causeway before their clanking armor or clopping horses' hooves attracted the notice of Aztec sentinels.

Priests keeping night watch at the teocalli heard the sentinels' cries from the causeways and added the wail of their conch shells. Drums soon added to the din.

Seeing a gap in the causeway, Sandoval ordered his men to bring out the portable bridge and place it over the murky waters. He tested its strength by riding across; then Cortes rode across with the treasure-loaded horses, their guards close behind him. Before the entire army could get across this narrow improvised bridge, however, a fleet of canoes approached with hundreds of warriors howling war cries and shouting insults.

Preceded by torrents of arrows, the Aztecs landed their canoes on the edges of the causeways and attacked the fleeing Spanish army with spears, three-pronged darts, and macuahuitls. The Spaniards divided their attention between fending off their attackers and getting themselves and their equipment across the twelve-foot bridge. Soon the vanguard reached another gap and sent a request to the rear for the portable bridge, but not all the rear guard had been able to get across the first gap. They were effectively trapped on the causeway.

In desperation, some cavaliers forded the waters by swimming through the gaps on the backs of their horses. In the second gap, Cortes found a fairly shallow place where some foot soldiers could wade through chest-high, though still subject to attack from canoes filled with shrieking enemies. The panicked porters dumped some of the boxes and baggage into the waters to make improvised bridges. Dead horses were piled upon the cannons and rubble to make footholds for the fleeing Spaniards, and the fallen bodies of some of the slain porters provided a similar bridge for their more fortunate comrades.

Alvarado, finding himself badly wounded, unhorsed, and driven to the edge of the water by furious enemies, used his lance to propel himself into the air and far enough across the gap to scramble to safety. Alvarado was met there by Cortes, who had come from the front to help those who still struggled in the rear. For most of them, help came too late, but the fact that Cortes had endangered himself by returning to the fray endeared him to the survivors.

The gold ingots so coveted by the Narvaez soldiers had proved to be their undoing, just as Cortes had warned. For as they struggled to carry these heavy encumbrances, they could neither run nor swim. Aztec warriors seized them, pulled them aboard their canoes, and gutted some on the spot, though they held some other captives for sacrifice in the temples.

The fighting and scrambling along the causeway lasted throughout the night. When the first gray streaks of daylight appeared, the exhausted survivors gathered on the shore near Tacuba. A few scouts sent to that town returned with news of an inhospitable reception, because Tacuba had been a sister city of Tenochtitlan and Texcoco in the Triple Alliance. So Cortes led the ragged remnants of his army to a village called Popotla.

In a small temple overlooking a plain, the soldiers dressed their multiple wounds as best they could and assessed their humiliating losses. They counted only four hundred and twenty surviving Spaniards out of an initial force of twelve hundred and fifty. Of the precious horses, only twenty-three remained. The losses to the Tlaxcalans were harder to estimate, but undoubtedly larger. Bernal Diaz guessed their dead to number around four thousand, about half the number they had started with, and he thanked God for providing the Spaniards with such fine friends. He also thanked God for those fine Tlaxcalan friends when he saw Marina and Luisa among the survivors. The two women had been well guarded by the Tlaxcalans in the vanguard, who considered Luisa their own princess and Marina their true friend. Marina also expressed gratitude to Juan Jaramillo, who had stayed by her side when the duties of command took Cortes away.

Cortes offered a prayer of thanks after his initial joy at seeing Marina alive alongside Jaramillo and his trusted captains Sandoval, Olid, Ordaz, Avila, and Alvarado. He was also relieved to see among the survivors Aguilar, Father Olmedo, and several shipbuilders whose skills he sorely needed.

Then he took time to grieve. The morning sunlight was revealing the sad condition of his surviving troops, with their black bruises and bloody bandages, their torn garments and dented armor, their salt-soaked hair and beards. Sadder still, on that night he later referred to as *la noche triste*, he had lost his loyal captain Juan Velasquez de Leon, his favorite page Juan de Salazar, his astrologer Botello, the fine horseman Lares, and his friends Francisco de Salcedo and Francisco de Morla.

The two daughters and son of Moctezuma placed in his care had also been killed, including Dona Ana and the child in her womb. Ironically, the rebel king Cacama, whom Cortes regarded as a worthy foe, had fallen to the indiscriminate spears of his own allies. The daughter of Xicotenga the elder, who had taken the name Elvira when she was baptized and given to Juan Velasquez de Leon, was gone; Cortes would have to take this sad news to his friend the Tlaxcalan ruler. The captain general, suffering from his own wounds of body and spirit, climbed a small hill, sat under a white willow tree, and wept.

* * *

The battered Cortes army struck out the next day to circle the northern rim of the great lakes and march toward Tlaxcala, where they hoped to find friendship, food, and rest. On the way they were harried by small bands of Aztecs shouting at them and slinging a few stones, but the efforts seemed pitifully feeble. Cortes wondered why, until he emerged from a mountain pass that his enemies knew he had to traverse on his way to Tlaxcala. There, on the plains near Otumba, assembled in all their feathery and glittering regalia, stood a force of two thousand Aztecs, confidently waiting to finish them off.

Chapter 26

The Final Days of Tenochtitlan

Metzli had never felt such loneliness as she did after Tlacoch left with the Aztec forces. Otumba sounded like such a faraway place, but he assured her he would not be gone long. The Spaniards would have to pass that way in a few days, and his captain had assured him they were in no condition to resist an army of Aztecs freshly recruited from neighboring towns.

Although she was lonely, she had no time alone, no time to be idle. Their small infirmary had been filled with wounded warriors since the night Moctezuma's forces drove the Spaniards away, a night blending victory and sorrow. Many other emergency hospitals had been established around the city to care for the wounded, and she had helped train other women as nurses.

The priests assigned most of their staff to community service, including the gardener Callipopoca and his wife Chihuallama from the temple of Quetzalcoatl. Caring for the dead took all the resources the city could muster after the able-bodied men had been recruited for the wars. The stricken bodies of dead Aztecs had to be gathered and cremated. The stinking bodies of Spaniards and Tlaxcalans had to be cleared from the causeway and canals, as well as the dead stags that had carried the false teules on their shoulders.

The bodies of enemies could not be cremated; there were too many. The workers stripped them of clothing and ornaments, loaded the bodies of Tlaxcalans into canoes, and dumped them among the rushes at the swampy edges of the lake. The Spaniards' corpses were set apart from the others, lined up in rows. Their naked bodies glowed white as the buds of the maguey, white as new corn. The naked bodies of the women, painted with their cosmetic yellow paint, looked like ripe corn on the cob. These would be offered to Huitzilopochtli for granting the Aztecs their victory.

By a generally recognized agreement, the cleanup workers were entitled to take any Spanish possessions they found. If they could carry something home on their shoulders, it became their property. They also collected many discarded weapons—not only the spent Aztec arrows and spears that could be re-used, but also Spanish steel and iron objects they might convert to their own use: helmets, coats of mail, breastplates, metal shields, cannons, and crossbows. The workers gathered up everything they could find, groping under water with their hands and feet to search the canals and lake.

The workers were told not to keep any gold ingots, gold disks, quills filled with gold dust, and collars studded with chalchihuitl stones. These were to be recovered, returned to the royal treasury, and placed under guard by the new emperor Cuitlahuac. There was no way to know, however, if all workers honored that command.

The work of cremation and ceremonies of mourning fell heavily upon the priests, who were exempted from military service, and who had the further advantage of being accustomed to smells of burning and decay. For many days after the Spaniards were expelled, the smells of burning flesh and hair hung in the air like a pall, and layers of smoke clouded the skies.

Priests from all temples were required to participate in funeral ceremonies for the late emperor Moctezuma, though they expressed some misgivings about the controversy it would cause. Some citizens said he should be regarded as a traitor and denied funeral rites; others demanded the full respect due an emperor who had fulfilled a strange and tragic tonalli without ever losing his faith in the true gods. As a practical matter, only a few elderly nobles were available to carry his litter through the streets, so the parade was kept short and the rites delivered somewhat hastily. Supposedly his body was interred in a crypt in the hill of Chapultepec, but in the confusion of warfare, few people took enough notice to be sure the crypt was properly marked. Ironically, his body disappeared into oblivion even as his name advanced into legend.

* * *

The month of Tlaxochimaco, the time of flowers, was normally a happy time in Tenochtitlan. The dances permitted men and women to join hands; the merchants often gave gifts generously to honor their god Yacatecuhtli. In the year 2 Flint, however, the mood was subdued. News came to the new Uey Tlatoani, Cuitlahuac, that his huge army of two hundred thousand Aztec warriors had been routed and sent away from Otumba in disgrace, with the dead numbering twenty thousand and the wounded innumerable.

One of the wounded was Tlacoch, who returned with only a stub where his left arm had been, the end covered with a mass of scars showing both slash wounds and burns. As soon as he had reported to the high council and obtained their released from active service in the army, he went to see Metzli.

Metzli disobeyed orders and left her post in the infirmary when she saw Tlacoch enter. The reunited couple walked along the canal and the lakeshore, which had been cleaned thoroughly since the night of victory over the Spaniards.

"I can't offer you a whole man now," Tlacoch said, "but I can still offer you a whole heart."

"Then take mine in return," said Metzli, her eyes glistening with emotion. "I'm so glad you're alive. Your wounds only make you dearer to me. Your father will see a hero in you now."

"I was almost a hero," Tlacoch said. "I recognized Malinche himself on the battlefield at Otumba. I'd seen him once on the battlements at the palace of Axayacatl, so I knew his face. I pulled him off his horse and had him in my grasp!" He emphasized his words by making a fist with his right hand. "I was trying to tie him up, when one of his soldiers slashed my left arm and knocked me down."

"Could you have killed him if you hadn't tried to tie him up?" As soon as Metzli asked the question she realized it sounded bloodthirsty. She would do penance for the dark thought, another thorn scratch on the earlobes.

"I've asked myself that a thousand times," Tlacoch said. "As I look back, I should have. Spaniards fight to kill, but we've been trained to take sacrifices alive."

"Then he was trying to kill you," Metzli said with her hand over her heart. "You came close to losing your life."

"You're right; you've been right all along, Metzli. War is for fools. I still can't see how we lost that battle. We had two hundred thousand men; the Spaniards had only five hundred or so, the Tlaxcalans only three or four thousand. They fought with a relish and a vengeance that surprised me—surprised all of us. I guess we were close enough to the Tlaxcalans' own territory so they put real passion into their spears."

"I can understand that," Metzli said. "Any of us would fight to defend our home territory."

"The Tlaxcalans, maybe, but the Spaniards didn't have any such motive," Tlacoch said. "They've fought us all along simply out of greed. What hurts most is, they destroyed us with our own military system. The only reason they didn't stop to kill me is that they saw a chance to kill Chihuaca."

"Who's he?"

"He was our quachic, our top commander. He came onto the field flaunting his emblems of authority: his golden net, the fountain of plumes over his head, flashy tilmantli with feathers and jewels. He even surrounded himself with attendants, and rode into battle on a litter!"

368

"He must've been quite easy to recognize."

"Yes, wasn't that crazy? The Spaniards had been looking for anyone wearing a topknot or a headdress, anyone with a high rank. They couldn't kill us all, so they concentrated on the leaders. When Malinche saw the entourage around Chihuaca, he and his captains slashed through them like a thunderbolt. Malinche fought alongside his own men, even in front where the danger was greatest. They always kept a group of fighters near him who came to his rescue if he stumbled or faltered. They worked efficiently, like priests lopping off the heads of sacrifices with one stroke. The Spaniards would slay each man with one thrust in the gut, including our foolish quachic."

"Was that the end of the battle, then, when the quachic was killed?"

Tlacoch looked disgusted. "A riot ended it. When Chihuaca fell, his attendants ran screaming away from the field, and soon all the other warriors started running too, thinking they were being chased. Most of the officers had been killed, so we had no one to give us directions, and the younger recruits panicked. They were trampling each other trying to get away."

"How did you get away?"

"When they saw me sprawled on the ground with my arm gone, everyone left me for dead. I took a thong from my sandals and wrapped it around my arm to stop the bleeding. As soon as it was dark, I sneaked into the village of Otumba. I found a ticitl there who sealed the blood vessels with hot coals and put some ointment on the burns. I nearly passed out with the pain, but I kept thinking of you, and how much I wanted to live."

Metzli touched the stub tenderly. "You've been so brave, Tlacoch. Does it still hurt?"

"Sometimes. The weirdest thing is that sometimes I get a pain in my hand—the hand that isn't there. Sometimes I wake up in the night sweating, but the worst pain is knowing I'm a failure, knowing how stupid I was to try being a hero. I wasn't meant to be a warrior."

"I'm glad you see that now," Metzli said. "You're really a gentle person, not a killer. Maybe that's why you couldn't kill Malinche when you had him. Some men seem brutal by nature; others are born with kindness woven into their souls. Be glad for what you are, as I am."

"You amaze me, Metzli," Tlacoch said. "You see goodness in me where others see only weakness. I've wondered many times what I could have done for my country if I hadn't been expected to kill myself as a warrior before I could live to do anything else. You've taught me to respect my own thinking."

"I'm learning important things from you, too," Metzli said. "You've helped me see how hard life must be for men. I've always thought women had no choice in their lives. I've felt resentful at times, but you make me see how few choices men have. You had only two choices: to be a foolhardy warrior or a cowardly wastrel. At least that's how it must have seemed."

"True. My father chose my school, my career, even a woman for me to marry."

"Didn't your father at least ask who you wanted for a wife?"

"Some fathers do, I know, but mine's more determined than most to have his own way. I don't mean to criticize him; I know he wanted the best for me, but Malinalli didn't respect me, and I wasn't ready for marriage either."

"Oh," said Metzli. "He wanted you to marry Malinalli? I've heard her say she never wanted to marry."

"She's the one he picked, but marriage would have been bad for both of us then. I'm a better man, now, Meztli, even though some might say I'm only half a man."

"I wouldn't say that," Metzli said. "It's one of life's ironies. You lost an arm, but you found your soul. You lost a part so that you could be whole."

"I won't be completely whole until you and I have tied the tilmantli," Tlacoch said gently. "I lost all my other friends and family, but I found you." He put his good arm protectively around Metzli's waist. "Should I ask your father's permission?"

"Let's not ask permission from either of our fathers. Let's just tie the tilmantli and tell them afterward." Metzli put both her arms around Tlacoch's neck, her cheek snuggling with his.

"How soon?" Tlacoch pulled Metzli close with his strong right arm, feeling the curve of her back, the warmth of her body against his.

"It better be soon," Metzli said happily, "or I may break my vows of chastity again."

* * *

Tlacoch inquired at the House of the Pochteca when Huatl would be expected to return so he could catch his former owner between trips. Luckily, Huatl was staying there, and the housekeeper directed Tlacoch to his sleeping chamber. In the morning light, Tlacoch could see stacks of tilmantli, baskets, and pottery piled against the wall. The rumpled cover on the petlatl showed that Huatl had just awakened.

"By the gods, what happened to you?" Huatl asked when he saw the stump of Tlacoch's left arm. When Tlacoch told him about the battle of Otumba, the cynical Huatl grunted. "I've seen some stupidity in my day, but this tops everything! You surprised us all with your fighting skills when they had you tethered to a disk at the temple grounds. Then as soon as your wounds heal, you limp off to war, as a volunteer, of all things!"

"You've always known I was a gambler," Tlacoch said. "I

took a gamble and lost, that's all."

"What were the stakes? Fame? Fortune?"

Tlacoch laughed. "Nothing like that. It may not make sense to you, but I was gambling on winning the respect of a couple of people I care about."

"Your father, I suppose. Don't tell me I'm the other one!"

"I'd welcome your respect;" Tlacoch said amiably. "I certainly didn't earn it when I was your slave. But the other person I had in mind is a woman."

"True, you were a lousy slave," Huatl said good-humoredly. "Lazy and scabrous, as I remember. Stupid, too, if you're gambling on the constancy of a woman!"

"Everything you say about me is true, but this woman is no gamble," Tlacoch said. "I want you to meet Metzli and come to our wedding, if you can."

"Metzli? Isn't she Opochtli's daughter?"

"That's right. She's also the priestess who nursed me to health. I know you and Opochtli have traveled together. If you're still on good terms with him, perhaps you'll carry the news to him in Oluta after Metzli and I are married."

"Hm," Huatl said. "I wouldn't mind seeing him again. Got kind of fond of the pot-bellied old frog. Trouble is, I'm not going that direction. I'm leaving tomorrow for Tlaxcala."

"Tlaxcala? Where the Spaniards are? Where the battle is?"

"It's not dangerous for pochteca. In fact, it's rather profitable. Since the Spaniards came, traders can go into the Tlaxcala territory. Tlaxcalans are always desperate for salt and cotton. Now that the war is over, they need lots of things."

"I wish you a profitable journey," Tlacoch smiled. "Before you leave, I'd like to propose a way to settle my debt to you."

"What debt?" Huatl asked, looking surprised. He wondered if Tlacoch had become suspicious of the way his life had been spared in the gladiator battle of Ochpanitzli, but he soon realized Tlacoch had no knowledge of the bribery.

"You gave me to the temple for sacrifice," Tlacoch said. "You'd paid for me, and you didn't get your money's worth. I should repay you for your losses."

"You were worthless to me when I gave you away," Huatl protested. "That was my poor contribution to the temple. We pochteca make donations instead of paying tribute, you know."

"I calculate the usual cost of a slave at 100 cacao beans," Tlacoch continued as if Huatl had not protested. He handed him a pouch of beans. "Here's what I owe you for that. This comes from my army pay, so it's earned money, not winnings from gambling."

Huatl took the pouch. "I can see you've changed, but I haven't. I'll take any man's money and call it a fair profit."

"There's another matter," Tlacoch said. "This is a debt of

honor, one I'm very embarrassed about. Remember the five pieces of jade I stole from you? I gave them to the temple without telling anyone where I got them. I want to make amends, as soon as I can earn the money."

"Tlacoch, you're making me uncomfortable with all this talk about honor," said Huatl in the gruff voice he always used when being especially cynical. "I've told you, that debt is paid. I can understand why a poor man steals when he gets a chance; it's the master's fault if he gets careless and puts temptation in the path of a slave. I can also understand someone making restitution to buy a friend out of slavery. What I can't understand is why you don't let well enough alone. Be glad for your luck, and be done with it."

"Well, then," Tlacoch said with a devious grin, "shall we talk about a business venture that might profit both of us?"

"Well, well!" Huatl grunted. "Why didn't you say so in the first place? I'm listening."

Tlacoch outlined his plan—to sell trade goods directly to wealthy clients in their homes, so trips to the market would be unnecessary. He had some acquaintances in Tenochtitlan—men he had gambled with previously. He knew what they liked and also what would please their wives and concubines. He could select some clothing and jewelry, show it directly to them, and make the sale right there. If the quality of the goods and the service pleased them, they would tell their friends.

Huatl nodded. "You could be doing that while I'm on the road collecting more goods. It makes sense; maybe you aren't as stupid as I thought. Tell me, though, would your old gambling friends tempt you into a game?"

"I have no friends," Tlacoch said. "Only acquaintances. They don't care who sells it, just so they get what they want."

"Okay, acquaintances, then. But those acquaintances once gambled with you. Would you be tempted to borrow a stake from our inventory—just a little loan, a debt of honor perhaps?"

The color in Tlacoch's cheeks deepened. "You'd have to trust me."

"Trust you? Why should I?"

Tlacoch's answer reminded Huatl of a bird circling a snake and moving in swiftly with direct and certain aim for the kill. "Because I'm promising you double the profits you get now, and you can't pass that up. Because I need to support a wife and child, so you know I won't run out on you. Besides, you've already been foolish enough to trust me, so you have an investment in me." Then he raised the stub of his left arm. "Besides that," he said, "how can you refuse a war hero?"

Huatl laughed, a deep and rollicking laugh. "By the gods," he said, "I think you can sell! No wonder you were a lousy slave—you were in the wrong profession!" Still laughing, he

tossed the pouch of cacao beans back at Tlacoch. "Take this for
a wedding present," he said. "Also, show me how you'd select
goods for a special client by selecting a huipil and skirt for
Metzli. She'll need something to replace that ugly temple robe."
He pointed to a pile of clothing on a mat in the corner.
"While you're at it, select a fine tilmantli for yourself to tie on
your wedding day. Take a few more for your prospective clients.
They might buy more from a dandified war hero than they
would from a ragged and dirty pochteca."
Tlacoch tossed the cacao bean pouch back at Huatl. "Sell
these in Tlaxcala where people are hungry for chocolate," he
said, "and we can split the profits. The clothing is more than
enough as a wedding present."
"You think like a merchant," Huatl said, laughing again, and
tying the pouch to his belt.
"I'm trying," Tlacoch said. He pulled a deep blue huipil
from the pile of clothing and held it up for Huatl's approval. "I
think this would be lovely on a merchant's wife, don't you?"

* * *

The tying of the tilmantli took place soon afterward in the
temple of Quetzalcoatl, in a ceremony conducted by Metzli's
favorite priest. Metzli's slender body looked enticingly feminine
in Huatl's gift—a deep blue huipil and skirt with red and yellow
flowers embroidered on the neckline and hem. Over her
shoulders she wore a shawl woven by Chihuallama, who had
happily put her creative talents to work on the loom again.
Tlacoch tied the corner of that shawl to his white tilmantli,
trimmed with a green border and fastened at the shoulder by a
clasp of green stones set in gold. Chihuallama marveled at how
different he looked from the bedraggled young man who had
come to them the previous year, ready to die. Gardener
Callipopoca was in a jovial mood. "Since I'm representing the
family far away in Paynala and Oluta, I should give a long-
winded speech like those Tlacateotl was noted for."
His wife Chihuallama discouraged him, as he expected she
would. "These young people don't need any advice from their
elders," she said. She was carrying in her strong arms the
wriggling three-year-old boy from the orphanage who had
trusted his caregiver enough to let her wash his hair that morning
and tie a blue ribbon on his little topknot. She had told him then
that Meztli would be his mother from now on and Tlacoch his
father, but he was still too young to understand that.
Metzli had decided to make this day a naming day for her
son, who had never been formally named but had answered to
the nickname of Citli or "Rabbit." Tlacoch had suggested the
name of "Quauhchimal," or "Eagle Shield," which would

combine the names of his natural father, Quauhtlatoa, and Metzli's dead brother Chimalli. Both men had died as warriors, Tlacoch said, and their names would be honored through this child. He and Metzli both agreed, however, that no shield or arrows would be placed in his hands to dedicate him to the life of a warrior. Instead, they gave him a small copper mirror, so he could lead a "life of reflection" as Metzli put it, and "see what he will become."

"I'd like to honor your father, too," Metzli said. "Tlacateotl might like a grandchild named after him."

"There's plenty of time for that," Tlacoch said with a grin. "We'll name another son after him."

* * *

When Huatl returned from Tlaxcala in the month of Teotleco, he heard more good news to carry to Oluta and Paynala: Metzli and Tlacoch were expecting their first child. If it was a boy, they planned to name him "Opochteotl," combining the names of his grandfathers Tlacateotl and Opochtli.

Huatl was highly amused. "What kind of a name is 'Left-handed god?' It'll sound strange to people who don't know the grandparents. I like it, anyway. I can hardly wait to see the faces of those two men who once were rivals and now will see each other in the faces of their grandchild." He laughed heartily.

Tlacoch had good news and bad news for Huatl. The good news was that their clothing business was thriving as they had hoped, and he paid Huatl's share in gold dust quills. The profits had also enabled Tlacoch and Metzli to afford the nice home to which they welcomed Huatl on his return. It stood in the Tlatelolco area, close to the marketplace, near a canal so that Tlacoch could transport his wares by canoe. It had a hidden underground storage area for goods or jewelry, accessible through a trap door hidden under a cotton rug. It had two sleeping rooms, one for them and one for little Quauhchimal, who still answered to the name of Citli or "Rabbit" as he had in the temple orphanage.

The bad news was that a terrible illness had struck in Tenochtitlan. The new Uey Tlatoani, Cuitlahuac, had died of this plague after only eighty days on the throne. Chihuallama had warned Metzli not to come to the temple and to keep little Citli away from the orphanage. Her skills as a healing-woman had failed to prevent two children from dying in her arms, and new orphans were being added every day as whole families became infected with the disease and many died.

"I was afraid of that," Huatl said grimly. "I was going to warn you. That plague has hit Cempoala and Tlaxcala, too. The Spaniards call it smallpox."

374

Metzli put the dried corn to soak for the next morning's meal and laid Citli down to sleep in his sleeping room while Huatl and Tlacoch talked business after the evening meal. Then she took some unfinished embroidery from a petlacalli chest and joined the men at the hearth while her fingers pulled a bright thread through the cotton with a maguey thorn.

Huatl was not displeased when Metzli joined the men's conversation. He had liked Metzli immediately, thinking Tlacoch had done well for himself with this intelligent and pretty woman, even though her earlobes were tattered from years of doing pious penances. Metzli's entering their discussion did not seem improper to Tlacoch, either, because he had been raised in a motherless home and had never witnessed the kind of deference most wives showed in Paynala by eating separately from their husbands. Metzli had lost her mother at birth and had never been taught how to be a docile wife. So she unsuspectingly broke with tradition, yet no one thought it ill-mannered.

"Is there a cure for smallpox?" asked Metzli anxiously.

"No one knows," Huatl answered. "The Spaniards believe in a cure called 'bleeding': they cut an arm open and drain blood from it. That seems like a curious remedy for people who are losing blood already, and it doesn't seem to work for Tlaxcalans. The worst cases vomit blood until they have none left."

"How awful," Meztli said, concern flooding her face. "What about the ticitls? Can't they divine the cause?" She stabbed the thorn through the cloth and pulled the thread out full length with a little jerk to make it taut.

Huatl looked disgusted. "Forgive my irreverence," he said to Metzli. "I know you were once a priestess and you may have faith in the ticitls, but I don't. For all their chants and mutterings and arranging of stones, they haven't cured one person and may have made some sicker. I'm getting away from this city tomorrow, and I'd advise you to do the same."

Tlacoch had been listening intently. "You said the worst cases. Does that mean some people aren't affected so badly?"

"Some only have a fever and a rash; they seem to get better by themselves, as if they had nothing worse than a bad cold. Others break out with painful blisters all over their faces, bellies, and limbs. I saw one man die of smallpox in Tlaxcala. The membranes in his nose and throat had swelled until he couldn't breathe. He thrashed and screamed, delirious with pain, until death seemed like a great mercy. In caring for him, his wife caught the disease, and there was no one to care for her, so she just lay on her petlatl and starved."

"The poor woman," Metzli said sorrowfully. "Couldn't you find some way to help her?"

"She's better off dead," Huatl said. "That may sound cruel, but those who survive sometimes wish they hadn't. They may end up blind and horribly disfigured. When the scabs come off, they leave holes like little craters all over the skin."

"I wonder if the cause is uncleanliness," Tlacoch said. "When I had a skin disease, Chihuallama said she saw it often on slaves or soldiers who couldn't bathe very often."

"I remember that skin disease of yours," Huatl said. "Smallpox is much, much worse, and bathing may spread it; I'm not sure. The Tlaxcalans are very clean people, always taking cold baths. The Spaniards laughed at them for bathing so much. I almost struck one Spaniard in his pock-marked face when he said the 'Indians' (as he called them) were spreading the disease by bathing too much. Even if what he said was true, it really galled me to see such a lack of compassion for the poor devils, just because the Spaniards seem immune to it."

"Are the Spaniards immune?" Metzli asked, aghast. "Could the gods protect such cruel people?" She took Tlacoch's hand, remembering Pedro de Alvarado, the cruel yellow-haired man whose soldiers attacked the Mexica at the Toxcatl festival.

"It's unjust, I know," Huatl said, "especially since the Spaniards brought the disease here. Life is often unjust; we all know that. The Spaniards don't seem to catch the disease, or if they do, they get light cases of it. They call it the 'small pox' because it doesn't bother them much. Apparently it's a common disease in Spain."

Tlacoch grimaced. "If this is a small pox, I wonder what their large pox is like."

"I hope we never find out," Metzli said with a shudder. "I feel guilty not being at the temple, where so many people are coming for help. Chihuallama told me they're coming to pray to Patecatl, the god of healing, or Ixlilton, the god of health and cures from ailments. Some of them who think they might die are coming to confess to Tlazolteotl."

Tlacoch shot a look like flint at Metzli. "Stay away from the temple," he ordered. "Someone who comes there with a fever could give you the disease. You could bring it to Citli and me."

Metzli returned Tlacoch's glare and said sweetly, "So could you, my husband. You could bring it home to us from the market." She tied a knot in her embroidery thread and reached into the petlacalli for a different color.

"You're both right," Huatl said. "The only thing to do is stay away from other people. Don't worry about the sick people with their desperate prayers, Metzli. Prayers aren't really doing any good. Some silly Tlaxcalans became Christians just because they thought the new god would protect them as well as the Spaniards. It didn't help; they died just the same."

"You don't believe in any gods, do you, Huatl?" Metzli

376

asked in dismay. "I've never heard so much cynicism before."

"I hope my unorthodox views don't offend you, my gracious hostess," Huatl said. "Your gentle and faithful nature does you credit, and I hope it will never be toughened by circumstances. If my hardness seems irreverent to you, I hope you'll see it as a kind of turtle shell—the weather-beaten hide of a creature who has endured too many storms. I do believe that the gods run the One World; they send us rain and sunshine, though I've never really understood why they torture us with too much or too little of one or the other. I'm a simple man at heart, and I accept whatever the gods send me, flowers or earthquakes. I don't think any prayers or penances will change their minds."

Meztli touched her ears self-consciously. "Don't you pray to the god Yacatecuhtli to protect you in your travels? I thought all pochteca did that."

"We do," Huatl admitted. "Personally, I see no harm in it, and some of my fellow pochteca swear Yacatecuhtli helps them brave the hazards of the road. I've noticed, though, that the caravans usually take human guards along, so I wonder how much confidence they've really placed in their god's influence."

Tlacoch chuckled. "Sounds to me like a gambler hedging his bets," he said. "If the prayer doesn't work, maybe the guard will. You both make good arguments, but I hope you'll save them for another time. I'd like to hear more about Tlaxcala."

"Ah, yes," Huatl said, stretching out his full length on the floor beside the hearth and staring into the smoldering ashes. "I've been meaning to warn you about that, too. You probably thought the Spaniards were just going to rest in Tlaxcala, then move on to the coast and sail away. I don't think they will."

"What are they up to?" Tlacoch asked, resting an elbow on his knee and leaning forward intently.

"In the last few weeks they've led an army of Tlaxcalans into Tepeaca and forty other small towns in the region. Once the towns were subdued, the Tlaxcalans went wild looting and robbing the villagers, taking everything they could carry. I know because they wanted to trade some of it with me."

"Maybe that's because those villages wouldn't trade with Tlaxcalans when the Triple Alliance controlled them," Metzli said. "That doesn't excuse theft, but it might explain it."

Tlacoch touched Metzli's shoulder understandingly, realizing that Metzli remembered her Tlaxcalan lover fondly and tried to defend his people. "We have more sympathy for Tlaxcalans than Spaniards," he said to Huatl. "Why do you say they won't leave?"

"They've set up a town of their own called 'Segura de la Frontera' which means 'security of the frontier.' The name tells us their intentions. They're securing a base of operations between their coastal settlement and Tenochtitlan. In other words, they're

377

planning to come back."

"I'm sure the new Uey Tlatoani can handle them," Tlacoch said. "Cuauhtemoc is a more capable general than Moctezuma was."

"I hope so," said Huatl, "but there's more." He turned to Metzli. "You aren't going to like what you hear."

"I've heard a lot of terrible things in the temple," Metzli reminded him. "I'm not easily shocked."

"Very well, then. The Spaniards have taken many slaves this time, mostly women and children. They've never done that before. They heat a metal rod with a design on the end of it and press it on the faces of the slaves, burning it into their flesh. I know only a little Spanish, but I do know the word *guerra*, meaning 'war.' They brand the slaves with the symbol they call 'g' meaning *guerra*. The Spaniards prefer women with light skin colors; those are kept for the captains or their king in Spain. The rest of the women are turned over to the soldiers, who pass them around from one to another to use sexually until the women are exhausted and weeping. In my opinion, that immoral practice does more to spread smallpox and other diseases than all the bathing done in all the villages everywhere."

"How cruel!" Meztli exclaimed vehemently. "War turns people into madmen." She bit off a piece of thread with her clenched teeth and pushed it through a hole in her thorn needle.

"Maybe it's the other way around," Tlacoch said. "Madmen turn to war."

"Exactly," Huatl said. "I think General Malinche has gone mad. He's taking slaves to sell, trying to replace the gold he lost fleeing Tenochtitlan two or three months ago. It isn't just greed, though. There's vengeance behind this."

Both Tlacoch and Metzli looked sickened by this report. After a moment of silence, Tlacoch spoke. "Branding slaves! I've never heard of it. Slaves don't have an easy life here, but at least their masters don't poke hot sticks into their faces."

"Moctezuma said the Christians objected to our using slaves for sacrifices," Metzli said wryly. "I've never liked sacrifices either, but it seems to me the Christian ways are no better. In some ways, they're much worse."

"I agree with you totally," Huatl said. "Maybe when you've lived as long as I have, you'll be a cynic too."

* * *

Huatl slept overnight beside the dying ashes of the hearth fire and rose early the next morning when the conch shells blew across the quiet city to herald the morning star. He glanced out the doorway. The water in the canals lay smooth and gray in the early pre-dawn light; a mist lay over the lake. A few birds called from the lake shores.

Metzli emerged from the sleeping room. In her arms she carried Citli, rubbing his eyes with a tiny fist. She deposited Citli on the floor beside the hearth and started to twirl a firestick to make a new fire.

"Let me do that for you," Huatl offered, taking from her hands the firestick, its base board with the hole to steady it, and a handful of dried moss.

"Thank you," Meztli smiled. "Citli would like to watch you." Citli scowled in disagreement and began to whimper. Then he jumped up and ran to his mother, clinging to her leg. "He's a little afraid of strangers," she said apologetically. "Tlacoch has won him over, and you will too in time." She began making the morning's corncakes, ignoring Citli's whimpering and clinging except when she had to move. Then she lifted the child and put him down again as if he were just a bag of beans.

"Have you and Tlacoch thought any more about coming to Paynala with me?" Huatl asked as he twirled the stick and flicked some sparks into the moss. "I'm concerned about the smallpox plague and the Spanish invasion."

"We didn't discuss it, but I doubt Tlacoch would leave our home here," Metzli said, slapping corn meal between her palms.

"Not even to save your lives? Maybe I should talk to Tlacoch some more." He placed the lighted moss against some small dry sticks in the hearth and began to blow on the flames.

Tlacoch then entered the room. "About what?" he asked, covering his mouth as he yawned. Citli ran to him, and he stooped to give the boy a one-armed hug.

"About the dangers here, my man! Smallpox. War. Retaliation by the Spaniards. Revolt in Tlaxcala." Huatl blew on the wood in the hearth to encourage the flames.

"I worry about the dangers," Tlacoch said as he tousled Citli's hair, "but I'm just getting the business started; I don't want to lose momentum."

"If you stay here, you may lose more than that. I'm not easily alarmed, but from what I've heard in Tlaxcala and seen along the way, I think we should all leave. This Malinche fellow could start another war and disrupt trade routes again."

Tlacoch looked puzzled. "I thought he'd opened trade routes to Tlaxcala by breaking the grip of the Triple Alliance."

"That's what Xicotenga the Elder says. He's an old man—almost totally blind—but he still commands respect in Tlaxcala and he's fiercely loyal to Malinche."

"So?"

"So the old man is at odds with his own son. Xicotenga the Younger doesn't like Malinche or trust him. Junior approached me because of my ties in Tenochtitlan, wondering if Cuauhtemoc would be interested in an alliance against Malinche. He was hoping to assemble the unhappy people from some neighboring villages, a few Tlaxcalans of similar persuasion, and people like me if he could. I made excuses, of course. I don't take sides in any conflict. Bad for business."

Tlacoch gave Citli a gentle spat and shoved him toward his mother. "I thought all the Tlaxcalans were bitter foes of the Triple Alliance."

"They were, but young Xicotenga thinks Cuauhtemoc might be more cooperative than Moctezuma. Xicotenga's father accused him in public of disloyalty and betrayal, and if I'm to believe what several people told me, he pushed his son down a flight of stairs."

"I hope he wasn't hurt," Metzli said, holding Citli back from the fire with one arm as she worked. "I hope he finds enough allies. We have good reason to hate the Spaniards, too."

Tlacoch added, "I've given one arm to stop those murdering dogs. I may have to give another."

"Brave talk, brave talk!" Huatl chided. "Brave talk can get you killed. Tenochtitlan is seriously weakened by disease. We can't save it, but we can save ourselves."

Metzli flipped some water from her fingers onto the comal. When the water broke into little dancing beads, she knew the comal was hot enough to cook the corncakes. The first one gave a little hiss as she dropped it onto the comal, and fragrant steam soon rose from it. "Huatl is right, Tlacoch. You've done your share; you have a right to retire from battle." Then she turned to Huatl. "Even if we did go away," she said, "we wouldn't go to Paynala or Oluta. Coatzacoalcos would be better; maybe we'd find sanctuary at the temple of Quetzalcoatl."

"I wouldn't advise that," Huatl said. "Pochteca from that region told us the Spaniards have built a permanent settlement there, even planted some crops and built buildings in the area."

"Then they *are* here to stay!" Tlacoch said angrily. "We can't avoid an all-out war. Which side are you on, Huatl?"

"The side of survival," Huatl said. "That's why I'm leaving. I've seen many people persuaded to fight or die for a cause, only to be enslaved by some other master when the fight is over. What difference does it make whether one king or another has his foot on your neck? Loyalty is always temporary. I may not come back, but I will take your message to your parents."

Tlacoch could say nothing in reply without insulting his business partner, so they ate in silence. Metzli fed the first corncake to Huatl, the next to Tlacoch. Then she tore one in half, giving part of it to Citli, part to the wooden images in the small shrine in one corner of her new home. She fed herself last. Citli ran outside with his half, eating it as he watched the canoes making shining lines in the water as they glided through the canal. Some of the canoes carried the usual produce for the daily market in Tlatelolco, but even more were carrying corpses toward the burial hill in Chapultepec.

* * *

During the heat and rain of summer, smallpox plagues raged throughout Tenochtitlan and the region of Tlatelolco, which once had been an independent city with its own rulers and palaces, its own temple and marketplace. Gradually Tlatelolco had become a trading center serving the entire Triple Alliance, but the growing city of Tenochtitlan had absorbed it. The marketplace had expanded into a regional trading center, and the temple's functions had shrunk proportionally, becoming subsidiary to the Great Temples in Tenochtitlan. As plague gripped the land, fewer customers came to market; fewer goods were offered for sale; more people crowded the temple praying to the gods of healing.

Tlacoch called on some of his former customers, only to find one household after another distressed. Obsessed with losses of family members and servants to the disease, or weakened by their own infections, his customers had no interest in new clothing or ornaments. Instead they asked for basic food supplies, so he took a canoe to Xochimilco where food was still being grown on the chinampas, although many of the farmers were too sick to tend or harvest their crops, let alone take them to market. Tlacoch also approached the official Woman Snake, second in command under the emperor Cuauhtemoc, for food supplies from the royal warehouses. As Tlacoch distributed food and medicinal herbs, he began to carry news from one household to another, and he brought some of that news home to Metzli.

Through this informal news network, Tlacoch and Metzli learned that Cortes had gathered another army, that more ships had come with additional soldiers, horses, supplies, and cannon, conveyed from Vera Cruz by way of Cholula. Supplemented by many Tlaxcalan warriors, Cortes had invaded the city of Texcoco at the eastern edge of Lake Texcoco and taken residence in the palace there. The city had been too weakened by smallpox to resist, and looting by Tlaxcalan warriors was widespread. Prince Ixtlilxochitl or "Black Flower" had hoped to acquire the throne of Texcoco after the death of his brother Cacama the previous year. He had even taken the name of Don Fernando Cortes in an attempt to flatter the conqueror, but General Cortes had only given him some backwoods provinces to rule, and the embittered monarch had retired there only to die of smallpox shortly afterward.

In Texcoco, Cortes built a high gallows and hanged Xicotenga the Younger, son of the chief of Tlaxcala, as a deterrent to traitors. He sent half his army to Tlaxcala to bring

381

back parts of brigantines that had been constructed in Tlaxcala. These parts were quickly reassembled on the shores of the lake, making thirteen brigantines that could hold twenty-three oarsmen; or the ships could be propelled by sails in a wind. Each brigantine also held a cannon that could smash a stone or adobe wall with one steel ball. These ships had given Spaniards and Tlaxcalans control over the lake. Cuauhtemoc, the valiant 26-year-old emperor, was preparing a defense, but his forces were already fighting two powerful enemies: disease and hunger.

Metzli, too, was having a difficult time, not only with her pregnancy, but also with Citli. Her main preoccupation had been to keep Citli well, but he didn't seem happy. In the orphanage he had been surrounded with other children; in Tlatelolco he played alone by the canal, floating small pieces of wood, or with his mother, stacking blocks into miniature pyramids. As food became more difficult to obtain, he became irritable, crying much of the day, making Metzli irritable too. As she grew large with child in the month of Huei Tozoztli, she waddled awkwardly and could no longer lift Citli.

"The baby is due next month, in Toxcatl," Metzli reminded Tlacoch. "Will you ask Chihuallama to stay with me during my confinement?"

"Is there any danger of her bringing smallpox here?"

"The plague seems to be over now," Metzli replied. "The cold weather stopped it, as far as I can tell."

"Probably so," Tlacoch assented. "I haven't heard of any new cases since Panquetzaliztli. Cold weather brings its own miseries, but it may have brought a blessing this year."

"Now we have the plagues of hunger and Spaniards," Metzli remarked wryly. "I wonder if Chihuallama and Callipopoca have been getting enough to eat at the temple."

"I doubt it," said Tlacoch. "People everywhere are hungry. Wealthy people are trading their jewelry and feathers for corn, but the poor have nothing to trade. I'm accumulating quite a store of luxury goods, jade, and feathers I can't sell."

"We can't eat them, either. Wouldn't it be ironic," Metzli said, "if we became wealthy and then starved right along with the macehualtin?"

"At least," Tlacoch said wryly, "we'd have some jade to put in our mouths for the journey to the Land of the Dead."

* * *

When Tlacoch arrived at the temple of Quetzalcoatl in the Great Square, a crowd had assembled in the courtyard below the temples of Huitzilopochtli and Tlaloc. He found Chihuallama at the temple orphanage, and she told him what was happening. A hard battle had been fought the previous day. The cruel Spanish commander—the man called Malinche—had forced a war party into the Great Square and set up a cannon on the block that was used for gladiatorial battles and sacrifices. The Aztecs had retaliated, driven Malinche out, and captured fifty-three of his men and four of his horses in addition to several hundred Tlaxcalan warriors. The celebration this day was to sacrifice these captives to Huitzilopochtli. Callipopoca, her husband, had been cleaning the temples and whitewashing them in preparation for the victory celebration.

Climbing to the temple rooftop, Tlacoch could see several brigantines anchored in Lake Texcoco. About twenty or twenty-five men stood on the deck of each brigantine, their faces turned westward toward the great pyramids. Gleefully he touched the stub of his left arm with his right hand and shouted to the Spaniards in the brigantines, even though he knew they could not hear him. "You're getting what you deserve," he said. "Watch while we kill your brothers the way you've killed ours."

In the afternoon sunlight, the symbolic time when Huitzilopochtli was descending into his own daily death, the priests began the sacrifices. The Spaniards on the brigantines looked on helplessly, because Cuauhtemoc had placed sharp stakes in the canals and along the causeways, and the boats could not get close enough to land.

First the fifty-three Spanish captives were led up the stairs one at a time, each firmly grasped by two Aztec warriors. Most of the Spaniards were screaming and wailing, but that only made it easier for their comrades to hear their keening carried by the lake breezes. The sacrifices were not given yautli powder or octli to dull the pain, so their cries pleased the crowd below as much as they did Huitzilopochtli. The crowd roared approval as each Spaniard and horse met his death.

Stripped naked, the captives looked like white worms, though some had brown arms and faces, tanned like leather. Each was spread out on the sacrificial stone at the top of the pyramid, chest upward, with a priest or a warrior holding each limb to keep him from struggling. Another priest deftly inserted a flint knife and pulled out the still-beating heart. The priest raised the heart to the four directions, then threw it into the stone chalice. Meanwhile, another priest garroted the victim and sliced off his head. The priests then mounted each head on the skull rack and awarded the body to the warrior or warriors who had captured the victim. The warriors carried their victim's body down the steps, or tumbled it ahead of them, knowing they were entitled to butcher it and feed it to their families.

When the fifty-three Spaniards had been sacrificed, the four horses were decapitated. The priests placed the horses' heads below the Spaniards' on the skull rack, and all agreed that the horses had met their death much more nobly than the Spaniards.

Many Tlaxcalans were also sacrificed that day, but their heads were not placed on the skull rack, and their bodies were fed to the jaguars and other beasts in the royal menagerie. The crowd began to dissipate as the Tlaxcalans were sacrificed, leaving the Great Square with bored expressions. The general mood, however, was jubilant. Tales of the heroic exploits of Aztec warriors passed from person to person, and satisfaction reigned.

Tlacoch walked back from the ceremony with Chihuallama and Callipopoca, discussing the events of the day and agreeing that justice had been done. None of the trio had especially enjoyed the bloodletting, but all felt anger toward the Spaniards. Tlacoch asked the macehual couple to come to Tlatelolco with him. Chihuallama agreed to come as midwife to Metzli; Callipopoca agreed to help with rowing canoes and making more wooden stakes to keep the brigantines out of the canals. There was little gardening for Callipopoca to do at the temple since the Spanish bombardment had largely destroyed the gardens, and he was eager to help with the war effort. The macehualtin would both feel safer, they said, away from the grounds of the Great Square where the Spaniards were concentrating their efforts.

After that time, however, the Spaniards redoubled their efforts. Cortes separated his forces into three divisions to attack from three sides, under Alvarado from the west, Sandoval from the east, and Olid from the south. His orders were explicit: smash every house into rubble, use the debris to fill up gaps in the causeways so the cavalry could ride over unimpeded, burn everything that would catch fire, take any food that the Spanish forces could use, and leave the city of Tenochtitlan as a flat, barren terrain that could hide no enemies and provide no sustenance. The final assault had begun.

* * *

By the time Metzli's baby arrived, Tlatelolco had become a refuge for many families fleeing the relentless destruction of Spanish cannons, trampling horses, and deliberate fires that filled the air daily with black smoke. Refugee priests brought the Huitzilopochtli idol with them, setting it up in the House of Young Men near the Tlatelolco temple. Every small house in Tlatelolco sheltered at least five people, some as many as ten.

The new baby girl was warmly welcomed by her parents and by Chihuallama, who insisted on the rites of the naming ceremony even as the cannons pounded and the war drums thundered not far away. Metzli and Tlacoch agreed; instinctively they knew that a ceremony can preserve a sense of dignity even under the most primitive conditions. They named their daughter Chicome Xochitl, or "Seven Flower," because seven was her birthdate and her lucky number. Chihuallama believed that every child brought good luck to a household, but especially those born on day seven. Four-year-old Citli regarded his new sister as a curiosity, but he became so jealous while Metzli was nursing the baby that Chihuallama had to hold him and sing to him. She had lost so much weight that her body no longer provided pillowy comfort, but her voice could still soothe a troubled child.

Food had become extremely scarce. The Tlatelolcans turned to catching lizards, rats, and swallows, extracting worms from the soil and insects from the marsh grasses. They were chewing corncobs to the marrow, eating salt grass from the lake, devouring water lilies and bitter weeds. They stripped the rooftop gardens to make stews of their vines, and when all other resources were exhausted, they chewed on deerhides or leather sandals for whatever nourishment they might squeeze out.

Cuauhtemoc had exhausted the supplies in the royal warehouses and did not even have enough food for his warriors. Water became an even greater problem after the Spaniards destroyed the aqueduct leading from Chapultepec. The besieged inhabitants began drinking the brackish water from the lake, but even that water turned red from the blood of warriors whose bodies clogged the lakes and canals after months of fighting.

* * *

Tlacoch was summoned to a meeting between the remaining lords of the Triple Alliance and the teules, who had set up headquarters in Nonohualco, west of the city. The lords were old customers who hoped Tlacoch could provide gifts to the Spaniards from the remaining valuables in his house. He took Callipopoca with him to row the canoe and carry bundles. At this meeting, he and Callipopoca saw their old friend Malinalli once more.

Cortes came into the meeting room with his interpreter Marina and his captains Sandoval and Alvarado, known to the natives as the dreaded Tonatiuh. Cortes seated himself on a carved wooden chair, though his attendants remained standing. Through Marina he addressed the lords. "I want to know what your emperor Cuauhtemoc is thinking of," he said. He pronounced the Uey Tlatoani's name as "Guatemoc," but Marina corrected it in her translation. "Can't he see that the kings of Tlaxcala, Huexotzinco, Cholula, Chalco, Alcolhuacan, Xochimilco, and Cuauhnahuac have joined forces with me?" He pronounced the name of Cuauhnahuac as "Cuernavaca," which meant "cow's horn" in Spanish, but Marina corrected it in her translation.

Tlacoch stepped forward with a small bag of jadestones and handed it to Cortes. "My lords bring you these precious stones," he said, "as gifts of goodwill." He looked directly at Marina as he spoke, again seeing an amazing resemblance to the girl he had known in Paynala. Her eyes flickered in faint recognition, but she could not remember exactly where she had seen this man before. She translated dutifully as Cortes took the gift and tossed it to Sandoval. Tlacoch was glad Cortes hadn't given it to Alvarado, because he still remembered the horrible massacre Alvarado had perpetrated at the feast of Toxcatl a year and a half earlier. That had started the war which was causing so much suffering.

Tlacoch returned to stand beside Callipopoca, who stood inconspicuously in the back of the room. "Could she be the girl we knew as Malinalli in Paynala?" he whispered to Callipopoca. Callipopoca was listening intently. The interpreter's face bore some resemblance to that of the girl he had last seen five or six years before. Yet her voice unmistakably stirred memories of a distant place and a happier life. He nodded solemnly to Tlacoch.

Cortes continued, "Is your chief a stupid, willful boy? Does he have no pity on your women and children? Must even the old men perish?"

One of the lords spoke up. "I've seen enough suffering," he said to the other lords present. "Why should the people of Tlatelolco pay for the foolishness of Tenochtitlan and Moctezuma? We should make peace with the Spaniards. They've clearly defeated us. We should get on with our lives."

Another disagreed. "The people of Tenochtitlan are our brothers, our neighbors. We can't abandon them now. I think the Spaniards have punished them enough." He turned to Marina and addressed Cortes through her. "Take the royal treasury, if that's what the general wants, but tell him to go away and stop slaughtering innocent people."

Cortes laughed when he heard that translated. "Go away? My men have fought bravely for the right to live in this land. We would have been your brothers, taught you to raise horses and sheep and pigs. We could have taught you to build ships and carts with wheels to carry burdens. Instead, you chose to fight us. If you still want war, we can teach you how Europeans make war! Tell your king Guatemoc the other kings have all abandoned him. I'm sending ships to Coyoacan to attack him."

With that, Cortes left the room, followed by Alvarado. Sandoval lingered, watching Marina protectively as she stopped to speak to the one-armed merchant. The Tlatelolcan lords had also left the room, and Sandoval would not leave Marina alone with strangers. "Are you by chance from the coastal region?" she asked. "Your accent sounds familiar."

"Are you by chance from Paynala?" Tlacoch asked.

Marina looked surprised. Sandoval instinctively stepped forward with his hand on his sword, but Marina held her hand up to stop him. "Yes, I'm from Paynala," she said slowly, remembering her mother's warning never to return there. "Are you from that place?"

Callipopoca stepped forward, dropped to his knees, touched the stone floor and then his tongue. "Don't you remember us, Malinalli? My master is Tlacoch. I'm Callipopoca. We thought you were dead."

"Old friend!" cried Marina, extending both hands to Callipopoca and helping him rise. "Don't kneel to me. I'm only a slave now, lower in rank than you."

Marina did not have equally warm feelings for Tlacoch, because her last memories of him were his drunken attempts to fondle her in the granary. Trying to protect him at that time, she'd gotten in trouble with her stepfather Anecoatl, the man she suspected of instigating the plot to sell her into slavery. She continued to address Callipopoca. "Where is Chihuallama now?"

"I'm so happy to see you alive, my lady," said Callipopoca joyfully. "Chihuallama is here with me in Tlatelolco. She's taking care of Metzli's baby."

"Metzli's baby? Is Metzli here too?" Marina sounded astonished.

"She's my wife," said Tlacoch. "She came here with a Tlaxcalan 'fair youth' sacrifice. Then she became a priestess and nursed me to health."

"So you married Metzli, and now you have a child," Marina said. "I'll send some gifts for the baby."

"Actually, we have two children. Metzli was raising little Citli alone when I met her here. He's four years old now. Our daughter is only a month old."

Alvarado reappeared at the door. "Marina, Captain General Cortes is asking for you."

"I must go," Marina said. "Can you bring Metzli and Chihuallama here tomorrow? We'll be leaving for Coyoacan soon."

"I'll try," said Tlacoch. "Our wives will want to see you again, I'm sure, but it wouldn't be safe to bring the children."

"I'll stay with the little ones," Callipopoca said as they left. While walking to the canoe, however, he said to Tlacoch, "I'm not as sure as you are that the women will want to see Malinalli. They may think of her as an enemy now."

* * *

Cuauhtemoc decided to try one more desperate ploy: magic. His troops had learned to dodge the cannon balls, muskets, and harquebuses by moving in zigzag lines or falling flat on the ground below the gunfire. His archers had learned not to cluster together where a single cannon ball could wound them all. Even the women and children had joined his army by throwing stones and excrement from the rooftops. The women had also tucked up their skirts and waded into the canals to place sharp stakes in the path of the brigantines or to rescue wounded warriors. They pounded small holes in the walls around the streets and canals so that only a man, and not a horse, could slip through. Never again would he permit his warriors to use the expression "they ran away like women."

He was gratified that his lords would not desert him and that Tlatelolco was still a loyal stronghold with a functioning, if seriously depleted, marketplace. Yet everyone in the city was weakened from disease or starvation, and the causeways had been filled with rubble, most of the houses to the south demolished. The temples had been hammered so often with cannonballs from the brigantines that they looked pock-marked.

Cuauhtemoc had stored in his palace the finery of the Quetzal-Owl costume once worn by his father, Ahuitzotl. He chose a brave captain to dress in this regalia and gave him an arrow with a long shaft and obsidian tip that had belonged to the great tlatoani. "The power of Huitzilopochtli resides in this magic regalia," said Cuauhtemoc. "Loose the sacred arrow at our enemies, for it is the Serpent of Fire, the Arrow that Pierces the Fire. Shoot it straight and well; it must not fall to earth. Wound the enemy with it, and divine power will drive them away."

Quetzal-Owl climbed up on a rooftop, his magic feathers reaching toward the sky, making him larger than life. When he came down, three enemies were captured while trying to snare the brave quachic. The fighting stopped for a full day, both sides watching and waiting, but then it resumed. Magic had failed.

The next day four Spanish cavalrymen rode into Tlatelolco, circling the marketplace and slaughtering everyone in their path. Aztec troops resisted for several hours, fighting bravely among the flower stalls and the vendors of snails and lime. Then the Spaniards fought their way hand-to-hand up the steps of the temple and set fire to the wooden structure on the top.

Then the omen came. Night had fallen, bringing a heavy dew almost like rain. Suddenly a great bonfire appeared in the sky, wheeling in circles like a whirlwind, giving off sparks like red-hot coals. It made loud noises, rumbling and hissing like something thrown into a fire. It moved through the sky to a point above Lake Texcoco, then disappeared.

Cuauhtemoc believed the gods were telling him the One World was coming to an end. Sadly, he told his followers to leave or follow him as they chose, but many followed his royal acali in their own canoes, ready to accept whatever fate their leader faced. Cuauhtemoc took three nobles and his wife with him in the royal acali, heading into the darkness and mist until he was stopped by a Spanish guard named Garcia Holguin. "I am Cuauhtemoc," he said in a voice filled with sorrow. "Take me to your Captain General, but do not harm these loved ones of mine."

* * *

When Holguin and Sandoval presented Cuauhtemoc to Cortes they were bickering over who deserved credit for the capture. Cortes dismissed them with a promise to settle the matter later. As Cortes welcomed him with great respect, Cuauhtemoc pointed to the dagger in Cortes' belt. "Senor Malinche," he said with deep emotion, "I have done my duty in defending my city. I can do no more. Take that dagger and kill me with it, for I come to you as a prisoner and would like a warrior's death."

"I admire your spirit in defending your city so bravely," Cortes replied. "I only wish you had surrendered earlier so more lives could have been saved, lives of your men and mine as well." Then Cortes ordered food for Cuauhtemoc and those who had followed him in their boats. He ordered comfortable quarters prepared for Cuauhtemoc. "Tomorrow we leave for Coyoacan," he said, "where I plan to establish my headquarters. You can help me rebuild the city we have both had a part in destroying."

As the two exhausted leaders fell asleep that night, the rain began to fall more heavily. It fell on the charred ruins of the temples and the marketplace, on the rubble of adobes and stones from shattered walls, on the thousands of broken spears and broken bodies that littered the once magnificent city. It fell equally on those who marked their calendars as August 13, in the Year of Our Lord 1521, and those who marked theirs as the day of 1 Serpent, in the ninth month (Tlaxochimaco, or "Birth of Flowers") in the year 3 House. For the latter, however, that wet and weeping night marked the cataclysmic end of an empire and the end of the One World as they had known it.

Chapter 27

Opochtli Takes Revenge

Attaching himself to another pochteca caravan, Huatl made his way along the trade route from Tenochtitlan to Oluta without being excessively searched or robbed. The Spaniards had blocked most of the roads, searching every refugee that left the area, confiscating any gold or jewels they found, and enslaving light-skinned women as prisoners of war. He had seen some women wearing rags, their faces plastered with disfiguring mud, but the Spaniards still grabbed them and branded their grimy faces with the letter "G."

As a precaution, Huatl carried nothing more valuable than cacao beans. If he should be stopped by a Spaniard or Tlaxcalan, precious stones and metals would only tempt them to search him further. He had sewn a number of cacao beans into the hem of his ragged robe, and he carried two pouches of beans, one to pay for lodging along the way, and a slimmer one to deceive any robbers into thinking its meager contents were his only money supply.

The journey confirmed what he already knew: that trade has its own universal language. The caravan leaders, by aggressively bargaining with any Spanish soldier who seemed inclined to rob them, presented themselves as potential sources of supply for scarce goods. With improvised gestures and a few Spanish words learned from previous bargaining, they indicated they were headed for the coast and would return soon with more goods for barter. Even a greedy Spaniard would see no advantage in destroying a potential market for his loot. As for the Mexica, they remained in awe of the emperor's past protection of pochteca. Because most villages had not heard of the impending collapse of the empire, they accorded pochteca their traditional respect.

As Huatl had promised, he stopped in Oluta to see Opochtli, taking leave of the caravan for a few days. He found Opochtli pursuing his latest passion—raising dogs for breeding or sale. For this purpose, he had constructed a gated pen in the back yard of his home, a light fence made of reeds laced together with hemp ropes. He was feeding his animals in the pen when Huatl arrived. Opochtli's weight had increased considerably—too much flesh to haul over the mountains—though his limbs remained strong. His girth, and the clean, undecorated maxtli encircling it, indicated to Huatl that Opochtli had retired from traveling long distances.

Huatl shouted in order to be heard over the yapping of the animals. "Fine looking dogs! Maybe I can trade some for you."

"Huatl! You old dog yourself! Come see my best ones." Opochtli opened the gate and invited Huatl into the pen. He affectionately picked up several dogs and stroked them behind the ears, showing Huatl their plump bodies and desirable features. "These are gentle dogs," he said admiringly. "They make good pets for children while they're being fattened."

"You're giving me a great idea," said Huatl. "I'll make you a business proposition later, but first I have some news." The two men went inside Opochtli's house where the yapping of feeding dogs would not disturb their conversation. Opochtli ordered a servant to prepare a meal for his guest and bring chocolate; then he settled on a petlatl beside Huatl to hear the news.

"Personal news first," Huatl said. "Your daughter Metzli has tied the tilmantli with Tlacoch. Remember him—that useless slave you came looking for when I first met you?"

"Chihuallama warned me that might happen," Opochtli chuckled. "Metzli was always a sucker for useless men."

"I know it's traditional to bewail the stupidity of young people," Huatl said, "but sometimes two useless things become useful when put together, like fire sticks and dry moss."

"True enough," Opochtli nodded agreeably. "Maybe there's hope. Are they planning to settle in Tenochtitlan?"

"Very near, in the market district of Tlatelolco. I've tried to get them to leave—the place is a shambles now—but Metzli was pregnant when I left and didn't want to travel. They plan to name the baby after you and Tlacoch's father if it's a boy. What do you think of the name 'Opochteotl'?"

Opochtli grimaced, but his expression revealed more pleasure than his words conveyed. "Left-handed god? Silly name! My old rival Tlacateotl probably wouldn't like having his name linked to a merchant's, but he'll be thrilled about having a grandson."

"It might be a girl," Huatl cautioned. "It's also possible the baby might not survive. Things are going badly in the Valley of Mexico right now. The smallpox epidemic seems to be over, thank the gods, but food and fresh water are hard to get."

"I've heard from other pochteca about the war; also about Moctezuma's death and Cuitlahuac's. So the Tlaxcalan warmongers are finally winning this time, are they?"

"They've teamed up with the Spaniards and had sweet revenge looting and burning the villages around Otumba; now they're doing the same with Tenochtitlan. The Spaniards built some new kind of boats with big cloth banners called 'sails' that catch the wind to push them forward. Or if there isn't any wind, they row the boats with long paddles. The Spaniards float these things around the lake, loaded with men and weapons. Each one has what they call a cannon. It shoots big balls made of metal—like copper, only much harder. Harder than any stone. Those balls can bust a stone wall to pieces. I saw lots of houses destroyed that way in southern Tenochtitlan. When I was there last, the army was moving toward Tlatelolco."

"Amazing. I'd like to get some of that hard metal to trade," Opochtli said. "Clearly those weapons are better than ours, but that puny band of Spaniards would've been captured and sacrificed long ago if it hadn't been for the Tlaxcalans."

"True enough; they provided thousands of warriors for the Spaniards, but Prince Ixtlxochitl, 'Black Flower,' helped them too. He hates Moctezuma for installing his brother Cacama on the throne of Texcoco. Moctezuma had other enemies, too; I realize now how many Mexica hated the whole Triple Alliance."

"Even here, we've felt the effects of the war," Opochtli said. "Cuauhtemoc has sent to every province to recruit warriors. Most of our young men have gone. The only males left are young boys and older men like me. Tlacateotl and Anecoatl are the only eagle knights left in Paynala, and Tlacateotl's not well—suffering from gout and losing his sight."

Helping himself to an avocado brought by the servant, Huatl peeled and sampled it before continuing. "Cuauhtemoc's getting desperate, all right. He's determined to fight to the death, but it's a losing battle. His warriors shoot hundreds of arrows and spears, but the Spaniards wear metal helmets and kneel behind the wooden sides of their boats. The Aztecs' canoes don't protect them from Spanish arrows or spears, and their cotton armor doesn't stop a bullet or a metal sword."

"Sounds pretty bad. Do you think Metzli and Tlacoch might change their minds and come here, if things get worse?"

"Anything's possible. More likely they'll head for the coast, *if* they survive, and *if* they leave. Metzli talked a bit about Coatzacoalcos, but I told her the Spaniards have been establishing farms in the region. It won't be the same as she remembers it from her temple days."

The servant returned with two cups of chocolate. Opochtli handed one to Huatl and took one himself. "So the Spaniards are definitely establishing settlements in this area?"

"Definitely," Huatl said wryly. "We may as well get used to new masters, because they seem determined to rule us. They'll need traders, though, and that reminds me of the business deal I spoke of. When the Spaniards take power, they'll want more horses for traveling and carrying burdens. We could breed horses here, just like dogs or turkeys. Horses eat grass like deer, or in winter they eat dried grass or grains. We'd have to bring the first ones from Spain, just as the conquistadors did, but think of the possibility for profit!"

"By the gods, Huatl, you can turn anything to profit—even a war!"

"Why not?" Huatl reasoned. "Pochteca always provide other people with things they need. It's war that creates needs, not the pochteca. They just fill the needs, in peace or in war."

"Maybe if you'd had a son, you'd be choosier about clients," Opochtli said. "Tlaxcalans killed my son Chimalli, you know. I wouldn't trade with Tlaxcalans for all the profit in the world."

"I've been accused of cynicism, my friend, and what I'm about to say may sound cynical to you. Your bitterness won't hurt the Tlaxcalans; your loyalty hasn't helped Moctezuma. Loyalty is always temporary. The Spaniards will probably dump the Tlaxcalans after they've served their purpose. The way to survive is to make yourself useful to the victors."

Opochtli bristled. "You certainly do sound cynical. If you had a son who died for his people, you'd honor him by making his enemies your own."

"And get into a silly feud, prolonging the killing for generations? What nonsense, my friend!" Huatl sipped his chocolate and continued gently. "I know your son was precious to you, but he's gone now. Honor his memory as long as you wish, but not at the expense of the living."

"What do you mean by that?"

Huatl looked embarrassed. "I've spoken out of turn. I have no right to give you advice. As you said, I've had no children of my own."

The servant returned with fresh corncakes and a stew of dog meat and vegetables. As both men began to eat, Opochtli continued to press Huatl. "I'd still like to know what you mean by not honoring the dead at the expense of the living."

"Very well, if you insist. You can't bring Chimalli back, but you have a living daughter and one or two grandchildren. Metzli wants her father's approval just as much as Chimalli did. When she talks about you, about coming here to live in safety, her voice sounds sad and painful."

"I've offered to make a place for her here," Opochtli said defensively. "She refused to come."

"Tlacoch told me she didn't want to come because you couldn't accept her child."

"You mean that Tlaxcalan's bastard?"

"There, you see? You're judging him and Metzli unfairly. She couldn't have tied the tilmantli with the Tlaxcalan. He was destined for sacrifice. His role was to give his seed to beautiful maidens to perpetuate the race with handsome people. Why can't you see Metzli's child as her contribution to the world, just as fighting a war was Chimalli's contribution?"

Opochtli gave Huatl a withering look. "You see nothing wrong when Metzli beds down with her brother's enemy?"

"I do know something about enemies; I've had a lot of them," Huatl replied calmly. "Some people can be enemies one year and friends the next. Since I'm your friend at the moment, let me speak frankly. Do you know who your enemies are? Why do you blame the Tlaxcalans for the flowery wars? Moctezuma was the first aggressor, looking for tribute, looking for captives to sacrifice. The Tlaxcalans have learned war from the Aztecs; now they take revenge by doing what the Aztecs did to them."

"What about the gods?" Opochtli asked patronizingly. "You don't sound like a religious man, Huatl. You may not believe in anything, but other people believe Huitzilopochtli needs human blood to bring us the sun. That's what Chimalli died for—to keep the universe running as it should."

"Did he? Or did he die to maintain Moctezuma's sources of tribute? Isn't tribute just a form of robbery? We pochteca don't pretend to be idealists, but at least we pay for the goods we get; we earn our profits. A conqueror just takes what he wants; he does nothing to earn it."

"You mean I should blame Moctezuma for Chimalli's death?"

"You don't have to blame anyone," Huatl shrugged. "All of us die sometime. I want to live a long life; Chimalli may have wanted to live a short one. It was his choice."

"Not really. He was ordered into battle. He wasn't a coward, but he wanted to live. No warrior wants to go into a hopeless situation."

"Who ordered him? Didn't his quachic know the battle with the Tlaxcalans was a lost cause? Maybe Chimalli's real enemies were those 'friends' who held his life so cheaply. Maybe they were people who sent him to fight so they could profit."

Opochtli remained silent for several moments, chewing on his stew meat, then spoke with a crack in his voice. "By the stars, Huatl, you're feeding my doubts just as surely as I'm feeding your belly. I've wondered for years why Anecoatl sent Chimalli into battle where he was almost certain to die. Anecoatl admired Chimalli, so I don't understand why he'd want Chimalli to die."

"Who's Anecoatl? Is he the villain?" Huatl spoke with his mouth full. "Pardon me, but this is the first hearty meal I've had in many days."

"You can have a bath here too," Opochtli said. "Consider yourself at home here. I've got some new robes in storage; I'll give you one."

"I can pay for it," Huatl said, pulling some cacao beans from his pouch. "I'd welcome a bath and a change of clothing."

394

"No need to pay me," Opochtli said, brushing aside Huatl's extended hand and spilling the cacao beans into his lap. "I'd rather ask you for a small favor. I'm thinking of a plan you could help me with. Will you bring me some special items from the Maya lands without letting anyone know who asked you to buy them? I'll pay your costs, of course; the favor lies in keeping quiet about it."

"I suppose I could do that," Huatl said. "If you have to trust anyone, you're smart to trust a cynic."

"You're cynical, all right, but you're wise to the ways of the world," Opochtli said. "For some reason I do trust you. I may have trusted the wrong people in the past."

"Maybe you mistrusted the wrong people too," said Huatl. "You can trust Metzli and Tlacoch more than you think. I've made Tlacoch my business partner in Tlatelolco. He's changed a great deal since you knew him as a spendthrift youth."

"Well, well," said Opochtli, stroking his chin. "What's this? A cynic gone soft? What made you change your mind about Tlacoch the lazy slave?"

Huatl smiled. "He's still stupid in some ways, dumb enough to fight the Tlaxcalans at Otumba. Cost him his left arm, up to here." He drew the edge of his flattened hand across his left upper arm.

"He lost an arm in battle? Some people might call that courage," Opochtli said. "His father would die more peacefully if he knew that. I'll tell Tlacateotl next time I see him."

"Please do. I won't have time to call on the old man and tell him about his son's stupid courage. You might also tell him Tlacoch's been smart in at least one respect."

"What's that?"

"He married Metzli. Knows a good woman when he sees one."

"I suppose you mean to complement me on my daughter," Opochtli said, "but are you implying that I *don't* see her worth? You think I've been too hard on her, don't you?"

"Well, since you ask . . . yes, you've been hard. I think she's wonderful; I'd have married her myself if Tlacoch hadn't beaten me to it. Tlacoch gets along pretty well with little Citli, and you could, too, if you don't let your bitterness blind you. I know your heart has a soft spot. Remember when you paid Tlacoch's debt to me and didn't tell him?"

"That was a favor to his father. Family honor. Community honor. Call it whatever you like."

"Very well. I'll call it a good investment in a son-in-law. You might like to know he's offered to pay it back also."

"You refused it, of course?"

"I refused the jadestones because he'd given them to the temple and I thought that was a worthy cause. I told him his theft had been repaid by a benefactor (I didn't tell him his benefactor was you). I did accept his payment of cacao beans to buy his own freedom from me, but only after he accepted a wedding gift of greater value."

Opochtli struck his forehead with the heel of his hand. "Huatl, you confound me! You always talk like a hard-headed businessman, but then you act like a friend."

Huatl smiled and burped. "Good meal," he said. "Sometimes friendship is good for business."

* * *

The next morning, when Huatl had bathed and gone on his way in a new mantle, Opochtli loaded several quachtli of fabrics and mantles on the backs of some aging tamemes, too old to be drafted as warriors, who carried them to Paynala. He also took a pair of plump dogs in a cage and three leather bags of octli as gifts for Anecoatl and Cimatl. By midmorning he reached the tecalli near Paynala where Anecoatl still lived with Cimatl and their son Xiuhtetl, "Turquoise Stone."

Cimatl was preparing the midmorning meal when Opochtli approached the tecalli. "How nice to see you again, Opochtli," she said as she came out to greet him. "I expect Anecoatl back from his office very soon. I'm sure he'll want you to join him at breakfast. I'll make some extra corncakes." She had aged since he saw her last, Opochtli thought. Dark circles shadowed her eyes, and threads of gray streaked the dark hair that hung loosely around her face. She moved slowly, uncertainly.

"Thank you, Cimatl," Opochtli said, setting the cage of yapping dogs on the patio. "Here's a present for you. I've taken up dog breeding since I saw you last. These should make good eating, or you can breed them yourself if you want to. These two are male and female."

Though she had no desire to breed messy dogs, Cimatl thanked Opochtli and invited his tamemes to sit in the shade of the huehuetl tree. She brought a jug of water for them to drink while she talked with Opochtli and finished preparing the meal.

"I'm hoping Anecoatl will store these fabrics for me the way Itzamitl used to do," Opochtli began. "First, though, I want to apologize for not coming to see you more often. I haven't felt much like visiting since Chimalli died. Perhaps you've missed Malinalli in the same way."

"Yes, I've never stopped missing her," Cimatl said sorrowfully, patting a corncake efficiently between her palms. "Have you heard for certain that Chimalli's dead?"

"I've learned there were no survivors in the battle against Tlaxcala. Today I have happier news, however. I've learned that Metzli got married and expects a baby any day now."

"How wonderful!" Cimatl exclaimed. "You're a grandfather!"

"I've been a grandfather for several years," Opochtli said candidly. "Metzli has a boy about four years old; I saw him on my last trip to Tenochtitlan. I'm hoping Metzli and her husband will bring the children here to stay."

"Oh, I hope they will," Cimatl said sympathetically. "Is she still in Tenochtitlan? I've heard there's a war going on there. Anecoatl's been worried about it. He can tell you more when he gets here."

"I'll be glad to hear what he has to say," Opochtli said. "Can you guess who Metzli married?"

"Someone she met in Tenochtitlan, I suppose."

"Yes, but he was an old acquaintance. Tlacoch, son of Tlacateotl, remember him?"

"My goodness!" Cimatl exclaimed. The sunshine of a faint smile lightened the shadows around her eyes. "This *is* news! I would never have imagined those two getting together. In fact, I thought neither of them would ever get married."

"I'm a little surprised myself," Opochtli admitted. "I haven't broken the news to Tlacateotl yet, but I think he'll approve. I'll call on him after I leave you today. I'm sure both of them have changed a lot since they were youngsters."

Cimatl withdrew quietly when Anecoatl arrived, swaggering in his elegant tilmantli, wearing a large lip plug. The gold-and-jadestone labret weighed down his lower lip so much that Opochtli found himself staring at Anecoatl's lower teeth as they talked.

Anecoatl greeted Opochtli with the brusqueness of a busy administrator reluctantly yielding time to a job-seeker. His manner softened, however, when Opochtli presented him with three bags of octli. He commented that the leather showed fine workmanship and he would enjoy drinking the octli in the privacy of his home. As the prospect of such indulgence lightened his mood, he invited Opochtli to share his midmorning meal.

Although Opochtli had not seen Anecoatl for seven years, he remembered instantly why he disliked the arrogant tecuhtli. With a pang he realized that Anecoatl had never seriously considered Chimalli as Malinalli's husband, and new suspicions arose about the deaths of both young people shortly after he had approached Anecoatl in hopes of arranging their marriage. Seven years he had lived with this gnawing doubt. It was time to set the matter to rest, at least in his own mind, but he would have to go about it cautiously. Anecoatl was known to be easily offended.

Anecoatl listened politely to the news about Metzli and Tlacoch and countered with news of his own. "My son is away from home too," he said. "Only nine years old, already distinguishing himself in swordsmanship at the telpochcalli. His

397

teachers say he'll make a fine warrior."

"Congratulations to you," Opochtli said sincerely. "Tell me, though, isn't warfare changing a great deal, now that the Spaniards are here?"

Anecoatl sneered. "I've heard the Spaniards are cowards. They didn't dare attack Texcoco until it was weakened by a plague. Didn't dare attack Tenochtitlan in a straightforward manner. Wriggled their way into the royal court by flattering Moctezuma. Cuauhtemoc will make short work of them."

"I'm surprised he hasn't called you back into active duty," Opochtli said, careful not to let his voice betray the sarcasm he felt. "I hear he's summoned warriors away from their fields all over the territory."

"I've sent all the men I can spare from Paynala," Anecoatl said with an air of sacrifice. "Of course, I can't be spared. Someone has to keep things running in the provinces. I've got my problems, though. Since the men have been called away from the fields, many women are working in the cornfields instead of doing their weaving. We might not meet our quotas for tribute this year if the women don't get busy soon."

"Isn't the corn more important?" Opochtli asked in surprise. "I've heard food is scarce in the Valley of Mexico. Surely the calpixqui will ask for contributions in food instead of fabrics."

"The macehual women can put forth a little extra effort in times like these," Anecoatl said. "Their husbands and sons are going into battle; it's not asking too much for them to help on the farms without neglecting their other duties."

"Let's hope the war ends soon," Opochtli said evasively. He realized Anecoatl had not heard the most recent news about Tenochtitlan, but there would be no point in upsetting the tecuhtli with unwelcome information, so he changed the subject. "I've come to ask if you have space to store a few loads of fabrics here. A friend of mine will soon be bringing more goods from the Maya lands, and I don't have enough room."

Anecoatl's eyes gleamed. "Perhaps I could accommodate you, for a modest fee, of course. Our guest house isn't used much, except when calpixqui come to collect tribute. I assume you'd contribute some mantles toward Paynala's share?"

"Of course," Opochtli said with forced heartiness. "We must all make an extra effort in wartime. What else can a poor merchant do?" At that point Opochtli had great difficulty keeping his voice from revealing the bitterness he felt. Hadn't he given enough? Hadn't he given his only son, seven years before? Would Anecoatl even acknowledge that?

Anecoatl didn't acknowledge it. Instead he rubbed his hands together and said "Fine, fine. Should we say one mantle of tribute for each ten I store? Then it's agreed."

Opochtli directed the tamemes to the guest house with their

loads. Then he turned to Anecoatl. "I know you don't have any extra men to guard my supplies. Should I leave a tameme here?" "No need," Anecoatl said. "Theft is punished severely in Paynala, as you know. No one around here would dare disturb any property left in my care." Opochtli nodded. "As you wish. Gotta go now. Tell Cimatl goodbye for me. I'll be back with more stuff in a few days." Then he led the tamemes back to Oluta with their empty baskets, thinking all the way about his plan. There could be no slip-ups. He had to do it right.

* * *

Over the next few months Opochtli visited the tecalli frequently, always bringing presents, sometimes bringing bales of mantles or cotton cloth to store. He never failed to bring octli, so the two men began to have a few drinks together at each visit. Opochtli encouraged Anecoatl to tell his war stories again and again, sensing that Anecoatl loved to brag even more than the average warrior.

One night Anecoatl was more talkative than usual because Cimatl was away, caring for a sick friend. He'd had two drinks of octli and was starting on his third. "Did I ever tell you I was an orphan?" he asked rhetorically, not waiting for an answer. "Well, I was. Never knew who my parents were. I was attached to a calpulli in a farm village where I earned my food by weeding the vegetable gardens. Hard work. Hated it. Only good thing was, it made me strong. When I saw the other boys playing with their wooden swords, I watched and imitated them. Made my own sword and practiced whenever I could. Got so I was better than any of the other boys. One day a telpochcalli instructor saw me fight at a festival and gave me a chance to be his student."

Opochtli refilled Anecoatl's cup with octli. "That was a lucky break," he said. "I've wondered why you never talked about your family."

"The army was my family," Anecoatl said as he took another swallow and licked his lips. "I belonged there. My teachers were like fathers to me. Taught me to be the best. I was a knight by th' time I was eighteen years old."

"You were certainly good at what you did," Opochtli said.

Anecoatl's voice was becoming thick as the octli took effect. "Have s'more octli, m'friend," he said to Opochtli.

"A little," Opochtli said, pouring some into his own cup. "Not too much. I have to walk home by myself." He refilled Anecoatl's cup. "But you're already home, Anecoatl, so relax and tell me what brought you to Paynala."

"I almost forgot," Anecoatl said, searching through his foggy memory. "An ol' buddy of mine named Omehuatl got killed. Used t' talk 'bout his beautiful wife, Papalotl. I came here to tell 'er he died a warrior's death. She was stayin' with Cimatl. Pregnant. Came here to have 'er baby. She was Cimatl's sister."

"So that's how you met Cimatl?"

"I didn't pay much 'tention to Cimatl then," Anecoatl said. "Really had the hots for Papalotl, but she was pregnant. She was headstrong, too. Would've been hell t' live with. Cimatl's been a better wife. No fuss from her about who heads th' family."

"No doubt Cimatl was grateful to get a husband like you," Opochtli said. He pretended to pour more octli into his own cup, then refilled Anecoatl's.

"I treat 'er like a queen," Anecoatl slurred. "She wants sumpin'; she gets it. Anythin' she wanted fer Malinalli, she got that too. I treated m' step-daughter better'n some men treat their own daughters, but Malinalli didn't 'preciate it. I knew she'd never amount t' much."

Opochtli began to feel uncomfortable as he recognized in Anecoatl the same patronizing attitude he himself had shown toward Metzli's first child—the child who didn't deserve much, who wouldn't amount to much. He changed the subject tactfully. "I had a good wife, too. She died when Metzli was born. Gave me Chimalli, though—a son to be proud of."

"Nothing's too good f'r my son," said Anecoatl. "Know what? He's gonna have all the things I never had."

"I believe that," Opochtli said. "I've noticed that you do whatever you set out to do."

Anecoatl tapped his head with one finger. "Takes brains," he said. "That's th' one thing my parents gave me. Brains."

"Chimalli admired your brains," Opochtli said. "You didn't just bash your enemies on the battlefield; you outwitted them."

Anecoatl grinned with his lips closed smugly, his lip plug protruding upward. "If you only knew, m' friend, how *much* I've had t' live by my wits!"

The coals in the hearth had turned gray, glowing a faint red in the cracks and edges. "It's getting late, my friend," Opochtli said as he rose to go. "Save those stories for another time." The plan was working. He had won Anecoatl's trust, but he mustn't appear too eager for it. Nothing must go wrong.

* * *

A few days later Opochtli returned to the tecalli with two tamemes, each carrying a load of mantles to deposit in Anecoatl's guest house. Then he sent the tamemes back to Oluta, planning to have some time alone with Anecoatl. Anecoatl accompanied him to the guest house to collect his percentage of the stored goods according to their agreement.

400

"I want to show you something," Opochtli said as he pointed to a stack of mantles made of maguey fiber. "You said a warrior lives by his wits, but so does a pochteca. These mantles aren't the best quality. Who'd want to steal them?"

"Who indeed?" Anecoatl said contemptuously. "Those cheap things aren't fit for anybody but slaves. I hope you don't intend to give me those as my share."

Opochtli laughed. "Not at all. I'm saving the best for you—these over here." He pointed to a bale of cotton mantles with elaborate woven borders, then he continued, "Since we have no guards here, let me show you how a clever pochteca protects his valuables." He counted down from the top of the stack until he reached the fifth folded mantle, then inserted his hand between the folds and pulled out a handful of jadestones, beautifully carved in shapes of flowers and stars and fish. "If I put these in a locked chest or a beautiful fawnskin bag," he said, "a thief would know something valuable was inside. Who would go through a stack of cheap slave garments looking for precious stones? Appearances can be deceiving, eh?"

"Very clever," Anecoatl said, rubbing his chin. "How do you remember where you put them?"

"Easy enough," Opochtli bragged. He held up his hand. "Five fingers on each hand, five garments on top of my treasure. At other times, I use other numbers."

"Why are you telling me this?" Anecoatl asked suspiciously. "Why don't you store these valuables in your own home?"

"Because that's where everyone would look for them," Opochtli shrugged. "They're safer here. I know you won't steal them, because then I wouldn't trade with you any more. You're smart. You know it's in your best interest to keep doing business with me. But in case anything happens to me, see that Metzli gets anything I've stored here. Don't throw out anything just because it looks cheap on the surface."

"I see," Anecoatl nodded. "Where's Metzli now, in case I have to find her?"

"Someplace around Tenochtitlan, probably the market district of Tlatelolco. You could always find her by inquiring at the temple of Quetzalcoatl in the temple square. Now how about a drink of octli?"

As the two men shared drinks and reminiscences, each one tried to impress the other with his cleverness. As the octli's power took hold, Anecoatl shared more and more of some secrets he had long locked inside.

"Y'know that Malinalli gal? She was turnin' into a real slut," he said to Opochtli after the fourth drink. He spoke in a low voice, though Cimatl was still away, nursing her sick friend. "At the naming celebration f'r her li'l brother, the slut tried t' seduce a guest—Tlacoch, it was. I've never tol' anyone else this, but I

401

saved 'im from her. He'd had too much t' drink, poor sap. I got 'im down to the river and soaked 'im in cold water. Don't tell anyone 'bout this."

"I certainly won't," Opochtli said emphatically. "Now that Tlacoch's my son-in-law, I'm grateful to you for saving his reputation around here."

"We men've gotta stick t'gether," Anecoatl said thickly, putting an arm sloppily around Opochtli's shoulder. Small red lines creased the whites of his eyes. "The next day, th' li'l whore tried t' seduce me! Imagine that, right in m' own granary, jus' after 'er mother'd had a baby!"

"I really can't imagine such a thing," Opochtli said in a shocked tone. "It must've been a hard thing for you to deal with."

"Hard, yeah," Anecoatl murmured. "It's been hard t' keep the secret f'r all these years. Don't tell Cimatl I tol' ya. Cuz she thought her rotten daughter was perfect."

"I never speak ill of the dead," Opochtli said, noting that Anecoatl's eyes flickered upon hearing the word *dead*. "I was sad when I heard Malinalli had died, but perhaps it's just as well she and Chimalli didn't get married."

"Yeah," Anecoatl slurred, pouring another drink of octli. "You didn't know 'er like I did. She wanted t' rule Paynala. Hated me when I got wise t' some of 'er schemes."

"Her schemes?"

"Yeah. You think she would've married Chimalli? She wanted Tlacoch. Thought he'd be the next tecuhtli, 'cause his father was a big shot here."

Opochtli's eyebrows pulled together in puzzlement. "I don't understand. You were already the tecuhtli of Paynala."

"Yeah. She knew I wanted Turquoise Stone t' rule after I'm gone. She tried t' team up with Tlacateotl and get Tlacoch appointed instead. Then she'd wrap Tlacoch 'round her li'l finger 'n boss 'im around, power behind th' throne, y'know."

"I had no idea she was like that," Opochtli said, wrinkling his forehead as if perplexed. His imagination wrestled with the images of Malinalli in his mind, trying to fit the personality he remembered into the pictures Anecoatl was painting of her. He recalled the young girl who had joyfully and appreciatively received his presents; the student-priestess and best friend of his daughter Metzli; the hard-working girl who had helped her mother raise Turquoise Stone for the first two years; the budding beauty who had seemed the perfect choice for Chimalli's bride. Could she have had secret ambitions she never shared with Metzli or Chimalli? Would she have used her beauty and her body to achieve those ends? He hoped the octli would loosen Anecoatl's tongue enough so that truths and secrets would spill out, but these accusations seemed totally improbable. In fact,

Anecoatl's description of Malinalli seemed to fit himself more than it did her. Truth comes in strange shapes, Opochtli concluded, sometimes in the form of a mirror a man would rather smash than look into.

Anecoatl was showing considerable effects of the octli, his eyes becoming red-rimmed and watery, his lips sagging, his words often unintelligible. His hands, stiff and clumsy, tipped over his cup as he tried to grasp it.

Opochtli wiped up the spilled liquid with a corner of his own tilmantli. "I'll get you some more," he said as Anecoatl stared dully at the inside of the empty cup. Opochtli opened another leather bottle and poured another cup for Anecoatl.

"Thanks, m'friend," Anecoatl said. "Y'r good t' talk to." He drained the cup of octli in a few rapid gulps.

"Tell me," Opochtli ventured, still hoping to get to the truth, "were you trying to save Chimalli from Malinalli when you sent him away?"

Anecoatl wore a glazed expression. "Sent him away? Oh, yeah. Had to get 'im away. Couldn't stay here. Not safe."

"Not safe?"

"Women out t' get us. Gotta get 'em b'fore they get us."

"Women are men's enemies?"

"Yeah, but we're too smart for 'em. I got ridda that bitch. Heh, heh. Cimatl never guessed. Heh, heh." Anecoatl swayed unsteadily on the mat, as if he were going to pass out. The empty cup tumbled from his loosening fingers.

Opochtli was growing more and more disturbed. He decided to ask his question bluntly, before Anecoatl became totally incoherent. "Did you get rid of Chimalli too?"

"Yeah, Chimalli too. Nobody ever guessed. Heh, heh."

Opochtli's heart sank. Now that he had his truth, he didn't want to face it. Tears flowed from his own eyes as he removed Anecoatl's tilmantli and hung it on a peg in the wall of the tecalli. Then he gently lowered Anecoatl's body until the tecuhtli lay flat on the petlatl. "Sleep well, Anecoatl," he said, and when Anecoatl's snores indicated he was sound asleep, Opochtli added, "Now I know who my enemies are. Do you know who your worst enemy is, Anecoatl? It's yourself."

Opochtli stumbled through the night alone on the path toward Oluta, glad his unmanly tears could be seen by no one except the inscrutable gods and the cold silent stars overhead. By the time he reached home, the morning star had appeared on the horizon, the conch shells were sounding mournfully from the local temple, and all the pent-up grief had been drained from his body. In its place had grown a determination that would lie like a stone on his chest until he had accomplished the one task that he believed could at last give meaning to his son's futile death.

* * *

Huatl returned from his trip to the lands of the Mayas with the goods Opochtli had requested, including coral jewelry, rubber balls, hemp ropes, chewing gum, and bales of cotton. He also carried three tightly-woven baskets with lids strapped on by leather thongs.

Huatl pointed to each basket in turn. "This one contains a coral snake," he said. "This one's a yellow chin. This one's the deadly nauyaka. Its bite can kill in a matter of minutes."

"Very ordinary looking baskets," Opochtli said approvingly. "Just what I wanted. Appearances can be deceiving."

"Every shabbily dressed pochteca knows that," Huatl grinned. Then he put on his shabby tilmantli and departed, saying he wanted to look into a settlement the Spaniards were establishing in the Coatzacoalcos area, hoping to do some bartering with them.

The next day Opochtli loaded some tamemes and took them to Paynala. They carried some coral jewelry for Cimatl, three leather bottles of octli for Anecoatl, and several things to store in the guest house: five bales of cotton quachtli, a tall basket full of hemp ropes, and three ordinary-looking baskets with tightly fitting lids.

Cimatl, at home once more after nursing her sick friend, greeted Opochtli and accepted the coral necklace appreciatively. "Anecoatl is still at his office in the village," she said. "Want to wait for him?"

"Thanks, Cimatl, and welcome back," Opochtli said warmly, handing her a leather bottle. "This octli is a gift for your husband. I'll leave some other things in the guest house. Tell him I'll be back in ten days. He can take his pick of the mantles I've brought, one for every ten I've stored here, as we agreed. But tell him I'm leaving three baskets with personal items; those aren't for trade. Tell him not to open them."

After Cimatl promised to relay the message, Opochtli stored the goods in the guest house. He sent the tamemes toward Oluta while he remained a few minutes to check the stack of maguey garments he had stored there several days before. Five folds down from the top, he inserted his hand and removed several small green stones. They were not the delicate carved stones he had hidden there earlier; instead they were substitutes of inferior grade. He smirked for a moment in satisfaction: he had been right. Only Anecoatl could have known those stones were there. Then he shuddered as he realized he had been in danger on those evenings when he had naively drunk octli with Anecoatl. Anecoatl must have intended to get rid of him before the theft and substitution could be discovered. Opochtli could have shared the fate of several others Anecoatl had gotten rid of. He'd have to be very careful, especially now that he knew too much.

* * *

A young boy who carried wood and water to the tecalli every morning brought the message from Cimatl to Opochtli in Oluta. Cimatl had found her husband dead on the floor of the guest house, the victim of a snake bite, judging from the imprint of fangs on his right hand and his swollen right arm. She and the servant boy had searched everywhere for the snake, but it had escaped. Or it might be hiding somewhere in the guest house. Her message asked Opochtli to come quickly and repossess his belongings, but also to be very, very careful because a dangerous snake was loose around there somewhere.

Opochtli rushed immediately to the tecalli in Paynala. Cimatl had arranged for the body to be removed and was preparing it for cremation, so he turned his attention to removing the stored goods and searching the guest house. He found one of his storage baskets opened and empty, but the other two were sealed as he had left them. Carefully he immersed the two remaining baskets in water. When they had been soaking long enough to drown the occupants, he cut the thongs of one basket with his flint knife and cut off the head of the drowned snake.

When Opochtli presented the dead snake to Cimatl, she wept in relief and gratitude. She also pronounced him a hero and told everyone how brave he was, to kill a snake by himself. The attention he received at Anecoatl's funeral service embarrassed Opochtli, but the more he attempted to minimize the event, the more people praised him for his modesty and acclaimed his heroism. At last he stopped protesting and accepted the accolades as if he deserved them.

Opochtli mused silently about the meaning of what he had just experienced. The snake that had really killed Anecoatl had disappeared never to be seen again, while a dead snake that had not bitten anyone received the blame. He, too, was not entirely blameless, for though he had not exactly killed Anecoatl, he had set the trap in which Anecoatl snared himself. Yet he could see layers of justice interleaving layers of deception and illusion. A guilty tecuhtli had been punished for his crimes, yet he had died with the appearance of being an innocent victim. A guilty pochteca had taken revenge on his son's murderer, yet he was being perceived as a savior of sorts. Still, he reasoned, had not justice ultimately triumphed? Was the illusion really as false as it seemed? Had he not, in a sense, helped to rid the world of a snake?

* * *

405

A few days after the cremation of Anecoatl, after her son Turquoise Stone had gone away to the telpochcalli, Cimatl walked to Oluta carrying a basket with a gift of cactus candy she had made for the hero Opochtli. Also she carried, carefully wrapped in a cloth, five precious carved jadestones. She found her old friend tending his dogs in his backyard pen, but he quickly finished his tasks, thanked her enthusiastically for the candy, and invited her into his house for rest and refreshment.

As soon as Opochtli's servant had served the chocolate drinks and departed, Cimatl removed the precious stones from her basket. "I found these stones among my husband's possessions," she said. "Can you tell me if they have much value?"

Opochtli stared at the polished green stones in Cimatl's hand. He instantly recognized the delicately carved shapes: these were the stones he had hidden in the stack of mantles to trap Anecoatl.

"They are extremely valuable," he said truthfully. Then he added a slight untruth, justifying it in his own mind as a kindness to Cimatl. "I traded them to Anecoatl myself. They came from an artisan I met in the Xicalango market long ago. His artistic skill has tripled the value of the stones themselves."

Cimatl sighed with audible relief. "Thank goodness! Could you sell them for me?" When she realized how her excitement might be misinterpreted, she muted it and explained solemnly, "I'm not sure how my son and I are going to live now that Anecoatl is gone."

Opochtli felt a pang in his heart and a tightening of his throat. For an instant before replying he silently upbraided himself. Why hadn't he thought of those consequences? He had been so intent on punishing Anecoatl for wicked ambition and callous cruelties that he hadn't even considered the needs of the wife and son who would lose the tecuhtli's protection. A sense of terrible guilt gripped him as he looked at the stricken, shadowy eyes of the once-beautiful, twice-widowed Cimatl.

"Cimatl, may I speak as an old friend? May I be very frank with you?" Opochtli asked the questions tentatively, conscious of the fact that Cimatl, as a tecuhtli's widow, had higher social rank than he.

"Of course," Cimatl said, an expression of gratitude temporarily transforming her sad face. "I'm turning to you as the person I trust most." She placed a reassuring hand on his shoulder as Opochtli knelt before her.

"Then let me pledge my friendship and offer you my support," Opochtli said, searching her face for approval. When a puzzled look flicked across Cimatl's eyes he rose and added hastily, "I wouldn't be so presumptuous as to offer myself in marriage, although I'd consider any man lucky to have you for a wife."

406

"Thank you, dear friend," Cimatl said softly. "I doubt I can ever remarry. I'm not a desirable woman at my age."

"Not true," said Opochtli firmly. "You'll be desirable at any age. But let's be practical. It'll be hard to find a husband of your same social rank and age, especially since so many men have been killed in the recent wars. Since our old friend Tlacateotl died a few months ago, there's nobody left in the local area who's attained the rank of eagle or jaguar knight. Even finding a new tecuhtli for Paynala will be difficult, but that may work in your favor."

"How so?" Cimatl sniffed, trying not to show the self-pity she was feeling.

"Perhaps your son could be given the title of tecuhtli and you could be named as his co-ruler until he's old enough to take on the responsibilities of the office himself."

"I've never heard of such an arrangement," Cimatl said in surprise, but clearly the idea interested her.

"I haven't either," Opochtli said, "but these are difficult times, unusual times. Normally the council in Tenochtitlan would appoint a younger brother of the former tecuhtli, provided of course he'd proved himself in scholarship and battle. But neither of your husbands had a younger brother. Anecoatl's son might be the next choice. He's about ten years old now, isn't he? I hear he's doing well at warrior school. If I could pay for his support and yours until he's eighteen years old, he could take his father's place in the tecalli."

Cimatl again held out the five stones in her outstretched palm. "Your offer is most generous," she said, "but we'd rather pay our own way. Could these stones be used toward my son's education?"

"No problem. These should bring a fine price. My friend Huatl is making arrangements to trade with the Spaniards on the coast. We might even trade these gems for some of their horses and begin breeding horses here. That's what Huatl wants to do."

"Horses?"

"The animals the Spaniards ride—four-footed animals like deer, but larger. They can carry men and heavy burdens, too. Huatl says we can breed them like dogs or turkeys. He sees real potential for profit in them."

"Is Huatl your partner?"

"Yes, and you could be one, also. These stones would buy you a share of the profits, and with steady profits you and your son could afford to keep your home and servants."

"Then it's agreed," Cimatl said happily, thrusting the gems into Opochtli's hand. "I couldn't accept your charity, but income from business is another matter. My son and I would have the satisfaction of doing our share."

"You must meet my other partner Huatl," Opochtli said with

a grin. "You've started to think and talk the way he does."

Cimatl picked up her empty basket and stood up. "I'd like that, but I must go now," she said. "I'll send a message to the Council in Tenochtitlan, asking them to appoint my son as tecuhtli. Thanks a lot for your advice and kindness."

Opochtli stood up, too, and walked her to the door. "The Council may not be functioning right now," he cautioned. "Huatl tells me the city's been devastated by the war. Talk to Paynala citizens first. I doubt the Council would make any objections as long as local people accept you and your son as rulers."

"Oh, I just remembered," Cimatl said, stopping in the doorway. "Is Metzli still in Tenochtitlan? Is she all right?"

"I've heard nothing for months—not since Huatl first told me Metzli had married Tlacoch and settled in Tlatelolco. I guess she's had her baby by now, if they're still alive. Huatl says the hunger and disease are killing hundreds every day."

"You must be worried about her." Cimatl started walking slowly toward the road.

"I am," Opochtli said truthfully, walking slowly beside Cimatl. Then he added somewhat defensively, "I've offered her a home here anytime she wants it. I can't make her come."

"I hope she'll change her mind," Cimatl said, swinging her empty basket casually, "but the gods might not will it so. Our tonalli determines our lives. Anecoatl's tonalli predicted a sudden death, but only the gods knew a snake would bite him. Life is hard, but things usually turn out for the best."

"I wish I had your unwavering faith," said Opochtli. "I can't help thinking some people cause others to die sooner than the gods intended. I'm thinking of my son Chimalli's senseless death in a senseless battle, all because a few powerful men wanted more power. I used to believe that the gods needed blood sacrifices. Now I think the rulers and priests manipulate us, using our faith and trust to their own advantage. But we make it too easy for them. We ought to control our own fate better."

"My faith is wavering too, as I grow older," Cimatl said, "but I cling to it because nothing else gives my life meaning. I, too, lost Itzamitl and Malinalli before their time. I've tried to tell myself these hardships were meant to be, but sometimes I feel angry. I feel cheated."

Even as he responded sympathetically, "I know that feeling," Opochtli thought it strange that Cimatl did not mention Anecoatl, her second husband, as one who had died prematurely. He sensed that Cimatl was not grieving nearly as much for Anecoatl as she had for Itzamitl and Malinalli. Was some of the anger she spoke of directed at Anecoatl? Perhaps she realized at some level that Anecoatl had been instrumental in Itzamitl's death; perhaps she understood that Anecoatl deserved to die. That thought gave Opochtli some relief from guilt, but he was still determined to make amends—to see that the widow Cimatl did not suffer from his act of vengeance against Anecoatl. Fortunately she was naive enough to believe that any money or gifts she received in the future were coming from investment profits. Opochtli sensed also that Cimatl needed illusions to make life bearable. She knew that Anecoatl was a lesser man than Itzamitl, yet she pretended to all her neighbors that her second husband had been as noble as her first. Even though Cimatl never acknowledged any conflicts between Malinalli and Anecoatl, Opochtli had serious suspicions that Anecoatl had killed Malinalli, too. Hadn't Anecoatl admitted, when he was maundering over his cups of octli, that he had "got rid of the bitch?" It was unaccountably strange that Anecoatl had exiled the macehual family who might have protected Malinalli or brought accusations against her killer—Chihuallama, Callipopoca, and their daughter Toto. Toto's complete disappearance was also a mystery, since Metzli had not seen her with Chimalli in Tenochtitlan shortly before his death. Opochtli thought it would be unwise to discuss his suspicions with Cimatl; if illusions helped to keep her sanity, he would not disturb them.

Cimatl, in turn, was sensitive to Opochtli's feelings. Sensing that he didn't want to talk about his deceased son Chimalli and his estranged daughter Metzli, Cimatl thanked him again, waved goodbye, and speeded the footsteps that separated her from him.

As she walked back alone to Paynala, the dry dust of the road rising and settling on her sandals, Cimatl thought silently how lucky Opochtli was to have a daughter whose whereabouts he knew. She worried about her own daughter Malinalli, wondering if she was still alive, hoping she had arrived safely in Coatzacoalcos with the Mayan traders nearly eight years before. Cimatl had maintained for all those years a mental image of Malinalli serving as a priestess in the temple of Quetzalcoatl, but she had to admit to herself that this vision could be a protective fiction through which she had sustained a frail hope. Would she ever see her daughter again? Now that Anecoatl was dead, Malinalli was in no danger from him, but Cimatl carried the guilt of having participated with Anecoatl in the lie about Malinalli's death. Even though it was Anecoatl's idea, Cimatl had dressed her servant Toto in Malinalli's clothing and presented that body as Malinalli's. She would have to live forever with that lie.

So she could never bring Malinalli back to Paynala, but Cimatl formed another fragile hope in her mind as she lifted her eyes to the distant blue mountains with a silver thread of river flowing through them. Someday she might be able to go with Opochtli or other merchants to Coatzacoalcos. If she could beg for some time alone at the temple, she might verify whether Malinalli was still there. She might even get a glimpse of

Malinalli, a blessed moment when she might be assured of her daughter's happiness and find peace of mind for herself. Meanwhile, she would give Turquoise Stone all the care she would have liked to lavish on two children. He was her only hope of ever having grandchildren, her only hope of someone to take care of her in her old age.

Concerned only with her own small world in the farming communities of Paynala and Oluta, Cimatl did not know how much her fate was becoming entangled with larger forces of destiny. The Spaniards' world seemed remote and inconsequential, for she could not have foreseen the eventual destiny of the five elegant jadestones she had removed from the tightly tied petlacalli that Anecoatl had forbidden her to open when he was alive.

The precious stones which had been the instrument of Anecoatl's downfall and Cimatl's liberation would become Opochtli's means of atonement. They were destined to pass from Opochtli's hands to those of Huatl, from Huatl's to the hands of the Spanish Captain Sandoval in exchange for breeding stock. Sandoval would give them to his Captain General Hernan Cortes, who would eventually take them to Spain as a gift for his bride. The queen of Spain would admire them and hint that she might like them for herself, but Cortes would ignore the hint and save them for his own intended purpose. The last destination of the jadestones, however, was fated to be at the bottom of the ocean on a sunken ship, where the indifferent salt water would wash over them and bury them in the shifting sands as if they had been no more than a piece of broken coral or a fragment of discarded seashell, crumbled by the leveling forces of time.

Chapter 28

After the Fall: A Wife and a Mistress

After Cuauhtemoc's surrender, a few weeds of doubt began to grow in Marina's garden of contentment. She told herself Hernan was just busier than usual, not intentionally neglecting her. Yet a different man was emerging, a man she didn't know: Cortes the builder, the planner, the civic administrator. She had been confident of her bond with Cortes the conquistador, Cortes the diplomat, Cortes the political strategist. Even in the furious days of battle he had made time to be with her; even when wounded or exhausted, he had given her energetic passion. Now his passions seemed redirected and dissipated, not only toward Moctezuma's daughter and the other women thrust upon him by various fawning lords, but also toward erecting buildings, demolishing monuments, and obsessively pursuing the gold he had lost on the Noche Triste, the "night of sorrows."

Marina's transition from her earlier philosophy to Christianity had been so interwoven with her love for Cortes that she had never differentiated between her physical and spiritual lives. To lose Cortes would certainly spawn a crisis of faith. She sought advice from Father Olmedo, but she asked only about loss of faith. He reassured her that most Christians pass through valleys of doubt, but he did not discern what was really troubling her. In the past she might have sought a healing woman and obtained charms to keep a lover from straying, but even if she could ask Father Olmedo what Christian women did under such circumstances, she doubted that a celibate, virtuous man like Olmedo would know. He, too, was busier than ever. He had requested more friars to help with baptisms, conversions, religious instruction, and other holy work.

Cortes had chosen Coyoacan, "Place of the Coyotes," as the capital city of New Spain, for several reasons. It had a convenient location not associated with previous power centers of the Triple Alliance—Tenochtitlan, Texcoco, and Tacuba. It was situated south of Tenochtitlan but connected to it with a causeway, accessible by either horse or boat, close to the lake where the floating chinampas could grow food, and close to the most direct route leading eastward through Cholula to Vera Cruz on the Gulf of Mexico.

As soon as the battle rubble had been cleared away, the causeways broadened and reinforced, and the wreckage of the great temple leveled, Cortes laid plans to build his headquarters in Coyoacan. Around a central square, facing inward toward a common garden area, he planned to erect four important buildings: to the south, a Christian church; to the east, government offices, with rooms where prisoners could be held or questioned. To the west, apartments that could be used in various ways: as temporary housing for Spanish officials and settlers, or as permanent housing for the friars and nuns Cortes hoped to bring from Spain. To the north, a two-story residence made of red tezontli stones, his most important gift to Marina. He assumed Marina would be pleased with her new home. Its prominent position attested to her importance, not only to him, but to the Christian faith she had helped disseminate, symbolized by the church facing her residence across the square.

From Coyoacan, Cortes issued a stream of orders covering civilian and military matters. Cortes banned gambling as morally corrupting, though he continued to enjoy it himself. He ordered his captains and soldiers to bring their wives from Spain or Cuba within eighteen months, or to find acceptable brides. Preferred brides were called "old Christians," those who had been raised as Christians rather than newly converted. Yet he did not send for his own wife, Catalina, who had remained in Cuba throughout the wars. He asked King Charles to send humble friars, not arrogant priests, to establish churches and schools in new settlements. He enjoyed playing the role of citizen-builder in the image of the god Quetzalcoatl for whom he had been mistaken.

But Cortes also maintained a warlike posture, keeping his captains on call to quell any rebellions in the conquered territories and sending scouts to report on the activities of other Spaniards who might encroach on his domain. One of the latter was Francisco de Garay, who had hoped to rule the Panuco region north of Vera Cruz ever since his first explorations in 1518. Men like Garay needed to be watched to see whether they were merely rivals or potential enemies. Letters from Spain informed Cortes that Garay's ambitions were being championed in Spanish court circles by Diego Velasquez, who had been Hernan's friend and mentor, then rival, and now his bitter enemy.

Before starting construction in Coyoacan, Cortes sent the popular twenty-five-year-old captain, Gonzalo de Sandoval, to establish a settlement near Coatzacoalcos. Four leagues inland, Sandoval established the town of Espiritu Santo, "Holy Spirit," where he maintained a garrison ready to protect coastal ports against any native uprisings. Sandoval had also been charged with authority to smooth the roads leading directly from the Valley of Mexico to the coast so that a steady stream of supplies could flow from Cuba, Jamaica, and Spain. Sandoval was also experimenting with new agricultural products and livestock to see if imported plants and animals would thrive in New Spain.

From his experience building plantations in Hispaniola and Cuba, Cortes anticipated that some imports might thrive in the Mexican soil and climate: sugar cane, mulberry trees for silk, vine cuttings for grapes. He also sent to Spain for plants that he guessed would fare better in the varied climate and topography of Mexico than in the West Indies: wheat and other grains, vegetables, and fruit-bearing trees such as olives, almonds, peaches, and citrus fruits. Even more important, he believed, would be brood stock for pigs, cows, sheep, goats, mules, and horses. These could be used as draft animals or to provide meat, milk, wool, and hides. He sent exploring parties into conquered territories searching for gold and silver which might be used in trade for imported goods or as tribute to win the king's favor.

In addition to bringing wives and families from Spain, Cortes ordered various weapons, iron, guns, powder, tools, forges for toolmaking, and other practical items. When his order for gunpowder was slow in arriving, he remembered the slopes of the volcano Popocatepetl and sent some men there to gather sulphur to make their own gunpowder. To permit easier unloading of Spanish ships, Cortes ordered his garrison at Vera Cruz to relocate the town two leagues from San Juan de Ulua, on a lagoon with inlets where ships could be sheltered from the northerly winds.

For most of these activities, Cortes did not need Marina. While the plans for reconstruction were being drawn and the rainy season brought showers every afternoon, she spent most of her time talking with Father Olmedo, asking many questions about Christianity and the Bible, but fearful of asking what was really in her heart. She also interpreted occasionally for Father Olmedo, but he was gradually learning Nahuatl to communicate directly with his new converts.

At the end of the rainy season, actual construction began. The air which had been filled with the stench of decay now carried the pleasant scents of fresh-cut pine and cedar logs or the whitish dust of recently-cut stone. Marina enjoyed watching the construction, sometimes bringing water and food to the native laborers, though she hesitated to do this too often lest Cortes consider it undignified.

Cortes declared the natives and their leader Cuauhtemoc at fault for the devastation of the cities, because they had been so foolish as to oppose him and prolong the battles when they had opportunities to surrender and become peaceful vassals.

413

Therefore, although his own architects drew the plans and his carpenters oversaw the work, natives were ordered to supply the labor and bring their own materials. Logs had to be brought from the mountains; building stones had to be cut out of nearby quarries or recovered from the city's demolished houses and temples. Laborers also had to bring their own food, in reparation for having killed so many Spaniards.

Although accustomed to hard work, the natives were also accustomed to short periods with frequent rests. Under the Spaniards they were made to work from dawn to dark, with no rest except to eat what little they could bring. Nevertheless the building proceeded quickly, because Prince Black Flower of Texcoco brought four thousand of his followers to do it, and thousands more were forcibly recruited from the lowlands. Many of the recruits, unaccustomed to the high altitude, suffered from the cold winds at night and became ill.

Marina felt sorry for the native laborers, especially those who fell sick, but she knew very well her master's theories of punishment and his ways of controlling people. Even if she had been tempted to intervene, she was beginning to doubt whether she had any power to influence him. Cortes was taking other women to his bed now, seeming to favor Dona Isabel, the daughter of Moctezuma, rumored to be pregnant by him. Although he treated Marina respectfully in the presence of others, and affectionately when they were alone, she wondered if he would continue to love her when he no longer needed her.

Cortes did need Marina to question his captive Cuauhtemoc, the last emperor or Uey Tlatoani of Tenochtitlan. Aguilar had been killed in a battle, so Marina ("La Malinche" as the natives called her), became Cortes' only interpreter. Cuauhtemoc, his family, and several courtiers were taken to the summer palace of Moctezuma in the mountain town of Cuauhnahuac, "Place of the Eagles," several leagues south of Coyoacan, where the weather was pleasant all year. Cortes corrupted the name of the village by pronouncing it "Cuernavaca," which meant "cow's horn" in Spanish, and he also continued to say Cuauhtemoc's name as "Guatemoc" no matter how many times he heard Marina pronounce it correctly.

At first the captive emperor was well treated and fed, because food had been harvested that year in Cuauhnahuac and other outlying provinces. Cuauhnahuac, having been conquered months earlier than the lake cities, had not suffered the ravages of bombardment and starvation that they had.

Cortes was still fiercely determined to recover the bars of gold and other treasures that his fleeing army left behind on the night of sorrows in June, 1520, when they had been driven out of Tenochtitlan. His soldiers were unable to find the treasure, either near the Tacuba causeway where most of it had been abandoned, or by probing in the mud of the lake. He hoped to persuade Cuauhtemoc, through polite speech and kind treatment, to tell him where the treasure was hidden. Cuauhtemoc always answered with deference, and his answer was always the same. He knew nothing about the treasure; the heavy gold bars must have sunk deep in the soft mud of the lake when the Spaniards dropped them; perhaps the cannons pounding the earth so noisily had shaken the heavy objects even further down into the muddy lake bottom. Cuauhtemoc also refused, politely but steadfastly, to hear the gospel or to become a Christian.

When none of these attempts produced the treasure, Cortes became exasperated. He ordered Cuauhtemoc brought to Coyoacan in chains along with two of his royal associates, the princes Coanacoch and Tetlepanquetzal. He asked Marina to bring the princess Dona Isabel with her, to see if she could persuade her uncle to relent. Accompanied by the two women and several guards, Cortes strode into one of the newly-completed government offices in Coyoacan. "Dona Isabel," he said, "tell your uncle what blessings you've received as a Christian."

As Marina translated Cortes' command, Isabel fell to her knees before Cuauhtemoc. The blue-green sheen of quetzal feathers ornamented her dark braids. "Please, Uncle," she said tearfully, "don't resist any more. It pains me to see you in chains—a great warrior, a great tlatoani. Christians forgive their enemies, as Jesus Christ taught them to do. Tell the teules what they want to know, and they'll treat you kindly."

While Marina was translating this for Cortes, Cuauhtemoc spoke directly to Isabel in Nahuatl. "You've sold yourself to your enemies for a quetzal feather," he said with withering scorn. "Now you'll be a slave to others, to foreigners who don't understand your way of life, to invaders who destroy your home stone by stone."

Marina had missed Cuauhtemoc's remark while she was translating Isabel's words, but she caught Isabel's reply. In a level voice, sounding as cold and unmoving as her uncle's, Isabel responded: "My father told me my duties. He gave me to Malinche and told me to obey him. When I obey my lord Malinche, I also obey my father Moctezuma."

Cuauhtemoc held out his hands and jangled the chains near Isabel's ears. "Hear this, my pathetic little niece," he said. "These chains don't bind me as much as the gifts of your lord bind you. The quetzal feathers you're wearing are a slave collar, a collar woven of quetzal feathers. Go back to your slave quarters and spread yourself like the rest of the tyrant's concubines; I have nothing more to say to you."

Isabel jumped to her feet and ran tearfully from the room, throwing a helpless glance toward Marina as she left.

The vein stood out on Cortes' neck. He did not wait for a translation, having heard Cuauhtemoc's sneering tone and having seen Isabel's reaction. "Bring me three braziers of coals from the kitchen fire," he barked to his guards.

When the braziers of hot coals had been placed under the captives' feet, Cortes addressed the three prisoners in mock courtesy. "I don't wish you to feel any discomfort, my lords," he said ironically. "You must understand my position. The lost treasure belonged not only to me, but also to my king and the other brave men who served their king and their god under me. You're all kings and men of honor. You'd help a fellow king recover his lost property, wouldn't you?"

The answers were the same as ever, though delivered through clenched teeth as the smell of seared flesh emanated from the braziers. The two princes writhed in agony, looking at Cuauhtemoc each time they answered Cortes' questions as if they hoped for a signal from him. Sweat poured from their faces; their bodies glistened in the dim light of hot coals. Marina, too, felt the heat from the coals and the tensions in the room; she steadied herself against a stone wall and tried not to reveal the nausea sweeping over her. She tried to keep her voice flat and unemotional, yet emotion surged within her as if it might boil over like a hot stew.

"Can't you tell them something?" pleaded the older of the two princes, looking desperately at Cuauhtemoc. "My feet are blistered; I may never walk again."

Through gritted teeth, Cuauhtemoc replied, "Do you think my feet are walking through a pleasure garden right now? Do you think I'm enjoying a bath?"

The questioning came to an abrupt halt when the younger prince fell unconscious. Cortes waved a hand, indicating to his guards to take the braziers away. One guard tried to shake the unconscious prince Coanacoch into consciousness again, but his head fell limply backward. "He's dead," said the guard.

"See what results from your stubbornness?" Cortes shouted at Cuauhtemoc. "Evil betide you!" Then he ordered the guard to bury the dead prince and stalked from the room. Marina leaned against the wall shakily as guards led away the suffering Cuauhtemoc and Tetlepanquetzal, limping on their blistered feet.

* * *

When Tlacoch and the people in the market district of Tlatelolco heard about the torture of Cuauhtemoc and the death of Prince Coanacoch, five or six of them gathered in Tlacoch's home, which was larger than most of the others and which had not been demolished before the surrender. The time of the Nemontemi had passed, though no special observances had marked the useless days. As many survivors wryly noted, every day of the calendar seemed like a nemontemi day, full of deprivations and fears. The year 4 Rabbit had begun with as great a sense of despair as that which had ended the year 3 House.

"What can we do?" the Tlatelolcans asked each other. Some of them took fierce pride in Cuauhtemoc's heroic resistance; others felt he should have given up any gold he knew about.

"What good is gold to us, anyway?" Tlacoch said angrily. "We need food and clean water. We've caught as much rainwater as we could, but the rainy season is almost over. We've learned to drink the brackish water of the lake, but it's making most of us sick. We have to repair the aqueducts."

"The Spaniards are in no hurry for that," said Callipopoca. They're spending all their time building in Coyoacan. Why should they worry about us?"

Metzli was holding her five-year-old son Citli, giving him a piece of dampened cloth to suck, but his forehead felt warm to her touch, and his listless eyes frightened her. "We can't hold out much longer," she said to Tlacoch. "Citli is getting sick, and I don't have enough milk in my breasts for the baby."

The formerly heavy Chihuallama, whose flesh now sagged on her bony frame, was holding Metzli's infant daughter, who slept fitfully in her withered arms. "Can't you repair the aqueduct yourselves?" she asked. "Why wait for the Spaniards?"

"They might not let us," Callipopoca explained. "They won't let us do the simplest tasks. Some of them are stopping every native male and searching him; they molest women and children even when they're only scavenging for food. I keep Citli with me to protect him when we go out looking."

"And what is there left to look for?" asked Tlacoch in disgust. "We've gathered every insect and blade of grass for miles around. We've stripped vines and plants from every roof garden in the area to make stews."

"The fish are all gone now," said a tired fisherman. "Even they can't stand these stinking waters."

"In my house," said a formerly wealthy lord, "we've taken to boiling our sandals and even some leather bottles and books we had, trying to get some nourishment out of them."

Tlacoch paced the floor, making a small circle with his steps in the crowded room. "They want gold and luxury goods, things we don't need," he said. "Let's give them whatever trinkets we can find—old rings or jewelry, even old copper axes or things made of seashells. All we'll ask in return is their mercy—to be let alone to repair the aqueduct and grow food on chinampas or rooftops. I'll start with this clasp." He removed the clasp holding his tilmantli and tossed it into the center of the floor, then tied his tilmantli in a knot at the shoulder, peasant-style. Soon a few

417

rings and noseplugs were added to the growing pile, pieces the citizens had been hiding and hoarding in hopes of being able to trade them for food. Tlacoch asked the other men to go from house to house in the Tlatelolco district, explaining their mission and collecting all the valuables they could get.

The Tlatelolcan leaders immediately went into action. They canvassed the area for contributions, appealed to every citizen's sense of community, and if that did not work they searched his house, his shield, or his clothing for any hidden objects. Tlacoch removed from his hidden storage place all the trade items he had been hoping to sell. Within two days, the men collected two baskets filled with gold and silver jewelry and household items. The group appointed Tlacoch their spokesperson, and three other leaders agreed to accompany him to Coyoacan.

The next morning, Metzli walked with Tlacoch to the edge of the canal, where the others waited for him in canoes. "I'll pray for your success," she said to the Tlatelolcans, and then to Tlacoch, "Hurry back, Dear One. Citli is still feverish today."

* * *

When the leaders of Tlatelolco arrived in Coyoacan and presented Cortes with the baskets of ornaments and art objects, he did not seem pleased. His black silk shirt added to his melancholy appearance, and his face wore the uncongenial look of a thundercloud. For a terrified moment Tlacoch wondered whether Cortes would recognize him as the warrior who had almost captured him at Otumba the year before, but Cortes showed no sign of recognition; nor did the half-dozen soldiers who flanked Cortes like a royal retinue. Marina stood beside Cortes, barefoot and clad simply in a white huipil, her dark hair falling loosely to her waist. Tlacoch searched Marina's face for some clue, but her expression was impassive, so he proceeded apprehensively.

"Great Captain Malinche," he said to Cortes, kneeling and touching the floor and then his tongue. "These lords, your vassals, the great lords of Tlatelolco, beg you to hear their pleas. They bring you these gifts and ask only for justice and mercy." He paused while Marina translated, searching for some sign of recognition in her voice, but hearing only the steady, unemotional tones of an interpreter.

Cortes grunted and picked up one basket, stirred its contents with his hand, looked at a few, then dropped them back indifferently into the basket. "Can you gentlemen help me find the lost treasure that fell into the Canal of the Toltecs?"

The Tlatelolcans exchanged distressed looks as they heard those words translated. Murmurs of denial accompanied the pained looks they turned upon Cortes. "None of us have seen the treasure," Tlacoch replied confidently. "We've collected all the wealth we can find in our poor district, to give to you. All we want is permission to rebuild the aqueduct, so we can have clean water again and citizens can return to their homes in peace."

Cortes scowled. "I'm not impressed by these baubles," he grumbled. "Why waste your time on these trinkets when thousands of pesos worth of gold have been stolen from me?"

One of the Tlatelolcan lords was also growing angry. "Ask Cuauhtemoc where it is. If he can't tell you, neither can we."

"Evil betide you for your insolence!" Cortes yelled. Then he turned to his guards. "Throw these people in chains," he ordered. "Maybe that will improve their memories." He turned and stalked out of the room, Marina following slowly behind him.

Tlacoch called after her as a guard grabbed him. He used her childhood name: "Malinalli!"

Marina turned briefly, looking to see if Cortes was out of hearing range, and spoke guardedly. "I recognize you, Tlacoch. I'd been hoping to see you sooner."

Another soldier entered the room, carrying several heavy chains. As the guards wrapped chains around the bewildered Tlatelolcans, Marina softened her voice and added, "The Captain General has been upset lately. I wish I could help him."

"Won't you see me for just a moment, Malinalli?" Tlacoch asked desperately. "We need your help. I can explain why I didn't bring Metzli to see you when you asked me to."

"It doesn't matter now, Tlacoch," she said, walking toward the door with a proud carriage that seemed incongruous with her bare feet and ordinary clothing. "I'm sorry, but there's nothing I can do," she said.

The combination of her queenly manner and unpretentious garments annoyed Tlacoch and infuriated the other Tlatelolcans, who muttered among themselves. Was she playing games with them? Did she have power to help which she was withholding from the people of her own race? Was she manipulating her master behind the scenes? Or was she just a servant, an underling, like the guards? If so, she was behaving with the self-importance of an insecure but ambitious subordinate, exaggerating her importance in small things. The more her behavior puzzled the unhappy lords, the more the ambiguity of it infuriated them. They couldn't figure her out. Where did her loyalties lie?

* * *

Metzli became worried when Tlacoch did not return. She nursed her baby, giving the infant both breasts in the hope that she would be satisfied and sleep a long time. Then Metzli left both her children with Chihuallama and took herself by canoe to

419

Coyoacan. When she arrived at the Spanish headquarters, she asked where she could find Dona Marina. Seeing that this woman in her faded blue huipil looked harmless and unarmed, the guard pointed toward the two-storied house on the north of the square, a red stone house with a wooden door and high windows covered by Spanish-style iron grill work. Metzli approached the house anxiously, yet she was certain she had been wise to come alone.

A servant woman opened the locked wooden door, looking quizzically at the thin woman with scars on her earlobes, wearing a shabby blue huipil and frayed hemp sandals. When Metzli identified herself as an old friend of Marina's, from Coatzacoalcos, the servant permitted her to enter.

The house smelled of new cedar; Metzli's sandaled feet padded across the polished floors and sank into a soft wool carpet, obviously imported, since nothing like it had been seen in Mexico before. Sunlight filtering through the windows accented the carving on the backs of four mahogany chairs with embroidered cushions, and colorful banners hung at the sides of the windows where they could be drawn closed at night. A few features of the house resembled her own: holders for pine torches protruded from the walls, and there was a niche to hold a family shrine. In this one, however, a graceful image of a mother and child replaced the squarish icons Metzli had become accustomed to. She was staring curiously at the image, wondering why the mother and baby both had something like a hat pasted behind their heads, when Marina entered.

"Metzli! It's you!" said Marina, approaching to embrace her with both arms open. Marina was barefoot, wearing the same white huipil she had worn the day before, but her hair was tied back with a twisted strip of cotton. Still, she held her shoulders erect and looked straight ahead with her shining dark eyes.

Metzli was uncertain whether to embrace the poised woman before her as the old friend Malinalli she had once been, or to kneel before her as Dona Marina, the powerful wealthy lady she had become. Metzli started to kneel, but Marina caught her hands and pulled her upward, embracing her warmly even though Metzli's return embrace felt awkward.

Metzli stared at Marina's face, seeking traces in her eyes and hair of the girl once known as Malinalli. She touched Marina's loose dark hair and stroked the side of her face. "I can't believe it's really you," she said. "Tlacoch was sure you were Malinalli, but my father said you'd died eight years ago."

"I'm glad to say I'm still alive," Marina assured her, leading Metzli toward the chairs and gesturing for her to be seated. She sat facing Metzli, clasping both Metzli's hands as she chatted rapidly in her native tongue. "I've had some amazing adventures. I'm not sure whether my mother sent me to the temple of Quetzalcoatl for my own safety, or whether it was a trick to send me into slavery and get me away from Paynala. I saw her pay the traders, so I suspect they may have kidnapped me."

Metzli's eyes widened with astonishment. "Why didn't you run away? Why didn't you come back to Paynala or Oluta?"

"A runaway slave wouldn't get far in the Maya jungles and rivers. Besides, I wouldn't return to Paynala, even if I could," Marina said. "I don't trust Anecoatl. He's an evil man, and he dominates my mother completely."

"My father doesn't trust him either," Metzli agreed. "Chihuallama and Callipopoca blame him for sending them away, and they wonder if he brought some harm to their daughter Toto. Remember her? She was Chimalli's auianime."

"I remember her well, my childhood playmate," Marina said. "When I left Paynala, Toto was very sick, but my mother was taking care of her. If Toto had died of that illness, though, surely Chihuallama and Callipopoca would have known. Toto could have met with foul play at Anecoatl's hands after he sent her parents away."

"Some of the villagers thought she'd followed Chimalli," Metzli said, "but Chimalli came to me at the temple here, and he'd lost track of her."

"I've been wondering what happened to all the people I knew in Paynala," Malinalli said. "You can see why I don't want to return there now, even if I could."

"I won't return to Oluta, either," Metzli said firmly. "My father offered to take us in, but my place is with Tlacoch, even if we starve here."

"Oh, forgive me!" Marina said in sudden embarrassment. "You must be hungry!" She yanked at a string of bells hanging on the wall, and the woman servant appeared again. "Bring my friend some chocolate," she said to the servant. "Bring tortillas and vegetables on a plate, and an extra basket for her to take home to her family." She turned again to Metzli. "The Spanish call corncakes 'tortillas,'" she said. "I'm learning their language."

Having anticipated her mistress' wishes, the servant had already prepared a quick meal for the guest. Metzli had eaten very little for several days, so the smell of frothy chocolate beaten with vanilla and honey almost made her dizzy. She sipped slowly, wanting to make it last, and nibbled her tortilla in tiny bites as if she would never have another. "I'll have to go home soon," she said to Marina. "I have a five-year-old son and a baby daughter. My baby will be getting hungry."

"Two children? That's wonderful; I envy you."

Metzli smiled, a proud mother smile, the first sign of happiness she had shown since she arrived. "They're sweet children," she said. "My son Citli was fathered by Quauhtlatoa, the Tlaxcalan prisoner of war I met in Coatzacoalcos. My daughter is Tlacoch's child. Citli isn't well, though. He's been

421

running a fever for three days. And now I'm worried about my husband. Have you seen Tlacoch? He came to Coyoacan with a delegation from Tlatelolco, and he hasn't returned."

"I've seen him and spoken to him," Marina said. "All I can tell you is that he's safe."

"That isn't enough," Metzli said impatiently. "If you know where he is, why won't you tell me?"

"If you insist on knowing, Senor Cortes is keeping the Tlatelolcans here for a while."

Metzli became visibly upset. "How could you let him do that?"

Marina, too, was becoming upset. "What do you mean, *let* him? Do you think I control my master? I've told you, I'm only a slave."

Metzli looked around the room, with its expensive imported furniture and beautifully woven banners. "Obviously, you're much more than a slave to Senor Cortes."

"Please don't get the wrong impression, Metzli. Senor Cortes has been generous to let me live in this beautiful home, but I don't own it—he does. He owns me, too, and many other slaves as well. We have nothing except what he gives us, not even our clothing, and we can't earn our freedom. Even if we have children, they belong to our masters. You may have heard that I'm Malinche's interpreter, and it's true, that's how I serve him, but I don't speak for him or tell him what to say."

"Surely you know that all the natives think you and he are partners who speak with one tongue. Many people think you have magic powers over him."

Marina sighed before responding. "I wish I did. But no, his magic comes from God, from his Christian family of the Chief God and his son Jesus Christ and the Virgin Mary who gave him birth. His critics exaggerate my influence. Sometimes Senor Cortes asks my advice, but if he doesn't, I don't offer it."

Metzli's eyes began to glisten. "I'm glad for your success in the world, Malinalli," she said. "You say you have nothing except what Senor Cortes gives you, but even that seems like a fortune compared to what my family and neighbors have. I have nothing except Tlacoch and my children, not even food or clean water to feed them. Please help me to keep the little I have."

"I do pity you, Metzli," Marina said sympathetically. "I'd help if I could, but Senor Cortes is angry with Cuauhtemoc and all his followers. I can't go against my master's wishes."

"You know it's unfair for him to punish all of us. Even Callipopoca and Chihuallama are starving. Did you know they're here with me and Tlacoch?"

"I've seen Callipopoca, during the fighting in Tenochtitlan. I hoped you'd bring Chihuallama when you came to see me, but of course, she must be watching your children." She motioned to

422

the household servant, who was standing in the doorway, to bring the extra basket of food. "Take these tortillas and vegetables to them; I'll try to get more for you if I can."

Metzli rubbed tears away as she took the food. "I have no pride left," she sobbed. "If I did, I wouldn't take any gifts from the Spanish conquerors. Tlacoch and I were at the feast of Toxcatl in Tenochtitlan when the Spanish soldiers slaughtered the innocent worshipers there. We've never recovered from that experience. It was horrible!"

"That was Alvarado's doing. Senor Cortes was very angry with him over that, but Alvarado is hard to control."

"Other Spaniards have been just as cruel. You can see why some of the natives hate all Spaniards. Even now, Spanish soldiers prevent us from scavenging for food. They rape and enslave our women; they keep our men from repairing the aqueducts."

"Some men on both sides have been cruel," Marina reminded her. "War brings out the worst in people. Haven't you and I seen many cruelties done in the name of Huitzilopochtli? Besides, not all Spaniards are cruel. For example, Father Olmedo is always kind and helpful. He says Christians often fall short of their ideals, but evil ones will be punished and good ones rewarded in the heavenly kingdom."

"So you've adopted their religion, too? Don't you believe the teachings of Quetzalcoatl any more?"

"I believe most of the same things, but now I know more. Quetzalcoatl taught people not to make human sacrifices; so did Christ. The priests of Quetzalcoatl taught people to be artisans instead of warriors; that's what Cortes wants to do now that we're living in peace. Christianity is a good religion, Metzli. I hope you'll let Father Olmedo tell you more about it."

"I'm not interested in Christianity," Metzli declared. "I'd feel like a traitor to my own people, as if I were betraying the priestesses who taught us about the gods and all the beauty they bring to the world."

"Christians have equally beautiful teachings," Marina said defensively. "They also preach forgiveness of others for their sins. When we can forgive others, God can forgive us."

Metzli stood to go. "You've changed, Malinalli—or perhaps I should call you La Malinche now, 'the Woman of Cortes.' You've been among the Spaniards so long that you talk like them and defend them. How can I forgive the unforgivable injuries done to my family and my countrymen?"

"If you can't forgive those who injured you, at least forgive me and try to understand why I live among the Spaniards. Don't blame me for the fall of the Aztecs and imply that I'm a traitress. I had no choice."

"I don't mean to offend you," Metzli said sincerely. "I came prepared to beg and humble myself to you if necessary. She kneeled before Marina's chair, touching the floor and then her tongue with her fingers. "I'm begging now. Everyone says Malinche listens to you. Tell him to release my husband!" Her voice raised to a high pitch; her eyes burned red as she looked upward into Marina's face.

Upset by Metzli's imperious tone, Marina stood up, like a queen indicating the interview was over. "Are you giving me an order?" she said icily. "I've told you, I don't give orders to Senor Cortes, and I don't take orders from others, not even old friends who presume on their friendship."

"I see you've become proud and vain," Metzli said, trembling with anger but remaining on her knees, settling back on her heels and looking up defiantly. "I was afraid you'd be this way. Now that you have money and power, you'll trample on your old friends and all your countrymen. You'll desert us for the enemy." She stopped abruptly; her lips tightened; her eyes closed as if she needed all her energy for self-control.

"Who are you to criticize?" Marina retorted. "Didn't you desert your family to follow an enemy—a Tlaxcalan? You accuse me of something you did yourself! Yet you followed an enemy of your own free will, and I was given away as tribute."

Metzli sighed deeply and sniffed as she wiped bitter tears from her eyes. "You're right, Malinalli. I just heard an echo of my father's voice in my own," she said unhappily. "For years he's been chiding me for consorting with the enemy, because I mated with a Tlaxcalan. Now I'm saying similar words to you. I have no right to judge you. Please forgive me."

"I hope you'll forgive me too, dear Metzli," Marina said tenderly, extending her hands and pulling her old friend to her feet. "I spoke too harshly. No one can blame you for trying to save your husband. Both of us know how it feels to be abandoned, to ache with loneliness, and then to find one man who cares for us." Marina cradled Metzli's head on her shoulder and stroked her hair. "The main reason I love Hernan is that he treats me like a person, even though he could sell me or give me away like an old rag. If I *were* free to choose, I'd still follow him."

"I spoke too harshly, too," Metzli said contritely as she embraced her old friend. "I know you aren't to blame for all the suffering, but I'm almost crazy with worry."

"I'd worry too, if the man I love was in chains, or if I had a sick child. I can't promise anything, but I'll try to talk to Hernan tonight. Sometimes after he's lost his temper, he cools down and changes his mind."

"Oh, thank you, Malinalli!" Metzli cried. "That's all I ask. I'd be so grateful." She hesitated for a moment, then added, "I'd prefer you didn't tell Tlacoch I came here to beg for his life."

"He'll never know," Marina said. "But remember, I can't promise anything." As she walked with Metzli to the door, she confessed to this former confidante what she had been unable to say to Father Olmedo. "I'm not sure Hernan still loves me." Metzli fell silent. It would not be wise to express to her old friend Malinalli the pity she felt for her at that moment.

* * *

That afternoon Marina walked to the government offices where Cortes was laboring over maps and letters. She said some sympathetic words about his working too hard and invited him to spend the night with her. She had just washed her hair and twined a sweet-smelling yellow blossom into the dark tresses. The thought of exploring the mysteries of her hair amid fragrant flowers tempted him; her candid seductiveness surprised and flattered him. He left the office early that evening, walking directly to the red stone house on the north of the square.

Marina had placed flowers and sweet-scented pine branches around the house and dressed prettily in a new huipil. When Hernan arrived, she tendered him all the comforts and pleasures he relished in a woman's art, beginning with a carefully planned meal she had cooked herself, ending with a playful pull toward the stairs leading to her bedroom.

"Do you remember your promise to give me a child when the conquest was over?" she asked teasingly. "I'm twenty years old now, and I'm still not a mother. My childhood friend Metzli came to see me today; she already has two children."

While still on the stairway, Hernan grabbed her around the waist and kissed her, exciting all the old passion, sending a gratifying thrill through her body. "If you get pregnant tonight," he whispered, "so be it."

Marina unbuttoned his black silk shirt and kissed Hernan's hairy chest. "I'd treasure your child even more than the beautiful house you've built and furnished for me," she said truthfully. For the rest of their night together, she nuzzled and kissed, stroked and soothed, cooed and sighed, laughed and wept with joy. And Hernan ran his strong hands over her body appreciatively, as he used to do.

The lovers grew excited and stimulated, then relaxed and amiable. Hernan was willing to listen to any appeal for justice, to hear any petition for the relief of suffering, to grant almost any favor. He no longer viewed the Tlatelolcans as important, and when his lover suggested that the prisoners might be more helpful to him back in Tlatelolco, he agreed. "Anything you wish, *mi vida*," he said. "They can leave tomorrow."

When morning came, Marina dressed and went to the cell where the Tlatelolcans were being held. She greeted the guard with a warm smile and told him she had a message from Cortes to release the prisoners. "The Captain General says he's grateful to you," Marina told the Tlatelolcan delegation in Nahuatl. "He's been considering what you said, and he thinks it's probably true that your people have been mistreated. You may leave now. Tell your people to return to their houses in Tlatelolco, to reoccupy and rebuild that quarter of the city. He offers you his protection to live in peace. But tell your other leaders that no one may settle around the temple area in Tenochtitlan. General Cortes wishes only the teules to occupy that quarter."

The following day one more rainfall came, blessing the Tlatelolcans with enough drinking water to sustain them while they rebuilt the aqueduct. The people gradually returned to their houses, unmolested by any Spaniards from that day forward, so Tlacoch and the other leaders considered their mission to Coyoacan a success. Still, they complained about the haughty La Malinche, not realizing she had secretly helped them.

Little Citli recovered with the help of the tortillas and vegetables his mother brought from Coyoacan, and Metzli considered his recovery a miracle. Chihuallama was fascinated with Metzli's tale about Malinalli's experiences in the Maya lands, but she had no interest in visiting Malinalli. In Chihuallama's view, though she never said so to Metzli, Malinalli had become and would remain a person who consorted with the invaders—a traitress.

Although she was losing any hope of gaining understanding or acceptance among the natives, Marina, too, had salvaged a miracle from the pile of events that had begun to restore normalcy to the devastated land. Soon after that night with Cortes, she began feeling sick every morning; her breasts became tender and swollen. Her friends Dona Isabel and Dona Luisa confirmed that she had entered a world where only women can go. She had entered a sisterhood of painful satisfactions and joyful sorrows, of unpredictable delights and unavoidable disappointments. She would be a mother before the year 4 Rabbit came to an end.

* * *

Catalina's arrival in Mexico that year spoiled many of her husband's plans. She arrived unannounced from Cuba in midsummer, bringing her mother, the domineering La Marcayda; her brother, Juan Suarez; and Juan's family, which by then included several children as well as his wife.

Cortes tried not to show his annoyance and to make the best of a bad situation, offering apartments to Catalina's family in the complex west of the Coyoacan square. He couldn't deny Catalina's grievance about his neglecting her. She had been embarrassed, she said, when the husbands of several of her friends had summoned their wives to New Spain. How could she admit to these women that her own husband, the great Captain General who ordered all the conquistadors to bring their wives from Spain and Cuba, had neglected to send for his own wife?

Cortes apologized to Catalina and his in-laws. He had been extremely busy, he explained, preparing an excursion to Panuco, the region north of Vera Cruz, to establish a settlement in that territory before Francisco de Garay, Jamaica's wealthy governor, could get a foothold there. Through the instigation of Diego Velasquez, by then Cortes' most implacable enemy, Garay had received authorization in 1521 from Bishop Juan de Fonseca of the Council of the Indies to settle in the Panuco region. Cortes' scouts had reported that Garay sent two preliminary expeditions. Then in June of 1522 Garay sailed from Jamaica himself, heading an expedition of nine ships, 850 men, and 144 horses. Garay was surprised to get fierce resistance from the Huastec tribes, who soon placed several bearded heads on the skull racks beside their temples. He appealed to Cortes for help, but Cortes debated whether to send help or discourage him from settling there.

Catalina's brother Juan relayed some gossip that had been floating around Cuba about Diego Velasquez and Bishop Fonseca. Velasquez had married the Bishop's niece, Petronila de Fonseca, who many believed was actually the Bishop's illegitimate daughter. Juan believed that explained why the Bishop of Burgos had sided with Velasquez in getting permission for Garay to settle Panuco. Furthermore, the conspirators Velasquez and Fonseca had persuaded a regent of King Charles to issue an order for the arrest of Cortes on grounds of disloyalty to the Spanish crown as well as the Cuban governor. Because Juan knew these charges against Hernan were false, he had severed all ties with his former friend Diego Velasquez and decided to leave Cuba. He hoped to start over in New Spain.

Catalina didn't want to hear about her husband's military or political problems and his plans to rebuild Mexican cities. She felt crowded in the small apartment Cortes had assigned her. She insisted that he show her the inside of the red stone house on the north side of the square. Cortes tried not to reveal his resentment as he sent a messenger to ask Marina to leave the red stone house. He reasoned that Catalina was asking no more than any wife would—living arrangements according to her husband's station. So he cleared the red stone house of its original occupant and, the following day, showed Catalina through it.

"This is a much better house for the family of the governor of New Spain," Catalina pronounced with satisfaction. "This is the one I want."

Cortes reminded her that his title was not *governor*, but

427

adelantado, and she should not put on airs.

"*Me* put on airs?" she laughed. "I've seen the way people treat you when you ride around town, like a king or a sultan, with a whole retinue of attendants—judges preceding you carrying their maces, four *caciques* on horseback, a whole parade of civil servants, chaplains, and petty officials of one kind or another. As you go by, all the Indians prostrate themselves. They seem to worship you."

"That's their way of showing respect, not worship," Cortes explained. "If you intend to live here, you'll need to learn more about the Indian customs."

"Nonsense!" Catalina scoffed. "They'll need to learn about ours! I think I'll throw out these woven draperies—too Indian looking. I'll get some damask drapes imported from Spain."

"Whatever you wish," Cortes said through clenched teeth.

"Then there's one more thing I'd wish," she said as she climbed the stairs to look at the bedrooms above. "Now that I'm here, I hope you'll give up your Indian women. My mother has heard that you keep several of them around here, which could be embarrassing for us all. I'm not complaining about your previous adulteries, assuming you made proper confession, of course. I can understand your need for women when you were far away from home. 'Any port in a storm,' as the saying goes. But I want you to know, Hernan, that *I* have been faithful to my marriage vows."

They had entered the main bedroom by the time her chatter stopped. She pointed to the petlatl on the floor. "We'll get rid of that thing and get a proper bed," she said. Then she turned to her husband and embraced him tightly. "I've missed you so much, my Darling," she said. "I want to be a true wife to you, beginning right now if you wish—right there on the floor if you wish." She kissed him passionately on the mouth.

Cortes returned her kiss by pecking her on the cheek half-heartedly. "Not now," he said, his hands on her waist gently pushing her away. "Let's wait until we can get a proper bed imported from Spain. I do think you're right about that. You may have to teach me how to be a proper Spanish gentleman again. I've been in the wars too long."

Cortes left the disappointed Catalina making plans for redecorating the red stone house. Walking back to his office with his eyes downcast, speaking to no one, Hernan felt a spiteful gladness that he had not allowed that obnoxious female, that totally disagreeable woman, that damnable intruder, to profane the petlatl he had shared so happily with Marina.

* * *

Three Flemish monks arrived that summer, members of the

realistic Franciscan order, but the Indians fled from them and couldn't understand their strange language. The friars set up a *doctrina* or school in Texcoco to teach religion, but they also perceived the language barrier as their most important challenge, and they studied as hard to master the native tongues as their pupils did to master Spanish.

Disappointed in receiving so little help, Father Olmedo continued his work in Coyoacan, asking Marina to translate. She was glad to keep busy during the early months of her pregnancy, and she wanted to keep as far away as possible from the Spanish woman who now occupied the red stone house.

Catalina began to suffer from asthma shortly after she arrived. Members of her household became accustomed to her sniffling and sneezing, attributing it to the high altitude or native plants. She eliminated all flowers and pine boughs from the house and ran up a medicine bill of 172 gold pesos by having an apothecary come to the house frequently. She spent most of her days inside, indulging in listless self-pity.

Catalina and Hernan quarreled about her treatment of the servants, her disdain for unfamiliar food, her tendency to feign illness and demand pity. Hernan also resented her extravagances, clothing and furniture all imported from Spain, and even the medicines she ordered—"just to get attention," Hernan said.

"Attention I never get from my husband," she sniffed in reply. But Hernan, as if to prove she was right, used every quarrel between them as a reason to leave the house and spend the night elsewhere.

By October, Catalina was dead. Officially, the doctors certified the cause as asthma, but suspicions abounded. Her brother Juan suspected the apothecary had been bribed to slip something lethal into the various medicines. Her mother, La Marcayda, accused Hernan of strangling Catalina during a quarrel. La Marcayda left for Cuba soon after, threatening to relay her suspicions to Governor Velasquez.

Cortes, after authorizing an investigation to clear himself of wrongdoing in his wife's death, resumed his plan to halt the incursions of Francisco de Garay in Panuco. In November he joined forces with Pedro Alvarado, who had gone ahead to fight the Huastecs and rescue the scattered forces of the Garay army. Garay, accustomed to the easy conquest of Jamaica and other islands, was stunned by the Mexican resistance and grateful for Alvarado's help.

* * *

While Cortes was away, Marina gave birth to a son. Hernan had instructed her to name their first son *Martin Cortes*, after his father. He had quietly re-installed Marina in the red stone house, where she lived until Martin was two years old.

Cortes had pacified Juan Suarez by giving him an encomienda, or trusteeship, that took him and his family away from Coyoacan. The encomienda system, established by Cortes in Mexico in 1522, was controversial even in Spain, where it originated. The king and many other Spaniards were horrified by the abuses in the West Indies, where whole communities had been given to individual Spanish encomenderos. Supposedly the encomenderos were entitled to extract labor or produce from the Indians in their encomienda, in return for "protection" and indoctrination into the Catholic faith. Yet the forced slavery that resulted had decimated the populations in the West Indies, and in 1520 the Spanish crown had declared all Indians free vassals of the king.

The Indians accepted the encomienda system at first because it resembled that of the calpulli, which meant "big house" in Nahuatl. The calpulli was one of twenty sub-groups of Mexican society that owned land collectively and distributed the wealth from the land among their members. Each calpulli had a war leader, its own god, ceremonies, and temple. Each member was expected to contribute a share of his crops for the good of the whole community, to maintain the temple and the telpochcalli. The Indians sometimes complained about the system, but on the whole they considered it fair. In the hands of the Spaniards, however, it became a means for robbing them.

Cortes wrote to King Charles in May of 1522 that, while he deplored the abuses he had seen in the West Indies, he saw no alternative to such an arrangement in New Spain. He argued that, since the conquistadors could support themselves only in warfare, they had only two alternatives: either enslaving the natives, which the king clearly deplored, or taking a small share of the tribute from the king's Indian vassals in return for managing the community and collecting the royal tribute.

Satisfied that he had made his case for the system, Cortes began giving out encomiendas in August, the first one to Pedro de Alvarado for Segura de la Frontera about thirty miles southeast of Tlaxcala. Others followed in rapid succession, with Cortes keeping the most fertile and productive communities for himself. But he also used encomiendas to reward his captains, some loyal soldiers, and even the enemies he wished to pacify.

By June of 1523, Cortes had assuaged Francisco de Garay with an encomienda, and the two were becoming friends. Although Cortes received a message from the king forbidding him to grant encomiendas, the system remained in place. His apparent defiance of royal orders, however, gave fuel to the fires of criticism that had begun to blaze around the name of Cortes.

In November, 1523, Cortes welcomed Francisco de Garay to Coyoacan. Garay liked Cortes so well that he agreed to an engagement between Garay's eldest son and Cortes' Cuban natural daughter Catalina Pizarro, named after his mother. Garay wrote out a will naming Cortes as executor, then accompanied his host to mass on Christmas Eve. On Christmas day, Garay died of pneumonia. As accusations of murder were again mounted against him, Cortes began to have dreams about circling vultures.

Chapter 29

The Last Expedition Together

By 1524 or 6 Flint, a new capital called Mexico City had risen from the ashes of Tenochtitlan. Many Mexicans considered it even more splendid. In the two and a half years since the defeat of the Triple Alliance, native laborers had built over forty thousand houses equal to the best the Aztec nobility had built and, for ordinary citizens, over a hundred thousand houses that everyone agreed were better than before. About thirty thousand families now occupied Tlatelolco, and the boundaries of formerly separate cities were beginning to blend into one metropolis encompassing Tenochtitlan, Tlatelolco, Tacuba, Coyoacan, and Xochimilco. The central square where the teocalli had once dominated the landscape of Tenochtitlan, bounded by its snake wall, had become a plaza mayor, or city center, for Mexico City. Where the great cues dedicated to Huitzilopochtli and Tlaloc had once stood, masons and carpenters had begun building a cathedral dedicated to St. Francis.

In those early post-conquest years, Cortes exercised freely the powers given to him by the Royal Court at Valladolid in October, 1522. The king's decision in his favor also granted him the titles of Governor of New Spain, Captain-General, and Chief Justice. Moreover, the decision represented a triumph over his enemies Velasquez and Fonseca, who had attempted unsuccessfully to discredit him in the king's eyes.

The Spanish settlers as well as indigenous people equated the government of New Spain with the personality of Cortes. He pursued strategies of benevolent dictatorship. Continuing the policy that had served him well in military campaigns, he placated his enemies and won their grudging loyalty by treating them generously after defeating them. He appointed many former Aztec officials to positions of authority with enough prestige to keep them from rebelling, though less than they formerly enjoyed. One of these was a grandson of Axayacatl, Huanitzin, who had held the prestigious office of Cihuacoatl under Moctezuma. The title *Cihuacoatl*, meaning "Woman Snake," came from a long tradition associating the emperor's chief adviser with the earth-goddess. Cortes allowed him to keep his title and rank, equivalent to that of a Captain-General in the Spanish army, and gave him responsibility for restoring population in the lake cities and reorganizing the calpulli system. Gradually the social organization regained stability and prosperity. Merchants plied their trade safely; canoes and acali barges skimmed the lake waters busily every day; fishermen filled their nets and sold their hauls; artisans, silversmiths, and stonecutters established shops in their homes and marketplaces. Farmers sowed their traditional cornfields and beanfields, but many also experimented with new plants and trees imported from Spain and the West Indies, such as wheat, grape vines, and sugar cane. In addition, some were learning to raise sheep, hogs, and goats, alleviating their fears of famine and thus reducing their anxious dependency upon the whims of rain and sun gods.

Controlling the influx of adventurers from Spain proved more difficult for the new governor than rebuilding. A swarm of predatory hidalgos, thirsty to share in the spoils of a victory they had made no sacrifices to attain, came to seek fortunes in precious minerals, land, and exploitable cheap labor. Cortes, having seen the effects of such greed in the West Indies, was determined to prevent settlers from destroying the Mexicans as they had the Arawaks and Tainos. He hoped at least to instill a philosophy of *noblesse oblige*, a paternal attitude toward the natives whose labor constituted the most genuine and permanent wealth of the country.

Some of the immigrants reminded him of La Marcayda and her ambitious daughters who had come to Hispaniola seeking husbands in 1509. Such a settler was Comendador Leonel de Cervantes, who established a virtual clan in 1524 when he arrived in Mexico with his seven daughters and promptly married them off to the most prosperous of the conquistadors.

Cortes himself remained determinedly unmarried, not wanting to repeat his unhappy experience in the West Indies when the laws and religious customs had bound him to Catalina Suarez, but his heart had bound him to a Cuban woman. This woman, whose name he could not even mention honorably in his letters to the king, had given him a daughter he yearned to acknowledge publicly. That daughter, Catalina Pizarro, was reaching betrothal age—around twelve years old, if he recalled correctly. The arrangement he had made for her to marry Francisco de Garay's eldest son would probably not materialize now that Garay was dead, but he hoped to find another prospect for her within a year or two. He was considering bringing her and her mother to Mexico, but he sensed that she and Marina might be uncomfortable with each other.

Cortes found himself again in conflict with the magnetic pull

433

of women on his heart and the dictates of his culture, reinforced by strong Catholic principles that he endorsed both publicly and personally. He loved Marina; of that he was sure. He also loved the son she had given him—little Martin, whose affectionate hugs brought him great paternal joy. Yet marriage was a different matter, so swathed in ceremony, so entangled with economic considerations, so dependent on social approval for its proper functioning. He was now free to marry Marina—or, for that matter, to marry his Cuban mistress or Moctezuma's daughter Isabel—and legitimize at least one of his natural children. Yet he saw himself as a man who could love many women and keep them all satisfied. He could marry only one.

In the previous year, Cortes had grown tired of pressures not only from single women seeking an eligible male, but also from parents seeking a man of wealth and connections for their daughters. He had already decided to resolve that problem by sending to his father in Spain a power of attorney with which to arrange a marriage contract. He specified the kind of bride his father should seek for him: attractive, educated, spirited, sociable, amiable, and raised from birth in the Catholic faith. She should also be connected with a reputable family in Spain, preferably possessed of a substantial dowry with which to advance his interests, yet willing to raise a family in Mexico.

It was a large order, but Martin Cortes de Monroy felt confident that his now-famous son would be considered fine husband material by the best families in Spain. Now that the mischief of Velasquez and Fonseca had been exposed, and Hernan had been vindicated in the king's eyes, the elder Martin could turn his energies toward arranging a suitable union for Hernan. He wrote to Hernan that he was making progress, but even if it took a year or two, he would personally interview each prospect.

Far more welcome than the fortune-seekers and husband-hunters in 1524 were twelve holy men sent by King Charles at the request of Cortes. As Cortes had wisely requested, these men were Franciscans, members of a mendicant order dedicated to poverty and humble service. Taking their vows seriously, they arrived in Vera Cruz wearing only coarsely woven, simple robes. Under the leadership of Fray Martin de Valencia, they obeyed a pious impulse that proved to be a brilliant strategy.

Nothing the friars could have done could have better served to arouse curiosity and veneration among the Mexicans. Refusing any assistance other than a guide and the simplest of food along the way, they walked barefoot in their coarse robes for three hundred miles from Vera Cruz to Mexico City. Not even on the steep, rocky mountain trails did they wear sandals; not even in the face of cold, biting winds in the mountain passes did they cover their bodies with more clothing than the humblest peasants would wear.

Cortes led a delegation to meet the friars, who had been affectionately dubbed "the twelve apostles" by messengers from the garrison at Vera Cruz who rode ahead on horseback to notify him. Cortes himself walked on foot to meet the Franciscans, though he dressed with his customary understated elegance wearing boots, his favorite silk shirt, and a broad-brimmed hat to shade his eyes from the summer sunlight. He took with him a crowd of attendants and soldiers, as many caciques or native leaders as he could assemble, and his prisoner Cuauhtemoc, assuming quite rightly that the emperor Cuauhtemoc and other Mexicans would be impressed with these unusual Europeans. As Cortes and his party moved through the city streets, hundreds of other residents, both Spanish and native, joined the procession.

When the twelve thin, ragged men appeared on the causeway, Cortes fell to his knees and kissed their hands. Cuauhtemoc and the caciques stared with utter amazement at this spectacle. These pale, tattered, wiry men, with their dirt-caked feet and partially shaven heads, seemed to emanate a radiance of devotion, a divine glow that awed everyone in their presence. Even the proud General Cortes, regarded by the natives with near-godlike admiration, showed deference to these beggars.

When the soldiers attending Cortes immediately followed his example, the awestruck Mexicans also knelt in profound respect. The friars passed among the crowd touching heads and shoulders, making gestures of blessing and gracious acceptance of the homage. Unlike haughty dignitaries of the former emperors, these men kept their heads at a downward tilt, their eyes directly looking into the faces of those who honored them as if returning their respect. In this way they accepted the crowd's devotion—not for themselves, for they were genuinely humble men, but as a sign that their mission in New Spain was accepted and welcomed.

Armed with nothing but their vast love for humanity, their energetic devotion to their cause, and a deep faith that enabled them to endure hardship without complaint, this little band of holy men began to conquer the hearts and imaginations of the people they served. Everyone present that morning, when the friars' long pilgrimage from the sea ended and their missionary work began, knew that this conquest would endure.

The friars set to work with zeal, walking from village to village conducting baptisms, confirmations, marriages, and religious instruction. Within a year they had baptized over a million natives and established three major doctrinas to train more friars and nuns. They had made considerable progress toward replacing the native priests and tecuhtlis as leaders of the villages. They tended and healed the sick, comforted the dying, buried the dead, and guided the living by teaching principles of monogamy, repentance, and forgiveness. They taught of a

Heaven in which virtue would be rewarded and of a Hell where evil would be punished, rejecting the Aztec hereafter in which good deeds played no part. Yet they also taught practical arts for daily living: European techniques of carpentry, masonry, weaving, dyeing, ceramics, and agriculture.

The friars organized the Indians of their parishes into brotherhoods or *cofradias*, similar to the calpulli with which the natives were familiar. They also became advocates for the natives in their disputes with Spanish landowners and overseers. Later on, some abuses would take place. Some friars would exploit native labor to build and maintain churches; some priests would abuse their power to inflict cruel punishments; some clerics would indulge in acts of corruption and hypocrisy. But the initial efforts of the Franciscans were labors of love. In those early years, the church secured its place in Mexican hearts so firmly that it became like a child conceived in rape but reared by an adoring family who never considered the child's origins once it was loved.

* * *

Marina witnessed the entrance of the friars into Mexico City carrying her two-year-old son Martin on her hip. Speaking in Nahuatl, she whispered into the boy's ear when Cortes knelt before the mendicants, "See, Martin? Your father's a great man, a tecuhtli of all those other men. Those men in the brown robes are fathers, too, fathers of the church. Even powerful tlatoanis kneel to them." Martin wriggled in Marina's arms and poked his fingers playfully into her eyes and mouth. He did not seem impressed with witnessing interactions between the powerful and the humble, or even with seeing some of those rare human beings who were shaping the destiny of the world.

"Oh, you want to play the face game?" Marina asked in Nahuatl, restraining Martin's fingers by enclosing them briefly in her fist. "Where's your eyes? Where's your nose? Where's your mouth? Your chin? Your ears?" With his gurgling baby laugh, Martin correctly pointed to each feature as his mother named it. Then she shifted into Spanish, asking Martin where he'd find his *ojos*, his *boca*, his *orejas*.

"You're getting so heavy," Marina said, continuing in Spanish. "Such a big boy! Want to get down now?"

Coming up beside them in the crowd, a captain of the Spanish army offered to help. "Want me to hold the boy for you? He really shouldn't miss this."

Marina looked into the full-bearded face of the tall, muscular Spaniard, observing how his brown hair curled around his ears. His sun-tanned skin showed faint pock marks, evidence that he had survived smallpox. "You can hold him higher than I can," she said in Spanish, handing the boy to the captain with a smile. "His name's Martin."

"Mine is Juan," the captain said to Martin. "Up you go, Little One!" He lifted Martin straight into the air with brown, brawny arms and held him there kicking and giggling, both of them clearly enjoying the boy's trust in the soldier's strength. Then he shifted Martin to one shoulder to let him watch the friars passing through the crowd.

Marina searched the captain's face intently, struggling to place it in her memory. "I think I've seen you before," she said. "Are you with General Cortes?" She fell in step with him as they moved slowly with the crowd following the friars along the causeway toward Coyoacan.

Juan shifted Martin's legs so they straddled both shoulders for balance. He clasped the boy's hands under his thick beard, tolerating the child's chokehold as a docile horse might tolerate an amateur rider's grip on the reins. "I hoped you might remember me," he said amiably. "You're Marina, aren't you? I had the pleasure of guarding you once."

"Of course! Juan Jaramillo!" Marina exclaimed, blushing. "On the Night of Sorrows. Sorry I didn't recognize you sooner."

"That was three years ago," Juan said understandingly. "The past two years I've been serving with Alvarado. Just got back from Panuco. I've probably changed a lot."

"You've grown a longer beard," Marina smiled.

"You've grown more beautiful," Juan said matter-of-factly. "Your Spanish has improved, too."

Marina realized that Juan must have overheard her baby words to Martin. "I know a little more than my son does," she laughed. "He's catching up to me, though."

"Martin's a cute kid," Juan said. "Has some lucky man married you since I saw you last?"

"I'm not married," Marina said candidly. "Martin is a love child."

It was Juan's turn to feel embarrassed. He had assumed that, once the conquest was over, Cortes would reward Marina by restoring her freedom. There had been enough time for her to marry and bear a child since he'd last seen her, so his mistake was understandable. He had heard that Cortes had brought his wife to Mexico, though she died shortly afterward, and he had also heard that Senora Cortes had sent her rival Marina away. But this boy must be Cortes's son, he concluded, and perhaps Marina had chosen to stay with her master. "Sorry; my mistake," he said awkwardly, then tried to explain: "I thought you'd be free by now, but I guess you're still serving General Cortes?"

"Martin and I live in the Cortes household," she said simply; then she fell silent, her mind too deep in thought to guide her tongue. Juan walked quietly beside her, stealing a glance occasionally at her lovely profile.

Martin was becoming restless by the time they reached the square in Coyoacan. The new friars were entering the church, followed by an even larger crowd than the one on the causeway. Marina paused at the red stone house facing the church across the square, then stretched her arms upward. "Come with me now, Martin." When her son fell into her arms with a playful giggle, she thanked Juan for holding him.

"Will I see you again?" Juan looked at Marina with intense interest that made her feel flattered. Yet she also felt sorry for this man, who showed signs of hope that would have to be discouraged.

"I don't get out very often," she said evasively. "Caring for my son keeps me busy."

"When do you go to market? Perhaps I could escort you, or even bring some things back for you."

Marina smiled at his persistence. "You're very kind," she said, "but I can't accept. Even if my master didn't object to my seeing you, my heart belongs to him."

That night other soldiers told Juan to forget her, because Marina belonged to Cortes in more ways than one. He could see the wisdom of not pursuing her, but he knew that forgetting her would not be easy.

As for Marina, she kept thinking of Juan Jaramillo after he had gone. He reminded her of someone else she had known, a long time ago. The thought teased her for many hours as she went through her afternoon and evening routines of playing with Martin, feeding him, and putting him to bed. It wasn't Juan Jaramillo's physical appearance that stirred old memories, but something in his manner, his interest in her, his desire to see her again. Then she remembered the young slave she had met in Tabasco who had sought permission from two masters—his and hers—just to spend time with her. He had walked from his master's plantation to hers after a long day's work, just to see her. He had spent many evenings patiently teaching her Mayan words, had even tried to buy her freedom after he himself had become free. What was his name? She chided herself for not remembering, as if her forgetting showed lack of appreciation for all he had done for her. What *was* his name? She remembered only bits and fragments about him. He had been born in the days of the nemontemi, when only the bleakest future could be predicted for him. How unjust, she thought. His name had branded that curse of low expectations upon him, just as surely as the "g" branded the war slaves of the Spaniards. That memory provided the clue she needed; his name was Nemon.

As she retired to her petlatl alone that night, she thought of both Juan Jaramillo and Nemon. She wondered if she would ever have a man of her own, as her mother did when she first married. Would she ever have one man who wanted to be with her every day, to belong to her as she did to him, to love her above all others, to forsake all others for her? Many times Hernan had professed to love her, but he kept his own apartment and visited her and Martin only when he wanted to enjoy their company. For the two years while she had been breast-feeding Martin, she knew it was best to avoid any chance of another pregnancy. But now Martin was weaned, and she could welcome Hernan to her bed whenever she could entice him there. Hernan could still be a tender lover; he could still rouse her passions; but she knew she was only one of many women who could rouse his.

Why could she not be content with her life, reconcile herself to the philandering ways of men as so many other women did? Many other women would probably envy her, not only for the fine house she lived in or the silverware and fine tableware with which she served her guests, but also for the opportunities she had for adventure and achievement far beyond the ordinary, more than most men experience in a lifetime. Even to have been loved at all, with such ardor, set her apart from most Nahua women she had known. Then the wise words of her father emerged from the depths of her consciousness, as they had done so often since his death. "Never want what you can never have, Malinalli. Wanting too much is the path to misery." She lay on her petlatl, staring into the darkness. Loneliness, she wanted to tell her father, was another path to misery.

* * *

Trouble was brewing in Honduras, trouble that would lead Cortes to make some uncharacteristically poor judgments and bad mistakes. It would also take Cortes and Marina on their last journey together and bring closure to the life Marina had known as a child in Coatzacoalcos.

Cortes was not a man to lead a sedentary life, even a prosperous one. In his heart's battles with itself, exploration and adventure would always win over comfort and stability. The age in which he lived was infused with a spirit of discovery; the excitement of new challenges and the lure of exotic places charged the very air he breathed.

News had reached both old Spain and New Spain that the crew of Ferdinand Magellan had sailed around the globe. King Charles wondered if a shorter route could be found, and in June of 1523 he had written Cortes asking him to look for a strait connecting the familiar Ocean Sea and the mysterious new ocean that lay to the west of New Spain. Cortes knew that another ocean lay to the west; he had explored the region of Michoacan, whose inhabitants had voluntarily become vassals shortly after Tenochtitlan fell. He had led an expedition to the western coast and even named an inlet there after himself.

The prospect of finding a strait or passage between the oceans intrigued Cortes. The coast south of the Yucatan also held some alluring prospects for colonization, though he had little hope of finding gold or silver in those limestone flats. Therefore in January of 1524, he sent one of his most able captains, Cristobal de Olid, to seek such a strait and also establish a colony in the territory vaguely known as Las Hibueras, or Honduras. Olid had served as a key commander in the siege of Tenochtitlan and had accompanied Cortes to Michoacan. Cortes trusted him.

Olid took five ships and a brigantine, carrying four hundred soldiers, and stopped in Cuba to pick up more horses and supplies for colonization. While there, Olid encountered Governor Diego Velasquez, whose bitterness against Cortes had reached the proportions of a vendetta. Velasquez's enmity was gnawing at his soul like an incurable disease consuming his body, and he acted with the desperation of a man with only a few months to live.

Velasquez had suffered a devastating blow when the court of King Charles at Valladolid had ruled against him and in favor of Cortes. To his tortured mind, Cortes had betrayed him by establishing the colony at Vera Cruz in the name of the king instead of Velasquez, the benefactor who originally sent him there. Still stinging from the ingratitude Cortes had shown him, and blind to his own history of double-dealing, Velasquez suggested that Olid might do to Cortes in Honduras what Cortes had successfully done to Velasquez in Vera Cruz.

Olid had been much attached to Cortes while under his command in the siege of Tenochtitlan, but he was tempted to emulate his commander. His dislike of being governed exceeded his ability to govern, yet he nevertheless craved an opportunity to rule. When he arrived in Honduras in May, he followed the advice of Velasquez, declared himself an independent agent, and established the settlement of Triunfo de la Cruz.

The plotting in Cuba had been overheard by Gonzalo de Salazar, a royal agent appointed by the crown to assist Cortes as governor in New Spain. When Salazar arrived in Mexico City, he informed Cortes. Angry over Olid's betrayal, Cortes immediately dispatched a kinsman, Francisco de las Casas, to go to Honduras and quell the rebellion. (Cortes' kinsman was not related to the Dominican Bartolome de las Casas, who had made a career of denouncing the mistreatment of the Indians by the colonists.)

Francisco de las Casas proceeded with two well-manned vessels, soon reaching the settlement of San Gil de Buenavista near the south shore of the Gulf of Honduras. This settlement had been established the year before by Gil Gonzalez de Avila, but Olid had captured it, imprisoned its founder, and killed Avila's nephew, among others who resisted. When a storm caused the ship of Las Casas to founder, Olid captured him and other survivors of the shipwreck. Olid forced the survivors to swear on a Bible not to oppose him, and since they had been kept out in cold weather for three days without water and food, many agreed reluctantly. Forced loyalty weakens quickly, however, and soon these resentful subjects, along with others, turned against him.

Olid took his two eminent prisoners, Francisco de Las Casas and Gil Gonzales de Avila, to the town of Naco, where he kept them in his home under the casual guard of household servants. He toyed with them by inviting them to dine with him as gentlemen, assuming that if they accepted his hospitality all would be forgiven. Instead, the two prisoners grabbed some table knives, pinned down their host, and stabbed him. Olid escaped, but his hiding place was discovered. He was arrested, put on trial, sentenced, and publicly beheaded in Naco a few days later. The two victors, having no ships to sail around the Yucatan Peninsula, decided to return overland through Guatemala, which had been recently pacified and was being governed by Pedro de Alvarado. When they arrived in Mexico City with their good news, however, Cortes had grown impatient and left to search for them, swearing he would deal with Olid himself.

Knowing what dangers would await Cortes or anyone else who braved the Yucatan jungles, Avila and Las Casas felt great anxiety for him. Even more disturbing, Cortes had left the city in the hands of two quarrelsome appointees of the king who were mismanaging the city and mistreating its citizens in his absence. The worries of Avila and Las Casas doubled and tripled as they observed the strife around them. Apparently the dangers extended beyond Cortes and his expedition to include all of Mexico City and the entire future of New Spain. Ironically, if Cortes had waited patiently to hear of the success of his envoys in Honduras, he might have saved himself the most disastrous journey he ever took.

* * *

"I need you, Marina, more than ever." Cortes's words rang with sincerity, but they had less effect on Marina than they once would have. She knew better than to behave petulantly, of course. Although she had felt lonely during most of the past two years, she knew her place, and she knew how futile it would be to exert any demands on Cortes. So she merely inquired, "What would you have me do, my Lord?"

"What's this 'my lord' talk? Call me 'Hernan' when we're alone." They were not entirely alone, because a servant was upstairs putting little Martin to bed, but they had the dining room to themselves. The bluish light of pine torches and the smaller flames of wax candles filled the room with a pleasant glow; their scents mingled with those of the roast pork dinner they had just consumed. Having brought some wine to the red stone house that night, Hernan was in a mellow mood. Candlelight glinted on the silverware and golden goblets graced the dining table, gifts Hernan had brought for use in the red stone house. Marina always used these symbols of refinement when Hernan had dinner with her. She had also learned to use forks, knives, and spoons as Hernan did, and she adapted quite easily to sitting in a chair with her knees under the dining table.

Smiling agreeably, Marina reached across the corner of the table, taking his left hand in her right one. "What would you like me to do, Hernan?"

"First let me say you can refuse my request if you choose."

"I couldn't do that. I've always done what you asked."

"I know, but now you have Martin to think of. You might not want to travel where you can't take him."

"Travel where?"

"To Honduras. It's been months since I sent Francisco to check on that scoundrel Cristobal de Olid. For all I know, Francisco might be captured or dead."

Marina wrinkled her brow and refilled Hernan's goblet. "You'd have to take the same risks, wouldn't you? Isn't there anyone else you can send?"

"Not really. Alvarado's in Guatemala keeping the peace. Sandoval's in Espiritu Santo, near Coatzacoalcos. Bernal Diaz is farming his encomienda somewhere near the coast. I'll pick up Sandoval and Diaz along the way, then march overland to Naco."

"You'd go by land? Why not by sea?"

"I want to take horses, more than I could take by ship. I've seen old maps of the Mayan territories, showing good roads."

Marina shook her head doubtfully. "That's jungle territory, south of Tabasco where I once lived. It's a hot climate, with lots of rain, deep rivers, thick forests. If the roads aren't used frequently, they quickly get overgrown."

"We have swords and machetes to cut away overgrowth," Hernan countered, his eyes gleaming at the prospect of a new challenge. "What I need most is an interpreter. I think you know that Aguilar has resumed his holy orders and left for Spain."

"You have many interpreters now, friars and pochteca who can speak Nahuatl and Spanish. I'd rather not leave my son."

"I know I'm asking a lot," Hernan said, using the direct gaze he had always found compelling with Marina. "Don't think I haven't thought about it. Martin is two years old now; he can drink goat's milk and eat tortillas. He'd be well cared for by your servants and the nuns here."

"You didn't seem to need me when you went to Panuco," Marina reminded him. "You said it was because I was nursing Martin, but wasn't it really because you'd grown tired of me? Did my body seem ugly to you, with its stretch marks where the skin split when my belly grew large?"

"You'll never know how much I missed you then," he said persuasively, kissing her throat. "It wasn't easy to go without you. Now I've got several friars who can translate Nahuatl, but they can't do Mayan, and besides, they make very bony bed partners. Even if you have ten babies, you'll always be a desirable woman to me."

Marina smiled, wanting to believe him yet knowing how he used words as tools to coax and seduce, just as he used swords and horses to conquer. She stroked his hair affectionately and questioned him further: "If I refuse to go, will you stay here?"

Hernan looked at her in surprise. He hadn't really expected her to say no. After a pause, he said decisively, "I've made up my mind to go, and this is the best time. The rainy season is coming to an end; the roads should be dry and passable."

"Something tells me you shouldn't go," Marina said. "You're almost forty years old now, entitled to some rest from the rigors of traveling and battles."

Hernan straightened his shoulders and expanded his chest with a deep breath. "I'm only thirty-nine, strong as ever."

"Still very handsome, too," Marina said, combining sincerity with flattery. "I didn't mean to say you can't handle it; of course you can. But other people could do that for you—the young hidalgos eager to prove themselves, or the adventurers still looking for gold and silver mines. The people need you here; no one else would govern as well."

Hernan sighed. "I've thought about that, but I really prefer campaigning to governing. I'm tired of the petty bickering between the four agents King Charles sent. After his bad experience with Cristobal and Diego Colon, the king doesn't trust any conqueror to govern without a bunch of idiot civil servants hindering him at every turn."

"I've heard Albornoz hates you. Does he?"

"He did at first, but I think he's changing his mind as he learns more about the rules here. We quarreled when he first came because I wouldn't give him some Indian slaves, even though King Charles expressly forbids us from taking slaves unless they refuse to become peaceful vassals. Albornoz took a fancy to the daughter of a lord in Texcoco, but I wouldn't let him have her. If he'd been willing to marry her, the king and I wouldn't have objected, but he just wanted a female slave."

"You know I'm on your side in that quarrel," Marina said. "Most Spaniards don't treat their slaves as well as you do."

"I know, Marina, and it troubles me," Hernan said. "Even granting encomiendas troubles my conscience a little, but some of my soldiers served the king of Spain for two years without pay, and there's no other way to reward them. The system works if encomenderos educate and protect their Indians as they should;

that's a fair exchange for a share of the harvest. But some of them overwork their vassals and treat them like slaves."

"I'm glad you're aware of it," Marina said with a sigh. "If you're concerned about natives who are suffering, doesn't that mean you should stay here and help right the wrongs?"

"I'll give the friars that responsibility," Hernan said. "King Charles has asked them to protect the Indians as well as minister to their needs." He pulled her to him so that she was sitting on his lap. "Enough of this talk. Shall I minister to your needs?"

Marina didn't answer directly, but nuzzled her face in his neck, smelling the masculine scent she loved, feeling the texture of Hernan's beard against her cheek. "You seem to have thought everything through, but I'm still worried about the danger."

"There's always some danger," Hernan replied. "That's why I wouldn't make you go with me unless you want to. You've served me so well, never complaining about dangers or hardships. You're entitled to stay here in comfort." He kissed her, more with tenderness than passion.

Tears flooded Marina's eyes; she tried to blink them away. "I remember those dangers and hardships fondly," she said. "How I prayed for your safety! How glad I was to see you come back to your tent, covered with dirt and sweat and blood, looking miserable and smelling worse."

Hernan tingled with the memory of their lovemaking after a victory, remembering the way his loins responded to the sight of her waiting by his tent in the campground, the way his blood raced through his veins with a new surge of strength despite his fatigue. "I must have been a revolting sight after a battle," he laughed, "but you never rejected me."

"I wouldn't mind reliving those days," Marina said, her eyes turned upward as if searching overhead for memories. "I didn't crave comforts, or gold, or finery. What I loved was being needed, knowing that my help and advice were important to you. Now I feel discarded, even if I sit on my garbage pile in a fine house surrounded by luxuries."

Hernan's face creased into lines of distress. "You aren't discarded! Don't you realize I still need you?"

Marina wiped an escaping tear from her cheek. "You removed me from this house when your wife came from Cuba; you never came to see me while she was here. You didn't need me then."

Hernan groaned. "By all that's holy, Marina, I needed you then more than ever. You can't imagine how I wrestled with my conscience. I thought it was my duty to give you up, to try being a good Christian husband, to set a good example for my soldiers and the settlers. Believe me, I tried, but those months were the loneliest I've ever experienced."

By the time he stopped kissing her, they were curling their

bodies together on the floor, on the wool carpet that had survived Catalina's redecorating schemes, reliving the hunger of old memories with new appreciation.

"I believe part of what you said," Marina whispered in Hernan's ear as his beard scratched her face in rough but affectionate intimacy.

"Not all?" He was kissing her all over, as if he cared more about her body than her answer.

"I believe you need an interpreter," she said between kisses on his mouth. "But I think the real reason for going to Honduras is that you're bored."

After their lovemaking, Hernan laughed happily and rolled over on his back, one arm bent over his forehead to wipe away the sweat. "You know me better than anyone," he said. "You're probably right about the boredom. I'm sick of the king's agents, disgusted with their meddling and quarreling. The pettiness of bureaucrats exhausts me more than a battle." Rising up on one elbow to look at her intently, he became suddenly serious. "It's true I'm restless, but you might be more contented in Mexico City than I am. I have no right to ask you to undergo danger and discomforts for my sake."

"You can always command me. I'm still your slave."

"Not tonight. Tonight you're the woman I love. You can command me."

"I can choose to go or stay?"

"Don't come unless you come of your own free will."

"Then I'll stay, because I want you to stay here, too. It's your safety I'm worried about, not my own."

Disappointed, Cortes rose and buckled his belt. "You can decide for yourself," he said firmly, like a commander speaking to a recruit, "but you can't decide for me." Then he walked stiffly out of the red stone house and into the fragrant gardens of the Coyoacan square, which looked strangely abandoned in the ghostly light of a half-moon.

* * *

In the next few days, Cortes made elaborate preparations for his departure. First, he drew up papers giving an encomienda to Marina, granting her title to a village whose residents would provide food and income for her and Martin if he should be killed or become ill on the journey. After his last visit to her, he realized that she had served him as loyally as any soldier, even without any hope of pay. Why shouldn't she be rewarded just as they had been? He chided himself silently for not realizing how painful it must have been for Marina to be ousted from her home when Catalina usurped it. He had two copies made of the legal document—one for Marina to keep, even though she could not read it, and one to be entrusted to the Franciscan friars for safekeeping. If he could trust anyone at all in Mexico City, now that his loyal friend Father Olmedo was in Heaven, he could trust them. They could read his instructions, and he was confident they would follow them.

He also composed a letter to King Charles, venting all the pent-up wrath he felt toward Diego Velasquez and his accomplice Cristobal de Olid. After explaining how they had conspired to thwart his project for colonizing Honduras, Cortes wrote, "This seemed such an ugly business and such a disservice to Your Majesty that I can scarcely believe it; on the other hand, knowing the cunning which Diego Velasquez had always practiced against me to harm me and hinder my services, I do believe it. I'm of a mind to send for the aforementioned Diego Velasquez and arrest him and send him to Your Majesty; for by cutting out the root of all these evils, which he is, all the branches will wither and I may more freely carry out those services which I have begun and those which I am planning."

Cortes had at last unburdened himself, and the relief he felt in doing so obscured the breach of propriety he had committed in that letter. Unwittingly, he had assumed an authority which only the king could lawfully exercise: to threaten the arrest of an offender. That letter would raise many eyebrows in Spain, convincing some of those who already entertained suspicions of Cortes that he had become more than a little drunk with his sweeping new powers.

As if to add more fuel to the fires of gossip in Spain, Cortes took a grandiose entourage with him. In addition to several hundred foot soldiers and half as many horsemen, he took several captains and other officers, three friars to preach the faith, a paymaster, two armor bearers, eight grooms, two falconers, a master of the horses, and three Spanish muleteers. He took household servants as well: a major domo, two stewards, a butler, a confectioner, a chamberlain, a physician, a surgeon, several pages, and a guard for the large service of goldplate and silverplate he carried for use at his table. To entertain this great crowd he brought five musicians, a stage dancer, a juggler and a puppet player. He arranged for a large drove of swine to follow the entourage about four days behind to provide meat for the marchers. He arranged for several thousand Indian porters to carry huge loads of iron tools, tents, gunpowder, horseshoes, and other supplies and trade items.

To guard against insurrection while he was away, he took the captured emperor of the Aztecs, Cuauhtemoc; the lord of Tacuba, Tetlepanquetzal; the deposed ruler of Texcoco, Coanacoch; and various other tecuhtlis who might be capable of stirring up rebellion in his absence.

He planned to add other important members to the

expedition later: his loyal captain Sandoval, now governing the settlement of Espiritu Santo; all hidalgos who had property to defend in that region and who could bring their own horses; some traveling merchants for guides; and if he could find one, an interpreter who could speak Nahuatl and Mayan, so he could, if necessary, have a three-way communication in Spanish, Nahuatl, and Mayan.

Just as he was mounting his horse to leave, however, another volunteer joined the assembly. Her simple huipil made her indistinguishable from the slave women being brought to make tortillas for the marchers, and like a slave being taken to market, she carried a small bundle of possessions wrapped in a shawl with the corners knotted. Her long black hair had been braided to keep it from tangling on the long march ahead. The only possessions that might differentiate her from the other women were her new fawnskin sandals with sturdy soles and a large pin that held a lightweight mantle around her shoulders.

Joy surged from his head to his heart as Cortes recognized that pin and the woman who wore it. "Marina!"

"I thought you might need me," she said simply. "Father Valencia told me about the encomienda you granted to me and Martin. Martin will be safe with him and the nuns for a while."

Cortes pulled her up on his horse, and she straddled his mount behind him, holding herself in place with her arms wrapped tightly around his waist. "The bonds of slavery are mere threads compared to the bonds of love," she said as they rode off on what would be their last trip together.

* * *

After only a few days of travel, Cortes began to admit to himself that Marina had been right. He was nearly forty years old, and the cold winds in the mountain passes brought aches to his bones, reminding him of old forgotten wounds. It soon became evident that he hadn't planned the march as well as he thought. He had to divide his army so that they could find food and places to camp near small villages along the way. He was also troubled in spirit, brooding over matters that, in his younger days, he would have dismissed flippantly or squelched easily. Not only was he still smarting with anger at Olid's betrayal, but his conscience pricked him to think that his most loyal follower had been the least well rewarded. Even with an encomienda to supply her with income, Marina still held the legal status of a slave.

One night, while walking along a mountain path thinking disturbing thoughts, Cortes stumbled and fell, bruising an arm. Chiding himself for his clumsiness, he tried to keep the bruise hidden from sight under his cape. When he reached his tent, Marina came and bound the bruised arm to keep the discoloration from spreading, but she could do nothing to assuage his bruised feelings. He fretted and stewed over whether those men he had sent to bring Olid down had instead joined forces with him.

Cortes did not tell Marina what a familiar pattern betrayals had become in the history of discoveries and conquests, but he had seen much evidence of it. Velasquez had been both betrayer and betrayed; Narvaez had tried to play both sides against each other; Moctezuma had shifted alliances whenever it served his purpose. Cortes himself could not claim total innocence in matters of double-dealing, but he reasoned that he had been forced into duplicity by Velasquez and other enemies. No one who knew Cortes could seriously doubt his loyalty to King Charles, but he knew the king's ears were being assaulted regularly with such accusations. As charges of betrayal mounted against him in Spain and suspicions floated around him in Mexico City, he wondered whether his turn had come. His very success had made him a target. For him, it was becoming easier to distrust others than to trust them.

Sensing that Cortes wanted to be left alone with his musings, Marina walked around the campground, enjoying the fragrance of pine forests and the brilliance of star clusters overhead. Hearing the sound of music, she walked toward the center of the camp where musicians and jugglers were entertaining an appreciative crowd.

Some soldiers had broken into small groups, playing cards or telling stories by the light of their campfires. She strolled from fire to fire, chatting and joking with the soldiers as she had done so many times before. The Spanish soldiers always removed their hats to her and respectfully called her "Dona Marina." After she had passed, some of those who had served with Cortes during the conquest told the newer recruits how she had won allies for them in Tlaxcala and saved their lives in Cholula. They also circulated among themselves the story Cortes had told them about how she became a slave, sold by her mother and step-father to secure the inheritance of her half-brother. Those who heard the story were moved to compassion as well as respect.

By the light of his campfire, Marina recognized the man who had held Martin over the heads of the crowd when the Franciscan friars arrived in Mexico City. "Why, hello, Juan!" she said. "I'm glad to see you again."

Juan Jaramillo's face and eyes reflected the firelight and intensified its glow. "I'm glad you remember me, Dona Marina," he said, removing his hat and struggling to his feet.

Acting on an impulse, Marina sat on the ground near the fire and asked all the soldiers there to tell her about themselves. They responded amiably, sitting in their circle and telling her one by one how they happened to be in Mexico, what adventures had befallen them, what dreams motivated them. As she listened intently to each in turn, responding by telling each man how valuable he was to the Captain-General, Juan watched her animated face and hands. She seemed even more captivating in firelight than in sunlight. Her hands formed graceful gestures, opening and turning, circling and pointing, touching her chin in thoughtfulness, opening in wonder like birds flying suddenly out of their nests.

Marina felt acutely conscious of Juan's eyes on her, though she looked at him only when it was his turn to speak. The shadows of the firelight molded his rugged features and the roughness of his skin into a statue to place on the pedestal of her memory, in the chapel of her private thoughts, where she could enter secretly any time she wished to remember him. The scent of pine smoke, the blue and gold of flames embracing the logs, the warmth of laughter and sharing seemed to surround and bind this band of adventurers. Two of them were beginning an adventure which they knew was forbidden, but which carried them like canoes on a swift current. They could envision the waterfalls such a current was pulling them toward, but they could not change course.

* * *

An unexpected lightning storm had muddied the trails, making the climb to the mountain town of Orizaba slippery and difficult, but the Cortes half of the army had at last arrived, exhausted and hungry. Cortes made camp just outside the little village, declaring that they would rest there at least a couple of days. The natives of Orizaba supplied them with tortillas and vegetables, and Cortes ordered preparations to be made for a feast. Feasting and music, he knew, would do much to keep morale high, and he wanted to justify the expense of having brought musicians and dancers along. Since the division would be there long enough to recover from hangovers, he decided to let the men drink pulque, the fermented beverage made from the maguey plant that the natives called *octli*.

By midmorning the day after they arrived, household stewards brought by Cortes had placed two hogs on spits to roast slowly throughout the day. The morning air, crisp and sunny, carried the scents of mountain plants after a refreshing rainstorm. Marina joined the other women, mostly domestic servants who were preparing tamales and chili beans for the feast. She worked comfortably among them, enjoying gossip about their children and families, sharing with them some amusing mistakes her own son had made when he was beginning to talk.

Juan stood at a distance from where Marina was working,

sipping his pulque and watching her longingly. He often drank too much, he had been told, but the world looked better to him through the blur that softened the edges of a harsh reality. As he watched her place an iron kettle on an improvised hearth of three stones, he thought how gracefully she blended the worlds of Spain and Mexico, keeping the ancient tradition of the three stones yet happily accepting a superior European invention.

He knew Marina had seen him; she acknowledged his presence with a smile and a quick wave of her hand before returning to her tasks. She must have greeted hundreds of people she knew in that way, he thought, yet he saw in the greeting a secret message. Because he was becoming obsessed with her, he interpreted her smile as an indication that the attraction was mutual.

Marina sensed Juan's eyes on her, and the feeling was not unpleasant. She had always welcomed soldiers' respect, knowing that soldiers did not always treat women respectfully. If the respect blossomed into admiration, it pleased her all the more. Cortes did not object to his men's admiring her; on the contrary, his status with them increased when they admired his woman. Yet there was an unspoken code they dared not violate. They could look at, even lust after, the birds in his cage, but they could not poach in his territory.

The pulque was making Juan bolder than usual. He picked a yellow flower from a wild bush near the camp and brought it to Marina. "This reminds me of the hibiscus blossom in Spain," he said. "It would be especially pretty in your hair tonight."

Marina blushed as the other women giggled, knowing they would tease her afterward, but she accepted the flower. "That's sweet of you, Juan," she said. "This kind of blossom won't last that long, but thank you for thinking of me." She hoped he would hear the message she was sending underneath her words, through the condescending tone of her thanks, like that of a mother accepting a flower from a child, not wanting to hurt his feelings. Her intent was to convey the tacit message, "This kind of attraction won't last; it wasn't meant to be, but thank you for thinking of me anyway."

Juan deduced a different message. He thought she was implying something like this: "In public I must say polite things and act as if your gift is unimportant to me, but I'm glad to know you're thinking of me."

That's why Juan took the boldest step any soldier had ever taken with his commander. He went to find Cortes, to offer to buy Marina from him. When Juan located him, Cortes was examining a hoof of his handsome chestnut mount to see if any burrs or other weeds might be causing the horse some pain. When Juan asked him whether he would consider selling his slave Marina, Cortes reacted first with surprise, then laughter, as he returned his horse's leg to the ground and slapped his own thigh. "That's the most preposterous thing I've ever heard," he said. "Are you drunk, Jaramillo?"

"No, sir," Juan replied. "I've had a few cups of pulque, but I know what I'm saying. I love Marina, and I want to marry her. I'll be good to her, you can be sure of that."

"Hang you, Jaramillo," Cortes scowled, "you've been here long enough to know that Marina isn't just a slave; she's an interpreter who knows three languages. I couldn't replace her."

"I know that, Sir. I saw her teaching her son both Spanish and Nahuatl. I don't intend to take her away from this campaign or prevent her from interpreting for you."

"Then you know about Marina's son?" Cortes stroked his horse's nose affectionately, but he delivered his words with a sting. He thought probably this upstart captain didn't realize he'd be taking on a bastard son.

But Juan was undeterred. "Yes, sir. His name's Martin. A wonderful boy. I'd raise him like my own."

"I don't know why I'm listening to you, Jaramillo," Cortes said gruffly. "Marina's not for sale, not at any price. I don't even want to hear how you'd propose to pay for her."

"To start with, you could keep my wages for this campaign as partial payment. I expect a small inheritance from my father in Extremadura. You could have that, too."

Cortes began to roar. "Go to the devil, Jaramillo! I've told you Marina's not for sale."

Juan persisted, deferentially but insistently. "Are you being fair to Marina, sir? I can offer her an honorable Christian marriage. I can offer Martin a home like those of other Christian children."

The vein on Cortes' neck was becoming prominent. "You've tried my patience long enough, Jaramillo. You think I'm unfair? Marina stays with me of her own free will."

If it hadn't been for the pulque, Juan might have been intimidated by his thundering commander. Instead, he drew a deep breath and asked a simple but devastating question. "Does she? Have you ever given her any choice?"

Juan saluted Cortes and withdrew. Then he went directly into the town of Orizaba and purchased more pulque from a vendor. He drank steadily that afternoon. By the time the feast began later that evening, he had almost succeeded in blotting out the pain of living in a world fraught with injustice.

* * *

The parting words of Juan Jaramillo continued to echo in Cortes's brain throughout the afternoon. His depressed mood inclined him to believe that Marina might indeed prefer

451

marriage, even to a wobbly sort of man like Jaramillo, to living in the ambiguous state of half slave, half mistress. But would she betray him with another man? If he couldn't trust her, could he trust anyone in the world? Yet his nature also possessed a disposition toward fairness, and Jaramillo's question taunted him. Was he being fair to Marina? She had never given him reason to doubt her loyalty, any more than he had given King Charles cause to doubt his loyalty. Was he treating Marina the way King Charles was treating him?

Toward sundown, as music began to filter through the walls of his tent, and the smell of roast pork began wafting through the cool mountain air, he summoned Marina. She had donned a clean white huipil and tucked a fresh yellow flower into her loosely flowing hair. She had never looked lovelier. Awareness of her beauty sharpened his sense of impending loss and increased the poignancy in their conversation.

"I have to ask you something," he said. "But before you answer me, promise you'll tell me exactly how you feel. The truth, that's all."

"I always tell you the truth," Marina said, bewildered.

"You look so pretty tonight," Cortes said. "Maybe you should always wear yellow flowers in your hair."

"Thank you," Marina said softly, but her eyes were making inquiry, trying to anticipate what he wanted.

"I'll come right to the point," Cortes said. "You've had an offer of marriage. Juan Jaramillo wants to buy you from me."

Marina looked stricken. "Would you sell me?"

"Of course not!" Cortes snorted. He touched her cheek gently, stroked the shiny black hair falling so prettily on her shoulders. "Ironically, however, I'm prepared to give you away."

Marina's anxiety intensified. "Why would you give me away? Have I displeased you? What have I done?"

"You've never displeased me," Cortes said, reflecting as he said it that, even if they had quarreled at times, these words were quite true. "But I've been selfish, and I want to please you for a change. I need to know what you really want."

Marina's comprehension was functioning on two levels. Hernan's words sounded clear and simple, but what did they really mean? Had Hernan finally come to realize how one-sided their love was, and would Juan's proposal stimulate Hernan into a similar offer? Or was Hernan angry with her, toying with her in some devious way? Had she exceeded the bounds of propriety by accepting a flower from Juan that morning? Had Hernan heard about it? She even began to question her own motives. Why had she decided to put the yellow flower in her hair? Was it to please Hernan, or to please Juan?

Her father's words came to mind once more. "Never want what you can never have, Malinalli." How unyielding was the

452

fence those words had placed around her life? Would she be throwing away a chance for happiness by never daring to reach for it, imprisoning herself by never daring to ask for it? For a few seconds she pondered her predicament; then she answered Hernan's question with her own questions.

"What do I really want? Can I tell you honestly what I want?" When Hernan nodded silently, she continued. "Hernan, my love, it's you I want. I've been hoping someday you'd ask me to marry you, in a church, with a priest."

Hernan looked down, concentrating on a few blades of grass trampled in the otherwise barren dirt floor of his tent. When he looked up, his eyes had lost their sparkle. "I do love you, Marina, but I can't grant your wish," he said. "I've given my father power of attorney to find a wife for me in Spain. He's arranged an engagement, as binding as a marriage, which needs only to be consummated. It's as if I'm a married man already."

Marina, too, looked down at the barren dirt floor, thinking she might find her heart sunken to the level of her feet. She listened quietly, arms dangling at her sides, while Cortes explained, as a lawyer might explain to a client, the advantages and disadvantages of a match with Juan Jaramillo. It would give her the legal status of a married woman; she would have a protector and provider in case anything happened to Cortes; and she could have more children if she wished, children with no clouds around their names, no shadows upon their futures. Yet she might be taken away from Mexico by her husband; she would have to go where he went, to obey him without question, to share his hardships, his failures, and his bed. Therefore, Cortes wanted to know, would Juan be acceptable to her as a man, as a lover?

Marina breathed deeply and painfully before answering. "The disadvantages you named are those I have already," she said slowly, lifting the flap of the tent and staring outside. "I obey without question, I go where I'm told to go, I share in hardships as well as triumphs, and I share my master's bed upon his command, not when I wish it. The advantages you listed are something every woman dreams of: protection, security, children, and a good man in bed beside her every night."

Cortes had been secretly hoping Marina would express a clear preference for him as a lover, but he admitted to himself that he had not been the devoted lover most women would want. "I meant to say also," he said, clearing his throat, "that Juan loves you. He'd probably be more faithful to you than I've been. Of course, he drinks too much—some say to a fault—and he gambles a little, like most soldiers."

Marina stepped out into the descending darkness and stared up into the heavens that control men's destinies. "Tell Juan he would be acceptable to me as a husband and a lover," she said, as she left Cortes's tent with an air of finality, dropping a crushed yellow flower on the path as she fled into the shadows.

* * *

The wedding took place that night, under the astonished stars, with a credulous friar officiating. Cortes made a speech about giving Marina her freedom as a wedding present, telling Juan Jaramillo how lucky he was to have won the heart of such a fine, chaste woman and devoted Christian. He also gave Juan a gold ring to place on Marina's finger, though it proved too large for her to wear. Marina carried a bouquet of yellow flowers Juan had brought her, but on her shawl she fastened the pin Cortes had given her, for good luck.

Juan's damp curly hair gave evidence that he had been hastily sobered up with bucketfuls of cold water, and some men gossiped that he was still too tipsy to know what he was doing. Yet Juan was clearly happy, and he found a way to convince Marina he knew exactly what he was doing. After the friar had pronounced them man and wife, for better or for worse, and after he and Marina had sealed their union with the traditional European kiss, Juan took a corner of Marina's shawl and knotted it to a corner of his own cape. "With this knot, I thee wed," he said to Marina, smiling a boyish smile.

"Oh Juan," Marina cried, throwing her arms around his neck. "I think I'm the luckiest wife in two worlds."

Cortes tried to make a joke, though to those who knew him well, his cheerfulness seemed forced. "That which hath been knotted together," he said, raising his golden goblet in a toast, "let no man tear asunder. Let this knot not be all for naught."

The musicians filled the night air with their happiest music; dancers and jugglers poured their energies into their work with feeling, soldiers drank pulque and sang noisily. The sleepy little mountain town of Orizaba resounded with merriment that night, but in the distance, flashes of lightning silhouetted the tops of a mountain range they still had to cross, warning them that many dangers still lay ahead.

Chapter 30

The Convergence of Lives

"So at last we'll get to see the famous Spanish general who defeated the Triple Alliance," Opochtli said to Cimatl as he seated himself on a petlatl at her tecalli. "It might be worth a trip to Coatzalcoalcos just for that, but I'll take you to the market, too, if you'd like to go."

"I still don't understand why we have to go there," Cimatl said crossly, grinding amaranth seeds to make a paste. It was the month of Tepeilhuitl, when she always made cakes made of ground amaranth grains. The cakes, shaped like people or snakes, would be offered to the mountain rain gods of Tlaloc, and then her son Turquoise Stone would eat them as special treats.

"Huatl says they're gathering all the tecuhtlis from the area surrounding the Spanish settlement called Espiritu Santo, a few long-runs from Coatzalcoalcos. He's made friends with a Captain Sandoval there, even traded with him for some sheep and goats and pigs, but Sandoval wouldn't part with any horses."

"All the tecuhtlis? Does that mean Turquoise Stone too?"

"Yes, he'll have to leave the telpochcalli for a few days and come with us. Would you like me to escort you to the coast?"

Cimatl placed a lump of the amaranth paste on a smooth board and began to shape it. "Yes, it's generous of you to offer." As she worked, she mused aloud. "I haven't been to Coatzacoalcos since the time you took me and Malinalli to see Papalotl, when she was still alive."

"You mean when both were still alive?" Opochtli took a steel knife out of a leather sheaf and began whittling a hollow reed, cutting out holes to make a flute for Turquoise Stone.

Cimatl's cheeks reddened when she realized her slip, but she adroitly shifted the discussion away from Malinalli. "Why yes, I was thinking mostly of my sister Papalotl. She lived on a farm near Coatzacoalcos, but she drowned."

"Chimalli told me she'd died," Opochtli said indifferently, examining the holes he had cut in the reed. "What do you think of this steel knife, Cimatl? I traded with the Spaniards for it. I'm making a flute for Turquoise Stone."

Cimatl examined the knife. "It has only one sharp edge," she said. "I prefer my flint knife with two edges."

"Steel knives sometimes have two edges," Opochtli said, "especially those made to kill. This one is made so it won't cut me accidentally. Steel knives don't break and chip the way flint knives do, but they do need sharpening. I sharpen this one by sliding it over a stone."

"I prefer the old ways," Cimatl said with a sigh. She put the amaranth cakes on the hearth to bake and watched Opochtli's carving with interest.

"We'd better get used to the new ways," Opochtli said. "The Spaniards are changing the One World forever. Some changes are good, like this knife and the sheep's wool weavers use in the cold lands. Some changes are bad, but they're here to stay."

"Even in Paynala? Why would Spaniards bother with a village like this?"

"According to Huatl, they want to change your religion. They wouldn't approve of those amaranth cakes, for example."

Cimatl looked surprised. "Why not?"

"They've seen amaranth used in ceremonies honoring the war god Huitzilopochtli. Eating the cakes suggests cannibalism to them, and they hate human sacrifices."

Cimatl sniffed. "Then why have they killed so many people themselves? Don't they do that to honor their god?"

"Good question; that's what Huatl says. He can't see why they object to our Flowery Wars when they don't fight wars fairly either. They like to knock over carved images of our gods, calling them idols, but they put up their own carved images. Their favorite seems to be an an earth goddess called Mary."

"I can't see how changing images would make any difference," Cimatl said. "They don't destroy the earth goddess Cihuacoatl by destroying her image or changing her name. Even if they abolish amaranth cakes, Tlaloc will still have his way, sending rain and lightning whenever he wishes. Religion isn't something we change like a garment that gets old and ragged; religion just *is*."

Opochtli was surprised to hear a woman discussing her beliefs so philosophically. He thought it would be interesting to see Cimatl exchanging ideas with the cynical Huatl. "We'll visit Huatl in Coatzacoalcos," Opochtli promised. "It's time you met him, since he's been trading for both of us. Your views may clash with his, because you're a mystic, and he's a worldly man, yet you're both interesting. Shall we leave day after tomorrow?"

"Could we leave earlier?" Cimatl asked, removing the finished cakes from the comal. "Tomorrow, perhaps?"

"If you wish, but we don't have to be there that soon." Opochtli stood up, sheathed his knife, and leaned the finished flute against the wall where Turquoise Stone would find it later.

"I have another reason to go to Coatzacoalcos," Cimatl said. "I've been wanting to tell you this for a long time, but I've been afraid, even a little ashamed. Now I trust you more than any other friend, and I hope you'll keep my secret." She paused, waiting for his assurance of confidentiality. When he gave it unequivocally, she continued, "I want to go to the temple of Quetzalcoatl to look for my daughter Malinalli."

Opochtli listened in fascination as Cimatl told him of the plot engineered by Anecoatl to kill Malinalli, and how she had thwarted her husband's wishes by sending Malinalli to the temple of Quetzalcoatl instead. At last the pieces of the puzzle were beginning to fit together—the simultaneous disappearance of Malinalli and the servant girl Toto, the banishing of Toto's parents so no questions could be raised.

"Now I understand why you didn't grieve long for Anecoatl," Opochtli said thoughtfully, and for a moment he considered telling her he'd set a trap for Anecoatl. Then he thought better of it, deciding that some things might be better left unsaid, just tacitly understood between friends. "Does Turquoise Stone know about this?" he asked.

"Nothing whatever. Now that Anecoatl is dead, you and I are the only people who know what really happened." Impulsively, Cimatl abandoned her usual poised demeanor to embrace her pot-bellied friend awkwardly. "You do understand, don't you, Opochtli?" she cried, squeezing him tightly. "I'll never have a moment's peace until I know she's still alive."

Opochtl gently patted Cimatl's back as her tears wet his shoulder. "I'll share your burden gladly," he said. "Neither of us will rest until we know the answer."

* * *

Opochtli left Oluta in the predawn darkness and arrived at the tecalli in Paynala shortly after sunrise. He and Cimatl picked up Turquoise Stone at the telpochcalli and gave him the flute Opochtli had made the day before. The three of them walked at a leisurely pace toward the rising sun, toward Coatzacoalcos and the great ocean. The two adults also sensed that they were walking toward an inescapable destiny.

Turquoise Stone practiced on the reed flute for awhile, then tired of it. Opochtli cut another reed along the roadside for him and made different tones by cutting holes in different places. This, too, satisfied Turquoise Stone only a short while; then he became restless again. Opochtli let Turquoise Stone use the knife, which amused the youth much longer as he cut marks in trees and slashed the stalks of flowers along the way.

Like most twelve-year-olds, Turquoise Stone liked to run

with his lanky legs. Cimatl and Opochtli made a game of his restlessness, telling him to scout the territory ahead and report back if he saw any bandits. He said he hoped he would see some, because he wanted to watch Opochtli dispatch them with the steel knife and the Spanish sword he kept sheathed at his side.

"Well, then, you'd better give back the knife," Opochtli said good-humoredly. "I should be prepared to protect us."

While Turquoise Stone was scouting the path ahead, Cimatl and Opochtli had an opportunity to talk uninterrupted by the boy's noisy flutes and chatter. Talking deepened their trust and understanding of each other. When they came to a crossroads, Opochtli took a few corn kernels from a leather pouch and dropped them into the soil, spreading dirt over them with his foot.

"Planting corn in the road for future travelers?" Cimatl asked, half joking, for his gesture seemed to make little sense.

"Merchants are superstitious at crossroads," Opochtli said. "I'm offering these grains to Cihuacoatl. Sometimes we fear her powers, hoping she'll devour the grain instead of us. She and her dead spirits haunt crossroads, you know." His face and voice took on a grimness, an unfamiliar dark quality that Cimatl had not seen in him before.

"I've never seen you do that," Cimatl said. "Or was I just not observant when we went to Coatzacoalcos so many years ago?"

"I haven't always done it, but now we're on a journey to hear about crosses. Huatl says Christians are superstitious about them; they tie two logs together in a cross wherever they go, usually after they've destroyed a temple's images."

"I understand sacred crosses," Cimatl said. "Does their cross represent the four directions, as ours does?"

"No, it's a different shape; not the same on all sides, but taller, more like the shape of a man standing with both arms outstretched." Opochtli demonstrated by holding out both arms. "Huatl says it represents death and resurrection, but I'm not sure why. Maybe they believe in somebody like Cihuacoatl, the giver and taker of life."

"That could be," Cimatl said. "Maybe all religions have similar basic beliefs. We only know the one we've been taught."

"My wife was buried at a crossroads," Opochtli said, his voice sad as a poet's when lamenting the brevity and randomness of life.

Cimatl took his hand sympathetically. "Buried, not cremated?" she probed. "Then she must have died in childbirth."

"Yes, when Metzli was born," Opochtli said, gently squeezing the hand she had offered. "I haven't told many people how she died. It's a terrible memory for me."

"If you want to tell me, I'll listen," Cimatl said gently.

"Yesterday I told you my griefs and anxieties about Malinalli. Today you can tell me what's been bothering you all these years."

"The midwife said it was Cihuacoatl's doing," Opochtli said. "I'm sure the midwife tried to save my wife, but Cihuacoatl sent a fever the day after Metzli was born."

"I'm so sorry," Cimatl said in deep sympathy. She could feel the tension in Opochtli's hand as he gripped hers.

"Perhaps the midwife was frightened; perhaps she felt guilty or incompetent, I don't know. But she didn't wait for any of the usual mourning procedures. She washed my wife's body quickly, combed her hair to hang loose, and put a new huipil on her. She and her attendants broke a hole in the back wall so I could carry my wife's body away without being seen. We left in darkness, with a whole entourage of midwives howling and shouting, waving shields to ward off Cihuacoatl's minions."

"Oh, Opochtli, that must have been horrible for you."

"That wasn't the worst of it. We were attacked on the way to the crossroads by warriors from the calmecac who wanted to steal parts of her body. They were desperate to get a piece of what they considered magically charged flesh—an arm, a finger, even a lock of hair. They thought the dark powers of Cihuacoatl resided in the corpse of a *mociaquetzi* who died giving birth. They thought they could use parts of her body as talismans to injure their enemies, to put spells on them and paralyze them."

Cimatl remained silent, thinking how that fate might have been her own. She remembered her own difficulties in childbirth, and how her midwife Chihuallama had cut up the child in her womb to save her life. She choked back tears, for herself, for Opochtli, and for the many mociaquetzi who accompanied the sun god daily in his descent to the dark womb of the earth.

Opochtli paused for a few moments; then, seeing Turquoise Stone approaching, he finished quickly. "I kept a vigil over the grave for four nights until the magic power slowly dispersed, holding a knife to ward off thieves and body-snatchers. Then I left her in that unmarked grave and tried not to think of her any more. Since then, I've avoided priests and calmecac students whenever I can."

Turquoise stone ran back to them, reported that no bandits were on the horizon, and ran off again.

"I'm deeply sorry," Cimatl said to Opochtli. "You had no real time to mourn, no comfort from friends or relatives."

"I had to keep on living, for Chimalli's sake."

Cimatl wondered why Opochtli had mentioned his son Chimalli, who would have been about four years old at the time, yet not his newborn daughter Metzli. "I suppose you had to find a wet-nurse for Metzli, too," she volunteered.

"Yes, poor Metzli almost didn't survive. She's always been

459

skinny and underweight. Probably didn't get enough mother's milk, having to share the breasts of a woman who had an infant of her own."

"Is that why you never married again?" Cimatl asked, "or is that too personal a question?"

"I've often wondered myself. Whenever I've thought of marrying, I see a vision of my wife's pale face, her loose hair around her shoulders. I feel her head flopping on my shoulder as it did when I carried her off into the darkness. And I hear those damnable howling women, those midwives, those minions of Cihuacoatl shrieking in the night, practically inviting those vultures from the calmecac to descend on us."

"I'm glad you're able to tell me this now," Cimatl said. "I've also known terrible losses, terrible grief—for a husband, a sister, a stillborn child, and even Malinalli, more than anyone could know. At times I thought the very sun shone darkness upon me, but each time I survived. You'll have to let yourself feel the pain, and then in time it will go away."

"I thought time had cured my sorrows," Opochtli said. "But I've never been able to reconcile myself to her death. Was it my fault, for getting her with child? Was it the incompetence of a midwife? Was it the sorcery of Chihuacoatl? I can't believe things like this just happen, for no reason."

"Blame Tezcatlipoca, then, the God of the Near and the Far, who toys with human destinies as if they were games of chance."

"The gods don't speak to me," Opochtli said bitterly. "What good does it do to propitiate them? Why do we foolishly try to buy their goodwill with offerings? Even those grains of corn I just left at the crossroads, I know the goddess will spurn them. Why do I pretend that what I do makes a difference?"

"We have no control over our tonalli," Cimatl said gently. "The gods can accept our offerings or decline them. You've done all you could. You mustn't blame yourself."

"Then I'll blame the gods and goddesses that make human lives so miserable. It was all Metzli's doing."

"Metzli?" Cimatl asked, surprised. "Don't you mean the goddess of childbirth, Chihuacoatl?"

"That's what I said," Opochtli said. "It was all her doing, her sorcery."

Cimatl fell into a puzzled but respectful silence. At last she understood, from Opochtli's slip of the tongue, why he had felt such antagonism toward Metzli and such need to control her. He had blamed his newborn daughter for the death of her mother, but he could not admit to himself what he was doing, and Cimatl could not tell him. He had trusted her enough to open the petlacalli of his pain after years of denial, enough to remove some grief and begin to make space for peace of mind. But the lid must not be shut too soon, or pain would stay locked in. She resolved to say nothing that might cause him more pain. Among friends, she thought, some things may be better left unsaid.

* * *

When the trio of travelers arrived in Coatzacoalcos, many Mexica were milling about the streets, some wearing the finery that flaunted their status as tecuhtlis. Opochtli was glad they had come a day earlier than necessary, since lodgings would be difficult to find. He took them to a merchant's inn he had frequented in the days when he had made regular buying trips; the rooms were not fancy, but they would do.

The following morning Cimatl asked Opochtli to take Turquoise Stone to the marketplace, saying she wanted to go to the temple of Quetzalcoatl for some quiet meditation. Opochtli understood she would try to find Malinalli, the daughter she had sent to this temple nine years before with some Mayan traders.

She approached the building she had seen only once many years before, hoping it would be the same as she remembered it, though she allowed realistically for a few of the inevitable changes time brings. Instead, she saw radical changes. The gardens showed signs of neglect, their grasses dry brown and their flowers drooping. The barren mound of an anthill stood where a tree had once flowered. As if to replace that tree, a crude cross had been erected on one side of the courtyard. Sand had blown into piles in the corners of the unswept stairs, and a few blades of grass were daring life in that precarious soil. She entered the open doorway, noticing that no statues remained. Walking down the empty halls, she could find no priests or priestesses. Only the sound of the wind, freely moving through the rounded corners of the snail-shaped building, gave any sign of the presence of the god Quetzalcoatl or his twin, Ehecatl, the god of Night Wind.

Disappointed, depressed, and heartsick, Cimatl sank at the foot of the cross—the barren tree with no branches—and wept. Her sobs expressed not only grief for a twice-lost daughter, but also for the death of her hopes, so tenuously held, and now so utterly shattered.

* * *

The next day that deserted courtyard came alive with people. Merchants hawked their wares to the crowds and the tecuhtlis sported their feathers and seashells. Spaniards mingled among them, carrying colorful banners and wearing puffy pants, leather boots, strangely shaped hats, and capes decorated with gold chains. Most impressive to Cimatl were the cavaliers on horseback and the horses themselves, snorting, drooling, and

461

tossing their heads as they clattered down the limestone streets. Their riders sat in leather chairs strapped to the animals' backs and held leather thongs attached to the horses' mouths, with which they controlled the animals' movements. After parading down the streets, the cavaliers formed a line with their backs to the sea, their horses splendidly arrayed against the blue of the sky and the white-edged gray of the waves.

One of the horses, with hair the color of a robin's breast, carried the man the crowd pointed to with a wave of shouting as Hernan Cortes. Beside his horse walked a Nahua woman about twenty-three years old and three friars, all barefoot. These five walked up the temple steps and stood where they could best be heard by the large crowd of natives.

Cortes bellowed his foreign-sounding words over the heads of the crowd, making dramatic gestures with his arms. Then he stopped speaking, and the Nahua woman translated into Nahuatl, not as loudly as Cortes, but clearly and forcefully, so the crowd grew quiet enough to hear her. Then Cortes introduced the friars, who told them they had come to teach all the Mexica about Jesus Christ, and to bring his blessings to all who would be baptized with holy water. Again the woman translated.

Then Cortes took many beads from a chest brought to him by porters, draping them around the necks of those tecuhtlis who seemed most finely dressed and most willing to cooperate. He said they could be of great help in spreading the Christian religion, for they were leaders in their communities. He told them to come forward in small groups, so that each could ask questions of the friars and arrange for baptism if they wished.

Opochtli and Cimatl wanted to leave as soon as the crowd began to break up, but Turquoise Stone begged them to stay. So they lingered a while longer, listening to one of the friars attempting to explain Christianity in his limited Nahuatl, making some mistakes and mispronunciations that Opochtli found very funny. While they were listening, a Spanish soldier carrying a large shield and a long spear approached the group, asking if anyone was there from Paynala. The friar translated this, and when they admitted they were from that territory, he said that Governor Cortes wished to see them. Filled with apprehension, they heard the friar's translation and followed the soldier.

The soldier took them, not to Cortes, but instead to the Nahua woman, who had climbed down the steps and stood at their base, brushing her loose hair away from her eyes with her hand. He spoke to her in Spanish, calling her "Dona Marina."

"Thank you, Bernal," she said to the soldier, and turned to search for recognition in the faces of Opochtli and Cimatl and Turquoise Stone. When Cimatl and Opochtli drew close enough to see her face, they recognized her. Her resemblance to her mother was so remarkable that the soldier, Bernal Diaz, was positive he had brought mother and daughter together.

"Malinalli!" cried Cimatl, falling to her knees and weeping for the second time in two days, this time in joyful relief. Turquoise Stone imitated his mother, kneeling and trembling in bewilderment, because he could not remember the older sister he had not seen since he was two years old. Opochtli simply stared, open mouthed, though he soon gained enough presence of mind to kneel also. He was struck by the resemblance of the two women; it seemed as if, in the past ten years, Malinalli had magically turned into the woman Cimatl had once been, before sorrows had traced their lines in her face and hair.

Cimatl's tearful delight in seeing Malinalli alive quickly turned to fear as she remembered the mysterious circumstances when Malinalli had been sent away. Trembling, she asked, "Will you have us killed, or may we speak?"

"Will she kill us?" Turquoise Stone anxiously asked Opochtli, hoping the merchant would draw his sword immediately. Turquoise Stone, too, began to tremble.

Opochtli put a quiet, reassuring hand on the boy's shoulder but focused intently on the scene he was witnessing. Malinalli had knelt to comfort her mother, her own cheeks shiny with tears.

"Don't be afraid," she said, embracing her mother. "I've never blamed you for sending me with the traders. You couldn't have known they'd sell me in Xicalango."

When he heard Cimatl's horrified gasp, Opochtli intervened hastily, "The one you should blame is Anecoatl." He too feared for his life, because Spaniards had a reputation for swift, harsh punishments. If Malinalli had lived among them very long, she might have learned to exercise the same awful, arbitrary power. If she had thoughts of revenge, his voice might be better than Cimatl's to plead for mercy. "The tyrant is dead now, so he's beyond hurt or hurting. Anecoatl wanted you dead; your mother tried to keep you alive."

Marina jumped up to embrace Opochtli and thank him for the news. Then she brushed tears from her cheek and turned again to Cimatl. "Knowing Anecoatl, I'm sure you had no choice, Mother, and I certainly forgive you," she said. "But wait—I have some gifts for you in my tent." Bernal Diaz summoned a page and told him to bring the chest from Marina's tent, so this touching reunion would not be interrupted.

"Tell me what happened, Malinalli," Cimatl said with intense curiosity once she had stopped trembling. "I paid the traders to bring you here, to the temple."

"They sold me as a slave," Marina said matter-of-factly, "but I think it was God's will. I've become an instrument in His hands, to help spread Christianity. I took the name Marina when I was baptized. I was born again to a new and wonderful life."

Opochtli would have felt suspicious if such sanctimonious words had come from a Spaniard, or even an Aztec priest, but Marina was so undeniably sincere that he could only listen in amazement. He pitied this girl for the wrongs she had suffered, yet admired her for climbing from a pit up to a mountaintop.

"Will you come back to Paynala?" Turquoise Stone asked anxiously.

Marina laughed affectionately and stroked Turquoise Stone's hair as she had often done when he was a baby. "No, never," she reassured him. "God has been good to me. Now I have a fine husband, Captain Juan Jaramillo, and a fine son named Martin. I'd rather serve them and Hernan Cortes than anything else I could do. I wouldn't change places with anyone, not even a tecuhtli. I'd rather be who I am than to rule all the provinces in Mexico."

"You have a son?" Cimatl beamed. "Is he with you?"

"No, Mother, I couldn't bring him. We'll be traveling through rough country when we leave here."

"Where are you headed, Marina?" Opochtli asked. He was careful to call her by the name she preferred, though his tongue stumbled a little with the unfamiliar sound.

"To Honduras," she answered, "but we need a guide. Senor Cortes thinks he can get a map of the trade routes in Xicalango."

"Maybe I can help you with that," Opochtli said. "My friend Huatl goes to Xicalango regularly. He knows several merchants who travel through Maya territory."

When the page returned with Marina's chest, she reached into it, bringing out a handful of jewels and gold chains. She gave her dazzled mother some gold rings with gemstones and some gold earcaps. She draped two gold chains over her brother's head, to his great delight. "These gifts are yours to keep," she said. "Think of me when you wear them." Then she turned to Opochtli and presented him with a handful of loose gemstones, knowing he could not wear ornaments in public. "These are gifts," she said, "for your friendship, and for taking care of my mother and brother. But if you bring a map showing a land route to Honduras, Governor Cortes will reward you even more handsomely."

* * *

Cimatl spent two more days in Coatzacoalcos, making the most of the brief visits she could have with her daughter when Cortes did not need Marina for translating. During that time, Cimatl decided to accept the amazing new religion that gave her daughter such radiance and poise. Before they left, Cimatl and Turquoise Stone were baptized, the mother taking the Christian name Marta, and her son taking the name Lazaro.

In the meanwhile, Opochtli located Huatl, who had taken a residence in Coatzacoalcos because from that point he could shuttle his merchandise back and forth between Xicalango and the Spanish coastal settlements of Espiritu Santo and Vera Cruz. The two merchants came to Cortes's tent bringing a map drawn on fine linen, showing the trade routes used by the merchants who regularly traveled from Xicalango through the Maya territories. Speaking through a friar who knew some Nahuatl and Spanish, the merchants also informed him proudly that they had found another interpreter who spoke Nahuatl and Mayan. Moreover, the man might also act as a guide, because he had lived in Maya territory.

Delighted, Cortes asked them to bring him inside, so they fetched an Indian with tattooed arms and intense dark eyes who had been waiting outside. He made a quick forward gesture of kneeling on one knee, but did not stay kneeling. His loincloth, embroidered in Mayan designs, dangled to a length below his knees, and he wore deerskin sandals with laces wound around his calves. He was no peasant, Cortes concluded. The Indian stared at the table in the tent, at the map spread out on it, and at the men's feet. The barefoot friar especially interested him.

"What kind of compensation would you require?" Cortes asked, facing the Indian directly. Huatl translated in Nahuatl and then interpreted the man's answer for Cortes in the limited Spanish he had learned from Sandoval and his men. The friar nodded his approval of the translation.

"This man saw Opochtli's steel sword," Huatl said, pointing to it. "He wants only a sword or machete he can use to cut back the jungle growth, and a few other items made of steel. He has no use for gold or jewels; he's a farmer."

"He sounds like someone we could use," Cortes said to Huatl and Opochtli. Then he stepped outside the tent and ordered a passing soldier to summon Marina. "If he can converse with her in those two languages," he said to the merchants upon returning, "we could use him in three-way conversations with me and the friars, the way we used to do with Marina and Aguilar."

Huatl conversed with the Indian as they looked at the map. Then he explained to Cortes the limits of the man's potential as a guide. "He says he knows the territory only as far as this river," Huatl explained, pointing a bony finger at a blue line on the fabric map. "Beyond that, you'd be dependent on the map."

The friar added, "He also seems concerned about the route you intend to follow. He says there are many trees and rivers full of alligators in that area."

"We know that," Cortes responded, "but the ancient Mayas built some excellent stone roads through that territory, level enough for the wheels of a cart. We just have to find them."

Before Huatl or the friar could translate, the soldier returned with Marina. Marina grasped the pole in the tent's doorway and stooped slightly to enter as the soldier held the tent flap for her. As she lifted her eyes, her smile of greeting turned into an expression of complete surprise.

"Nemon!" she exclaimed. "Is it really you?"

* * *

Nemon looked as surprised to see Marina as she was to see him. "Malinalli?"

"I'm called Marina now." Unsure exactly how to greet him, she tried to put warmth into her voice and smile. She spoke in Nahuatl, knowing it was his native tongue. "Nemon, I'm so glad to see you, so glad you're alive."

Nemon did not kneel or bow his head, so she could not act the part of an officer's gracious lady as she did with soldiers. Kneeling to him would be inappropriate, too, since he had no recognizable rank entitling him to deference, and such a gesture might be seen as mockery. His manner of dress and colorfully painted body suggested that he had become the prosperous farmer he had dreamed of being when he was still a slave working to pay off his family's debts and earn his freedom.

Nemon looked at her coldly, his face as stony as an Olmec statue's. His eyes traveled over her unshod feet, her plain huipil, her shining loose hair and the nervous hands brushing it back over her shoulders. "Forgive my looking directly at you, Malinalli—or Marina," he said in puzzlement, "but I'm unable to discern your rank. Have you gained your freedom since I knew you in Tabasco?" He made a sweeping gesture around the circle of men in the tent. "Perhaps you've married one of these men?"

"Oh, no," she said quickly. "My husband is feeding his horse, making preparations for our march to Honduras."

Nemon nodded icily; his brows had lifted slightly when she said the word *horse*. "I have a wife now," he said, "and two children. We have a farm, keep a few bees, raise a few crops."

Cortes had been listening to the flow of the conversation without understanding it. He spoke to Marina, "Try some Mayan now, Marina. Does he speak that as well?"

Dutifully, Marina shifted into the dialect of Putun Maya. "I'm glad for your happiness, Nemon. I have a child, too. He's two years old now."

Nemon responded in Mayan. "You've come far in the past five years. I've come far, too, but not so far as you. Please tell Senor Cortes that I'm no longer interested in being his guide." Then he knelt suddenly before her, springing up as quickly as he had dropped to the ground. He had left the tent before Cortes could hear the translation.

466

The perplexed Cortes told a guard to follow Nemon and bring him back. Huatl looked at Marina, who explained in Nahuatl: "Nemon was a slave who befriended me and taught me to speak Mayan," she told the merchant. "He earned his freedom and came to buy my freedom, but my mistress Ix Chan refused. He asked me to run away with him, which I wanted to do, but Ix Chan would have had him arrested and killed. So I told him I didn't want to run away with him or marry him."

"Yet you didn't really mean it?"

"I would've married him gladly, because he was the only person in Tabasco who cared about me. But my tonalli decreed a different destiny. Or, as a Christian might say, God had other plans for me."

"I see," Huatl said. "How can we convince him of that?"

"Just tell him the truth," Marina suggested. "There was no time to explain why I said the words that hurt him, to save his life. Even today, I didn't have time to explain."

"I'll try to explain for you," Huatl said. "I think I know where I can find him."

Two days later Huatl returned to the Spanish camp with Nemon. "He's agreed to guide you as far as the fourth river on the map," Huatl said to Cortes through Marina. "He wants one steel sword in advance, which he can leave with his wife, and two more when you reach that point."

"Very well," Cortes said, "he can have a sword now if he'll bring corn and honey to help feed my army. What did you tell him that made him change his mind?"

"The truth," Huatl said soberly, "only the truth." Then, with a sly smile, he departed.

Which truths Huatl had imparted he never did say, and Marina assumed he had just cleared up the misunderstandings. But the untutored Nemon guided the Spaniards so adroitly through Maya territory that they passed within a few miles of an ancient temple containing buried treasure and art objects which would have been consigned to the melting pots if Spaniards had discovered them. Centuries later, archaeologists would marvel over a beautiful Mayan temple, name it "Palenque," and consider themselves lucky that the abandoned ruin had been so buried under vines and obscured by trees that the Spaniards had not even noticed it when they passed.

Chapter 31

Circle of Life, Circle of Love

"Remember the first time you sailed on a ship?" Juan asked Marina on the second morning of their voyage to Spain. "You got seasick then, too."

She stood at the railing, feeling queasy as the ship bobbed up and down and the wooden deck shifted under her feet. "I remember," she said, trying to laugh without choking. "We were sailing from Honduras to Vera Cruz. I was already weak from hunger, and I hated to lose what little food I'd eaten." The feeling of nausea intensified beyond her control, so she leaned far over the rail to expel the contents of her stomach into the waves. Even her nose felt the sting and bitter taste of vomit.

"You'll get used to it," Juan grinned. "The first few days are the hardest. On my first ocean voyage I was afraid I was going to die; then I was afraid I wouldn't."

Marina smiled at Juan's joking, but she felt too weak to laugh. "Is Martin all right?" she asked.

"Fine. He's at the bow watching the helmsman steer. Seven-year-olds adapt to the sea pretty well. They don't know enough to tie themselves into worry knots. Fear makes it worse."

Fear. Again Marina wondered, as she had when they set sail from Vera Cruz, what was causing her irrational fear. She looked up at the sails, radiant with sunlight as they billowed against the clear blue sky. "It's a beautiful day," she said, clinging tightly to the rough wooden railing.

"Beautiful," Juan agreed. "The rainy season should be over by now. We probably won't hit any storms in the crossing, but even if we do, we'll just pull in the sails and ride them out." He wrapped his arms around her from the back and kissed her neck. She liked the way he expressed his love with touching.

Marina leaned her head back on her husband's shoulder, touching her forehead to his bearded cheek. "We can't see Mexico any more," she said, rubbing her hand affectionately over his arm, enjoying its masculine hairiness. "Not even the peaks of the volcanos."

Juan kissed her forehead to assuage her fears. "Imagine how scary the first voyages from Spain must have been, when the sailors didn't know what lay ahead, and they couldn't see anything but water."

Marina shuddered, though she was beginning to feel better. "They must've had incredible faith," she said with a sense of awe. "Faith in their captain and in God." When Juan murmured agreement, she continued, "I think my faith is strong enough. I'm not afraid of bad weather."

"Are you afraid of something else?"

Marina lifted one of Juan's hands to her lips and kissed his fingers, just as he had done with her many times. "I'm not afraid of a new life in a new country, because you're with me," she said. "I feel sad about leaving Mexico, though, leaving so many memories, and never being able to talk about them again."

"Maybe I frightened you with the warning I gave you yesterday," Juan said apologetically. "I didn't mean for you to forget everything you've cared about here; I just hope you won't dwell on the past so much that you get homesick."

"My home is where you are, and it always will be," Marina said sincerely. "I think my sickness this morning is not just seasickness. I think I'm going to have your child."

Juan turned Marina around by the shoulders to read the pleasure in her face. "Honestly, Marina? Are you sure?"

"I've had all the symptoms I had with Martin," she said. Then she searched his face. "Juan, are you happy about this?"

"Happy?" Juan exploded. "I'd shout it across all the rooftops, if we had any rooftops here."

"Can you love both children, this new one and Martin too?"

"Of course!" Juan said emphatically. "You know how much I enjoy Martin. Is that what's been worrying you?"

"Maybe. I remember how my own life changed when my step-brother was born. A man sometimes favors his own child over another man's."

"I'm not Anecoatl," Juan said firmly. "I have no ambition greater than being a good family man and a good provider for my wife and children."

"Oh, Juan," Marina said, tears in her eyes. "I believe you mean that. I'm so lucky to have you."

"What about you?" Juan asked. "Are you happy about this, and can you love my child as much as Hernan's?"

"I can love all the children you want to give me," she assured him, gratified by his look of relief. "Tell me, if you can love two children, can you love two countries?"

"I suppose so," Juan mused. "I never thought much about it, but I've grown fond of Mexico. It's an exciting, beautiful country, but so is Spain."

"Then I'm sure I'll love Spain too. It's given me two

469

wonderful men to enrich my life."

At those words, Juan felt a surge of hope. "Can you ever love me as much as you loved Hernan?"

"I think I can answer that question now," Marina said. "I used to think a Christian woman could love only one man, yet in my heart I knew I loved two—or maybe even three, because I loved Nemon too, in a way. I used to feel confused about that, but I also felt angry that Christian men like Hernan could love many women without guilt."

"Some Christian men are perfectly faithful to their wives," Juan said. "I'll never want any other woman while I have you."

"But if I should die, I'd want you to love again," Marina said earnestly. "And if you don't ask me to choose between you and Hernan, I'll love you both forever, just as a widow might love two husbands, even if one is just a memory."

"Fine with me," Juan said; "in fact, I'm glad to hear it. As long as your other loves are only memories, I'll be content."

Marina looked out across the sunny waves, drew a deep breath of salt air, and felt the breeze and the sunlight caress her face. She felt deliciously alive, glad that another child was coming, knowing how busy she would be and how much the child would need her care. A smaller satisfaction, she smiled to herself, would be the comfort of wearing huipils during the pregnancy without seeming to reject the tight-waisted dresses most Spanish women wore. Thinking about the Spanish women she had seen in Mexico, she suddenly realized what she had feared.

Juan took her hand and started to walk slowly with her along the deck. "Let's get some exercise," he said. "It will do you good, and the baby too."

Happily Marina squeezed his hand and walked beside him. "Juan," she said, "I know now what was bothering me. I'm not afraid any more."

"What were you afraid of?"

"Becoming useless," she said with conviction. "That's all it was. I don't want to be like some Spanish women I've seen, spending all their time fussing over their hair and clothes, sipping tea and talking about trivial things."

"I've seen a few Mexican women do that, too," Juan said. "You couldn't be one, not in this country or any other."

"May I raise our children myself, not hire servants to do it?"

"Whatever you wish," Juan said, pleased at her maternal feelings. At the bow of the ship he saw Martin asking questions of the helmsman. So Martin was going to be like his mother, Juan thought, remembering how Marina liked to ask questions. "Let's see if Martin wants to take a tour around the ship now," Juan said, sounding like a proud new father.

Seeing Juan's jubilant mood, Marina thought of asking again

if she could learn to read and write. Juan might grant even that wish while he was in good spirits. But she decided to wait until another time, after she had fully mastered the spoken language.

If she could learn to write words down on paper, she thought fervently, she could paint pictures with words. With written words, she could speak through the centuries, to her children's children and beyond. She could be a voice telling them of their origins in a magnificent world full of magic and powerful forces, a world of enchantment and omens, a world where life was tenuous but joyful in the face of harsh realities.

She could write down the words to the poems and songs that had once floated around the temples and infused life into rituals and ceremonies that brought meaning to existence. She could tell them the stories of gods and goddesses that had given her own childhood such flavor, even if the gods were now considered primitive or false. With words, the curiosity of future generations could be satisfied when they saw ancient deities gazing at them inscrutably from the silence of their stone sanctuaries and tombs. She could explain why stories of the gods and goddesses had to be invented to satisfy the deep human craving to know and understand. She could write about the rhythms of life and the worship of nature's creatures by a people whose way of life was rapidly disappearing, changing so fast that even the wisest old woman could not remember everything about it. She could tell her progeny how to honor the old ways even when replacing them with something of greater value.

For those progeny who might someday walk through an empty tlachtli ball court and wonder how the players had bounded a rubber ball through the high ring, she could fill the stands with the shouts of spectators and the babbling of gamblers. She could enliven deserted marketplaces with the sounds of yapping dogs, squawking birds, and haggling shoppers. She could stock the merchants' stalls with marvelous products—things like rubber, cotton, chocolate, tomatoes, chilis and corn—that her ancestors developed for themselves yet gave generously to a needy world.

She could restore the arts of the ephemeral, the featherwork that decays, the dance that evaporates in time, the music that fades in the wind, the love that passes from parent to child or from man to woman leaving no trace.

She could people the empty temples with the souls of priests and priestesses who flowed through the sacred halls like life's blood. She could put fire not only in the abandoned temples but also in the forsaken hearths with three stones that now lay in disuse wherever a thatched hut had once stood.

She could tell them of men and women who had lived lives of greatness and smallness, committing evil deeds and heroic ones, singing poems of tragic death or keeping life alive by

471

living it. She could recount tales of loyalty and betrayal, striving and survival, humility and pride, cruelty and kindness. She could write of the calamities of nations and the aches of individual hearts. She could speak of the inventiveness of commoners, the sensibilities of slaves, the aspirations of women, and the divinity of those human souls who uplift the downtrodden.

She wanted to tell the stories of two civilizations that had collided in a particular place and time in such a way that the rest of the world was changed forever, in such a way that they strengthened each other even as they tried to destroy each other. She yearned to tell of her own small part in those great clashing events in history.

But that yearning was a dream, a dream for her own future and her family's future. Perhaps it was a dream that could never be realized, a futile desire for what she could never have. But it was also a dream for others in the human family, wherever a ship might sail or a wind might blow. It was a dream of building a legacy of love, to preserve her native country's intriguing and glorious past, the past that she now had permission to remember.

The End

About the Author

Helen Heightsman Gordon, Ed.D. is Professor of English at Bakersfield College in Bakersfield, California. She has taught freshman and sophomore literature and women's studies courses, specializing in "Women in Literature." She has a compelling interest in seeing history afresh from the viewpoint of women who have played important roles but whose stories have not been fully told. Although she has published several textbooks, many professional articles, newspaper features, and some poetry, this is her first novel.

CENTRAL TENOCHTITLAN

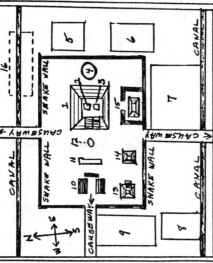

1. Great Pyramid with two temples
2. Temple of Tlaloc (Blue trim)
3. Temple of Huitzilopochtli (Red trim)
4. Temple of Quetzalcoatl
5. Palace of Axayacatl (where Cortes stayed)
6. Moctezuma's Zoo and Aviary
7. Palace of Moctezuma II
8. House of Song
9. Palace of Moctezuma I
10. Ceremonial Tlachtli Ball Court
11. Skull Rack
12. Stone of Tizoc
13. Temple of Xipe Totec
14. Eagle Temple
15. Temple of Tezcatlipoca
16. Ruins of Palace of Ahuitzotl

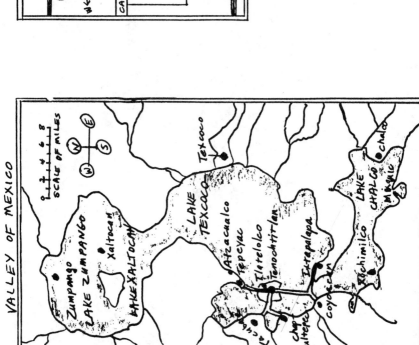

VALLEY OF MEXICO